FEAST OF DARKNESS
PART I

✳ ✳ ✳

A Novel of Geadhain

CHRISTIAN A. BROWN

For Zeus, my furry muse, and for all the creatures of Earth and Geadhain that comfort, nurture, and inspire us as our companions.

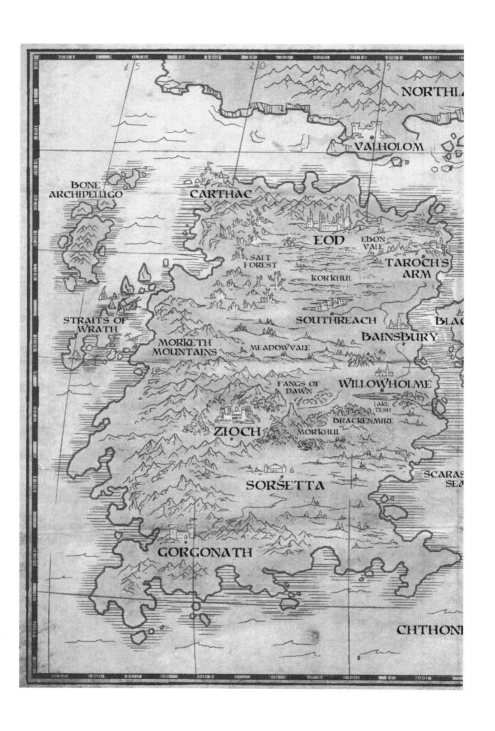

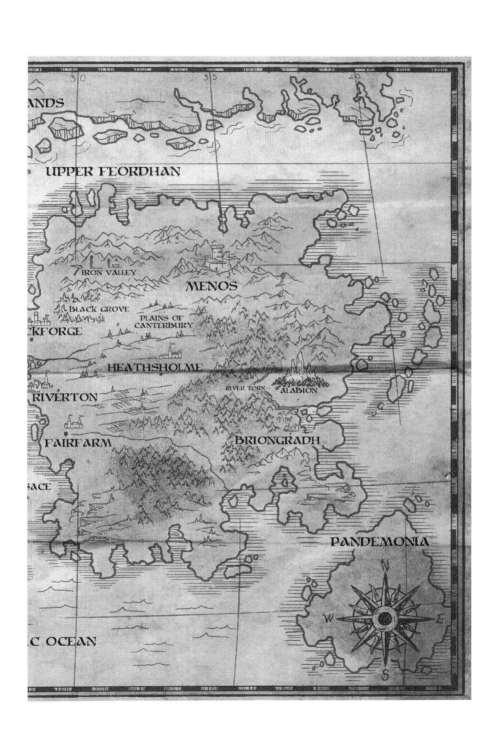

CONTENTS

ON GEADHAIN (GLOSSARY)

I: Paragons, Wonders, and Horrors

Brutus: The Sun King. Brutus is the second of the Immortal Kings and ruler of the Summerlands in southern Geadhain. Zioch, the City of Gold, shines like a gold star on the southern horizon and is the seat of his power. Brutus is the master of the wilderness and the hunt. His magik has dominion over the physical world and self. He is victim to the Black Queen's whispers and falls far from his nobility.

Lilehum (Lila): Magnus's bride. Magnus sought her when learning to live as a man independent of his ageless brother. Through the sharing of blood and ancient vows—the *Fuilimean*—she is drawn into the mystery of the immortal brothers and imbued with a sliver of their magik. She is a sorceress and possibly eternal in her years. She is wise, kind, and comely without compare. However, she is ruthless if her kingdom or bloodmate is threatened.

Magnus: The Immortal King of the North. Magnus is one of two guardians of the Waking World. The other is his brother, Brutus. The Everfair King—the colloquial name for Magnus—rules Eod, the City of Wonders. He is living magik itself, a sorcerer without compare, and the master of the forces of ice, thunder, Will, and intellect.

Morigan Lostarot: A young woman living a rather unremarkable life as the handmaiden to an elderly sorcerer, Thackery Thule. A world of wonder and horror engulfs her after a chance, perhaps fated, meeting with the Wolf. She learns she is an axis of magik, mystery, and Fate to the proceedings of Geadhain's Great War. In the darkest days that she and her companions must face, her heroism and oft-tested virtue will determine much of the world's salvation or ruin.

Thackery Hadrian Thule (Whitehawk): An old sorcerer living in Eod. Thackery lives an unassuming life as a man of modest stature. However, he is a man with many skeletons in his closet. He has no known children or family, and he cares for Morigan as if she were his daughter. Morigan's grace will touch him, too, and he is drawn into the web of Fate she weaves.

The Black Queen, Zionae \\'Zē-ō-ˌnā\\: A shapeless, bodiless, monstrous entity without empathy who seeks to undo the Immortal Kings and the world's order. Her actions—those who perceive these things sense she is a she—are horrific and inexplicable.

The Dreamstalker: A vile presence that haunts and travels the waters of Dream as Morigan does. She is the Herald of the Black Queen, Zionae's voice in the physical world.

The Lady of Luck, Charazance \\'SHer-āh-zans\\: The Dreamer of serendipity, gambles, and games. Alastair is her vessel.

The Sisters Three—Ealasyd \\'Ēl-ə-sid\\, ***Elemech*** \\'El-ə-mek\\, and ***Eean*** \\'Ē-en\\: From youngest to eldest in appearance, they are Ealasyd, Elemech, and Eean. The Sisters Three are a trio of ageless witches who live in the woods of Alabion. They are known to hold sway over the destinies of men. They can be capricious, philanthropic, or woefully cruel. One must be careful when bartering with the Sisters Three for their wisdom. There is always a price.

The Wanderer, Feyhazir \\'Ph-āe-āh-ˈzi(ə)r\\: The Dreamer of mystery, seduction, and desire. He is Morigan's father.

The Wolf, Caenith \\'Kā-nith\\: A smith of Eod. His fearsome, raw exterior hides an animal and a dreadful wrath. Caenith is a conflicted creature—a beast, man, poet, lover, and killer. Caenith believes himself beyond salvation, and he passes the years making metal skins and claws for the slow-walkers of Geadhain while drowning himself in bitter remorse. He does not know it, but Morigan will pull him from his darkness and make him confront what is most black and wicked within him.

II: Eod's Finest

Adhamh (Adam): An exiled changeling of Briongrahd. Noble, loyal, and loving, his only hatred is for those like the White Wolf, who abuse and punish life. Humble Adam has a destiny beyond what he or others would ever expect.

Beauregard Fischer: A waifish, lyrical young man lost in the Summerlands with his father. In his past and soul lies a great mystery. His cheek is marked with the birthmark of the one true northern star.

Devlin Fischer: A seasoned hunter and Beauregard's father. He is as gruff and hairy as a bear.

Dorvain: Master of the North Watch and Leonitis's brother. He is a brutish, gruff warrior tempered by the winds of the Northlands. He is dependable and unflappable. He is an oak of a man who will not bend to the winds of change or war.

Erithitek \ˈĀr-ith-ə-ˌtek**:** More commonly referred to as "Erik." He is the king's hammer. Erik was once an orphaned child of the Salt Forests and a member of the Kree tribe, but Magnus took him in. Erik now serves as his right hand.

Galivad: Master of the East Watch. The youngest of Eod's watchmasters, he is seen by many as unfit for the post because of his pretty face, foppish manner, and cavalier airs. He laughs and sings to avoid the pain of remembering what he has lost.

Jebidiah Rotbottom: A flamboyant spice merchant from Sorsetta. He sails the breadth of Geadhain in a garish, crimson vessel—the *Red Mary*. Currently, he uses different aliases, for reasons no doubt unscrupulous and suspect.

Leonitis: The Lion. He is thusly named for his roar, grandeur, and courage. He is the Ninth Legion master of Eod (King Magnus's personal legion). Once Geadhain's Great War commences, he will play many roles, from soldier to spy to hero. Leonitis's thread of destiny is long and woven through many Fates.

Lowelia Larson (Lowe): The queen knows her as the Lady of Whispers. Lowelia seems a simple, high-standing palace servant, yet her doughy, pleasant demeanor conceals a shrewd mind and a vengeful secret.

Maggie Halm: Maggie is the granddaughter of Cordenzia, an infamous whoremistress who traded her power for freedom from the Iron City. Maggie runs an establishment called the Silk Purse in Taroch's Arm.

Muriel Bochance: Simon's precocious daughter.

Pythius: A shaman of the Doomchaser tribe of Pandemonia. A mystical, two-spirited being as adventurous as he is pragmatic and traditional.

Rowena: She is Queen Lila's sword and Her Majesty's left hand. Rowena's tale was destined for a swift, bleak end until the queen intervened and saved Rowena's young life. Since that day, Rowena has revered Queen Lila as a mother and a true savior.

Simon Bochance: A scholar and geologist whose quiet life is hijacked by the Sisters of Fate.

Tabitha Fischer: The sole magistrate of Willowholme. She has assumed this role not by choice but through tragedy.

Talwyn Blackmore: The illegitimate son of Roland Blackmore (since deceased). Talwyn is a kind, brilliant scholar and inheritor of all the virtue that escaped his half brother, Augustus. Talwyn lives in Riverton. His thirst for knowledge often makes him cross boundaries of decorum.

III: Menos's Darkest Souls

Aadore Brennoch: An Iron-born survivor. A woman whose strange lineage comes from the far, far East. Once a handmaiden to the Lady El, she will leave that meager station behind and rise into a woman of prominence and legend alongside her brother.

Adelaide: Mouse's childhood friend from the charterhouse. The girl's fate is the cause of much torment for Mouse.

Alastair: A mysterious figure who acts seemingly in his own interests. He greatly influences certain meetings and events. To all appearances, he is the Watchers' agent and Mouse's mentor. He almost certainly, though, serves another power or master.

Beatrice of El: Moreth's pale and ghastly wife. After a glance, a person can tell this ethereal woman is not wholly of this world.

Curtis: An athletic young man with a shameful criminal past trying to make a better life for himself in Menos. He is taken with Aadore, though will prove himself more than a doting suitor.

Elineth: Son of Elissandra.

Elissandra: The Mistress of Mysteries. She is an Iron Sage and the proprietress of Menos's Houses of Mystery—places where a wary master can consult oracles and seek augurs regarding his or her inevitable doom. While she is wicked, she is also bright with love for her children, and she fosters a hidden dream and hope no other Iron Sage would ever be so bold as to consider.

Elsa Brennoch: Mother to Aadore and Sean.

Gloriatrix: The Iron Queen and ruler of Menos. Gloriatrix single-handedly clawed her way to the top of Menos's black Crucible after her husband, Gabriel, lost first his right to chair on the Council of the Wise and then his life. Gloriatrix has never remarried and blames her brother, Thackery Thule, for Gabriel's death. With her family in shambles, power is the only thing to which she clings. Gloriatrix has ambitions far beyond Menos. She would rule the stars themselves if she could.

Iarron (Ian): An abandoned child, unnaturally calm and still, who was discovered by the Brennoch siblings on Menos's darkest day—he is a star of hope to them.

Kanatuk: A tribesman of the Northlands who had been stolen from his home and placed into a lifetime of abhorrent slavery, serving as a vassal to the Broker. Morigan rescues him in Menos.

Lord Augustus Blackmore: Lord of Blackforge. A deviant power-monger with grotesque appetites.

Moreth of El: Master of the House of El and the Blood Pits of Menos. He traffics in people, gladiators, and death.

Mouse: More of a gray soul than a black one, Mouse is a woman without a firm flag planted on the map of morality. She knows well life's cruelty and how best to avoid it through self-sufficiency and indifference. As a girl, she escaped a rather unfortunate fate, and she has since risen to become a Voice of the Watchers—a shadowbroker of Geadhain. Mouse's real trial begins when she is thrust into peril with Morigan—at that time a stranger—and Mouse is forced to rethink everything she knows.

Sangloris: Elissandra's husband.

Sean Brennoch: Brother to Aadore. Once a soldier of the Ironguard, now a one-legged veteran. Sean wants no pity, however, and is more capable and clever than most other soldiers.

Skar: An ugly, ogreish mercenary whose heart is kinder than his looks. Fate sees his path cross with the Brennochs, and to them he will become a sword not for hire but bound to protect them through respect and duty.

Sorren: Gloriatrix's youngest child. Sorren is a nekromancer of incredible power who possesses the restraint and moods of a spoiled and petulant child. He shares a pained past with his (mostly) deceased brother, Vortigern.

Tessariel: Daughter of Elissandra.

The Broker: All the black rivers of sin in Menos come to one confluence: the Broker. Little is known about this man beyond the terror tales whispered to misbehaving children. The Broker has metal teeth, mad eyes, and a cadre of twisted servants whom he calls sons. He inhabits and controls the Iron City's underbelly.

The Great Mother: Her Faithful are multitudinous. Her elements and the shades of her divinity—Green, White, Blue—are prefixes to her many names.

The Slave: An unnamed vassal purchased in the Flesh Markets of Menos. A dangerous creature; more than a man. Although property, he later became a free man and substitute father to the Lord El. Together, the men traveled into the wilds of Pandemonia on a most dangerous safari.

Vortigern: Gloriatrix's second son. This pitiable soul lives in a state between light and dark and without memory of the errors that brought him to this walking death.

IV: Lands and Landmarks

Alabion: The great woodland and the realm of the Sisters Three.

Bainsbury: A moderate-sized township on the west bank of the River Feordhan. Gavin Foss lords over it.

Blackforge: A city on the east bank of the Feordhan. It was once famous for blacksmithing.

Brackenmire: The realm outside of Mor'Khul. It is a swampy but pleasant place.

Carthac: The City of Waves.

Ceceltoth: City of Stone.

Eatoth: City of Waterfalls.

Ebon Vale: The land around Taroch's Arm. It has fiefs, farmsteads, and large shale deposits.

Eod: The City of Wonders and kingdom of Magnus. Eod is a testament to the advances of technomagik and culture in Geadhain.

Fairfarm: The largest rural community in the East. With so many pastures, fields, and farms, this realm produces most of Central Geadhain's consumable resources.

Heathsholme: A small hamlet known for its fine ale.

Intomitath: City of Flames.

Iron Valley: One of the richest sources of feliron in Geadhain.

Kor'Khul: The great sand ocean surrounding Eod. These lands were once thought to be lush and verdant.

Lake Tesh: The blue jewel glittering under the willows of Willowholme.

Menos: The Iron City. It is hung always in a pall of gloom.

Mor'Khul: The green, rolling valleys of Brutus's realm. They are legendary for their beauty.

Pandemonia: The large island continent across the Chthonic Ocean and separated from most of Geadhain's other landmasses. Three Great Cities of immeasurable technomagikal power serve to bring order to this realm of chaos, a land where topography shifts and changes day by day from tundra to desert to lava field to wastes. Only these three Great Cities stand permanent in Pandemonia's constant flux.

Plains of Canterbury: Wide, sparse fields and gullies.

Riverton: A bustling, eclectic city of lighthearted criminals and troubadours. The city is found on the eastern shore of the River Feordhan, and it was built from the reconstituted wreckage of old hulls and whatever interesting bits floated down the great river.

Sorsetta: In the south and past the Sun King's lands. This is a realm of contemplation and quiet enlightenment.

Southreach: A great ancient city built into a cleft in Kor'Khul.

Taroch's Arm: The resting place of a relic of the great warlord Taroch: his arm. The city is also a hub of great trade among all corners of Geadhain.

The Black Grove: The forest outside of Blackforge. It leads to the Plains of Canterbury.

Willowholme: A village located in Brackenmire and famed for its musicians and anglers.

Zioch: The City of Gold and kingdom of Brutus.

V: Miscellaneous Mysteries

Fuilimean: The Blood Promise. It is a trading of blood and vows and a spiritual binding between two willing participants. Magnus and Brutus did this first in the oldest ages. Depending on who partakes in the ritual, the results can be extraordinary.

Technomagik: A hybrid science that blends raw power—often currents of magik—with mechanical engineering.

The Faithful: Worshippers of the Green Mother. They exist in many cultures and forms, and the most sacred and spiritual of their kind, curators of the world's history known as Keepers, often lead them.

The Watchers: The largest network of shadowbrokers in Central Geadhain.

FOREWORD (A RECAP)

Four Feasts till Darkness is an expansive and complex work—even I lose track of things without my notes! It would be unreasonable, then, to expect perfect recall from my readers. To that end, I set one of my dear editors—Kyla—to scribbling down all the important bits of the story. Here you are: a refresher of the events of Geadhain's Great War leading up to *Feast of Darkness, Part I*.

— Christian

When first entering the world of Geadhain, we encounter a realm of magical smoke and metaphysical mirrors reflecting the darkest and lightest that its inhabitants have to offer. But as the pages of *Feast of Fates* turn, a deeper understanding of this mystical realm emerges, one that parallels the universalisms found in our own very real experiences in this, our own world. Geadhain is a world unlike any other, where science and magic form a mysterious force known as technomagik. It is a land born of a Green Mother earth, but ruled by the wills—both conscious and unconscious—of kings and queens that wreak havoc on their world. But there comes a time when even a mother must teach her children the hard way, even if it pains her. And so *Feast of Fates* sees the start of the Green Mother's tough love, depriving them of her protection for the anguish they have brought to her with their violence; it is the world's inhabitants alone who can save themselves.

Our story begins with the weavers of fate themselves, the Three Sisters—Eean, Elemech, and Ealasyd—who make their homes in the forests of Alabion. The Sisters represent life, death, and all its various contortions and permutations in the world. There, they both give birth to, and usher death upon, themselves and the world. With each renewal, they shape the twists and turns of our players' journeys, for better or worse. They represent destiny's infinite loop in a twisted sibling rivalry that will determine Geadhain's future. But even the Sisters of Fate cannot control the rumblings on destiny's horizon—the harbinger of destruction to come in the stormy and ethereal form of the Black Queen.

The scene shifts to the city of Eod—Geadhain's cosmopolitan metropolis. Nestled within Kor'Khul's oceans of sand, it is known as the City of Wonders for its host of technomagikal advancements and a skyline filled with flying carriages ferrying Eod's cultural and social elite. There we find Morigan, a young woman of character and strength who is traveling toward a destiny forged ages before her birth, and one that is intimately entwined in tapestries of the Three Sisters.

Morigan lives a simple life as a handmaiden until her world is thrown into tumult as she is drawn to the literal animal magnetism of Caenith, a wolf-man changeling whose initial gruff appearance belies his ancient origins and unimaginable power. The two are instantly bonded, each of them knowing that their attraction goes well beyond "love at first sight," and is more akin to having been written in Geadhain's starry skies. The two cannot deny what has been preordained, and the ripple effect of the Wolf and Fawn's union (as they come to know each other) as bloodmates begins to be felt throughout Geadhain. Their coming together stirs ancient powers of sight in Morigan and inspires the beast in Caenith to reclaim its role in his life.

Morigan's nascent visions are a near-constant reminder that whenever there is joy, sorrow remains but a half step behind. She is witness to waves of destruction and death shadowing the realm, making their impending presence known not only to her but to all of Geadhain. In her mind's eye, she sees that just as we humans wage war against ourselves and the earth that has borne us all, so too does Geadhain face a battle against evil forged in blackness, smelted from the depths of all the worst the world has to offer. Chief among Morigan's visions is the emergence from the pitch of the Black Queen.

This foul black entity exerts her power chiefly by wielding the bodies of others like puppets. Morigan is forced to watch as the Black Queen overtakes Magnus's body to mete out a brutal attack on his wife. She is also witness to her exploitation of the Sun King, Brutus, to wage war against his own people, pitting him against his brother in kingship and immortality, Magnus, the Everfair King. The incorporeal figure of the Black Queen has set the wheels firmly in motion to bring drought and death to the Green Mother's world.

A witness to Morigan's symbiosis is Thackery Thule, a sorcerer who guided her in her youth and through the painful loss of her mother. Thackery forms another piece of the puzzling group that will either pitch Geadhain forward into light or see it crumble before them into darkness. For years, Thackery's past was concealed from Morigan, but unwittingly, she begins to reveal tragedies long buried. His is a history filled with loss at the hands of those closest to him, the details of which will play out over the tapestry of time. He quickly realizes that Morigan's powers extend beyond simple fortune-tellers' tricks; she may hold the key to Geadhain's future. In an effort to safeguard this knowledge, Thackery takes them to see Queen Lila. There, in the royal palace's Hall of Memories, Morigan reveals that the threat that Brutus poses to the queen, the kingdom, and the entire realm is also manifest in Lila's spouse, Magnus.

But the sudden emergence of Morigan's long-repressed powers has not gone unnoticed by other powers that be, and fear that she might pose a threat to the hierarchical order of Menos quickly makes her a target. In those moments where Caenith and Morigan are pledging their blood to each other, others are plotting to capture the Fawn and subjugate her before the Iron Queen of Menos, Gloriatrix, a woman so driven by grief at the loss of her husband that she has ruled her kingdom with a fist worthy of her title. Never content to do her own dirty work, she instructs her son, Sorren, to become a party to the destruction of Eod and capture of Morigan. He sets off a number of explosions that destabilize the city not only physically but also politically and socially, and Lila is struck with the realization of Eod's vulnerability. For Thackery, Sorren's indifference to inflicting pain comes as no surprise. As his uncle, the sorcerer was not only a witness to his past violence but a victim as well. As the mysteries of Thackery's past continue to be untangled, we learn that not only is Gloriatrix his sister, but his nephew was responsible for the death of his wife.

Before the dust can settle, Morigan is spirited away to Menos, a city that breeds its own brand of filth born out of fear. She is to be held captive there until she is subjugated under the whims of Gloriatrix. But even with her newfound powers still in their infancy, the Fawn is a worthy match for her captors. So, too, is her new companion, Mouse, a member of Geadhain's underworld network of spies. This diminutive woman has been shaped by the mean streets of Menos, the ones paved with slavery, exploitation, violations, and hate. Mouse had done her time in the city and sought out a new face from a fleshcrafter, only to discover that there truly is no honor among thieves, landing her in the same captivity as Morigan. Like the city of Menos itself, Mouse's moral compass is one that, accordingly, wavers with the magnetic pull of the tides.

The unlikely pairing of these two women is a reminder of how difficult it can be to cut through the obscurities of a world in which appearances are never quite as they seem. Our impulse to simply dismiss the "bad guys" is constantly challenged by being privy to perceptions of individuals both within and without the relationships of all our players. Good and evil are never as simple as they appear. Each player is "othered" by those in opposition. Good is never just good. Evil is never simply evil. Perception is everything.

Neither does "dead" always mean "dead." There are brokers and flesh-crafters who deal in the undead and nearly dead, and these ruined vessels are holding the women in custody for Gloriatrix's interrogation. But even the zombielike slaves of these nekromantic death dealers have deep within them a spark of humanity waiting to be rekindled. For no one is this more true than Vortigern, the dead man whose shackles of catatonia are broken when Morigan's psychic bees pierce his mind. Buried deep below his death mask is a past and present inextricably linked to the group. He was no random victim of Sorren's psychopathy—they were brothers. Vortigern's present death was the consequence of having once loved Sorren's wife and fathered a child with her, Fionna, the mighty Mouse who is now a witness to his deliverance from un-death.

But these women are not stunned into inaction by their newly gained knowledge, for the world of Fates is not one in which women are the meek observers of the world's affairs, passively allowing events to simply happen to them. And so their escape comes not at the hands of Thackery and Caenith, who have ventured into Menos's dangerous underworld to rescue them, but through the women's own ingenuity and intuitive powers. In the process of their escape, they rescue yet another prisoner, Kanatuk—once a malevolent, mind-thralled servant to Menos's underworld kingpin, the Broker. Although before being enslaved and brought to Menos, Kanatuk had been a peaceful wanderer of the frozen North. Through Morigan's grace and natural proclivity toward reweaving broken souls, he is rescued from his darkness and restored of his past.

Elsewhere, in their efforts to rescue Morigan, Caenith and Thackery also encounter a young changeling girl being exploited at the hands of the seemingly insane Augustus and free her of the bonds of child bride-dom. A skin-walker without a skin, Macha is a sister of Alabion, and like her changeling brethren she is possessed of visions of other worlds. Her dreams are ones that foreshadow the presence of an unknown, fanged warmother who has ushered an era of conflict and violence into their homeland. They form a troop of undeniable misfits that eventually makes its way out of Menos toward a destiny whose grandeur and importance is made increasingly clear through Morigan's visions and buzzing mind hive. She alone bears the full weight of those visions and the horrors that unfold within her mind's eye. Even the mental and spiritual link with her bloodmate does not fully spare her of that burden.

In an effort to secure what she believes is her rightful place in the halls of power, Gloriatrix has formed an alliance with Elissandra, a powerful sorceress and seer. She believes that the prophecies have foretold that when brother rises against brother, she will find her place in the resulting power vacuum. But even the Iron Queen is unaware that the powers that run deep in Morigan's veins also run in Elissandra's; we learn that they are both Daughters of the Moon, sisters in the providence of Alabion. And so Gloriatrix's plan to wage war against the immortals may be undermined and her suspicions of Elissandra warranted.

Meanwhile, King Magnus and his hand, Erithitek, have been leading the troops of Eod's Silver Watch forward toward Zioch, the City of Gold and host to Brutus's throne. Magnus begins to appreciate the scope of his brother's burgeoning depravity, how much terror and chaos Brutus has unleashed upon his own people. It also becomes clear that there is every chance that his journey is one from which he might not return. He thus elicits a hard-won promise from Erithitek to return to Eod and keep safe his Queen Lila.

But not unlike the two women who use their strength and cunning to escape Menos, the queen that Magnus left behind is no manner of shrinking violet. Shaken by Morigan's prophetic revelations, she is no longer certain that the man she loved is as virtuous as she once believed, and whether the choices she made were truly guided by love or something more sinister. Upon Erithitek's return, she sets out on a dangerous journey, steeled to protect her people against any offensive from Gloriatrix. Yet love of husband and love of kingdom drive her to commit acts of terror against those who would threaten either, reminding us that each one of us believes we are "the good guys."

As Magnus continues the Watch's advance, he knows that his brother is lying in wait, hunting him. Once the two are face-to-face, Magnus comes to understand that just as Brutus has transformed his kingdom into a wasteland, so too have the feelings of fraternity they once shared been transformed into intense hatred. Empowered by the Black Queen, Brutus overtakes his brother in a firestorm of destruction. Lest mortals and immortals alike forget—even with all the accumulated powers of the world, complete control over one's ecosystem is always an illusion. Magnus's vanquishment by his brother shakes the foundations of Geadhain, and the land spews forth a natural disaster, a storm of frost and fire that sweeps the world from end to end, triggered by the outcome of the battle between brothers.

It is a battle that produces no winners, since it takes place in a realm where the very concept of death is malleable. And death, or that which resembles it, is the destabilizing force it always is, bringing with it both chaos and clarity. Thus the Black Queen's reign of terror begins with the fall of Magnus and the rise of her corrupted avatar, Brutus, from the ashes of that climactic battle.

When the smoke clears, a world lies in ruin. The line between coincidence and fate is wholly blurred. And the Three Sisters reveal that they are adding a new sibling to their fold—one by the name of Morigan.

In *Feast of Dreams*, we are greeted by the Three Sisters of fate who reveal that despite their best plans the threads of fate have been broken, and by none other than our own Hunters of Fate: Morigan, Caenith, Mouse, Thackery, and Vortigern. We join the pack as they venture through the land of the Untamed, deeper into the protracted quagmire of a great war.

Morigan's mind has become a virtual hive of visions. The bees of her dream-walking are beating out a nearly incessant rhythm of prophecies that are becoming ever more burdensome. Her waking dreams show her that she is, indeed, of immortal origin, and that the woman she called her mother, Mifanwae, did not give birth to her but rather was a willing pawn in destiny's game. In many ways, Morigan has become a silent Cassandra, blessed with a second sight full of images she cannot, or dare not, share. With every passing day, she comes to realize that much of what she sees is unchangeable. She also peeks behind fate's curtain to reveal more about the woman in Caenith's past who once held his heart. Aghna, herself a wolf-changeling, had long ago ended her life when faced with a future of untold suffering. Morigan herself felt she had little to fear from a shadow of the past until she and her friends suddenly found themselves surrounded by an even greater legion—led by the long-departed Aghna.

Once again, it appears that death represents little more than a temporary transition for the lycanthropic being who now governs Briongrahd, the City of Fangs. She is no longer wrapped in the loving glow Caenith remembers from their last moments together but by a shroud of violence and hate. The changeling to whom Caenith had once devoted himself bears little resemblance to their glorious past, and he is forced to reconcile the woman he knew in life with the woman she became in death. Aghna has become the warmother of which Macha had warned, leading her species toward a battle against the Immortal Kings in which victory will represent the domination over other species in the realm. And much like Brutus allowed himself to be moved to slaughter his own kin, Aghna now appears possessed by a power that lives only to satisfy its carnal desires and lust for domination.

Unsurprisingly, there is little honor among those who are singularly focused on the advancement of their own—a kind of species-based nationalism—and Aghna betrays her former lover, killing Vortigern in the process. This is a death from which he will not return, and while the survivors escape, Mouse is scarred by the untimely loss of a father she had known only in his afterlife.

All the while, the indefinable, ethereal evil of the Black Queen continues to overshadow the land, reminding Geadhain's inhabitants at every turn that in the battle of man versus the forces of the universe, they are always the underdogs. Yet the machinations of the Black Queen and her cabal are not the only threats to peace in the realm. With Magnus either missing or dead after the battle with his corrupted brother, the Iron Queen, Gloriatrix, intends to launch an offensive against Eod, using all the forces of her technomagikal arsenal.

Gloriatrix's past has been so marred by loss that when her son Sorren suddenly disappears, she takes it as a signal that she is destined to live a life bereft of love, cementing her ire against anyone who would deny her the singular pleasure remaining to her: power. But Elissandra, who shares Morigan's gift of insight, knows that Sorren's disappearance was not of earthly origin. His essence has been given over to a power greater than anything Gloriatrix could imagine—that of Death itself. And while Gloriatrix is almost singularly focused on capturing Morigan and her fellow travelers, she is blinded to the dissent that is fomenting in the halls of Menos in her absence. The Iron Sages begin staging a revolt, targeting Elissandra and her one vulnerability: her children. The sorceress barely escapes with her life and fails to impress upon Gloriatrix the growing futility of waging war against Eod.

Queen Lila, Magnus's wife, has left the kingdom with her husband's hammer, Erithitek. She leaves in her stead her hands, Lowelia and Leonitis, who will serve the kingdom in her absence, both wrapped in a spell of illusion that tricks whoever looks upon them into perceiving the appearances and voices of their departed queen and Magnus's hammer. Believing Magnus to have perished at Brutus's hands, Lila has taken it upon herself to acquire a tool of untold power: the arm of Taroch. Conjured out of the ashes of Magnus's despair, the ancient relic, like every tool of magik in the realm, possesses power that is easily abused and will exact a steep price from its user.

Approaching madness, Lila gives barely a thought to her once-beloved Summerlands or to those she left to safeguard its borders. She is blinded by her loss and pain, and Erik—her silent admirer and stalwart protector—is the only thing keeping her physical and spiritual being safe, as she wrestles with a faltering morality that is dizzied by grief. Both she and Erithitek—who is increasingly struggling to keep silent his intense feelings for the queen—are unaware that Magnus, in fact, exists in a kind of purgatory. There, Brutus has opened a window into his mind through which Magnus can view his rampages, in the hopes that he might seduce his captive brother into joining him as a vessel for the Black Queen. And so visions of Magnus that push Lila to the brink of sanity represent more than simple nightmares from which Erithitek must awaken her.

All the while, Rowena and Galivad, Queen Lila's sword and the master of Eod's East Watch, respectively, have been watching Moreth of El—a trafficker of all things dark and depraved in Menos. Also under their purview is his new bride, Beatrice, a woman not unfamiliar to Galivad. Beatrice, with her angelic appearance and glowing aura, is more akin to a viper in her actions, her need for self-gratification finding purchase in the indulgent devouring of bodies and souls—one of whom was Galivad's mother. The couple are kindred spirits with Gloriatrix, both reveling in exacting their own sick torments on those who have the terrible misfortune of crossing their path—and Lila's envoys are exactly such misfortunates.

Also caught in their web is one working for an invisible authority, guided by forces unknown in the corporeal world. Alastair, a man who had once granted Mouse her freedom from indentured service, appears to have a mission that extends well beyond that of underground trader of goods in Menos. His intrigue with Maggie, the owner of the Silk Purse tavern, leads him to pull her into his plots as well—the goals of which seem to shift along with his loyalties. While Alastair is another of Geadhain's citizens for whom dying simply represents a bump on the road toward his next death, there is little question that he takes no pleasure in seeing Maggie tortured at the hands of their captors.

As the pack's journey continues, Caenith comes to see that Aghna's treachery is but the first of many shocking truths he must absorb. Deep in a cave, the pup that grew into a great Wolf is reunited with his mother. There in the darkness, the great Mother-wolf divulges a secret about his father's identity that eclipses all that the Wolf thought to be true about the world and his place in it. Face-to-face with the woman/beast who bore him, he learns that his father is none other than Brutus, the creature who would see the world's destruction as a vessel of the Black Queen.

But while the immortals are faced with challenges of an otherworldly nature, most inhabitants of Geadhain cannot shake their mortal coil. Amid Menos's murk, there are civilian casualties of a war they are simply trying to survive. A simple observer, Aadore does not see herself as a party to the jingoist frenzy into which Menos is being whipped. She seeks only to reunite with her brother, Sean, a man who has been ravaged not only by time but by life's savagery. At the moment of their strained homecoming, the city is rocked by explosions, and rising from the detritus these new players reveal themselves as the sole survivors.

Another unwitting player in fate's grand theater, young Beauregard has a past that remains a mystery. But in the present, he and his father, Devlin, have been entrusted with knowledge that may secure the future of Geadhain's most precious and beautiful region: Sorsetta. They leave the Summerlands—a land now scarred by Brutus's fury—to act as messengers of the war that is bearing down on Sorsetta's peaceful land. But more than that, they bring with them a tool of magik that offers one of the few glimpses of hope for defense. As Brutus appears to them, he is cloaked in the shadow of Magnus's trapped spirit. Knowing that his son is strong enough to survive the hardships that await him, Devlin sacrifices himself so that Beauregard might wield their weapon: a wonderstone—a shard of condensed, ancient magik. Doing so releases Magnus from his purgatory, banishes Brutus, and propels Beauregard forward from peaceful poet to warrior of fate.

Meanwhile, as our travelers venture through the Pitch Dark groves of Alabion, they are met with three sisters of another kind. The three red witches whose taste for blood would see a meal made of each of them can sense Morigan's ascendant power. They foretell that hers will not be a path paved by peaceful light but with crimson. They also sense within Mouse a growing resentment toward a fate that would drive her further into darkness.

The immutable nature of that which is preordained becomes ever more apparent as the Hunters of Fate finally meet with the Sisters whose shaping of destinies makes them both friend and foe to all they meet. There, Morigan's true calling as a Daughter of Fate is confirmed, born of Elemech and sister to Eean and Ealasyd. But the Sisters also reveal that the darkness overtaking Geadhain is more terrible than the anthropomorphized version of the Black Queen could have led them to believe; she is the Great Dreamer, Zionae, whose roots run deeper than anything in their world. She is devouring Geadhain, and even immortals cannot halt her frenzy. Their only hope is to return to the cradle where life began to find a trace of Zionae's fall from grace that might reveal a weakness. Despite the incredible losses they have incurred during their campaign to find the Sisters, Morigan and Caenith know that their destiny is to take up this mantle.

Recognizing that he, too, bears a burden for Geadhain's fate, weary Thackery strikes a bargain for time. As an old man nearing the end of his days, Thackery declined across the miles, an effect made even more glaring in the company of immortals and beings who are seemingly beyond death. Each night as the travelers rested, he was enveloped by a vigil of companions wary that each breath might be the one that ushered in the end. But to add time to one life, it must be taken from another's. And as a now youthful Thackery emerges from negotiations with the Sisters, the origins of his newfound years are unknown.

Mouse—seemingly unable to deny the dark roots that were nurtured during her life in Menos—also readily accepts a deal, albeit from the three Red Witches, that would see her avenge her father. She is so blinded by her grief that she fails to realize that even for the purest of hearts, it is all too easy to be led astray when the desire to exact revenge rears its head. There is always a price to pay for such caprice, whether in this realm or another, and early indications are that Mouse may pay dearly for acting as the messenger for a spirit of retribution.

Even knowing that much of what lies ahead is unchangeable, the Three Sisters pull at wefts and warps here and there, keeping the fabric of fate intact, but all the while subtly changing its pattern. They cannot help themselves from crafting deals designed to test the travelers' characters and push the limits of their virtues. Nor can they remain untangled from the affairs of beasts and men, even when their own existence may depend upon it. Even as sisters of fate, they make these bargains, largely unaware of the impacts they might have on the final tapestry for the future. But then again, these are not concerns for beings who are reborn as easily as a snake sloughs off its skin.

The only certainty that remains is that the Green Mother is angry, and What She Wills, She Wills...

Having partially lifted the veil of secrecy surrounding Morigan's place in the universe as a Daughter of Fate, the mysteries of the Black Queen, and even the dark revelation that Caenith's father is none other than Brutus, the stage is set in *Feast of Chaos* for our travelers to go beyond illusions and visions, to facing their foes up close. Still, as a blood moon rises over Geadhain, worries grow that Morigan might not live up to the savior status the Sisters have bestowed upon her. A shadow of hate is overtaking the realm, its gloom affecting even the impermeable willpower of the Sisters Three.

In their midst now, is Sorren—whose role in ushering in this immutable blackness leaves the Sisters conflicted about their hospitality in allowing him to recuperate under their auspices. What vestiges of his old life as a psychopath and murderer might remain within the mangled skin-suit of one who once acted as the vessel of Death is a mystery to all. And he is sent on his way, his external injuries not so much healed as stayed, while uncertainty remains as to whether his newly professed humanism is simply a guise to conceal his fevered and angry internal wounds. As a parting gift, for reasons unknown, the miscreant Ealasyd gives Sorren custody of three "old stones," whose providence and future utility are equally cloaked in obscurity.

Unaware of Sorren's resurrection, Morigan, Caenith, Mouse, Thackery, Talwyn, and the unlikeliest of allies Moreth of El have set their sights on a region whose shifting landscapes and mysterious creatures that populate its climes do honor to its name: Pandemonia. It is a land of dreams and nightmares incarnate, wherein a million manners of death exist. There, even those accustomed to wielding magik are left agog and aghast at its unpredictability. The borders bind this land in a perpetual spell that warps the laws of nature, rendering even the most skilled sorcerer virtually impotent. Survival in this land requires that most difficult and elusive of skills: the capacity to truly listen and humble oneself. Simply to survive, let alone thrive, travelers of Pandemonia must be able to filter out the din of the world—to distill from noise its greater meaning.

As they venture deeper into Pandemonia's frigid terrain, Morigan is newly besieged by visions of such ferocity that they leave her begging for the easement of her incessantly humming hive. For within this dream world, she has been transformed into a witness of, and prey to, a Dreamstalker. As the herald to Zionae, this hunter lives with Brutus in the physical world, as well as inhabiting that ethereal otherworld of blackness and potential that is Dream. Together these villains realize that to vanquish the Daughter of Fate and return Caenith to the protection of his father, they must find and capture an arkstone, one of Fate's cornerstones. In the dawning of the world, these wonderstones hurtled down to earth as a single meteorite forged from Zionae's essence before shattering into four pieces. They are known to work miracles beyond imagination and horror, but so too is their power easily corrupted.

Meanwhile, having absconded to Carthac, Erik and Lila temporarily safeguard themselves from the ever-expanding fields of battle by hiding as a sellsword and a peasant woman. But their newfound isolation is bittersweet; they find no joy in the meeting of flesh, and their passions play out painfully and joylessly as though a punishment for their crimes against Menos. Their lustful encounters are cloaked with Erik's anguish over his once-hidden desires and Lila's intense guilt over the holocaustic rampage she set in motion. But when the sanctity of their temporary refuge is violated and their identities exposed, everything changes. Their attempted escape sees Erik grievously injured, and Lila—reluctant as she is to use magik, knowing how cruel a path it has led her down—seeks to heal her lover. Little does she know that in knitting his wounds, she inadvertently weaves their essences together, enmeshing them as bloodmates. Bound together, Erik's strength surges, and Lila reclaims her former name, Lilehum, and her former strength.

The marriage of these two souls marks the terminus for the illusory spell Lila had cast upon Leonitis and Lowelia back in Eod. As all magik is born of, and powered by, emotion, the spell had been weakening with every moment of bonding between Erik and Lila. So in that peak moment of spiritual commingling, the incantation dissolves before an angry Magnus's eyes. Thus alerted to what Magnus perceives of as a betrayal of his and Lila's vows, he annuls what tatters remain of Lila's illusion and the two—soldier and servant—are restored to their erstwhile physical forms. The revelation to Gloriatrix that for lo these many weeks she has been speaking to impostors unleashes in her a fury that sees a tenuous truce with Magnus strained to the limits. Together, he and the Iron Queen agree to a bargain that would see Lila punished and Erik executed.

There are those, however, who are still entrenched in the detritus of Menos's fall, such as the siblings Aadore and Sean, whose miraculous survival is made all the more astonishing by the fact that they have emerged from the quaking waves of destruction that leveled Menos with a babe in arms. The landscape grows more treacherous by the minute, with ragged, infectious shadows of former beings mindlessly amassing as legions to fight for one of the many omnipotent alien forces seeking dominance in this war. The Queen of Bones, however, is no one's ally. For she is *Death* herself, and her swift resolution to the conflicts at hand would see all life transformed into ashes.

Joining their small but formidable contingent of warriors braced for battle against the source of Menos's dark infection are Aadore's bodyguard, Skar, a former mercenary whose physical dimensions harken back to a world where ogres roamed, and the man long-enamored of Aadore, Curtis. It becomes apparent to their compatriots that Sean and Aadore share a resilience toward the violent strain of infection that sees its victims transformed into monstrous undead slaves to the Dreamer of Death. They and the others are also left to wonder what other strengths their shared legacy may reveal that renders them immune to Death's powers. Their external fragility seems to belie an incredible inner strength. Sean's wounds are not strictly the by-products of a battle well-fought as a former soldier in the Ironguard. Rather, his many painful scars and aberrations are the product of torture beyond that which anyone could imagine and remain sane—the cicatrices from his incarceration by myriad fleshcrafters and demented men of medicine are fused to his soul. And despite a primarily peaceful past as handmaiden to the Lady El, Aadore is no coward, either, and steels herself to become a fighter alongside her brother.

Back in Pandemonia, Mouse, Talwyn, and Moreth are spirited away through dreams and somnolent magik—the tools of their supposed ally and Morigan's father, Feyhazir. They are taken away from the safety of their pack and into the regions ruled by Indigenous inhabitants of the region known as the Amakri. Here they must learn to abide by the rules of these people and discover the reason for Feyhazir's machinations. The hulking, blue, and horned Doomchasers—a unique and powerful race of the greater race of Pandemonian natives—are a people focused on treading the path toward reclaiming their place in this land. And to that end, Mouse's debt to the Red Witches comes due, and the being with whom Mouse must share her corporeal power makes his presence increasingly known. Feyhazir, the starry father of Morigan, begins regularly inhabiting Mouse's body, and without her consent.

Once, as a vessel in times immemorial and as an adoptive member of the Amakri, Feyhazir had shared with the fierce blue warriors a drink from a chalice, and with them made a covenant that gave them the strength to resist the influence of Zionae's and all other magik. For as soon discovered by the ever curious Talwyn, the Amakri's strength is waning, and quickly; children are being born plain as any man, without horns, scales, or a resistance to dark forces. The promise of the chalice is a restoration of the tribe to its former strength. Feyhazir, claiming to play peacemaker while acting as abductor, takes pains to appear to Talwyn and Moreth in Fionna's skin, and to commune with Morigan, to assure them of his intent to use her vessel to vanquish their common enemy. But Mouse's inability to recall Feyhazir's actions when in her fugue state leaves them with little to go on as to his trustworthiness. She cannot fight off Feyhazir's violations, and she feels those infractions changing her piece by piece, beyond tinges of gray appearing in her hair or small wrinkles about her face that appear after her possessions.

Newly pledged to assist in vanquishing the Black Queen, Moreth is one of the few who is able to navigate Pandemonia's terrain, and he becomes a valuable asset, adding to his already considerable contribution to the group in the form of tutelage on magik and control to the companions with whom they are now separated. The unexpected vulnerabilities of this once Menosian overlord are revealed to his traveling companions. While his proclivities induce cringes among those who lend an ear to his story, beneath the depravity lies a soul that still knows a simulacrum of love in the form of the blood eater Beatrice. His sexual sadism did not preclude him from a deep desire for comfort hard-won through years of inflicting pain on others who were—mostly—willing. The twisted creature that is Beatrice, a blood eater, was propitiously suited to meet his needs. But the ability to tame, or at least train, the blood lust within Beatrice through music and visitations to the Blood Pits, is not something that is shared with others of her kind, a lesson the Amakri encampment soon learns. And as Moreth teaches them of the true nature of these blood beasts, separated from her partner in bloodlust, Beatrice, now returned to Eod, stalks Alastair to reveal a near incomprehensible truth to him. The man whose dalliances numbered in the countless is forced to face a painful memory from the past—one that repudiates his long-held belief that he was infertile. In fact, a woman named Belle had the unique magikal physiology to propagate with an unnatural creature such as Alastair. The harrowing truth is that this woman—who eventually became one of Beatrice's victims and whose ghost now acts as a faint beacon of humanity within the blood eater—begat Alastair two sons, one of whom is none other than Galivad.

As Talwyn communes with the Amakri's leader, Pythius, he comes to believe that at the very least this people's intentions are honorable, even as his faith in Feyhazir's motives wavers. Through this cultural exchange, Moreth and Mouse also grow to more fully appreciate the scholar as they realize that his desire for knowledge extends beyond intellectual curiosity. They learn that his intellectual curiosity is both a blessing and a curse. His mind's absorption of information is pathological; he has little control over the information that filters into his mind, forcing him into an incessant state of analysis and calculation. The strength of will required to harness it all often pushes him beyond his emotional capacity. But even Talwyn's intellectual prowess cannot wholly forewarn them of the fact that Feyhazir's promises are predicated on deceit; the chalice they have long sought is cursed, and he has manipulated others into coveting the arkstones for his own nefarious purposes.

Elsewhere, with distance in space but not spirit between them, the rest of Morigan's pack continues its journey to Eatoth. This quest, bestowed upon them by her father who claims the city will be under siege from Brutus, is his justification for cleaving their fellowship in two. However, Morigan is beginning to resent the callous manipulations of Dreamers, increasingly believing that her father isn't too different from his flock. Meanwhile, Adam struggles with the beast within and without, shamed that while he is considered one of the pack, he is not *of* the pack—no great sorcerer or warrior. Yet as time wears on, a newly developed talent within the young changeling rears its head. Desperate for a way to connect with his adoptive pack, Adam had previously begged Elemech to bestow upon him the gift of communication. Little did he expect at that time, however, that his gift would also allow him to decipher and communicate in languages once completely unknown to him. This realization provides him not only with a greater connection with his compatriots, but renders him an invaluable ally in working to achieve their greater goals.

Their arrival at the glittering city of Eatoth takes all the travelers aback. It is an expansive vista of prismatic glass, its towering panes reflecting sunlight onto the landscape in every direction, concealing the dark foundations upon which the city was established. Once there, the secret behind the Herald's resurrection in darkness is pulled from deep within Eatoth's bowels. Its Keeper, Ankha, is so attended with hubris that she believes she holds dominion over everyone and anything that exists within the city walls. And so it is only after much resistance that she is forced to explain that Zionae's consort and Herald—Morigan's Dreamstalker, Amunai—was her sister. Once a woman of peace, she had trained to be a Keeper alongside her. When Amunai had professed her expanding views on the equality of all and the Green Mother's one true voice, her sister deemed her a heretic. She punished Amunai by killing her unborn child and mutilating and banishing her lover. It was in these darkest of moments that the Black Queen engulfed the former Keeper, embracing her with dark promises of revenge and shielding her from the pain of her past. So now, not only is Amunai an accomplice to the Black Queen's rampage, but she is an assassin with her sights locked in on the sister who tore from her all the joy she had ever known.

But the Herald's goals extend beyond sororicide, as Ankha is also the unlawful keeper of an arkstone. As with all of the self-declared "cultured"

Amakri—these grotesque technomagikophiles who wall themselves away from Pandemonia's influence in great bastions of comfort, who have built an entire religion to sustain their hubris—Ankha's abuse and misuse of the wonderstones has made her a clear target. Realizing this, and that Brutus will be the weapon to strike Eatoth, Morigan and Caenith forge a plan to bind Brutus in technomagikal chains or, failing that, to end him completely, in order to protect Eod and the world beyond. Alas, on the eve in which they gather to await Brutus and to execute their plans, Amunai appears and overtakes Ankha's body. In those moments incarnated in flesh, Amunai challenges everything Morigan believes to be true about her role in Fate's plans. Not least of which is the assertion that Morigan herself is responsible for the city's fall, by weakening her sister's will through her incessant prodding of the past and hunt for the truth—it was through those kinks, formed by Morigan, that Amunai at last slipped into the Keeper's mind. Knowing they have but moments to act, Morigan and Caenith are forced to kill Ankha in an effort to banish Amunai and protect the arkstone. But their efforts come too late, and Amunai—the Lady of Wind, she calls herself— escapes as an incorporeal ghost with the stone in tow.

Lilehum, in the meantime—through coordination via farspeaking stones with Lowe, Leonitis, Rowena, and Dorothy—has fomented a rebellion. Lilehum's evolving identity, one that is increasingly predatory, is now also entwined with that of an ancient relic found on the ancient Menosian ship she and Erik used to escape Carthac. It is an orb she calls the Mind—an entity whose genius connects her to an expansive network of knowledge spanning all manner of space and time. All the while, her spiritual metamorphosis is being mirrored by a physical transformation. Lilehum is changing at a molecular level into a being whose fearsomeness is bound up not only in her resolve to denounce and punish those men who would subjugate women and the marginalized, but in her newly discovered reptilian form, replete with poison sacs and feline-like incisors. She is emboldened to advance against the man who betrayed her; she sees clearly that Magnus's rape was, in fact, what drove her into a madness that saw her overtaken by the powers of the Death, which loosed upon Menos the destruction from Taroch's Arm.

In the nick of time, and just before Eod's gates are sundered, Aadore and the others arrive at Eod to inform Gloriatrix of all they have witnessed; their revelation of a new and wicked Dreamer's role in the destruction of Menos brings with it the possibility of reprieve for Lila and Erik. But as with all political negotiations, success is always predicated on the existence of good faith between the parties. This is something that is sorely lacking on both sides, and there can be little question of the presence of backroom machinations on both sides of the table. Gloriatrix's longing to see a Geadhain bereft of Immortals is hardly in line with Magnus's vision for himself or the realm. As Lilehum's troops breach the city of Eod's walls, a moment of silence, of listening, allows a peace between Erik, Magnus, and his former queen that holds back the fog of another impending war.

In the east, however, the theft of the arkstone sees another storm brewing quickly behind, promising to breach any peace that might be found in such moments.

"Mercy's Mirror"
I came across a slash of blue
Under shade of ancient yew
Silver glittered most playfully
A trail, which I could see
I followed the coin,
To a rasping shadow,
A highwayman
Fallen, blood reddening the ground
"No further," he said
All trembles and aches
Gashes and shakes
His robbery had only stolen from him
His life
Soon, at least
"Will you play for me, as I die?" asked he
Mine instrument declared my talent
I'd held lute like blade,
Whilst making my approach
A song seemed cleaner than my minding
—to take his coin, without a song
Thus, I sat and I crooned
Plucking every fair tune
For this fading soul and the moon
To which his light slowly rose
A twained star gone home
Till it was dark
And silent
I closed his eyes, kissed his cheek
Not a tear of mine did creep,
As I picked red coins from the ground
I wouldn't feel shame
Nor ponder his blame
For I wished for an end
Selfsame

—From the private journal of Kericot

BEFORE THE WAR

The horses were beaten—puffing, bowlegged beasts more likely to be made into meals by their barbaric riders than to be further burdened by the journey home. Winter shrieked against the helms of these conquerors, seven men and one beast of a man in a cape of wolf's fur who seemed as if he would break his shivering horse. All were mantled in furs and warmed further by the meat and sinew of warriors; none more than the great rider, though. He who had thrown his hood back to the weather so that he could scowl at the stubbornness of it; his face was hard, chipped, and so glowering as to render ugly whatever stateliness his heavy features might have held. A simple iron circle of rule ran across his brow, though his power in the earthly realm was more manifest through his posture, through the ungloved hand that held most of his horse's bridle—small as strings in his great fist. A tiny shivering woman was lost in the saddle behind him. She had been blindfolded and tied at the wrists, and her fear would have run warm down her legs had her kidnappers fed or nourished her properly during the long ride north.

They had gathered in a rimed pass dripping with icicles and crackling like a land of broken glass. Shadows, clotted and moving from sheets of snow, swirled through the air in monstrous currents. Even here, beneath the weight of mountains glaring down into the crevasse, the wind reached. It could not be stopped, this rage, the anger of Mother Winter at their having pushed so far into her domain. There was farther to go, however, if the legends of where the manifestation of Winter—her witch, priestess, and avatar—sat upon a throne of ice were true. But they needn't travel that far, the men had been told by their master; here they could summon her, too, in a site of the old magik of the land. They couldn't see this place, though, until their master, kin to all and lord of the North—Kinlord—pointed a mighty finger across at a tiny opening in the ice walling the crevasse.

There, he said in mindspeak, and his soldiers heard him and spurred their horses.

As they galloped, their captive had the sense of passing from the cold into a quieter passage in which the men dismounted. She was almost thrown off the horse by the hands and strength of the Kinlord. He barked at her to march, which she did. A knowing captive, she righted her standing before she was thrown around. A wise captive, she realized that they had come to an ending—for once these men were slow, reverent, and plodding, not the frenzied beasts they'd formerly been. An ending—the end of the road. Facing death wasn't as difficult as the starvation, insults, and abuse she'd suffered being dragged across the Northlands by these barbarians. Sweetly, she thought of her life back in Valholom, regretting most that she hadn't settled for rosy-cheeked, gin-loving Seamus, thinking him and his offer of a life as a cobbler's wife droll. No, she had decided upon a better life and greater opportunities working as a charwoman for the Kinlord's staff. What a life that had turned out to be: a sack over her head while sleeping in the night, kidnapped, and soon to be dead. They stopped, and she waited for the moment when he would end her life, swearing that she wouldn't scream when the knife or sword brought her to the next world.

What is this place, Kinlord? asked one of his mindspeaking warriors.

Their master could sense the awe in each of them, pumping through them like the lust they often shared with each other. They were men of rude passion and carnality, creatures of his basest instincts, and he wondered how much they understood of this site of ancient promise and ritual. The warriors understood the scope of this sculpted hollow, where Winter's bluster came as a whimper through the passage where they'd left their mounts. Toward the back of the chamber, they noticed the layered altar, like flat and smaller plates of obsidian laid over themselves. Closer, and everywhere across the floor and recesses of the place, they saw the scattered relics, trapped under snow as an ancient trove under dust and cobwebs, but they had no idea as to what culture these carved sticks—some quite large—baskets, and masks that looked like animal faces belonged. Strange, primitive-seeming drawings they noticed on the ceilings, too, though deciphering the exact images beneath the ages of murky ice was impossible without an ice pick and time, neither of which they had. Their master's urgency was their urgency, his blood their blood, his desires their desires, and while they might have wanted to know more about this site, their master had decided they need not.

The Kinlord startled his captive with his grumbling, angry-bear voice; so much of her captivity had been spent in dreadful silence, but this was no better.

"Hear me, Spirit of Winter," he said, throwing back his cloak, revealing a dagger more fitting as a sword in the hands of men. He drew forth the blade. "We have come north, as far as we can go without stepping upon your sacred lands. My father has passed, his remains—" The Kinlord stumbled on the word as his father still existed in a cursed state of existence. But the crown had been passed, and his father was dead in memory. He continued. "He has been buried in the Halls of our Ancestors. He drinks in the afterlife with heroes of Vallistheim. However, he has told me all that I know to be kin to all and lord of this land. I know of the children I must have: three. I know of the sacrifices that I must make: three. Without doubt, I stand and declare that there is nothing—no sacrifice—too great for me to rule this land. In the tradition of old, through which the first Kinlord of the North offered his own flesh and blood, do I bring you flesh and blood to anoint our sacrament."

Don't scream, thought the captive, as the Kinlord's shadow fell upon her. She choked on that pride a little when swift, cold, then burning steel was drawn across her throat. She collapsed, and heat and life bled from her quickly, forming crimson veins on the ground. The Kinlord's men watched the patterns and stared at the whorls and gentle mist hiding the reaches of the chamber, searching for whatever force their master had sought to summon here. The warriors strained their animal senses—the senses of men augmented through blood-rites and magik—and all perceived it together: a creak, a shuffle, a footstep. The creaking withered the balls of these frostborn warriors, and even shuddered the Kinlord, for a doorway had opened between this world and the beyond, and something had taken a delicate step through. They drew blades, instinctively, and waited to see what this creature was.

"Put down your blades, outcasts of Menos," said a voice from behind the altar, a distortion in the mist.

It sounded female, with a tone that buzzed in their heads. So, too, did sudden, frenzied visions attack them like pecking crows: of snakes circling a green globe—could that be a world, their world, which sages said was round?—of a golden-haired woman eating a glass apple then contorting and hissing at them, of a spray of blood over snow, all while the thundering of murderous combat rumbled in their ears. Even the Kinlord gasped once the visions and auditory hallucinations left him spinning. Wary, he did not call forth the creature lingering behind the altar. He had the sense that this creature wasn't so much hiding as refusing to reveal itself, and there were other shapes now lurking around the chamber—monkeylike and multitudinous, speckling the whiteness, these pygmy demons with hunched backs, long arms, and smiles filled with gnashing teeth so bright that they shone—spreading and growing quicker than he could count them. The Kinlord waved down his men's weapons. Bowing to a knee, he spoke to the Spirit of Winter.

"I have come as my forefathers have come," he said, "and offered you this first of many sacrifices for the treaty you and I shall swear."

"This is not what I want," said the spirit. "Three children I am promised. Three children you must give, their blood spilled in this chamber where your forefathers first outwitted the original keepers of the North. That has always been the bargain."

"You shall have these children, once they are born."

"Do you know *what* you offer?" The chamber rumbled and groaned, loosing snow and ice. The demons in the dark shuffled, and for a moment he heard their baboonish howling. "A child is a seed watered by love and time. You would strip your tree of any fruit. You will live a life without kindness."

"Kindness." The Kinlord snorted. "Three lives for three times my lifespan is a fairer bargain."

"You will live longer than that," warned the spirit.

Pondering, the Kinlord considered his greatness, his legacy and legend, and also thought of the glistening pudding into which his father had degraded at the end, as his power—the power once bestowed by this very ritual—had passed from parent to child. They'd had to pool father into an urn, and his swimming matter lay now in the undercroft. The Kinlord remembered an eye looking out from the fleshy stew and winking, before the urn was sealed. Was it worth it? Three centuries of supreme might and lordliness for an eternity of suffering? Could he bloody his hands with his own children's essence as easily as he had that nameless serving wench dead on the ice nearby? Could he not say no, here and now? What would that do to him?

"Three of your beloved sons," demanded the spirit. "That is what I take in exchange for your power: your sons and the love you might bear with them. Accept, or...*return* my power to me, to the North, and live and die as a man should."

He would not die as a man should. He was a warrior, a giant. He would die as a conqueror. And what was a son but another of his soldiers who happened to have come from his own seed?

"I offer my sons, my seeds, and my love," said the Kinlord, rising and haughty. "I need none of it when I am lord and king of all."

"As you wish," said the spirit, with a nuance of sadness that this corrupt lord would never discern. He had continued the cycle, and the North would swallow another lifetime of his blood and sin. But as always, and as the spirit faded and allowed her raging demons to howl and beat their chests at this new king of the land, she held on to a hope—that cycles would be broken, wiser choices made, and one day a sacrifice, the right sacrifice, would save them all.

PROLOGUE

F rom the snowy cave atop Alabion's highest throne of rock, there shone an unearthly light. A hum too could be heard, as well as felt, through the whole of the great edifice, and its tremble resonated far and wide—down through the bastion of stone, into the soil and the bones of the animals who walked upon the earth, who paused in their scavenging amid the bramble-and-boulder garden below the aerie of the Sisters Three. Scared of the great magik they felt, these creatures abandoned their foraging and predations to scamper off into woods.

Elsewhere, deep within the Sisters' labyrinth, the buzzing and emanation of light had grown strong. It was a greenish radiance tinged with heat, as ominous as a spell bringing forth a plague or the conjuring of something forbidden. Deeper still, in the hallowed sanctum of the Sisters Three, nothing could be clearly discerned among the throbbing fantasia of emerald magik and blurred, twisting shapes. Still, three presences, notable for their stature of large to small and humanoid semblance, surrounded the silver ripple of what might have been a font, and from these three Sisters was born—in ribbons of ether and green fire—the shuddering hum and thunderous crackle of awesome magik. Whatever the invocation, fair or foul, it ended with a bang that shook the oldest rock in Alabion. Outside the natural fortress, snow and rubble sloughed from the mountain and assaulted the forest. Animals and trees were crushed, and the land trembled before finally grumbling to a hush. The spell had failed again.

"May I have my hands back, please?" asked Ealasyd, as she tried to wriggle her fingers out of her sisters' painful grasps. Together, the three stood in a triangle at the edge of Elemech's witch-water pool. Their abode looked as though it had been ransacked, as if by a hurricane; baskets were strewn everywhere, cots had been tossed into heaps of sheets and straw, a shelf of arcane wares had tipped over—its jars shattered and precious contents scattered. Only their great stone table and immovable benches had successfully weathered the wrath of their spell. "Sisters," she continued, "I did as you asked and concentrated. You know that isn't easy for me. Everything is such a terrible mess now, and since I can tell from your sour expressions that you two aren't going to use your own hands to play maid, give me back mine. Please."

Eean and Elemech released her and waved her off. While Ealasyd intended to tidy up, a piece of chalk rolling in the debris distracted her. She claimed the chalk instead of a broom and wandered over to scrawl drawings on the limestone table, which had been unmoved by their failed spell. Elemech knelt by her pool and retreated into studying the intimations that fluttered in the mists wafting off the water; to her, failure was becoming par for the course. In the recent days since she'd witnessed the catastrophic events in Pandemonia—namely, the foiling of her daughter's efforts by that wicked Keeper, Amunai—she'd grown gloomier and gloomier.

Watching her frown from a distance, and pondering Elemech's sadness, Eean was certain that her sister's hair had grown darker, her frown somehow deeper, and that her eyes had now hardened and sharpened into splinters of green glass. Alone in that moment, abandoned by her sisters, Eean stood for a while, watching her Sisters give in to despair and feeling her frustration rising to a boil. She would not become forgetful like Ealasyd, or beaten down like Elemech. She was the foundation of their family. She was the source of their wisdom and courage. Surely there must be another way to still achieve something they had never before dreamed possible in their eternal lives: freeing themselves from the invisible shackles of Alabion.

"Elemech, we must try again," said Eean, walking a few steps before placing her hand upon Elemech, who shook, faintly, with anger.

"We tried, Eean. We tried with all of our might and magik, and we failed. It is our destiny to watch the world, to influence it, yet never to shape the clay ourselves. To have even considered we had a right to defy that order was purest hubris, as vainglorious as the Lords of Carthac were when they struck the White Mother. They were cursed and turned into hungry, bloodlusting things for their sacrilege, those hideous Kinlords—living monster-men. Likewise have we seen our darkest selves in the Red Witches of the woods, and may Mother help us all if we birth a second brood. No more. I shall watch my waters. Ealasyd will craft her toys. And *you* will wander the woods. But we shall never do so beyond the bars of our cell. Such is the fate to which we are bound. You should seek no other."

"I do not accept that, Sister." Eean knelt and snatched Elemech's hand and pulled her to her feet. She forced her into a stare, her gaze bearing twice the sting of any of Elemech's disgruntlement. "Our shadows, the Furies, have left these woods. The Red Witches, those vilest aspects of ourselves, have allied with Aghna, and you know what red monster she serves: the Dreamer of War himself, come to feast on the blood spilled by man and Dreamer alike. If Death does not eradicate Eod, and if Brutus somehow fails, then those witches and Aghna's army will succeed in the genocide of man. We can stand by and watch no longer. We cannot simply plant our suggestions and wait centuries for our garden to once more bear rotten fruit. There's no time left. There will be no more gardens. No more chances or centuries. We have to act. We have to become soldiers in this war."

Elemech sneered. "Have we not done enough? All our meddling and tricks! If we are no longer Mother's favorites, if we are no longer needed to guide her flocks and tend her lands, then we should allow ourselves to pass as all things do—into dust."

"Yes, Sister, such has been our way." A memory came to Eean then, of three children, crawling in the dirt like worms. She remembered the stench of ripped earth, the dripping sound of water, and a great fuzzy warmth, as though a fire were lit and near, though she saw no light. They'd been born from a placenta of moss, muck, and mulch. "Our creed since a birth that none of us can wholly remember. Do you remember anything of it? For I do. Pieces, at least. I've seen us crawling in this cave. Over time, I have assembled, reasoned together, the fragments of a code of duty and sisterhood to which we are bound, a reason for our being—to serve the Green Mother who made us. For what other meaning could we have? What else would be our purpose? What would distinguish us from the mindless golems—men of mud and muck—that sorcerers conjure to serve them? Is that what we are, Elemech? Automatons? Brainless creatures bidding the Will of our maker? Is it?"

Elemech flinched and stayed silent.

"As we've seen with the Kings," continued Eean, "destinies are not immutable. Bonds that once seemed eternal can be broken. As Amunai has shown us, as your daughter has shown us, the future cannot be faultlessly foretold by even the grandest seer. The wild elements of free will and chance are each forces that can devour all certainty. Is it not time to become such forces ourselves?"

"Your words sound like heresy," hissed Elemech.

Eean spat back. "Heresy against what? We have no religion but what falsities we have purposed for ourselves!"

"This isn't you," said Elemech, softening. "It is not our role to intervene. I was remiss in having allowed you to even suggest something as rash as breaking our chains to the forest, to Mother. And why? To betray everything that we are?"

"And what are we, Sister?" asked Eean.

The silence trembled, as did Elemech's lip, though no reply came forth.

"Who are we?" continued Eean, grasping her sister's shoulder. "Earthworms? Golems? Sisters? Witches? We are ghosts to our own world. We have been given life and power beyond reckoning, and yet as I look back over our lives, memories that I once held dear seem like echoes of real life. We love each other, though we've never had to test that love. We love our world, though we've never risen to defend it. So what are we, Sister? Other than ghosts and whisperers?"

Rage flashed through Elemech, and she threw off her sister's hand. "Morigan has done this to you! Her magik. It's infected us all!"

Eean wrestled with her sister a while and, being the stronger one, soon forced her into an uncomfortable hug. She whispered, "Indeed. But it is the best kind of infection: one of love, bravery, and sympathy. We no longer need to envy these traits in others; we can embody them. Your daughter fights alone. She needs you and us, her family, more than ever before. Would you abandon her again? For you know how close to breaking she will be. In fact, were it not for that one wretched vision that you shared with me regarding her fate, I might not have changed so greatly and deeply, or in so short a time, myself."

Days ago, it had come to Elemech—the vision. She hadn't been seeking a prophecy. On the contrary, she'd been sulking by her pool and pickling herself with wine from their ever-flowing jug. She'd been fighting a slowly creeping toxic mix of despair, restlessness, and a yearning for her daughter. Numb and lost in this emotional fever, the vision had entered her head like a rusted nail. She'd jolted to her feet, thrown her drink, and screamed.

A woman stands far away on a hazy horizon. Sharp rocks and buried dunes rise up around here, black and curved as the talons of a great eagle now dead and lying on its back, partly entombed by the sand. Murky clouds flood the skies, while breaths of thick dust tumble over a land that rasps as it decays. A jagged point ruptures the razor-backed ridges dominating the distance; perhaps it is a tower, though what lord or lady would ever dwell within is likely to be avoided. Given the sandy smoke and ruin, there is the sense that the whole world has been burned, then doused; to further bolster this notion, the air is rank with wet ash. However, there is no heat source apparent that could have caused a fire. It could certainly not have been sparked by the cold, gray, unholy sun that struggles to light this land.

What is this place? Elemech wonders. Perhaps it is a realm between realms, for it is too surreal to be real. Indeed, and on the heels of that thought, she senses it is a limbo, a border between what is and what is not.

There is enough reality, though, in the expression on Morigan's face: a contortion of grief reined in by pure grit. A mother knows the moods of her babe—no matter their age. A mother who is also a seer, however, feels the same wrenching pull as any parent more deeply and with every nerve, as if strings have been made of her guts and plucked like some abhorrent Mortalitisi cello. Morigan's sorrow is a hollowness so deep that it has gone beyond grief. Elemech knows her daughter has lost everything: her bloodmate, her friends, her world. Elemech wills herself forward, as though her spirit could embrace this phantom of her daughter. But Morigan flashes away into a stream of time and space like a school of silver fish, and even if Elemech were to Will herself into a chase, she knows Morigan will soon tread roads no power can reach. Morigan shall go beyond death and time. She will never return.

Eean shook Elemech who, given her horrified expression, had surely been revisiting the original haunting vision. "Answer me!"

"We have no idea what the vision means," said Elemech, unsure and defensive.

"We do," muttered Eean. "No bloodmate...No soul-bound friends. Not even a living creature in that realm of dust and decay you saw. Just a woman who is more ghost than we, lost in a place that might as well be nowhere. Whether this is the cost of the war, or another price she must pay for being a hero, everything has been taken from her. The Thule who was among us taught me that men don't have to be selfish for themselves, as we are—hiding away while the world crumbles. Thackery taught me that you can be selfish for another. Which is what we must do. We must protect your daughter, our Sister, and the seed of hope that we brought into the world. Words and prophecies are not enough. We must stand with her."

The two Sisters did stand at that moment, and then held each other at arm's length, exchanging frowns and twists of emotion that ran like currents between them. Drawn by their intensity, Ealasyd drifted to her Sisters. She pried apart their grips and claimed their hands again. Ealasyd, the innocent, who remembered nothing, who was purity itself, was somehow able to recall the importance of the spell she and her Sisters had tried only sands ago. They'd wanted to free themselves from the wood. They'd wanted to help Morigan. This truth grew as if it were a mystic seed growing into a tree of fire in her mind. While her Sisters fought their weaknesses and indecision, little Ealasyd determined what was to be done.

"It's time to free ourselves, Sisters," said Ealasyd. "I'm ready. I think that Mother is, too. She's quiet, uneasy, as we are. One more time. Let's ask. Nicely. Let's take our fates—our lives—into our hands. I'm not afraid."

Neither were her Sisters, they realized. Their pulses raced from excitement, not fear. The three shut their eyes, squeezed tight their hands, and Willed their desire to the Wood. Once more, the sun shone in the Sisters' abode. Alabion fell silent—utterly and truly still—for a beat. When the animals breathed again, when the trees swayed in the reborn wind, it was with fervor and passion, with *freedom*.

PART I

I

THE MEDICINE OF FORGIVENESS

I

"**M**uriel! Not so far, please," called Simon.

Raising his hand to act as a visor against the sun, he squinted to find her. He was doubtful that his daughter would heed him, though she couldn't be faulted for her carefree behavior given the magnificence of the day. Even though winter was supposedly howling away somewhere in Central Geadhain, the beaches down from the port of Taroch's Arm were year-round, among the finest in the land. Great stretches of warm, white sands rolling beneath him had demanded he bare his feet. A sweet and stringent breeze blew in from the east. And so much sunshine surrounded him that everything was encircled by halos, as though kissed by the divine. Simon's vision had been reduced to a haze.

He squinted at a nearby wall of shattered rock speckled with fragments of emerald green; it lay far enough from the River Feordhan's great blue tongue that it would never be licked. Simon wondered how the wall had been created, and if it had ever been part of the ancient clay hills into which Taroch's Arm—that second embankment looming beyond the black wall towering over the beach—was built. They seemed to be of different ages entirely—different elements, even. The fragmented wall's stones were densely dark and seemingly igneous, not like the sedimentary formations that surrounded Taroch's Arm. Indeed, the formations seemed almost to have been unearthed and thawed from the legendary Long Winter.

As a geologist, Simon often pondered the differing lithologies of the foundation here and beyond in Taroch's Arm whenever he and his daughter came to the beach. However, he'd never gotten around to actually taking a sample of the wall—not even a smaller fragment. This morning, as he did whenever curiosity tugged at him, he decided against it. The black wall was old, he decided, older than Taroch's Arm, and from an age in which nature, not man, had held dominion over Geadhain. As a scientist he preferred to examine fossilized mysteries; he rarely wanted to participate as a subject in active wonders. Perhaps his old friend from college, Tal, would have leapt at the opportunity, but he had never been as brave.

However, the mystery as to where his daughter had run off was certainly a concerning one. Again he called for her, and Muriel's high and excited shriek echoed back to him. Simon swung his sandals as he sauntered toward the radiant silhouette that waded and splashed along the shore up ahead. The first thing he did upon reaching his daughter was lead her out of the shallows. A father's primary instinct was one of safety, and he had to be twice as diligent since Muriel had no mother to compensate for any of his own potential negligence.

Whenever he glanced at his daughter, he felt the spirit of his departed wife; it was in his child's laugh, her auburn hair, the stare that twinkled when she was amused. However, he admitted that Muriel's tanned complexion and haleness—still slighter than a boy's—came from his side of the genetic trade. Supposedly, there was old Swannish blood in his veins, which accounted for his persistent beard and the well-placed hirsuteness of his chest, forearms, and legs. Ideally, Muriel wouldn't be burdened with those particular traits and instead might inherit her mother's voluptuousness, once she'd added another ten summers to her dozen.

"Papa, why are you staring at me?" asked Muriel. Her hazel eyes widened fishlike, and she frantically wiped at her cheeks and brow. "Is there something on my face? Sand? Seaweed? A lady is nothing without her looks."

Simon laughed and assured her that her countenance was impeccable, then insisted that a proper lady was about much more than her looks. She blew him a kiss and began to hunt for shells in the sand. Simon plopped himself down on the beach, keeping a lazy watch on his daughter while propped on his elbows. Muriel was patrician with her play. She paused at intervals to ask her invisible friends to "behave," to straighten her two-piece solari suit and shawl, or to shake the sand from her glittering wide-brimmed hat—an accoutrement that was adorned with rainbow-colored glass beads, and befitting a mad duchess. Simon couldn't recall whence the glitzy hat had been purchased.

Muriel's obsession with society and "ladyisms" had soared to new heights since he'd been able to afford a finishing school for her, but he'd never placed such suggestions in her head. Some women were naturally inclined toward lace, restrained laughter, coiffed hair, and powdered faces. Of all men, he would not compel his child to conform to the trappings of any gender. She'd simply gravitated toward these comforts—possibly because she was familiar with her mother's proclivities for perfumes and dresses. Or perhaps she'd picked up on her father's, though as parents he and Mary had been careful to shield their child from bedtime activities.

He missed Mary. The loss created a dull throb of pain he carried with him every hourglass. She hadn't judged him, but rather loved him *for* his tastes. When she'd caught him plain as a criminal under a spotlight in her closet, wearing her garters and uncomfortable shoes, she had only smiled. There'd been no wrath, no decrying of betrayal. Indeed, she'd been grateful to learn that her intuition regarding his moments away and secret-keeping weren't related to another woman. Well, perhaps in a sense it was—the woman he'd wanted to be. It became their secret, another reason to love what made the other special. Thereafter, Mary had always told him, "I'm the luckiest woman in Geadhain, for I have a sister, a mistress, and a husband in one."

For a time, drifting through memories of his wife was as pleasant as watching his child's play, or the gentle beat of surf onto sand. Then the crimson flashes of his last moments with Mary threatened to ruin his calm. Simon kept them at bay for as long as he could with kinder remembrances of her smile, her violet perfume, or the feel of her—the silky graze of her fingers upon his chest. He loved her too much to allow memories of her to be darkened by her savage murder. Although, even as he claimed this imperturbability, another self—a forgotten self—sat coiled in the corner of his skull. There, an emaciated, mad-eyed, and ghoulish version of him clutched an improbably long, curved dagger in each hand and muttered about finding the man with the two-colored stare. At that moment, Simon heard that inner demon whispering, and unwittingly followed his lead through a doorway into his deepest, darkest memories.

"Mary?" shouts Simon.

Riverton, a place once so familiar, has abruptly become both bewildering and grotesque: the lights strung between masts glare down at Simon like floating milky eyes, the permanent pall from witchroot smoke feels as smothering as a pillow upon his face, the cheese and wine laid out on their table smell as sharp and foul as vinegar; around them, the circus of people and music seems violently animated. Simons feels as if he spins in the center of a cackling funhouse of horrors. Where is Mary? She had been there a moment ago, in the distance just beyond the eatery's cheap metal fence. Now she's vanished. Why had she risen from their meal so abruptly? Who was that cloaked and shadowy figure she'd spoken to before becoming lost in the crowd? Simon, trembling, places down the napkin he's been clutching, pushes back his plate, and stands before helping his tiny daughter off her seat.

"Where's Mama?" asks Muriel—she's only just learned to speak, and the innocence of her fear makes her question all the more jarring.

Simon snatches up his daughter and clutches her to his chest. An animal can sense the presence of doom, and suddenly, Simon has such nausea inside of him. He's sure that Muriel feels it as well, though at least she doesn't cry as they begin to scour the outdoor marketplace. Simon stumbles into tables, spilling people's drinks. He nudges his broad shoulders into bearded, chip-toothed brutes who are standing around drinking ale, men who would've nudged him back none too kindly if not for the second glance at his child. At the exit of the eatery, he argues with the maître-d' about his wife, who must have walked right past him. The man claims to have seen nothing and turns his back to Simon. On his way out into the thoroughfare, Simon kicks over a street-beggar's can of coins. The scrawny man cries out and barks at Simon, who apologizes, squats, and hastily tries to collect the man's scattered wealth while holding his daughter and spastically craning his neck back and forth for signs of Mary.

"Wot you lookin' fer?" says the beggar. "Stop messing wiv me coins!"

Indeed, Simon is only scattering silver about, returning little of it to the can. "I'm sorry. My wife. I am looking for my wife," he replies.

"My Mama," says Muriel.

Muriel's charm warms the old beggar, and he gives her a gummy grin. "Wot she look like? Pretty like you?"

"Prettier," says Muriel. "In a red dress. A lady's dress. She looks like a queen, my Mama. A red queen."

"Oh, her." The old man points a yellowed fingernail toward an alleyway momentarily obscured by foot traffic. As the passersby clear, Simon sees a narrow lane driven between two tall black ships snugly parked next to each other. It looks like a portal into the afterlife, and Simon's stomach inexplicably drops. The beggar continues nattering as Simon lurches up and crosses the wooden road. Simon makes it into the alley, and his daughter clings to him—her head buried against him—as they wander a place evocative of a haunted port: Riverton and its collage of naval refuse, ships, bilges, and barges, wherein constricted paths such as the one he now wanders can slither deep into underbellies of crime. Much is quiet but for the subliminal sloshing that occurs beneath the great deck upon which all of Riverton is built. He can hear nothing but wood's groan and water's whisper. He can see nothing more ominous than *the suggestions of maritime relics such as crates, spooled rope, and barrels. He sees no dim wifely shadow. Perhaps the beggar was mistaken.*

There is a blaring wet shriek. "Gaah!"

The scene Simon then enters, running, will only ever reassemble as a montage of shattered memories. After chasing the scream, he arrives deeper down the alley. A gleam of moonlight or radiance from Riverton's strung-up lighting has slipped between the ships. But such pitiable light is still enough to see fresh red paint glistening across the boardwalk. The paint is oozing from a wrapped, heavy twist of fabric, like a sopping crimson dishrag wrung into a tube, lying on the boardwalk. It's the hunch of the shape, what could be shoulders, and the single shoe tossed nearby—his wife's, one that he's squeezed into before—that identifies Mary's body. From the smell, he knows she has to be dead; blood and shit and fear clog his nose. Simon's body turns as cold as Mary's will soon be. His body convulses, propelling him to crawl on two knees and one hand toward his wife. Muriel stays buried against his body, clung like a barnacle, twisting his tunic into knots—bless the Kings she does not look, or knows not to. He can't cry; his brain has separated from his body and will not bring logic to this situation. When he reaches Mary and turns her, and sees her blood-speckled face—her now cataract-like stare—the awful, unavoidable reality finally slams into him.

He chokes on a sob. He begins rocking over his wife's body and holding their whimpering child. Simon glares at the moon, then at the swirling dark gathered past the scene of the body, demanding with all his soul a reason for this insanity. An answer arrives; a man stares back at him from the blackness. Simon sees only his face: thin, vulpine. He is hooded, though the eyes, one an emerald and one a sapphire, are an indelible and striking trait. That look will be a wonder and a torment for Simon in all his years to come. Whoever this watcher is, he beholds Simon for a beat, then mumbles, "I..."

Simon waits for more.

"I did not mean for this," the stranger adds.

Simon whispers to his child to be still and quiet, to keep her eyes shut. He places Muriel, sobbing, onto the tacky ground. He leaps with the ferocity of a Swannish warrior toward the man. But the blue-and-green-eyed shadow has moved without moving, like a ghost or a nightmare's illusion, and vanished. Alas, Simon's nightmare is not one he can wake from, and he knows he must turn, step over his wife's corpse, and collect his daughter. He doesn't know what to say as he returns to his shivering child. In fact, simply touching her shoulder shatters him like he's made of crystal. He falls, and on the sloppy ground he remains, curled around Muriel, holding her fragile body with bloodied hands, and whispering, quite wrongly, that all is well.

Simon resurfaced from the memory. Perhaps his remembrances were the cause, but the day seemed suddenly darker. Time had passed, and a chill had crept over the beach. A stink, too, had blown in from the Feordhan: sour and wet, as from seaweed and sewage. Simon crinkled his nose and perked up to scan the waterfront. A few threatening thunderheads floated in the sky, and more appeared to be moving in from the west. Simon's skin prickled, and he retrieved the light shirt he'd tucked into his waistband and threw it on. The shirt didn't repel much of the cold, which felt *wintry*.

"A bit cold, Papa," said Muriel, echoing his thoughts. She had sat down a while back to put on her shift and trousers. She talked while arranging her shells in the sand. "I thought we never got weather like those poor folks in Heathsholme. I don't have proper winter clothes. We'll have to move if it persists. I'd rather not. I don't like to move, as you know."

"I know, my flower. And we shan't be moving."

They'd moved several times since Mary's passing. He'd given up his post with the Royal Geological Institute in Menos, abandoned his landmark work on the primeval substrata found along Riverton's shores. Who cared what the world was like before men and Kings recorded their histories? Who cared about the importance of the monstrous fossils they'd found, the bones of nameless terrors rich with geo-magikal minerals—mysteries he had once been eager to decipher? Simon only cared for one history now—his family's—and his time with Muriel. Sadly, there wasn't much work for a highly specialized intellectual who no longer wanted to work in his field of expertise. He'd worked a few seasons as a farmhand in the highlands. It was there that the locals had claimed that a back broad as his, and looks swarthy as his, surely came from Swannish blood. The families were kind there, and caregivers for Muriel came easily. He wasn't certain why they'd left, other than his growing restlessness and a feeling that they'd needed to move on, and to build something better for his child. After that, he'd made do with slightly better paying work as a miner in Blackforge, until the Iron army had shown up and those mining operations became suspect.

The job had been simple enough; the crew would set out for a couple weeks at a time and survey the lands north of Blackforge and south of the old mine. Wherever their instruments detected feliron in the granite mounds and natural quarries scattered over Black Grove, they set up camp. Then Simon and his pickaxe-wielding fellows would excavate the area. There was never enough feliron to constitute a real mining operation, only lingering flaccid veins of a once grand feliron heart that had beaten through the region in ancient times. Nonetheless, the meager deposits would be collected and taken elsewhere by Ironguards—Simon was smart enough not to ask where.

Augustus Blackmore, lord of that realm, was often on-site, preening like a vainglorious but vicious black dog in his fur and regal adornments—a hand always on his sword and ready to use it. Simon hated him, even more as he knew of the abandonment and excommunication that had been forced upon a dear personal friend by this vile lord. It seemed strange to Simon that a man of Augustus's arrogance and status would lower himself to squatting in a tent at the edges of a dust-belching ravine, but he clearly did so for a reason. Asking about that reason had seen an inquiring colleague vanish. Another fellow who'd wondered about the whereabouts of his missing friend was suddenly "lost" to wild animals. When the crew returned for their occasional reprieve in Blackforge, Simon had decided that enough was enough, and that he wouldn't chance leaving Muriel without a father. He picked up his daughter from her caretaker and paid for passage on the first ferry to the lands on the western side of the River Feordhan.

In the five years since Mary's murder, Muriel had experienced a transient and unsettled life. At least here in Taroch's Arm she and Simon had found a moment's peace to heal, to be a family again. Their time in the city had indeed been peaceful, aside from that recent incident at Taroch's Crypt, where a sorceress and her rogue allegedly broke into Taroch's sacred resting place. Thereafter came murmurs of walking dead haunting the graveyard, and if one believed the outlandish stories, the small horde had supposedly been incinerated by a deployment of the Fingers' finest sorcerers. Furthermore, the destruction of the Iron City remained fresh in his and everyone else's mind. Nothing felt fully settled after an event like that.

Simon dusted himself off and stood over his daughter. *The world is all shite, sin, and garbage, my little flower. In the least, I have you, and your innocence—somehow preserved. I shall see that it stays that way.*

"Papa?"

"Yes, little flower?"

"Did you toot?"

"Pardon?"

"I smell a fart."

Simon laughed. "It wasn't I."

"Are you sure? You do toot quite often. I hesitate to say anything. Being a *lady*, I shan't discuss bodily exercises and evacuations. If not you, though, Papa, then something has a terrible smell." Muriel returned to her make-believe—chatting with invisible patrons at her imaginary boutique, discussing what piece of shell jewelry would best accompany which attire.

Simon noticed the stale, wet reek again, stronger than before. He hunted for it, and while shuffling and gazing eastward, noticed a strange buoy on the horizon: a green sphere—or was that two—sticking up like a frog's head. Only this wasn't a public beach that needed safety markers but a quiet and unused stretch of nowhere, far away from habitual vacation spots. It was a secret spot to which he and his daughter enjoyed retreating, and where they'd never met another soul. A second "buoy" appeared, quite close to the first. Perhaps it was simply flotsam from a wreck, he postulated, approaching the Feordhan to inspect. Since the objects weren't far from shore, and his curiosity had been piqued, he started into the water to get a better look. Goodness, the water was frigid! Simon yelped and leapt back onto the sand.

Danger. Death. Wickedness. Simon's stomach twisted in a familiar knot of instinctual fear. It was the same visceral wrenching that had afflicted him when Mary had vanished. The green sphere began to rise, then another rose, and another, and still more beside and behind, these shapes juddering into bipedal forms. Men? It seemed a generous term for these horrors of bone and seaweed, draped in vestiges of clothing, with leaking ribcages and mangled water-bloated heads, with unspooled guts and lesions seeping eels and crabs and rot—these motley, moaning abominations risen from graves and time and animated with unholy life. Gasping, dizzy, though still in the grip of something resembling sanity, Simon realized he was observer, perhaps even first watchman, to the advance of an army of the walking dead.

And an army it was, he realized. Beneath the water, and beyond the smattering of rising dead, he now noticed the ripple of a shadow, curving and stretching toward the piers and terracotta dwellings of Taroch's Arm. Not only here but elsewhere, the horde was still unfurling under the waves, and in mere sands the dead would cover these shores. In moments, they would be scrabbling across the docks of Taroch's Arm or pulling boatswains and their vessels into bloodying water. The smell overtook him like acid being poured down his throat, and he gagged and coughed. Only a dozen dead had risen here, and those few sloshed and snarled toward the living pair on the beach.

"Papa!" cried Muriel.

"Close your eyes," ordered her father.

Without a sliver of uncertainty, Muriel embraced him. His arms lifted her up, and even as the angry, garbled hisses and roars echoed around her, she felt—she had to believe—that he would keep her safe.

II

The shadowy man stood among the mountains of sand bordering the radiant pearl that was Eod. The hawk-eyed scouts along the Great Wall hadn't yet spotted the figure, and he would vanish before they ever did. Night concealed and swaddled the stranger as though he were her child. He could have been a night-spawned creature, too, with his solid black gaze, his white marble flesh, his mop of ebon hair, and the raggedy comportment of a man risen from his grave. Rags adorned him, his once fine shirt and trousers eaten away by the elements to the scraps of a pauper's attire. His feet were bare, though he felt none of the wicked cold of the desert at this hourglass.

One of the only perks of being unliving, Sorren found, was that the elements were never a bother. The sand in his eyes and whipping against his face was more akin to a spray of mist—enough of an irritant only to the degree that his body acknowledged the sensation. He didn't remember the nuances of pain or pleasure, and couldn't say which this was. To feel something, anything, against his dead flesh was a sublime delight. Although he saw better as a dead thing; he saw truths painted into technicolor hues and auroras. Thus did the great city before him, cascading with rainbows and syncopating with a drum symphony of a million heartbeats and murmurs, almost break Sorren's unbeating heart. *What colors*, he remarked, of the gold and the silver twists, the lambent maroon arcs of energy, and the hundreds of blue-green stars floating within the grand nexus of the living. The colors told a story in a language in which the dead man was slowly becoming versed: shades of gold for bravery, silver for hope, purple for fear, green for doubt.

For a while, Sorren watched this borealis of souls, was awed as a child, and pondered which, if any, of those lights belonged to his mother. He anticipated their reunion. He'd come to save his mother from herself. He'd come to reunite their family.

However, somewhere within his withered mind, the rational and calculating sociopath that he'd once been snickered and plotted against this new upstart holding the reins—this man who believed in hope and redemption. *You'll have none of that*, said his monster. *You're a selfish beast, through and through. You think you can be a hero, though it's as the young Sister said: you're rotten through and through. Outside as well as within. If not today, then tomorrow, you'll be back to carving up women; you'll be back to worshipping at the altar of arrogance and conceit. Everything that you touch rots. Embrace that. Embrace the horror that you've become. You're free of death; you can be a champion for whatever cause you choose. We can twist the world to our desires. We can make ourselves new playmates, new family, new mothers and lovers. You'd like to think that the bit of meat between your legs is about as useful as tits on a spinrex now, but you're wrong. Listen to me, and I'll show you how to get that mast rising again. All you have to do is cut, and feel the red on your fingers—*

"Shut up!" snapped Sorren.

We'll start with your mother, continued the monster inside. *Cut, cut, cut. Stitch, stitch. One good operation and we'll cure the bitch! Then we can get that bit of yours working again. Raise that flag and set sail! For our next destination, I think the whore from Heathsholme—*

"Silence," he hissed.

Rhiannon might have been a woman of the night, but she was a woman of character; she had been kind and sincere with him, and her aura of crimson bravery spoke to her virtue. Sorren would not harm her, ever. Perhaps the monster within him knew this, or it sensed his resolve on the matter. It did not speak of Rhiannon again. Rather, it faded back into ghostliness and recited into his ear the menu of tortures it had planned for his mother: an appetizer of shock treatments, a main course of amputations and surgeries, and a dessert of marble-mouthed screams as her soul was shoved into a jigsawed, misshapen, many-limbed centipede of human parts. Sorren could remake her perfectly, it promised. Gloriatrix hadn't been a good mother, but a wicked one, and the voice had a new template in mind for her.

Babbling to himself, and sometimes swatting at the whisperer inside him, Sorren glided across the dunes and slunk toward the city of a thousand lights.

III

In the dimness of Magnus's royal chamber, an unearthly golden hearth flickered light like a fire-serpent's tongue, moved by the morning's blustery temper. Today, the pearly stone décor and calming friezes of the chamber's walls were cast in shadows, rendering the handsome figurines carved into the stone as hideous gargoyles. Over at the king's bed a flowing silk canopy had been parted to reveal a chair in which the Queen of Eod sat. She was all the shades of the dawn: amber, yellow, tan, and gold. Indeed, she was a creature so sunny and graceful that the sadness she experienced was masked behind her splendor. Also concealed was the shadow hovering at her back: a man, dark and motionless. Next to this nymph of summer, his skin was as black as obsidian.

As for the king, he lay on the mattress before them, his beauty cocooned by a fever-soaked white bedsheet, leaving only his head exposed. Magnus was still enough as to appear dead, or locked in an enchanted sleep, and only Erik heard the gentle rasping of his breath. Often, Lila imagined touching her former husband, though she never did. Instead, it was the copper light from the fire that played across Magnus's features like the fingertips of a lover. To behold Magnus at rest so peacefully and beautifully made it hard to perceive the terrible torment he was suffering. It was a maelstrom of agony he held somewhere behind the dam of his countenance and Will, wherein nothing escaped but beads of sweat—glittering like dewdrops—from his ultimate control. Erik had also noticed the king's subtle spasms. There had also been fits where Magnus was torn between fever and chills, soaking the sheets with sweat, piss, and once even blood from the clenching of his fists so tightly that his fingernails had torn into his palms.

Twice, Magnus had shaken his caregivers from their placid stupor with shrieks that had surely ripped his throat raw, and thrashing that only Erik, with his incredible strength, could contain. These fits ended abruptly, though, with the last seeing him touch his foster son's face while gasping, "Forgive me," before falling back into the sheets. Since that last incident, he had neither spoken nor awoken. Since then, there had been only deep bouts of sleep—getting deeper, heading toward a depth Erik feared. Built with a soldier's chronex inside him, and the acumen of an Immortal, he recalled that the last fit had occurred on the third day after Magnus's tumble before the Great Wall. It was Sevensday now.

Soon it will have been a week, my Queen, he whispered into the mind of his beloved.

I know, she replied, reaching for the dark hand that rested upon her shoulder. *How queer for us to be here...for us to have come full circle through our gauntlet of grief, rejection, pain, and love. I had once thought to denounce Magnus, to loathe him. However, I realize I cannot. We have greater works than the casting of rage. We must rebuild. We must forgive. Not even for ourselves, but for those less fortunate who have been trapped in the cruel games we remorseless tyrants have played. We all have so much for which to atone...*Visions, imaginings of shadows twisting in flame—victims of the genocide she had committed—shrieked in her head. *So much...I don't want him to slip away like this.*

Nor do I, admitted Erik.

A deep, shared breath and a sigh. The bloodmates fell into each other, beating their heartbeat, each feeling the essence of the other's soul. Lila was teased away from the condemnation of her thoughts by the throb of a grand surf and thoughts of cold, gray, calming shores; in that solace the screaming of the ghosts of Menos was dulled by the ocean's wind. In contrast Erik's veins filled with the brandy-venom of the queen, and his head with dreams of golden fields and sunlight smooth as the fall of her hair through his fingers. A primal creature, enticed by these scents and sensations, Erik fought a battle with his decency. Given the circumstances, she hadn't been with him physically since Magnus had fallen, and he realized that much of his end of their union was nourished by desire, and he wished that these emotions didn't have so fierce a hold upon him. Even now, he felt jealous of the attention she had heaped upon his father. Since becoming his new self, an Immortal of stone and passion, his moods felt muddled even to him. At times, happiness and love could blend into an unfocused passion, lust, or even rage. He did not always feel in control of himself, a flaw he hadn't borne as a man. The hand he'd kept on Lila's shoulder dipped toward her bust, his rough fingers running over her collarbone like sandpaper on silk. They each shuddered, and before he realized what he was doing, Lila seized his hand to stop.

Forgive me, my Queen.

There is nothing to forgive. We are without shame—for this act of loving the other, at least. Although Sister Abagail of Carthac was right in that we are bound by duty until Magnus, you, and I settle our bloody past for good.

She returned his hand to its place upon her shoulder, and they settled into their bedside watch. Morning started to fade, and the usual parade of curious and concerned persons trickled in and out of the king's chamber. First arrived the physicians and fleshbinders, who checked the king's perfect physique for signs of trauma or healing. As was the routine, they left with pardons and hollow, obsequious foresights into how Magnus's condition—one for which they had yet to attribute a name, cause, or course of treatment—would eventually improve.

After the doctors left, the serfs came. They changed the sheets and swapped out the meals that only Erik really nibbled on. In all her long years, Lila had never tested the result of famishment on her immortal self, but since Magnus's incapacitation she'd lost all her appetite and thus had settled that ancient quandary. For Immortals, she realized, eating was an epicurean delight, much the same as enjoying art. Eating wasn't a function that was necessary for her—or Magnus's, or even Erik's—continued preservation. Thus the serfs gathered up Magnus's sweat-soiled bedding and replaced the picked-at tray they'd brought the day before, then exited with similar blindly optimistic sophisms echoing what Lila had already heard today. She couldn't be angry at them, however, for they were as frightened as she was and worried that an invulnerable cornerstone of their world was somehow crumbling, and that with Magnus's demise, so too would the frail shield of peace that protected Eod collapse. As sycophantic and wishful as Lila found the doctors' and staff's brittle optimism, she found it encouraging, too. They had flames of hope burning behind their tight faces, and they treated her with the respect due a former queen of Eod, and none had ever possessed either the gall or courage to challenge her decision to watch over her husband.

For she was now Lila: Ruiner of Realms. And behind what respect was given, and whatever hope was held, fear gleamed in the gazes of men who beheld her. One day, she assumed, questions of her guilt would return, and her crimes against Menos would need to be balanced by justice. No longer on the run or beguiled by the whirlwind of her passion and revenge, and in the silence and solitude of Magnus's chamber, which lent itself to rumination, at last the breadth of what she had done struck her. No matter her reasoning, no matter her coercion by supernatural forces, she had murdered a nation. She faced a jury of tens of thousands of ghosts, glaring at her from the shadows. In the waking dream-state of an Immortal, she was never certain if a ruffle in the dark would emerge into the horror of an incinerated, shambling, reaching victim. Apparitions remained in her mind, however, for the moment, and she stashed her self-loathing so deep that even Erik sensed her as merely conflicted—and likely over Magnus. He shared none of her guilt, for Menosians had always been enemies to him, and he was—for better or worse—a man of stone and stony feelings. There were moments, also hidden, where she wondered if the trade from a lover of ice to one of stone had really liberated her at all—a decision she was to now live with forever.

At the moment, though, on this morning, her internal and known woes were superficial to the wounds of the world. The leader of the world's only remaining bastion against chaos was in some manner of coma, while an unholy star descended closer and closer to Geadhain's orbit with each passing hourglass, and nearly all the townships and civilizations to the east had been devoured by a ravenous undead horde. Despite the complications of communication, news of that tragedy had carried in from the east—such ghastly rumors couldn't be contained. Horror stories of Fairfarm, Bainsbury, and all the fiefs of the Swannish Highlands being virtually erased from existence were common terrors discussed around Eod's tables. Where buildings and cultivate-lands once stood, a dark artist had painted long strokes of tar over home and green, a vision of ashen razed wastes. Through a farscope's view, Taroch's Arm now appeared to be as quiet and collapsed as an ancient ruin. A brown and white haze shrouded the place: filth and snow. For somehow—because of the broken balance of the world, perhaps—the winter that had always stayed penned in the north, beyond the borders of Magnus's kingdom, had now reached southward.

A more harsh winter had now beset the lands in Central Geadhain that had known only spring, summer, fall, and slightly cooler days that dusted diamonds on the fields, transforming trees into pretty glass things; winter had simply been a season used as an excuse to put on knitted garments and sip spiced coco drinks. However, this winter was unlike any other remembered in Lila's thousand years of life; it battled the desert heat, and it forced the Silver Watch to bundle in furs as they patrolled at night. Northern winds rattled her land like a specter of frost pounding on a window. It was a dire thought, but she knew that if Eod was to fall, and all of Magnus's magik with it, that this wrathful season would sweep across Central Geadhain. Already, the evidence of the many cities and homesteads on the northeast of the continent had been completely erased by snow. Should Eod fall to war and ruin, in a thousand years no remnants of their world would be found; her history would be sealed in a tomb of ice. As though her people, her past, had never been.

She understood that next to these universal fears and terrors, the genocide she had committed was easily overlooked. Rumors of her possession by an unholy force during the commission of these acts had also leaked out, thanks to utterances from Rasputhane's lips. She didn't understand why he so deeply loathed Menos and its subjects, though he took every opportunity to incite against the Iron empire. Regardless, she knew forgiveness was earned, and not something to be twisted into another's mind. She'd earn the people's forgiveness. She would be a Queen of Mercy—not of Death. Never again would she repeat the ruthlessness she'd shown toward Gorgonath and Menos.

As soon as she'd heard Beauregard's report of the dead swarming Bainsbury, she'd ordered the *Skylark* and every other vessel of its size to begin transporting the caravans of vagrants who'd escaped Taroch's Arm, and the many other places assaulted by the unliving, to safety. These ships swept the land from day to night looking for wagons or the flagging arms of survivors wandering below. Lost, filthy, and terrified, some had come from Fairfarm or farther, and some shared terrible stories of ferries that had not survived the journey—whole fleets of flaming ships, decks milling with ravaging dead, survivors hurling themselves overboard into waters as thick with the clawing dead as the decks from which they sought escape. Many ships vanished and no more answered farspeaking stones. Whole families had been separated or lost completely. The toll of war and the first of the greatest scars were now being felt acutely.

Now the refugees from the east and elsewhere were being shuttled farther west. Some hid in Southreach, hoping that the unliving horde wouldn't spill down into the valley like a waterfall of ants, hoping that Southreach's towering fortresses and earthspeakers were a safer bet than Eod. But Lila wasn't certain that the city's natural defenses would protect it, and men had forgotten that before Southreach stood in glory today, Magnus had smashed that realm to a powdery abyss in another age. Other refugees had been placed in great tent cities erected in the untainted fields of Meadowvale. The City of Wonders, despite the miracles it produced, simply couldn't hold anyone else. Truly, she'd never heard Eod so loud, so full of unease. As the sun crept around the sky, wavering the room in white, then yellow, then orange, the noises from outside became a rumble. Eodians, Menosians, Arhadians, men of Riverton, Meadowvale, and Ebon Vale. Aside from Carthacians, who were the safest distance from the war, in Eod a representative could be now found from every corner of Central Geadhain.

The warmasters told her that many would fight. A surprising number of the mercenaries who Magnus had given the offer to conscript remained; mercenaries understood death and balance, business and sense, and if the City of Wonders were to fall, there would be no realm left on Geadhain that would stand for long thereafter, or in which their services would be needed. The mercenary army was bound to Eod's army by desperation. Lila felt that was as strong a tie as honor, if not as virtuous.

The embodiment of true virtue came by that day around noon. A gentle knock announced Beauregard—as punctual as ever—and with a swing of the door he stood there, shining in silver and white armor against his black hair. Lila equally admired and was irritated by the young man's unbreakable conviction and gallantry. He seemed bound to an old code, one of untarnished beliefs where warriors always had a pure cause, where evil always lost and blood was only spilled with purpose. It was mostly horseshite and idealism, she felt, though he believed in it, which mattered more than reality in this situation. Whenever she saw Erik and Beauregard standing in the same room, as they were now, and as they gazed upon one another like a panther to a white stag, she appreciated that they were from similar, albeit rival, schools of chivalry. A white knight and a black knight, each defending their ruler.

The lad broke his staring contest with Erik and bowed to the queen. He took off his fencing gloves, approached the king's bed, and dropped to a plated knee—with a veteran's practiced elegance, noted Erik. Beneath his soap-scented exterior, the lad smelled of exertion. He'd clearly been drilling himself hard for the sweat of his labors to have distilled into a musk of battle, and must have washed himself before coming to see his king.

"Has there been any change?" asked Beauregard.

"No," replied Lila. "However, the fleshbinders have said that his vital signs are stable."

Beauregard reached out and touched the scars upon Magnus's lips—left by a cage once clenched over his head—that blended into the king's iridescent complexion.

"Yes," said Beauregard. "His body is nigh impervious to damage. Only the greatest magik can harm him. It's his mind for which I worry." He laid his hand upon the king's brow, the coldness of the flesh prickling the spellsong's hairs. Shivering, he took the king's hand then turned to Lila. "Is there nothing you can do? You and he were..."

She beheld the romantic knight, with pity. "What we were, we are no longer. Love can be eternal, but ours was only long. I cannot wake him with a kiss, the way you've heard spoken of in the tales of yore. I cannot stir him with shout, plea, or even shaking. I have tried each of these remedies, save placing mine lips to his. You can try the kiss, if you'd like."

Beauregard blushed. "I don't know what I was asking of you. My pardon." He stood. "I should get back to the Warpath." Such was the old and rarely used colloquialism for the palace training grounds, a path that leads to war, which evoked in Erik a fondness for his time there. That fondness was further stoked as the young knight stared at him keenly and asked, "Would you join me there? The men could use a display of your leadership and support. You are, historically, the only man next to the mad king to have matched the king in combat. We would be honored."

"When the king wakes, perhaps I shall join you," replied Erik.

"When the king wakes," repeated Beauregard, before he slipped away.

Time continued its creep, and the bloodmates shifted little in their moods or positions. After all, Erik was rock—more and more each day. He hadn't felt an ache or pain since the king's bashing and slicing of his flesh during battle; the finger he'd lost and other wounds he'd suffered had healed within a day. Without Lila ever having to ask, he fetched her water for her thirst, and he ministered to her fatigue by channeling his strength into her: jolts of spirit and magik that had her sitting up as straight as if her seat had suddenly been charged with lightning. Most sands trickled past with him at her side, unmoving, as devoted as she needed him to be.

That afternoon, Leonitis disturbed their perfect solitude, creeping into the chamber as would the lion for which he was named. Still, Erik heard his soft steps—even in full, bulky plate—and turned.

"Soldier," said Erik.

While Beauregard and Galivad had assumed command of the rank and file of the king's forces, Leonitis, his brother Dorvain, and Rowena spent their days beyond the Great Wall. There, the three commanders and their ragtag militia of civilians and mercenaries fought until their hands blistered from weapon play and their skins peeled from the heat. Leonitis spilled a bit of sand as he walked toward the bloodmates, his once pale face nearly as golden brown as Rowena's. The queen didn't hide her disappointment that her sword wasn't with him—she'd seen little of Rowena since her return, and the reason for the queen's frown was obvious to Leonitis.

"Rowena sends her regards and prayers," he said, as he strode over to the bedside for the customary stand-and-stare at the king.

"I do not want her regards and prayers," said Lila. "I would like to see my desert flower. Tell her that I miss her. I need her. She is as much my child as you and your brother."

Leonitis's voice hitched from a pang of emotion. "I shall, Your Majesty. I shall see that she comes with me soon. She cannot avoid the palace forever." *Or avoid Galivad, for that matter*, thought Leonitis, who knew something of their entanglement, though neither Galivad nor Rowena would speak of it. Avoidance and body language often spoke louder than words, and with those actions the two were practically screaming at one another.

"Your report?" asked Erik of Leonitis, who seemed lost in his thoughts.

"Right. Better than expected. Greatly on account of those whose trust we were so leery of—the swords for hire. Next to food and board, the only thing we've offered them is a chance at honor. I'm humbled that so many have aspired to such a reward. They're among the sharpest warriors I've met. These folk don't play by the handbook of clean warfare, which makes them invaluable assets since our enemies do not fight with decorum, either."

"Civility is futility at this point," said Erik. "The sword is mightier than the quill."

"Indeed. And it's no surprise that mercenaries would be handy with a blade or bow. A rare few, even, were already sorcerers-for-hire, and I've sent them to Gorijen to brush up on their skills. It remains to be seen if those sorcerers will do more than blow themselves up, though I have hope. I believed you would return. I believe in justice. So I believe in my recruits: cobblers playing soldiers, virtue-blackened warriors, rogue sorcerers about to wield their spellfire against a monster...I believe in them all. Regardless of their skill or checkered pasts, they all seem to share one commonality: they want this war to end. I think that will keep even the most mercenary of men united and following orders for a time."

"Yes, but will they be ready to face the army of Death?" demanded Erik.

Leonitis swallowed. Brutus had been demoted to secondary apocalypse. Villages, farms, and civilizations from east to west were disappearing under the black march of an unliving army—a force that did not suffer casualties or weaken with each mêlée, but rather grew fatter with swollen corpses and rotting generals. Leonitis, the Iron Queen, and aides from each kingdom had been present for Queen Lila's frank disclosure of the madness that had crept into her mind and possessed her for months. With biting clarity, he remembered that moment, for she'd warned them of their enemy.

Queen Lila, pale, stricken, has told her tale. Now only the roar of the Chamber of Echoes is heard, though its noise seems far away and muted by the long white branches of the ancient yew that hangs over the gathering today like a shadow. Aside from the confessor, Lila, and her stone knight, most everyone's nerves have propelled them from their seats around the stone table and affected them with nervous pacing and chatter. Leonitis feels unsteady after learning of this strange, spinning reality in which he and the other confidants of the Kingdoms, East and West, now exist—a world wherein Death has taken corporeal shape and marches to war against humankind. Beauregard presents a strong front, though his hand shakes like a rickety old man's—rattling the hilt of the scabbard he clutches. As for the actual old men in attendance, Rasputhane and Gorijen Cross whisper to each other, their faces waxen with fear. Neither man has ever known such terrors as those that now threaten Geadhain. Gloriatrix appears the most unfazed, and her ghoul guardian, leering at others from behind her, seems no more bothered than his mistress. The Iron Queen claps her hands together, the sound possessing a startling puissance, which snaps the gathering from their gloom.

"A little iron in your spines!" she says. "We speak only of the walking dead."

"What of this one who leads the horde?" asks Rasputhane as he straightens up and releases Gorijen; he is, after all, the default head of the chain of command next to Lila, and needs to demonstrate some authority. "The nekromancer?"

"Death," corrects Erik from his post behind the queen. Everything about the man seems deeper and darker now. His voice is a dusty grumble, his skin the shade of polished shale—for such a familiar face, he's rather terrifying to Leonitis.

"This Dreamer has claimed a vessel," mutters Gloriatrix, who—from her discourse with Magnus and Elissandra—knows more of the celestial terrors waging war on Geadhain than many at the table. She begins to pace and think aloud. "While Magnus recovers, we need to figure out how to break this vessel of Death. Our efforts in defeating Death should be a good test for whatever measures we might employ against the mad king when he returns. For reason would dictate that if we can cast out one cosmic entity, then we shall have found a weapon that could do the same to Brutus's parasite. Rasputhane, I believe our technomancers should work together in this venture. Menos's less ethical practices may provide an edge; we are less afraid to get messy with our sciences."

"Your tortures and experimentations on human subjects, you mean?" snipes the spymaster.

"Our courage to cross boundaries," replies the Iron Queen, in stride. "And by the same token, Menos may gain a few insights from Eod's more measured principles. I believe we can find a way, together, to shatter this vessel. If that feat alone does not disassemble the unliving army, then any walking corpses that remain thereafter can be dealt with easily enough through fire. 'Twas *always the remedy in Menos when the reborn broke from their leashes, and the Furies have the fire of all three suns once said to float in our skies."*

"Simple," says Rasputhane. "And lacking foresight into the many terrible things that can go wrong with any and every plan."

Although, with no better stratagems to lay out, he sighs, and asks everyone to sit once more while discussions commence. Many questions are raised regarding the terms nonchalantly thrown around by the monarch and the spymaster—terms of which not all of the gathering have been enlightened: Dreamers, vessels. Begrudged by these imbeciles, Gloriatrix barks out an unpleasant lesson on these great entities that are often formless themselves but have found other forms with which to wage war, and doesn't stay afterward to answer questions.

Leonitis feels twice as bewildered by all the extraordinary facts now whirling in his skull. Too many times this past year, his understanding of the world has expanded too fast for his sanity to accept. In a mad, storming world, he looks to the only woman who has ever been there to ground him. He gazes at Lila, and in that instant half-remembers her reaching hand and radiant outline against a harsh sun, or the glow of a fire, her soft voice whispering to his brother and him a greeting, a promise of safety. What was the heat? Torches? A pyre? And why did he always envision flecks of snow in the half-baked memory? As usual, he can't grasp the memory, and that tenderness in Lila he recalled isn't present now.

Instead, his Queen Mother's expression is hard and sad, like a bystander watching a man hang. Her detached candor stuns him. She shakes her head at something being discussed by the circle, and says to him, "I share the same doubts as Rasputhane. It is unreasonable to think that Death can be banished easily by fire and cleverness. We shall need a miracle. Even then, the cost of this exorcism will be a king's ransom, to be paid in blood."

"You didn't answer me, soldier," said Erik, and he strode over to the contemplative warrior.

Leonitis took a deep breath. "My pardon. My mind runs away with itself. My men will be ready. The rest now hinges on Gorijen and his Menosian allies. Have they made much progress?" *Of banishing an everlasting incarnation of Death, however that would work?*

"No," replied the queen. "And I do not see us conquering Death with simple stratagems or clever tricks."

"You speak with certainty." Erik gazed long and true at the queen. "As you did in the Chamber of Echoes. I have not forgotten that moment. Do you know something, my Queen? Have you seen something? A premonition?"

Lila looked away, reflecting on something. "I was given one vision in all my years, and that I shall share with my former husband when he wakes. I only know what was inside of me, when I was driven to destroy the Iron City and it was...*relentless*, monstrous, all-consuming. I was not even one of its vessels, merely a witless puppet being twisted to its Will. I cowered in the shadow of that force, and I do not see how mere men or their magik could ever stand against it."

"We are doomed, then?" asked Leonitis.

"Dear boy..." The queen stood, drifted over to him, and cupped his cheek; he blushed at her compassion. "We are not doomed. I said we need a miracle. I believe in miracles. I have seen my own wounded heart healed and transformed through love. I have seen enemies made into allies. I have met a woman who has touched the souls of every soldier in this Great War. I believe that Magnus will return to us through that same inexplicable agency."

Leonitis wasn't confident in the power of miracles. It was flimsy logic, and he'd have spat at such words coming from any other woman. In this case, however, he smiled, bowed, and left the bloodmates, feeling slightly lighter in his troubled heart.

Do you believe that? asked Erik, as they settled once again into their roles of watchful minder and stone guardian.

Not as I spoke it. Miracles are made by the hands of men and women— people provide the foundations for the impossible to become possible. No divine hand will directly save us, though perhaps we are all fragments of the divine, all small Dreamers ourselves. In that case, we shall create our miracle and cast this unwanted shadow back into the depths of space. She paused, and Erik felt her emotions grow tempestuous. *I am no seer, as I've said. However, I think that after touching Death, after being her priestess, I can sense her immanence.* She paused again as she looked around the chamber for shadows ready to leap at her. *I sense it all around us, Erithitek, and in others. Death surrounds Leonitis in a shroud.*

You think he's in danger? Erik leaned down and slipped his arms around his queen.

We all are. Again, I have had no vision, only a sense that Death is closer to him than most. It could mean anything, my knight.

Or anyone, he thought.

IV

Throughout the morning and afternoon, Lowelia had been taking carriages and strolling promenades all across the city. It was tireless, this most unwanted duty to which the queen had assigned her, playing guide for the strange tourist with whom she'd been saddled—this spherical sentient mass of black crystal that had been wrapped and hidden in the shoulder sling she now carried. While the Mind had no eyes that she knew of, it wasn't sightless. On the contrary, it saw *everything* in Eod, and Kings knew how much farther beyond the city's white walls. Since becoming its guide, she'd abstained from physically interacting with the Mind as much as possible. It couldn't speak unless she pressed her flesh to its crystal skin, and that was a small mercy.

For today's itinerary she'd planned an interesting adventure. First, she went to Eod's extraordinary Royal Botanical Exhibition, sprawling beneath the bottom tier of the palace and walled by towering shrubberies. A layperson, or anyone who had decided against engaging the chatty guides who strutted around the great gate of the gardens, might be lost inside the maze of greenery for days, but Lowe was familiar with enough routes to wave away their insistent pandering. She walked amid crystal hedgerows, paused to admire flowers with petals of cold fire, took breaks on benches made of misting ice, studied the arboreal hedge monsters that seemed to have been pulled from Alabionic myths, made wishes into the pools that dazzled like windows to the afterlife, and listened to the harmonies of soothing birdsong on breezes that smelled of a natural, thick syrup that made her stomach growl. Lowelia felt at peace while they were there, though with war stirring, she knew such peace was false. She wondered how many of the gawking children—dragging their parents by the hand from wonder to wonder—would be ruined corpses in a week. That dismal thought made her instinctively reach for the life-form with which she'd been entrusted; her fingers slipped through the fabric and brushed smooth, oddly warm matter.

The Mind's voice entered her with a jolt. *I have completed my examination of the Royal Botanical Gardens of Eod. The fate of the children for whom you feel sadness has intrigued my network. I would like to see other relevant socio-anthropological behaviors common to west-central Geadhain.*

I'll show you sadness, you over-curious little beast, she thought, taking her hand off the object. Lowe hurried through the labyrinthine gardens, through the crowded square outside the root-and-starlight gates, and leapt into the first carriage she saw. She asked to be taken to the memorial on Carpenter Street.

"Lose someone in the Storm of Frostfire?" the driver shouted down from his perch.

"Haven't we all? Or won't we in the next?" she replied.

Momentarily, while she was gazing out the window during the ride, the strangest apparition appeared in her view. It was of a brown-skinned woman in a white dress standing in the alleyway of a home that was being raided by

Eod's Silver Watch. A man was being savagely hauled out of the dwelling while she gawked. *Dorothy?* she wondered. The man she couldn't place. The woman soon vanished from view, and Lowelia was no longer sure of what she'd seen. Perhaps she'd ask Dorothy the next time she saw her at one of the teas they'd promised each other... although she hadn't seen her more than once, many days ago, when she'd caught her talking to Rasputhane in one of the palace's shadier alcoves. Upon seeing her, the pair had broken apart and vanished like burglars spying a watchman. What had that been about?

Your telemetric current continues to shift toward frequencies I believe represent sorrow.

Be quiet. Many days prior, after the first passerby had given her the telltale "is she crazy?" look for speaking to the lump she carried, Lowelia had learned not to speak aloud, to merely think her responses to the Mind. Still, she had to remember to stop touching the thing—a hard impulse to ignore when it felt so much like the weight of an infant. Cecilia. She sighed and was able to continue the journey in peace.

Soon the coach stopped outside an ugly, pitted, burned out ruin possessed only of the bones of a once-grand, many-winged structure. This was what remained of the old carpenter's guild. There was nothing left of its majesty other than the occasional carved nymph or gloriously detailed faery to be seen in the blackened trim visible to Lowe through the passenger window. Soot had twisted those figures into demons. As she stepped from the carriage, she immediately bowed in silent respect toward the memorial ahead—a river of colorful wreaths and potted flowers flowing along the great blackened steps. In a moment, she frowned at the façade of scorched stone behind the lovely dedication and glanced down the street to where a newer, more modern guild stood. Sadly, that structure would never have the charm of its predecessor. She could recall all of the old guild's beauty, for her husband—before the injury that had led him to unemployment and drink—had once been among the finest carpenters in Geadhain. They'd been in love once, though whatever love there'd been was now dead as the ruins of the guild upon which she gazed. Thinking of that long-dead passion stirred in her gut a cocktail of brimstone and broken glass.

Funny how feelings twist, she thought. *Or endure.* She gazed again at the memorial. She smiled at the kneeling mourners who looked her way, and she pretended to be one of them as she walked. For a while she eavesdropped on the murmurs of conversations that passed between these loving folk and the dead. She felt the Mind buzzing with magik against her chest, and it was surely spying on them, too. She left. Once they'd entered a quiet carriage en route to the Faire of Fates, she fell into the familiar habit of cradling and caressing the Mind again.

Your matrix appears unbalanced.

Drat. She needed to wear gloves. *My matrix?* she replied.

The collection and collation of your neural, spiritual, and emotional essences. At the present, your matrix oscillates with sadness.

Not sadness. Lowe spread her free hand against the cool window and envied the happy crowds outside. *Disappointment in how life plays out. Disappointment in what a poor choice I made in marrying.*

Disappointment is a division of sadness? A sub-state of the parent affliction?

Yes.

Curious. This ache in you is old. You have healed it. As much as a wound mends to a scar—not perfect, though functional. How did you do this? How did you restore yourself to functionality?

I castrated my husband, she thought—then realized that the Mind might consider that to be a literal response. *Disregard that. I was being callous and cynical. How did I "fix" myself? Well...I found a new reason to live. I found a duty. I suppose that I drew strength from the people who had forgiven me: Magnus and Lila.*

Is it fair to state that your matrix was reinforced by the telemetric impulses of other, stronger, more complex matrices?

If you say so.

Thank you for this information.

The Mind was quiet then, and the carriage rolled on. In time, the Faire of Fates declared its proximity, as the noise of the marketplace rattled the carriage more than the bumps in the road. More than ever, Eod was at capacity, and its famous market was thick with refugees, ruffians, and pale masters and Ironguard. Among the wave of bobbing heads, breaking against stages, stalls, and stands, there were no signs of the upheaval and damage caused by Lila's arrival only a week past, which saddened Lowe since she wanted to see some of the ruin and repercussions of her little rebellion. Eod seemed eager to forget grudges—too eager, she felt; too complacent.

The carriage was quickly mired in crowds, at which point Lowelia paid the coachman and braved the traffic by foot. There were curses and apologies aplenty, some in languages and with accents that puzzled her. Finally she reached the first stalls and tented shops, where folk knew to behave themselves and operated more agreeably, at a browsing pace.

Lowelia spent the afternoon examining baubles and things that interested both her and the Mind. For only a few fates, she treated herself to a truefire bracelet. Truefire could be woven into the loveliest jewelry, and the piece she'd selected was a relief of two fire-twined maidens twisted into a spiral, lit from within by golden light. She felt as though she held a relic of the sun. Moreover it was a symbol that represented women, freedom, and fire—all elements she believed surrounded and guided her. As if it were manifest, this secret sisterhood of flame, she then spotted two lean Arhadian women in dusty gray tunics slinking through the crowd like wolves amid a flock of nattering goats. They were warrior women of the queen's army, and they nodded at her as though she too was part of their circle. She lost their faces to the crowd, though she carried the pride of that encounter with her in their wake.

Interesting.

As usual, the voice startled Lowelia—naturally, she'd been fondling the damned thing again. Choosing to ignore it for a time, weary of its curiosity, she paused at a stall that hawked hickory-flavored smoked meats and ordered a slice of the dripping red hunk that spun on the rotisserie before her. She walked and nibbled for a spell before she asked, *What is interesting?*

The matrices of you and those bipeds shared a strong telemetric impulse.

Telemetric impulse. Second time I've heard that, and I'm no clearer on its meaning than I was the first. I'm a handmaiden, not a scientist.

A metascientist or empath would be the required vocation to understand the intricacies of that of which I speak. Nonetheless, in rudimentary terms, I speak of the feelings, thoughts, and histories that constitute the living creature's aura in the subatomic mesh of the neural network; meshes that interact and react with each other many millions of times each microspeck and across any distance, great to small. When you and the desert bipeds noticed one another, there was a reaction. As a result, your matrix changed. I have observed this process before, though rarely in as advanced an adaptation as yours; akin in principle only to my observations of the shifting matrices of Mother Lila and Father Erik—though a mutation nowhere near as severe.

Hmm. The concept that her spiritual makeup, her *being*, could change in a microspeck, or even that there were millions of such processes occurring every moment, intrigued her. Lowelia's stick of meat trembled in her hand. *How can I change? So quickly? How is that possible?*

Your species is ever-changing. You are never the same as you were a speck ago. Not physically, emotionally, or spiritually. Your existence is one of chaos and flux. Even my advanced matrix is not exempt from the rules of chaos theory. My matrix expands and develops with each new telemetric impulse it encounters, as it has today, handmaiden. I have learned much from you on this day in particular—and on other days in which you have unwillingly acted as my caretaker. I know you do not care for the duty, which says much about your dedication to our mother figure, your willingness to do that which you are not wont to do. We are all small and delicate parts of a larger machine; some gears function more efficiently than the others, more willfully.

With her head strained by these concepts of universal energy and unity, she desired a less busy environment. She passed her food to a hungry-looking urchin, before negotiating her way into one of the quieter streets rambling off the Faire. Sweet shops and bakeries dotted the neighborhood, and the scents of sugar and butter were instant comforts. She wandered, and did not handle the Mind. She paid heed to her surroundings and not to the alien creature she held. It was easy to distract herself in the City of Wonders. Eod's silver-roofed villas and glimmering towers engaged in a battle of lights with the pearl shield covering the sky—the Witchwall erected to protect Eod from the Iron Queen. In contrast, the soft-yellow desert sun was a dull and boring eyesore. Chatter rumbled in Lowelia's ear like the burble of water; the voices were loud—though jubilant—wherever she went. It was as though they'd already won the war against the unliving hordes and a mad king. *Fools*, she thought. Citizens of Eod seemed oblivious, as well, to the intermingling of black-shelled, barbed men and warriors of rough trade who casually strode among them. A few of Menos's elite had even shed their garish gothic masks and revealed their pale faces, unblessed by the light, to the day. With such sunless complexions, they'd be burned and red as roasted crawfish come nightfall, and their impending discomfort pleased her. She knew she was bigoted against their new "allies," but felt no shame for it. Their alliance was a farce, and Gloriatrix would stick the dagger into Magnus's back sooner or later. Going back to the Mind's theories on interconnectivity, on the importance of each being, how could Menosians be a part of the grand universal balance? Other than to tip the scales of creation with their darkness.

During her ruminations, she'd been rubbing the Mind as if it were a sphere into which a seer might gaze—wanting answers to the great questions of life. It sensed her need and spoke.

I do not know of scales, or a great cosmic hierarchy, other than the Dreamers, which are matrices of interminable complexity. Even they, by what you would judge fair or foul, are part of the world in which you live. Faith on this world is fractured, and many worship only themselves. When you think of divinity, you think of the actions of the devout and kind against the actions of the cruel. Yet on a molecular scale, I see only matrices and patterns, swarms of atoms and movement—a poetry, I suppose. I see beyond the values and confusions that mortals—and Dreamers—lay over their perceptions to constitute and define their reality. You have a strong matrix, a strong Will, to realize some of the underlying truth in chaos theory.

I do? wondered Lowelia, awed.

You question what is beyond what your eyes see, and have yourself undertaken actions both divine and evil. Yes, I have seen your truths, all of them, and they have not stunted your evolution. You continue to evolve, to enrich your matrix with unforeseen mutations. A textbook case for chaos theory. Great Iron Sage Euphorius Maxis, originator of said theory, would have been delighted were he to have seen your specimen—were he still living, and had he not perished as a madman in disrepute—and to have seen himself and his theories ratified. I am amazed by you, biped #2,123,893, the "Lowelia Larson," and I have only recently discovered the capacity in myself for amazement. You are as bright a star, as unpredictable a flame, as Mother Lila or Father Erik. Your adaptability is what makes you so unique; it is a cycle self-replicating, a mutation without end.

A blush consumed her, and then a smile. She needed to sit on the nearest step to recover from the kindest compliment she'd received in some time. She patted the crystal entity that throbbed at her breast.

Thank you.

Again, thank you for our many days of explorations and exposure to this vast environment of matrices. As I mentioned, Lowelia Larson, your company has been a boon in my efforts to solve the problem of how to free the Magnus from the oppressive matrix that seeks to subdue him. I believe I have a theory on how to protect the king's matrix from the telemetric energy of the entity you call the Black Queen, though only through implementation can the validity of my theory be tested.

Lowelia blinked, her slower matrix digesting what the entity was saying.

I'm sorry, are you saying you know how to wake the king?

I have found a way to strengthen his spirit, so that he might resist the invading presence of the Black Queen. Like an immune response to invading bacterium, we must amplify the antibodies in his system. With an appropriate telemetric—

"Deary mittens!" she shrieked, leapt up, then flagged the first available carriage to return her to the palace.

V

"Wasn't that the queen's maid who caught that coach?" asked Aadore, then scowled at a thought. "Or rather, the maid who once played at being the queen and then led a rebellion to reinstate the real queen?"

"People say that Menosian politics are a quagmire." Curtis chuckled.

"Were," corrected Aadore. "There are no Menosian politics left to discuss."

Shadow was cast over their features, perhaps from a cloud drifting above the shimmering Witchwall, falling only upon their small company and seemingly on none of the others around them who were enjoying a sunny afternoon repast at the café. Grumpily, the four refugees of the Iron City played with the embroidered tablecloth and the gleaming tea set and passed around scones, savory desserts, jellies, and ham sandwiches. *Tea time* is what Eodians called this supper-spoiling feast that took place after lunch and before one sat down for a meal. In Menos, one ate three times if they were a master, twice if they served such men, and maybe once if they were among the luckier slaves. Aadore felt she would get fat if she stayed here much longer, but sadly, there was no other city to which she could return.

A frown, half-hidden under the wide cavalier's hat he now wore that kept out the sun and made him resemble a brutish frontier lawman, suggested that Skar shared her discomfort. Under his short coat he even carried two heavy hammers, hooked and made for pummeling flesh and not machine; they sat in holsters like pistols. Skar always sported some degree of a frown, though it had deepened since they'd been taken in by Eod.

She could tell that Sean wasn't content, either. Like Skar, Sean had chosen a hat to combat Eod's perpetual sunshine, and the Arhadian seamstress Dorothy, who'd recently cozied up to the royal household, had fixed for him a tunic and trousers of deep purple brocade. It was a garment that Aadore felt gave her brother a handsome, lordly appeal, though Sean decried it as being "fit for a Sorsettan princess." Then again, Aadore knew he had only gratitude for the enchanted wooden prosthetic that the king's sorcerers had fashioned for him. Since the wood had been enchanted for lightness and balance, Sean walked with a far less noticeable gait than he would with any common prosthesis. And because the magikal limb was only attached by plain old straps, it didn't react unfavorably with his—or hers, she supposed—resilience to arcane powers.

When requesting the prosthesis, the suggestion of fleshcrafting had arisen, and he'd stressed that he was simply more comfortable with a prosthetic. No one had bothered him further, and the object was soon made and ready. There was a lot more than the Brennoch siblings' resistance to magik that they'd brushed under the conversational rug lately. After their confession to Magnus and the Iron Queen, no one within their numbers had discussed the events prior to Eod: the ruin of Menos, their odyssey through a living hell, their encounter with the nekromancer and embodiment of Death. Aadore sensed that they were all healing hidden wounds from these events. As she studied the gloomy fellows, she considered saying something to cheer them up.

Curtis interrupted her thoughts, clearing his throat and telling the suddenly manifested waiter that they weren't yet ready to have their meal cleared away. Aadore glanced his way as he spoke; Curtis was holding up well. An initially horrid sunburn had now peeled to a bronze-brown. Unlike the other Menosians, he seemed to have embraced Eod's brightness and charm. His attitude was further testified to by his gay white outfit of padded cream vest, slacks, and studded bracers, more decorative than defensive. Complementing his noble admiral-come-to-port image was a scarf tied about his thick neck. On any other man, this attire and the laid-back grace of his manner might be interpreted as dandyish, but to Aadore he seemed a man comfortable with himself. And comfortable with *her*, she realized, as he caught her glancing at the cleft of his meaty chest and gave her a wink. She blushed, secretly wondering when she might have the opportunity to caress that cleft.

Ian's ongoing giggles became too sweet to ignore, and she looked down at the lad in her care. Ian had taken to their move as happily as Curtis, and was dressed like a tiny sailor of the former's imaginary armada, wearing a white jumper, blue scarf, and a sennit straw hat circled in navy ribbon. He was too darling for her not to smile. Aadore stopped bouncing him, pinched his cheeks, and told him he was a darling. Eventually her stomach grumbled, and she picked at the sun-warmed sandwiches and tarts.

"Is this about it, then?" Skar said, then waved at the ambling crowds. "War's over. Nothing to see here. Not as if hordes of the dead are roaming the land, razing villages. I'm sure the mad king is just having a poke and a sun bake with the murderesses of Terotak, too—the ones that aren't wandering these streets, that is. He'll return to Central Geadhain eased of all troubles and ready to talk peace."

Skar leaned in his chair and spat; a few folks looked at the ogre ruining their tea, though his demeanor scared them back to their pleasant delusions.

"You're right: clueless, the lot of them," said Aadore, once the silence between them had congealed into discomfort.

Even Ian's burbling petered out. Aadore rose and passed him across the table to Skar. He had become the regular nanny for the boy, replete even with a leather chest-hammock in which to hold the lad. Aadore instinctively slid her hand to the hilt pressing into the bottom of her corset. People stared at her as if she were about to wield her weapon, and she returned glares that said she just might.

"I'd like to get back to my swordplay lessons, of which I've only had a few. I don't expect I shall be swashbuckling or selling my mercenary services any time in the foreseeable future, though I would like to feel as though I'm endangering my opponent more than myself."

A pittance of hourglasses had been spent on the Warpath on her martial education. She'd found herself embarrassed by the young, athletic women sparring in the royal training grounds who upstaged her at every opportunity. In Menos there had been no female Ironguard, and women were trained to fence and defend themselves privately, with tutors. Curtis and Skar—both sellswords in their way—made fine instructors, though they hadn't yet found an environment conducive for her learning. The royal training grounds would again prove too intimidating and distracting. They needed a comfortable space, which so far she'd struggled to find anywhere in Eod.

"Are you intending to set out?" asked Curtis, eying the woman as she chewed her thoughts. "You seem irritated and ready to dash off."

"Not irritated," she replied, adjusting the awkward metal object tucked behind the lace and leather of her bodice—a piece of jewelry she hated thinking about. "I want to get out of the city, though; I find its resplendence repulsive."

"Ha!" laughed Curtis. "You long for cold iron and black walls. I feel my inclinations shifting toward different places; however, I shall go wherever her Ladyship pleases." She gave him a deadly glare at that honorific. "If the comforts of Menos are what you seek, then we are in the wrong place."

He raised a finger to call for patience. After a bit of rummaging in his pockets, he tossed a generous payment upon the table and rose to kiss Aadore's hand. Aadore blushed once more and slipped an arm into Curtis's. Snickering, Sean and Skar followed the pair out through the gate and into the streets, turning left toward the Faire of Fates. Soon, their small family merged with the living river that wended its way through Eod's mercantile district. Twice they stopped so that Ian might gawk, goober his delight, and clap his hands for an artist swallowing a snake of flame, or a pair of harpists who levitated themselves with the thick currents of music conjured by their Wills.

Impressive sights, to be sure, though Aadore was canny to Eod's ways. Cities, however grand, could crumble. All Eod's wonder meant nothing to the forces that strode this world. Knowing that, she struggled against thinking back into a chilling past. Try as she might, she was brought back to flashes of a dead city thick with the putrescence of the dead, of the hot tingle that came from stepping into an infernal fire to save her brother. She smelled corpses on several occasions, when truly there were no scents more redolent than spun sugar and roasted meat around her. She wondered how long these phantom impressions would haunt her—or the others, she assumed.

Later, they paused outside a public lavatory, a squat sandstone building that played peaceful water trickles and wafted a spicy musk from hanging braziers—the sounds and fragrances designed to mask whatever defecations happened therein. Skar left them leaning by a shaded wall and went inside to change Ian's nappy.

"We're going to change your dirty bum. Your dirty widdle bum," he whispered as he disappeared.

Aadore smiled at his manner, while strangers gave the ogre and child looks of the greatest concern. It didn't help the queerness that under the child's sling, Skar carried a nanny's haversack that looked like a spinster's cluttered purse, brimming with rattles, spare nappies, and bottles for both water and milk.

Sean left her and Curtis and went to lean near the men's lavatory entrance into which Skar had passed. She suspected that Sean had taken that position not to leave her and Curtis to their flirtations, but in case he was summoned to protect little Ian. He wanted to be closer to any conflict. Through observation, she'd learned that her brother watched the world like a predator and protector: head titled slightly toward the entrance, examining every person coming and going into the building; body held tight; his new cane trapped in a white fist; ready to strike at any moment. While less gaunt and more rested these days, a darkness hid around his eyes like smudged makeup. As she stared, Sean unexpectedly broke his watch, moved forward, and grabbed her hand. They shared a dread-soaked gaze that flickered with memories of a black city, smog, and a cold, immortal terror that had attacked them—and squeezed one another's fingers.

"We'll get through this, sister," he promised.

They shivered over what had been promised, or what remained to endure. Somehow they knew they would see the entity again. It was an instinct, a summons as clear as if heralded by a clap of thunder. They needed to be ready for that confrontation. Their hand-holding grew tight and painful.

"Indeed we shall," agreed Curtis, interrupting and nudging Aadore. "And there's Skar."

Aadore and Sean turned to the ogre and his pampered charge as they emerged from the lavatory. "The day grows long, and I'd like to be there before dusk."

"Be where?" asked Aadore. Neither she nor the others knew where Curtis intended to take them.

Curtis beamed. "To Camp Fury, my Ladyship—"

"Aadore," she said quickly.

"Lady Aadore."

"If you weren't so handsome, you'd be a bother."

"I'm glad you think so." Curtis and the others left the lavatory, and the Faire of Fates enveloped them. He continued, louder, over the crowd. "You wanted what remains of our Menos...well, we have a store of its technomagikal genius, architecture, and culture only a few spans outside this city that so grates on your iron nerves. We can visit our countrymen, or use their encampment for your swordplay lessons. I doubt that they will deny our company given your heroic stature."

Cheeky and clever, thought Aadore. When Curtis stopped in the middle of the Faire and suddenly reached for her chest, she nearly exchanged enchantment for rage and virtue. However, Curtis had only traced her neckline so that he could fish out a chain from between her breasts, upon which was attached an old iron cross with a circle around it. It was a cumbersome, austere piece of jewelry, reminiscent of a relic a priest might have used in ancient times to cast out evil spirits. Despite the stature associated with the medal, Aadore preferred to keep it private; Sean, who wore a similar medal under his shirt, must have felt similarly. She thought of when the gift had been given to her, the night after their meeting with the Iron Queen. Without ceremony or the customary celebrations often present for appointments to nobility, she and Sean had been elevated from servant to master by one sweep of the Iron Queen's quill upon a paper. Notes had been delivered, one apiece, to their respective quarters by an Ironguard, who'd waited like a murderer in each of their bedrooms as they'd returned from supper in the White Hearth. The messenger for Aadore had bowed, apologized for startling her Ladyship, then handed her a velvet-sewn box, in which lay the medal as well as a note:

> *Aadore Brennoch, champion of the Iron City, I have considered the story of your survival and recognize you with one of the highest honors our realm can bestow: a title and a tithe—the latter to be bequeathed when Menos's wealth has been reestablished. Here is a relic of old Menos, an Iron Cross from when men knew to worship the institution of the Crown and not only the men who wore it. I bequeath to you this Iron Cross, and bestow the same gift upon your brother with the expectation that you will stand with me as did the old nobles of the Iron City: with pride and loyalty.*

> *I believe that a woman creates her station, and you, through your actions, have cast off the shell of what you once were. You serve Lady El no longer. I shall see that the Lady El is informed of your rise into Menosian aristocracy.*

> *Regards,*
> *— G. Bb.*

PS. You will be provided with funds to properly outfit yourself and your servants.

A personal missive, autographed by the Iron Queen herself—Gloriatrix Blackbriar—as though they were equals. It could shatter a lesser woman, the reality of how quickly life could change. Standing there, in the swell of Eod's obstreperous and garish human circus, she was nearly overwhelmed by the unreality of it all. She kept on walking, though, revealing none of her inner turmoil. But it was *a lot* to consider. When they'd asked the Ironguard messengers about the promised funds, she and Sean had each been given a disgustingly generous allowance—more coin than they'd ever seen in a purse. The next morning, after a gathering of their small family in which they could talk of nothing but this incredible turn in their fortunes, she'd hurried to a boutique and attired herself in a corseted black dress with a short train. It was the kind of gown the Iron Queen herself would wear.

Aside from that purchase, in the aimless days thereafter she had no idea of how to live this new life. She was a Menosian aristocrat? Is that what had happened? Had she gone from sewing hemlines to ordering hemlines sewn? It was hysterical. What did her new status even mean in an empire without a stake of land? What was she to rule, govern, or influence? She was torn between glee and ingratitude at the mantle of privilege that had been bestowed upon her and Sean. She'd been happy being a lady's maid. One in service never considered they would ever achieve anything greater than a higher level of servitude. Menosian service girls knew not to dream of being ladies, for the closest they'd ever come would be mistresses...or corpses if the master's wife discovered an affair. She couldn't imagine what Sean thought of all this: the promise of riches, a medal of honor, a title, and possibly lands in the new empire. While much of it was vagaries and dreams, the Iron Queen seemed not a woman to break her word—at least not with those she favored. Why had she chosen them? And what would they make of it? They hadn't even spoken to the Iron Queen since their appointment, to address their myriad and pressing concerns.

Aadore finally faltered and stood dumbstruck in the roaring crowd. Sean, sympathetic to these same issues, grasped his concealed amulet in a knot of fabric and wished he had anything to say to his sister about a situation he himself found so bewildering. People began to elbow the seemingly intractable strangers standing in their path. Skar and Curtis shoved them off, though as pleasantly as the guards to Menosian nobility should be. Even little Ian gave a pout of indignation toward those expelled from the company of his masters. They could not stand there foolishly forever, however. At that moment, Curtis—decisively and with a boldness that would have seen him killed in the old empire *or* the new—pressed himself into Aadore and shattered her icy ruminations with a kiss. It was sweet and savory as the tea and tarts he'd eaten a while ago. It was warm as the sun, though slightly cold, too, as his tongue probed deeper and she tasted the back of his mouth. It was their first kiss after the years of tension masked beneath glances, brushes of flesh, and the alchemy of desire had flourished between them. As their passions rose and shivered into a fever, they grasped harder at each other's flesh. It was everything the two had waited for and expected. They didn't want the heat between their bodies to subside, and pulling their mouths apart was painful. Before that moment, it had been safe to say that neither of them had been kissed before with such force.

Aadore slapped Curtis across the face, more with passion than vigor. "Next time, you should ask. I am your master. I am your lover only if, and when, I choose."

"I shall remember to ask, my lady." Curtis bowed and stepped back. He rubbed his cheek, grinned, and offered his arm like a proper valet-cum-courtesan. "The day wanes, and we shall have to ride in the desert for a time. Come, Lord and Lady Brennoch, our countrymen await."

Aadore and Sean stiffened, raised their chins, and glared at the day with the defiance of ones who knew rule.

VI

The woman rose from her knees and stood. She was tall, brown, and as firm as a young tree. A tumble of sand-bleached hair fell from the single shaved mane she kept upon her naked skull over her unkind, hard-hewn face. A chain ran from a small nose ring to her ear—representing another component of her ferocity. She wore less colorful, less padded leathers than the other warriors in Lila's army, and a tattered cape fell from her shoulders before it was swept back by her hips and the capped silver fangs that were her daggers. In the glow of dusk, Kali shone with a threatening radiance appropriate to her transformation. Once she had been a cowed, sewn-up woman, and now she was a proud general of Lila's army. Only they weren't called generals, the women who led, but *Makret*—mother-warriors.

"*Hamārē janajāti kō surakṣita rakhanē kē li'ē, bēṭī dhan'yavāda. Maiṁ jalda hī unakē sātha hōṅgē,*" (Thank you, daughter, for keeping our tribe safe. I shall be with them soon), said Lila.

Burning with resentment, Kali glanced at the pale, perfect, sleeping man near her queen. "*Rājā uṭhatā hai?*" (When the king wakes?)

"*Āpa krōdha kē sātha kahatē haiṁ ki. Maiṁ usakē li'ē intajāra nahīṁ hai. Mujhē lagatā hai vaha kyā pratinidhitva karatā hai kē li'ē pratīkṣā karēṁ,*" (You say that with anger. I do not wait for him. I wait for what he represents), countered the queen.

The reproach instantly sobered Kali. She lowered her head. "*Kṣamā karēṁ, mām. Maiṁ apanē jñāna kā sam'māna.*" (Sorry, Mother. I honor your wisdom).

"*Bidā'ī.*" (Travel well). Lila nodded as she said her farewell. Kali reciprocated before sliding from the room like one of the chamber's creeping shadows.

She is stealthy, strong, and proud. A fine warrior in your army, said Erik.

Our army.

He grinned, broke his stone pose, and bent to kiss the back of her neck. He moved up to her ear and finally to her candy-red mouth as she turned her head to the tune of his passion. When Lowelia entered in a fuss, she saw Erik—huger, blacker, and as imposing as an Immortal brother of Brutus himself—twisted around and groping her seated liege. The carnality of the act and sudden heat and strange smells of cinnamon, rock-dust, ocean mist, and man-sweat in the air disarmed her.

"M-my Queen!" she said, at last.

The bloodmates continued their erotic tussle for a moment before reinstating their formality. Soon, Erik returned to being a guardian, and Lila was again a composed, watchful ruler.

"My friend," said Lila. "A secret burns in you."

"It does!" Lowe hurried forward, unwrapping the crystal sphere she held. "The Mind. At first I was a bit burdened by its company. I haven't had a child in my care since my daughter, Cecilia. And it asks so many questions, like a child—a vexingly inquisitive child. Only I don't usually have the knowledge or skill to answer any of its questions. Mostly I take it around, like a pet, even though I feel I'm more on the leash than it. I show it the world and all its wonders; *matrices* would be the term. Well, I didn't realize what it was doing during our wanderings. Thinking, always thinking. Unraveling the mysteries that we cannot see—and working on one problem in particular I hadn't imagined it could fix."

From Lila's circumspect expression she could tell she'd been rambling. "King-be-damned, it's done it. It's figured out how to wake him! Oh, bother. Here, it can tell you better than I."

Lowelia took a few steps and then shoved the Mind into the hands of the queen. Both Erik and Lila froze as the jolt of the Mind's words flowed into them. *Mother Lila and Father Erik*, it began (they'd changed the nomenclature for their relationship with the Mind naturally and without disagreement). *After extensive examination and collation, I believe that I have found a remedy for the Magnus's condition. As you know, the Magnus's spirit lies under assault from the viral energy of the Dreamer classified as the Black Queen. In order to slow the infection of his matrix, he has retreated within himself—shut down the essential functions of his body to stem the pathways through which the infection is carried. The simplest and most physiologically obvious solution would be to inoculate him. However, in this case, since we are dealing with a spiritual infection, traditional medicine cannot provide the answers. A spiritual inoculation, then, is required, a fortification of his Will through the application of magik from powerful and pure Wills that share similar telemetry. Such telemetries will ensure a successful bonding of the magikal vaccine, while at the same time their variance will provide an added deterrent against the viral matrix of the Black Queen.*

You want us to heal Magnus? asked Erik. *With magik? I am no sorcerer, and the luminaries, sages, and the whole of the royal college's circle have attempted every known remedy to wake him.*

He does not sleep; he has suspended himself and his higher functions, contested the Mind. *Magik is a part of you, Father Erik, and you are of a sorcerer's matrix even if you would not apply yourself to that discipline. I believe the crudest and rawest application of metascience is necessary. Blood and oaths. Promises and an exchange of power. Reweave into him the threads of the matrix that you have sundered, and I believe he will receive—from you and Mother Lila—the immune response necessary to fight his infection.*

"A blood oath?" roared Erik; Lowelia pounced away from him like a terrified cat. "With him?" He pointed at the tranquil king as if he were an ominous object of worship. "We broke such ties once, Lila, and I have come far in understanding my hate toward him...but this...What is being asked of me, of *us*...?" With a shake of his head, he stormed around the chamber, his steps creating a small earthquake.

Lila sat still and mysterious. She cradled the Mind, which had grown silent. Behind her composure and grace, her mind was on fire. Each in this room knew what she'd suffered, and the grand, terrifying steps she'd since taken to walk a path of love and life—though actions of darkness and wickedness she had done, too. Was this penance? Was this the agony of events reaching their natural climax? For a person's past could never be escaped, only confronted. What a wretched mess it would be to bind the three of them to all their hatreds and faults. And yet Lila, ever brave, having vowed to think of others—her queendom, her children in the desert, her victims in Menos, and the children of tomorrow—once more put aside her fears.

Erik loved her more for her bravery, and knew what she wanted of him before she stood, leaving the Mind to rock in the warmth of her vacant chair. She shimmered with the golden-green scales of her hidden spirit, and bit into her hand with two sprouted fangs. In a speck Erik was at her side with a lazily bleeding wound of his own: after making a fist, his fingernails slicing into the meat of his palm. He thrust his hand into Lila's, and their fingers formed a slippery, sensual entanglement. Next, the queen bent at the side of her former husband, pulled down the light sheet that rested upon him, and leaned over his body.

Farther back by the wall, and huddled into herself, Lowelia watched the Immortals. She felt her smallness in that instant. At once, the room swam with a strange potpourri of magik and musk, and her vision began to drunkenly ripple. She couldn't be sure of what she was seeing in the dusky room—her queen, who'd become part serpent, or Erik who'd turned so dark that he gleamed like polished stone. Despite her disorientation, however, she was sure that Lila—a fanged Lila—had bitten into the alabaster wrist of the king. Lowelia watched the queen and Erik take Magnus's hand as if to share in a prayer, while the knight rubbed the king's wound with his thumb, mixing their blood into a glittering paint that coated all their fingers. She could not tell whose blood belonged to whom, or if that starry paint was even blood, or why there seemed to be so much of it. Something was whispered, though by whom was another mystery, for there were no words—rather a power that warped the pressure in the air to lead. With a whimper Lowelia fell to the ground. She remained in a wheezing heap, until the throb of whatever words the Immortals had shared in their minds and souls stopped trying to shatter the world.

Father, lover, wife, and brother. Bleed into me, see into thee. Three pains, three souls, are bound once more. I swear to you, until the end: lover, father, mother, and friend. I hate you. I love you. We are one. Did she imagine the strange rhyme repeating in her head? Was this her mind trying to construe what could not be construed? Suddenly, Lila—now fangless and scaleless—was lifting Lowelia to her feet. Lowe's knees felt like quivering pudding, and she couldn't remember anything other than that circular incantation. She must have passed out.

"My dear," said the queen. "Come, have a seat."

Lila led Lowelia to the nursemaid's chair, where the Mind had been laid. Lowelia took the Mind back into her swaddling sling before sitting. It took some sands before she regained her bearings, before the golden light from the fireplace dispelled some of the haze and fog in both the room and her mind. Lowelia's skin tingled for a time, as though a lightning storm had occurred. Erik and the queen stood behind her while she recuperated. She'd had her share of their strangeness, and looked to the exotic king instead. With her sense as a caregiver, she detected a change in the king's health. He was moving, for one. His pink-shaded hand, which lay above the sheets, was twitching, and he was gasping fitfully. She couldn't see any injury; perhaps he'd healed as quickly as Immortals were rumored to do.

"Did it work?" she asked, at length.

A crash of thunder cut across the sky outside. The curtains whirled from a wind that tore through the chamber, a wind as cold as the heart of a glacier. In the whipped hearth, the fire flared from gold to a heinous, sickly emerald and spat a flurry of sparks. Lowelia screamed, and it was perhaps the sound of her terror that shook the vestiges of Magnus's long, cold fever from the king's head. He too awoke, screaming like an infant pulled from loins and into life. The thunder and wind died down. Magnus, bathed in sweat though quite lucid, looked past Lowelia at the figures behind her. She saw only agony and sorrow in his face, and as such, Magnus's first words shocked her.

"Thank you," he said, and then wept from whatever new pain consumed him.

VII

While loath to ever admit it, Gloriatrix had grown to enjoy the wondrousness of the King's Garden. Granted, the flowers could have been blacker, the trees thornier, the birds given to more shrieking caws and clattering claws, but those were Menosian flourishes and inspirations. For now, the calm and enchantment of the King's Garden sufficed. Gustavius made a fine, quiet companion for her evening constitutionals. He hooked his cold, armored elbow into hers and walked in perfect stride without glancing at her. Indeed, his gaze was ever ahead, peering into the murky corners of the wood, scanning for threats against his queen. The King's Garden, however, was a place freer of danger than any other woodland in Geadhain, and there were but night larks and peaceful fauna to test Gustav's attentiveness. As they followed the silver ribbon of road twisting through the dense forest, the oft-silent man surprised her with his words.

"Forgive any assumptions as to the worth of my opinion, but may I speak of the new nobles?"

Aadore and Sean Brennoch, thought Gloriatrix; he was probably wondering what she planned with them. "You may," she replied.

"I admire what you have done. As a man who has come from nothing, and one who earned his title and status the iron way, I think that power is best earned and taken—and they clawed their way through a dead city for theirs."

"I agree," she replied. "I know that you know how power is earned in life. The *iron way*, as you say. It is a road taken by the brave. We have so few men and women of real character in the world. Thus, to find two persons—brother and sister, even—who share the same fortitude as you or I is rare. I can see leadership and cunning in them. People think I am without feeling or mercy, when in actuality I reserve my pathos only for those who've bled, crawled, and fought their way through life. I thought deeply of how to reward these clever heroes for their truth, fealty, and service. Wealth and power are the easiest rewards to give, so it may seem that I played my hand frivolously. However, what interests me more is how their ambition, when paired with that influence, will shape their next steps in this war. Whether to be greater or lesser than what we were the day before—that is the choice we all face."

"Ah. You have a plan for them? These Brennochs?"

"I always have a plan."

Gustavius nodded. Naturally, his queen had strategized her next move. He would be informed of it when it became necessary. They continued to saunter down the trail. They wandered by enormous swaying perennials that chimed as their crystal bodies clattered into one another. Once, a white elk trotted over the trail, and they paused—the Iron Queen thinking of how much nicer it would look with an ebon coat, while her ever-savage companion felt the urge to shoot the beast and eat its delicious flanks. Farther down the path, over a woven-glass bridge, something from a faery princess's domain, the pair spotted another white blot in the darkness ahead. The twist of gay color about the figure's head—a scarf—identified her.

"Elissandra!" cried Gloriatrix.

She dropped her companion's arm and rushed over to a bench planted slightly off the road that had been twisted together from leaves, glass roots, and silver veins. There sat Elissandra—hand and wrist-stump on her lap, knees together, and gazing up through a hole in the forest's roof at the inscrutable canvas of space. At first, she didn't notice the Iron Queen, or at least she failed to respond as if she had. But as soon as Gloriatrix sat beside her, Elissandra took her hand, palm to palm and with their fingers interlaced like young friends. It was terribly awkward for the Iron Queen—she hadn't spoken to the seer since her damning revelations and the subsequent vanishing act she had performed on the day of Queen Lila's return. While she tried to shake off the seer's hand, Elissandra restrained hers with awesome force. Gustavius had caught up and lingered behind, knowing not to interrupt this embarrassing reunion.

"Release me," said Gloriatrix.

Elissandra snickered. "Sometimes we need a bit of love shoved down our throats. It's the only way bitter medicine can be administered."

"I'll not ask twice. I shall ask Gustavius to separate us in a speck, and you won't care for his method."

"As you wish." Elissandra sighed and let go.

Gloriatrix slid down the bench, away from the grabby seer. "Where have you been? Almost a full week and none of my soldiers, or the king's forces, have seen either hide or hair of you or your children."

"We've been preparing."

"For?"

"For Death."

A chill passed over the Iron Queen. "As have I, and I could have used one of the few remaining resources left in the Iron Empire—you and your gifts."

Elissandra shrugged and then turned to give the Iron Queen a macabre smile. "I'm already a ghost, Gloria. You must focus on those who are to remain in our world. Do not bother yourself with me, beyond your promise to see to the safety of my children."

"Where are they?" Gloriatrix looked around, as if they might be cackling and lurking in the dark, which probably wasn't far from the truth.

"Practicing, readying themselves for the Pale Lady," replied Elissandra. "They have to hone their skills and Will for what is to come. I have to prepare you as well, which is why I've sought you out."

"I *am* ready," declared Gloriatrix, as she envisioned Death's rotten army incinerated beneath the might of her Furies like a horde of wax figures left in a roaring kiln. She wondered for how long the Dreamer and its vessel would withstand her Furies' wrath before melting. Specks, she figured, since even a Dreamer in the body of a man was limited by a certain weakness of flesh. While Magnus had been playing the princess slumbering under enchantment, she'd concluded this battle in her head, and it ended with a desert licked in flames and reeking of atomized corpses, with the Dreamer's vessel somewhere among them.

Are you really ready, though? thought Elissandra, caressing her wrist-stump at a sudden ache. The illusion of such simple domination flickered in her head. *Do you know that the great iron ships in which you have placed such certainty will betray you, as will all your iron machines and machinations? Do you know that the blood of heroes and the sacrifices of noble souls are all that is capable of halting the withering hand of Death? The sands you have left to save your soul are running low, Gloria. I shall have my chance to redeem myself for my crimes. I pray to the Fates, to their daughter, that you will have yours, too. I wish that I could tell you the futures that I have seen, or give you the guidance*

*of a friend; to do so, however, might alter the beauty and chaos ahead. I shall
not risk my children's lives or the sanctity of this world for selfishness—you and
I have done that too much in our lives.*

"Why are you here?" snapped the Iron Queen. Elissandra stared at her,
eyes watering. Gloriatrix wanted none of that pity. It infuriated her. "If you
have sought me out, I assume there is a reason, which isn't to sit on a bench
like widows waxing on the charms of our dead husbands."

"I am here for a meeting," replied Elissandra. She stood and drifted
away from the bench and a bewildered Iron Queen.

"Meeting?" exclaimed Gloriatrix. "What meeting, if not this one, here
and now?" She bolted after the seer, but somehow Elissandra was ever out of
reach, fluttering almost, several steps ahead, and moving deeper into the
woods.

"Not with me," she whispered. "But a voice. One that I heard above all
the other echoes of Fate I have been subjected to in recent days. One man's
voice shouting over the din. One that called for his mother. I found him—or
he found me—crawling up the side of Kor'Keth. Like a baby maggot, or a
worm. He's a bit of each. *Death* is inside him now, though he owns a piece of
her power, and she cannot take it back. You mustn't be frightened, though he
is rather frightening. I thought it best for you two to meet away from the eyes
of Silver Watchmen or Ironguards. Men who would judge without seeing
beyond the skin."

Elissandra had stopped near a tall black tree with fingered branches that
clawed at the moon; it seemed entirely out of place in Magnus's garden. By
this gloomy forest giant, she stood, beckoning and billowing, as much an
apparition as the second shape that suddenly reared behind her, peeling out
of the tree's shadow. Gloriatrix's breath ceased as that new shape slithered
around Elissandra and into the starlight. Her hand flew up to her mouth to
hold in a scream.

"Iron Queen, watch out!" Gustavius had seen the ghastly creature as
well—a man risen from soil and death. He wielded his pistol in its direction.

"No!" cried the Iron Queen, as she bit down on her fist to stop the tears.
"It's my son. It's Sorren."

The dead man caught his mother as she fainted.

II

STAINED HANDS,
ACHING HEART

I

"Mama, what's that light?" asked Reginus.

"What light?" Octavia had no answer for the golden-brown boy tugging at her hand about the flash in the sky, the ripple of sapphire power that had shot out like lightning from a rod in reverse from one of the towers—the greatest, the Keeper Superior's tower—in the ring of the Faithful. Eatoth had trembled from its core, and now a shroud of darkness had overtaken the sky. All of the city's white stone and gold-tinted beauty looked as dull as old bronze, as though it were a moldering ruin. Octavia felt the deepest dread in her heart. What had that been? Along with the other timid denizens paused on the Ramble or gawking from the loggias that bulged onto the street, she stared at the Keeper's silver tower. Like them, she was waiting for more light, or another shake of the earth—symbols of the divine, she felt. Despite the curious event and its accompanying grim thunderclouds, she approached the others who were filling the street and fretting, and tried to set them at ease with the words of their order: "What She Wills, She Wills."

Octavia was a Keeper of Words, and thus knew every old phrase and prayer from the era of Teskatekmet and onward. As one who did the busywork of cataloging the histories, mysteries, and sciences of each and every age—the work with which Keepers themselves were too holy to be bothered—she knew much of the world's workings. In the back of her mind, she searched her knowledge for a similar historical event to explain a flash of power, the tremble, and the suddenly darkened sky.

"What does she Will, Mother?" asked Reginus, who was as curious as his mother.

"I think she Wills for us to get home."

Octavia's smile was genuine despite her nerves, though her grip on her son was tight. She wondered about the wisdom in leaving the safety of the towers today. Her husband, Longinus, would be cross with her for having taken a trip into the Ring of the Repentant without telling him, especially if he knew she'd come looking for Amakri trinkets to teach their half-born son about the other side of his heritage.

Longinus had been assigned as guard to those incredible strangers: the Daughter of Fate, the son of Brutus, and the other two powerful men. As he told it, they'd been nothing but a bother to him, especially Morigan and Caenith, with their running off to the Exhibition and causing all kinds of mischief, and she realized that she adored these disruptive beings, even if they'd never met, and even if one of them was the son of a mad Immortal. For Eatoth had needed a shake to its tradition and over-indulgent worship, and these bloodmates had brought with them that change. Again, she'd never speak such heresies aloud, except perhaps to her husband, who entertained her ideas because he loved her so, because he knew where she'd come from— the wilds of Pandemonia. Indeed, he'd done the unthinkable and married an Amakri woman. Her origin was a secret, of course, though they kept few friends, and strangers were naturally hesitant to ask a legionnaire of Longinus's standing too personal a question.

Taken by sudden nostalgia in a busy street not unlike the one in which she and Longinus had met, she remembered the moment of their meeting. She'd been rifling through the pockets of Eatothians for valuables they'd likely never miss. He'd caught her by the hand, their eyes had met, and his grip had gone from hard to soft; emotion moved across his face like ripples on a lake. Love, lust, then the lighting of a spark, between old tribes and new.

"Mama, please stop squeezing my hand so much."

"Sorry."

Happy memories dissolved, danger swirling in the acid of her stomach, slithering like one of the great rock snakes from the wilds outside these walls. Thinking of walls, she stopped, turned, and gazed at the grand, ever-flowing barricade that protected Eatoth from incursion. A queer noise further cautioned her: another rumble, long and rising in pitch, as if a machine somewhere were grinding unhealthily to an end. And then the wall and the technomagikal power behind it did end. Like hammers of lightning striking the forge of the heavens, flashes of blue power dazzled the sky. People shrieked at the spume rising from the enormous wall, throwing its shade over the city's highest roofs. People gasped as they saw glints of the tangible copper surface that had been hidden by water for thousands of years, something they'd always thought was crystal and pure magic, but was merely a simple wall. Over the hissing and thundering heavens, next to the fury of nature being unleashed from her long imprisonment, the cracking of that frail man-made barrier was heard as clearly as an egg dropped in a hurricane. Those nearest Octavia screamed in ragged madness as one of the theikispor— a silver egg-shaped carrier of the divine that was flying over the wall— shivered and abruptly dropped into the writhing mess beneath, its impact swallowed by water that frothed and rose.

Octavia knew that staying frozen upon her spot any longer would spell her doom. She was an Amakri by blood and thus had inherited their fleet-footed instincts. She ran with her child, who neither questioned nor protested. Perhaps the tribal blood within him had also been triggered, and as she reached for him, he leapt into her arms like baby to mother ape. She loped toward any sign of safety, shoving stunned fools out of her way. Behind her the city was creaking, and she imagined its ancient bridges swaying like loose strings in the wind. Beneath her, the ground gurgled as if it were a hungry throat, and a chaos of bystanders, gawkers, hair-pullers, and shriekers threatened to swallow them before the earth had a chance. Praying to the Green Mother for guidance, she noted a seemingly solid building from an older era appear on the street. A portico led up into the pillared façade of an ancient building, which had a banner over its arch announcing itself as the Spoiled Goat.

How appropriate, she thought, referring to the baying, senseless creatures wandering about the steps and staring into the cacophony of a city unraveling. They did, indeed, seem like spoiled and brainless goats. Although goats would have had more sense. Bullish, still carrying her child, she threw herself up the steps and through a crowded doorway just as more fools came flooding out. All her supposed kindness and mercy was cruelly shown to be false, for in that moment she thought of saving no one but herself and her son.

Dashing through a door, then a foyer, then a hallway, she emerged in the tavern's heart, her vision spinning from the adrenaline. She tore around tables and their discarded, steaming lunches to behind the bar, where she hoped a cellar or basement entrance could be found. The oldest buildings, like her own home, had storm-rooms from the time when people still worried about the elements out of habit and hadn't yet grown complacent under the arkstone's watch. Praise the Green Mother, who must have led her here, for behind the bar was a metal-banded door, set into the flagstone floor. Whoever was tending the tavern had clearly left to watch the disturbance outside, and there was no one to stop her or her boy. She set him down and they worked together to hoist open the heavy door. A waft of cold mist hit their faces, and they stared for an instant down a ladder that might've led to one of the religious purgatories for sinners about which Octavia had often read. It would be cold, damp, and quite unpleasant, though nothing compared to the worst of all disasters that was currently befalling Eatoth. She hesitated.

CRACK! HISS! BOOM!

The sounds shook the land like cries of agony being ripped from the throat of the Green Mother—the worst *was* happening, here and now. If she had any remaining doubt about jumping into the cellar, it vanished with the flurry of shakes, rumbles, and terror storming outside. It was possible they were sealing themselves into a tomb, and yet Reginus, unquestioning, descended the ladder before his mother took the same precarious trip down, slamming shut the hatch and bolting it above her head before joining her son in the dark. There, she sat among crates and fusty piles, holding her child near. However much Doomchaser blood flowed within the lad seemed to be keeping him from crying.

Outside, keening slabs of foaming blue flesh toppled upon the city, wave after wave, one of which crushed the entire building above their heads and tested the seams of their stone prison. The old bones of the cellar resisted, bleeding a bit of dust—for now. It was dire enough for Octavia, once Octavikta of the Doomchasers, a child sent to Eatoth for her lack of scales, to harken back to her roots and sing to her child the songs of his people.

In darkness, he listened to her music, and she to the music of the world collapsing: a vile music that settled gradually into soft percussions. Then it was still, and there was only her voice and a gentle whoosh, as if they were hearing water from a cabin below a ship's deck. When all seemed as quiet as it could be, she answered the question she knew was burning in his mind.

"Eatoth is gone, my son. Our age of arrogance has ended. What She Wills, She Wills."

He could not see her expression, but she sounded happy.

II

Did you feel that?

Amkhapet awoke from her trance and stared at the man, hooded in red and gold fineries with sleeves draped long as a funereal priest, who hovered near her side. She could not read his expression through the mask he wore—an ornamented silver plaque of a man's bearded face. However, she watched him look around the chamber for threats. After a speck, her ward shook his head and replied with a mind whisper.

I felt nothing, your Eminence.

She wished she could say the same, though the sensation, the shiver she'd felt while wandering the valleys of Intomitath with her mind, lingered. It was a revulsion, as if a dead eel had been dragged along her thigh—sickly sexual and horribly unwanted. Still shuddering, the Keeper of Intomitath rose from her crimson settee and walked softly on her naked feet across the golden tiles of her grand cupola. Golden monsters wrought into the metal dome seemed to snarl from the dancing light of the copper braziers that stood about the room. Breezes twisted the gossamer of her thin shift tight across her lean frame.

She was dressed more seductively than Keepers usually were. That was her right, however, as Keeper of Intomitath. Consumed with vague notions of danger, she reached the railing, leaned upon it, and pondered what she knew of threats to the other Great Cities. Foremost was the legend, the atrocity, of the City of Wind: one sister usurping the liberties and rights of another, then a dark deal struck by Amunai in revenge. But how could Intomitath be in danger? Who would betray her? She was loved by all. Except, perhaps, by the usurper now sitting on the throne of Pandemonia, who loved nothing but herself and her misery.

Annoyingly, politics were not within the purview of Keepers, and each great city was an institution unto itself, and any threat of Ankha's was distant. Why this feeling of fear, then, as though what she had built could truly be undone by an enemy? Against the intractable foundations of her realm, she had made great strides in civility and social engineering—moves that would seem small to the cultures of the west, though revolutionary in Pandemonia. Long ago, Aesorath's survivors had come here seeking sanctuary after being turned away from Ceceltoth, Eatoth, and the wandering tribes, as their beliefs had cast them as heretics against all three factions. Over half their company of hundreds had been lost in the trekking back and forth across Pandemonia, and if turned away again, the nomads would not survive another season. So rather than cast them out to continue their wandering attrition, Amkhapet had surprised these refugees and her own people by opening the fiery gates of Pandemonia's most austere and ancient city to them, and ushering the trembling masses into her realm.

For she wasn't like her sisters, or the Keepers before her; she was her own woman. No more did she choose to wear the itchy, unflattering garments of a Keeper, but donned herself in silks and sensuality. The arkstone had maintained the beauty of her youth: her unblemished countenance, her figure, her long black hair, streaked with golden highlights from Intomitath's endless heat and light. For this feature, her ward called her a *tygris*, after one of the jungle beasts from the western islands. Power was not simply the freedom to choose one's attire or to act with few consequences; it was a flame through which change was forged. In Intomitath, in Pandemonia's greatest forge, she'd continued the work whispered of by Aesorath's exiles: breaking down barriers between faithful and faithless, between those in towers and those below. In order to discern the blueprint for this society, she had given these exiles homes and comforts that at first they had believed to be traps to expose their heretical ways. But she was no betrayer, and this was merely an exercise in patience for her. She would wait years, or in some cases generations, until the survivors of these exiles spoke of the legends of Aesorath they'd heard from their parents. Then, along with her own ideas, she'd nurtured the concepts that Amunai had struggled to implement: freedom, love, unity. Thus, while Intomitath was not the city Amunai would have made, it was even brighter, for it stood as a testament to that dream—a flame never to be doused.

As she gazed from her pinnacle—a red metal fortress forged from the oldest of alloys and veins found only in Pandemonia—past the floating red eggs that patrolled the sky, past the metal bridges banding the sky and crackling with fire and magik, and down onto a landscape of crimson towers, black buildings shingled in cherry red, many-piped factories puffing technomagikal smoke, and the multitude of dark, glittering swatches of the walking gardens, she could neither see nor sense what had pulled her from her meditations.

Beyond the awe of Intomitath's construction—the awesome, roaring greatness of the City of Flames, at which one could gawk for hourglasses— there simmered in the cauldron of steadily puffing forges and cast-iron domiciles a *peace*, which lured the Keeper from her wakefulness. It lent gentleness to a realm that should have been a devourer of life. Indeed, and at this time of day, many would have left the forges, closed up shop, and wandered the lamplit threads of light weaving through the sootiness below. With her Keeper's mystic ear, she heard the laughter, songs, and woes of her people. Although even their grievances were no more the simple conflicts of Amakri versus Lakpoli, but of people heartbroken, or doubting their worth.

That these men and women could now consider their smallness, or desired greatness, meant much in a city where one's magnitude had long been predetermined: you were a Keeper, a Faithful, or you were lost or a heretic. Never should those classes cross or intermingle.

And yet, she had mingled traditions and truths. Slowly, carefully, to not upset the social balance, she had first allowed Amunai's disciples to continue with the customs that had come from Aesorath. Many seasons later, and when left alone, their neighborhood, the outcast's quarter, had flourished. Aesorathians were master tenders and eked greenery from plots where no green had grown in a thousand years. Most notably they became known for the trees and their fruits that were cultivated: golden spheres of fleshy sweetness that literally dropped in abundance to the ground. Apples...From what she knew of the dead Keeper, Amunai would have been pleased that her offering of peace to her sister had at least brought peace elsewhere. With these fruits, the outcasts baked rolls and pies, and the aromas of dusty spice and buttery sweetness borne on a hot breeze were an enchantment to many.

The quickest way to a nation's heart was no different than to a man's: through the stomach. Fear of the outcasts had lessened day by day, bite by bite. Likewise were the other unfortunates of the city, the Amakri, slowly welcomed as members of equal society. First, by the people from Aesorath, then by those who visited the Spice Quarter and saw these natives being treated as compatriots.

Amkhapet had named the outcasts' neighborhood, whispered it from her mind into the common parlance. This was one of many suggestions and whispers she was to give to shape her nation. Another was to slow, then eventually stop, the tolling magikal bells that crippled people to their knees for daily worship. Many moving parts, whispers, small rebellions later—brutally, silently crushed—and the city had taken on its new form. Within the cauldron of Intomitath glimmered green swaths where apple trees bloomed, or outdoor encampments lay amid the metal trees where the Amakri continued their wild traditions: hunting vermin, which had grown quite large and fearsome in the magik-soaked sewers of Intomitath. Ratchasers, many named themselves—a twist on another and quite prestigious tribe from which some had been exiled.

Peace had come to the City of Flames, and it was all that she sensed as she looked over her great work and remembered that she had been looking for danger. Perhaps the fires in the factories burned brighter, angrier, and she could almost taste their industrial tinge on her tongue. Perhaps the skies over Intomitath appeared redder than usual, as red as raw flesh veined in purple. Still, she could not separate fancy from truth, which left her with a sense of lingering, displaced fear.

Her ward stood beside her at the balcony, observing his mistress. Since he knew they were alone, he gripped her waist, and she pictured his large tanned hand and the smile that surely rested behind the embossed metal mask strapped over his face—she'd taken to many of Amunai's heresies, including the rumors of rolling with her servants. But what leader didn't know love? How could she preach for or against such a concept without first understanding it? So much of what Amunai had been punished for was simply part of being mortal. Amunai's curse had been her instinct for rebellion, for seeking hidden truths. Amkhapet supposed she suffered from the same problem. Which raised the question of how many women trapped in these metal towers and suffocating in ritual and silence had thought the same as she and the dead Keeper? Amunai's sacrifice had given a woman like her hope that change could happen. In the secret shrine of her heart, she honored the mad Keeper for that sacrifice.

She would make Pandemonia see differently, behave differently. She did not fear the Keeper Superior's wrath, and if it came down to a clash between water and fire, the flames of Intomitath would fizzle Ankha's might to steam. While considering that potential clash, from out beyond the smoking city, its iron wall, and the brazen circle of fire that surrounded it, there came a whisper, a rustle to the ear, leaves and dust-laden wind over stone—the voice of nature. She'd heard it before, more recently and clearly as her compassion had grown and her devotion to ritual and arrogance had faded. It was the voice of the Great Mother, and she arched, enraptured, as she was spoken to by the land.

Dead, said the voice, and the rustle of leaves went silent, the scent of loam and soil that filled her head suddenly redolent of rot. She stiffened, coughed away the ethereal smell, and shook off the sensation of the blood in her veins turning to ice. It was no summer whisper, no tune of change and love from the Great Mother. It had been a message of death that had come to her—a warning.

Ankha is dead, she said to her ward, bewildered. *Eatoth has...fallen?*

Choking on the thought, at first she could only gasp. Another of the ancient cities had fallen? How, and by what power?

Then came another thread of music, and not in the Great Mother's melancholy temperament or tone. Drums. A song of war. It echoed to the Keeper's mystic senses from somewhere out in the blasted, black-encrusted mountains surrounding Intomitath. It came from a thousand throats and instruments or more, all in sync with a hideous maestro: a king of lust, fire, and depravity. She knew it was the mad king, for his name was both the lyric and chorus to their song, rolling and rising throughout the march of their approach: *Brutus! Brutus! Brutus!* Her premonition was a warning from the

Great Mother. Her ward had not yet heard the heinous song, though soon all in Intomitath would shudder from the music. She leaned over the balcony and screamed with her psychic might to all those in her army.

Brutus marches to our city! We must protect our people. Every child and animal is sacred. The only blood that must be spilled is that of the mad king's army. We shall incinerate them with our fury. Call down the fire. Unleash the ballistae of the sun. We cannot allow him to enter our city, to defile our dream. Go! And may righteousness bring us victory.

After her proclamation, she stumbled back from the window and was caught by her ward. For a moment, he held her, staring with his deep blue eyes through the expressionless husk of his mask. Then he removed it, showing the measurably more handsome countenance beneath, and kissed her.

"I would die to protect you," he whispered.

And so he shall, came an insidious murmur from the window, a whisper of the Great Mother. Amkhapet, reeling, coldly pushed her lover off and called to her other wards to bring her armaments for battle.

III

Sun rose over the glass towers of Eatoth, providing light for an otherwise dull, doomed city. In a place where so much music once played, there were no songs but for the howl of desolation, and broken instruments lay scattered amid great embankments of refuse. In the week since the city had gone dark, a swampy and ashen stink had settled into the city's bones—remnants of the flood that had come as the wall of waterfalls was unmade, smashing the city in a tsunami of death. The flood had long since abated, flowing into the holes surrounding Eatoth, or those made as the skyroads had snapped and careened into the city, cleaving wide fissures in the ground. Here and there, small lakes and tracts of road remained flooded. Should one wander too close to the magik-stripped, coppery wall, an insufferable trickling and groaning could be heard. Sometimes the wall creaked as if it were a wounded frigate and seemed ready to topple on what remained of Eatoth.

Within the ruined outer ring of the city, quiet buildings hid in the hazed amber mist of dawn, though much was alive within that obscurity. Only a few days after Eatoth's fall, Pandemonia's buzzards—rubbery-looking birds with spiky heads and jarring caws—and packs of wild horrors had infested the city's ruins and picked at the many trash-mounds or through the buildings submerged in mortar and wreckage. In time, the many sinkholes would widen and pull more of the neighboring buildings into the earth. Soon the land that had endured, unchanged for millennia by the arkstone's power, would at last submit to the will of Pandemonia. It would erode and transform. It would swallow the copper tiles, marble statues, and other elements of hubristic grandeur of which the city was made.

What persisted of the Ramble, an often shy glimmer that circled the ruins, seemed to have been torn up by giants. Waste and abandoned goods that couldn't be eaten by the wildlife were strewn across its once bronze and beautiful skin. Discarded clothing flapped from bent streetlamps, superfluous declarations of the empire's demise. Moldering, waterlogged theater stages cowered in smashed heaps, abuzz with flies. The Ramble's many fountains, at least those that hadn't been entirely destroyed, had been raided for their water and left with only their coins. Beside the Ramble, a few of the grand, old-boned taverns that had once warned away the Amakri with their rococo opulence, stood defiantly. Their vine-wrapped pillars, however, were splitting, their loggias bleeding bricks and wood into the street, and their myriad windows shattered, the wind whistling across their shards and through shredded silk curtains. In the end, though, it hadn't been the disaster or even savages who'd sacked the city; rather, it was the "civilized" people of Eatoth.

For when true darkness fell upon Eatoth, the citizens of Paradise had been anything but civilized. After the screaming, flooding, and crying in the night had calmed, these professional aristocrats had grown wilder than any of their Pandemonian relatives. Having never known strife, they'd descended into desperation. Upon realizing food would no longer simply appear or be delivered to them, street wars had begun over what edible resources remained, which weren't many as the nation had never considered or planned for the dismantling of its society in a single day.

Further from the conflict, the legionnaires couldn't be dispatched quickly enough to settle even a portion of the disputes. Moreover, those warriors were already engaged sorting the business of a dead Keeper Superior and a missing arkstone. The divine seeds used as transit around the city-state, vehicles powered by the arkstone, had also become as useless for flight as boulders. When the arkstone was taken, many of the seeds fell from the silver highways in the sky. Fires had broken out, and it was only on account of Eatoth's old infrastructure and reliance on stone buildings that the City of Waterfalls wasn't completely razed by flames. For a few nights, and from afar, the streets had glowed with watery mirrors and flares of light—each one a small pocket of floods, fire, pain, and destruction. Whatever wonder and cleanliness Eatoth had once possessed had been eradicated by the hand of chaos. There was no society left, no order remaining. The head of the great snake, Ankha and the arkstone, had been removed, and the body of Eatoth thrashed and floundered. A few wards, seeing no path forward, took their own lives, leaping from the silver towers to their doom.

Chaos wouldn't win, however, and from the Keeper Superior's tower a battered legion arose, united under the wisdom of a soldier named Longinus. A soldier who thought more freely than his fellow warriors. A man who fought to find a harbor from this storm for his countrymen and his family. Longinus sought to find them first—his missing wife and son—and his fight would inspire Ankha's other lost servants.

IV

After Ankha's death, and with Morigan and Caenith covered in the crime's blood, the bloodmates and their company had been placed under arrest. Their jailers, however, secretly knew that their imprisonment had been consented to by the prisoners. Even one-armed, the Wolf could have stood against the pitiable wards in whose care they were left. Instead, he and his pack chose to behave while Longinus advocated on their behalf to the remnants of Eatoth's rulers. Morigan couldn't be stirred from her remorse, anyway. She was content to be imprisoned, to suffer for her foolishness and hubris, and be punished for her crimes—among them, the death of Ankha weighed the least heavily.

In the hourglasses following the Keeper Superior's death and Eatoth's fall, the compatriots remained in a gloomy crystal and metal chamber, watching their own sad faces twisted in reflections on the wall. No matter how much sense the Wolf tried to whisper into his bloodmate's mind, she couldn't forgive herself for her mistakes. She stood apart from the others, who sat on the floor, and leaned against the wall as if it was the only thing preventing her from falling. When she was not sulking, she fondled the fragment of stone hidden in her pocket—Ankha's necklace, which the Keeper Superior had been wearing and which Morigan had inexplicably stolen off the corpse when her bloodmate was looking elsewhere.

At one point, the Wolf stormed over from his huddle and slammed his hands against the wall beside her, hoping that the shock would startle some sense into her. His aggression scared only Adam, Thackery, and the jittery legionnaires guarding the holding cell. At once, the Wolf felt sorry.

We have committed no crime, my Fawn, he mind-whispered to her, softly. *She was a monster, and Eatoth a society of sinners.*

Morigan's silver glare cut him like a cold winter blade. *Do not slam and stomp around and expect that I shall bend to your will. I am not as much of an animal as you. You would do well to heed that fragment in you that is mine, that is mortal. I would have seen the tortured Keeper Superior live. I am neither judge nor executioner. Nor are you. I would have liked her to have had the chance to explain herself to some authority, to heal herself—or her sister— through admittance of guilt. As it is, I almost pity Amunai now, knowing what I do. Her child, her lover, her life was taken away—*

Do not pity her!

I don't. I said almost. She pushed him away from her, with a stunning demonstration of bestial strength. *I pity the people of Eatoth the most; these ones you call sinners. They are innocents, fattened and dumb from a life of pleasant imprisonment. Their screams are echoing in my head.* She grasped his arm and, in doing so, sparks crackled through his body, and his head exploded with psychic sensations: howls, explosions, and drawn, gurgling death rattles. These noises so powerful that the room faded to black until Morigan removed her hand and let him drop to his knees on the floor. There he huffed, and she continued. *Take a moment to see what and how much we've ruined. Use your great ears to listen to the chaos happening outside these walls; use your nose to smell the piss, fear, and blood of a society undone. I don't know how we shall fix this. I don't know that it can be fixed.*

"What was broken here was broken long before you, I, or my father were ever involved," he said. "We are not the seeds of destruction. At best, we are the rain."

Rain, she thought, safely, behind a shield of her Will. *Shall it rain here again in a hundred years even? Or will this chaotic land decide to blight this place in desert and lifeless tundra? Do you realize what we've done, my Wolf? We've ended a society. We've ripped through Pandemonia's peace. All because we believed too much in ourselves and our power. Arrogance. Would Amunai have won without her tricks and our conceit? Would I have been less violent? It was my blade and your claws that gored her sister first; we were the instruments of Amunai's vengeance. I remember the feel of her warm lifeblood spilling over my hand. More and more, I see how we are weapons. Weapons so rarely bring about peace.*

She watched her bloodmate's great bronzed back heave and yearned to share their feelings, or even his sensuous, primal touch—the simple warmth of his nature. Although she knew on this matter they were of different minds. To her, she'd murdered someone. To him, he'd been hunting. She had committed genocide. He had protected his pack.

While she pondered, the Wolf rejoined the fellows on the floor. Angry, he hunkered down, shifting his weight back and forth, foot to foot, looking ready to leap, his back to Morigan. The Wolf believed this was what mortals referred to as "having a spat." It was agonizing for him to fight in such a way, to feel so torn from and yet connected to her. The Wolf wanted to kiss her, or lick the blood from her hands—which he'd earlier attempted to do before she stopped him with a look of disgust. Still potent came the rusty waft of the Keeper Superior's murder from her hands. While she detested what they'd done, he felt more indifference toward the execution than when hunting an evening meal. Ankha had been wicked, and the wicked were predators, and also prey for greater killers. Ankha's end was a just end for the life she'd lived. If he were to die, then he too would likely die in battle. However, after considering Morigan's words, he realized that there were also many other lives at stake, especially those enslaved by Ankha's madness. For those innocents, his mortal side was repulsed by Ankha's cruelty.

Thackery broke the Wolf's spell by placing a hand upon him. "Is she going to be all right?" He'd attempted to speak to Morigan since Eatoth lost its light, but she had been as cold and dark as the city itself. "She won't talk to me. I've never known her to hold back her feelings. Except when it came to you."

A flash of memory of the men's tempestuous introduction on the doorstep of Thackery's tower in Eod, where they had met snarling lover to growling grandfather (of sorts), brought each of them a small flicker of joy. They grinned.

"*Element breaker.*" The Wolf sighed. "I cannot believe I slandered you so. How far you and I have come from the bitter, wary wolves we were."

He continued, bold and loud, caring not if his bloodmate heard. In fact, he wanted her to.

"As for the woman to whom we have devoted our service and hearts, she is stronger than any metal, a rose forged of fire and steel. Remember, friend, it is through her adaptability, and her extension of that gift for change to us, that we have become friends. I am better now, and stronger, though I am still myself. I am still an animal, and almost I wish I could be more of a man for her in times such as this, which require the kind of empathy and sensitivity I struggle with. I feel no pity for this wicked woman, Ankha, but I feel for the people of Eatoth. I also feel how deeply my Fawn has been wounded by these trials, and I am ashamed that I cannot be the remedy for her heart."

"You are," replied Morigan.

She had drifted from her sulking by the wall and, as she came near, Caenith stood and they adopted a familiar copper and pearl embrace. As Thackery and Adam beheld them, again united, the men sighed. One could not be in their presence and be unaffected by the majesty and charisma of the giant Wolf and his most elegant, silver-eyed Fawn. They were unshakeable; they could change the world.

The Wolf hammered true this fact as he said, "We do not break."

"We do not break," repeated Morigan.

Hungry from their separation and torments, the bloodmates kissed, and the men looked elsewhere until, in a moment, Morigan and the Wolf sat once more with their companions.

"We have broken something, though—the Wills and hearts of the people of Eatoth," said Morigan. "I know time is pressing, and wars do not wait, but we must lend our hands to help these people before we continue our quest."

No one would dispute this, even though the wick of time felt short—the Black Queen's maw was poised to consume Geadhain. Morigan knew that when she gazed heavenward, Zionae's wretched star would appall her with its presence. However, Zionae's triumph wouldn't happen today, and she and her pack had amends to make and not many sands in which to do so.

V

Longinus arrived when Adam summoned the guards. The man seemed pale, if energized. His helm was off, his sandy hair tousled, and sweat beaded under his anxious brown stare. The man seemed in need of a good shave, too. He'd stripped down to his tunic and sandals. Such dishevelment was forgivable given the night's events. Not to mention that with the climate control of the technomagikal city now as dead as every other modern amenity, the tower—like most others—was beginning to heat like a tube of glass on a sunny day. The heat would become nauseating by midmorning.

Longinus pointed at Morigan. "Your crimes have been somewhat pardoned," he said. "I made a case for your innocence before the council of the wise, and a bargain was struck in exchange for your help."

"Her help?" asked Adam.

"Who better to help us find the missing, the wounded, and the needy than she?"

Extending the olive branch further, Longinus then shared with the company the waterskins he'd slung on his belt, along with his tale of his missing wife and child, who had been somewhere below when the city collapsed.

"I would know if they have died," he declared to Adam, with shivering conviction and a hand to his heart. "Octavia, my wife, is a Keeper's archivist—a woman of many wiles and secrets. Of all the people of Eatoth, she would be among the most likely to survive—she and my son. I've had scouting parties look for them in the ruins, though that's as hopeless as it sounds. I need to know if they live, and where they might be found. Please, ask her."

While she wasn't anywhere close to fluent in Pandemonia's tongue, Adam's translations weren't necessary to stir the powers of Fate in Morigan, and a cloud settled in her mind. Through that dreamy mist, she spied a woman and a child somewhere precipitously dark—like a tomb. Only, they weren't dead; they were very much alive. Morigan knew she could trust this vision, and that it wasn't a trick of her senses. While Adam was explaining Longinus's situation to the seer—she didn't appear to be listening—she returned from her Dream with a jolt and a gasp. "His wife...and son," she said to Adam. "That's what he was asking you about, yes? I can lead us to them. Tell him. And there are others, too, who haven't been found. I shall lead us to them, as well."

Morigan smiled and nodded to the weary legionnaire, and he took this as a signal of hope. His family was alive. Praise the Green Mother's kindness. In haste, he gathered the strangers and led them from the dark chamber. A group of battered warriors, their armor tarnished and imperfect, their faces grimy, awaited them in the crystal hallways outside the chamber where they had been kept. Somber blue wards were there, too, though they also wore the same fatigue as their companions, expressions drawn ever grimmer by the duskiness of the tower. None of them scowled or raised arms against those who had killed the Keeper Superior. Somehow, somewhere, a truce had been reached.

Morigan, following this fate, then saw in her mind's theater a scene wherein an animated Longinus had stood in a grand candlelit hall and shouted for reason among blue robes and terrified-looking warriors—none of whom seemed to possess the wisdom, practicality, or leadership to orchestrate Eatoth's next movements. Longinus had stood then, and declared himself and his willingness to lead; not a soul around him had contested his announcement, as he was the only shepherd in a city of sheep. She admired his bravery and felt him the leader the city most needed. The bees had more to say on this new leader's aptitude, too, and another rippling looking glass in time appeared. Peering through, there stood Longinus in another era. The legionnaire was older, his blond curls twisted with white. She watched him orate to a captive audience around a campfire, telling legends of times past, of a city bloated by its own greed, and of the cataclysm that had freed it. Behind him thrived a green and strange woodland that hooted and shuffled with the noises of beasts alien to Morigan's Geadhain. Beside the elderly Longinus was a handsome man who looked much like the leader and was surely his son, and an elegant woman who wore her gray features with the majesty of a silver queen. Surrounding the family of shepherds, hidden in greenery, were buildings entwined, almost hidden, by nature. Here was a vision of a place, knew Morigan, a realm that could possibly be standing in many years: a new Eatoth.

At least all is not lost, she thought, as her vision of a forest shredded to nothingness, and she was again in the crystal chamber with her companions, who were all waiting for her to stop dreaming. Now she had another future to protect by winning this war.

VI

During the long descent from the tower, Adam spoke with Longinus about the state of the city. Longinus and his men had first organized themselves and then made several small excursions toward the outer ring of the city, where the damage was most severe. Survivors were few, and they'd been brought back to the safer region of the ring of rule, where the crystal towers presided...although that safety was a thin illusion, since there were few to no supplies of which to speak. Even in ideal circumstances, they could have sustained themselves and a pittance of refugees only for a week.

"What of Ankha?" Adam whispered as they descended a crystal stairwell as thick with heat as an Alabion summer. "What has been done with her body?"

So little had been said about the former Keeper Superior. Longinus wrung his hands and shook his sweaty head. "The Keeper Superior's body was brought out from the depths of Purgatorium, and we discussed what to do with it. In the end, she was wrapped, anointed, and will be buried— somewhere among the earth and stones, and without the formalities due a normal Keeper. We know that she was not herself, that her spirit had been taken by another. We believe that the mad Keeper of Aesorath controlled her actions. We also know partly why such vengeance was enacted upon her...The wards have heard strange whispers since the darkness fell. Whispers from a voice they believe to be divine, from the Great Mother of many colors and manifestations. We have been blind and deaf to so much, for so long. Our people are not how you've seen them; we are Pandemonian in our hearts, and therefore creatures of change. So it was that the wiser, cooler heads among those left to govern our city prevailed with common sense and declared you free. We shall ponder the mistakes of Ankha's rule for many generations to come."

"You mean *your* wiser, cooler head," said Adam.

"I was one of the most vocal, yes," he replied. "Although, between you and me, my wife is responsible for destroying much of my prejudice toward outsiders and outside beliefs beforehand. And while I may be a leader today, as we've seen, nothing is permanent. My station is not guaranteed."

"Thank you for being our advocate," said Adam.

Longinus acknowledged this with a grunt, and they continued down the winding well of stairs. The procession down the crystal tower took on the mood of a funeral ceremony as sad songs began echoing up the stairwell toward the party. The Wolf was first to notice the scents wafting up: pungent, pepperminty oils slathered over something once dry and now greasily shifting. *Bandages*, thought the Wolf. He knew they would be passing the Keeper Superior's funeral procession before the wards bearing a palette emerged from the haze as he peered over the railing. In time, they caught up with the four bearers and the body on a landing.

Because of the heat, the wards had slipped off their cowls and revealed beautiful faces. It was these ritually silent men who sang with clear a cappella voices. Apparently, when honoring death the tradition of quietude was broken; either that or the rules were changing entirely. With morbid fascination, Morigan gazed at the body, to the pits that were shadows of eyes and mouth under the slick wrappings that had been thrown over Ankha's remains. She felt none of the remorse she'd expected to. The Wolf was right; they'd performed a mercy killing of a sick animal—even if their hand had been if not forced at least influenced by Amunai. Still, Morigan's staring and her appearance here startled the singing wards, whose songs broke. As the weariest of the four stumbled, the oiled mummy slid off its pallet. The Wolf astonished and humbled his companions with his thoughtfulness, leaping over Adam and Longinus in a breeze and snatching up the corpse just as its bound toe was about to graze the crystal floor. All of the pallbearers were scared, trembling and afraid to ask him to return the body. Without any objection from Longinus or the wards, the Wolf decided to give these men a break, and he carried Ankha's body from there on. The pallet was discarded and the procession continued, with the Wolf separated from his pack and solemnly holding the corpse in his arms as if it were a delicate ritual object.

How gallant and mortal of you, my Wolf, whispered Morigan.

We have amends to make, as you have said.

Amends. Octavia's spirit called out to Morigan from the desecrated edges of the city, past ruins, floods, beasts, and other dangers. Once Octavia and all the other survivors had been found, there would be another pilgrimage to undertake. Morigan knew she must lead them to the scene of that verdant hope pulling at her chest: the woods at the city's core. There, much stood unchanged by the disaster. There, men and women hummed old

Pandemonian tunes and carried on with their work as if all in Eatoth hadn't ended. Those people were pardoning of mistakes, and understanding of the cycles of growth, life, and death. They would welcome her and the divine rulers now outcast from their heavenly thrones.

VII

Octavia and her son lived as moles in the dark, and in due time no longer bumped into shelves, sacks, or each other; they saw hues and shadows for what they were. Because there was nothing to do when the world ended, and since they were trapped beneath hundreds of thousands of tons of stone, they spoke, ate, and worried about Longinus's fate. If he lived, he would find them, somehow, and that much they knew. There would be no escape on their own; Octavia had climbed the ladder and tested the hatch. The trapdoor absolutely wouldn't budge upward, and collapsing it inward through hacking or force was a damnable idea, as there was no telling how much detritus had sealed them in and might collapse in on them at any time. The hatch leaked a bit of water, though not enough to drown them before they died from starvation or misery. The former was less likely to happen than the latter, since the hideaway they'd found was stocked enough to feed the tavern patrons for many a night—more food than was usually on hand for people so used to a rotating, unending supply of wants. From cracks in the wall they couldn't see, wind hissed in. They wouldn't be dying of asphyxiation or starvation, it appeared. Which left them with the game of patience and hope.

And so, to make the near unbearable less grim, Octavia told her son the bright and valiant tales of his people—his real people, not the witless lambs of Eatoth. The telling of his heritage was a duty to be done on his sixteenth nameday, she and Longinus had decided, once their son had become a man. Yet she wasn't sure that day would come, and a person must go into the Great Mystery without uncertainty.

She began by telling him of a girl, Octavikta, of the Doomchaser tribe of the Amakri peoples, a girl who'd come with other weak-skinned children to the wonders of Eatoth, where a life of petty crime awaited her. She stole to survive, and was quite good at pilfering from the fattened masses of the Faithful. Until one day when Reginus's father, and her truest love, caught her in the act. Since Reginus was cut from the same honorable cloth as his father, he didn't judge his mother for her thefts, nor become upset at the truths she'd kept from him. Instead, he hugged her, and said, "I am glad, at last, to know thee and me, Mother. Thank you."

After all, here was a child who had walked through an apocalypse with her, a real blood-child of the Doomchasers. There would be no more secrets, not when they'd known such disaster together, not when they had to piss and shite a few paces from each other, trying to ignore the smell until it faded into something more tolerable. They were mother monster and baby beast. They slept a while and had no idea how much time had passed when they woke to insensate darkness. But they did not fear, for they had each other. They strolled about their cell, examining and checking supplies, while she continued to tell her tales. Soon she imagined that they looked like the wildest hermits of the Amakri: all bolls of hair, filth, and nattering teeth. Eventually, they would circle back to a comfortable spot they'd made for themselves upon the sacks, and she would recount for her son the most ancient legends of her people: tales of the Wanderer who both fractured and enlightened men, stories of the Cradle—from where all life had begun.

"That tale was horrible, Mother," whispered her son, as she finished one of the Wanderer's tales. In the story, he had tricked the man out of his last bit of food for a shiny, extraordinarily pretty bauble—which the man promptly broke in his excited handling and then proceeded to slowly starve to death. Confused, he asked, "But I find the story confusing. Was the Wanderer a hero or a villain?"

"Why can he not be both—light and dark—as all men can be?" She shuffled closer on the bags of potatoes that they'd turned into a beggar's cushion, and tapped his breastbone. "The heart is never one emotion, Reggie. We are both weak and strong, chivalrous and terrible, many, many times in our lives. Why would this be any different for the Dreamers?"

"Because Dreamers are above us; they are divine."

Now Octavia tapped his head—a bit roughly, as if his skull were made of wood. "Think harder, as if you were Amakri and not drowned in false verses and egomaniacal grandeur as you have been, my son. I have had to protect you by not telling you all the truths, though I have always encouraged you to learn, see, and feel for yourself."

This was true, and his mother had often challenged him when he—by reflex—would disdain the Amakri they passed on the streets. Likewise had she always reminded him at every meal of how the food they ate had arrived at their table—from the Amakri serfs who toiled in the green, forgotten arm of their city. By *their* lifeblood was that food present, and thus were they included in any prayers for their meals. With a mother's subtlety, she had already prepared his mind for the truths and stories of his people. Thus, it didn't take long for Reginus to reach the same conclusion as his mother.

"I suppose a man can be each, as you say...If we were made in the image of the Dreamers, then, we should have been given their weaknesses—along with all of their strengths."

"Exactly, just as you've inherited your father's stubbornness."

"I have not."

"You have."

"You're wrong."

"See, there it is again, Reggie."

He opened his mouth to continue his rebuttal, then realized it was as if his father and mother were arguing, and he was watching Longinus throw the final word at the door slammed by mother. Holding his tongue was harder than holding a hot coal in his mouth, and he ached to spit out that last rebuttal.

"Well done," said Octavia, when he'd been silent—albeit grunting a little—for a sand. "Let's have some lunch and do a few more circles around this crypt to keep our legs fresh. Our rescue can't be far away."

They returned to some pickled goods they'd found earlier on a shelf, ate a few handfuls, then walked to the vase-shaped cistern that sat at the back of the cellar. Why such an old means of storing water was present, and full, in a city that had depended upon technomagik for everything, was one more blessing which Octavia attributed to the Green Mother's divine grace. But the relic was there, and filled with cold, untouched water that tasted only a little of the clay in which it was kept. She and her son shared a tin cup before getting to their feet again to walk through the cellar. In the dark, and with only gray boundaries of mist, Reginus make-believed the obscurity into mountains, monsters, or ruins near which they were passing. It almost felt like a real walk somewhere. Almost. His curiosity over monsters, ruins, mountains, and adventures outside this purgatory brought to the surface of his mind a question still unanswered from his mother's stories.

"But why did Feyhazir do that to the man?"

"Hmm? Pardon?" Octavia had stopped, and was hunched over, poking among objects on a shelf. Beneath a swath of fabric, she felt a row of solid, sharp objects with handles: knives. With no particular reason other than that she and her son were living in a post-apocalypse, she instinctively took two and startled Reggie as she stood, faced him, and thrust one of the handles toward him. "Take this blade; you never know when we might need it."

"For what?" he asked hesitantly, claiming the knife as it was shoved at him again.

"Protection. Animals might creep down here somehow."

For us there will be no creeping up *out of here*, he thought, and wondered if they'd ever be desperate enough to use the knives on themselves to end their torment. They knelt on cold stone, and slow and talented as a blind weaponsmith, Octavia explained to him how to fashion a makeshift sheath by repeatedly folding and knitting fabric until it became a twisted, lumpy ring in which a knife could nestle safely. While little of her motions could be seen in the dark, she had her son feel with his fingertips the twists she made. Finished, she then had him stand while she fixed the corded sheath to his belt. Once done, she fitted herself with a sheath, too.

"The lessons of the wild never leave us, my son," she whispered, then ruffled his greasy hair. They began to make the short weave through the shelves back toward their potato-couch.

Reginus was more and more amazed at the serenity and canniness of his mother. Indeed, she appeared as a different person in his mind, and he pondered the change even as they finally sat beside each other on their thrones of root vegetables. In the murklight, he could partly discern her strong chin, her thin and exotic eyes, her tanned skin, and her deep black hair. He'd taken all of his father's comeliness and gotten none of hers, except for the same silvery green eyes: the eyes of a hunter, his mother had once told him, which made sense now that he knew he was a distant descendant of a tribe of Pandemonia's greatest. He wanted to know even more about these people and their divine patron, so for a second time he asked the question that had slipped by his mother.

"Mother, why did Feyhazir trick the man?"

"In the story that I told you?"

"Yes."

"It wasn't a trick, my son; he gave the man what was asked of him. You see, Feyhazir cannot help his nature. Perhaps of all the Dreamers, he is the most prone to wants and to serving those urges, for he is the Dreamer of *Desire*." She said the word as if it were magik, or held power beyond simple, mundane wanting. "Desire is among the strongest forces in the world. Man desires another. Man desires power. Man desires to defeat death, to reign forever. Even the simplest act of eating, sleeping, or breathing is bound to our desire to prolong our existence. When one removes desire from existence, the fire of life is soon extinguished.

"Feyhazir is that fire itself: ever-burning. Thus, in the story, when the outcast Amakri—who'd lived alone for so long that all he knew were rocks and monsters—asked the divine being for a thing of true beauty, it was Feyhazir's compulsion to serve that want, even though he knew the despair of breaking that delicate object would, eventually, snuff that man's flame of life. Feyhazir is the most invested of the Dreamers in our kind, for we are naught but vessels, machines that produce endless want and intoxication for him. Give a man infinite wishes, and it still won't be enough. We are beautiful to Feyhazir, and tragic. We are the endless romance that he seeks and can only touch in rare moments when he is summoned to our world. Is he wicked? I don't know, my son, for he is giving. Is he cruel? How cruel is it to be eternally bound to the service of bequeathing unto us what we desire? I think that very selfless of him, and I wonder if there was ever anything the Dreamer himself wanted, or needed even, other than being a courier of our sinful desires."

In school, Reginus had only been learning Teskatekmet's cants and the histories of Eatoth, so he wrestled with the grand concepts spoken of by his mother. From what he knew, Feyhazir had granted Teskatekmet the knowledge to use her Will for magik powerful enough to control the arkstones, and—less commonly acknowledged—the Dreamer was patron to many of the tribes of Pandemonia, as well. A friend to both, neither, or himself? The Wanderer was a gray and cryptic force, and thinking any more on this legend he'd never witness and in which he wasn't even certain he believed felt fruitless down here in the musty dark.

"The snake in the garden," mumbled his mother. With a sigh, she wandered off to piss, and her son tuned out the hiss of her excretions and stared at the few eggshell-like cracks in the cellar through which light teasingly stole. If only he could be a beam of light, or breath of wind, he wished—his mother, too. They'd fly to freedom. *That's all I would ask for, mighty Dreamer: to be free of this tomb*, he said in silent prayer.

The ceiling rumbled.

Dust fell into his eyes and mouth, and he coughed. Water spat and burbled from hidden fissures; the boy could soon see the black lines from which it came glistening in the dark, and cold wetness touched his sandaled foot. Then the entire chamber began to tremble as mass was moved around above them. *This is the instant in which we shall be entombed.* Whirling, his mother came upon him, clutching him and brandishing her weapon as if it could magikally deflect the thousand tons of stone quite possibly about to fall on their heads. Dragging scrapes followed by shattering thuds rocked their united and courageous front. Reginus buried his head in his mother's skirts and squeezed back the tears; he was a warrior, an Amakri, and if he were to die, it wouldn't be while weeping.

They weren't crushed immediately, however, as they expected. The dragging and thudding continued, rhythmically, as if a machine were working overhead. Mother and son—hearts hammering, breathing ragged— wondered what new terror had arrived.

CRACK!

The ceiling split, and sizzling golden light poured down with a shower of dust. They were blinded, and Octavia crouched with her son, hissing like a lizard and shakily swinging her knife.

"Raaggh!" came a man's cry. Or not quite a man's, for it had the timbre of a beast ripping through flesh.

In the haze of falling sand, Octavia saw a massive shape blocking the light along with other heads surrounding it, like the dread hydra of Pandemonia.

No, those were separate shapes—people—who were moving away from the greater mass and beginning to shout. Whereas the largest person shouted something in that beast-bellow of his that she mildly understood in her bewilderment, with what languages she knew from reading the vocabularae fantastica—codices of language from across the globe—in the Font of Knowledge.

"I see people!" roared the massive figure. "A woman and a child. Adam, we have found Longinus's mate!"

Her husband's name couldn't be mistaken. She leapt and called for her husband, and her son joined her in croaking for his father. The enormous shape that was certainly a man of some sort leapt into the pit, and Octavia raised her knife, as one does when faced with beasts. He was grand. Lean and yet so thick with muscle that every line of his body could have been forged by the ancient metalsmiths of Eatoth, a man of sun, gold, and wild shadow—the hair on his chest and head. And though his eyes were cold with winter chill, gray too, there was still an element of warmth to his manner. A gentleness in how he extended his crushing hands slowly toward her and the boy.

She lowered the knife.

"Caenith," said the man, and she realized that this was the son of Brutus, and likewise that the woman who flickered into being beside him in a silver twist of light must be the Daughter of Fate.

"I am Morigan, and I promised your husband that I would find you," said the exquisite vision, this woman of fire, raw beauty, and sorrow. Octavia understood more of that last characteristic than words could express. She dropped her knife, straightened herself and her son up, and allowed the divine creatures to lead them from the gloom.

VIII

In time, the soldiers, outcasts, refugees, and stragglers converged into a small horde, as Longinus's quest to recover many of the city's missing and dead continued. Their plunge into the ruins became heart-wrenching as they were witness to devastation. Buildings had been reduced to shapeless mounds of brick, emptied houses were mired in wet filth, the whole of the Ramble had turned into a slogging trough of mud and was populated by strange rabid beasts—ones savage enough to risk an attack even when the Wolf was around. Bodies floated in the rank, flyblown pools that surrounded the shattered landscape; the corpses evoked little hope that further survivors were anywhere to be found in this city of death.

Still, their woes were misplaced, and Morigan and the Wolf's senses led them to the few barricaded homes where survivors had gathered. Longinus had wept for sands after his son and wife were raised by the Wolf from a hole in a mountain of trash. Other rescues were less heartwarming, and the bodies of those unable to hold on were left in ruinous tombs, much to the despair of the scant survivors with whom they'd been interred. Few of Eatoth's lost souls would have a proper burial. Most would be left for scraps over which the hunting cats, scaled vultures, and hissing, horse-sized lizards that had invaded Eatoth would fight.

On the third day of their rescue mission, Morigan heard no more cries for help in her head; that dissonance had been a constant headache since they'd set out. That morning, she woke with her bloodmate, watched the ratty flaps of her tent billowing in the white vapors of early morning mist and smoke, and heard nothing aside from the chatter of early risers and the calls of Pandemonia's beasts. Blessed silence. The Wolf nuzzled and kissed her, and they made love with their mouths for a time, though she kindly pushed his hands away from elaborating on that. Their companions were sleeping nearby. Adam and Thackery had been admirable support through this mission—Thackery mending what wounds he could with his magik, Adam lending his strength to excavations as well as tirelessly translating and speaking on behalf of his friends. Aye, their spirits were as tired as spirits could be. They needed this moment of rest.

Besides, a buzzing in her skull told her that there was some place for her to be. The bloodmates left Adam and Thackery to their deep, deserving slumbers and snuck outside.

Mist hung over the sun and city, hiding Eatoth's ugliness behind billows. The morning was neither too hot nor too cold, and the hickory sweetness of campfires concealed the lingering stench of Eatoth's demise. Gangly survivors and golden legionnaires appeared in the dreamlike swell of the morning. She knew most of their faces and names by now, through either visions or camaraderie. As she strode about the camp—the Wolf trailing like her shadow—she waved and nodded hello to those gathered around weakly fluttering fires made from the city's scraps. Truly this was the best of what they'd salvaged that hadn't been ruined past usefulness. There wasn't much more of a supply reserve beyond their wood collection, the hunting contributions of the Wolf and the legionnaires, and the strained supplies they'd brought with them from Paradisium. But the Wolf only hunted when not acting as the Keeper Superior's pallbearer, and even his best efforts wouldn't feed the hundreds of mouths they'd saved from chaos.

Soon this legion would need to join the other legions and the thousands of survivors already headed toward Eatoth's green heart—an operation set in motion by Longinus's runners some days past. It had been a hard decision at which to arrive, for the prideful leaders of Eatoth to go begging to their servants for aid. But Adam's quiet diplomacy and a few mutterings from Octavia had certainly influenced Longinus's mind. Many survivors would have already reached the green heart of the city. When Longinus's legion arrived there, they would bury the magikally preserved corpse of Eatoth's old ruler and both symbolically and literally lay this chapter of the city's history to rest. That journey would begin today, Morigan felt, and then her quest to stop mad Dreamers and kings would resume. She paused and sighed, lost for a moment.

"Daughter of Fate," hailed Octavia in a loud, clear voice.

Longinus's wife sat upon a toppled pillar by one of the fires. Tribulations and filth had dimmed none of her dark beauty. She looked as fit as a midnight stallion, as rested as the misfits huddled around her campfire seemed beaten. Although Morigan hadn't spoken much with Longinus's wife, she appeared to have a strong grasp of Western Ghaedic. In the hive of Morigan's mind, the bees buzzed with excitement; this was who she was to meet.

"Octavia," muttered Morigan, sounding dreamy and in the thrall of Fate.

"Please, sit with me," said Octavia, and the bloodmates joined her.

Bystanders watched them, trying to be inconspicuous; men seemed in awe of the size of the Wolf, up close, and took him in from head to toe as he stood behind his bloodmate.

"You speak our tongue well," said Morigan at last.

"I was an Archivist to our realm," she replied, "a woman of words and letters in the Font of Knowledge."

Morigan wore a puzzled expression as the bees continued to pollinate her with psychic information. She was unsure of what, exactly, the images of a grand churchlike building with mezzanines and terraces brimming with gilded shelves and sterling desks might be.

Octavia sensed the need for an explanation. "The Font of Knowledge was a library and museum for all of the world's secrets. Every language, story, and history known to the Great Mother."

"Ah," said Morigan.

"Are you seeing it now?" asked Octavia, for there was a cloudiness and distance to Morigan's gaze.

"Yes, I believe so."

"I should expect nothing less from the Daughter of Fate." Octavia smiled. "Perhaps it's redundant for me to further detail my duties to you. Still, I spent my life within those walls, where I learned, scribbled, and spoke of infinite things upon which our divine ruler wouldn't deign to ponder."

"You sound indifferent to her death," stated the Wolf, bluntly. He sniffed. "And you are one of the few who does not carry the stink of old flowers and fall rain: the scent of sorrow."

"Why would I bear such a scent?" Octavia matched his boldness with her own. "I am glad she is dead. I am glad that we are once again free to struggle, hurt, and know all that it is to be alive, that long fight against death. My husband and son are hunting together. Longinus was always reluctant to take him hunting—perhaps afraid to enkindle the wild blood that I have given the boy."

Octavia turned back to Morigan.

"Since you see and know everything, I shall spare you the need to divine this, and tell you that I am not like these lost lambs." Throwing back her tattered shawl, proudly, she gestured toward the peering masses. "I am an Amakri. A Doomchaser. I am a child of chaos, and at one on the seas of change. We must always adapt."

She humbled herself once more. "Although I am speaking wisdom to the masters themselves. For I have seen how you, son of Brutus, are nothing like your father. While a beast, you are also penitent and wise. Kind enough to carry the body of the woman who enslaved and tormented us. Likewise, Daughter of Fate, have you spent your precious hourglasses helping us unite as one people again. I am honored that each of you has stayed with us and given your strength and time."

"We have places to be," said the Wolf. *And we have companions who need an Eatoth to which to return.* Wistful, he gazed off toward the ghostly sun. "And I should find my burden, whom I left with the wards last night. Morigan?"

"I shall be along in a while."

While the Wolf's hide prickled from Fate or magik, he felt no danger and left his Fawn to chat with the unusual woman. The ladies, alone, expressed shyness at the other's presence—Octavia a bit more than Morigan as she wrestled something from her pride.

"I should thank you," she whispered, "for finding my son and me. Until that day, I didn't believe in miracles, or in many of the wonders of which I've read. You are a wonder, and you have been my miracle. My truest thanks."

Her gratitude brought Morigan warmth; looking around at the ruination of Eatoth, she questioned what penances would be enough to absolve them. "It is a miracle of your own that the two of you survived," replied Morigan, "considering a place as deep and dark as where we found you. My bloodmate had to remove a whole building's worth of wreckage. What did you do? How did you survive?"

"I felt a sense of danger." Octavia gazed westward, as though the Doom-chasers were riding on the horizon. "My people all have it—we're children of Feyhazir, too, though not as special or purebred as you. In the dark, it was those tales that sustained us—the stories of our history, our patron, your father. They were more fattening than any food, more nurturing than the sun—without them we would've died."

"You know of my father?"

"Of course. How could I not, as both Doomchaser and Archivist of the Font of Knowledge?"

Octavia recalled the brass glory of her old workplace: the chandeliers of crystal and pulsing light, the leaning chambers, wall-to-wall shelves built into buttresses, the sheer echo of a place so grand that every step and shuffle resonated, the wafting scents of must and leather from a million books and parchments—it had been a cathedral of wisdom. She assumed it was all rubbish and flooded ruins now. It would be what she missed most of Eatoth, and not only for the wasted, irretrievable knowledge. It had been her familiarity with societies outside of Eatoth's strictly preached theocratic beliefs that made her a candidate for the position, as her job had been the one in all of Eatoth for which an open mind was needed. And, endorsed by her husband who'd risked his status by suggesting that a woman not of Eatoth should be given such a sacred appointment, it had become like a second marriage. Longinus's gambit had succeeded, aided by her dazzling capacity for retaining facts. She'd learned much in those halls, even made a few friends, none of whom had been found in rubble, as far as she knew. They were as dead as the Font to which they'd pledged their years.

"Sorry," she said after her long silence. "I was remembering the lost."

"Could you tell me more of my father?" asked Morigan, as the hive inside her mind went wild from hunger; this was the nectar they desired.

"I believe I was meant to," declared the Archivist, feeling the trembling of a buzz off the woman.

Thus the seer and the Archivist of all Eatoth's secrets, perhaps the wisest in all the realm, began to speak of the Wanderer, the Dreamer of Desire, the Snake in the Garden, the Tempter of a Thousand Names. Many sands later, after Longinus and his son had returned and as the encampment disassembled and the inhabitants began to move, did the Wolf approach the women. He was holding Ankha's body and standing at a distance as if he were a golem of death and trying not to eavesdrop on what was a private and clearly intimate conversation. It was evident from the fluttering of her heart, which he felt, that she was hearing nettlesome truths.

"Remember," said Octavia, reaching for Morigan as she rose, "the Wanderer is not evil. He is just like us, flawed and broken, his actions as obscured by desire as our own. Remember that, but be aware that desire can lead us deeper into damnation than anything else."

Overhearing that tidbit, the Wolf shivered.

IX

Through the green wild they went, the legion a glimmering line in the darkness like a long tear wept by the moon on high. Longinus, Octavia, and young Reggie walked at its head. Behind them moved the shadow of the Wolf—still bearing the embalmed and preserved body of Ankha. Behind him walked, almost drifted, the ethereal seer. Then a haunted and comely man covered in tattoos, and finally and a striking miracle-worker, who had healed so many with his rudimentary though helpful fleshsculpting. Thackery was more clearly seen since he'd lit the end of a walking stick with a star seemingly pulled from the fabric of space. Indeed, Thackery's light shone brighter than the dull sapphire effulgence emitted by any of the blue robes' weapons: armaments—and men—that Thackery figured were losing what power remained in them without the arkstone's energy, as these men had been unable to mend the simple wounds he'd treated. These sorcerers would have to return to the basics of their craft. They'd have to learn how to tap into emotions and passion again, then temper that against Pandemonia's temperamental nature, and all without the crutch of using a relic of obscene power. Perhaps here, in returning to their sorcerous basics, was a lesson in which Thackery could appoint himself as teacher.

Throughout their days of searching, the pleasant death dirge of the blue robes had continued off and on, like the flickering magik of their staves.

Ankha's original pallbearers walked behind the Wolf in a somber quartet. This morning Adam had surprised his friends by joining the choir, with a voice as pleasant and trained as any other to be heard.

"My mother and I used to sing together," he explained after many an inquisitive glance, adding, "The whole woodland is sad, and excited, for this time of great change—you should hear their songs."

At that, the Wolf returned to noticing a harmony to the chatter of life around them: tweeting night birds, clacking bugs, barking creatures. It was almost unified in its beats of high and low, the shrill animal flutes and delicate nattering, with threads of even more lyrical sound—words, prosody— between. As the Wolf lost himself in nature's song, he lost himself in time and distance, too. His feet moved, and Ankha's body felt weightless in his arms. It wasn't until the spice of soil and leaf mingled with smoke and sweat, and metallurgy's singed-tang hit him, that the Wolf woke from his reverie and noticed the trees bent aside to the wide field, and saw the one bright place left in all of Eatoth.

Come, all ye faithful, beckoned the land, and Longinus's procession of disheveled outcasts wove through a moonlit woodland toward the flock of lights blinking through the trees. The forest was thick with growth and droning flies, and the air weighed the men down more than the sweat on their stripped skins. Nevertheless, they raced against their discomfort and toward the lights. At last they'd found a home.

X

In the days that followed, the company worked themselves, their disciplines and spirits, as they had never done before.

The Wolf was put to work in the fields, now that more food was desper- ately needed for the suddenly swollen populace. In the mornings, his silhouette could be spotted by workers clearing lines amid the golden maze of maize. Later, Morigan could see—with mind's eye—her beloved plowing barren fields like a technomagikal workhorse. He moved in a blur, spraying earth and wielding two tills while dragging a plough behind him usually fastened to a machine thrice his size. Mostly, the workmen either watched, awed, or waited until the dust had settled to tend to whatever irregularities in the soil the Wolf's work had missed. Then seeds were planted, a task with which the Wolf helped as well. Truly, there wasn't one span of terrain, one tree, or one tract in which his hands hadn't been immersed. As days bled into nights, and his love and sweat poured into the soil, the realm became richer for his toil. Perhaps, as his father had in Zioch, his strong, virile Will was instilled into the dirt—Immortals were magikians whether they learned theory or not. After only a few days, hardly enough for normal germination, sprouts had peeked from the brown, and flowers on long stalks appeared by the week's end. When the Wolf and Morigan met in the evenings, she kissed his earthen hands. She understood the Wolf's *siogtine*, his penance, was all in her honor.

Morigan was no less busy in the rebuilding and had focused her skills on uniting Eatoth's fractured peoples: the outcasts, the once-vassals, and those who had ruled. Bringing together three radically different cultures and expecting them to live in harmony was a monumental task. Morigan's days were exhausted through supporting Longinus and Octavia in their move to disassemble the old rule and to create a new order. Although the blue robes were without a compass to guide them, and their magik was weakening, that didn't stop certain dissenting voices from rising in opposition. Wards were angry and also leery of any changes that removed their stature as leaders, and saw themselves serving a community of earth-tending heathens and Amakri dissidents.

Often Morigan sat in on the meetings held in the great shell of an ancient temple. It was a spectacular ruin, a crater lined with weary pillars, a few of which were trees. At the outskirts, under the pillars, slithering greenery burst through a solid granite ring of descending stairs—that such a ring had stood since the dawn of this city spoke to the ancient masons' talents. The stairs, though partially succumbing to wear and decay, were strangely handsome with their runners of dirt and leaf. Heaps of grass and flowers obscured ancient crumbling benches. People had guessed that the place had been an amphitheater. No one but Morigan knew that it had really been a site of worship for the Green Mother—or Great Mother, as Octavia seemed to refer to her—before her haughty children had abandoned the ancient ways.

During her visits to the site, Morigan and her two arbiters, Adam and Octavia, remained near the stage of the grand hall, listening to arguments while either the Archivist or the changeling translated for her. She was less interested in physical language, though. Rather, she bided her intercessions, she disassembled men's auras when they clouded in dark red—the shade of intolerance—then she plumbed them for their secret fears. Finally, Morigan shared these secrets with Octavia. After which, bearing the seer's insights, Octavia would tiptoe down the verdant tumble and then paraphrase Morigan's words to the council of New Eatoth: a gathering of farmers, smiths, and blue robes who'd been nominated by their peers to negotiate the rules of the new city.

The goal in these women's minds was to create a realm where the three different—though at once the same—cultures could exist. Nothing could be the same as it had been. Though to achieve harmony came the dirty work through which weaknesses had to be exposed, pride shattered, egos broken. At these tasks of calling out men for their failures, Octavia seemed, perhaps, a little too enthusiastic. A smile on her lips as she reminded the blue robes that their power and authority had come from the arkstone and had not been earned. A laugh at the man who asked why she was even speaking, before she reminded him that she held all the remaining knowledge of their culture and of the systems and technomagiks they might one day reclaim. Truly Octavia was a force to be reckoned with, and soon when she came down to the circle of debate there was silence and respect for whatever insightful wisdom she might bring.

The resolutions were easy, as no tyrants had been elected. Most men wanted peace, though they rarely knew how to strike it. Morigan, through Octavia, outlined what concessions were to be made. The women's edicts were clear and simple. *We shall give the blue robes the lands to the east of the farmsteads. In those wilds, they may again hear the whispers of the Green Mother, or see her grace in the flutter of a butterfly against the sun. They will remember and strengthen their magik only once they've thrown off all that they were. Much like that butterfly, they must molt and change. Thackery can teach them how to connect to their magik again—he is our bargaining chip; he is what we shall offer.*

Thackery, who had mostly been helping out with mending and magik elsewhere, was shortly informed of his new duty. And while the earthly holdings of the woods beyond the farmlands where the wards could continue their practices were a far cry from the tall buildings in the heart of the green city that the blue robe appointees had thought to claim, these terms were not contested. The blue robes had all heard of—or in some instances seen—this man who could work magik without the crutch of an arkstone and had conceded to the wisdom of Octavia's proposal.

Other conflicts were similarly resolved. There was a reallocation of half the legionnaires' martial forces into rural responsibilities to support the strained productivity of the city. The remainder of the soldiers would keep watch, as normal, or rotate back and forth between the duties of soldier and serf, and those complex schedules and divisions took many days to settle. As for the original inhabitants of the green city, Morigan had to rely on little in the way of machinations to make them comfortable with the sudden change in their lifestyles. These folk hadn't forgotten the Green Mother's wisdom, and the magistrates that were present for these people—the foremen of farms, armories, and general laborers—watched their former superiors struggle to embrace the new reality with naught but wry expressions on their faces and amused whispers in their heads. When everyone had tired of civic debates, or when situations appeared civil enough that Morigan could remove her intimidating presence, she left to lend her hands to simpler responsibilities.

She would walk the streets of the green city under the emerald and brown arches that wept damp autumnal leaves. Throngs surrounded her wherever she went, and while she kept herself hooded, nearly everyone recognized her. Wide berths were given, nods too, and occasionally a smiling child, grimy from play or work, would run up to her or whisper about her being "the Lady." As Octavia translated it, she was the Lady who'd destroyed the old order. The Lady who'd cast them from an age of technomagik and back into an era of candlemaking and frontier survival. People didn't have a spark of technomagik to light their fires, so they picked up two stones and cracked them one off the other. Simple as that, and what the people in the center of Eatoth were already mostly familiar with. Indeed, technomagik had made many things easier, though they still had many primitive mills and forges about. Thus they shut down anything too newfangled or busted it apart for parts; these technomagikal contraptions worked only sporadically now anyway. They cleared the cobwebs out of the old mills and factories and again brought them roaring to life.

However, most people weren't ungrateful for being taken back a few centuries—unlike a few of the sour and still-settling legionnaires seen blundering about. Of all that had changed, the once working-slaves, these Amakri who had been vassals to the rulers of Eatoth had only been brought nearer to their natures, nearer to the earth. Nearer, especially, to the outcast ancestors now wandering among them—a class of wastrels who they had shunned out of a fear of becoming as destitute as they. Now everything was shared, and everything of past value had been destroyed.

Day after day, it humbled Morigan to walk down a busy lane and witness the slow healing of the people. Life thrived as though the apocalypse had never come. Grunting beasts hauled bumping carts down mud-splattered roads. What passed for domesticated dogs in Pandemonia—furry quadrupeds with horns, talons, and occasionally dragonfly wings they used to soar small distances—chased down the carts and were shooed off from ransacking them by the jovial farmhands riding in the back. Rows of stone and metal houses leapt out from the hollows between roots, and from the coziest of cottages Morigan's half-wolfish nose caught the buttery tease of baking bread.

Later on, she would walk beside long rows of columns fully sheathed in ivy and flowers. Statues were buried under the green as well, and persons congregated in these spaces, chatting. She greeted the tired workmen and workwomen enjoying a cool break under the shade. Elsewhere, marketplaces opened in time-deteriorated buildings with clay, thatched, or bronzed and green roofs, and carried on vigorous trade. Resurrected windmills, once apartments or inutile structures, had been retrofitted with groaning wooden blades, and their churning provided a feeble pulse to the old technomagikal lamplights along the street. Thackery's genius, and Octavia's perfect recall of technomagikal sciences from the Font of Knowledge, had been responsible for creating a rudimentary grid and rewiring the city quickly to run on natural resources. As afternoon came, and men relaxed or finished work, not even the labored groaning of these great wooden fans could stymie the glorious panoply of handclaps, laughter, and jangles that overtook the city.

When these folk finished for the day, Morigan's second shift was just beginning. She would arrive at one of the few places in New Eatoth where the toil was ceaseless. Here, grungy black tenements burped smoke and curses from their empty windows. Within, she would find more smoke, noise, and the loud curses of legionnaires at last learning an honest trade from bossy smiths. And for those who knew nothing of her industriousness, she'd roll up her sleeves, throw on an apron, and grab bucket, plier, hammer, or unfinished blade and regularly surprise a few newcomers with her astonishing metallurgy skills. For the Wolf was with her, even when he was not, and she, as her own woman, could call upon that love and knowledge to serve her.

Meanwhile, and also working hard and late, Thackery yoked his strength to the downcast blue robes who, without their umbilical attachment of the arkstone, had forgotten their ties to magik, Will, and Pandemonia itself. Sad, but these great invokers had been reduced to the level of novices. Every spell they cast was dangerous, every invocation of Will left them overexerted as though they'd passed a stubborn stool—though often with contrasting and messier results. Thackery spent the majority of his hourglasses over at the hedge-guarded encampment in the woods claimed by the blue robes training these men on how to be calm—and not calm in the arrogant microcosm in which they'd existed but calm in the sense of being open and available to magik. Teaching them how to be a vessel and not a master, just as a poet was a channel for their muse.

Then came the necessary teaching of the ritual control that sorcerers of the West practiced, which these poor ducklings had never had to learn. To call upon the arkstone's power and very little of their own had been as easy as suckling from a teat. However, they all had the gift, and minds so disciplined could be shaped, so Thackery's efforts were far from futile. Each blue robe was already trained in mindspeak, at least, which meant there were no communication issues between teacher and students. Adam joined him in the late afternoons after council meetings to ensure nothing of the day's lessons had been lost in translation. Nothing was, and their mindspeak allowed them to share successes and information among themselves a little like a hive would do. Mistakes were rarely repeated from one man to the next. Thus, the blue robes learned the basics of magikal control faster than any student of the West would.

In the days and nights since Thackery's arrival at the sorcerers' encampment in the forests outside the city, strange lights, explosions, rainbows, fogs, and—once—a pelting of sizzling toads appeared over the trees to the east of the green city. When working the land, the Wolf would look up from his labors, sniff the sulfur, and hear Thackery's laugh or admonishment, then return to work with a grin. Teaching these adults how to be men was tiring, even for Thackery, someone who enjoyed being a pedagogue. He started to split their time between instruction and excursions into the city, where he and a few other sorcerers who needed to learn would check on the water reserve—a huge technomagikal sphere planted in the middle of a barren lot—and the other subsystems whose dying technomagikal currents had been temporarily suffused with supplemental strength from the windmills around the green city. His tourniquet-style approach would only stem the bleeding of magik for so long, and then what faltering currents remained in this place would disappear like the light in the blue robes' staffs. It was his hope that the wards of Eatoth, once trained, would power the city with their own Wills. But first they had to master themselves and their egos, and learn not to rule but serve; he didn't think that such humility could be achieved in a single generation, though he figured they would be able to squeeze enough magik out of themselves to power the most necessary conveniences of the city.

As for the fate of New Eatoth beyond his time here…The magik in this place was strong. It felt as immutable as the ground beneath his feet, as if the arkstone's power had a secondary well here that hadn't dried up. Such a sustaining Will had grown beyond the nourishment of the arkstone, a Will he believed came from the people themselves—a collective consciousness, a great spell of joy and hope. He knew of the Caedentriae, of nightmares that collective madness and pain could conjure, and it wasn't outside the realm of possibility that the inverse sorcery could be made. Perhaps that magik, once strengthened by wards, would be enough to prevent this kingdom from perishing from the encroaching chaos of Pandemonia. Mayhap New Eatoth would remain a whole but smaller and more humble simulacrum of the original.

Once the reservoir, windmills, and other critical infrastructure had been seen to, he'd dismiss his chosen students and go for a wander. Later, after he'd had his fill of smoked meats, children's laughter, and the crude jokes of workmen he struggled to understand, Thackery would join his company where they met each night: at Ankha's grave.

✳ ✳ ✳

XI

The maiden of dusk laid her head upon New Eatoth, spilling threads of her crimson and golden hair through the streets, fields, and woods. Rowdy evening music had replaced the slow heave and burble of the day, though it was quiet on the rise, with only the wind to sing to the strangers, and the distant thud of windmills but a few could hear. The hourglass was as heavy and calm as the great sigh a body took when told its labor had finally finished.

The four companions gathered on the small hill looked happily beaten down, with nearly imperceptible smiles on their faces and a dappling of sweat on their brows and temples. Adam, arms crossed, leaned against the plain unmarked stone under which Ankha's body rested. He was careful not to kick about the wreaths and bundled herbs laid there by pilgrims throughout the day—no one visited here at night, which made this spot ideal for the strangers to gather. Thackery stood down the slope from the changeling and cupped his hand over his eyes, peering at something in the dazzling distance. Behind their two companions, and on the opposite slope, the bloodmates lay together on the itchy, sun-sizzled grass. Its discomfort couldn't penetrate their absolute contentment.

In their solitude, the four strangers each pondered the distant city. They'd helped to build New Eatoth every bit as much as the thousands of other toiling hands. Farther east of the mound, a long ways through the gold-shaded trees, there murmured the encampment of reformed blue robes. Only the Wolf and Morigan could sense that achievement; he the noise of men contented, she the shivers of hope they gave, as if hovering near little flames. The land was at peace. The people were at peace.

The bloodmates wondered when they should tell their friends that their work was done, assuming the others did not sense the same themselves. It was time to leave; the mad king and vengeance awaited. Mouse too, apparently.

Morigan bolted up and out of her bloodmate's embrace. "Mouse!" she cried, and looked to her Wolf with tears. "She's here! My sister's here. I have to go."

A flutter of wind and in the twist of silver air she vanished. Thackery and Adam rushed to join the slowly shuffling Wolf, who seemed both gleeful and sad.

"Mouse has returned," he said, and the men embraced the great fellow so passionately and unexpectedly that he toppled over.

III

SLIVER IN THE EYE

I

"Not the most promising vista," said Moreth.

He finished his squinting, and still had no words for what lay before them. Eatoth's majesty was indelible in his memory: a wall of foaming water; crystal towers piercing upward from the heart of a maelstrom; sunlight scintillating over so much moving, magikal water that the city resembled a quicksilver bauble. The unpleasant hump he beheld right now, including the valley pocketed in an acne of dangerous dark holes, was *not* the city he'd known. The coppery wall, once veiled in mist and water, once thought to be an edifice of crystal, looked like a worn, rusted canister. The towers teetering beyond the barrier shone meekly, dim as cloudy quartz, while dull, broken, and collapsed arches hung like dead spiderwebs over the ruination. Were those not great bridges once? What of the silver pods that had soared through the sky? He couldn't have imagined it all. Eatoth had been a city of extravagant majesty and magik—a place unrivaled even by Eod.

But there was no magik here, and Moreth didn't need to be a Sage or sorcerer to divine that truth. Eatoth had been destroyed, its majesty the stuff of legends now. Whatever crisis Morigan had attempted to avert hadn't been averted. Moreth's stomach sank. Three of his companions stood on a slab of cold black stone behind him and shuffled forward to gawk at the silent ruin.

More determined than the others, the tall, blue, and frighteningly charismatic shaman of the Doomchasers—Pythius—strode to the crumbling tip of this disk of land and leaned his shoulders and horned head out like a nosy bull. "*Óchi mageía*," he said.

"No magik," translated Talwyn, saying what everyone suspected. The scholar joined Pythius to stare, pinching his sharp face, setting his square jaw, and looking as if his every nerve were on fire. Thoughts fluttered from his mouth. "It doesn't appear to have been sieged. I see no ladders, catapults, or remains of those grotesque worms Alastair mentioned having been summoned by Brutus in his siege against Gorgonath. Although...the city looks dead as far as technomagikal currents are concerned. As if someone has flipped a switch and shut everything off."

"Are you sure what we're seeing is defeat? Were we too late?" asked the willow of a woman wrapped in ebon furs that shrank her stature. Mouse. Wisps of dark and white hair flickered from her hood, remnants from her last summoning of Feyhazir's power. Still, she proudly wore her ivory as a mantle. The whirl of wind and a shimmer of blinding dusk did naught to cow her, and she gazed down the eerie valley and upon the dead city. She searched for a speck of life. She listened for a single note not owned by the pining breeze.

"If it wasn't attacked..." pondered Talwyn, who'd done a broader sweep of the expanse, his deductions the result of compiling a million factoids and details. "Definitely no signs that it was, no scarring to the exterior wall. A wall that, from what Moreth has said, should be roaring with elemental magik—"

"It should," said Moreth.

Talwyn nodded. "Yes, and we can see that it is not now. From the smoothness of the volcanic stone upon which we stand, and the withered lichen around, one can speculate that this porous plain, too, should be cascading with water." He tapped his foot and a puff of dust rose. "As you can see, the land is desert dry. Factoring in environmental variables—heat, light, winds, Pandemonia's accelerated decay—I'd say it's been this way for many days, more than a week, certainly less than a fortnight, give or take. Those clouds look as if they won't rain anytime soon. For a city of waterfalls, there seems to be a drought."

Pythius pointed toward the city. "*Prasinach.*" (Green.)

"Yes," agreed Talwyn. "I noticed that myself. There's green down there."

"Green?" asked Mouse.

"A forest, probably," replied Talwyn.

"A forest?"

"You know—a large area covered chiefly by woodland and under-growth?"

"I know what a forest is, you twit." Mouse hopped over a small crevice and onto another stone disk. "If there's life—green life—still in Eatoth, that's where our friends will be. Hurry up."

Friends. The word danced in her head as her feet danced over the land; the men followed her, though in her eagerness she made good distance ahead of them. Adam, Thackery, Caenith, and Morigan were as much her friends as these fellows with whom she'd crossed this hellish continent. As she summoned faces into her mind, she nearly wept. She had never thought she could miss anyone so much that her chest ached at the thought of seeing them once more. She even missed the Wolf's handsome smell, and reflected fondly on his warmth from whenever she and the others had huddled together to weather another long, cold night. As of late, there had been many of those fitful sleeps on snowy, sandy, spongy, or otherwise inhospitable beds. Talwyn and the Amakri shaman tended to *warm* each other, then wake the next day looking as embarrassed as schoolboys hiding their first erections. That left only Moreth—a frigid, stiff substitute for the great hearth of the Wolf. Not to mention her Menosian companion had seemed achy and out of sorts since facing the terrors of the Forever Stones.

She shuffled off that memory and returned to thinking how nice it would be to wake with her family again. To Thackery's familial kindness and Adam's doting. Tomorrow, Fates willing, Morigan's red-gold beauty would greet her and inspire her to rise, wake, and step more lightly into this wicked world. Mulling it over, she knew she missed Morigan the most of all her friends. She felt the same sense of longing for Morigan—that of a deep, twisting knife in her chest—that she felt whenever she thought of her father. But Morigan wasn't dead; she was somewhere down in the quiet ruin below—of that, Mouse was certain. She'd have known if her best friend, her sister, had passed, as much as she'd know the severing of one of her own limbs.

Morigan, I shall see you very soon, she thought.

"Mouse," said a voice.

A silver light flashed at Mouse's side, accompanied by a ruffle of wind and the sound of glass chimes and faery music. A strong hand grabbed Mouse and pulled her back from taking a dangerous step over a wide crevice. Mouse froze in astonishment and heartache. Morigan seemed older, and instantly Mouse knew her friend had been hurt deeply, in her heart. They would each figure out how the other had suffered and what had been lost once they'd hugged, wept, and hugged still more.

"I missed you," whispered Morigan into the shoulder of her clinging friend.

"And I you," replied Mouse, squeezing tight.

In time, they stepped back and beheld each other. Untold stories roiled behind their faces and were cast in their gazes like flickering storms.

"We have so much of which to speak," said Morigan.

Their reunion was disrupted, and Fate pulled Morigan into a sort of trance. Forgetting her friend, she stared at a crude, weighty object hanging from a sack at Mouse's waist. Morigan saw that this object was somewhat angular and sharp—descriptors that were mere impressions of its prominence. A mace felt apt, though, for she felt what her friend carried was as dangerous as a weapon. Another item hummed a song of destiny to Morigan from the left side of her friend's belt. That was indeed a weapon, a dagger, and its song was like the screech of a flaming star blasting through space. It wasn't a weapon forged of Geadhain, but a manifestation of celestial power.

Mouse slapped Morigan's cheek, lightly. "I see your habit of gazing vacantly hasn't abated. I'd like to tell you about our time apart, rather than you picking it out of my head."

"Of course. I have much to share with you, as well."

Talwyn, Moreth, and a strange, blue, and slightly reptilian man had caught up to the pair. After a speck, Morigan recognized Pythius from the description Mouse had given her when last they'd met in Dream. Suddenly, Talwyn threw himself into Morigan's arms.

"It is good to see you," he whispered.

"And you." Morigan took a moment to enjoy the baby-scented perfume of the man, which even Pandemonia's foul conditions couldn't repress. As they made contact, the bees stung her with images of Talwyn's journey, his maturity beyond that of naïve scholar and perpetual watcher, into a man of action and courage. *You smell of innocence and honor now*, she thought. While they were wrapped up, she noticed the Amakri man staring at her with an air of possessive caution. *An innocence he would like to claim for himself, it seems. What brings you here, shaman of the Doomchasers? You have not come for the mad king. You have come for this man, and...*The answer eluded her.

"Where are the others?" asked Moreth.

Glancing at the Menosian, Morigan noticed a fiery shimmer to his aura, a confidence and courage radiating from him that was similar to Talwyn's. His journey apart had refined his character; he wasn't necessarily a good man, but he was a stronger one. There was, however, a queer black fringe resonating at its edges. She'd never seen anything like it. What was it? Illness?

"Morigan?" Moreth snapped his fingers.

"Come, I shall take you to them," said Morigan.

✳ ✳ ✳

II

The women moved ahead of the group, holding hands and jumping pitfalls as if they were sisters skipping through puddles on a rain-soaked street. Their gaiety was infectious to the men who watched and followed; even Moreth clucked his tongue at their silliness. Talwyn and Pythius returned to their habit of quiet discussions between themselves and in the shaman's native tongue—in which Talwyn had perfected his fluency.

They had much to talk about, especially now, and Pythius had many questions about the daughter of the patron Dreamer of his tribe. How did she know Talwyn? What kind of person was she? Talwyn's narrative of his relationship with the bold, not-to-be-trifled-with Daughter of Feyhazir was one that was so lengthy it dried his throat during the long hike down the valley toward Eatoth. In telling their story, he realized how much had taken place in the few months since his meeting Morigan and her fellows, and soon his mind darkened with thoughts of how much was to come. A black star shone somewhere, hidden by the autumn serenity of the sky. With a bit of stargazing, he was sure he would find it. Talwyn wondered when the Black Star would become impossible to ignore, when it would be revealed to all, and if he and his company would be able to stop the rise of the Black Queen it heralded.

"West Sun, what troubles you? Your mood turns black as the creeping night."

"Time. I'm thinking about sands and hourglasses, opportunities and losses."

Pythius's austere brow wrinkled into a more fearsome twist than usual.

"I've confused you with my Westernisms," said Talwyn. "As we've been over before in our discussions on our culture's view of impermanence: *sands* and *hourglasses*, which you seem to have forgotten about, are smaller measurements of time. Your people use only broader terms: days, sometimes weeks, even rarer, seasons."

"I have forgotten because your 'measurements' are attempts to chain a drakagor with a string. Time cannot be controlled or contained. Why break a day down into anything smaller than dark and light? In those two shades we live and breathe all there is to be known."

"Order. We need order. We need to divide our days further to assist us in accomplishing tasks. We need to ensure all expectations and duties are accomplished to the best of our ability within that allotted time. Days are finite. Greatness is accomplished in degrees. I've been hopelessly disordered since arriving in your land."

"Turning away from old habits allows us to find what is new. Your Western world sounds like a very busy, unsatisfying place to live. Being ruled by"—Pythius paused to recall the Ghaedic word Talwyn had used—"chonxes."

"Chronexes."

Pythius dismissed him with a flip of his hand. "Too much counting of grains of sand, which not even the desert does, and then hurrying hither and thither and pretending to be birds with your metal ships—not unlike those of my prideful ancestors, the Lakpoli. One who lives by dawn and dusk is not stupid, though he sees and hears the world's simplest mysteries because he is one with nature's beat, he is uncomplicated himself. A simple man fears death by appreciating the wonder of day rise and the descent of night. A simple man knows his place on Geadhain, as a part of the chain of life, not by surrounding himself with mirrors and effigies of his greatness. His greatness will crumble like even the hardest of metal does in time. Accepting our impermanence allows us to live each cycle of dark to light with the passion of the fire moths who breed, birth, dance, and are snuffed out all in the passing of a single day in Pandemonia. It is better to live like those wise creatures than it is to live under a burden of self-imposed restraints. To live with...*pyrkagos*."

All of their exchange, Talwyn had understood, barring that word. Something about fire? Or heat? Now it was his turn to be puzzled.

It was a short leap to the next platform, and Pythius was there to catch him after a slippery attempt. The man helped him up, forcefully, and held his wrists while their sea-green and hazel gazes crossed and twinkled. In that instant, Pythius's dry, herbal body odor and heat affected Talwyn like an animal's musk. While Mouse was convinced they were already lovers, it wasn't true, though they did sleep side-by-side and often touched when they rolled into one another during sleep. Talwyn also liked to pretend that their strange infatuation with each other's species was only a diversion, a fantasy. Yet here was Pythius, who'd left his tribe so that he might follow Mouse, her Dreamer, and the Dreamer's artifact as far as those tales would weave. Eventually, Pythius thought he would see that artifact returned to his people and used to restore the strength of their lineage. Or so the story was told, though Talwyn finally admitted to himself another reason for Pythius's devotion to this quest.

The shaman released Talwyn's wrists, wandered his hands up the sides of the man's torso, and paused to stroke the soft, dark-golden hair exposed by the man's unlaced tunic. Pythius's face softened into the tenderness of a child bearing witness to a blooming flower; Talwyn was a fascination for him, encompassing both the wonder of life and light. He was his rising West Sun. It wasn't trivial. It was a curiosity that had driven him away from his people on a doomsday quest to see what would come of that affection.

"Pyrkagos," muttered the shaman, again.

Pressing close into an embrace, Talwyn grasped at straws as to the meaning of the word. A fire stirred from under their clothes, their boiling blood, flexing arms, sweating skins, and swollen pricks. They tightened against each other as only men could, as two slowly yielding walls of meat, muscle, and need. They kissed and writhed like pugilists: messy, rough, and unsure, though still adroit. Hands fell and moved across groins, backs, horns, and hair. Each man was both mystery and dream to the other, and that exoticism heightened the desire. Moreth watched from afar, having turned around at first to harangue the slowpokes. But their passion had rather disarmed him.

Fanning himself with his bowler (which he'd miraculously borne all this way), he said, "About time, and great show—it's not often that a man can get a rise from this master. Brava. Perhaps you could deflower each other later, though, since we're losing those fleet-footed lasses?"

They ignored him, and Moreth lost his amusement anyhow, wincing and bent over slightly as if he'd developed a stitch in his side. Cursing, he shouted, flagging down the ladies ahead, who were in as much of their own world as the fellows he'd left behind.

"We must seize our happiness," said Pythius, his lips hovering next to Talwyn's ear, his hand on the firmness in the scholar's pants. "I have seized you. I would have more of this happiness." His hand came to lie over Talwyn's breastbone and thudding heart. "And what fire you keep here."

"I would have the same," answered Talwyn.

"Pyrkagos."

"Pyrkagos," repeated the scholar. Whatever the meaning—an oath of brotherhood, heat, sex, love, or zeal for savoring every speck from dawn to night—Talwyn agreed with it. In this journey he'd learned that the best things in life came when one leapt blindly and with faith that others would catch him. He and Pythius walked onward, helping each other over the whistling fissures to the underground—a subterranean realm no longer traversable and sloshing with water. The men were unashamed of each prolonged touch they shared. They spoke less and watched more of themselves and the world. Talwyn knew that tonight or soon after, their pyrkagos—their flame—would roar once more. And he would allow it to burn off his clothing, sear away his inhibitions, and consume him.

III

Nightfall had made travel more dangerous, and the company stuck close together. They were ready for accidents, though none occurred. Everyone was being vigilant, with Talwyn and Pythius taking special care of each other—their affection now on clear display. Their contrasting physical appearance, cultures, and behaviors reminded Morigan of the complementary archetypes she and the Wolf shared. She felt her bloodmate was up ahead, in the dark, moving toward them; the two had been communicating their intentions to one another.

Rather than creating a fuss over their leaving, the Wolf, Thackery, and Adam had used night as their cover to slink off into the woods and head north through the ruins of the abandoned metropolis. It would have been harder to say farewell to Longinus, Octavia, their son, and all of the other countrymen they'd come to know if they'd stayed for a proper farewell. While the Wolf could have carried Thackery as he had back in Kor'Khul, it was an easy enough trip to make by foot, and he had another burden: in a woven sack he bore clanked the feliron chains meant for his father—Ankha's one and only selfless gift to the world. If all went well, the Wolf, Morigan, and their companions would meet outside the eastern side of Eatoth's wall by sunrise.

Morigan wouldn't rest until then, and neither would he. She sensed little fatigue in her companions. To her wolfish nose, they all had a whiff of travel stink, and under that, a tang of warming metal—the scent of determination.

While they hiked over darkened pitfalls, being careful to form a chain when the moon winked behind unseen clouds, Morigan at last heard the tale of Mouse's terrible adventure, the quest undertaken at the behest of her father. Mouse was the storyteller, and the others listened, occasionally shouting out an amendment. As Mouse spoke, Morigan's bees pollinated her mind with additional images and feelings from all three of her companions. At times, it was as though she'd taken those horrific steps out of the blood eater's domain herself.

White slop surrounds her: on the floor in guano-mounds, from the roof in waxy, dripping icicles. A sizzling rancidity burns the hair from her nose, gags her throat, and fills her skull with pain. At least her mouth is covered by a rag, though that feels as flimsy as all else in the trembling cavern. Sloppy stalactites fall, though their descent is precipitated by so much raining goop that the hazards can easily be avoided. What happened beneath in the chamber of the

Brood Queen has begun to undo the whole of the Second City. When the Brood Queen met her flaming death, stones set in place for thousands and thousands of years were blasted, and the foundation of the city now shifts and oozes downward. Many of these tunnels will soon be plugged with the ivory ichor that flows knee-deep around the company—a river that pulls at them with the weight and tenacity of a rapids made of glue.

In the other world, the waking one, Morigan feels that her hand is being held in a similar way to how these escapees cling to each other's. They are hauling themselves upward, and following the shouts and instructions of the scholar who has somehow mapped this deteriorating place in his head. They refuse to die graveless and in vain. They will see the light of dawn. With that determination carved into their sweating faces, they grunt, curse, swim, and throw themselves against the increasing tides. What they've come to claim—the chalice—Mouse holds in her sack, aloft from the white river. Whether it's this talisman or the Dreamer's blessing that keeps them safe and unseen by the blind, wailing blood eaters madly flapping for cover above them or splashing down and flailing in the incredible heaving flotsam, the companions do not stop to question. No, they push and trawl themselves toward the light, at first imagined, then real: a fluttering pale star that will be an exit. They've found the way out. They've almost survived. A bit more wading and the cries and swarms of infuriated blood eaters will fade into an unsettling memory as with all they've known of the City of Ghosts.

A chalice, thought Morigan. It was that image that stuck with her most from the story of Mouse's underground escape. She could envision the object as clearly as if she were holding it in her hands. It was made of bone—so antediluvian as to be grayish-black—and covered in an orgy of writhing, scrawled, agonized shapes that bore no semblance to mortals from her age. Instead, the figures were gaunt and hunched, with attenuated limbs and elongated peaked skulls. Twists of tentacles, razor-backed jellyfish, and other undersea or deep-space horrors filled in the rest of the chalice's relief. A few tiny red gems, precious stone deeper in shade and richer in color than rubies or bloodstones, were nestled amid the grotesquerie. The whole picture chilled Morigan. *Evil and dark,* was all she could think, and knew not how or why her father was involved with such a relic.

Mouse realized that Morigan's silver eyes had taken on that sheen she knew well. She squeezed Morigan's hand to summon her back. "Shall I continue?"

"Yes."

"Shall we talk about what you've just seen?"

"In a moment, perhaps." She wanted to know what other resonances of Fate Mouse's tale would next stir in her.

"Very well. As I was saying, after we made it out of that infernal pit..."

Mouse's story continued from when they had emerged from the lair of the blood eaters. What monster-women passed at the mouth of the cavern, ones that should've been invigorated after their nightly hunt, gave no bloodthirsty chase. Rather, they lay there, letting the new sunlight glide over their blank prune faces and hideously jutting flesh. Or they turned their sad black gazes to Mouse for a moment, recognized the Dreamer in her flesh, and let loose a sorrowing cry. A few of the most lucid screeched and managed enough strength to scuttle away from Mouse. No one knew, specifically, the fate in store for the blood eaters who lingered on or what had happened to their communal psyche; even Talwyn hadn't openly postulated on the future of the species—other than to say it had diametrically changed.

After leaving behind the City of Ghosts, and following their long trek across the icy wreckage of the snow-stuffed clefts of the Forever Stones, they'd spent an unpleasant night preemptively hiding from the blood eaters in a subterranean pocket, though the creatures were silent that night and didn't hunt—perhaps they were tending to their shattered home, or were indeed all withering away with their connection to their queen now severed. Could the whole race really be gone? The question consumed them all, particularly the puzzle of the logic behind it. But no one spoke of their fears or theories, although Pythius ominously mentioned a "great stillness" he felt in the land. A death.

In the morning they'd struck out, hard and fast, and reached the Doom-chaser encampment beneath the Forever Stones. The Amakri had been overjoyed to see their champions return, and the warriors who hadn't survived the descent were honored that night with bright fires, more of the somber piled-stone effigies the Doomchasers made for the dead, and loud voices and drum-songs in the names of the deceased. Beyond the mournful celebration of life, meetings occurred in whispery tents. Pythius had gathered those closest to him and the tribe, and told them of his intent to travel with the strangers, who'd proven themselves friends of the Doomchasers.

Mouse stopped her hike and her tale, brooding. "Pythius believes that the chalice is holy. He thinks it can remake people. Once we've won our war, he intends to use it to restore the strength and ferocity of his people, which have steadily diminished since their ancient pact with Feyhazir."

She and the seer brewed their thoughts. Finally, Morigan said, "What do you think?"

"I think it's wicked."

"As do I."

They exchanged uncertain though comforting smiles. Mouse continued. "I'm certain I saw it used in a ritual with Teskatekmet—the First Keeper

Superior, I've since learned from Mr. Knows-everything, who heard it from his beau. Used on her and the straggling tribes who wouldn't leave the City of Ghosts—err, Second City. Our world is too old and has too many damned names for things!"

"Teskatekmet?" exclaimed Morigan.

"You know of this woman?"

"I do. I do, indeed."

Mouse and Morigan now whispered and hunched as if either Pythius or the Dreamer inside one of them might catch their scheming.

"I had a vision, you see," said Mouse, "when I touched the chalice. A vision as clear as the ones you have, I think. Teskatekmet made a pact with your father—she was his vessel once, too. However, this was her second pact. A new pact with him for another chance at life and greatness, which he accepted, in exchange for her and the people of the Second City guarding the chalice."

Shrieking visions whirled in Morigan's mind: a sand-banked city, a woman kneeling before an assemblage of people in an earthen chamber. Then of Teskatekmet's midnight gaze staring upon the glowing vessel of Feyhazir holding the chalice. She had such a hunger in her eyes, a desire that marked her as a bride to the Dreamer of Desire.

"He turned them into blood eaters," whispered Mouse, "to protect his treasure for all time."

Morigan gasped, though Mouse snatched her wrist and stopped her from reeling away. "I'm not done—that's not the worst of what I know. When Feyhazir was finished with them, when they'd sat in the dark—breeding, hunting, and living mindlessly to serve his needs for thousands of years—he had me act as Teskatekmet's executioner. I killed Teskatekmet, who had been turned into an abomination and driven insane by her endless servitude. And I think that the whole of the race—tied to her need and sacrament—are dying now, too. Or just mad and lost. Either way, I'm responsible."

Mouse shook her friend with both hands as she spoke what neither of them wanted to say, and they looked to the lumpy sack tied on her belt. "With this relic he bred an entire race of monsters to serve him. I worry now for Pythius, for you, for any of those bound to his whims—even more than I worry for my own fate, really."

They'd been still too long in their conspicuous huddling. Moreth called out from up ahead, and they put on a pretense of normalcy. Morigan would speak to the others about what Mouse had shared once they could make decisions as a pack. Distractions from the duplicity and danger posed by her father were easy to find; in her mind she could see the Wolf and her other companions tackling the rubble and perils of Eatoth's ruins. Thackery brandished a staff that shone light to make the going easier, though at this point they were all adept journeymen. A few times, she had visions of the Wolf and his company encountering a wild inhabitant of Eatoth—a hissing, scaled thing that had claimed territory within the city. However, these animals were warned off with one of her bloodmate's fists, a flash of light from Thackery's staff, while a few rabid horrors simply turned after meeting Adam's gaze and no one could explain why.

Dawn's shimmering dissolution of the night and her own neglected fatigue made her visions of the men so tangible that when she saw the three dots down and across the riddled valley she wondered who they were, feeling certain all the members of her pack were already with her. But they weren't, and those three were indeed the remaining of their number. Hastily, she dashed into Dream, becoming a silver gleam in dawn's fanning radiance. She reappeared before the loping man-beast who had sprung ahead of his fellows to reach her, and they clashed in a tumble of softness and strength, pearl and copper, kisses and mind-whispers.

Morigan broke their embrace and tapped his pouting lips. They each knew what she was thinking. *Now we must turn to our company, to their great minds and courage, and determine how we can win this war. The Black Queen will fall, and we shall be the hand to swing the axe that cleaves off her head.*

Although the yearning to lay with this radiant warmother struck the Wolf like a full-bodied itch, he resisted it. Instead, he stole a few more sands of affection while their companions caught up with them. They'd make camp and the war council would begin.

IV

They climbed out of Eatoth's basin onto an eastern slope where a swath of purple bushes overtook the shale, spreading itself far and wide. Watery roads twisted through the undergrowth and around stunted fists of pale rock. An abundance of squawking crimson herons foraged along the black sand beaches of these streams. Stopping at a large embankment, the Wolf dashed off to quickly, and humanely, snap the necks of a pair of the birds, chasing away the remaining flock. In specks, the birds had been gutted and strung up by Morigan before being roasted over a fire conjured by Thackery's Will. Adam did not eat the birds; rather, he foraged from an empty nest he somehow knew had been theirs and drank from the eggs therein. It felt kinder to him, now that their parents were dead, and the eggs didn't speak or squeal their pain like that boar he'd killed before coming to Eatoth—the thought of which made him ill while he sipped the yolk.

Thackery chose a spot next to Morigan as the conversations began, and couldn't be moved even when the huge Wolf attempted to circle his great body around her. The two men made do sitting on either side of Morigan, each taking a hand of the woman they loved. Moreth and Adam formed an opposing tableau across the fire with Mouse between them—an image of friendship and duty. Following their meal, Pythius was formally introduced to the company. A proper introduction and not Mouse's succinct hailing given hourglasses ago when the parties had met: "He's a good fellow. A bit of magik. Quite strong. Won't stab us while we sleep."

When necessary, Pythius spoke through Talwyn. He was cautious of the Wolf—a predator to predator leeriness, felt the scholar. Caenith brought out the Amakri's possessiveness, and he kept Talwyn close to him, a hand always somewhere on his flesh.

The company only newly reunited, Morigan loathed the task before her. As day settled into dusk, and another day to stop the mad king had been lost, Morigan could be complacent no more. At last, she recounted the fall of Eatoth. She told them of her mistake in believing that her prophecies were infallible, of the Keeper Superior's murder, and of Eatoth's destruction, as wrought by her hand.

"By *our* hand, my Fawn," said the Wolf.

"*Amunai's* hand," snarled Mouse.

Pythius gasped at the name and more as Talwyn, quietly and furiously translating, relayed Morigan's story.

"Amunai wanted her sister dead," continued the Wolf, unwavering. "There were few other outcomes in this situation. Had it not been by our hand, the twisted woman would have slit her sister's throat herself while wearing the Keeper Superior's skin. I have no regret for Ankha's death. She reeked of roses, rot, and old wine: the stink of guilt. She yearned to die, to be free from what she had done, which, as my Fawn has told you, was far greater than our crime. It was a mercy, I say."

As the cold-cast faces digested what was said, Pythius shifted and whispered something to Talwyn. The scholar spoke. "Pythius agrees with your dispensing of justice. He claims that all those in the great cities have abandoned the ways of the Green Mother. They preach greatness to conceal their venality."

The Wolf gave a thoughtful nod to the shaman. "The snake-man speaks truth. Although not all of Pandemonia's children are neglectful of the old ways. There are those who understand our pact with the land, those who earn their bread at the Green Mother's table through toil and sweat. We stayed with them for a while, so that we could repay our debts. It is good that you three arrived when you did, for I am not a man for contrition, but rather one of action. We have been still for too long while my father wreaks terror unchecked."

"Amunai's threat..." Talwyn said slowly. "Did Brutus succeed? Did he take one of the great cities?"

Without contact with the other great cities or the power of the arkstone to call upon to successfully traverse Pandemonia's volatile ether for the simplest of farspeaking messages, none of the survivors of Eatoth's fall knew if Brutus had breached another of their domains that were once considered impregnable.

Mouse was the first to look at Morigan with respectful regret.

"Well," she said, "do your weird work. We need to know what we're up against."

Although still wary of peering into Dream, Morigan knew that the past couldn't be altered or obscured like the future. To this point, the Fates had been silent about the downfall of any other cities, which could be a positive sign. Or it might simply be a sign that hope was already quite lost for those cities and their people. Morigan knew only that she didn't want to know of any more dismal fates, failures, or tricks she was powerless to stop. But it was time to face her monsters. She sighed, breathed deeply, and leaned against the hard shoulder of her bloodmate. Magik scattered from her like silver confetti, and she slumped into a trance.

Show me where my bloodmate's father has been, she commanded of her hive. *Follow his steps, hunt his madness.*

She is floating, birdlike, on a single black cloud amid many, all of which are angry and rearing like a herd of nightmare ebon steeds. The storm is magikal, its heart flashing red and blazing a rain of cinders. The fire has been fanned by the hideous blackened men with their glowing staves below. In Sorsetta, fire was met with flame. Here, the mad king has wrought that elemental conflict once more. An army is marching against Intomitath, the City of Flames. A horde of misshapen, metal-fused, mutated soldiers worms its way down a charred valley and under their smoldering storm like a river of sludge. They each chant the name of their puppet master and king in a maddening burble.

The iconoclasts of Intomitath do not fear Brutus. Why would they? They have a queen who fights with the nobility Amunai once extolled. Morigan senses their Keeper's great light somewhere atop the wall, in one of the towers overlooking what will be the field of battle. The people have no fear; their hearts are loving and set on life. They've conquered the untamable soil of Pandemonia and forged their now ancient city from the seared wasteland. Morigan loses herself in its astonishing size, this metropolitan heap, ringed in a wall of iron, circled with a moat of leaping fire, and surrounded at its limits by cruel brackets of rock, like the blackened remains of a Dreamer.

Inside that colossal rib cage, she sees thousands of residential towers or fortresses, with numerous windows and smokestacks. Elsewhere rise bizarre bastions for the wise—the crystal towers of Intomitath—that twist like corkscrews into the smoldering firmament and are fanned at their spherical apexes like suns, by opulent, rippled blades of metal. The city shines, smokes, and coruscates as if it were one large forge. It threatens to blister any traveler in its heat-shimmering valleys. And if the desiccating haze, the iron gates that could be breached only by an army of colossi, the moat of liquid brimstone, and the menacing valley around the city weren't enough, then the whirling, glowing pods hovering over Intomitath are a final, seemingly unnecessary deterrent. The ships are not outfitted for cultivation or cargo; they're made to fire concentrated, invisible blasts of solar heat through magik gathered from the sun-towers, and magnified by the arkstone. Such violent sorcery will evaporate flesh like water on a grill.

As the army of horrors continues flowing toward the moat of fire, several fleets of ships detach from the armada and zoom toward the flaming riverbank. The spherical vessels pulse gold at their bows, and gusty rifts are carved into the mad king's army. The gaps in Brutus's ranks quickly fill with more blackness, and more ships are sent forth.

Still, you will fall, *thinks Morigan.* No matter how much might you send their way.

Once again, artifice has served the mad king well. He's outwitted his foes by lighting a fire in one place while preparing to strike from another.

While the warmasters of Intomitath think to thin Brutus's horde before commanding the moat of fire to flood the valley and turn the hideous men into statues of ash, they have not tracked the actions of the instigator of this assault. They believed him to be with the horde that chants his name, and his presence, seed, and soul was so threaded through the bodies of his horde that only a seer of Morigan's power could ever have untangled one pattern from the next to isolate Brutus. Such a pattern Morigan finds, and follows deeper into this past.

The wise Keepers of Intomitath had forgotten that Brutus was a beast that breathed the deepest ash of the Age of Fire, one who'd shielded his brother from the astral rains that seared Geadhain. While ancient tribes hid in darkness, Brutus thrived in fire. He'd wed himself to the element by blood-binding himself to the Father of Fire himself—a monster that, even though it now sleeps beneath the charred ring of Zioch, is as present in his blood as his urge to rape, devour, and conquer. Thus, before his army had even been noticed by the farthest seeing of Intomitath's instruments, Brutus crept so slowly as to avoid magikal detection, as though he was soil itself, slithering to bring himself to the moat of lava. Like a salamander, he slid into its stream. Once on the other side he rose, naked, crawling, shedding magma like scales, and skulked toward the walls of Intomitath. Those he could breach, alone and with subtlety.

Far away from the smoldering valley, he hears his army chanting his name and moves deeper into the city's grated channels, and soon into sewers and filth. In a moment he'll rise to claim the arkstone. He'll need the Keeper to open the vault in which it is kept, bound by their mistresses. He is without Amunai's ability to steal a woman's body for the task, but as a master of horrors, he knows that there are other ways to puppeteer mortals, and that Wills are not only bent by magik. Terror is a far stronger force in his hands. Explosions ring out, drumming out his ascension as he rises from below to feast.

Screams, ripped up visions of mutilated men, women and children as crimson as shattered dolls cast under a blood rain, and the juddering picture of Intomitath, cold and lightless as a dead forge, jolted Morigan out of her vision. She leapt up, shrieking until the Wolf wrapped his arms tightly around her.

"I didn't see the very end of Intomitath; I was spared that horror," she told her companions. "Brutus snuck into the city and planned to force the Keeper into surrendering the arkstone. I saw a city without magik, so we have no reason to believe he would have failed. The City of Flames has fallen." As there was no point in softening the blow, she added, "Whomever Brutus's horde hasn't killed will have been converted into fodder for his army. Most dire is that he and Amunai possess a second arkstone now."

"Another?" exclaimed Moreth.

"Why would they even need such power?" asked Talwyn. "Furthermore, why amass so large a force here when he has no way to return it to Central Geadhain, where the war with his brother awaits? Even the best armored ships sailing in open water would be like shooting bottles at a Heathsholme fair to the technomagikal might of Eod and the Iron City. I understand that Brutus is *mad*, but I cannot see a motive for his or this dark priestess's designs."

They looked to Morigan for answers. "I'm not sure," she said. "I felt, in that vision, that the beast of fire to which he's bound himself was dormant, and very far away. Under the ashes of Zioch, I believe. So yes, he would need to return to Central Geadhain. I think he intends to wake the beast beneath Zioch once more, to call upon its power as he did when facing Magnus. I still remember that battle, which I saw clear as this circle before me. I saw a writhing sun emerge from under the earth, a power that could burn everything green and civilized in our realm..."

As Morigan trailed off, Thackery thought of the bloated dragonfly leviathan he'd seen in Pandemonia, the mountainous worm of diamonds and dirt that had nearly eaten him and the Wolf in Kor'Khul, and of Morgan's description of another creature, long ago. She told him of a pact Brutus had made with ancient powers: a beast of pure fire, like a snake—if a snake could be the size of a mountain. She'd been speaking of an elemental, then and now, even if she hadn't used the term.

"Elementals..." he mumbled, then spoke more boldly. "Their kind cannot be bound to a man's Will. I don't think even an Immortal has that power. Somehow, though, Brutus has tamed the untamable...How could he have performed such incredible magik? He's no raw sorcerer—"

"He'd need a source of *incredible* magik then," said the scholar.

"An arkstone," the two exclaimed in tandem.

"Well, we know something of his plans then," said Mouse, much less excited. "He'll summon this elemental—"

"No," said Morgan, sternly. Something snapped and hummed behind her ears, a resonance of fate. "It is no mere beast of its kind. It is..." Suddenly, Morgan's mind was stormed with images of smoke-blasting tears in igneous shale. Upon her breast burned a phantom heat as though she stood naked and incinerating before the sun. A silver static crackled through the air and prickled the bodies of the men near her. She spoke, at last, the true name of the elemental.

"Brutus has bound himself to Ignifax: the Father of Fire."

Fate left her and her companions hanging, and her insight and silver aura dimmed. Pythius was far more confused than the others, since Talwyn had failed to translate their most recent discussions, and he was more troubled by his grasp of the one word he'd understood: *Ignifax*. The shaman sprung up from the fire, paced a bit, and then motioned Talwyn over. They chattered back and forth with increasing animation. Soon they drew the others' attention with their noise and arm-waving. Talwyn was aglow with the mad gleam of scholarly pursuit, and Pythius raged with an angry fire. The company sensed an argument was imminent. Then came a moment of peaceful romanticism, as the shaman held Talwyn by his shoulders and whispered a single, sensual word—"Pyrkagos"—which Talwyn returned. Still, Pythius appeared to have had enough of whatever Talwyn was saying, and he stomped down the beach to kick stones into the burbling river and startle the cranes that had only recently returned.

Perplexed and out of sorts, Talwyn didn't immediately address the others. Instead he chewed his face while studying the distant, angry Amakri.

"I'm guessing that was a fight," said Mouse.

"A disagreement," replied Talwyn.

"About?" asked Mouse.

Talwyn held his tongue, though; instead of speaking he knelt and poked around in the fire with a stick.

It was Adam who'd grasped the words from their exchange and spoke up. "They were arguing about a place," he said. "A dangerous place. Talwyn wants us to head there, and the other one disagrees. Pythius knows of this Father of Fire. Not by that name, but by something similar."

"The First Flame, *Ignifaks*—a nominal variant with identical meaning," explained Talwyn. "I have learned a great deal from Pythius as my fluency with his tongue has improved, and I believe his people are perhaps the oldest of mortal kinds. That means that they can tell us much. But he remains guarded against certain suggestions, and staunch against insinuations that would shake his world. Stubborn…"

Talwyn sighed and continued.

"As we've learned, many legends were born here, in Pandemonia, when the Dreamers first came to Geadhain. However, before the Dreamers came, the forces of nature were what man considered Divine. The elementals were once our divinities, and they were worshipped as greater beings usually are by lesser ones. They were giants, though friendly giants, to our minuscule selves. We had peace with nature before…Well, I'd like to see that part myself, since seeing trumps believing. Only my blue friend isn't being forthcoming with his folk tales or magik anymore…Ow!" His poking stick had caught fire and Talwyn threw the wood away before he was further burned. "I have something in mind. A plan. Give me a moment, and perhaps Pythius will stop being so stubborn and lend more weight to my proposal than I can alone. I shall sound insane if I just spit out what I'm thinking."

Leaving his companions bewildered, Talwyn dashed down to the bank where he and the shaman engaged in another verbal mêlée. This time, Talwyn seemed to win, and he returned to the fire dragging Pythius by his hand. The pair sat together, as before, and Talwyn coached his scowling friend on whatever action he needed the other to perform—first through soft whispers, and then with a touch and turn of his head, a movement that brought them eye to eye and eased every angry line in Pythius's face.

Love in bloom, thought Morigan. She wondered if they would kiss, here and now, in front of everyone, and was so enchanted by the notion that she imagined Pythius's hand ending up somewhere on Talwyn's body. In fact, the prospect aroused the bestial side of her soul, and she was surprised when the shaman slipped his fingers into one of the small brown pouches at his belt before throwing a white dust onto the fire. The flames roared and twisted high, and a flash of smoke blinded them all. It was a magikian's trick, however, and the smoke vanished as quickly as it had come. A fragrance with hints of festive spices, apples, sage, and a sweet and floral oil from whatever had been tossed into the fire persisted. The scent slithered like a serpent into their nostrils and skulls, filled their heads with a buzzing song, and slowed their blood to a crawl. Of all present, the Wolf most resisted this imposed docility, as was his nature, until the shaman, wavering, spoke to him in clear Ghaedic.

"Calm yourself, mighty warrior. It is only the peace of the quiet herb. Its spell will not last long. If you wish to hear the stories of my people, to truly live them, as West Sun has suggested, then to this magik you must submit."

While the Wolf could never fully drop his guard, he did take in a deeper breath, daring magik to do its worst. With that, Pythius seemed to grow and waver into a hulk twice his normal size, while Talwyn shrank to a small golden wisp next to him. The sky peeled back like torn paper, behind which was a gray cloud. The ground, too, faded into a cottony inconsistence. Soon everyone and everything around the whispering flames floated in a sea of clouds.

Said the shaman, "We Amakri share our stories through magik and memory. What you see will be echoes of all those who have come before me, echoes of the life of every Keeper of my tribe, back to the days when Dreamers and worms of fire were seen as no less extraordinary than the faded stars that gaze down upon us today."

The golden light beside Pythius pulsed and purred in a kittenish way, and he nodded toward it.

"Like any memory, what you see will not be complete, and I know not how well this will serve hunters so set on truth. Still, West Sun has asked that I share with you the tales of my people. Tales that the six of you are determined to not let remain in the fog of time. You have come here, seeking the most dark and beautiful treasures of our ancient land: our truths. So I shall tell you of *Orach*—the Scar—from the memory of one who lived in that time."

Scribbles of color appeared on the mist, like the blurred lines of water-color strokes. Other blots festered on the gray like mold, whence shapes and scenes emerged. As the vestiges of a forming world surged around them, those gathered felt as if they stood and were spun to take in an enveloping panorama of amazing sights. While aware that their bodies weren't moving, they knew that their minds were wandering then, within the story-magik of the shaman's tale.

"Long, long ago the heart of Pandemonia wasn't called the Scar, for Zionae had not yet fallen, and her vessel hadn't torn apart the world," said Pythius. "Claeobhan, the Cradle, was what the ancient wanderers called that utopia." They had heard that term before from the Sisters. "It was a realm unlike any in Pandemonia, or any elsewhere on Geadhain. For there the chaos had achieved an equilibrium. There, chaos was balance."

How can chaos be balance? they all thought. Then upon the smoky theater they saw the glory of this ancient realm. It opened up to them like a wave falling inward, pulling them out of their bodies and into the current. From there, they floated higher in the air than birds could go. Beneath them, the multicolored carpet of Pandemonia was split by a raw crevasse, the tail of which peeked out from under a dense shield of cloud. The split in the earth seemed as fuzzed, fertile, and sensual as Geadhain's womanhood about which Kericot often waxed. The earth, moss, fern, sulfur, water, and animal aromas were a wind of spice and life that were smelled by all. The ghosts of the travelers descended into the earthen channel and floated along a river of mist. Their senses continued to be aroused by the richness around them: the salts, sweet effusions of flora, and minerals on their invisible skins and palates. This was *life*, as they'd never known it.

The Wolf had now surrendered to the illusion, for it was so alluring. He'd chase every hideous and glorious shadow that moved in the mist. Whatever part of him existed in this place roared as the haze retreated in tatters and they emerged from the channel, which had only been a passage to true wonder, into a ringed archipelago. There, upon exiting the crevasse, the Cradle of Life lay beating before him like the most succulent heart imaginable—small continents of mountains, forests, ice floes, and deserts.

There were too many shades and hues to declare any single one dominant. Jungles straddled golden streams that the Wolf's senses told him, impossibly, were liquid fire. Cold blue buttes, spooled in mist, pierced the breast of a distant plain that looked glazed, though not in ice. It was water, the Wolf realized. He had seen Eatoth's ever-flowing wall; here, though, nature had not been subverted by man, and this distortion of elemental physics—stones made of liquid—was somehow natural, for a marvelous ecology flourished and wandered in the region. Birds soared through the mists screening the pools set into the foot of the waterfall mountains, and in the billowing whiteness below dazzled white-yellow beasts that the Wolf saw in tantalizing flashes. The creatures moved like sparks, leaping from one spot to another, dancing over the skin of water in pairs and herds that reminded him of watching a storm.

Lightning and water, while present in one place then, were not at odds. The fulminous horses did not electrocute the great sharp-headed fish he saw leaping through the skin of water, fish that in some cases continued into the sky with tribbling cries and anemone tendrils that they somehow used for flight. Indeed, a flock of silvery swordfish fluttered up into a tawny airspace spotted with a glassy asteroid belt that hovered in countless places above the land, and the Wolf lost interest in the former wonder. Some sky-rocks seemed on fire. Other belts were muffled in storm clouds, thunder, and rain. For once the Wolf could discern few details. His senses were scattered, with too much to see, sniff, and know. His animal was wild in this psychedelic zoo.

A million beasts with different cries sounded across the islands below. Aside from the mechanical bleating coming from two families of gargantuan dragonflies—distant ancestors to the monsters floating in the air like chubby clouds he'd seen in Pandemonia—he recognized none of them. While this world made no sense, and its sounds, sights, and scents colluded into perfect confusion, the Wolf had never felt such a desire to belong. Were this not an illusion, the Wolf could've lived and hunted here, forever, with his mate. In a land such as this, Morigan and he would never grow weary.

"Great hunter," said the voice of their spirit guide. The Wolf realized he and the shaman were now alone. "I feel in you the love of the untamed. This would have been your land, your glory, only it is no more. You could have run free and praised life with my ancestors below. You could have carved fire and ridden wind. You would have been as close to a king as any man can be in a realm that knows no worship but of the laws of nature. That which is can be undone; that which was will be remade. Chaos. I think you still practice that religion, as a smith, as a lover, as a hunter. Let me show you who else once believed as you do."

A black sliver stuck in the Wolf's eye, jarring him from his dream. Far, far past the archipelago lay a green and sapphire shore cloaked by rolling fog. On that distant, rugged continent, the black line flickered. Having a sense for dark things, the Wolf cringed.

"What is that?" He pointed at the land beyond the sea that embraced the beautiful archipelago.

His spirit guide pondered; this was not his memory, and the memory of whichever ancestor this was had no recollection of that object. "I do not know, and it is not what we have come to see—I can only show you that memory."

"Hmm. Very well."

With that, the wind he'd become swept downward. The Wolf thought for a moment about his companions, and how this shaman spoke so truly to his spirit. Perhaps his bloodmate and the others were having their own private hallucinations and conversations with Pythius. Into one of the jungles bristling on the nearest island to the archipelago he plunged.

Past trees with fanged blowholes and scales, through vines that crawled and looped themselves into sentient nests, past man-sized caterpillars chewing and tearing whole living birds he went, emerging above a place where civilization had been wrought. Tents and skin-houses stood pitched on the sinister shifting roots of monstrous trees. More often than not, a furred hammock or sleeping roll was all that the natives who wandered beneath claimed as possessions, aside from their weapons. People wandered around, and from their sly gaits—an ingrained dexterity and threat—he could tell that these people had been made for the hunt. They were so thickly and vibrantly tattooed that along with their camouflage paint they could blend with any crimson, brown, or green thing of the woods as only another daub of the realm's painterly muds. They wore bones and fetishes as savage persons did, yet there was where their pretense of incivility ended, for as the Wolf ebbed from elder to child, from mother to father, to daughter and son, he saw evidence of this peoples' superiority to modern man.

While floating on the outskirts of the encampment, he noticed a young boy carrying a clear, quivering fluid in a flimsy pail. Water? From the shimmer and movement, the Wolf suspected it was magik of a kind. The child, far away from any adults, walked alone to the rocky, slippery bank of a dashing stream that carved furiously through the wild. There the boy knelt, lifted what seemed to be a sphere of water out of the bucket, and placed it upon damp stone. The contact of the water thing with a moist surface sparked a reaction, and the sphere unfurled into a large, glistening, transparent salamander—revealing itself as an elemental. The being repaid the favor of its return to the river by squawking and spinning in a circle with glee before spitting a stream of silvery fluid into the bucket. Whatever it was the creature spat, it wasn't water; the Wolf knew this from its honey-sweet and medicinal odor.

"The ancients had no magik other than the magik of the land," said the spirit guide.

No magik? A time before magik? The Wolf was awed.

"Feyhazir had not yet come to teach us how to call upon miracles with our Will," explained Pythius, as if his patron had been the bringer of all knowledge to the world. "Without him, we had to negotiate with Geadhain when we needed Her protection or care. Our respect was our currency."

"You were richer then than ever," said the Wolf.

Pythius didn't respond, and they were brought to another scene, whisking through flaps of one of the few patchwork tents in the village. Therein, a woman knelt and tended to a grievously wounded, sweating man. He bit on a stick while she applied a poultice to his freshly mutilated leg; with a rag the Wolf judged, by the smell, as soaked in some of the elemental ichor he had just seen. The Wolf watched the man's shredded calf reweave itself like a knitted sweater. Less than a sand, and the mending was complete. The man spat out the stick and thanked the healer. In another sand, he'd be out hunting again, and he swore—in a clacking language that the Wolf could somehow grasp in this mystical dream—to get the better of the beast next time.

Another breeze, and the Wolf and his guide found themselves at a circle of hunters—men and women who dipped their spears and arrowheads into small pots of radiant red liquid. Once the coating had dried, they struck the weapons against the rocks on which they sat and were satisfied by the profusion of sparks created from the simplest of taps. A serious impact with warm, living flesh would send a jolt of fire through a creature that would sizzle its insides, Pythius explained.

"A gift from the fire elementals, the children of Ignifaks," continued the shaman, "who were harder to appease but offered gifts for the hunt, like the power to conjure a sun's wrath in a single blow, as you've seen with those sparks. Or crushed scatterings of their scales could be thrown that would blind any creature turned their way."

They moved on to the next scene where people sang, harmonizing while they toiled using mortar and pestle, and knife and flat stone, to make medicines and food. Men and women served equally, the Wolf noticed. There seemed to be no division of responsibility based on sex. A group of children, who were too young and not dexterous enough for fine work, were tending to an incredibly ancient man. He was old and nude as dirt, and his smile—while toothless—shone with all the charm of a child's worn stuffed bear. It took the usually observant Wolf a speck to note his black eyes, then the throat that reached past a toothless mouth-hole. Truly, this simulacrum of a man was nearly without imperfection, and only as the Wolf drifted closer did the sun reveal the small cracks, like weathered clay, in the golem.

The Wolf was also mistaken in thinking that the children weren't working. Those kneeling were busy picking through the wild grass at their feet and harvesting wriggling, black-shelled creatures—some larger than their hands. The insects were passed on to other children, who grunted a little in their songs as they ground the bugs to paste in a bowl, wincing afterward as they pricked their fingers on any manner of thorny flora, adding a bit of their blood to the mulch. Finally, a young girl—the quietest of those who seemed to listen to nature's tune most profoundly—brought the bowls of offerings to the dirt-man and poured the meal of earth into the golem's suddenly widened mouth.

For a moment, the Wolf thought the elemental would swallow the child whole. It was only the sweat, service, and love that it desired, however. And it gave in return; at the elemental's feet bloomed silver mushrooms and flowers with buds of gems rather than petal. These fruits of the earth would be used for the tribes' weapons and tools, could be shaped with the facility of clay, and once set upon by smiths would be as unbreakable as the people's love for their land.

"I shall show you Air, now. And then the fall of this beauty. The end of the Garden of Life." Pythius sighed heavily.

Up soared the Wolf's wind through the forest's fingers, swooshing through gem-scattered heavens and psychedelic clouds. As the Wolf howled at the exhilarating speed, his spirit guide's voice boomed.

"Air could not be caught nor shaped. Air offered fewer blessings to my ancestors, since it was fickle and unpredictable. In times of emergency, Air might be asked to soothe the wickedest storms, though these supplications sometimes made the storms angrier. Occasionally, an elemental would be asked to carry a man as my magik carries you in this Dream—faster even, from one moment in time to the next. Air's gifts were called upon less than those of the other elements. Even so, my ancestors paid Air with one of their greatest tributes. They offered it the dead."

Abruptly, the wind stopped. They had crossed the multicolored sea over to the farthest island and the domain of the water mountains. Beneath him, a huge stone flatland of shimmering jade appeared to float on the surface of a vast lake. Smaller land-plates, like stepping stones, led off into drifts of thick mist toward a looming monument. Lightning horses, which he had spotted when first coming to this memory, wandered through the grayness, issuing cries best equated to those of the loons of Alabion. Mesmerized, the Wolf watched the flickering herd weave about in the mist, prancing on the lake from one spot to the next. But he was not the only one whose attention the beasts held; a gathering of tribesmen on the jade plate below were similarly captivated. The tribesmen began unwrapping a body they'd brought with them—an old shell, withered as walnut, which no elemental magik could restore. The tribesfolk—differently painted from the tribe the Wolf had previously seen, with blue turtle markings—sang songs to the crackling herd in the mist. Once the bindings had been removed, a woman carried the withered body to the edge of the plate, bowed, and eased it into the water. It didn't sink, as one would have expected, but drifted as a leaf upon a stream, until the mist veiled it from the chanting mourners it had left behind.

"Where has it gone?" asked the Wolf.

"It was in this one duty that Air never failed the ancients," said Pythius. "Air bore our dead away. Air protected us from the indignity of watching our dead burn or be eaten by worms. Air carried the bodies elsewhere—into fire, into clefts, or into the deepest waters. It delivered our flesh back into the elemental cycle. Thus our return to the land was complete; we are but borrowed life."

In the ethereal stillness of the moment, as the mourners swayed and chanted with the songs of the lightning herd, there came at last a distant gulp as the body was swallowed by the watery throat of Geadhain. The Wolf had seen and heard enough now; he grasped the honorable traditions of these ancients, and he knew that what came next would sicken him.

"Show me the end of the Garden of Life," he said, reluctantly.

The Wolf's consciousness whirled, and a force fired him as an arrow into the sky. Once high above the vista of the Cradle's majesty, he hovered there. Pulsing ruby-crusted meteorites threw blinding dazzles his way, and the flocks of crooning manta rays weaving through the air with their swishing tails, spines, and transparent fins gave the Wolf a last vision of the glory and miracle that was to be destroyed.

A shadow darkened the valley. His stare was drawn to the east where he thought he saw the vertical line again—a tower?—before blackness rolled over the horizon. As he twisted to peer upward, glaring down upon him was a doomsday eye, an ebon planetoid circled in a furious white flame—blazing either from its piercing of the atmosphere or from a rage and hunger all its own. Geadhain bent and wailed from the weight that was about to consume it. Crystal asteroids were pushed back from the crushing of gravity, these great objects hurled on fire into the paradise beneath. Right before the roaring thunderstorm and atomic flash that would first envelop then consume the First Land, the Wolf was sure he saw a line running across the catastrophe. It couldn't be fully perceived through the sudden flames, the distortions of heat, the noise, the shattering pulverization as the enormous celestial fragment, the Black Star itself, crashed into the Cradle of Life and whitened out the landscape.

The Wolf's vision was atomized. Throbbing gave way to hurricane winds, then rumbling clouds, and finally a churning sea of white ash and smoke was revealed to be all that lay beneath him. The land moaned and banged, shrieked and crumbled. At least the untold horrors below were shielded from his vision by the sea of brume, though flashes of light and crackles continued to roll through it. What a remarkable horror, on a scale astonishing even to the war-weary Wolf. It had been the end of their world. The first one, at least; they still had a second one to contend with.

Suddenly, the Wolf realized his companions' consciousness now floated alongside him in the apocalypse, as Mouse whispered, "Holy fuk..." The six now appeared to have phantom bodies in the ether.

Their guide continued as a disembodied voice. "And so you have seen the first of many falls. Here we were not undone by our arrogance, but rather by our innocence. We trusted in the elementals and our land to protect us, yet they were powerless against what descended from above."

"Why did you want to show this to us?" asked Mouse.

"Answers remain in the Cradle," said Talwyn, as he pointed into the cauldron. "More answers than we could conceive of in a thousand lifetimes. What we see now—this ruination—fades, though never heals, into a gruesome scar. The Scar. There were survivors, and they move on. Others remain. Some are among the first mortals in history to meet with the Dreamer who destroyed their paradise."

"Zionae?" exclaimed Morigan.

"The Mother of Light and Darkness, she was called," said Pythius, and the watchers believed that they spotted a glimmer, impossibly, in the chaos. Everything began to wane, tear, and fall to tatters. Stars shone through the holes wearing in the gray tapestry of their surroundings. In a moment, flashes of flesh, fingers, and faces spotted the phantoms' bodies like an illness. They were returning to their world while the shaman continued to speak, though his voice sounded gruff, and many felt him to be skipping or confusing a word or two. "So was the name she took when she inhabited her first vessel: Zeeonae." With his accent, he said the Dark Dreamer's name more sharply than they were used to.

"However, I do not have the history of those who met Zionae to share with you, travelers, as my line and the Keepers from whose memories I weave this Dream did not remain in the Scar. Her fall was when the Age of Fire began, the rule of Ignifaks who burned our world clean of its corruption. And I am told that Geadhain burned for ten thousand seasons—though as my people did not keep time, it may have been longer. Likewise, not all of what I know or have shared may be true. Like anyone's memory, these visions may be an illusion, hope or terror of what has been rather than true history.

"Nonetheless, Zionae pitied what her descent had done to the world, as though she had not meant to destroy it, and she gave to her children fragments of her divine body, the arkstones, which would protect them from elemental terrors. Then she told them to go north, through the world of ash. She bade them leave what I believe must have been the First City, or realm, and to find what we call the Forever Stones. Those stones would be as eternal as her love throughout Geadhain's turmoil. At the Forever Stones, the first people could be safe. Thus did the first people make that pilgrimage and build what we would know as the Second City. Later, the City of Pride, or City of Ghosts. That, my friends from afar, is the history of our world, as I, and all who have listened before me, know it."

No one spoke over the whisper of the fire, or the whispers of the world to which they'd been returned. Life felt rudimentary after the colored extravaganza of paradise lost. Their heads were heavy—and slightly sore— from the quiet herb and the visions.

"Amazing," gasped Thackery, at last having recovered some composure. The sage's questions couldn't be compiled quickly enough to exit his mouth in an orderly fashion. Life had begun in Pandemonia? Such was always the convincing theory, as more mysteries came to light. Although what the shaman had shown them was a legend that spoke of first people with lives, cultures, and interactions with the Divine, that came before the great ages of fire, frost, dust, and drowning that had blanketed the planet. Those catastrophes must have come about as a result of Zionae's celestial impact.

Mouse mulled over different thoughts. After she and her companions had witnessed so many of the Black Queen's manipulations, the image of Zionae as mother of both light and darkness was horridly incongruous. "The Black Queen? Benevolent?" she muttered.

Pythius glanced at her. "She was no spleen of heartless darkness, then, not the man's hair you crib."

The others looked at him in confusion. Talwyn touched Pythius's lips before the man embarrassed himself further.

"The quiet herb," said the scholar. "Its effects can only be employed for so long. You won't be able to understand him in a speck, at least those of you not fluent in his tongue. There's also a nasty headache on the horizon, for all of us. *Regardless*, as Pythius tried to explain, Zionae was no queen of heartless darkness; she was not the monster you've described."

"I suppose we knew that," admitted Mouse.

"But there's so much more, don't you see?" In the thrall of discovery, Talwyn leapt up and flapped his arms as if he were on fire.

"The Cradle of Life...The First People...The history of our world. It all began *here*. Your mother knew that we would have to take this journey." He pointed in Morigan's direction, while consulting the stars more than she or the company. "She mentioned the Cradle, once or twice, and those women never speak without innuendo. She wanted us to find a relic of Zionae. That's why we're here. We must remember that. We have to travel to the Cradle of Life and unearth the ancient secrets. We simply have no choice."

"What about the arkstones? Or the City of Stone as a new, potential target of Brutus?" protested Mouse. "I would not want to see us once again divided, so we must consider our next moves carefully."

"The arkstones and the City of Stone are not our problems," barked Talwyn. "Brutus has two of the arkstones, and if he wants another I'm certain he'll just take it. We can't focus on him anymore, he's merely the symptom of a disease we have yet to treat: Zionae. In order to defeat Zionae, we must understand her. That was what Elemech said, and I believe her. I believe that every answer we seek, and more, can be found in the Cradle—or Scar, rather. I mean, the land itself should have resonances, impressions, left by Zionae.

She walked there, as a vessel, touching, interacting...Imagine, even, what Morigan could do if she were to lay her hands on the *bones* of the first vessel."

Gasps and curses exploded among the company when they realized Talwyn wasn't being loose with words. Bones. Remains. Zionae's first vessel.

Thackery whispered, "Bones?"

Talwyn sprung over and crouched near Thackery, gripping the man's hands. "Yes! Pythius never reached that point in the conversation, which was the fact over which he and I had been fighting earlier—the one thing I wanted his permission to share more than any visions of the old world. Pythius has been so cagey about the details of his people's sacred history, with it coming out only in dribs and drabs or slips of the tongue—but it's been more than enough for me to turn into something useful. But none of this is information that an outsider should ever know, even if we're not really outsiders anymore. I finally put this murky puzzle together, and confronted him with my suspicions, which was the argument you all witnessed. First Ignifax; well, his olden name: Ignifaks. Then the elemental's origins, then the origin of all elementals, and with more prodding and the natural flow of conversation we arrived at the Scar, Zionae, and the *remains* of her vessel, which legend says lies within those lands. I mean there are a few obstacles to our success in this adventure, I'll grant you."

Moreth gave a most unpleasant sneer. "Obstacles?"

"Yes. Small ones," claimed the scholar.

"Such as?"

"The usual! Nothing that can't be dealt with by any of the hands and Wills sitting here. Monsters..."—the next word he intentionally mumbled—"cannibals, sandstorms—well, ash-storms—"

Mouse hissed. "You said cannibals."

"Did I?" Talwyn said, flustered, wringing his hands.

"You did," grumbled the Wolf. *Only I shall eat you,* he mind-whispered to his mate, and while it was inappropriate for the gravitas of the subject matter, Morigan laughed. She wasn't scared of flesh-eating madmen as much as she was of losing this war. She summoned her swarm and called to the Fates. She asked them if the body of Zionae's vessel still lay in the dreaded Scar—she wouldn't risk misadventure without knowing if it did. The answer struck her like a hammer: *yes.* Its truth lit her every nerve on fire. As her companions began to bicker, she donned the crown of leadership and cleared her throat. Everyone turned to her, silent.

"I have felt it, the pull of fate," she said. "What Talwyn suggested seems true; at least a piece of the body that once housed Zionae's soul remains in this land. Whatever it may be—finger, tooth, bone—I shall lead us to it. We shall use this night to pool our insights. Talwyn, I need you to glean from your Amakri friend every detail on these remains, and of the dangers we shall face journeying into the realm where they reside."

The scholar nodded, a bit too enthusiastically in light of the mission they were embarking on.

She pounded her fist into her palm. "We were foiled in Eatoth. Our options are few. I care not of any dangers in the place where Zionae's secrets lie. I've had enough of this war, though. It's time to end it."

They agreed with her, for they felt it, too. An end.

IV

Once the relevant discussions had been had, the plan seemed simple enough: get from point A to point B, find a long-dead body, have Morigan work her magik. The Cradle, or Scar, was the same distance from where they'd come to where they intended to go; it would take a few weeks to reach it. Myriad potential issues were foreseen in the increasingly hostile environment near Pandemonia's core where terrains had been mutated by the catastrophic celestial effluvia of Zionae's crash. Apparently, magik had never settled in Pandemonia's interior, even when judged alongside the unstable laws by which magik in this realm was ruled. They could expect skin-blistering heat, sandstorms laced with metal rain, and lakes of oil, acid, and other toxic matter that could consume them in mere specks. And that was just the first part of their journey.

In the interior, said Talwyn, speaking for his lover, there lay a plain and then a mountain range as unflinching as an ebon wall. There, the land's capricious terrors dwindled, revealed as false and foolish things to fear, and animals living beyond the barrier were colossi of a primeval era, since mutated by the chaotic magik ripping through the area. Wild elementals, warned Pythius, beasts of brimstone and poison called *drakagor* that circled the skies and were fast as hawks, though ten thousand times the size. Occasionally, when the oldest of these beasts, which mostly slept in the deep strata of the earth, stirred, their blubberous shifting moved the earth for spans or brought tidal waves in from the Chthonic Ocean to devastate the far-off shores of Pandemonia. Beyond these terrors, fools who persisted and entered the Scar were faced with magik that induced sickness, blindness, and delirium, illnesses against which Pythius could offer a few protections, though he doubted many of them would work. As no Amakri had dared set foot in that cursed yet sacred valley for eons, their potency was now unknown. The Cradle had already been claimed, by the Magmac: the Stick Tribe.

The Magmac were the tribes of yore that stayed amid the worst of the destruction when the Mother of Light and Darkness bade all living men flee the Cradle. Legend said they'd hidden beneath the earth like worms, as magma washed over the land above. It was here, in the first of the four long seasons of the world, and in the absence of anything green or living to hunt, that the Magmac began to turn on their own herd for sustenance. First the eldest, and then the extra young—the ones for which they didn't have excess meat to spare. Thus the practice continued from the Age of Fire throughout the wettest and driest eras of Geadhain. In the great winter, they stained the hollows in the glaciers in which they lived with the crimson blood of their kin. When the leviathans that swam in the sea couldn't be caught with their primitive tools, the meat of a man became easier fare; they stayed in their reefs—pockets that hadn't filled with water as with the rest of the world—like carnivorous hermit crabs, *feasting*. And when all of Geadhain had withered, the font of blood from a man's slashed throat was as nourishing and sweet as a dribble of water, and there was no hesitation about how to feed. No man could live without water, believed Pythius, and it was through black magik that this atrocity actually preserved the Magmac. At last, when the Green Mother's rage had subsided, and the wound in her heart had started to heal in hardened tissue, the Magmac emerged from wherever they'd been hiding.

The Magmac were unrecognizable to the people of Pandemonia—who'd lived out the millennia since the apocalypse in the wilds or in their sacred cities. The Magmac had become monsters, speaking a husky tongue robbed of any of the grace or lyricism of their once native language. The Lakpoli pretended the Magmac didn't exist. The Amakri attempted contact, though any parties that ventured into the Scar to engage in reconnaissance or attempted diplomacy never returned. It was whispered around the campfires that the Magmac had taken the skins of the Amakri emissaries to make cloaks, and used their skulls for bowls, and bones for fancy flutes. Or so it was told.

Despite the paucity of contact, there was one rumor that persisted, which told of a ruin, perhaps the First City, that had been built within the devastated natural sore in the land—the site where the ark had fallen. These were simply more nightmares and legends to add to the Magmac legend, though, until many lifetimes past, a wanderer in Pandemonia, an explorer, took the journey no wise native of this land would dare to embark on. He sought to find the heart of this world, which he too believed was the birthplace of all life. He reached the Scar. He saw the ruined heap of rock and ash, climbed the cauterized mountain, and discovered the pit it housed leading to the oldest grave in the world: that of Zionae. While there, he managed to meet with the Stick Tribe, to somehow live with them and prove himself more than cattle. Thus the explorer ultimately returned to civilization with extraordinary tales of the Magmac people. He said they were peaceful, which seemed insane to those who listened. He said they were kind and knowing, a sentiment that was also dismissed, especially when others learned that the legends of *what* the Magmac ate had not been embellished.

A new story that stuck in the Amakri consciousness, however, was that of the resting place at the wound in the world. He had described it in such detail that its existence was harder to question. It was a chamber, calcified in dust wherein, upon a primal altar, did rest the ossified remains of a person. A person, claimed the Magmac, who'd once held the greatest of divine beings within their flesh. It was the body of a vessel: Zionae's vessel. At the end of the long telling, Talwyn uttered a final shocking twist to his audience.

"The wanderer's name?" he said, counting the beats until he sensed their anticipation had grown as hot as the fire. "Kericot."

Such a revelation shed fresh light on the depth and meaning of the ancient bard's poetry. Kericot had written about Pandemonia, so it was not entirely surprising that he'd been here. Although his poetry had always seemed reflective and romanticized, more fictional than autobiographical, much like the rest of his work. It was a shame Kericot wasn't there to guide them with his wisdom, or that they didn't have a tome of his works on hand, thought Mouse, who remembered a great deal of the bard's poetry from Alastair's drunken ramblings—he knew Kericot's whole catalogue. She tried to consider all Talwyn had shared with them, but those words were soon clouded by Alastair's phantom blather, and eventually she decided that sleep was probably the best journey to undertake right now.

Mouse sighed and shuffled around, trying to find part of the ground without stones to stab her. "I'm going to end up in a bloody stew. I know it. Talwyn, your plans are quite possibly the worst."

"It'll be grand!" declared Talwyn with a grin.

"Cretin," she spat, then threw her shoulder to the ground, rolled over and forced herself into what could quite possibly be the last pleasant sleep she would ever enjoy. Mouse was as tired as the rest of her company and was asleep in sands. Adam curled up with her, sharing his warmth with his friend. Moreth remained sitting in an upright position, looking stressed or strained, a pistol on his lap. Thackery had soon fallen against the Wolf's arm and snored and slept like the old man he used to be. As for the shaman and Talwyn, they snuck off into the purple bush. The Wolf didn't mind, so long as they didn't journey far.

In pensive quiet, the bloodmates had listened to Talwyn's legends and pondered the course he strongly suggested with his words. Alas, there was no other path to take. They sensed the fear of their friends. That emotion would have greater hold of their minds in the ordeal to come. However, now that they were a united pack again of coyotes, snakes, wolves, mice, and witches, neither bloodmate feared the future.

We're nearly there, my Wolf. At a future not ordained in legend.

Then I shall hunt you, always, he replied as he nuzzled her hair, kissed her ivory neck, and succumbed to her sympathetic fatigue. Moreth would watch over them tonight. For the solitary wolf, one hardened through centuries of disappointment in the virtues of mortals, a man once so untrusting of the honor of others, he didn't consider for a speck that the coyote would fail in his duty to guard them. He did wonder what was causing a nearly undetectable sour smell, though; one that seemed to waft from Moreth. Perhaps the scent was bothering his bloodmate as well, for she was looking at the Menosian, frowning.

My Fawn?

Past Moreth, over the vegetated terrain, rose a weedy lavender hill, with a miniature butte jutting out toward the moon. There she saw a large brown dog of a handsome breed, if now mangy from the wilderness. Its appearance wasn't itself a shock, aside from the queerness of such a familiar species somehow roaming here rather than Central Geadhain. As the beast stared at her, the shine of night off its pelt grew to a brighter shimmer, its fur and form softening with light. With a hum, the light rose, and she soon had to turn her head away from it just as the dog itself shifted on the rock. The sharp hum faded. She looked back and saw nothing but the rock; Moreth remained hunched and ignorant of the manifestation, her companions slept, and not even her bloodmate looked concerned about anything but her. She raced from her bloodmate's arms to explore what she had seen, sensing this as some important prophecy—her bees whirling and stinging the inside of her skull with sparks. After a time, her intuition and excitement dimmed with disappointment. There was no trace of a dog, not even the smell of one as she leaned over the boulder it had stood upon.

The Wolf had followed her, watching her. *My Fawn?*

I saw a beast, clear as my hand before me. A vision so real that my mind threw it into this world.

A vision of what?

A dog, she replied. Perplexed, she turned to him. *A dog of light and mystery.*

A spirit animal? A guide?

Perhaps.

Then you must heed it and see where it leads you.

It had turned east, she recalled, the same direction she and her companions were set to travel. While she did not trust the Fates to have suddenly provided her with a spirit guide after all her scrapes and fumbling for mysteries, she would keep an eye out for this creature. She felt, however, that it would find her.

V

Pythius and Talwyn didn't go far, instinctively remaining close to their armed company. Softly smiling and linking hands, the men slunk through the purple underbrush. The gibbous eye of moon cast the men in golden light. It made Talwyn shine like the man of sunlight and wisdom he was, and it made Pythius stop to catch his breath.

"What is it?" asked Talwyn.

"You are a vision of light," said the shaman, and they kissed with passions that fluctuated between tongued invasions of the other's mouth and the most innocent churchyard pecking. Pythius parted bushes and pointed out stones upon which his lover might otherwise have tripped. Talwyn could be a clumsy man, since most of his might lay in his head. He was only graceful when he focused his mental energy outward. He wasn't doing that tonight and suffered a few nicks and bruises despite Pythius's efforts to shield him. Surely, Talwyn was scared a little, too, of what lay in their future, tonight and beyond.

Some of that fear was what had propelled the Doomchaser shaman to seize his pyrkagos's hand and dash to privacy. They were about to embark on a grand hunt, and who knew if their small, though bright, flame could withstand the winds of doom ahead? Pythius believed it would. For he was a man of blinding conviction and made no secret of that. A man was ruled by two powerful tides of emotion, one kind and wise, the other cruel and passionate, and he'd never thought to temper them. His elders had called him two-spirited, a man of both darkness and light, a man of ultimate precision and balance—like one of these western compasses Talwyn had told him about, which could never point the wrong way. Likewise, Pythius's heart never erred untrue; he and Talwyn were destined.

Having led them far enough, he stopped an ear's whisper from camp, at the edge of the gravelly beach where the sand blended in to a tract of grass and wiry purple blooms. Pythius promised that the ground would be soft as he guided them both, kneeling, into the bed of flowers.

They undressed each other, slowly, revealing each tanned or blue shoulder, each lined ridge of hard abdomen as though they were delicate archeological treasures. Pythius once more admired the golden-red trail running from Talwyn's trousers to the patch of strange fur upon his chest; the Amakri were hairless, and the contrasting textures of the man's body hair and satiny skin were wondrous to him. Likewise, the raw contours and slightly textured feel of Pythius's scaled but still slippery-smooth body held a tremendous fascination for the scholar. He would have been curious—possibly concerned—about their other anatomical differences had he not already felt for and found the tumescence risen between the man's thighs. At least they shared the important attributes, he knew, and fumbling with desire he brought forth the thick, turquoise, and angry-looking rod from Pythius's pants. He pulled the man's large blue balls out, too, cupped them and prepared to kiss the fat, glistening head of this new seductive snake. Pythius stopped him, however, bringing him up for a kiss, and they leaned back together, rolling on the flowers.

After a speck they separated, gasping. Pythius sat up to remove the scholar's boots, then moth-eaten socks, then trousers, before removing whatever articles remained on his own body. Against the moon, he remained, standing: a frightful, horned intimation of a powerful creature, like a spirit of a bull and the hunt from Ghaedic legends of yore—even puffing little white breaths in the night. Talwyn sensed the other side of his lover, the violently passionate creature that might ravage him.

He wanted to be ravaged. Talwyn reached for the square hunk of the man's calf, let his hand climb farther, draw him higher off the ground and to his knees. He'd never wanted to swallow a man's cock so hungrily. With a shudder of passion, he wondered what else they might do together tonight—he hadn't touched flesh with a man for years now, not since his favorite pay-for-play lad in Riverton. Even then, he'd never been a particularly passionate man; he had sex every few years only when the need had whipped him to such a throbbing frenzy that it interfered with his concentration. At this moment, though, he wanted this man, and not just for a release—although he'd start with that. Opposite his wandering hand, he kissed his way up the Amakri's leg, he licked the musky crack of vein, muscle, and resplendent aquamarine scales that lay next to the hot, slapping weight of Pythius's testicles and shaft. He turned his head and prepared to kiss that treasure next. Yet for the second time, his greedy mouth was thwarted. The Amakri took his hands and brought him to standing, too. Pythius's gaze was darkened with inner conflict.

"Am I doing something wrong?" asked Talwyn.

"No. I like what you are doing very much," said the shaman. "However, I am not a man of one desire, but many. Nor do I see you as a conquest. I would like to fan our flame, West Sun, to grow it from an ember into a fire worthy of drum-songs and feasting. To do that, we must know each other. We have only just learned how to understand one another. Now we must press close and blend our heat into the other—the fire not only of our passion, but of our minds, our desires, our souls."

"Oh..." said Talwyn, and his face flushed. Embarrassed at his zeal, he cupped his deflating manhood and looked around the clothing-strewn sward for something with which to cover himself.

"West Sun," said the Amakri. As Pythius thrust his body against his like two pieces of stone, Talwyn's lust was instantly rekindled. "No clothes," he whispered, and he briefly stroked the scholar's hard, hairy meat. "We can touch. We can bare ourselves, though we must be patient, for men do not come to know each other in those tiny increments by which you measure life. Men must fight, sleep, speak, and learn of the other's soul. The process cannot be rushed. It cannot be assigned an allotment of your hourglasses in which to be completed. When we have forged that fire over so many days and nights together, then, when I enter you, or you me, when we taste the seed and sweat and blood of the other, it will be a heat, a pyrkagos, which will make the sun seem feeble. That is the way of my people. That is how I would like to love you."

"How you'd like to love me?" exclaimed the scholar.

The world spun slightly, though only Talwyn felt it. Perhaps the shaman did too, for they tightened their lean arms and rocked for a moment. That ephemeral science, that damnable, unquantifiable disease had finally afflicted Talwyn: love. He didn't believe in it. Not epic and true. Not for him. And yet here he was, on the adventure of any and all lifetimes, kissing not fuking an extraordinary creature, yearning for him and not wanting that moment to end. Eventually, their embrace waxed passionate and settled into the softer allure of discovery, of touching scales, horns, and hair, of watching the twinkle of brown eyes to serpent-green ones. Then that also dimmed to an ember—the start of the great flame of which Pythius had spoken—and the men made a quick nest with their garments and lay down.

With that, they began to share their stories, the tales they'd compiled since their youth. Pythius heard of Talwyn's queer family of "working women," which included discussion of the concept of persons who sold sex for coin, something the shaman couldn't fathom at first. Talwyn learned of the first time Pythius had conjured magik—he'd called a bird from the sky to his side with a song, one that he then sang for the scholar in his throaty, undulant voice. No birds came, since no Will had actually been used, but

Talwyn felt a certain magik regardless. They wanted to know everything about the other, all the ugliness and beauty, all lies and truths.

As they lay, basking, golden and laughing from Talwyn's often funny stories of his youth, a shadow fell over Pythius's face.

"I feel as if I may have lied to you," he said.

"Oh?"

"I understood you, even before I yearned for your heat," he admitted. "Like the West Sun, you desire to chase away the darkness, the old, shameful legends of my people. I tried to hide these things from you, knowing what you are, though I wanted to scream them to you all the while. It hurts, to hold so much knowledge. You must know this."

"I do."

"I am glad that we can banish the darkness of my people's history together." Pythius reached over and stroked his lover's cheek. "I knew, at the moment of our meeting, that our fates and flames were crossed. That you would be...a redemption."

"Did you?" asked Talwyn coquettishly, with a flick of his hand.

Pythius snatched his hand, and the small, secondary fangs set amid his normalish row of teeth were revealed in a snarl of passion. "Yes. I wanted you soon after we met. Our differences are like an eclipse: dark and light, though like sun and moon we are drawn to the other."

"I don't believe in love at first sight."

"Love is built. I shall build that with you. A man can know his destiny before laying the stones of that road." Pythius ended the discussion by running his hand roughly through the autumn tangle of the scholar's hair and wrenching him in for a snarling kiss.

Through the twinkling and cool night, they held each other, their legs and fingers entangled, staring at the stars. Slowly and diligently, they uncovered the secrets of each other's flesh and histories. It was the seeding of true friendship and, if the shaman was to be believed, love.

Pyrkagos. Talwyn thought of this strange word that was both noun and action, often thinking and mumbling the word aloud. Whenever he did the latter, the wind died, his heart raced, and in a moment he and Pythius would kiss and shiver from heat—a fire between the two men that, now lit, might never be extinguished.

VI

"Ha! The shamble of shame!" teased Mouse, as their missing companions emerged from the bushes. A fire had been started, around which the group was huddled, skinning beasts hunted earlier by the Wolf to cook over the flames. It was that smell of the food that had drawn the two men from their half-sleeping bliss. Talwyn ignored Mouse's jest and went straight for the food.

"I would have thought that a roll in the bushes would have left you in better spirits," said Moreth, as he watched the grumpy-looking gents wander near; the Amakri always had some variation of a scowl, though, so his appraisal on that one's mood might not have been accurate.

"It wasn't like that!" snapped Talwyn. He dipped and snatched the two pieces of shaved beast sitting on large leaves for himself and Pythius. "Pyth and I—"

"Pyth?" Mouse chuckled.

"We've moved into the realm of lovers' sobriquets now?" said Moreth. "How sweet. I wonder if they've set a date for the nuptials. Who will the bridesmaids be? I don't know that I can pull off a dress, depends on the shade of pink."

"You're horrible," said Talwyn, and he retreated to the outside of the circle, where he and Pythius sat. The Amakri was incorrigible with his attention, and neither cared nor concerned himself with such jibes. Pythius really couldn't be shaken, and whenever their eyes met or knees brushed as they ate, the sparks leapt up between them, and they would pause, stare, and reminisce over words, kisses, and promises traded last night. It wasn't love at first sight, Talwyn kept repeating in his mind. It was something, though, and it was possessing him by degrees.

I am impressed at the ferocity of love, whispered the Wolf, as he and Morigan nestled together. *It blooms in the blackest muck, the most wounded of gardens. It will not be enough to win this war, though it will be one of the weapons we can wield. The Black Queen and her allies do not have that grace, or strength.*

They do not.

The bloodmates sat for a time, patient. As soon as the men were finished eating, it would be time to leave. Their respite had been well and good, but now, refocused, they needed to set out into the ruined heart of their world. Morigan had visions of that darkness, phantasms that fluttered in her mind like birds at a night window—impressions that wouldn't clearly manifest either truth or terror. *No matter*, she thought, as the sun burst through the clouds and blessed them with glaring, golden light. It was as good an omen as she could expect.

It is time, declared the Wolf. On that thought, he stood, stamped out the fire, and led the pack down the black sand path of the shore. No one thought to ask for more time, for they'd been given more moments of rest than weathered heroes ought to expect. The eight souls wavered into yellow twists on the horizon and vanished.

VII

So this is the sound of the world ending, thought Amkhapet of the gonging sounds of her metal towers striking the plated streets; somewhere under that noise were a hundred thousand screaming voices. But they couldn't be heard over the shattering architecture, the reverberating buzz, as divine seed after divine seed was shot out of the sky by the fiery magik of Brutus's horde—who were, somehow, far more organized and tactically oriented than she and her cabinet of wise wards had assumed them to be.

Earlier, after the initial bombardment from her armada of divine seeds, which had left the valley beyond Intomitath twirling in fumes, the horde had continued its advance—whatever great holes blown into the massed ranks filled quickly by new bodies. Knowing more firepower was needed, she descended via seed to the forefront of the battle. Then, as the horde had approached the moat surrounding Intomitath, she and her coven of esteemed wards watched the repugnant stain's crawl toward their city calmly from the battlements. She'd felt great distaste that this affront had come to be in the first place, though she certainly felt no fear. Once the army had filled the valley, she mind-whispered and marshaled her wards, and crimson lights splayed out from the top of Intomitath's wall. United in mind and spirit, whirling in a rapturous ether, she commanded the great consciousness they had all become to speak to Fire, to call its blood from the moat surrounding Intomitath. Fire obeyed, and the magma below bubbled, rose, crested, and crashed upon Brutus's minions. The warriors attending the Keeper and her coven peered about the battlefield with spyglasses, believing nothing could have survived in the boiling expanse below.

These creatures, however, were born from the loins of their father—a beast of fire and lust—and as creatures of those aspects, they were more resistant to the heat than adamant golems and were driven to push forward into danger where normal men would not. Thus, as the wave of lava receded, the legionnaires saw through the great steaming billows below that Brutus's army still stood.

Astonished, Intomitath's defenders watched these husks, burned like the ashen statues littering the base of a volcano, continue forward. Then came a great cloud as the sooty flesh of thousands of these creatures cracked, their blackened hides shedding in the wind, revealing underneath gleaming pink and metal forms that seemed to have been newly refreshed and recast by Intomitath's assault. Many knew of how another horde had been repelled in the far west at Gorgonath, and how fire had somewhat worked on that occasion. But to Intomitath's horror, these monsters seemed to have evolved.

Brutus's sorcerers—the monsters with the glowing staves and auras of fire—had resumed their chanting. Now, however, rather than Brutus's name, they called out something old and magikal, their bodies glowing as red as the blood jewels in the crown of their infernal king. There were too many Redeyes to count—tens or hundreds. As the ancient war incantation reached its height, the still-flowing lava slowed its retreat into the moat—raising into a hump, twisting as though it were a titan's tentacle, then calming, cooling, and setting into a bridge over which they could now stride to reach the heights of the great wall, the rampart where it connected: a road directly into Intomitath.

In the thrall of a sorcerer's circle, Amkhapet and the other wards saw none of what was occurring, though they felt the tug-of-war between their Wills and the Wills of the soulless army's sorcerers over the moat of fire's power. As that struggle ended, Amkhapet and the others were pulled violently from their connection. She knew they'd lost as she stumbled toward the edge of Intomitath's rampart. One ward, then two, then three, flew up and over the edge as if they had been pulled by strings. By the Green Mother's mercy, one of the doomed wasn't Samael, her lover. Indeed, her golden-masked and special guardian, who had not taken part in the ritual so that he might watch her, was the one to catch her firmly as she flailed and others died.

"You lost control," he said, panting. "We must get you to safety. We cannot predict this battle."

Samael threw off his mask and kissed her before thrusting her into the arms of a nearby legionnaire and screaming at the man to take her to safety. She could have objected. She could have overruled any command, but she no longer felt any certainty in her choices. The last she saw of Samael was his face shining with tears, lit by a sunset beyond the wall. He roughly shook the emotion off, gritted his teeth, and then was lost in a shuddering eruption of smoke as Brutus's vile sorcerers launched their first assault on Intomitath's wall.

She wasn't sure what had happened to her lover, and her mind was reeling too much for her to worry over the fate of one man when all of her city was in peril. Screams. So many screams came to her: psychic echoes of her people being decimated. Now that she'd been shuttled back to her tower by a divine seed, the screams were fewer—torturer's echoes happening outside her walls. She refused to go to the window, to be faced with the destruction happening outside; hearing it was enough. What sense she had she kept for the frenzied mind-whispers of her wards as they updated her on the status of her city and the location of Brutus.

The mad king hadn't been leading his army; the wards hadn't seen him on the smoldering battleground—the slag heaps and mountainous canyons of scorched waste surrounding the hole burrowed through Intomitath's wall by the magik of Brutus's firecallers. The demon sorcerers with the reddest eyes possessed flames hotter than those of Intomitath, hot enough to melt the ironwork of the city. Now the city had been breached, and not just from one bridge-to-rampart, but from several similar bridges and breaches around its perimeter. As for Brutus, he did not fight on those fronts. The Keeper sensed him, like a speck in the corner of her mind's eye. The Immortal was as fast and fleeting, though, and her trained, perceptive mind couldn't catch wind of him.

No, he must have slipped into the city before his army had arrived. Intuition told her that was true, and that he had been sowing horror in her city right under her nose for some time. At last, the Immortal cast off his stealth and began dispensing his brand of violence fast and loose, wreaking havoc and leaving bodies in a trail that led to one place: the Pinnacle of Fire.

It was the tallest and greatest tower in Intomitath, and it represented the Paradisium of Intomitath—her sanctuary. She imagined he'd climb it with the facility of a demonic ape, leaping through her window in a single bound. She sensed his imminence as a hiding animal perceives the rustle of a predator. What did he want? Other than to ruin another city? Had he come for the arkstone? She would never surrender it. Amkhapet's pride was greater than her fear, and she stood, glaring angrily around her pristine chamber, the music of her crumbling city rising around her. She waited for the mad king to show himself, to make the demands that she'd refuse.

I shall never surrender my city, our souls, or the arkstone, she swore. *I shall take them all to my death.*

As though in response to her challenge, there came a bestial bellow from the chambers beneath her sanctuary. Clashing sounds and wet screams nearby caused the Keeper to doubt whether she could hold more than a weak-kneed front against what was coming. She heard his footsteps, each as loud as the heartbeat ringing in her ears. She smelled his buttery animal stink wafting up from the archway at the end of the chamber, where winding gold stairs spun down into darkness. Brutus was coming. She wouldn't flee, for really there was nowhere to hide. She would face her fate and death with dignity.

"Brave," came the purring voice that shook her entire frame. He'd smelled the stringent puff of her courage, and it teased him like fresh blood.

Suddenly aware of the Immortal's presence behind her, Amkhapet spun around. She gagged from the Immortal's smell, her eyes tearing at once. Blinded, she thrust out her hand in a conjuration of Will summoned by her righteous fury. Howling light whirled around her, and a fiery detonation of her conjured magik, a meteor-punch that should have shattered a stone wall, thudded limply into the gargantuan black-and-gold shadow, tarred in ash and blood, which towered over her. Knowing she'd achieved nothing, and screaming with hate, she called on another burst of power, but Brutus seized her hand, crushing its bones and meat to paste; she'd have nothing left now but a shapeless claw. Then, with the strength of a baleful Immortal, he threw her as easily as if she were a toy. Soaring, she flew twenty or more paces into the dome of her antechamber, struck the gaudy fresco with a grunt and a spray of gore, before falling to the ground. Brutus, moving faster than magik, caught her before she could take another breath in her broken body.

Amkhapet returned to consciousness, dizzy, her sight clouded, gripped in the Immortal's embrace. He held her like a lover, and she wondered if she was to be defiled before being murdered. However hard she tried, she couldn't move anything below her neck and was forced to stare into the hungry face of her destroyer. Alas, he was beautiful, much like a fire was beautiful: raw, vicious. While she was numb with the coldness of death's blanket, and ready for that long sleep, Brutus hadn't yet released her, and, as he explained, he wouldn't.

"You have so great a spirit for such a tiny bird," said the Immortal. "I have clipped your wings, though. You are too weak to fly, or to call upon your power. However, I have a duty for you to perform, before I end your suffering. A single task."

"Nebber..." she dribbled, through a swollen sore of a mouth.

Laughing, the Immortal shook her body as more of her insides churned and snapped. "I can keep you here, on the brink, forever if I must. I can feed you my blood, my seed." He licked the side of her face with a tongue as long as an elephant's trunk. Broken neck be damned, she wriggled her head from him as best she could.

"Ah...I think your breed is strong against the torments of the flesh. Even now, even armed—barely—with words, you resist me. I can smell the steel of your soul. I would offer you a place in my army, as I shall all the people of

Intomitath, yet I can see that you would rather die. As one strong soul to another, I shall grant you that. But first, there is your task. I need you to open the Purgatorium. My mother's stones do not belong in the hands of mortals, they never have. You must Will the gates to open. I cannot rely upon Amunai to twist your body to her will, for you are so strong…"

Since she was paralyzed, neck-down frozen as a woman in ice water, Amkhapet couldn't tell and wouldn't imagine what Brutus was doing to her with his giant hands and rabid lust. She closed her eyes and imagined the tugging and squelching was something else. At last, that horrid storm passed.

"Mmm…your blood is sweet, and I've given you a drop of mine, which should keep you alive for a while. Still, I have promised you freedom from my rule, and release into the hands of Death. I shall not resurrect you as a child of my mother. Retrieve for me the arkstone, and I shall show you mercy. Deny me, and there will be consequences."

Consequences? Her city was ruined, her people likely dead or of the undead. She would not walk, shite, or even be alive beyond today. He had no power over her. Purgatorium could remain sealed for all time, and her ghost would relish Brutus's infuriated bellowing as he banged on doors so steeped in magik that not even his terrible strength could shatter them. She smiled her defiance, since she felt words would again fail her.

Brutus, snarling, dropped her body on the tiles and stomped away. With her head turned toward the floor, she saw Brutus's giant feet moving in flickering shadows across her dim field of vision. Although crippled, her ears worked perfectly fine. It was the gasp she recognized, a sound she'd heard only in the throes of pleasure. It was Samael's whimpering she heard.

The mad king explained himself. "I smelled you upon him, and him upon you. I smelled your rich desire for one another as ripe as the first turn of spring soil. It was that desire that I chased first, knowing how you fleshlings value love, how you surrender everything for it, when I arrived before my forces. I have watched you both for hourglasses. I considered how to break an unbreakable mind. Amunai does not believe I can do it. But men and women are mere clay to the hands of the Immortals. We shape you, we make you; you are as we desire you to be. I shall teach you that lesson, Keeper, and then we can discuss Purgatorium once more."

Praying for Samael in her heart, weeping silently, she listened as Brutus tore the man apart. Not as an animal would, which would've been kinder, but instead as slowly, steadily, and as wetly as though he were making love. At times, from Samael's gurgles and the slapping spasms she heard, she hoped he was dead and these were but reactions of his corpse. The moment seemed eternal, and she wished her frozen body would simply die. Yet she felt a wriggling worm—Brutus's blood and Will—chewing a hole in her stomach.

The worm slithered up her intestines and around her heart. In moments when her sight spotted and she felt the pull of the void, the worm squeezed, pumping her heart for her, and dragged her back into this mockery of existence.

When she returned from almost falling into the abyss for a second or third time, Samael's bloodied face was before her, his neck twisted like hers, and gaping at her with the startled look of the suddenly dead. His mouth had been ravaged into a toothless pit that dribbled thick, white fluid, and he was as wet with secretions as a newborn. She knew what Brutus had done to him; he reeked of sex, shite, and death. While her stomach clenched and tried to expel itself, the worm of Brutus's blood tightened her throat and prevented even that release. The king of rapists and horror squatted beside her, flinging her around so that she looked straight up into his shadowed majesty. Samael's blood spilled off the king's flesh and pattered down on her face in a drizzle. She tried to blink it away. She'd moved beyond fear, pain, or horror. Again, he smelled her courage. He savored its scent with a long open-mouthed inhalation—an animal tasting ether.

"You could have been my queen, once—fierce as you are. And I know his death means nothing next to your values, which makes me desire you more."

Brutus's blood worm was giving her unholy fortitude, and as a bit of her magik trickled back, she mind-whispered, *I shall pray for Samael. I shall miss him, though I shall surrender to you nothing. Purgatorium will be sealed for an eternity. May you and your conquest be denied and damned forever.*

"Yes." Brutus snorted. "A creature of your prideful ilk would not surrender her possessions so easily. I know pride. I am pride. I understand you and what it will take to break you. The end of your lover is not enough, for you love your people, your dream even more. So I shall threaten that dream. I shall turn it into a nightmare unless you do as I say, and willingly open the gates to Purgatorium."

Brutus looked away from her, his jaw subtly working as though he was chewing on words. Mindspeaking, she realized. By his command, others were brought into the room, and with the drop of vitality infused in her by Brutus's blood she was able to turn her head to see them. A dozen or so captives, legionnaires and wards, had been seized by Brutus's soldiers. They were beaten, bloody, and babbling. More silent were the wards who'd been blinded—cruel rents and gouges across their eyes—and whose hands had been gnarled into lumpy meat like hers; they were sorcerers who had been numbed by their defeat and were incapable of summoning any Will.

Almost worse than their treatment, though, was the horror that was Brutus's children. Things that were more horrible to behold at a shorter distance, these almost-men with exposed skulls, grimaces forced by golden triangles of scrap metal shoved into their jaws, and arms that twisted into blades or lazily forged maces. It was hard to say which keratinous plates upon them were metal or which were scarred flesh, as they were armored like piecemeal insects. At least one hand and arm on each had been left mostly operative for tasks such as herding the people they'd captured. In each of the Blackeyes' stares was a flicker of malice, but nothing more than the perceived evil of a gargoyle; they were as empty and lifeless as those stone effigies. Whatever souls they'd once had were gone. There was one glowering, red-gazed sorcerous being, however, who led them and glared at the ruined Keeper with an intelligence that blazed bright as the runes engraved upon his blackened, withered face. Not all of his army were mindless, then.

"I shall start by showing you the price of your defiance," said the Immortal. "I shall start by turning your men into my men." The helpless prisoners struggled as Brutus strode toward them. "I shall fill them with my seed and my grace. You will watch as their souls are consumed in the fire of my passion."

Brutus caressed the cheek of a trembling legionnaire, then seized the man's head, lifted him off the floor, and kissed him. The soldier choked as though his guts were being siphoned out through his throat, his body convulsing, and the king moaned. With a grunt, he cast the legionnaire aside and the man, invigorated by whatever churning nest of maggots Brutus had passed into his body, crawled toward Amkhapet. The soldier hadn't reached her before he slumped over and a rooty malignancy hunched his back, split his clothing, arced his body, and swelled his head until it bled from his mouth, ears, and eyes. Then, from that sputtering, bleeding, flailing end, from a pool of his own juices, he rose: strong, proud, and with a stare as black and empty as the rest of the metal-fused unliving things he'd soon be outfitted, at one of Brutus's infernal forges, to match.

"You will watch. And as you watch, know that my generals are rounding up the women, children, and elderly of your city. I have not ordered their deaths. I have ordained them to be blessed and reborn to serve my mother and me for time eternal."

Brutus whirled and suddenly was before her, snarling. "Think, you who loves your people and your dream. Consider whether your pride is more important than the souls of the hundreds of thousands who've depended upon you for sanctuary, for the divine release of which I shall deprive them. There will be no paradise, no reward for their life of piety; they will be my vassals for all time. Once I am done with these men, we shall see if you have come to your senses. If not, I'll start with the infants. A soulless babe still makes for an agile grub in my army. I shall find a use for *every* body, this I swear to you."

Making good on his threat, Brutus walked to the circle of prisoners and began his molestation of their bodies and expunging of their souls. The men whose sight remained shrieked as the king stormed toward them. Nothing she could do would save them; they, like Samael, were to be a lesson for her. However, the children and women, especially the wailing babes whose plaintive echoes filled her mind, were not beyond salvation. She could release them, if only she chose among the least vile of her wicked options. Do nothing and damn her city and the souls of its people? Or give Brutus what he desired and receive his mercy, though possibly damn the world? Could a monster like him be trusted to keep his word? She believed a perverse code of honor still ruled him. Thinking of honor, were there not still noble heroes who could stand against him?

As she watched her brave warriors being mauled and raped of all decency, baptized in blood, semen, and sin, as she saw these noble men reborn into shells that would know only an honorless, endless existence, she knew what choice she must make.

VIII

Rain thrashed the winding road and carved up the land like broken glass. Simon's ramshackle, Romanisti-style caravan, with its small door, drawn curtains, and the look of a miniature witch's cottage on wheels, somehow withstood the tempest. As did his brave steed, who Muriel had named Patience, a commentary on Simon's animal-handling ineptitude. Patience tended to follow her own lead, which sometimes ran concurrently with the direction in which Simon reined her.

Though he was grateful for her self-navigation, especially in tonight's storm. Occasionally, Simon could see the road quite well through one parted veil or another. Most of the time, however, he and his horse were left guessing—and cursing, in his case. There wasn't much to see, anyway, just lonely humps of foothills beside the precipice-thin trail that shimmered in water along which his horse trotted.

He had barely seen another soul since stealing the horse and buggy from an abandoned farm south of Taroch's Arm. As they'd slid open the clawed-up barn door and peeked into the dark, brandishing broken sticks, they were astonished to see the beast resting at the back of the shambled place, quiet and standing. They couldn't figure out how the beast remained alive when the rest of the farm was splattered in blood. That is until Simon had spotted the bags of salt used for preserving, which had been slashed and spilled all over the barn floor during whatever tussle had taken place. Salt, which had formed a spiral about the horse: a circle. A circle of salt, fortuitously laid, and which he'd always heard the wise women say was an ancient ward against evil. The horse had seemed so indifferent to the destruction surrounding it. From then on, it had been Muriel, Patience, and him traveling the Southern Thread—the webwork of roads winding through the green spans south of Kor'Khul.

One morning, they'd passed near Bainsbury, but he hadn't proceeded into its quiet, dark ruins. Instead, he'd parked the caravan distant, told Muriel to stay inside, and gone ahead to peer at the crumpled fences, scorched houses, and general pall of decay that had fallen over the once picturesque town, gathering enough of a tale.

Days later, Simon had caught up with a few survivors hiking along the Southern Thread. "Into the survivors camps deeper in Meadowvale, perhaps even as far as Eod," they'd said, and offered to take him and his girl along with them to Eod, to these places where all of civilization had since gathered. But he knew of a place safer than anywhere they were headed, and he wouldn't risk his child's life in these encampments that he felt would be targets for hungry dead, or in traveling through the blasting heat of Kor'Khul to reach Eod. After seeing the end of every gathering of humanity from Taroch's Arm to here, he doubted that these people would live for more than a week. No, he had a better idea for him and Muriel.

He had seen and come to know enough about what was happening in Geadhain. A Sun King reborn as a mad king. The City of Iron razed to ruin. And that awful assault on Sorsetta. Hiding in the larger cities had seemed like the dumbest of ideas when clearly they were the exact places being targeted by evil. Simon wasn't a coward; he'd been tested and ultimately judged during his wife's murder to be quite brave in the face of doom. But he wasn't stupid either, and a smart man knew when and where to hide.

He would seek out a remote hideaway like an old cabin south of Meadowvale, nestled in the crags of the Straits of Wrath, where a man and his family could fish, could boil the seawater and capture the steam for condensation to drink, and most importantly, hide from an apocalypse of the undead. In another day or so, they would turn west onto a wild road that deviated from the Southern Thread. Then it would be another few days ride until the gloomy rock towers of the Straits marred the skyline. Muriel could sleep in the caravan as she had been, and he'd continue to take only the occasional involuntary nap in the mornings when he felt it was safe to sleep. Muriel always woke him if he dozed for more than an hourglass or two, or if she heard even the smallest noise. He didn't mind the sleeplessness, aside from the delusional, hyperactive state into which this run from death had placed him. Such jitteriness startled him more than any dangers they had recently faced.

Often, he thought he was seeing things, like tonight as three shadows materialized in front of him on the rainy road. One of them, holding what appeared to be a staff, shouted and a flash of white boomed from above.

"Hold!" said the shadow.

Patience stopped before Simon even pulled on her reins. Three figures came forward—two tall, one short, all dressed in dark riding cloaks. Simon believed in that instant that he was still partially asleep, or imagining things, for the figures seemed to move through the rain as if separate from the element, like dry phantoms of Dream. They were on the soaked rider in a speck. He felt smaller in his saddle, as if he looked up, not down, at the oldest. She with a voice of stone, time, and thunder addressed him.

"You're shivering like waterfowl in winter. You shouldn't be out in such weather."

Simon noticed the face beneath her cowl. Her hair flowed black and white, around features so stern that their beauty was painful to behold, her eyes gleaming like a raven's, only green instead of black, and far more canny. Another tall beauty stood beside this one, and her gaze sliced Simon to the marrow so thoroughly that he shuddered from toe to groin. The third woman—*they must be sisters*, he thought—was actually a child, not a dwarf. She pulled back her hood a little and greeted him with a blast of sunny comeliness and a smile. In an instant, she had restored all the warmth to his blood that the other had stolen from him.

Simon noticed that they were all as sopping wet as he, and thus must also be subject to the laws of reality, and not be the spirits he'd thought they might be.

"What can I do for you ladies?" he asked, as he wiped the rain from his gawking face.

"We are on a journey," said the oldest.

"A pilgrimage," said the saddest.

"An adventure!" the golden girl exclaimed, clapping.

Simon couldn't explain the queer buzzing he heard in his head, or the echoes their voices seemed to create. He tried to shake off the strange fog.

"Where are you headed? On a dark night like this? Wandering the road during a storm? You too must find shelter. Surely you know, but it's the end of the world."

"Not yet," said the oldest. "Although we'll need you to take us to where that end will take place."

"P-pardon?"

Rather helplessly, Simon watched as the young child hopped over and knocked on the door to the coach. Muriel answered, armed with a frown and a stick she hadn't let go of since Riverton, but she dropped both weapons as soon as she laid eyes on the young girl. *She's not a girl*, came a thought from Simon's primal core, from an ancestral wisdom buried in his blood. *She's a force, as elemental as this storm. She's a vessel of sunlight and innocence donning the shape of a girl. She—*

"Oh, you're clever," said the iciest woman. "I can see why Mother Geadhain led me to you." The woman reached her pale hand through the air as if stealing secrets from around his figure. Simon cringed in the saddle as she also held a long cloth-wrapped shaft in her other hand, and he worried she might smite him with it. "The resonances of Fate flicker around you like an orgy of firebugs, ready to mate and die. Perhaps that lies in your future: love, passion, and death. That's all you mortals seem to worry about. It wouldn't surprise me." She shook the bundled object at him. "Worry not over this, little firebug, it is indeed for smiting, though it is not aimed at your end— you'll wield it sooner than you'd prefer."

Mortals? Simon was flabbergasted that this witch had somehow managed to read his thoughts. He was further unsettled by his acquiescence when that woman, too, left him to climb inside the open door to his only sanctuary.

"Muriel!" he cried, though with little fear.

"You know you don't have to be afraid," said the oldest witch. "A part of your soul understands who we are, what we are, and why we've been brought to you this eve. We all have roles to play in Geadhain's great war. Yours, my dear rock-tinkerer, my warrior with a heart of lace, has only begun. This is not the time to hide your daughter from these events; she will need to be shaped by them. As will you. I shall prepare you as best I can for the unimaginable things you and your daughter are to witness. Consider it your reward for your part in this pilgrimage: information. You'll have the wisdom that kings and wise men have all sought since they first learned to dream."

"Pilgrimage?"

"Man's steel is better tested in battle, so be patient until it's time for you to know fear; your role will uncloud itself in time. For now, turn around and head south. Allow the journey to reveal itself to you."

The witch petted Patience's wet muzzle, at which the horse whinnied in glee and stomped her hoof. "Patience knows the path. I see that Geadhain has already blessed our journey with protection, fortuitousness, and nourishment. Do not fear for your daughter. Fear for the future if we do not complete our tasks in time to intervene."

The woman swept over toward the carriage. There she hung on to the handle of the door, one foot on the step, waiting. Simon hadn't broken his stare, and his mind was a wildfire of dread and curiosity. "Go on," she said. "What is it?"

Simon struggled to understand even a fragment of this grand mirage. "Who are you?"

"You know the answer to that, Simon Bochance." She smiled as she declared, "We are three sisters."

The carriage door closed, and laughter echoed over to Simon through the pattering rain. His hands, clenching the reins without purpose, grew colder. Without guidance, Patience trotted in a slow semicircle, turned to the southeast, and set off across the foggy dales.

IV

EVIL WITHIN

I

Dawn glowered, red and furious. It foretold an ominous day, felt Gustavius, who winced as he looked out the window of the crowe and watched a wave of bloody light baptize the dunes. He stopped sky-watching and slumped into the plush comfort of the couch. Unsettled for no clear reason, he counted the studs on the black metal ceiling. He tried to let his mind wander, which, being a man of action, wasn't a pursuit at which he excelled. Perhaps he was simply troubled by the return of the Iron Queen's dead son last night.

Was that the proper term? Dead? Reanimated? Undead (as was quickly becoming the vogue over "unliving")? Gustavius was a man of iron and strength, not Will and magik. These strange miracles did not settle well with him. In any event, Sorren had returned and brought with him news that confirmed what was long suspected: Death had come to conquer Geadhain, and she'd raised an army to do so. Across the desert, the dead would soon shamble, and if Death succeeded in her plan, Eod would become the world's largest graveyard. Gloriatrix had shooed him away like a gnat before he'd been able to hear anything more from that meeting. Sorren's appearance had caused her to express emotions he'd never before witnessed from her. *Humph, tears from the Iron Queen.* Too much was changing. It seemed as though all that he knew was being redefined and that myth had become reality.

Although his people—those who had been from the North—had spoken of times when spirits walked the land wearing the flesh of men. As if through a veil of lace, a distant memory returned to him of a longhouse, its walls hammered by cold. He and others surrounded the only fire willing to be lit on the frozen earth. A wise man had been speaking of the legend of Beira, describing her avatar. At the pinnacle of his tale, he'd thrown something in the fire that made it flare white mist, and in that haze Gustav had seen a phantasm of a woman as white as snow, gold of hair, and dressed in a crown and sash of gossamer ice. In her hand had been a spear of crackling golden light—the same that shone in her eyes. Beira was real, not myth, the shaman had claimed. She was a manifestation of the North. She was the spirit of Winter. Men would pray to her before going on a hunt. It was a habit that Gustav himself had taken up for even the most menial of duties—milking, skinning, and tanning—to which he was assigned. He couldn't remember the last time he'd thought of his old life and religion.

Strange ruminations these were, and yet if Death could throw on a body and walk around, the notion that Winter could do the same wasn't totally without reason. *We need order and civility. We need an end to the age of immortals and madness. Legends must die for the sake of progress.* On that note, he wondered if they'd made any progress on eradicating the caged dead they'd secretly brought back from the frontlines.

It was a wise and fair judgment from the king that the survivors of Menos would be taken, first and foremost, to Eod. There, they would receive the finest care available. On the surface, the Iron Queen had seemed to honor this arrangement. In secret, she'd had a shipload of Menos's refugees flown to Camp Fury, made up of those found wandering the black fog, too feverish or wounded to speak, or who had been ravaged by festering wounds or burns. They'd arrived days ago and been instantly quarantined. By then rumors and postulations that postmortem these people could rise again as servants to a dark power was far more fact than fancy. They took no risks with these patients. Indeed, they allowed many citizens to die in their iron cells while under the grim watch of Menos's remaining Iron marshals and nekromancers. When the first of the damned had passed, then twitched and leapt up slavering, snarling, and clawing through his cage bars for whatever soft, living flesh he could find, the Menosian physicians applauded. Gustavius hadn't been at Camp Fury for that heinous eureka moment; however, he'd heard his fill of their macabre joy courtesy of farspeaking stones.

Soon, he was told, they had nine of the living dead caged like rabid wolves, and the study of these autonomously made unliving had been given a name: Project Animus. A few of the reborn hadn't survived the various environmental and toxic extremes to which they'd been exposed for the purposes of science, and the Iron lord wasn't sure how far his countrymen could progress in their research with a thinning supply of lab rats. Only once had Gustavius visited the makeshift laboratory at Camp Fury. It was a large, fetid, and humid tent filled with iron kennels and cage-rattling dead, like a zoo of horrors. Quite quickly, the putrid stench of ammonia, roasted rotten flesh, and the damp rankness of compost had driven him off. He wasn't relishing a second visit. Alas, that time was upon him, as "discoveries" had been made according to the latest communications.

The crowe touched down with a soft shudder. Gustavius remained in the cabin, peering out the portal at the dusty soldiers hustling through a whirl of white grit and the dozens of tents peaked on the wavy back of the land. Once those tents had been as black as the Ironguard, too, though they were now painted in sand. *In another week they'll be as pale as this desert. In two more, they might be buried entirely, after Death has stamped out Eod and all of mankind's glory*, thought the Iron lord, gloomily.

Rap-rap-rap. An Iron lord, particularly the queen's favorite, was never to be interrupted without courtesy. Gustavius didn't see himself as entirely superior to his fellow man—just stronger, wilier, and luckier, he supposed. Thus, he didn't make the nervous Ironguard knock once more. He stood, opened the submersible-style handle with a spin, and startled the man who stood listening at the door. He had a wick of red hair, a face spotted with freckles, a piggish nose, and seemed as feckless as he was stunned.

"Oh! That was quite fast," said the soldier. "Not that you wouldn't be fast, on account of your age or anything." His eyes went wide as the Iron lord frowned. "Do pardon."

"Who are you?"

"Irongrunt Davy. Sir!" The Ironguard saluted. He'd forgotten that in order to eavesdrop, however, he'd removed his helm, which he now held in his dominant hand. And so as he swung up his hand, he thwacked himself in the face with his helmet. The blow threw him against the wall of the narrow hallway, with the power of that impact propelling him forward like a rubber man into another topple, this one ending at Gustavius's feet. From there he looked up as a dribble of blood ran from his nose and into his smile. "It's an honor to serve you, sir! Doctor Hex has moved, and I've been assigned to take you to him."

Gustavius glanced from side to side to check for hidden snickerers, though no one would be so daft as to play tricks on him. This idiot appeared to be his guide.

"A man only stays on his knees if he's been bought by a pleasure house," spat Gustavius. "On your feet and in your uniform. Fall again and it will be by my hand or rifle."

"I'm so sorry, sir." Davy scrabbled up, dropped his helm, apologized, and then dropped it once more, forcing him to chase it down the hallway and around a corner. Gustavius pondered shooting his simple face the speck it peeked around the bend, though he heard Davy making prostrations as objects and insults were thrown at the lad by the captain and crew—whom he'd offended somehow while recapturing his helmet. Gustavius decided to let the world punish the fool, as it surely would.

When the bumbling lad returned to him, they walked out of the dark ship, down a small ramp, and into the sweltering kiss of a day barely stoked in its glory. Sand whorled through the encampment in howling apparitions. No matter how early the hourglass or how desolate the welcome of Mother Geadhain here, soldiers were up and ready—filing weapons, polishing rifles, and marching. Gustavius silently commended the metal-clad men who strode around, fully attired in their cruel suits of twisted, spiny darkness. Scarcely a man was about who wasn't prepped and dressed for war. Alas, while an Ironguard's vestments were constructed for facility of movement and possessed the tenacity of metal, they weren't especially breathable. Almost immediately upon leaving the ship, sweat had trickled down Gustavius's spine. He did not don his helm, since the face—even sweating—of an Iron lord was something men should see and fear, and so he and Davy set out.

Soon he realized that Davy wasn't leading him to the sprawling sandy compound of tents, but past those tents and campfires and toward the three ebon monoliths: the Furies. What majestic and terrible things these ships were: sharp hulls that could be ravens' beaks, the enormous and seemingly throbbing bodies, the rows upon rows of razor plumage tipped in pulsating red—like the quills of a poisonous, magikal beast. Each of those quills held a mine's worth of truefire. Only to himself did Gustavius admit that he was glad Gloriatrix hadn't unleashed these monstrosities; their power would scar the world as terribly as the sundering of Menos—or worse.

"Impressive and dreadful," commented Davy, as they wandered the barren sandscape in front of the Furies. "I think we could win the war with those. Could win any war with them, really."

"We shall."

"Shall! Of course."

Their walk felt long in the shadow of the behemoths. The encampment was behind them. On that point, as he'd walked through Camp Fury on previous occasions, Gustavius couldn't recall having seen the smaller compound that had been erected to house the unliving. It had been encircled in barbed wire and was too conspicuous for him to have missed, like a heap of bristly trash thrown on Eod's white lawn. He wondered what the mad doctor had decided to do with his specimens.

"Where are you taking me?" asked the Iron lord.

"To the *Morgana*!" replied the lad. "Master Hex has taken up residence in one of the supply bays. It's better for containment, now that there are so many subjects."

"Pardon?" Gustavius halted Davy with a stone hand on his collar and spun the lad around. "There were only a few *victims* upon my previous inspection. Has the plague, illness, or whatever the medicine men have deemed to call it, spread?"

"I'm not the best resource on such matters, Iron lord. I believe that Doctor Hex will have all the explanations you will need."

Surly, Gustav shoved Davy ahead, and they moved at a faster pace toward the nearest and largest of the three Furies, which was parked at the armada's head. Kor'Khul had done little to bury the vessel's great hull, and yet the men who appeared tiny beneath the giantess spent tireless, sweaty sands simply hiking up and then down the awesome sandbank into which she'd been beached, so that they might reach the starboard side. There, a slanted bridge had been thrust from a hole in the *Morgana*. The men reached it, huffing, and leaned for a speck upon the furled feliron railing of the grand walkway before conquering the next ascent.

"What remarkable stamina you have," said Davy.

The grunt was keeled over and hyperventilating as Gustavius shook the sand from his cloak and clanked his metal boots up the bridge; Ironguards were ahead of him, and he would not show them weakness. As for how the infantile soldier gasping to catch up had ever passed the most lenient of military exams, Gustavius was left to wonder. Distracting somewhat were the subtle, blinking, bloodred lights along the bridge that had been embedded into the metal relief of the railing. Gustavius wondered what their purpose might be, though he knew many of these ships' designs were ostentatious only for the purpose of insulting any advocate of moderation. When he absentmindedly touched one of the red crystals and received a withering shock through his gauntlet, he instantly recalled a snippet of a sleep-inducing debriefing on the warships. These were part of the electromagikal defenses of the *Morgana*, small conductors that contributed to a larger grid. As though she—and her sisters—were one of nature's lethal defenders, the shell of each vessel could be wreathed in a field of magik to repel invasion from outside. *The most impossible weapons ever made*, he remarked. *We don't need Immortals with your dastardly ingenuity, my Queen.*

Ironguards stood at attention down the center of the bridge, offering salutes to Gustavius and his attaché as the pair passed by. Davy seemed to receive the salutations with pride, as though he'd earned them himself. He still hadn't decided whether Davy was an idiot he should kill or whether he should keep him around for his antics. At that moment, the man somehow managed to trip on air and sprawled rump to the sun, exposing pink undershorts through the crack in his faulds. Gustavius was unable to hold in his cruel laugh. The lad stood and adjusted his armor, making sure everything was tucked back in where it was supposed to be, smoothing down the flexible plates of his armor.

"You're laughing about the color of my drawers," he said, trembling with emotion—not fear. "Or from my fall, or both. I'm a fool, and I know it. But please don't laugh about my shorts. They're from my mum, you see. She was a weaver in Taroch's Arm and made them herself." Gustavius exploded with another laugh. "They're pink from blood that wouldn't wash out. Her blood—I was soaked in it when I found her body."

Gustavius frowned.

"Do pardon me for boring you with the details of my life," said Davy. "You, of all persons, have more important things to hear. Doctor Hex awaits!"

Davy resumed his march and didn't falter again or offer any more comedy from his misadventures. Gustavius would no longer have appreciated the humor, anyway. For if he looked far enough back in his memory to that gray distortion that burbled songs and bore women's perfumes, he'd remember a mother in whose blood he, too, had been bathed. Thanks to the advancements of Menos, and a privileged life drawn beyond what span of years the luckiest Northman could ever claim, the past was easy for Gustavius to forget. Age and spiritual cataracts had lent a misty blur to that time. It was perhaps not so queer that the memory would come to him then, after hearing of a dead mother, as he stood in the wing of the *Morgana*, this grand mother of metal and darkness, who would herself drench Geadhain in gore.

"Astrid," he muttered.

He spotted a shimmer of dark hair in the shadowy vault that lay ahead. It belonged to a ghost, a delusion of the heat, yet still Gustavius ran toward it.

II

Gideon Hex had been a busy man, Gustavius realized. The shipping dock at which the Iron lord and his attaché arrived resembled nothing befitting its old purpose. There should have been crates piled sky-high to the metal rafters of this interior cathedral. However, most of that technomagikal and martial equipment had been moved, shoved against the walls, and hurriedly covered with tarps so that the massive floor could be used for something else.

Worship, perhaps. Idolatry of mankind's madness and genius. He and Davy hesitated in crossing the floor of the menacing chamber, which flickered from the electromagikal flares of live static crackling from protrusions thrust into the floor. These objects failed specificity in make or purpose: some resembled wire trees, others iron crosses with heavy spheres affixed to their heads. Nearly every conductor—he could think of no other phrase to describe them—was many times grander than a man.

They moved slowly, gawking upward and around and minding their steps to avoid the charged pools that had flooded portions of the floor. The presence of so much water surely wasn't safe—not that Gustavius was even certain it was water. And as they crept toward the center of this masterpiece of madness, more deviancy revealed itself: a jumbled iron lab with boiling alchemies, cauldrons that might have been stolen from a witch, and metal tables painted with blood and body parts attended by masked doctors wearing the faceless garb of welders. Beyond these chattering doctors, who picked through organs like primal soothsayers, loomed stacks of kennels, three high by dozens long. Within weren't dogs, but people. Or at least, what had once been people. Railing, slobbering dead—many who had only just begun to green and bloat from their conditions—slammed against their prisons. Neither Gustavius nor Davy could appreciate the true volume and fury of the reborns' incessant wailing until they drew nearer. It was the unholiest of symphonies. It was—

"Madness," exclaimed Gustavius. What had Gideon been doing? As a servant to the crown and to madmen who ruled, the Iron lord felt experienced in the shades of his countrymen's lunacy. This, though, seemed abominable.

"It's...well..." mumbled Davy. "Quite unbecoming."

A short man hustled over from near the tower of cages. They were so immersed in the horror that neither Gustavius nor Davy noticed him until he'd approached quite close. The man's entire appearance was a lie; with a bushy white beard and a small belly that bulged from behind his rubber apron, it was as though he were a warm grandfather upon whose lap one might sit. And when he said hello, his voice was cheery and high. Although the blood on his spectacles and in his beard, and the pinched, concentrated disregard—a glowering abjection as if whatever he beheld had no soul, no name, or no purpose other than interrupting him—warned of his true nature.

Incorrectly reading Gustavius's expression as befuddlement—stupidity before all this science—the doctor decided to escort them around the new facility.

"Here, let me show you gawking fools around," he said, grinning.

Gideon's courtesy was a false pageantry of emotion obscured further by his perfect gleaming teeth. That a man that could be so tidy in one regard and so haphazard in another was a telltale sign of madness. Gustav followed the madman for a tour of the new facility, listening to the lunatic point at this apparatus and that while explaining a science that neither the Iron lord nor Davy could possibly fathom. Gustav pondered not these devices; rather, he regretted that Gloriatrix had assigned this scholar to oversee Project Animus. It wasn't as though she'd had her pick of the academic litter since so many minds had been lost in Menos, but Gideon had at least come highly recommended for his work in metasciences. Prior to the war, he'd worked at the Iron College before getting expelled—for a scandal involving reanimated wolves who'd devoured a headmaster with whom Gideon had been feuding. As was the way in Menos, justice was often blind, and could be implored to put on an even heavier blindfold for a substantive payment to the crown. Thus, the military had scooped Hex up and ferreted him away, and in the years since the scandal, Gideon had been applying his genius as medical officer abroad—working on Kings knew what diablerie—and then on to the *Morgana*. Doctor Hex had been the first learned man to leap at the opportunity to study the soon-to-be-unliving victims of Menos's plague.

"Cat snatch your tongue? We have of those plenty to spare,"the doctor jeered, once the tour had been completed. Most of the horrors he'd seen Gustavius allowed to fade into a dreamy delusion. He and the ever-dutiful Davy—surely having wetted his pink undergarments by now—stood before kennels, a wall of trapped dead. Gustavius sensed too much: red, peeling, and rotting fingers wriggling through a cell wrapped in wire mesh (most of these kennels were doubly protected as such), the gurgling farts and opened-gut stench of the recently dead. However, few of the unliving were anywhere near as decomposed as they should have been.

"I thought you'd lost some of your specimens—to experimentation," said the Iron lord. "How are there now so many? Are these more unfortunates who've been dragged from the black fog?"

"Something like that," replied Hex, obtusely, before folding his chubby hands together, as if in prayer. "Shall I tell you what I've learned of our subjects? It's extraordinary metascience. Stuff that bridges the theoretical and the divine."

"We need to know how to kill what is already dead."

"Oh, that's simple. May I have your firearm?"

"Absolutely not."

Clearly excited despite the Iron lord's scorn, Hex hurried over to the cages. Gustavius was disappointed to see that when the doctor stepped into a few electrified puddles on his way, he wasn't sizzled; the reasoning behind the madman's latex boots finally made sense. A collection of instruments that could have been forks or cutlery used at a demon's dinner party had accrued in a heap laid before the wall of cages. Mumbling to himself, Hex sifted through the pile and threw aside whatever items didn't entice him. Disembodied hilts that Gustavius knew from his armament training would burst to swords of flame, large-game rifles, pumps attached to handheld hoses, and backpacks that sloshed with chemicals all bounced across the floor.

"Aha!" Hex exclaimed, grabbing a simple pistol—so tiny it was almost a lady's pistol. Given the mad doctor's limp-wristed brandishing of the weapon, Gustav kept a hand on his own firearm. Something else niggled at him, too, a thought chewing paranoia into the base of his spine involving the doctor, newly undead, missing soldiers, and experimentation. He'd figure it out in a sand. At the moment the doctor had returned, and Gustavius was more concerned with what the man intended to do with that pistol. Hex aimed it toward the nearest cage.

"I shoot like an old maid," he confessed, and shuffled up a bit. "Even with these Talwynian models and all their fanciful technomagikal adjustments—I met the man once, and he's a foppish pedant." As he approached one of the cages, a snarling face pressed against the wide mesh of its prison. The creature's frenzy rose as the distance between them shortened. It shredded its gray flesh against the cage, and the doctor placed the muzzle of the pistol against a gleaming white patch of skull surrounded by peeled, brownish meat. Gideon cocked the pistol and fired. The beast fell, wheezing out a final snarl. It did not rise.

"See?" said the doctor, and turned, smiling with his smoking gun. "Easy as baking a Vallistheim pie. Killing them, I mean. We've tried fire, acid, and classic hacking and slicing. An interesting aside: that old wives' trick of heaps of salt scares them, but only when cast in a traditional witch's pattern—a circle of power. And who has the time for that, given how fast these creatures can be? Can't drown them, obviously, and saltwater, which you might be mistaken to believe has magical properties from my previous findings, only makes them wet. However, for killing, not containing, anything works, so long as the connection between brain and the body is severed or severely crippled. Decapitation is the safest bet, however." The doctor threw the gun in the direction of the heap of armaments. He rubbed his hands together with insufferable delight. "However, that's not the most fascinating part."

Gustavius didn't persist with an inquiry. The thought from before continued its chewing. Had it been in the south? That incident...

"Why are they so quiet and watchful?" he asked, suddenly. All the yellowed eyes focused on him and the doctor. Even the creatures in the kennels behind him Gustavius sensed turning their rent faces toward and sniffing with their gaping nose pits his presence.

"Ah, you've noticed, yes." The doctor strolled along the cages, reaching out and almost touching the creatures. "They have moments, usually when one of their own is killed, where their focus becomes a single eye of unity. On these occasions they evolve from machines concerned only with killing and consuming. In case you were wondering, that's all they care to do when they're put in contact with a living man: eat him." Gustavius had not been wondering, though he was now curious as to how the doctor could state that with such vehemence. "What you're seeing at the moment is what I believe to be the suppression of their consciousness for the Will and mind of another—whoever it is that controls them."

There were few officials and members of the inner circles of either kingdom, East or West, who'd heard that Death herself marched to conquer civilization. The mad doctor, sequestered in this farce of investigative research wasn't privy to those whispers, and nor would he be, decided Gustavius. What experimentations would he pursue if he knew who the real master was behind these puppets?

"I see that you're as stumped as I am," sighed the doctor. "Likely more, since you meat-and-sword types have such a dim flicker of intelligence, though more than these creatures, I'm sure. But a fraction of whatever brilliant Will still commands them."

"None of that is of interest to Menos," said Gustavius. He wanted this meeting to end. In fact, he actually longed for the bright, clean, garish wonder of Eod to cleanse him of this stained memory. "From the number of subjects, I'm assuming that you've discovered how this illness or curse is spread, then? Should we be preparing a quarantine?"

"The growth in samples has been intentional."

"Intentional?"

"To cure or conquer a metascientifical quandary, one must replicate and reproduce certain variables in order to define a course of treatment. I assure you that all that I have done is in the interests of Menos. The disease, as you call it, can be spread through the active biological matter of one subject getting into the bloodstream of another. It can be bile, sweat, feces, blood—secretions of any kind. A deep cut will often do, from what we've observed, as long as enough biologically active matter enters a wound. From there, infection sets in. We're still collecting data on the incubation period and speed of the virus since it varies so much from subject to subject. Thus far, we've approximated the windows of infection to reanimation with a mean average of eight days—so over or under a week. After ten days, death then reanimation is guaranteed. No magik or medicine at our disposal has been able to cure the black fever once it sets into the brain."

"Black fever?"

"Here, I shall show you."

Gesturing for them to follow, the doctor strode alongside the wall of watching rot and turned left. Gustavius and his silent irongrunt proceeded to follow the doctor down past the front two rows to the last, and smaller, line of cages. Here, the dead seemed less gangrenous than their brethren. Unlike the naked dead they'd just seen, a few of these wore the tatters of whatever clothing had survived their moments of rampage. Only a couple of these specimens tracked the men with a bloodhound's alertness, as with the others they'd left behind. It was the senseless behavior of these other subjects—their sweaty writhing, muttering, and dribbled swearing—that made Gustavius realize they weren't yet dead. Very pale, with as much meat on their bones as a sparrow, though they were alive.

"These men, why are they in here?" demanded the Iron lord.

"They're sick, obviously!" snapped the doctor. "Can't let them out or they'd be dining on the *Morgana*'s crew before sundown. I wanted to show you the progression of the illness." He tapped the crossed bars of one cage, and a naked man looked up; he was quivering in fear, blind from agony, and he screamed at Gideon. "Silence! The wailing will pass in a speck. It always does. Subject PA-57 was exposed on the Sevensday of last week. The black fever should bring him to cessation rather soon..."

Exposed, thought Gustavius. PA-57: Project Animus, number fifty-seven. There'd been fifty-six before this one? Unless the doctor had begun kidnapping savages, or Arhadians, of which the sunless skins of these subjects spoke otherwise, then he was using Menosians, Eodians, or civilians for his experiments. "Queen's mercy. What is this?" he exclaimed.

The doctor sneered. "Metascience!"

Into the other's shadows, the men stepped; fists clenched, sneering. Davy willed himself as tiny as the pus-green toenail popped off one of the reanimated soldiers beside him that floated in the wet stagnancy of the chamber—it was a gruesome, though ideal distraction. Meanwhile, the doctor stood, legs apart, fists balled, and wouldn't be cowed by the Iron lord.

"Metascience," said the doctor. "That's what it is, you fuking cretin. We could be on the verge of breaking the barrier between reanimation and true resurrection. For here we have creatures reborn, truly reborn with life."

"Dare I ask from where your subjects have come?"

"Surely you know."

"I'd like to hear you say it."

"Rank and file," spat Hex. "Men that were on their final merits. Men who we were forced to endure simply because Menos's iron milk has run so thin." Hex turned his piggish gaze on Davy who, admirably, wasn't trembling, babbling, tripping, or pissing himself. "Men like that twit. I remember when I sent for a page and *he* arrived, green as the shite from a seagull's arsehole. He's not worthy of the iron way. If you haven't any need of him, I could use his flesh for the service of Menos."

"Never!" roared Gustavius. A few rubber-garbed acolytes of the mad doctor paused in their operations, holding limbs like they were curious butchers, squinting behind their goggles or welding masks. While the Iron lord was cold and cruel, he was fair. Soldiers were expendable in war; they died for their leaders. But this perverse end to their military service certainly could not have been approved by the queen. She would hear of this. That rage shattered a door in his memory, and he recalled Hex's previous assignment.

"You...the Blood Moors...I remember now."

Hex grinned.

"I couldn't place you. I couldn't recall whence arose the shudder of revulsion I feel when in your presence. You've done this before. Taken men and turned them into objects for your experiments. It was that missing legion, found tied and executed in the most brutal of ways in an underground bunker. One man lived..." He shook his head. "I can't recall his name since those dossiers have long since burned. I'm no soft-heart, either. I'm not opposed to metascientifical engineering, or mortal experimentation, but with limits. You have no limits, Hex. You are a warped child of infinite curiosity, and this whole wretched playground of yours meets its end today."

Hex leaned up on his tiptoes and reached as if to strangle the Iron lord. A dismissive slap from the giant Northerner threw the man against the nearest cage. Hex screamed and quickly scrambled away, although the previously shrieking man had collapsed in the corner and hadn't moved during the commotion. The doctor doubled over, heaving protests. "Imbecile! Y-you can't—"

"I can," declared the Iron lord. He pulled out his pistol and fired around the chamber. Surgical tables were dinged by bullets and beakers shattered; cauldrons were pierced and spewed caustic vomit. The Iron lord's well-aimed bullets skimmed the ankles of the abruptly fleeing doctor's cohorts. Within a sand, the cathedral of horror was empty and quiet, but for the burbles and creaks of settling destruction and the doctor's whimpers.

"I shall be sending in a force to contain and incinerate this area within the hourglass," Gustavius warned. "I doubt the *Morgana* will suffer more than an unseemly scar to her honor from your diabolical workings here. Cry and feel shame, for you have shamed the Iron City. When this war ends, I'll see you sent to the Iron marshals. They'll educate you on humility while you plead for the suffering to end. It won't, not for weeks, each of which will feel like a decade." Deeming the sobbing madman no more of a threat, Gustavius holstered his pistol. "Good day, Doctor Hex. Be certain to make it a good one, since it will be one of your last before the marshals take you."

Spite energized the doctor and he leapt up. "Eod has made you soft!"

With that, the Iron lord spun around, dipped as gracefully as a black swan, and struck the fool. His fist hit the doctor's abdomen with a force that left him choking on spittle and blindly crawling on the ground through a field of imaginary stars. Last night, Gustavius had seen his great queen weep from mercy and love—and he felt her to be no weaker. In these trying days, he'd seen his nation fall and knew that when it rose once more it wouldn't be the same as before. It couldn't be. Surely the iron-born children would never be as weak as Eodians; surely they would still evolve. They would recast themselves like the metal of their souls and become stronger through new alloys: loyalty, family, and trust. Only virtues shared among themselves, and all others would remain lesser. Somehow, Gustavius knew or wanted to believe in this new ideology. Gideon Hex, this repugnant boil of a man would never be one of the new iron-born.

He had half a mind to cave in the man's head right there, but he embraced temperance—a quality of new Menos—and the loyal fealty that he should carry out no executions without his queen's command. To exact at least some vengeance, he spat on the man's head and kicked him a few times, before squatting over the cringing creature. "I've changed my mind. The Iron marshals have worthier victims to torment than you. You are a waste of even our hatred. I hereby cast you from the queen's service. She would not want you in the world she intends to build. You're a monster, the kind that eats its own pack. Flee into the desert or into Eod, though do not be here when the firecallers come, for I shall leave them with orders to set flame to you, too."

Gustavius cracked the man's head off the ground, stood and left. He didn't care if the doctor bled out from what was surely a fracture of his skull. It would be better for him to burn with his menagerie of terrors. Davy and his master walked slowly from the chamber.

"Thank you, sir," whispered Davy.

"For?"

For being the bravest, noblest iron soldier he'd ever seen? For showing him that men of Menos were as righteous as all the other knights of the world? What could he say that wouldn't sound pathetically fawning?

"For not leaving me to turn into one of them," was what Davy settled on.

"I have few choices that I regret," said Gustavius. "Don't be one of them."

In a moment the pair had vanished, silently, into the dims of the chamber. Gustavius had to find men to expunge this experiment and then report all that he'd seen to his queen. Far from them, the doctor continued his squiggling on the ground. He'd begun to regain his sight, although none of the throbbing in his stomach or skull had subsided. He was fairly certain that he'd wet himself, since his rubbers were slippery against his thighs. A rib or three were surely broken. He crawled for a time, aimless, and found himself back at the cage of his slumped subject. On his knees and like an angry inmate he shook the bars.

Everything was ruined—his career, his status, his life. While he figured he could rebuild, it would be nearly impossible to have the same access as he'd been given through the Iron Crown. Furthermore, who would sanction his work? Work he could no longer turn from, now that he knew how fine a membrane was the skin between life and death, and how easily one could prick it and milk those secrets. He'd been so close. He'd nearly solved the mystery of all mysteries. It was far more of a puzzle than that lad in the Blood Moors who had been naturally resistant to every form of magik on Geadhain. That was an anti-mystery. Almost a year of excruciating research—for him, not that scrawny invalid—and the threads had run nowhere. That ungrateful shite, who could have contributed so much more to man's understanding of the universe, had surrendered nothing. One morning, his laboratory had been raided, all the metascientists who weren't as important as him rounded up and shot, and he never learned what became of the vexation.

Thus had ended that chapter of the opus he'd been working on about life, death, and the cosmos. Now another chapter had ended. Gideon didn't know how many more he could write. He supposed that he should pick himself up and move on, but the agony of this defeat was too raw. It was a sweet and welcome gesture, then, the hand that suddenly patted his shoulder as he hung, sniveling and slumped, against the cage.

"Thank you," he said. "Wait—"

The hand clenched, digging its fingers like railway spikes into his shoulder. He looked up into the cage he'd stupidly clung to as refuge, and there was a face echoing far more evil than his petty weaknesses: subject PA-57. Rather, the reborn version of him. The naked thing had thrust its hand through a rip in the grill, and another one followed before the doctor could respond. Shoulder by shoulder, it grabbed him and beheld him with its resonantly dark, deep gaze. It smiled its approval at whatever it sensed in him.

"**Little maggot**," it said. This was no dead soldier, but a being that withered what frail sense of self the doctor possessed. Instantly, he understood how insignificant he was to this creature. He fathomed his meekness so completely that he stopped struggling and gave himself to the creature's thrall. "*I have a task for you.*"

"A t-task?"

"*Yes, little maggot,*" said Death. "*My army waits beneath the sands of Kor'Khul, hidden—thousands upon thousands of rotting knights. Soon, we shall rise across the desert like a black sun, though we cannot cross Kor'Khul without trouble from these irksome weapons, these arrogant toys, these ships made to delay my coming. I shall need you to disable these warships.*"

"The Furies? I can't disable a Fury." Even in his trance, the idea felt absurd.

"*You can, little maggot; only the parts that bring the fire mankind should not possess—Feyhazir should never have given them that gift. So strip them of their canniness, their armaments, and we shall leave these vessels to become new mounds of ash in the desert I shall sow. Swear your service to me, and I shall give you a glimmer of my power to see that you do not fail. I shall anoint you as my champion.*"

It had found him: the mystery of all mysteries. Gideon hungered for it. "I swear!"

Death threw him back, and he cowered and knelt before the cage and her vessel. As she rose above him, for an instant Gideon sensed the full black glory of Death in a cataclysm of shadows, explosions, stars, and thunder that enveloped him. He didn't look up at her, into the force crackling at the eye of this hurricane; he couldn't. He knew not that the crackling came as Death ripped open the dark veins on the wrists of her meat-suit, and from these poured an ichor of the storm, a liquid ebon flecked in starlight. Her blood fizzled as it fell down on Gideon, and sparked on his skin. Like a slave to pleasure, he turned his face into that unholy rain and lapped it up. Whatever the anointment, it tasted so bitter that his mouth was numbed, his tongue shriveled, and his body retched to reject it. For this was unlife, the antimatter of creation, and it wouldn't be placed into a vessel not made for its power. Too late now to be refused, Death reminded Gideon of this caveat, as he grinned, puked, writhed, and consumed his own vomit...and received her blessing.

"*You are not made with the fortitude of a true vessel. You are a weak, soft maggot, and my gift shall eat at you as sand devours stone. You have three of your mortal nights, at most, until your flesh and soul are forfeit. Succeed, and I shall extend my gift. I shall give you the true blessing of the Daughters of Xalloreth: eternal unlife.*"

Her voice shook the chamber with thunder and flickering black and gray lights: "*Fail, and I shall show you every suffering I have learned across eternity*."

"I shall not fail, Mistress."

"*Death*," she corrected.

Death's meat-suit stumbled as the Dreamer left it in a sigh of vapor. Like the other penned dead, it looked at Gideon—sopping in oils—and waited for its general to rise. He did, after a time. He stood as though he were a man half his years and ten times his strength. Gideon squeezed the lock of the cage in front of him and bellowed as it relented like an aluminum trinket. The doctor of death then walked down the line, twisting and tossing feliron locks aside with a glee that foretold none of the reaping he had planned.

III

Today was momentous; every mouth in the palace of Eod was whispering that King Magnus was awake and well. Further still, the gossipmongers clucked that Magnus had reunited with his estranged wife. Perhaps, and even more astonishing were the rumors that he'd made peace with the man—his former and honored guard—who'd since wooed his wife. A cloying mist of scandal had so thickened the air that people choked upon seeing the two royals and the man of obsidian walking together down the hallowed halls of Eod that morning.

Erik was as dark and glowering as Magnus was pale and cherubic. Mayhap it was only the palace's starry lights, twinkling down from the canopy of verdure in this realm, which rendered upon them these qualities. Certainly Erik's black clothes and Magnus's cream shift and sandals—the clothing of an emperor of the old world—heightened the extreme disparity in their appearance. Between the men, Lila shimmered like a spirit of beauty and rule. She certainly ruled these men somehow, and while only Erik tended her arm, Magnus appeared similarly in step to Lila's tune. There was a distinct magik that had to have been created by the synergy of the three. They walked, stride in stride, perfect as royal court dancers, and the most discerning and captivated observer believed that they breathed with the same rhythm, too. Serfs and Silver Watchmen alike bowed to and greeted what felt like three royals, not two, who passed them that morn.

Gossip buzzes through these halls like bees, remarked Magnus. *I can only imagine what they're saying.*

Each of his bloodmates heard him, and Erik, the gray spirit that resided within Magnus along with the familiar summer spirit that was Lila, surged.

Erik replied. *They're thinking of how strange it all is. I can't say that they're alone in that.*

It is only temporary.

Temporary, repeated the three joined souls.

A fourth voice inserted itself into their heads. Lila had been fondling the Mind in the sling in which it slept. She often did this for comfort now; the gentle buzz and prickle it emitted when exposed to its magik was like a tonic to her anxiety. *Mother Lila, Father Erik, and the Magnus, I would not want to lead you to believe that disentangling your matrices from one another will be a process without complications. What's been done has never before been attempted, and each day the telemetric currents will transform, evolve, or perhaps dangerously mutate your matrices in unpredictable ways.*

We can't stay this way forever, grumbled Erik.

Magnus's soul expressed its sympathetic distress with an abrupt chill that wracked his two bloodmates.

How irritating that is, having my balls wither every few sands, complained Erik.

My apologies. Magnus's handsome face twisted in anger. *Your tempestuous moods are no better. As soon as you get into one of your petulant sulks, I feel as if I'm seasick for the better half of a day. How can a man be so miserable so often?*

Erik stopped and turned to Magnus with clenched fists and a snarl; Lila stepped back. Magnus faced him, equally furious; the air cooled to a shivering crispness, and a crackle of thunder came from somewhere far outside this deep vein through rock—Magnus's anger manifesting. They bickered mentally, and affected all three in their blood-circle with shudders, twitches, and fevers both hot and cold.

I could have been perfectly happy. Until we had to return, growled Erik.

I was for once perfectly alone. Without a bloodmate, without my brother's base urges. I was myself, until you and she returned and ruined my one moment of individuality, hissed Magnus.

We could have let you die.

You should have.

Cradling the Mind like a worried mother in the midst of a family argument, Lila didn't intervene. It had been this way since Magnus's first morning out of bed, when her two bloodmates had the first of many meaningless conflicts—one over what would be had for breakfast, which neither of them really needed or ate. From then on, arguments between Magnus and Erik had erupted over the silliest turns of phrase or perceived slights. Lila knew their vitriol was attributable to each man being the equivalent of an elemental force: one of the sea, stone, and duty, and the other of intellect, raw power, and the crippling authority of a storm. She hadn't learned how to minimize their differences, and a part of her—that small lockbox of secrets that bloodmates could withhold from one another—*wanted* them to fight.

After the reunion with Magnus, the memories of her love and ghosts of her feelings returned to haunt her. Erasing one thousand years of blissful matrimony wasn't easy, although his desecration of her body on the night about which they never spoke surely gave her an anchor. She could have fought with Magnus herself, though Erik tended to do that for her. She wondered if her feelings of vengeance weren't influencing her knight, and possibly her former lover as well. If she could surreptitiously stoke Erik's rage, she too could affect Magnus's guilt. Adding reason to the situation, however, she knew that she loved Erik, with all of her heart and without pretense. She wanted to return to loving him and only him, and wondered how long this three-headed snake could exist without biting itself.

Mother Lila, said the Mind, reading her most secret thoughts (it was growing in power). *As I've warned, it is possible the matrices will develop cancerously, putting all three of you at grave risk. Alternatively, and a theory that I have lately pondered—with a result equally as lethal to your three matrices—the virus against which this unification is being used as an inoculation may fail, and simply breed a stronger illness. I have been diligently monitoring the telemetry of the three of you at micro-intervals so that I shall be abreast of any alarming new patterns in your matrices immediately.*

It had spoken to all three Immortals, not just one, and ahead of her the men had stopped their mind-whispering bickering and gazed back at her, then the lump she held, then each other. Their expressions transitioned from anger to fear. Horrified by the revelation, Magnus leaned against the cold, comforting, eternal flesh of Kor'Keth. He made sure that the hallway was empty of persons before he spoke.

"Is it saying that we could all die, or have our souls subsumed by the Black Queen?"

"We understood that there would be risks," said Erik, quietly.

Magnus shuffled his feet and looked at the ceiling. To Erik, he seemed minuscule in that moment: frail, weak, and propped up only by their strength. It wasn't far from the truth. Suddenly, Lila's sense of compassion for all weak, wounded creatures bloomed and rose in each man with refreshing ebullience. The men smiled from her warmth.

She said, "We bound ourselves to you, Magnus, knowing that there would be a cost. If we look at our pasts, our mistakes and regrets, they're all so similar—missed moments, missed confessions, terrible acts we can never undo. We've ruined marriages, kingdoms, and lives. We've been the greatest of despots and the sweetest of loves. One would think that we should not have regrets in lives as full as these; however, the longer the life, the longer that list. For too often it is pain that rises above joy."

The queen drifted closer to Magnus, and Erik followed, sniffing the intoxicating incense of her sorcery. It was a scent that thrilled Magnus as well. She placed a hand on his smooth white chest, then clasped Erik's hand, too. Magnus shivered, since she was loath to touch him these days, and whatever remaining aggression he might have felt vanished like night's darkness in the sunrise of her beauty.

"And so we are tied," she continued, holding each man, "in ropes of pain, to the other. We cannot break them. Not now, not without risking more selfish, rash circumstances. It is time to stop fighting each other. We must submit—for a time—to this unwanted fellowship of hearts."

They were overwhelmed in that moment by every sensation and memory of Lila's love. She was as great a force as any pure-born Immortal. For a while, at least, the men would be at peace with each other, and Lila's empathic venom still flooded their systems. A bit drunkenly, the men shook hands and returned to escort the woman of their affection. They each claimed an arm this time, and Lila didn't recoil from Magnus's icy touch. With her warm knight of stone on her left, and a wintry king on her right, they proceeded to their meeting with the generals of East and West.

Today was the day they would unveil their freshly hatched plan to end the threat of the mad king and the Black Queen once and for all. A journey lay ahead for the three, and it would be cold, fierce, and long. But they would be united. They would be the hope for which mankind could pray. More than once, the trio wore the same smile, or laughed at the same ripple of memory that passed through their heads.

IV

The war council had gathered beneath the great yew that drank in the roar of the Chamber of Echoes. Around the stone table, though, emanated enough noise to combat what was missing. An assemblage of all the leaders, luminaries, tacticians, and prominent sages of Eod and Menos were present. They had been cordially summoned by the king, via messenger, for his first appearance since falling during Lila's siege of Eod. Some feuds were beyond repair, and not unexpectedly, Gloriatrix and her cabinet had claimed one half of the table, while the Eodians took the other. The Iron Queen had taken the largest seat available on her end—the tall rock throne of an ancient king, acting as counterpart to Magnus's throne opposite her. Celebratory in her way, she had chosen to wear a high-collared black chiffon mourning dress.

Next to Gloriatrix was Elissandra, swaddled in gray silks and appearing utterly spent. Today she seemed more ethereal than normal; her garish head wrap of gold, navy blue, and silver was the most tangible aspect of her. The rest of her seemed faded as an old paper phantograph. Elissandra's dapperly dressed children hovered behind their mother's chair; they peered around like ghostly owls, seeing who knew what in the ether and auras of the assembly. The manner in which they lurked on the periphery reminded one of the great pale gargoyle Gustavius looming over the Iron Queen's shoulder.

The ghastly Beatrice, adorned in white upon white that looked eggshell again her flesh, held the chair to the Iron Queen's right, and her carved-in-ice face didn't hide her detachment or some other worrisome experience—possibly pain, given her squinting expression. Indeed, the sharpest of observers would notice a dappling of sweat along her cheeks and chin, and the near imperceptible presence of a shiver to her body, as if she might be succumbing to a cold. She'd spent the waiting period exchanging stares with Alastair. As for that wily shadowbroker, he shrank in his hooded garment next to fair Maggie. She, like Beatrice, seemed almost haunted by a secret or pain—pinched and bothered in her face, too—and was constantly stealing glances at Alastair. That pair of wayward and rogue sat in the curve that separated East and West, emphasizing their allegiance to neither; an uncomfortable region of the table's hemisphere.

On the king's side of the table, Magnus's rock throne sat empty, as did the queen's. Beside the king's seat, and while waiting for his master, Leonitis avoided the stares and whispers at the table by fiddling with the hilt of the grand hammer that rose up between his legs like an indecent metal erection. Dorvain sat elbow to elbow with his brother, his skin as tanned from the desert days as a golem of leather; he fiddled with his worn hands and worried about how old they'd begun to look. Nearly lost beside the two large men was the shriveled, though alert, Gorijen Cross. He wasn't fiddling with anything, but rather was thinking about why they'd all been summoned. Rounding out those attending, and flanking Lila's seat, was Beauregard, who glared at his secret brother sitting next to him, when he thought no one was looking; choking down that secret was as hard as swallowing nails. Elsewhere on Eod's side of the table, and straining to look past the wizened heads of the city's oldest cabinet members, Rowena spied on the spellsong and the watchmaster, who were so rarely spotted in each other's company. But here they were, side by side. With their pretty jaws, pouty mouths, and slender faces, their femininity and flashes of stubble, the two were as stunning as the prized jewels of a male harem. They even wore matching tunics of silver and white; they could have been—

"Friends of East and West," boomed the king. "Please, do not rise."

The gathering nearly did leap to their feet, however, as a dash of thunder had surely been added to Magnus's voice. A thick late-morning mist had breathed up from the precipice that encircled the Chamber of Echoes, and only dingy silhouettes at first appeared. Through the vapor three shapes emerged to join the assembly. No one had expected to see Magnus, the queen, and Erik appear together, or as such a seemingly intimate company. Both king and knight ushered the golden Lila into her wild throne, before the king took his. The obsidian knight—he honestly was *black*, Rowena observed of his sheen and impregnable pigment—held a frowning vigil between the two rulers. Like a small gray tail to this magnificent trio of Immortals came the spymaster, Rasputhane. He'd met with them prior to the gathering to provide a report on Death's movements, or rather, on the lack of information regarding her movements. Nearly invisible, he slunk over and lingered behind Erik, to wait until he was called upon.

"I see that you have recovered, Magnus," said the Iron Queen, and tipped her chin down in respect.

"I have," replied Magnus. When the happy murmuring at this news had calmed, Magnus continued. "My return to health has not come without a price, however. Nor is this cure permanent. We can celebrate nothing, as you will soon hear."

With a whirl of his hand, the king summoned forth the spymaster. Rasputhane shuffled away from the Immortals toward the empty arc of the table to face the calculating gaze of the man who also dealt in secrets: Alastair. Put in the spotlight, the spymaster was as outgoing and charismatic as a humpbacked jester. A tight wince of a smile from the queen stirred sufficient courage in him to tell them the dire news.

"Our skycarriages and the crowes of Menos called in from Fort Havok's reserves have lost track of Death's army."

"Pardon?" exclaimed the Iron Queen. "How does one lose track of an army of walking dead? It's not as if the gate to the cattle farm was left open, though the incompetence could be excusable in a shitepot like Bainsbury—in which we are not."

"Bainsbury is no more; we should not speak glibly of the dead," said Magnus with a chilling sadness. "Continue, spymaster."

Rasputhane nodded. "As you may or may not know, the horde—as it were—has been protected by incredible magik, or, rather, by someone wielding such power. Our skycarriages can only fly so close to the creatures before they are seized by sorcery and hurled to the land. Our instruments and farscopes have also been encountering extreme etheric interference, and in most cases very little can be sensed, or seen, of our enemies' movements."

"You are repeating information we have covered in previous meetings," warned Gloriatrix, "and wasting my time."

"I would not want to waste Her Majesty's or anyone else's time." Rasputhane pulled at his collar and adjusted his glasses, which were slipping on his sweaty slide of a nose. "I simply wanted to explain that while Death's army is being monitored, it is not a perfect watch. To engage in such surveillance would require assets that we simply do not have to waste. Furthermore, the size of the force had only begun to make itself apparent once it had crossed the Feordhan and amassed its troops around the ruins of Taroch's Arm. From then on, we had an army that we could monitor. I say 'army,' because that is what it is now. It is a force of thousands, which we believed—as would be the natural assumption—could not easily evade our notice."

"What happened?" demanded the Iron Queen.

"Somewhere between Taroch's Arm and Eod, the entire horde vanished," said Rasputhane, to a collective gasp of those gathered.

He continued. "We don't know where to. Perhaps into the deep crannies of Ebon Vale. Perhaps into a subterranean river as of yet uncharted, through which they swim like a school of rotting fish. Given our enemy's age, and that it is a force of incomprehensible might, we must remember that Death could know things about this world that exceed anything our king or historical memory might recall. It might know ways to travel or hide that subvert any detection. So, for the moment, we've been outplayed. Until we discover the horde's location, any summoning of the Furies' wrath will be as pointless as shooting cannons into the wind."

Gloriatrix slammed her fist on the table. "Inexcusable!"

The plan that had formed while the king was incapacitated had been to wait until Death's army revealed itself in full, and then to drop a payload of magikal truefire on all the Dreamer's toy soldiers. They'd end Death's war quicker than it'd started. Now, it seemed that Gloriatrix's potential triumph had been stolen away from her. The spymaster was glad that the Iron Queen possessed no magikal abilities, for in that moment she looked as though she could set the Chamber of Echoes on fire with her rage.

"You may want to save your anger for what I've next to share," he said. "Despite this setback, our forces—jointly—have continued their reconnaissance missions to scour every realm along the western Feordhan for signs of Brutus. In the South, in Zioch's warm ashes, some terrible power still sleeps there that sends our technomagikal instruments into spastic fits. And while we haven't found the cause of that disruption, there are signs of another troubling development: a second army."

Rasputhane had to plead for silence in the raucous chamber before he could finish. "Lords, ladies, and protectors of Geadhain, please, settle your unrest. Take solace in knowing that, for now, the second army is weeks away from being any threat to Eod."

"What other might would dare to thrust itself into this struggle?" asked Alastair.

"Indeed," agreed the Iron Queen. "East and West, and the Immortals themselves have written the rules of engagement for this war. We have no room for other players or their interests."

"Yet they have materialized," said Rasputhane, "and from the pages of legend."

"Legend?" pressed the Iron Queen.

"Changelings," replied the spymaster; more gasps and murmurs followed and soon settled. "I didn't believe it myself. Changelings...wolves, actually. I flew to the South yesterday morning to confirm what was being reported by our scouts. An encampment has been erected, up at the northern outskirts of Brutus's kingdom, near Willowholme, or what remains of the ghosted city..."

"Spymaster," says the watchman.

Rasputhane isn't the best on ships—water or airborne. Although the long hallway, softened by padded wainscoting and eased in gentle yellow pot lights, brings an impression of being somewhere on land and not thousands of spans in the sky. After a few deep breaths, he continues his drunken crawl along the walls of the skycarriage. It seems to be shaking more violently than when he lay queasily tossing on the couch in the passenger cabin. In a speck, he's forced to ask the kind, pretty, short-haired watchman with him for her arm. She obliges and carries him along as if he were her aged grandmother. Soon they've taken a few topsy-turvy turns through the skycarriage's claustrophobic halls and arrived at a space of seemingly vast expansiveness. It's only the cockpit of the vessel, however, and in a moment the steel walls close in on the spymaster. The kind young woman sits him in her chair beside the captain's almost hovering glass seat—supported by many thin, enchanted strings of metal that are nearly invisible—and he realizes that she's a pilot and not a watchman at all.

She leaves him with her silent copilot, and he watches his own contorted visage in the reflection from the cockpit's various crystal panels, which pulse with subdermal runes of magik and give his and the captain's faces a ghostly glow. The captain shows none of the spymaster's fear while peacockishly sitting in his chair and glaring through a narrow, clouded visor into the atmosphere. In fact, he hums a tap-worthy tune as he interfaces his mind and magik with the floating shell of steel and crystal. He's a windsinger, and to him this craft is his instrument, and the runes that pulse to the tune of his mind are the notes that he plays. Surely, the faintest of faint music, more tingle than note, can be sensed thrumming through the seat, the cockpit, even in the gasps of air Rasputhane breathes into his lungs. He wishes he had the captain's constitution, and that he wasn't such a coward in these circumstances. He could strangle a man with a garrote made of table napkins, but he has the seaworthiness of a young girl with food poisoning and vertigo.

"You're not a sorcerer," says the first copilot, startling Rasputhane as she appears at his side bearing a clean silver tube with a lens at one end, "so you'll have to use this."

It's a farscope, which a normal man would need to see anything on the ground from this height, while windsingers like she and the captain can simply remain in their seats and peer out into the clouded ether—above, below, beside— as if they've the sight of great flies. But the spymaster has his own queer blessings of perception. He can probably see better than either of these sorcerers. Regardless, he accepts the gift; his secrets are his own. He also takes the offer of the woman's arm to rise, which he certainly needs. They play old lady and helper again, as she guides him to a section of the viewing screen beside the tidy podiums and levitating seats.

The copilot taps the glass. "We're thirty spans over Lake Tesh. If you use the farscope and look down, at an angle, you'll see an encampment."

"Encampment?"

"If you can call it that," says the woman, and her tanned Eodian complexion suddenly pales. "It's best that you see and judge for yourself, spymaster."

She steps aside, and Rasputhane, dangerously curious, pushes up his spectacles and applies the cold tube against his eye socket. The instrument assists his shimmering silver cornea, and his mystic sight, combined with the technomagik's power, slices through the cloud vapor and across the rippling brown water and through the sighing, surely rancid flotsam, cold animal corpses, and floating logs. At least the worst environmental decay has been hidden by the kiss of winter, and under a shield of ice. Whatever cauldron of infernal heat Brutus keeps roaring in the South seems not to have reached this far. At last some order to nature has returned to his field of vision, and at the frozen shore of the lake he sees a garden of icicles—possibly reeds—though beyond that smoke, movement, and shapes.

"Wolves?" He gasps.

"That's what I thought, too, at first," says the copilot.

He takes a second look. Again, he sees great shadows of fur and shining teeth wandering the icicle garden. They're larger than any wolves known to prowl Ebon Vale and don armor like the ceremonial war hounds at a master's hunt: plated muzzles, iron chitin on their shoulders, spiked cuffs at their ankles. Their uncanny ferocity holds Rasputhane's attention even as the haze weakens, and behind the stalking shadows manifests a sprawl of campfires, tents, and two-legged men who walk alongside these war wolves. The encampment reaches far across the tired, snow-fallen canopy of Willowholme, and in that powdery landscape is a frenzy of activity. Rows of nearly naked and cringing people are being driven around by the lash or bark of tribal masters, who are also dressed in piecemeal garbs of metal and fur. These masters walk the bridge and flood the houses of the home-bearing willows. Beneath the trees, fires fueled for war and churning out more metal harnesses, spears, and weapons lend an unholy light to Willowholme. At last, he realizes the truth and secret of this new threat as he watches a circle of nude persons twist and howl into beasts. The orgy of transformation is primal and terrifying, and he can watch no more after he sees a mucous-covered muzzle split a man's face in half with snapping teeth.

"Straight out of myth," reiterated Rasputhane to the war council.

"The children of Alabion," whispered Elissandra, and thought of the book she and the children of her line had read to prepare them for the inevitable return of legends. Eli and Tessa each took and shared their mother's one good hand.

"At the king's behest," said Rasputhane, "we shall send an emissary to meet with this power, and to see what its purpose is in Central Geadhain."

"Always the diplomat." Gloriatrix glared scornfully across the table at Magnus. She found all three Immortals there, staring eerily at her, even blinking as one. It occurred to her that something rather strange was happening between king, queen, and hammer. "Do you really believe that your branch of peace will work on beasts? With dogs, branches are only good for fetching and retrieving. However, if they could be made to behave, they could serve us well as foot soldiers. It is far more probable, though, that they intend to ride on the backs of our enemies and finish off what was begun. We face war on two fronts already; *three* fronts could pose a serious problem— even with my support." Indeed, her warships' truefire reserves were finite, and much as she wanted to, she couldn't bomb the world into obedience.

"We shall try peaceful methods first," declared Magnus. "A wise man speaks before he swings his blade."

"When dealing with men. Not animals," protested Gloriatrix.

"Peace," muttered Elissandra. Everyone looked at her, summoned by the dreamy song of her voice, and none felt it queer that she appeared to be haloed in silver light. "In thirty days from this night, the Black Star will shine bright, and all futures save for the darkest will reign. If we are to win, if we are to live, we must make peace with the old ways, religions, and peoples. We must show our weaknesses to the Green Mother and ask that she forgive us.

We must embrace each and every child from her womb. After everything man has done to ruin their kind, the vengeance we fear from the wolves we have persecuted will resolve itself. An emissary is unnecessary."

"It is?" asked the king.

Elissandra's form rippled like a woman of water; she'd almost entirely submerged herself into a Dream.

"One has already been sent," she said, her voice a shivery echo. "Three, actually. I told you not to concern yourself. The matter is done. Our sands are waning. Thirty suns, thirty sleeps. Peace with the Green Mother or we die."

With that, Elissandra's silver hues and otherworldly intimations passed.

For a while there was only silence.

"Thirty days..." muttered Magnus. "At last the doomsday chronex has been set."

He mustered his regality and straightened. "Iron Queen, and champions of Geadhain, we face new terrors at every turn, this is true. I shall trust in the words of the seer at our table that this new force to the south doesn't desire to add destruction to the feast of darkness we face. Although I shan't soften your mettle with too much optimism. Since the hourglass is so fleeting, and victory so unsure, I should tell you—utterly—the reality of our circumstances."

He glanced at his bloodmates for their agreement on this disclosure. Lila and Erik nodded their assent. He resumed. "I am awake and whole for the moment. The army of the dead does not pose an immediate threat, and my brother still remains in hiding. But this is merely the calm before Geadhain's great storm. In this calm, we must build, plan, and prepare. We must make our nations strong. We must have our technomagikal weapons ready for those that will soon be at our gates. Sadly, I am a weapon for our enemy. I am a danger to my kingdom for as long as I remain here. Some of you are uninitiated regarding the true goals this Black Queen has for our world. My brother and I are at the root of her designs. She has set herself on claiming our bodies and our powers, and has already succeeded halfway in her goals. However, the metaphysical and elemental consequences of her seizing hold of my power will make the storm of frostfire that struck our world not long ago seem like an apprentice's first spell. I shall be without my senses. I shall be without my mercy. I shall terrorize this world by my brother's side. Imagine two mad Immortals, and what magnificent atrocities we two, together, could commit."

Snow began to fall and Magnus rose, looking skyward through the whiteness. "Magik and life, sadly, have been tied to my body. I weep, and winter descends. I rage, and clouds black out the sky. I try to use this symbiosis wisely, and kindly. Every sand I spend in contemplation of my actions, which makes for a very long list of misgivings...I used to believe that my union with the Green Mother was a blessing, though I see how power is the blade with the poisoned hilt—a curse whenever it's wielded. I once believed, blindly, that all my ties to life and mystery were wondrous threads of glass, and that I was to care for these secrets. I did not see how their frailty was mine, too. I cannot be destroyed without unleashing the shattered torment of all that I am: thunder, wind, might, love, doom. My end will result in catastrophes beyond the scale of anything we currently face."

Lila and Erik shivered as Magnus flushed their souls with a queer, quiet chill, as though winter were whistling through the cracks of a lonely mountain. Magnus's sadness vanished in a speck, and he locked it in that secret box of which none of those in his soul-circle could partake. "I have thought of sleep...deep, dark, and formless," he whispered. "I have thought of removing myself from this world so that I cannot harm or be harmed. However, even if I can be subdued, put into a comatose state, I would not be safe from the Black Queen. She would find me, *helpless*, and claim me.

"*Zionae*—that is the name of our enemy. Hear it, know it, and cultivate for her your deepest hatred. Now that you know her name, and my weakness, we must decide how to conquer them both. One half of the equation has my queen and our knight already construed. We shall get to that in a moment. But what I require from you, at this table of enemies turned cautious allies, of men and women whose virtues and weakness have been rendered inconsequential before the shadow that threatens us all, is a promise."

"A promise?" Beauregard whispered, and it was so quiet that all heard him.

"A promise," said the king.

Magnus flexed his authority, his unity with the elements, man, emotion and, if one followed that current far and deep enough, to life itself. Without words, with only the melancholy of his spirit, Magnus made them understand what would be lost should each man or woman, wicked or good, fail. And once he'd cast that spell, and their chests had pounded to the tune of his, their skins had prickled with his cold compassion, and their gazes had drowned too deep in his stare to ever be released, he said, "You will defend Eod, our one final bastion against the dark. Iron and silver, darkness and light, will become defenders against unholiness. Should you fail, we shall be devoured along with all life. First by Death, then by the Black Queen who would eat Geadhain and beyond. I cannot be the champion in this war. Even a man as great as I, am but one of many soldiers in the army of hope. And I am weak. So you must be my strength. All of you. A family of heroes. Swear this to me."

Mouths moved, all stood. Some persons wept. Others mumbled oaths or made the fisted salutes of their Iron and Silver nations. A power as great as any magik—honor—would see this pledge through to its bloody and terrible end. Irascible to the core, Gloriatrix was able to dispel the queer enchantment first.

"Wait, where will you be, if not defending your own city?" she asked.

Magnus looked off and far away, as if looking toward the journey. "As I have said, I must prepare myself. I must be a weapon for Eod, not the Black Queen. Our allies wandering the ancient east are working to discover her secrets. However, it is up to me to defeat my brother and the beast of fire that serves him, the thing that surely sleeps in the cinders of Zioch: an elemental named Ignifax. There will be many wars, and we need an army for each. I shall be the army that rises against my brother, each of you will be the protectors of Eod, and the Daughter of Fate will topple the Black Queen. If we can succeed in our tasks before the Black Star rises, and my body is claimed, we may just eke out an impossible triumph."

"Where will you find this power?" asked Beauregard. "To stand against your brother and his beast?"

"I must head north," replied Magnus. "Fate has bestowed upon us a revelation. Where there is fire, there is ice; the universe cannot exist without balance. So my brother has claimed one power; I must claim the other. If he has chained a beast of fire, then I shall chain winter to my Will. Deep in the North, beyond most known names and places, there is a tomb in which that power sleeps. I must travel there to awaken the ancient elemental of ice, the Father of Winter himself: Nifhalheim. So Queen Lila has been told, through visions and magik, after consorting with the spirits of the damned—"

Elissandra suddenly burst into wrenching cries.

"He loved you, Elissandra," said Lila, who had not forgotten her promise to Sangloris's ghost to speak to his wife—though where but now had that happenstance to meet occurred? Regretful, Lila reached across the table even though their hands would never touch. "You've known he was dead for weeks. You must no longer let that secret devour you. Know, too, that you were his world, and united in almost as much blood and promise as I to the men I've loved."

As Elissandra's children huddled around their mother to comfort her, the council moved on to discuss in earnest Eod's final gamble: Lila's visitation with the dying witch-man, a quest to wake one of the world's oldest legends, to bind it to Magnus as Brutus had done with the Father of Fire. Only then could they stand against Brutus. Fire against ice, brother to brother. It was how things must be. In that glimmer of opportunity, with Death and Brutus at bay for Fates knew how long, and with the uncertain force haunting Eod from the south, the king had to act. Eod's destiny, the destiny of civilization itself, lay now in the hands of its champions: children of iron and children of steel would, together, defy the Black Queen, Death, and whatever new horror next dared to announce itself.

V

Before his exit, Magnus embraced the spellsong and spoke sophistry about honor and pride. "You should speak to your brother," the king whispered. "Thirty days might be all we have left, and you dishonor yourself and the blessing of brotherhood by keeping your secret."

Beauregard remembered little else of what his liege had expressed. Further words were shared, before and after that statement. Beauregard remembered none of them, though the image of the king and his black and golden consorts dragging him away was indelible in his memory. Magnus disappeared, and Beauregard stood shivering in the Chamber of Echoes. Everyone else appeared to have vanished, too, aside from Rasputhane and Leonitis who sat at the table seemingly embroiled in schemes. Beauregard cared not for such strategizing. He wanted to sulk. It seemed as if every time he found a father he loved, that man was taken away—first Devlin and now the king.

As Beauregard dragged his feet through the palace halls and day-dreamed his way back to the Warpath, he pondered what family meant in this unsteady age. What was he even to do with the remnants of his family? He and his mother had grown distant since the wave of Death had crashed over Bainsbury. Although, he'd only witnessed so much of that devastation before the Iron lord had settled him with a punch to the face. Remembering that event, he was sure Tabitha had allowed him to be struck and dragged aboard the skycarriage. Beauregard wasn't the naïve and trusting child she'd known, and he wasn't fooled into believing her an innocent. As a man, he'd seen mad kings, armies clashing, nature weeping fire and ice, and a father die. Beauregard knew a lie when it was being spun. Lately, Tabitha had stopped feigning confusion over the whirlwind surrounding their flight from Bainsbury. Now she simply spouted adages about how "the past is the past" or, quite curtly, that she'd rather not discuss the matter. Beauregard had started training later, and arriving back at his chamber even later, so they rarely saw each other even though she had been given accommodations down the hall from him.

In the mornings they would encounter each other in the White Hearth, where she seemed to lurk, and exchange pleasantries while he stuffed his face with jam, meat, and cheese—anything that he could quickly and effortlessly consume so that he could hurry off to the Warpath. It was shameful behavior for a son to ignore his mother like that. Truthfully, he couldn't say the first thing about how or where she spent her days. Although she had mentioned tailoring once, and he had seen her in the company of that woman, Dorothy, so perhaps they'd started a knitting circle or the like. Curious habits considering the impending world's end. Whatever the case, he and Tabitha had gone from estranged to strangers, and the journey back to mother and son wasn't one he was prepared to take.

The clang of steel and thuds of men striking sandbags, shields, or one another, stirred Beauregard out of his ennui. Noon scorched the red slate of the Warpath, and a fine dust blew across the escarpment. Soldiers clashed with one another, or darted in and out of ivory tents. The day was awash with light and movement. The thunder of hooves from mounted knights and the boom of thunderstrike archers practicing their marksmanship against a distant rock wall lent the day an inspiring beat. Beauregard couldn't feel down when on stage in the theater of war—he could only feel alive. Watchmen saluted and greeted him as "commander," and he nodded to his brothers-in-arms. He appreciated how candidly they had accepted him, and how patient they had been while he learned the rigors of being a commander while acting under that title. Respect did not come easily in the military, but these men and women had given him theirs. Hence he had to repay that gift by becoming the leader they believed he could be.

These men and women were better kin to him than that irritating blond waif Galivad, whom he'd only ever seen fight once. In that matchup, and willingly disarmed against a blade-bearing watchman, Galivad had first thrown sand into his opponent's face and then kicked the soldier with the flat of his heel, for maximum spread and force, in the man plums. The sparring ended in mere specks, with Galivad as the victor. Beauregard admitted that his brother was an adept, if dirty, fighter, as well as a fine tactician, judging from the orders and formations he issued.

However, none of that genius was on display today. While checking the lines, counting supplies, shadowing legion masters, and reading reports from Rowena's and Leonitis's respective forces (the driest of all duties, he felt), he kept an ear tuned for his brother's lyrical laugh. Later, as he stood with the drill instructors and studied the strength of his soldiers' swings, timed the charges of his knights, then eventually engaged in combat himself, he'd still seen no trace of his brother. Galivad wouldn't be visiting the army today. Were he to have shown up so late, a wispy woman, more ghost than flesh, would've come to whisk him away anyway: Beatrice. Sometimes, if Beauregard forgot to eat on the field and wandered to the White Hearth hungry as a flesh-crazed reborn, he'd see the pair of them sitting and watching the night's performers. Occasionally, his brother would sing to the Menosian woman. He believed that they were having an affair, and left as soon as Beatrice turned her gaze of frozen knives upon him. It was only a suspicion, however, but Beauregard felt she wasn't quite mortal. No woman, without magik, should be able to leave a man shivering with only a look.

Still, Beauregard couldn't even muster more than a wheeze of disappointment as the sun bled down and confirmed his brother's absence—he must have left for a tryst with Beatrice after the king's meeting. Thirty days remained until all that was green and good on Geadhain could be no more, and his brother had decided it was more important to wax his candle than to defend his city. It was a miracle that they were cut from the same cloth.

Beauregard was toweling the sweat off of his nude torso in the private shade of a tent when in peeked a watchman—*watchwoman or watchperson*, he thought, *should be the corrective term*, for women in the service of Eod. She was distressingly pretty, tanned as a Sorsettan princess (were they to have them), with brown-sugar skin and hair as black as his, that fell in loose coils over her face. The watchman's lips had a tint of tawny brown, like copper, and her eyes twinkled with the comeliness of the sea even from afar. Beauregard felt as if he was swaying, enchanted. In that drawn instant, Beauregard wondered how it was possible that he'd never spotted her before. His hand froze while wiping his stomach.

"Sorry to disturb you, spellsong," she said.

"No. I am not disturbed. As in flustered—not insane." He threw the towel away and recovered his lost graces. "What may I do for you?"

"A missive for you was delivered a moment ago; the sender, a shrouded woman, wouldn't stay to deliver it herself."

"Mysterious." Beauregard made his way over to her and claimed the piece of paper she'd extended. She didn't remain to watch him read the note, and turned to leave. "Thank you...Miss?"

The watchwoman glanced over her shoulder, bespelling him with her exotic and heavy sensuality. Beauregard leaned forward in animalistic fashion, to catch a whiff of whatever sweet licorice scent spilled from her presence.

"*Missus* Edina Cross of the thunderstrike artillery. My father is my commander, and almost a second husband if you will, since we spend so much time training these days. Poor Paracelsus, my beloved, plays the second fiddle. As for me, I'm not a messenger, though most men tend to stand around with dumb stares on their faces, not unlike yours"—she smiled, and he melted like a man of butter—"when it falls upon them to deliver or serve. Women, sadly, have the instinct to labor set into their bones, and it's taken advantage of far too often. The lady asked for this to be taken to the spellsong, and here we are."

"Gorijen's daughter?"

"Yes, and my husband is master of the west watch." She realized he was stalling, perplexed and allowing his unread missive to flutter, as if it might escape his fingers at any moment. "You might want to watch that note, spellsong. It's about to drift out of your dreamy hand."

Beauregard flailed at and crumpled the note, and as though she were a cruel spirit of seduction and trickery, Edina disappeared amid a gust of laughter. He reprimanded himself for behaving so stupidly in the presence of that woman. He frowned while trying to place her husband, though, and mostly construed a tall, imposing lump of muscle and bad opinions that he believed to be the man. One should not judge a person by their appearances or lack of graces, admonished his inner saint. It was best not to waste another thought on Edina, as tempting as those thoughts might be when he was alone this evening. Moreover, he had a note that had been delivered through Edina by a suspicious stranger, which he uncrumpled and read.

He dropped it in shock, then fell to his knees and retrieved it, frenzied to read the missive again and again. The words resonated in his head and heart like the vindictive echo of Edina's laugh—teasing and charged with fate. No matter how many times his eyes scanned the paper, he couldn't understand the promise of what was written: "Come to the King's Garden, tonight, and meet your father."

VI

The hourglass had waned past the noonday sun when Lowe arrived at the Chamber of Echoes. Although the talks had been long, the gathering had broken apart when driven by grumbling stomachs and exhausted minds that knew better than their owners when to stop, eat, and rest. Thus, Lowelia entered the hallowed quiet under the yew and discovered that only Leonitis and Rasputhane remained. The men sat close together, a bit like fellow hounds all tired after a day of herding and chasing, though leaning on the table on elbows not paws. As she waved to them, they looked at her with long faces. Though their countenances had been made sunken by fatigue, their voices held a happy note as they returned the greeting.

"Gents." She claimed a stone seat, then sighed. She appeared to be as invigorated as they were enervated. Her sand-beaten leather trousers, vest, and brimmed hat lent her an adventuresome charm—even the sling in which the Mind rested whenever she had possession of it looked like a conscious part of her apparel. "Seems I missed a long assembly," she continued, putting her feet up on the table.

"I would have come sooner, but it took me forever to track that woman down. You probably know this already, but Rowena's been running back and forth between the queen's army and your sword-and-spells-for-hire militia, Leo. I can't imagine the headache. Understandable that she was so curt with me this afternoon when I finally caught up with her." Lowelia wore the unmistakable pout of the sword of the queen. "'King's summons,' she said. 'I'd rather milk the lizards.' Dorothy usually plays carrier pigeon, though she hasn't been around recently—suspicious. Though what isn't these days? I told Rowena that I would attend in her stead, but it seems I missed the meeting myself."

"She refused to come?" asked Leo.

"Indeed, though I can't blame her..." She drifted into thoughts of the kiss of sun, the gritty desert wind whipping at her clothes, the dusty musk of spinrexes, and the nutty fragrance of the oils with which Arhadians treated their leathers, weapons, and even skins. Some of that oil remained on her hands from touching something at the Arhad encampment earlier that day. One couldn't easily wash or sweat the emollient away—that was the point—and it gave her knuckles a sheen. Rubbing her supple hands together, she continued. "Rowena's a Makret, now, which I suppose is a bit like a marshal and mother to all the children of the desert rolled into one. Comes with a lot of duties that make for good excuses. Still, rather incredible...I'm sorry, my mind is drifting today. What did I miss?"

"A great deal of news," said Rasputhane. "While you've been lollygagging your way here, you—Rowena, really—have missed the most divisive and decisive strategizing session of this war. I don't even know where to start."

"Start with what you told us, about the army of changelings," suggested Leonitis.

"Changelings!" Lowelia took her feet off the table and gave Rasputhane her full attention.

What followed was a seemingly implausible story, even in a time where she thought every impossible truth had been traded for fact. She listened but couldn't remember everything. She couldn't expunge herself of the gut-wrenching news that Lila was leaving. Not only that, she was leaving with the king, a monster whom Lowe had never really forgiven. A beast to whom Lila had bound herself again just to save his miserable life—an existence over which this whole bloody war was being fought.

"I must take my leave," she said, when she'd heard enough.

Rasputhane assessed something of her intent. "If you hurry to the anchorage, you'll be able to say goodbye."

Lowelia bolted from the Chamber of Echoes. Only Rasputhane with his silver sight noticed the tears streaming from her eyes as she left.

VII

Dusk fell over Eod as a wave of red fire that consumed the clouds floating beyond the Witchwall. Beneath the flaming heavens, the tiny houses with their metal roofs glimmered like rubies. *Such beauty.* Though Lowe minded none of it for more than the fleeting moment of awe she felt as she stepped out onto the anchorage. Indeed, as she searched, the dazzle became bothersome, and she had to squint and bark for directions from the sun-glazed impressions of watchmen to find out where the queen and her companions were. At least the Immortals hadn't left yet, as far as any soldier knew, although the three could have been in any of the shining carriages lifting off from the anchorage.

Lowe worked up a sweat as she hurried between parked skycarriages, stealing moments in their warm shade when she could. After popping out of one dark pocket, she saw four figures in the distance against the crimson sunlight and recognized the three Immortals from their radiant carriages. She rushed toward the trio and was soon upon them. A watchwoman was with them too, engaged in a confidence with the queen while the men stood off near a purring silver skycarriage. The three Immortals turned all at once to greet Lowe with smiles.

"Oh, she's here," said the watchwoman. "I suppose my services shan't be needed."

"Indeed," replied the queen, retrieving the leather parcel she'd been about to hand to the woman.

The soldier left. Lowelia noted that they were all dressed in traveler's clothing: thick boots, and cloaks with furred rims and a heaviness that was of no use in Eod. Lowelia was so flustered from her run that she neglected her manners.

"What's this? Where are you going?"

"This is a much nicer farewell then a secondhand goodbye that soldier was about to deliver on my behest." Lila came forward and traded a spherical object into the empty sling Lowe carried. "Along with this, our anxious-to-please and curious child."

The Mind.

"Where are you going?" repeated Lowe.

"Carthac to charter a ship to Valholom," replied Erik, who grinned—great and white—as if he'd been there before or knew what to expect. "It's a vast kingdom at the edge of the Northlands, about as far as we can travel, by vessel, before the etheric currents interfere with navigation; a skycarriage landing there would be more of a crash, akin to us announcing ourselves with trumpets. Hence the voyage along the Feordhan. From Valholom we shall strike out into the deep north."

"Yes, but *why*?" Lowelia hung her head in despair. Details of Rasputhane's debriefing beyond the fact that her queen—her noble, honorable queen for whom she'd committed treason and rebellion—was about to leave Eod were lost to her.

"To do our part in this war," said Magnus.

Lowelia couldn't restrain her contempt for the man; it boiled her face red. Lila glanced at the men in her company, then took one of the woman's shaking hands. They walked around the skycarriage and faced the night as it descended, gracefully, in a shivering purple caress, at last, snuffing out some of Eod's twinkle. They stood there for several sands, though it felt as if only a moment had passed when the queen said, "Night falls fast, which is why we must leave. I have had a vision, Lowe, and when Fate reaches so far as to whisper into the ear of one who is not born to receive prophecy, we must heed that voice."

The women leaned upon each other. "You've served me so well, Lowe, as well as the sister I never had. You, Rowena, Leonitis, and all those who were loyal to me even when I wasn't worthy of your praise."

Was there ever a time? thought Lowe of this strong and terrible woman.

"In my heart, I still bear the bloody weight of what I did while under the influence of Death," confessed Lila. "The screams and suffering of hundreds of thousands. If I use slippery morals, I can justify the bloodshed I caused to free the daughters and sons of the Arhad. Although, with the children of the Iron City, persons we have come to trust with the future and hope of our nation, I see how blind my rage had made me when I murdered so many of them."

Admittedly, the genocide hadn't been one of Lila's finest moments, even if Menosians were—or had been, until very recently—monstrous. Lila's forgiveness of her husband of one thousand years, who'd beaten her to an unrecognizable heap of meat and agony, Lowe couldn't as easily pardon. "Your rage had reason; that seed of darkness was planted by Magnus," she said.

"Oh, dear friend," whispered Lila, and as she kissed the handmaiden's cheek a waft of her curious, impassioning new spice enveloped Lowelia's senses. In the heady haze of cinnamon and serpent's rattles in which Lowelia drifted, she understood all of what the queen said, the fullness and the pain of it. "We are all made of glass. I realize that now. We are all breakable and too often broken. I was shattered by the punishing yoke of my people, whose suffering I shall always feel, even if I claim Eod as my home. Magnus was shattered long before he thought I would be the power to repair him. Magnus was half a man when he wreaked that unspeakable violence upon me. It was that violence that forced me to look at the illusion of our happiness, and to realize what we had shared for a millennium was not love. Rather, it was an elixir of escape—he from his brother, me from my people.

"We are not whole until we accept whence we've come. Magnus was never mine, and I was never his. I have taken that great leap toward acceptance. I've walked through fire and blood—quite literally. My fair and once beholden king has only begun to step upon the flames. Strangely, I feel closer to Magnus now that he's aware he's imperfect. Do remember, too, how he was kind to you when you were so broken. It was his mercy that brought us to this moment today. And do not fear for me, my friend, for I have you, and Erik, and gratitude for who I am—all of my wicked and wonderful bits. I have made it through the greatest war already. A Black Queen I do not fear. I shall not be conquered. As much as your clemency protests, let us worry for the immortal wounded child who has never known true love, true peace, or true self. For if he breaks further, if he doesn't learn how to master himself, we are bound and doomed from his failure. Take care of the Mind. Take care of yourself. Pick up your broken pieces and become something new. I believe in you, my friend. I believe that you will be greater when next I see you."

Lowelia awoke; the queen was gone, and time had been ripped away from her. The queen's words echoed in her head. Night tarnished the silver city, and it wasn't clear to her for how long she'd stood, rocking and weeping, wrapped in the spice-and-sorcery invoked dream of her queen. Her queen had left, and the vacant lot that had harbored her skycarriage now exposed her to a harsh wind.

One hourglass and thirty-two sands have passed since the skycarriage bearing Mother Lila and Father Erik departed the anchorage, said the Mind. Then with a pause—out of sadness or worry, Lowelia thought—it added, *Where will you go, Navigator Lowelia?*

"I shall stay with you," she said, "and we shall have a grand adventure."

Lowe had been clutching the crystal thing, and it tingled in pleasure from her reply. She was its parent now. Lila and Erik were gone to the Northlands. Lowelia wanted it all to end: the chase, the terror, the constant threats. Nevertheless, the journey *had* shaped her. Lowe was no more a cheery, blithe handmaiden or reformed mutilator. She'd worn many hats:

queen, soldier, anarchist, and spy. What would she be next? She didn't think she would find that answer here. Rather, the desert beckoned her back with fragrances of nut, sweat, and the labor of strong women. Perhaps she could become one of them—a warrior-maiden, or even a Makret. The future was more forgiving and exciting than the past. Lowelia smiled, bade goodbye to what remained of her old self, and strode through the quiet anchorage on the lookout for a watchman. She had spent too much time here, and she longed to return to the daughters and sons of sand. People who, like her, Lila, and Erik, had been reformed by their trials and agonies. As for the king, Magnus's penance and transformation had just begun. Perhaps she would grow to like, and not loathe, the man who returned from the Northlands. She hoped for that.

VIII

"Thirty days," muttered Gloriatrix.

The slick, luxurious interior cabin of the crowe was empty aside from herself and the shade of her son. Shadows hugged Sorren, naturally, as he lurked down the bench from her, somehow able to avoid what scant light entered the cabin through its portals. In case he was spotted, they'd attired him in the voluminous garments of a Carthacian priest—a hooded priest's frock and a metal theater mask trapped in a toothy, maniacal grimace to cover his face. The masks unsettled her, though they were perfect for hiding her son's strangeness. Curious minds simply assumed that in the shadow of doomsday she'd taken to the crutch of religion. Wiser minds would know that she would never be so weak as to rely upon the graces of a time-veiled divinity to absolve her of her sins. She knew nothing of that religion and couldn't even say to what spirit, lord, or lady the Carthacian priests offered their eaten sin, or how the process was conducted. No one would challenge her beliefs, however, and what she understood today of celestial forces was that they weren't a benefactor one should pray to, ever, for anything—they had their own ruthless ambitions and cared not for humanity's bleatings.

"Thirty days?" asked Sorren.

"Till the end of the world, my son."

"I see."

"Although, it shan't come to that." She tapped the upholstery and summoned her son closer—he slunk down the bench. "We won't have much to rule if it is all laid to waste, and this world will still be mine."

Gloriatrix smiled. The end of the world brought people together, she had realized. Although she wouldn't degrade herself with soppy professions of love. Sorren was here, and he'd crossed Death, battled Death, for that right. Pride in oneself and one's family was a greater virtue than love. Now that he had become a living dead—an undeniable horror—she felt, for the first time, respect for him. There was, however, a bolt loose in her son's head, a flicker of wild violence in his eyes that she recognized from the madmen and moguls of Menos. She interpreted that as potential for greatness. She was certain that he possessed the same ruthless fire, the same ability to snap out judgments of life and death, as she did. Mother and son, at last. Gloriatrix patted his cold knee.

Do you like it when she touches you? whispered the monster in Sorren's head. *We'll touch her soon, too. Cut her up, hollow her out, and have a fine puppet that can touch us whenever we like. Wherever we like. What a good mommy she'll finally be. Perfect, with only a few stitches.*

Enough.

We need a toy. It's been too long. I want a meat-puppet. I want red on my hands. Deny me this and you'll rue your resistance.

You are not real. You cannot bend me to your will.

I am you. Thou art I. We cannot be denied.

A firm knock on the chamber's metal door sent the monster in Sorren's head scurrying into the shadows. Before permitting entry, Gloriatrix nodded to her son and he slid back to the respectable distance a man of faith should maintain toward a woman. The Iron Queen bade the caller enter, and the hatch opened. Enough of the hallway's light had spilled upon the taut shoulders and lithe silhouette of the woman for Gloriatrix to easily identify Aadore Brennoch. It was the first she'd seen of Aadore since Eod's civil war, and she had been meaning to speak to the young noble. So naturally, when she heard of Aadore's sudden visit to Camp Fury, she'd extended an invitation to the encampment on her personal crowe.

Aadore bowed as she entered the cabin, and Iron Lord Gustavius did the same—though due to his height as well as respect—as he followed Aadore. The Iron lord had vanished a while ago, to check on the fledgling aristocrats. Perhaps they'd chatted, for Aadore and the Iron lord were quite comfortable with each other as they moved to the benches split by the entryway, Gustavius guiding her—a hand upon her back—to her seat. He then sat on the other half of the bench. Displaying a natural sophistication, Aadore smoothed out her ebon lace and beaded gown, slipped off her gloves, and tilted her scabbard so that it lay over her lap prior to addressing the Iron Queen. She'd quickly mastered or watched the actions of her betters enough to have picked up such poise so soon, noted Gloriatrix. While the presence of Aadore's sword was off-putting for a lady of class, the Iron Queen considered it part of what made this woman unique.

"Thank you for your hospitality," said Aadore. "My brother and his men are all asleep." They'd taken to referring to Skar and Curtis as their manservants so as to permit them admittance into her inner circle. "I'm astonished that so much snoring hasn't woken the baby, and I didn't want my conversation with Gustavius to wake him, either."

"In times of war the peace of an infant is a profound blessing," replied the queen. "As is the joy of communication in the company of equals. Do continue your talk."

"Oh." Aadore appeared to crack in her graces for being deemed *equal*. "Well, perhaps your knowledge would be of service here. I wanted to know about the heraldries of Menos—old and new. The families, their histories, and their respective industrial contributions. We are a nation of progress, and it behooves me that I know very little about the stones upon which Menos was built."

"Why would you care about the lineages and traditions of a dead nation?" Gloriatrix asked, slyly.

It was evident this was a test of character or wisdom, and Aadore replied at once. "If we are all that remains, then our history, our culture, and our identity is honored and perpetuated through us. If I am to be noble, then my brother and I must embrace the fullness of the gift we've been offered."

"You believe that power is a gift?"

"More of an opportunity—or series thereof. Although power must be claimed before it can be of any use. It must be wielded by the strong. Power in the hands of a weak man is a dangerous weapon."

"And you believe you are strong?"

"I do. And I'm not a man."

In what was a rare shock, Gloriatrix laughed. Aadore had passed the gauntlet of her first inquisition. "So you wish to curate what we have lost?"

"I wish to respect and renew what we still have," replied Aadore. "If I may romanticize for a moment?"

"You may."

Aadore gazed through a glass-and-iron portal and into the white forgetfulness of the moon—memories of Menos assailed her. "When we were lost in Menos, I thought of what we had lost, and of how much we had lost. Many times, I thought of your speech—which I heard on the day Menos fell—and I thought of your own story. I thought of how one woman could claw herself from disrepute, could reinvent all that she was, could become the first queen in a city in which women were only suffered as whores and housewives.

Rather than envy that crown myself, I took from your tale the moral of determination, of rising from the ashes.

"We can do that. Through you, I have been given the opportunity to shape what will be, and that I shall not waste. I believe that Menos can and will be remade—grander than any city before it. I feel that you too share that vision. I feel that's why you are so unafraid of wars and Immortals and all the troubles that plague our lives, because you know that they are fleeting compared to your dream."

"You speak bravely," said the Iron Queen.

Aadore couldn't say whether this was meant to be menacing, and she replied with honesty. "I am brave. As are you. As is the Iron lord, I feel. I cannot speak for the Father of Carthac."

"He is," declared the Iron Queen.

"Four brave minds and Wills can shape more than a hundred thousand meek and ambitionless souls." Aadore raised her chin as if enjoying a cleaner, lighter air than what men usually inhaled. "The future starts here."

"Perhaps it does..." mused the Iron Queen. She'd been clenching her shoulders and jaw, quite taken with the young woman, and finally relaxed into her seat. The crowe soared along, ruffled by the eastern winds of the Feordhan. From a density in the air—the weight of doom and death—she sensed that they were near the ruins of Taroch's Arm, and she picked herself a spot at a viewing portal. Clouds parted to reveal a sea of blackened ruins and glimmers of a furious river looking ready to swallow the charnel-house memory. Indeed, memories were the sum of what remained of Taroch's Arm. There were no signs of movement.

Before their departure from Eod, Gloriatrix had ordered her vessel to take one more circuit along the eastern front, and for her windsingers to commune with whatever ethereal spirits were required to scout a single dead, flagging arm in the desert. She was convinced that incompetence always lay in the hands of others. Alas, their voyage had revealed nothing, and soured by regret she sat and pondered how the army of the dead had so efficaciously evaded the combined technomagiks of her and her allies. It mattered not; Death was but prolonging the defeat of her forces and of her exorcism from this world. Next to her Furies, the Iron Queen possessed a secret feint of which no one was aware aside from Sorren: the wonderstones.

He'd been very cagey about how he'd acquired the wonderstones, and twice as obscure as to how the relics were to be used, and utterly inscrutable regarding the details of his harrowing adventure after leaping from the window of the Blackbriar estate while *possessed*, the latter detail of which he had revealed. Still, Sorren had trusted her enough to show her the stones and to explain that they would be used to "save their family," whatever he meant by that. Even in remembrance, the wonderstones shimmered with the tantalizing beauty of stars. For they were power incarnate: raw, pure miracles in the shape of tiny glass rocks. She was well versed in all the legends. In reality, she knew what one wonderstone had done to repel the mad king and to free Magnus in Sorsetta. For the time being, Sorren was keeping the wonderstones somewhere on his person, and she had no desire to steal or otherwise remove them from his care. These relics were better off in the hands of a devout, immortal child of hers anyhow. Perhaps she'd use a stone or two to inseminate herself with divine power and finally become the sorceress and Will-shaper she was meant to be. If she allowed her mind to wander the garden of possibilities, she might be lost forever.

Time passed, and she was here and there stirred from ruminating by a peak in Gustavius and Aadore's conversation, wherein the girl was grilling the man for every historical nugget he possessed. Gustavius, however, was not as engrossed as his pupil, and due in no way to her lack of charm. While he answered the young aristocrat with his brusque civility, the other passenger, with his molasses-sweet fragrance of wilted flowers and death, often unsettled his nerves. Moreover, there was a haunting, a chill to the night that was inexplicable beyond the dead man sharing the cabin. Gustavius was a wild man, and wild men were but beasts in two-legged skins. So when the call of danger came, it ran like the cold tip of a knife traced up his balls and caused him to leap, run to, and peer out the window.

They'd made it back to Eod in good time; the Furies lay close, prickling with crimson lights. But something was wrong—the image was twisted. Smoke wriggled up from campfires scattered across the dark scab of the Menosian encampment. The evening made difficult the separation of what was simply darkness from the smoky tails that rose from the backs of the Furies. "Fire!" he exclaimed.

Sorren was suddenly at the window beside the Iron lord. Sorren couldn't see the details beheld by the other man; instead, he viewed the field of souls in the sands beneath, and the three great souls that were his mother's furious warships. Within those gargantuan bodies, and moving through their mass like an infection through blood, he saw black, squiggly things, like men of barbwire: the auras of unliving servants.

"Mother," he said, forgetting himself, "your ships are under assault from Death."

IX

Beauregard entered the King's Garden like an assassin. He slipped in through one of the palace's tunnels that Lowe had once shown him from a hall near the king's chamber. He snuck around a grill camouflaged in vibrant red flowers that reeked of festival spice, before closing the access. He skulked into a woodland glimmering with northern auras cast from trees wreathed in crystal, flowers budded in emerald flame, silver-and-glass bridges, and the other wonders of the King's Garden. Adrenaline, coupled with playing a game of wolf-and-deer with the Silver Watch who patrolled the garden, kept him alert and fully engaged in the night's espionage. However, after much wandering, and many pricks from glass thorn bushes and other pretty but prickly flora, he began to feel annoyed more than intrigued by this clandestine arrangement.

The letter hadn't told him where precisely he was to go. In fact, it couldn't have been more vague, as the King's Garden was as huge a wilderness as certain uncultivated regions of Alabion. At least it was less dangerous, being inhabited by only gentle, furred creatures, he supposed. Realizing his guard had dropped, he began pondering whether or not he'd been set up. After deciding that this was all too suspicious, and that he'd had enough of wandering, he left the bushes and stood on the road. There he picked the various twigs of glass off that had attached themselves to him, along with a few of the large, harmless, and shimmering green bugs that had found their way into his hood—star-beetles, as they were known. For a sand, he allowed one of the horned things to crawl along his palm. He studied the flicker upon its back as if it were a wishing star or the sparkle of Edina's gaze; he wished the thought of her hadn't lingered in his mind all day. Then he dipped and set the bug free to wander the weaving crystal road. "Safe travels to your home," he whispered, and turned round to head home himself.

"Galivad!" he cried.

A man dressed in dark clothing stood down the path. The gold shimmer of his hair and the posture of condescending appraisal—arms crossed, one hip jutting—revealed the man's identity even in the dim light.

"The one and only," said the watchmaster, and swaggered forward. "What brings you to the King's Garden? Other than having a private conversation with yourself?"

"I wasn't talking to myself."

"Certainly looked that way."

"It was an insect, a pest, like you."

Galivad chuffed.

With that, Beauregard's anger abated; this was his brother, after all. Perhaps the fates had arranged this, for the moment felt almost perfect for a confession. They were alone, and a silver bench glimmered down the road behind Galivad where he and his brother could sit and share their stories and bare their sorrows. Being a romantic, Beauregard nursed that fantasy while the sands dribbled onward. In his mind he thought of everything he wanted to say. *You're my brother. We were separated soon after my birth. I don't know that you know that I even exist. Here we be, a part of our mother: two sides of her nature—black and gold. I try to see difference, I try to tell myself that where we've come from doesn't define who we are, and yet...with each repetition of that deceit, my heart twists a little more and tells me that I'm lying. I am afraid that I'll be nothing but pain and regret, come the end, a debt that may come due in thirty days. Magnus knows the pain of being betrayed by family, though I think he wanted me also to understand the joy of knowing brotherhood. Can we try to be brothers? We only have so long.*

"Well? What are you doing here?" Galivad poked his shoulder. "I know you're the king's new pet; however, that doesn't absolve you of suspicion. Magnus has had plenty of pets before you, anyway—doting boys and girls—and there'll be more after you. I saw you sneaking about. Followed you for half an hourglass before I got bored of your stomping. It's good that you abandoned your skullduggery when you did—you're terrible at it. Your swordplay may have improved, but you track through the woods like a bear in iron boots. I want to know what you're doing here, *now.*"

"Perhaps you should answer that yourself," said Beauregard.

Flustered, Galivad backed away. *I don't have to explain to you any of my comings and goings.* He had excused himself from lunch with Beatrice to quickly make water, and when he'd returned the Lady El had disappeared, and in her place was a tented note. She had written it herself, and it had especially tugged at his heartstrings since the script was in Belle's ornately looped handwriting—as if it were something his dead mother, living within the monstrous Beatrice, had wanted to say. It read: *I am feeling unwell, my child, and need a bit of rest. Do not look for me; let me recuperate. Instead, meet me tonight, in the King's Garden. There's something there that I must show you.* But he hadn't been able to find her, only this fool.

"I must tell you something," said Beauregard. The spellsong stepped across the distance between them and reached for the man's hand. Galivad, a romantic in his own right, wrongly intuited the nature of the gesture and shied from the affection.

"I'm not...I mean, I'm honored, humbled even, though you must understand that I don't willingly lie with men." He frowned. "For honesty's sake, there was that one incident during my first summer with the Silver Watch;

however, it's not what you may have heard. She was a *sensuate*: exotic dancers, spun like a divine caterpillar in silks and perfumes that are born through blood-magik rituals in the far west. She was of both sexes, and too pretty for me to care about a bit of wood down below. There was an overabundance of wine to be had that evening, as well...So while I'm flattered—"

"What?" Beauregard shook his head. "I'll ignore your remarks and the insight into your recreational activities, and simply take it as fortuitous that you and I are here, and have met, as we have. I need you to shelve your arrogance for a moment and listen. Fate favors the bold, and so I must be—"

"*Fortune* favors the bold," corrected Galivad.

"Does it matter?"

"Language matters. Grace matters. Without those qualities we are mere savages shrieking into an incomprehensible bedlam."

Beauregard puffed and shook his fists. "Why must you be so insufferably pretentious? I'm trying to give you my heartfelt confession!"

"Confession?" Galivad stepped back, his hands and body clenched with aggression. "Aha! I knew your country-boy ignorance and charm was a façade to wheedle your way into the king's soft heart and good graces. What's the truth, then? Are you a spy for the Iron Queen? I know she can't be trusted, no matter how dumb and fat the council of Eod has grown on her sour milk. I wouldn't blame you if you've realized that Eod would be a kinder master."

"I'm no traitor!"

Galivad reverted to his prior assumption. "Are you in love with me, then?"

"King's mercy, you're an idiot!" Beauregard dropped to the ground, on his arse, exhausted by this entire queer confrontation. "I was given a note, to meet my family here. My father, and you, too, it seems. I can't believe we're related."

Their stares met, burned, and revealed the secret before he added, "I'm your brother."

At least the truth had slipped out in the least cruel manner: as a breath, an expression of frustration and freedom. A tenacious truth that each man— despite their denials—knew within the shadows of his heart. Once it had been uttered, Galivad did a half-swoon. Beauregard leapt up and caught his brother by his frail, girlish wrists—not unlike his own, though Beauregard's were thicker and rough with a dappling of dark hair. The spellsong helped his kin to the bench he'd spotted earlier, and they sat. For the first time they faced each other, as kin, as brothers. A fire unfelt before that moment licked flames inside their ribs. It was fear, wonder, and joy that they felt. Their passion came from marveling at the miracle that was each a half of Belle poured into a cast of flesh: two men at last staring, whole, into a mirror. It seemed silly to have ignored their similarities before this. They were nearly twins, only rougher and darker when it came to Beauregard. They drifted out of the moment. They were holding hands now, lightly, almost sisterly, though such effeminacy wasn't an affront to either man. It was a solace.

"You said something regarding a note?" asked Galivad.

"Yes, brother." Beau smiled. "Should I call you that?"

"You may. Don't overuse it though, it's gauche."

"Gauche? You're ridiculous. Although...it's nice to finally meet you."

Galivad looked at his brother sadly. "You've known for a while."

"I have. Since Sorsetta."

"I've known that I had a brother somewhere in our great green world. I hadn't imagined—or wanted to believe—that it was you. Who told you?"

"My father—stepfather, rather. Who told you?"

"Our mother."

"Belle?" Beauregard jolted up to his feet. "She's dead! Or so I was told."

The brothers froze, a melody flowing to them:

"Through the rye, under evening sky, the hills are alive with flame..."

A song had enchanted the night; the trees shivered, the animals harked, and the children of Belle recognized the summoning from their mother's voice.

"'The Wheat and the Barley,'" whispered Galivad. "Her favorite tune. She must have arranged this. Come, brother; it is time to meet your mother. Are you ready?"

"I am."

Belle's boys were brave; they were passion, art, and life. Like swaying nymphs to music, they raced toward the mystery. They held their hands fast; they were love, and they were about to meet one who had conceived them both through love. As they entered a deep glade in the wood, a sanctuary blessed in moonlight and bloodred in posies and roses, they were slapped viciously back to reality. There they saw a stone island in the crimson sea, a sitting woman with two figures surrounding her.

"Belle?" asked Beauregard, of the white woman who'd suddenly ceased her singing—his mind required several specks to associate the lovely voice with the Menosian witch who was present.

"Somewhat," she replied. "And here, Galivad, is the surprise I wanted to share with you—with each of you. The man who conceived you with Belle."

"Our father?" Galivad gasped, for no man was present to have seeded them save for that wicked shadowbroker, Alastair. He had known there was a man, somewhere, who had spurted his responsibility into his mother then vanished, though this revelation hardly softened the shock. He reeled and clung to his brother, each of them trying to digest so many exposed secrets and ties.

Alastair stepped forward. "My sons."

Slowly the four family members estranged through death, deceit, and distance waded through the flowers to be reunited, leaving one last and lost person in their wake: Maggie. She was the most confused and least abreast of the ties and of who knew what from whom. She still grappled with Alastair's most recent confession that he was instead a man named Stevoch, or another named Lucien, among his many and varied existences. Just how old was he? She wished he hadn't roped her into all of this, as she was a woman who only wanted an uncomplicated life, and all he seemed to create was convolution. Alas, there had been no one else trustworthy enough and at least somewhat knowledgeable enough of this tangled family tree who could have delivered the message of this meeting to Beauregard.

She stood outside the whispering coven of persons beholden to Beatrice and, she supposed, Belle and grew more and more uneasy about her interloping until one of the lads, the dark-haired one with a golden heart, ushered her forward as well—inviting her further into the mystery, into this queer family, from which she knew she might never be released.

V

LANDSPEAKER

D awn was a sword that cleaved the sky and split the clouds with golden blood; uncommon brilliance for a Pandemonian morning. The company hissed and grumbled as they began to stir. They groaned and massaged their sore elbows and hips, which had rested on stone last night. All except the Wolf and Morigan, who had long been awake. After that great flash of dawn, the sun faded away, swallowed by fog. Sleepily, the waking company cast stares into the obscure reaches of the mist that flowed about the shattered carpal outcrops and mossy bridges of the land.

It was a strange and quiet realm to which they'd come. It was a change from the rent flats around Eatoth, or from the region of purple fields and rivers through which they'd subsequently hiked. Sleek, hairless, wet creatures, some legged, some clawed, snuffled and hunted in the fern gullies that grew in the shelter of stone arches and hills. Winged eels, relatives of this leech ecology, fluttered through the mist in flocks, while the basest of the species—eyeless snakes—swam the many creeks and pools. Those creatures were easily caught and edible, with a tasty pink meat enjoyed after they were skinned and roasted.

While the company shuffled around, pissing and shaking off sleep's heavy hand, the Wolf and his bloodmate prepared the morning's meal. Morigan looked road sore and haggard, which was unusual for her. The dreamscape she and her Wolf had shared had been an invigorating hunt across an ethereal forest of smoky trees. At one point during their dream-hunt, she had stopped, her sixth sense caught in a waft of movement, and she'd stared off into the distance while he raced ahead. Now he wondered if she had seen something troubling last night, for she was looking away from him, her expression tight and haunted.

What is it, my Fawn?

That dog again. I thought I saw it last night in Dream as well.

Where is it now? The Wolf looked around.

Morigan paused her preparations, laying down eel and blade. Last night she had seen a glint of the creature—its mothy form leaking light—through the trees in the forest of Dream. She saw it again at this very moment, as it stared down on the company from atop a curve of green. But she hadn't tried chasing the apparition either then or now, for she knew it could not be caught, for it was not real. It was a presence that existed outside of life and time. Dead. As if it were—

A memory, she spoke, without truly understanding the depth of her statement. *A memory of something grand. I feel as if it is leading us somewhere.*

Then we shall follow this guide.

I believe we are, as we head toward the Cradle. She had taken her eye off the mongrel to address her bloodmate and was not shocked to see it had disappeared when she looked back. She returned to her work, and the Wolf watched her, cautiously, as he prodded the fire to life.

It wasn't long before the smell of food lured Talwyn and Pythius from wherever they'd spent the night over to the fire. Arms slung around each other, with clothing still ruffled from recent robing and disrobing, the scholar and shaman emerged through a damp, green veil and joined the others without questions. Those who might poke fun had already been informed that Talwyn and Pythius were "courting," as was the Amakri custom. As Talwyn had informed them, they weren't having sex—not that anyone would have been overly prudish after Morigan and the Wolf's displays of public carnality. Really, the only concern the Wolf had was that the men stay near enough to camp for safety, which they did.

After gorging themselves on leech-fish and water, they set out. Adam had breakfasted on hard-shelled nuts, and still, rather selfishly, none had heeded or asked about his complete transition from omnivore to herbivore.

Although the Wolf had vouched for the safety of their breakfast, the food had not agreed with Mouse, and she stayed at the back of the travelers, passing well-timed gas whenever the thick ferns thwacked her and her friends as they dove into the land's chirruping dells. Down in these pathways that ran under the green-shagged arches of rock, the mist gathered in dense breaths and wet everything around it, and eventually she stopped shivering whenever a leech-beast of the peaceful quadruped variety—like a hog without hair, eyes, or features of any kind except for a mouth—brushed into her and squealed in fright. There were places where the greenery rose over her head, and the swish and slap of the wetlands became a mesmerizing music to which she drifted, as if sleepwalking. Then they would climb the land, they'd emerge from the dell, and she'd breathe that first breath of the awake. She'd felt somnolent too many times on this journey, she realized. As though she were a helpless passenger in this dream, or nightmare. And there was an awful sense that their journey was coming to an end, one that she feared. Would they know peace or doom? Would Brutus know justice? What would she do with herself if she lived? So much was uncertain.

While hiking up a battered hill tumbled with weeds, pebbles, and sheets of moss that tore to brown flesh, Mouse realized that Morigan was now at her side. It hadn't been one of her silver magik tricks either; Mouse had simply been too absorbed in her brooding to notice her friend's approach.

"How strange. I smelled your unease; and I'm not talking about your making wind," Morigan said, nudging a laugh out of her friend. "I can smell things that I never could before: the spice of the soil of which Caenith always speaks, some dung over yonder, and the scent of your fear. It's a bit like lemons and sweat. I have changed so much; I even feel my speech reformed with the poetry of my mate, sometimes so much that I cannot recognize my own voice. I don't know when it happened, but I've lost my fear of that transformation. We are on a most amazing journey, my friend. We are following a path that no one else will ever take. They will write songs and tell inflated tales of our triumphs—and we shall triumph. We have each found something on this journey..." Morigan pointed ahead to Moreth. "Even humility. So whatever end we create to our tale—even if it's bittersweet—our timeless souls shall always have the memory of our pack."

"I know," replied Mouse, though she remained filled with doubts.

"Does that not please you?"

"It does. It's just that I've changed, too. I've seen the deepest cruelty of man. I've bargained with a Lord of Creation. I've slain horrors with a sword of light. It's all very epic, we can agree. And yet, it's the smaller things that have affected me most. My father. My uncle. The friendship that you and I share."

"You've come to know love, and family."

"I have. I never believed—not once—that I would experience such blessings. I thought they were porcelain dreams, made to be broken, and yet I've held so many, so soon, and only a few have shattered. I can't bring my father back, although..."

Something sparked in the honeycomb of the seer's head; the bees began to buzz and whisper their secrets to her. She heard a baritone laugh, felt a beard against her cheek and something soft glide over her skin—a man's touch. Then, a small hand suddenly grabbed her pant leg, and a power kicked in her stomach. Morigan gasped.

"Ah..." said the seer, as silver fire flickered in her eyes. "You want a dream that belongs only to you."

"I do."

The women had stopped and were now holding each other by the forearms, as though in expectation of either wondrous or dire news. Neither woman could form Mouse's vague fantasy into a desire. Instead, they bit back their tears, grinned, and celebrated Mouse's absurd, vaporous future and family that wasn't and might never be.

"I think that after all this queerness," confessed Mouse, "I only want something normal. A stone to honor my father's grave. A home away from all the iron memories that haunt me. Maybe even—"

Morigan pulled her friend close and kissed her upon the cheek. "Shhh. I know. Say no more. Your dream is a treasure, and I shall protect it. My life is not destined for normal things. It can never turn that way again. I know that. I must and have accepted it. You can be my dream of a normal life, then. I love you, Fionna, as my one and dearest friend."

"Oh, I love you too!"

Like foolish old widows, they embraced and shuddered with happy sobs.

"Women," muttered Moreth, who'd paused to glance down the hill at the ladies and sighed. Casual disdain was a mask he wore well, yet he winced from holding the expression—*or was that pain?* wondered the Wolf. Moreth seemed as moved as the men standing beside him, also watching, and were it not for that stink the Menosian carried, the Wolf would have been convinced. In a sand, red-eyed and raw-nosed, Morigan and Mouse rejoined their companions.

"Look ahead," said Mouse, "and mind your business."

Below their small peak, the vale of green hillocks swimming in the mist seemed as deep and forlorn as a mysterious archipelago. A flock of black worms soared overhead in an arc before diving into the mist, their wet warbles lingering in an echo long after they had vanished. Morigan and Mouse shoved past the men and descended, as if they'd somewhere important to get to.

✳ ✳ ✳

II

Another few sunrises and the realm of leech beasts and mists had faded to a gray smudge on the horizon at their backs. The company's time there had afflicted nearly everyone's constitutions, and they were grateful to be free of it. Even Moreth seemed sapped of his usual gibes once the cramping—or another pain, the Wolf suspected—started to twist his innards into a cat's cradle; he'd spent his final evening watch in that place shitting himself pale in the ferns. The bloodmates were unaffected by the gamy diet; in fact, they rarely went to the bathroom anymore as far as their companions had noticed. Adam, too, was sound in constitution, though he hadn't shared any of the meat with them, sustaining himself like a peaceful hermit living off berries and fruits.

Morigan and the Wolf led their compatriots across the latest realm: an unstable, shaking flatland of high valleys and perilous gulfs. While the land could be relatively easily traversed, a brutal wind threw crumbled earth into their faces, though not one of them flinched. When, on occasion, a skittering herd of hissing, blue-shelled lizards crawled toward them, the Wolf and Morigan's barking, as well as a spectacle of lights from Thackery's newest staff, scared away the horde. They tempered their aggressions against what seemed gentler creatures meandering the clouds. Those beasts were beautiful twisting impressions that shone with colors as they wove in and out of the firmament. What they were, none could declare. Only the Wolf had a keen enough stare, and his frown told others that they wouldn't find the reality as lovely as they'd imagined.

At times the clouds would darken suddenly, and they would be forced to hide under rocky humps that leaned out and overhung the land, where they'd stay for a while watching lightning strike in dazzling spears. During these storms there was rarely rain, only rage, and a few times dissolved gobs of pulsing light came down smoldering from the heavens. Wandering out after the storm, Talwyn examined a glowing puddle left behind and concluded it constituted the remains of sky creatures who'd been struck by lightning; in death they seemed like radioactive pastels melted, mixed, and spat upon the earth.

Another sharp turn in the weather saw a snowfall of crystal knives and pellets besiege the company. They had no stone hideaways available to them this time and sheltered themselves as best they could in a copse of twisted trees. For the remainder of their journey, they rested in these way stations of rock or copse, conserving as much food and water as possible, while the land provided them with an unpleasant feast of beetles and large, hairy spiders—the lizards and sky beasts had since vanished. There wasn't a drop of water to be found, either. However, Adam had deduced that the trees could be tapped for a pungent sap filled with nutrients and thin enough to ingest like treacle.

One afternoon they stopped for Adam and the Wolf to milk the trees while their thirsty friends huddled in a cold circle. Creatures hissed in the canopy yet didn't make good on any threats.

"It's out of balance," said Pythius to his chosen.

"The land?" asked Talwyn.

"Yes, this hostility and clashing of elements is unusual—even for my land. We must be nearing the Cradle."

Soon, Caenith and Adam came over with canteens filled with the nourishing sap. While they waited for a storm to pass they sipped, watching winter ravage the trees and coat the land in snow, wondering not for the first time what the chattering things were that roosted above them in these forests. Again, the Wolf kept his own counsel on this matter. Indeed, he could have told the others of the hundreds of monkeys staring down at them, with spiderlike eyes bulging out of their faces. Or of their starving, ragged grins distorted by rows of sharp baby-cannibal teeth. Perhaps he could have also mentioned their irregularly positioned arms and legs, pink and curled like mouse tails, which they used to cling to the treetops against winter's cold winds. However, he decided that his companions didn't need be advised of these little carnivores, because despite all appearances, they would not attack them. Judging by the insect husks and bones of animals strewn across the woodlands, these creatures were aggressively hostile. However, around the company these behaviors had changed to docility and patience, as if the small monsters were held at bay by his low-throat growl and nothing else. Dumb carnivores should be dumb, not obedient or wary of death, considered the Wolf. No matter, proper cannibals were only a few days away, and certainly smarter than these vermin. It was wiser to save his grit for those nightmares than these petty, oddly behaved horrors.

Are you afraid, aroused, or hungry, my Fawn? Morigan's curious scent pulled him away from brooding; it was a bittersweet mix of wine and chocolate.

Morigan leaned in to her standing mate, kissing him deeply. *I am ready to put this cosmic monster into her grave.*

We shan't have to wait long, my Fawn.

Beyond the woods, he'd seen shadows to the east, a jumble of nonsensical shapes—cones, hooks, pyramids, and towers that formed a messy playground of chaos scribbled overhead by lambent markings that could be thunder or stars. It would be the greatest storm they had ever known, one to put the frostfire to shame. They would be walking into it to claim their weapon to end the Black Queen. He was ready, too. Though his thirst extended beyond that vile queen, to his father and Amunai as well. No tree sap would slake his desire to be quenched by their blood.

III

They continued their march through dim days and darker nights. The sun teased them, never revealing itself for more than a few sands. The weather didn't improve, but in fact grew more temperamental, launching hail at them before sheets of rain to wash it all away, which turned to glassy ice, before furious lightning storms smashed it all asunder only to begin the cycle again. Ash despoiled the land after every cycle of brutal weather, a rage meant to destroy whatever life might adamantly decide to call this dread realm home. They passed great potholes, filled with snow or water, depending on the season of the day. Slag of what might have been wood or even stone warned them how lucky they had been.

Since entering this territory, the Wolf had forbidden anyone, including Talwyn and Pythius, from separating themselves from the group. For a time, all they had to worry about was the declining number of woodland circles from which to harvest drinkable fluid, and the fact that they had only many-legged, antennaed roaches as large as housecats to consume. Mouse couldn't bring herself to put a single piece of their squashy meat to her lips. When Morigan made them into a more digestible "stew," as she called her abominable, uncooked, squash-stringed porridge, Mouse tested her bravery but was forced to swallow her vomit. She imagined the paste wriggling back out of her mouth, and got one, maybe two swallows down before passing the communal bowl along. Mouse eventually asked Adam for some of the nuts he'd preciously hoarded; she'd noticed him stuffing them into his cheeks like a sneaky squirrel. She'd finally realized that he had been eating nuts, roots, and foraged scraps of the earth this whole time.

Their concerns over food and sleeping arrangements quickly diminished in importance once their streak of "good" fortune ended and their nightly shelter was set ablaze by a bolt of skyfire. Running for their lives, with the Wolf smacking and hurling flaming debris aside to clear a path through the inferno, Mouse glanced up to catch sight of the long-hidden spider monkeys as their sizzling corpses dropped from the trees. *Screaming, flaming spider monkeys*, was all Mouse thought, and was reminded of Menos's inferno.

Once out of immediate danger, they continued through the night. Here more than anywhere else in Pandemonia, they realized, they were at nature's mercy, and she was ruthless. She would punish them even more as they reached the final stretch. But they knew that at the end of that gauntlet was a prize, something sacred and protected. Thus, they marshaled their fortitude against the elements, drove themselves forward.

It wasn't long before the gatherings of white trees had vanished, and thus their reserves of sap were exhausted. None of them had washed for days, though the smell of the land—that of scorch and bitterness borne in every windy fart blown into their mouths—concealed their unwashed odors. On the last day of their march it rained, and the pack cheered. The Wolf roared, lapping at the raindrops, thrashing his wet mane and wildly kissing his bloodmate. Chaos ruled in Pandemonia, however, and hourglasses later that jubilation transformed into damp discontent—the rain would not cease. Many muddy footsteps and a shivering sleep huddled under a downpour hence, and the realm of thunder, snow, stone, ghost trees, and spider monkeys was drowned by a swamp. In a miasmic dawn, a mire unfolded before them, of a scope and grimy splendor not even Alabion's swamps could match.

From end to end, the land bubbled as a brown stew, stirred by teetering claws of driftwood hung in black nets, and thickened by forests of reeds that one would need a plow to clear. Without a doubt, the turbid water would suck at them like quicksand, and they'd join the rotting hulks of the behemoths whose cavities rose in filth-barnacled stalagmites, and which could only be partially blamed for the rotten-vegetable stink of this swamp. Other muddy corpses, much younger and smaller, rose and fell lethargically on the mucky tides that washed to the shore, which really was only a section of mud in which the company's feet left deep impressions.

A few more steps, and they would be ankle deep. A few more after that, and they'd be up to their hips and fortunate to make it out. There was a chain of landmasses in the distance of varying size, some tiny enough for a single person to inhabit, forged from the fossilized remains of dead animals, which could be seen to form a lunatic's route through the mire. It was the only option forward; to the north and south the waters were just as stagnant, if not deeper and more dangerous. And the Wolf had heard bugs that buzzed like machines of razorblades and chitin in those regions and knew they must've been of formidable size, or numbers, to have taken down some of the dead titans before him.

"This is worse than that mud pit in Alabion," complained Mouse, before emitting a quiet yelp. Streaming filth, a huge, undulating mass flapped out of the swamp and flew off into the shroud of the horizon. Though it was daytime, the sun made no appearances here, and Mouse was spared illuminating details of the monster aside from its enormous size—vehicular—and waggling body and wings. It had a call like a ship's horn, only wetter. "I don't know what that was, either. Definitely worse than the last swamp."

"Definitely," agreed Thackery.

"We can get some footing on those greenish masses ahead," said the Wolf and stamped forward till his knees were swallowed before surveying the movements and lay of the land. "Be careful where you step. Hardly anything is solid. Follow my footsteps, and do not chance to step outside the path I make."

No one moved forward, and nor did he move himself. The whip of unease had struck the beast in his soul. He adjusted the bag of irons slung over his shoulder, which ever so slightly sizzled their magik through burlap and into his back. Lately their weight had been troublesome, though he knew that was from psychological and not physical strain. Perhaps that was what troubled his mate, too—this bag, its burden, and what they would do with those chains if given the opportunity. Would they even use them? Or would ripping out his father's throat be the more merciful solution?

'Tis not that, my Wolf, said Morigan, whose heart was also flickering with fear.

He turned to see his bloodmate still and staring at the sky. *Then what?*

Can't you feel it? A woman had been standing beside her only a moment ago, a phantom of white with a scarf of colors, and she'd spun for a speck amid a room of murmuring people—sages, kings, queens, and noble people all with faces wan from terror. Fate was tearing apart reality to show her the screeching velocity with which her demise was approaching.

Can't you see it, my Wolf? Look! she commanded.

He did, as did everyone else, though they knew not wherefore until her magik, her prescient thrall, trained their eyes on a dot in the gray sky, a fleck that was nothing and everything—antimatter, incalculable darkness, the end of all life. The Black Star. It would reveal itself in all its vile glory soon, to those who didn't have oracular or wolfish sight, and to that slimy shivering realization the others returned while Morigan and the Wolf continued to gaze upward.

"Thirty days," she said, and somehow, they all knew what she meant.

IV

Three weeks until the world was to end; this was the spark needed to get the company's fire roaring. Pythius and Talwyn were a bit slower in following as the scholar had to explain the convoluted calendar of Central Geadhain: seven to twelve days per week (depending on holidays and civic dates, with an average of ten), three to four weeks per month, thirteen months in a year, four hundred and some days each year to account for the long spinning of

Geadhain's mass through space. Their preoccupations made the plunge down the wobbling, mud-sluiced stone path into the eternal bog—one that the Wolf had assured them was *safe*—a little less taxing. The Wolf wouldn't allow them to wade further than into the shallows they'd crossed earlier, though he didn't say why. The warm mist of the bog gave nearly everyone rashes on their faces, hands, and any other areas of skin that were exposed. As if that weren't alarming enough, black shapes glided in the sea of slop, occasionally rising to seize a glistening frog-like creature, the size of a dog, from its grand lily pad.

The strange thorny tangles that hissed like cats when torn gave them more than enough troubles on the relatively dry land to even consider the threats in the water. Even following Caenith's path, their footing wasn't sure. They walked in pairs to bear the burden and care for the other: Adam and Mouse, Talwyn and Pythius, Moreth and Thackery, and the bloodmates who led them.

When Mouse—who was still quite a terrible adventurer—slipped, her walking partner saved her from taking a brown bath. Her boot was soaked through, and shortly afterward her shin began to feel quite warm. When the warmth persisted for a few sands and she began to feel woozy, the group paused on one of the tiny islands and laid her in a bassinet of moss and hissing twigs—it offered as much comfort here as anything else in this ghastly place. The Wolf rolled up her pant leg and took a look. Mouse glanced also, at least until the terror and blood loss made her faint. For attached to her leg was a parasite—brown, blubbery, and with a centipede's many appendages, all fixed like hooks into her white flesh. The creature's beaded head suckled at her skin and swelled red from her blood. By the time she'd been fanned back awake, the creature was a dead, splatted mass next to the Wolf's sandal, and Talwyn had finishing bandaging her ripped leg. Blood dotted through the fabric.

"My thanks, you two," she said. "I hate bugs."

Small legs skittered on her fingers, and she leapt up and audibly shuddered.

"'Tis best that we continue and do not dip into the water again," said the Wolf. "There are far worse creatures around us than those pests."

Indeed, this was one of Pandemonia's wickedest realms, a place not meant for mortals, but for primeval and terrible beasts engaged in an orgy of hunting. A horde of the armored mosquitoes the Wolf had heard from far away flew in that afternoon. The whirling mass detached itself from the sky as if it were a child of the storm clouds. At that, the Wolf motioned for the company to be still, waited to see where the buzzing breeze would blow, and watched with his huddled friends as the clacking, clattering, droning flock of things that were as black and excitable as magpies whirled above them. The Wolf hissed at Thackery to kill the light in his staff, lest it draw attention. They prepared for the worst.

"Go away," whispered Adam, annoyed.

The horde gathered and funneled off like living smoke. Farther out in the fog a shape lumbered: one of the horned armadillos that could trample a house, and which the company had so far only encountered from a distance. The stream of demon-mosquitoes whirled toward it and then descended upon it. The armadillo's bleats were heard until the insect swarm had fully masticated its throat. After its death came an eerie quiet, where naught but the buzz and bubble of the cauldron was heard.

As they moved on, the Wolf dismissed the notion that Adam had magikally Willed the horde away; he'd felt no sorcerous static and smelled no waft of ozone. It was surely a coincidence. Perhaps their constant terror was breeding paranoia in him, between this fancy with Adam and the notion that Moreth was growing somehow paler—and smellier, even—than the rest of them. His odor had, however, transformed from the sourness of rot and disease into the briny scent of afterbirth. Without a doubt the odor came from Moreth, and it was getting stronger—so much so that the others might soon notice it.

What troubles you? whispered Morigan.

I am not sure yet, my Fawn, though I believe Moreth's health may be in question. Morigan started to turn, and the Wolf stopped her. *It is the same condition as before, I feel: an illness or disease. Although...the fragrance: there is a scent of life to it. I cannot explain. Do not ask him, my Fawn. The Menosian is a creature of pride and honor. He would not want us to draw attention to his weakness. If he is ill, it will be clear, soon enough. Allow him his dignity until then. Perhaps he will tell us before we must demand it of him.*

In mild protest, Morigan crossed her arms. *I shan't lose another companion. Moreth has proven himself as one of heart and valor. My patience goes only so far, my Wolf, and there are times that I dislike these manly virtues of yours that seem so much like fickle pride. If his health worsens, or he doesn't share with us his trials in another few hourglasses, then I shall ask him.*

As you wish.

Their feud felt as gloomy as the weather and affected the pack behind them. Later, and in a welcome reprieve from the bloodmates' silent spat, Pythius remarked on the great cycle of decay and birth that surrounded them. Talwyn passed on his theories about the environment to the company, as well as his own observations, shouting over the sound of the swamp so that everyone could hear.

"Close to the Cradle, the magik becomes so dense that you'll actually find lands that are less mutable in their environments than other places on Pandemonia. Places like the Forever Stones. While he's never been this far, Pythius believes that we're wandering the Swallowing Sands."

"But there's no sand," noted Mouse, scuffing the wet rock with her boot. "I wish there were."

"Not now," said Talwyn. "These fixed points of elemental power still suffer from the whims of Pandemonia, and they tend to veer from one environmental polarity to another. Just as Moreth recalled the Forever Stones being a lush, tropical jungle, while what we saw was a world sealed in ice. Likewise, in time, all of what we see here will waste and wither away to damning dryness. Only that change will occur slower than Pandemonia's other transitions, and it will repeat itself, *cyclically*, not chaotically as we see everywhere else. We should be grateful, really, that we've come during a wet season."

"Yes, how wonderful," she replied.

At that snark, the conversation felt closed. The realm was hostile to conviviality anyway; leave a mouth open for too long and something would fly into it. Nor could they talk away their doom, and thus they hurried down the path chosen by their grunting leader, who cleared whole logs and thorny obtrusions as though they were but twigs and twine. The Wolf appeared to all to be angry, though no one felt brave enough to ask what had stirred his temper. A few times, he glared at the slowly rolling dusk, as it bled the horizon grayer and grayer into what would be pitch darkness. It was as if he were counting sands, or was watching the Black Star rise from behind.

In the dark it would be difficult to proceed, and the floating wisps of yellow light that appeared in the swamp were temptations meant to mislead rather than guide the travelers. When they came to a large stone platform that was mostly free of entanglements, the Wolf bade them halt. They cleared themselves a space in which to rest while the Wolf skulked off to find food. Thackery gathered together the driest weeds and reeds he could find and treated the company to a fire—sparked with a glance and a burst of his pure white Will. The flames retained that pale hue and bathed the companions in warm, dry air. In no time at all, the seven of them were relaxing, and even testing their mud-smeared faces with smiles. The world might be nearing its end, but it was companionship that had brought them this far, and it was that fellowship that would be celebrated come what may. The mood remained cheerful until Mouse, curious, kicked the bag of chains the Wolf was rarely without, the clatter shattering their bliss.

"What's the idea with those?" asked Mouse.

"Chains," replied Morigan.

"Clearly. Although you and the big man haven't been too chatty on the matter. What are they for?"

"For his father."

Talwyn gasped. "We're expected to subdue Brutus and put those on him?"

"Once we find Brutus, yes, that would be the plan," replied Morigan, realizing they had formed such an anemic strategy for dealing with Brutus, having discussed nothing of that battle other than the chase to reach it.

"Don't scoff," she continued. "Those chains are wonders of Eatoth. They will turn his own magik against him and render him powerless. They are one of the tools with which we shall win this war. Now it's only a matter of hunting him down. We know he's here, somewhere, and he knows we're here. A confrontation is inevitable." Her eyes glimmered—wishful or portentous stars in the dark. "He will come for me, and his son, and we must be at the ready for when he does. We cannot hesitate. Hopefully, by then, we shall have a remedy for the parasite that has infected his soul. If not, we shall leave him in chains until we do."

"You sound so sure," said Thackery, who was anything but.

"I am. I must be. We cannot fail. There is no time left for alternative tactics. We strike down the mad king, bind him, and cleanse him."

"What of the Dreamstalker, Amunai?" asked Thackery.

"I shall end her myself. I owe her a slip of the knife that took her sister." Morigan slunk her hand to the cold hilt of her promise dagger, and caressed it as tenderly as the cock of her lover.

THWACK!

The sudden splatting of carcasses upon stone startled even the most steadfast of those gathered. The Wolf had returned, with fortuitously grim timing, and had cast dead, wet things upon the ground for them to eat. Only Morigan had not been surprised by his sudden arrival, having sensed him; she knelt and began gutting their dinner. People were afraid to ask what was being served from the bloodmates who were both quickly covered in blood; Morigan and the Wolf were sharing their sentiments, feeding off each other's rage. Mouse wished she knew what it was all about. Rather than ask, Mouse and the others humbly slurped from the communal bowl as it was passed around, gagging down their questions along with the blubbery hash. Keeping with custom, Adam chewed on what berries and roots he'd carefully scavenged. Not since before Eatoth had the metallic sweetness of blood wet his lips; even watching his companions eat animal flesh made his stomach contort. No one but Mouse had noticed his change in appetites. Indeed, no one seemed to notice much about him these days.

As the others ate, Morigan and her mate descended upon the bony remains of the carcasses and tore apart what was left like dogs gone wild. Mouse barely recognized her friend in the snarling red countenance that whipped up from the carcass. Suddenly, Morigan remembered her manners; she wiped her face and hands and returned to the graceful, fearsome woman Mouse and the others loved.

"I am sorry," she said. "Caenith would like to press on through the night. We can have a proper rest once we've passed beyond this region. He says that it isn't far."

"Can he speak for himself?" asked Mouse. A secret, or two, or three, was being kept by the bloodmates. She walked up to the Wolf, who was hunched over and glaring into the gloomy sea with its strange bobbing lights, and poked him in the back. "You there. I know your tells, and you do nothing to hide them. You've caught wind of something, or it's caught wind of us. What is it?"

"Danger." He snarled. Mouse waved her hand flamboyantly for more information, which the Wolf didn't divulge beyond vagueness. "I sensed a presence while I was hunting. Nay, I sensed it even earlier. I'm sensing too many things these days for me to react to everything; my instincts are strained and strung. Still, I felt a shiver when you spoke of my father. A flutter of your whispers came to me during my hunt. I have also sensed a watchful evil since we came here, though I cannot say from what well it springs."

"Your instincts are never wrong." Mouse threw back her cloak. "Let's move."

Thackery snuffed out his fire, and blackness swallowed them once again. As they assembled behind the bloodmates, Morigan considered asking Thackery to conjure a bit of his witch fire to light the swirling murk ahead, in which she saw naught but nightmare whirls. Such a beacon might further endanger them to whatever peril her bloodmate had sensed, and the going would be perilous, regardless...

At that moment, Adam made a noise, like a whistle but longer, and a miracle happened.

Beyond, misty yellow spheres floated in the night abyss, and upon the changeling's whistle, they began drifting and rearranging themselves. With a chaotic elegance, hundreds of these stars bobbed against one another like blindfolded but trained dancers in a ballroom. After a moment they began to synchronize, and the lights spun nearer, circled, and nudged themselves into a formation: a lane of stars, which rambled off into the dark. Gatherings of the wisps perched on driftwood and reed, acting as lampposts; the companions could have been staring down one of Eod's most enchanted streets. No one could explain it, or Adam's involvement, and nor were any paranormal senses tingled by magik. It was as if Pandemonia, the cruelest of all the Green Mother's children, had suddenly decided to delight its victims with faery-tale mystery and charm.

"Do we take the path?" asked Talwyn, his scientific mind automatically conjuring distrust for this serendipitous development.

It was Adam who moved first, walking down the wet stone road, which seemed to be even more perfect than the ones the Wolf had found. Adam said, "This is the path."

Everyone else followed, finally aware that a strangeness, a shift in confidence—perhaps power—had taken place in the young changeling. The delicate glass creatures that lit their way were remarkable. With all the horrors beyond reckoning they had witnessed, these creatures possessed a beauty that stirred the friends deeply. About as large as sparrows, with the pale bodies of crayfish before they matured, and with the most delicate lacy wings, these were small wonders. But it was their tribal headdresses of lucent filaments that gave them their shining beauty, these matching threads of magik to the gold whorls seen within their immaterial shells. They ruffled their glass and feather wings and peered upon the strangers with their beaded rows of crimson eyes—the only solid color visible within their auric forms.

They whistled to the travelers through cruel-looking curved beaks that likely never snapped at anything more than a fat spider, and were now being used as instruments for their soft, whistling chorus. The light these creatures shone was more than physical; it inspired the travelers with visions, memories, and the passion of hope. Never did the companions scare the hundreds upon hundreds of singing things, nor did they feel worried, or in the slightest way beguiled by them, as they walked their path. These creatures were, in fact, leading Caenith away from the danger he had sensed was approaching.

I cannot explain this, my Fawn. I feel as if this is magik, though I see only the grace of nature, which I did not believe Pandemonia could have. In Pandemonia, we have been stalked, left alone for easier prey, or been the biggest predator in our domain, yet never have we been guided and blessed by nature's hand.

Adam is the source of our blessing, said Morigan, and the bloodmates stared—as one force—at the ivy-scribed back of the lad who had now assumed the role of guide. In the bloodmates' minds swelled a cloud of memory that crackled with flashes of the changeling's many silent achievements: slaying a boar that pleaded for its life, courting a flock of butterflies, glancing to bloodthirsty spider monkeys that clamored for the flesh of the company, or chastising a swarm of black razor-jawed beetles. Adam had touched Nature, and she had embraced him back. Somehow, each entity with which he'd communed had respected Adam's calm, understated diplomacy, a skill he had honed in his discussions with the council of New Eatoth, a talent honed as an artist—they who listen to the world and hear how it wants to be shaped. Adam was a child of peace, and among the shadows of the great beings with whom he walked, his elegance, as delicate as that of the light-bearers now surrounding them, and his aptitude for communication had metamorphosed into a divine gift. Adam had told Elemech that he wanted to hear and know all the voices of the world. It seemed those voices, great to small, would hear him, too. Suddenly, the bloodmates understood, and gave themselves to the thrill of being present for a grand mystery. They did not share the changeling's secret. As a humble man, he wouldn't want them to announce his greatness.

As the group wandered on, however, everyone began to notice Adam's new confidence. They noticed the enormous three-headed serpents that spooled on the path and slithered off into the steaming bog as Adam neared. They watched the constant shifting dance of light-bearers that flew in flocks from behind to ahead to repave and spotlight the road through the bog. All the while, they still fought against reason to accredit these miracles to this modest man as he strode though a phantasmagoric hallway of nature, occasionally giving a queer whistle of thanks to the creatures who illuminated the darkness. Eventually, Adam's grace was irrefutable, for the politely slithering snakes, migrating flock of lights, and even the reptilian whales and rhinoceroses that swam in the brown sea and shifted rotten trees and rocks up ahead to extend the golden road shattered any of the company's lingering doubts.

They walked faster and more excitedly than before. They were no longer afraid of what was ahead or of what they'd left behind. A few times, Pythius muttered a phrase with which Talwyn was unfamiliar: *Gaeomina*. After a few passes, Talwyn worked out the expression meant "Landspeaker," and he spoke it aloud.

"What?" hissed Thackery, turning from up ahead.

"Landspeaker," repeated Talwyn. "It's some kind of Amakri term associated with the wise persons we saw in the first age—those who dealt with spirits and elements. I know not what it means beyond that, though his reverence feels no less than mine at what we are seeing."

Above Adam circled a terrifying creature that resembled a prehistoric bird hung in a shredded sheet; it cawed triumphantly. With a rustle, a new flock of light-bearers soared over the travelers, too, and fluttered down the long golden road to rest on sunken trees and sliding mud shacks to light the night anew. Whatever else Thackery might have asked was abandoned in his wonder.

"Gaeomina," muttered Pythius. He was sure what they were witnessing, and he drew Talwyn close to whisper. "When we are young Keepers and learning about our powers, the land speaks to us. It tells us secrets: where danger lurks, where water can be found, which pits bear fangs, and which are safe to shelter in for the night. When we accept our power, when we become the caller and not the listener, that pact changes, West Sun."

"Changes how?" asked Talwyn.

"Like the child who grows from wrestling drakagir to the warrior who hunts drakagor, the balance of power shifts, and so, too, does the balance of respect. Do you remember the stories I told you as we lay together, West Sun? Of the lords of wing and scale?"

Those memories had grown hazy from lust, though Talwyn never had to dig too deeply for information. As Talwyn recalled, the drakagir were the infant variant of drakagor, the enormous chasm-striding lizards covered in hard scales and horny protrusions that could rear up and walk on two legs, or fly on massive cartilaginous wings. The oldest of their species—they could live for a thousand years or more—were said to spit toxic phlegm that could dissolve a man on contact. The adults of the species showed no paternal or maternal instincts, abandoning the eggs of their young after mating—a ritual that was shrouded in esotericism, since studying the dangerous creatures wasn't a vocation one pursued. The abandoned clutch, even with the nigh-iron shells of the drakagor's eggs, was only safe in Pandemonia's ecology for so long before animals or natural disasters eradicated the brood. And so for all the doom brought by the adult creatures, the young, the drakagir, were thought of as a great fortune and discovery among the Amakri. Finding a brood was akin to striking feliron in the West, for the shells could be forged into weapons, and the beasts themselves, once born, secreted marvelous oils and shed scales that, once mixed and ground, could treat illness and wounds.

By Pandemonia's queer design, these infant beasts did not despise the Amakri but rather loved them. However, a young shaman, not yet a Keeper of his tribe, was needed to keep the lizards' warring instincts under control. Without a young shaman around, the beasts turned as violent as their parents. For every legend about the graces of the drakagor, there were horrifying anecdotes of a young shaman developing his adult talents early, or passing away in a tragedy, and the beasts of scales and poison who had been under the child's care unleashing their grief by terrorizing the tribe. In any event, were drakagir broodlings ever discovered, they were let loose in the wild before their adulthood, or before the rites that turned their Amakri caregiver into a Keeper—the inheritance of memories from the previous shaman, and the realization of the gift of Will. The transformation from a novice to a Keeper, from innocence to control, corrupted whatever spiritual bond a young man had shared with a drakagor.

As fascinating as these beasts were, Talwyn scratched his head to find Adam's connection to the shaman's analogy.

"I'm stumped," he said. It was an unfortunate Western colloquialism that confused Pythius, but once sorted, Pythius explained.

"When we are young, we hear the earth, we feel her, and know her as only a child—full of hope, light, and wonder. When we are older, when we seek to control, rather than be at peace with, our land, the contract that we've made is written over in charcoal." He paused and reached out to one of the light-bearers whistling from a nearby drooping branch, and sighed as the creature crawled away from him.

"I could summon it, you know. With the fire in my soul. I could command its tiny mind to obey me. I told you the tale of when I first called a creature of the sky to me. Well, that was the moment where I broke my trust with the land. One can listen, one can ask, one can hunt as an animal of the land and return blood and bones to the soil without consequence, though once one takes, truly *takes* from the Green Mother, she will never forgive. She has not forgiven any of us since we ruined the Cradle—Geadhain's heart and soul."

"Are you telling me that all of this...?" Talwyn wanted to believe that Adam, the simple, uncomplicated changeling, had evoked some hitherto unknown and incredible power that made light-bearers, crocodile-horrors, mud whales, snakes, and carnivorous insects bow down to him. Nothing aside from untenable magik could explain nature's obedience. Adam had simply *asked*? He had asked the land to yield? Inconceivable.

"The softest voice is the one Geadhain hears," muttered the shaman, as he and his chosen held hands and beheld the shadow that guided them through the bog—the ivy on his back appearing to writhe in the light. "He is so soft, that boy, like a child of feathers and light. Long ago, the softest and sweetest souls spoke to nature, communed with her, and in respect, she answered their humble voices. I showed you this in the dream of my dead ancestors. When we cared for Geadhain, she cared for her children. Not since before the Cradle's destruction have I heard of anyone like this young man. I know why he has hidden his secret, for its beauty is of a frailty that must be hidden. What we are witnessing, West Sun, is the birth of legend. A Landspeaker. An avatar of Her voice; a spirit untouched by vice, deaf to every voice but the one—the most green and ancient. He may be the first, and last, of his kind in ten thousand of your Western years...or however long it has been since we were cast out of the Cradle. He is a miracle, but he should not be."

Talwyn watched Adam weave in and out of light and shadow, saw him move with Caenith's grace through water and reed. He felt as if he should bow to him like the silent beasts that bobbed in the bubbling brown sea, and knew that everything Pythius had said about the young man was true.

V

"What were we running from? Back in the swamp?" asked Mouse. She felt that posing a simple question, rather than attempting to tackle all the various complex thoughts that consumed their minds at the moment, would serve to break the insouciance that had fallen over them all.

Morning wrapped them in a cold blanket of musty dew, and they sat amid a sticky graveyard of fractured trees and hard mud. Farther on, green swaths and glimmering patches of water appeared on the land's rising, spotted quilt, and beyond lurked the shadows of spires, claws, and waves of rock that looked too impossible to be mountains. Peaks of Doom notwithstanding, the scenery was a pleasant change from the swamp. All that murk lay behind them, though a few of the light-bearing creatures had followed them out of the swamp. The creatures gathered by Adam where he sat, like a wise spirit-tender, on a tall rock near a watering hole.

Adam seemed to be watching the pale fish that swam in the water—*or talking to them*, thought Mouse. She asked her question again.

"Red Riders," said Adam and the Wolf at the same time.

The men stared at each other.

The Wolf rose from his place where he was crouched near the fire. "After considering, I recognized the scent of my father's fodder: burned and spoiled. How did you know?"

"I was told."

Adam went to speak again, then thought better of it. Supernatural empathy wasn't required to understand when a man was suffering from choices or fate, and Morigan, as a caring confidante, went to the changeling. She hunkered down near his feet and waited for him to look at her. Eventually, he cast his deep brown stare her way: these jewels of the woods, an amber of innocence and life.

"It has been happening for a while," confessed Adam, "this strangeness with animals. Ever since I stayed too long in my other skin. For weeks, I haven't been able to eat meat. I cannot when I can hear their voices, pleading. It would be no different from murdering a child. I know you haven't noticed my queer habits. No one has. I never wanted to trouble you or the others about the voices in my head."

Morigan took and caressed his trembling hand. "Adam, we are your friends, we share troubles. A pain to one of us is a pain to all."

"I did not need to be special," whispered Adam. "I came on this journey to walk with great men and women, to know the world. That was enough for me."

"We do not choose our gifts. I believe that my mother saw that within you—a seed of the wondrous, which she nurtured with her magik. Elemech's talisman was the key to unlocking your gift. I don't even know what to call what you've done, for it bears no whiff of magik nor weight of Will with which magik is associated. Thus, I shall say that you've discovered a precious gift, Adam, a secret of the old world, an inheritance that I, of all people, can understand carries with it a burden. Still, your gift has come to us when we need a guide, at a time when our sands are few, and the shadow war grows longer by the hourglass. I've learned that we must seize on a miracle when it presents itself. We must embrace it, and love it, for tomorrow it may be gone. That's what you did back in the swamp. You surrendered, and it was beautiful to behold. But do you know *how* you did what you did? Can you tap into that power once more?"

In the swamp, he'd fallen into a walking sleep; the dark and dreary march had rather subsumed his mind. When he had closed his eyes, he'd begun to think of the olden tales his mother wolf had told him, of when changelings honored both the land and the Ancients. He had begun to daydream about the feel of working stone with his hands; he'd even scratched his nose once or twice as though he might sneeze from a phantom itch of mason powder. He'd felt peaceful, drifting on the same steady sea of consciousness as when he crafted, when he touched nature. Nature had always understood him. She was his oldest friend, and the parent to whom he'd run once his mother had been taken by Aghna. And then, somewhere in that dream, he'd seen one of the beautiful glass birdlings, and he'd realized how, despite all the decomposition and muck the swamp was filled with, other glorious creations lived there too. Perhaps, he'd called out to a birdling, and then it came. He had simply seen it, reached out with mind, word, and emotion, and not only had he summoned the one birdling, but rather all the hundreds of its flock. Still in his hazy state, and abetted by the silent amazement of his companions, he'd floated outside of himself until morning's golden sting had woken him.

As he pondered Morigan's question, he thought of the birdlings and enchanted paths, and one of the creatures flew up from the ground and wrapped its dozens of legs around his forearm like a happy caterpillar. It gazed at him, its many crimson eyes bright from emotion. It was love, he felt, a raw unconditional love of him. Such was what he expressed and what the land was expressing to him in turn.

"I see that you have some understanding of your gift," remarked Morigan.

"But I cannot explain it," said Adam, smiling and stroking the soft wings of the creature that had landed on him.

"You don't have to."

Morigan left the changeling to contemplate both himself and the living wonder on his arm, and returned to the others. "Red Riders," she said, and set the mood to grim. "So they've followed us, then? Or they are aware of where we intend to go?"

"Both, I believe," said the Wolf.

"Rest up," commanded their warmother. She sniffed, her nostrils flaring and nose wrinkling wolfishly. "The water seems fresh—smells that way, at least. Let's refill our waterskins and wash some of the swamp from our hides. This may be our final repose before taking on the Scar."

They scattered from the fire, gathering water, counting and rationing out food. The latter became a depressing exercise, as they'd relied so heavily on the provisional skills of the Wolf, skills that would only eke so much blood from the stalwart land of stone into which they were headed. As Pythius had warned, the Scar was a land so angry that every animal was toxic and every stream polluted. Thus it was that the natives who lived there turned to one another for fluid and meat. While concentrating on their preparations, everyone tried to push those terrible thoughts aside, time and again. Regrettably, when they'd finished counting their stores, their bags only carried so much sustenance—the few scraps of dried meat and salted vegetables that they'd acquired in Eatoth. However, once Adam shared the contents of his haversack, they discovered he'd been an assiduous hoarder. He'd collected roots, berries, and fleshy nuts during his existence as a shadowy thief within the company. He didn't tell his fellows that he'd simply known which ones were safe to eat or that, at times, the plants had whispered their desire to be eaten so that they might sustain him. Adam's store would last them a while, if they were stingy with the dispensation. They could sustain eight persons for a week or thereabouts, and really, if they were in the Scar for longer than that, they would have spent too much time there anyway.

After they were packed up, the Wolf promised to try for one more good meal before they entered the shadowy pinnacles to the east. The company often stared at that cold vista, and when he returned, the meat he had hunted blanched in their mouths to a distaste as gray and forbidding as the smoldering fog that clutched at the distant towers of black, fragmented rock.

How old and destroyed was that place to seem so dead from afar? Dealing with their nerves aside, they ate all they could, knowing that there wouldn't be many more substantial meals in their future. Then they drank till their bellies ached, and a few of them stripped off their shirts to wash in the pool.

Talwyn and Pythius seemed more enamored with each other than they were intent on washing, and made Thackery—who washed with them—a trifle uncomfortable with their rough handling of chests, hands, half-tented trousers, and sloppy kisses. Adam didn't seem to take offense, and he idly splashed near the men while watching, and once waving to, one of the light-bearers perched on the rock he'd abandoned. Caenith snickered as the little thing waved a wing in return. On the other side of the wading pool, Mouse kept herself turned away from the others. No matter how much they had been through together, she was still embarrassed by her scars. Often her fingertips hovered over the spiderwebs of tissue that ran up from her loins. Only the bloodmates remained by the campfire, for other than the Wolf's handsome smell, and at best a fineness of dirt in their fingernails and hair, they were clean and stink-free. The providence of being an Immortal, remarked Morigan, who lay against the hot, hard chest of her bloodmate and petted the fur there. They folded into each other, he surrounding and entangling her with his limbs. She couldn't tell the start of her heartbeat or the end of his, and felt supremely content.

She didn't wonder why Moreth, his once white shirt now sewer-brown from sweat and filth, wasn't joining the others in a splash. Instead, he stayed nearby, huddled in his garments like a beggar, and rocked back and forth as though surrendering to a madness. He lacked his usual elegance. The slightly foul smell was as noticeable as a fart of spiced apples and compost. When she was sure none of the others were listening, she asked him, "You're ill or wounded. Which is it?"

Contesting the matter with a seer and a glaring wolf-man who'd surely smelled the decomposition happening in his body for days seemed pointless. Moreth darted his gaze around, then opened his jacket and pulled his shirt up from his waistline. He gave them a peek at the swollen black scrape across his abdomen, and they caught a strong whiff of the sweet and mulchy odor of his wound. Then he quickly tucked in his shirt and buttoned up his jacket.

"Thackery or Talwyn should take a look at that," said Morigan.

Moreth stabbed a finger at her and hissed. "No! Neither of those men should. There is nothing that they can do for me—"

"Moreth—"

"I thought you were all-knowing?" He heaved himself to a stand and leered at the bloodmates. They saw a sweat-beaded man battling terrible pain, an agony so severe that only someone with a strength of will such as

Moreth's could hold back the primal impulse to scream and writhe. Surely it was his Will—magikal or not—that had kept this grand fate from the seer, his end. Moreth was dying; he had to be.

Proud and menacing, he continued. "My wound comes from the talon of a blood eater. I must have suffered it when we recovered your father's damned chalice. I thought nothing of it, since the wounds from a blood eater are efficiently fatal. I should have been dead many weeks ago, and yet here I stand. I shall not die the shameful death of a cripple or an invalid. I shall walk, then crawl, then slither if I must, until this tediously slow death takes me. I see that as a blessing, this long death. For I still have time to march and die in battle. You will grant me this, bloodmates, as well as your silence, after what I have given of myself to be here. I would ask that you each swear on your honor. My impending death is our secret."

"You three having a tiff?" shouted Mouse as she dressed by the pool. In a speck, she would come over to attempt some manner of peacekeeping, they knew. Sands dripped fast as the sweat down Moreth's fevered face. His appeal had been passionate; it was the wish of a dying man, and they wouldn't deny their companion that.

Still, Morigan made one last entreaty. "Moreth, you must give your friends a chance." She stood, reaching for Moreth's chest and pressing her hand to his heart. She felt its spasmodic flutter, she felt—

"What is that?"

Morigan fingered a small, tough object hidden under Moreth's clothes. It felt like the irregular head of an amulet. Had he always worn a necklace? Her hands wandered his neck, pulled on the leather cord, and out popped a dull piece of ebon tied in animal gut. The bloodmates gasped.

"I'm sorry, but what is going on with you three?" asked Mouse. She'd wandered into a scene where the Wolf squatted and bared his teeth, Moreth seemed ready to weep, and Morigan looked torn between repulsion and awe. The seer was pulling at jewelry still around Moreth's neck. It was the necklace he had been given from his Pandemonian foster father of sorts, if she remembered right, and all three of them were spellbound by the item. Morigan's hand, as if possessed, thrust into her pocket and pulled out an almost identical necklace to that which hung on Moreth's neck.

Power electrified Morigan as the necklaces swung near, like pendulums of fate. Like a macabre magpie, she'd taken the necklace from Ankha's belongings, hoping to read a destiny from it. However, in her hands, it was simply a cold piece of stone with an evil history into which she'd been unable to tap. She knew now that the talisman's impotence was a result of it being only one half of a whole. She felt her cleft-stone thrumming its desire to be united with Moreth's. She drew the two nearer, before finally touching them together to the roar of a thunderclap in her head. Clouds of time gathered, secrets rained, and she understood, at last, the heart of the Herald and the glorious wickedness she had sown.

"All this time," muttered Morigan as she emerged from the tides of Dream. Everyone had gathered around her, and the Wolf stood purring heat and power against her back. She hadn't fallen, fainted, or lost herself. In fact, she now had crystal clarity regarding a great many mysteries now.

"This necklace was in the keeping of Ankha—former ruler of Eatoth," whispered Morigan. "She stole it from her sister. I stole it from her corpse."

Moreth clutched back his talisman. "This belonged to the Slave, my father, and teacher in all that I am."

"Amunai's lover," she said, and prophecy's bell rung a name in her mind. "Know the man who loved you, Moreth. For his name was Rom, and he loved you as a true father loves his son."

"As I loved him." Moreth shuddered and hid his teary face from the company.

Humming with purpose and fate, Morigan turned to her pack. "I hold a stone from the Cradle of Life from the ages before humanity fell from grace." She grinned ferociously. "I can use it to follow the footsteps of our prey. I can use it to hunt Amunai to the ends of Geadhain. She will never escape us. Indeed, her ghost will be what leads us to Zionae's crypt. Her tragedy is the path to our victory. Rejoice, my friends, for we have nearly won."

Had they? It was a day of staggering surprises, to be sure. Mouse felt their celebrations should be guarded. A burning madness in the eyes of the bloodmates, and the black twists to the east gave her every reason to doubt their triumph. Something had already been lost, she felt. The bloodmates left Moreth sobbing and strode down the muddy flatland toward the heart of the world.

VI

Morigan and Caenith were hunting. After the recent developments, Morigan had claimed to have much to think about, though she was silent about what those thoughts might entail. She raced ahead of the others, consumed by her thoughts; Caenith matched her—sometimes flickering—speed. The others struggled, huffing and puffing, to remain in the dusty trail the bloodmates carved. For the land was soon dry and rolled in a carpet of fine sand. Wetness dissipated, life grew shy, and aside from the mammoth slugs they saw wriggling from one stone garden to another—and the slurp of their slimy movements—there wasn't much to see or hear. Even the air was dulled by an absence of profusion. As if the land itself had grown wholly gray, still, and pregnant from the terrible dread that roiled in the Scar. There, a thunderhead had crested over the spires of the realm, and dim noises of beasts that rode the air echoed. Those grand shadows glided so slowly and sinuously that at times they looped into symbols of eternity.

"Drakagor," murmured Pythius as he followed with the others.

Mouse didn't ask what he meant, and the way he drew Talwyn to him and sneered at the far-off horizon thereafter snuffed her curiosity. *All terrible, unholy things, which I'm sure we'll have to face,* she thought.

Along with the lords of air, other shapes ruled heaven and earth. They had to creep nearer and reach what approximated noon on this ashen day for her to construe the matter floating in the firmament. Belts of rock were strung over the land in wicked festive wreathing. Some of the debris pulsed an ominous orange and red, as though the sun had been shattered and these were its dying remains. Such was the sense she had of the land—that it had shattered, was ruined, and filled with violent ghosts. At last, the day outpaced the fevered bloodmates, and the rest of the travelers caught up with the pair at a desolate plain, the start of which was marked only by a tree half-degraded into ash. The land beyond was tinged with soot. The fire that had destroyed the Cradle had never been healed by the Green Mother, or by any of the Long Seasons. There was nothing to burn for a campfire, although the throbbing asteroids above them provided a sufficient if eerie light. In a circle they sat, and shared nibbles of Adam's provisions as well as a strip of preserved meat. It would have to do, as the giant slugs that roamed the land were said by those wise to fauna to be as poisonous as jungle frogs.

Morigan didn't help their dispositions when she said, "Before we enter the Scar, there is something I must do." The Wolf signaled his permission to share their secrets, nodding. "Caenith has agreed that you must know the true soul of our enemy—and not merely that of the Black Queen for whom we've come, seeking to understand. When my amulet met with Moreth's, the tides of Fate parted, and I witnessed the entirety of Amunai's madness...and of Brutus's corruption. You, too, must see what I have seen. Moreth, I shall need your talisman." He shrank, clutching at the lump under his clothing. "Only for a while," she promised, and with that he slipped the twine necklace off his neck and passed it to her.

Morigan fiddled with the objects until the two fragments of stone slid over and together as if they were puzzle pieces, making a *snap* once locked into place. The talismans prickled her fingers with static. She was wracked with tremors and shrieking visions from within. She held the visions at bay with her Will, and continued. "Join hands, please."

Mouse sighed and shuffled over with the others. She took one of Adam's hands and one of Moreth's. "Your hand is so cold," she said to him.

Moreth looked at the ground.

Once all were bound together, hand in hand in a circle, Morigan took a final deep breath before setting the talisman on her thigh and beginning her séance. As her hands joined the circle, a current passed from Morigan through the chain of bodies. It was more pleasant than her usual jolt, and the world was softened with strokes of mist and dulled of noise. The cries of the drakagor came through the clouds like distant rolls of thunder. Her ability to conjure a lucid dream dispensed with the need for Amakri spices and ritual, and those gathered succumbed wholly to her magik. She opened her mind and her heart. She drew from the land its ages of torment and spurned trust— its sympathetic suffering to Brutus's—and she spoke to the seven ghosts that hovered around her. Already images had begun to form for them.

"Amunai came here once, with Brutus," said Morigan. "Along the same road we shall tread. She led Caenith's father into the heart of the Scar, and through her trickery broke his once noble spirit and filled him with the Black Queen's poison. I shall show you that journey, and what came before the Immortal's fall. Know that you will pity Brutus for what you are to see. You may pity him, though he is not pitiable now. Until the Black Queen is exorcised, he remains Geadhain's greatest threat."

Morigan glanced at her bloodmate and then twisted herself like a coiling snake, irreverent to the laws of physical being. Suddenly, everyone was facing east where before them was a road of golden tracks that wandered off and between the phantom mountains: Brutus's path.

Open to me, gates of time. Wash me in your waves. Drown me in your memory, your pain, your love, your folly. Show me the Sun King's truth.

Was she speaking, or were they? No one had an answer. The voice of the ages rent open the land, and into that chasm they tumbled and fell. When they woke, it would not be here, in this time, year, or place. They would awake in the Court of Roses, and in the era of the Sun King.

VI

WHAT WAS LOST

I

O leander bloomed year-round in Zioch. Truly, though, the city's gentle tropical clime served to cultivate every genus of flower, and not a road could be taken that wasn't as rich in hues as a sunset over Gorgonath. Indeed, it was almost too much vibrancy, for a city already paved in golden alloy. It was not gold, but rather a Mor'Kethian mineral with all of the sparkle yet none of the softness of that ore. Come dawn or dusk, and Zioch became a dizzying panoply of color. Here, any traveler could see that nature ruled alongside man. Old-fashioned carriages traversed rustic lanes, their wheels traced in moss, and occasionally their roofs burdened with beds of grass where families of birds were annoyed at the jostling of transit. Vines and rosebushes entwined the clockwork skyscrapers built of rods and church-windowed spires that puffed magik into the sky: clean vapors that filled the heavens like a thinner veil of clouds. Flocks of fair creatures soared through that gossamer haze; they could have been birds, or creatures of bird and beast, bird and green, or windup owls, for such harmony between the forces of nature, magik, and man were hardly uncommon in Zioch. True, verdant passion had threaded itself into every golden brick and metal shingle of the city's many grand and steepled keeps that stood stoutly, not hidden, in the shadows of taller structures. It would have been a mistake to believe that the realm wasn't without design, or had been left to the whims of nature and artisans; order was plainly obvious in the placement of the golden towers and keeps spread out on radial tracks of road surrounding the looming ziggurat—more tower than pyramid—at the heart of the city.

To a wayfarer, the many keeps might have seemed to exist in antithesis to the dark ateliers of the Iron City. Perhaps a likeness, too, could be drawn between the king's ziggurat and the Crucible. However, Zioch's keeps and towers were houses of serenity, learning, and lodging—not factories for evil.

The king's grand, jutting edifice of gold, cast in banners of sunlight and clouds, portrayed only the purest mystery and benevolence. Tolling songs rang out from unseen belfries, or mayhap from the gentle hammering of the city's technomagikal industry where metal-and-magik craft was at peace with nature. Indeed, in Zioch, the greatest arts of metallurgy and engineering in all of Geadhain were practiced. The smiths knew how to coax the oldest secrets from ore and wood. Speak to any such tranquil craftsman or woman, and she'd stop her singing to metal and timber, and explain how here the elements were shaped by a discussion, a romance with the material, and not merely by hammer and grit. Things wanted to be shaped, wanted to be used. One only had to know how to ask—which these sorcerers did.

It was the way of Zioch to find nature's tune, to dance to her song, or with her as a partner. Still, Zioch was not a wanton society, lacking in discipline or morals. Earthspeakers and watersculptors tended the great gardens surrounding housing and keeps. Firecallers toiled in the lofty forges atop the great towers with the metalsmiths and windsingers, who removed the toxic qualities borne on the smoke of industry. The smoke was sweet, if one were to taste it, and full with the nutrients of love. For the people loved their city, and in loving it, their magik and toil became an expression, a manifestation, of their love. It was said that one could never be unhappy in Zioch, and this was very much true, for the air was affected by the people's bliss, and it roused in men passion, vigor, and desire.

People lived in what houses they chose and were tied not by taxation or duty. For in addition to his brother's Nine Laws, the Sun King had set forth an astonishing edict for the modern world. Amid all of this progress, an anachronistic grace persisted where men and women worked for the land, and sought not to denigrate their city with skycarriages or a proliferation of self-aggrandizing ingenuities. Aside from their homes, their plant and animal husbandry, and their constant attempts to achieve a perfect balance with the land—how to purify water and waste without exhaust, how to light their homes without burning wood, how to grow the largest bloom, how to cultivate the prettiest sculptures and songs of fire, ice, and wind—the people wanted for nothing. Their humility and gentle pride could be observed, less transcendentally, in the city's numerous parks, wherein the king's words had been inscribed on podiums set with plaques. People flocked to these monuments, where they sometimes slept in the warm grass beds surrounding them. In their dreams they murmured the adage upon which every man, woman, and child of Zioch was weaned.

When once I loved, I ached with greatness of my heart. So, too, shall the keepers of the Golden City cherish soil and stone, water and loam, as if each were a child of their own. Love this garden as you would love me, as I have loved her, as I now love you. Love is the flower that we share, the ache that we bear, and the beauty that endures beyond stone.

Since it was known that Kericot had summered a season in Zioch—the era in which the Nine Laws and Brutus's edict had come to pass—the romantic innuendo within the king's prose was never taken at face value. Undoubtedly, Brutus had spoken broadly, and Kericot, being Kericot, had floridly interpreted his words. No one believed that Brutus had loved or would love another as much as he did his brother and the people of Geadhain. Even an Immortal's heart could only be so full.

II

Yet Brutus ached for them: his she-wolf, his unknown child. From the Court of Roses, and its bloom and ivy throne, the most beautiful seat in all Central Geadhain, the king couldn't find peace. Brutus's somber decadence seemed to have infected his court. Uneaten feasts now decayed and congealed on the hall's many gilded tables, this food once sculpted into pâté-swans, wreaths of spring greens and herbs, and flowers cut from exotic fruits. While there was an overabundance of food and game in Zioch, the king's feasts were more frequently enjoyed by the blowflies than by him or his despondent court. Against colonnades grown down the hall like pillared rosebushes leaned buxom courtesans and half-nude men who appeared to be drunk on the sweet humidity of the chamber and who pricked themselves on thorns while staring sulkily at the king; he hadn't played with any of them lately. More courtesans lay along the steps ascending Brutus's great throne. As if they were partly aroused, partly bored cats, they rolled on the bloodred satin that spilled down the ascent, pining for his attention. Sages and city men lingered near the braziers and shadows along the walls, too scared to approach their scowling liege—a man whose moods, while tempestuous, in the past had always been predictable.

Every so often, a sage would test their courage on the courtesan-strewn stairs and bother Brutus with one request or another. He'd bark at them and terrify everyone in the hall, even though he never meant to scare them; it was the animal within him. It was deprived and vicious. He could barely hold it in. Although he tried to temper himself when dealing with these poor creatures who had—willingly—given themselves to the service of his city or his pleasure, he could barely look at any of them without suffering a pang for the musk of fur, the bite of fangs, or the memory of his mate's heartbeat.

Once he'd left Alabion, he had faced an extraordinary dilemma: how to tell the world about his strange love and his incredible child. With his brother sojourning and quiet, silently building his desired kingdom and collective of ideals, Brutus realized he would have to continue to sort out his own problems for a time. He'd simply wandered without aim from Menos to Terotak, to the ruins of a nameless, horrid culture to the west. He saw the machinations and twisted minds of men, and he worried how a world with souls stained as dark as these could ever accept his family. Later, upon returning to Central Geadhain, he'd swum the Straits of Wrath and then reveled in the happy songs of the seafarers in Carthac—people singing glory to a storm that wanted to smash them to ruin. Their passion was as inspired as the herds of wild deer in Meadowvale with whom he spent a season running, or the white bears with whom he hunted seals along the salt shores to the south. Eventually he left, to chase a new quarry, and when he returned, it was to the bones of his bear-family—killed by hunters for their pelts.

It was the way of life, he'd been told by his brother. Man could be a friend to nature, though often he chose not to be. He considered tracking down and slaughtering the hunters, whose sweat he could follow to the ends of Geadhain. However, the echo of his brother's mercy arrested the urge, and even pondering that clemency brought forth the man in his spirit. In the cave of bones, he had wondered: could man not change, not learn to be less selfish? And he realized that as a creature who would live forever, he would have an eternity in which to teach man the error of his ways. Perhaps this had been what his brother had meant about being and growing apart. Thus he had used this inspiration to guide him, and his travels took him south to a land of green wonder somehow untouched by man's burning curiosity and greed. *Here,* he had thought. *Here I can build a temple to the Green Mother and a realm where all her creatures—including my son and his mother—can come, worship, and be.*

With that dream, he had started Zioch, which was first a rough stone temple, a vale, and a garden watered with his sweat and power. Once, a wandering minstrel had come, lured by the flourish of color he had seen through a farscope while trekking from Sorsetta. The traveler was charming and humorous and went by a Romanisti name that had since receded in the king's mind—and ages later the king would come to swear he'd met an ancestor of Kericot, for the two men, met centuries apart, were so much the same. For a season, the traveler had stayed with him, eaten the fats and fruits of the land, partaken in the stories and kindnesses of an Immortal who'd been living since the dawn of time. He'd repaid the king's hospitality with songs, both newly written and some of the oldest the Immortal recalled. In the fall, the traveler left and carried with him on the autumn road songs of bounty and wonder—odes to the fertile counterpart to Eod's austere glory, this secret that lay to the south. From then, they had come: vagabonds and artists, sages, rangers, tired warriors, and the destitute but eager, who only needed a soft meadow for a bed, of which Zioch had valleys full. They had ambition, though, and were inspired by the glory of the Immortal and of his land. Thus, what they made was to honor him: buildings coaxed from raw soil by earthspeakers, streets laid with stones the color of the Immortal's skin, and arts that worked with nature instead of against her, as all of Brutus's agriculture and animal husbandry had shown. They called Brutus a king, since they knew not what else to call a man who was thrice their size and who had lived through ages of fire, ice, dust, and drowning. And for the first time, Brutus learned of both the humility and responsibility of power, of protecting the weak. He had not forgotten about his family, though, for whom all this work had been done.

His utopia was soon to be challenged, as the dread warlord Taroch appeared, claiming to be an Immortal, declaring himself Geadhain's newest king, and amassing an army of clansmen to back his claim. These warriors were adamant about submitting to Immortal rule, and already ostracized by their unaligned values of men and strength over freedom and culture. Then, as Brutus had been rallying his riders and huntsmen for the first wave said to have crossed the Feordhan, did the first mind-whisper in lifetimes echo southward from his brother. *I need you, my brother,* the cold side of his soul had said. *We must strike this tyrant down. We must be the hammer for my realm and the wonder that I hear you have made in the South—a wonder I must see.*

More than the war, it had been the promise and an opportunity to confess to Magnus the source of his newfound philanthropy that had transformed Brutus into a typhoon of terror against Taroch's forces. Thousands were slain, and few of his men or Eod's were in that tally as the dominant armies met on the soaked sands of the desert and their commanders congratulated each other with a long-overdue hug. While this should have been a triumph, however, Magnus had seemed unsatisfied and even sullen at their conquest and brotherly reunion. And still, once the warlord was fully rerouted and found hanged in Southreach, Magnus's petulance had him damn that poor city to a devastating demise—regardless of who in Southreach had been complicit in Taroch's concealment. Afterward, before the dust and quakes had even settled, Magnus's banners rolled north, away from the smoking valley he had created. Since then, his brother had not come to visit Zioch, as sworn, nor had Brutus told him anything of his time in Alabion.

Decades crept past, and while the kings' relationship withered, their cities had flourished in the prosperous peace after war. Winter came to tickle the balmy streets of Zioch with coolness, and perhaps this had presaged his brother's desire, for Magnus had suddenly reached out to him. It had been seasons upon seasons since their minds had last spoken—Magnus had wanted privacy as much as his brother. What had he been doing all these years? Brutus had wondered, as his sense of logic and time returned to him. About this, Magnus had asked that they should meet and speak, face-to-face. Soon, with his brother's frosty compassion filling and shivering him from within, Brutus remembered all of what they'd been together, and he set off to hunt down his brother. They were to meet in Kor'Keth, Magnus's mind-whisper bade, near the place where they had picked the first stone—used for a pulpit, from which Magnus had preached—of Eod. Brutus ran and did not stop until he reached his destination, for this was to be their true reunion, and the day when all secrets would be shared.

Drifting back to the present in the Court of Roses, and as he remembered that meeting, rage became his world. The Sun King hammered his throne with his fists. Courtesans scurried off the steps like mice running from hawks. The memory played before him unremittingly with cruel vivacity, more real than ethereal, for such was how the eternal mind, the mind that rarely slept, and to which all sands and time blurred into a soft smear, remembered.

The desert winds howl like the excitement of Brutus's heart. He has longed to see his brother, and so too does his brother yearn. For the treaty of silence between them, signed ages ago, has weathered of its ink, and Magnus's cold sentiments and longing trickle to his brother. Love—theirs is interminable and impossible. Theirs is a love that will understand any inconvenience of fur and fang. Magnus will accept his brother's child and lover, this he knows. Why have they been apart? Why force this agony on themselves when they could exist in the bliss of brotherhood? Faster than the wind, he crosses Kor'Khul. He sees his brother's achievement shimmering like a pearl—Eod, which has grown astronomically in scale and grandeur since its birth in the meekness of sand and a single pulpit—the stage from which his brother could sermonize on fellowship, fraternity, and philosophy. Brutus wonders if any of that ancient relic of brotherhood remains, buried somewhere under all the stone, steel, and technomagik.

Away from that grandiose display, on a quieter bluff, upon which a cairn and a woman's bones will one day be placed, he and his brother meet. Brutus arrives draped in a savage's primal loincloth and not the garments a civilized king should wear. He would be awesome and horrifying to anyone other than the pale Immortal who waits and studies his slowing approach. Their nearing is the dance of lovers, and it ends in an embrace of fire and thunder: passionate, and with the larger almost crushing the smaller. It's almost sexual, as is everything with Brutus—that is how his body loves. Whatever ardor possesses him dies in a fizzle as a woman, quiet and insignificant until now, manifests behind his brother. She's wreathed in white silks, and her appearance comes as a trick, an illusion. She slithers, he feels, as if she were a snake, and exudes the same such insidious beauty and alluring poison. He can smell his brother upon her lips and breasts, and knows that they have been together. In instants, the flame of his jealousy struggles against the cold storm of his brother's feelings for this nameless woman.

"Lila," says Magnus, while eating his brother's thoughts.

Although that is the woman's name, she recognizes it not in the prehistoric chattering in which the brothers engage. It will be the first of many slights given to her over the marriage through which she has signed away her dignity. So she looks on, bewildered, at the wild giant and her waifish king as they embrace and whisper their secrets.

"It has a name?" mocks Brutus. "Is this the prize for which you cast our eternal brotherhood aside?"

Magnus rises to his tiptoes and appeases the giant with two cold fingers to Brutus's curled lips. "I cast nothing aside, brother. I sought strength outside of myself, outside of our circle. Lila is everything that I am not: warm, charitable, sensual, and kind. I want to be with her, as I am with you."

"You summoned me here to shun me?"

"To welcome you, brother, into a new family."

Brutus strides ahead, softly shoving his brother, and looms over the woman. She impresses him by holding herself proud and without a shiver of fear, even if she reeks of it. Crudely, he examines her hair, smile, limbs, and scent as if she were a Menosian slave being auctioned. Magnus allows this to continue, and Brutus himself knows he should be kinder, though his jealousy subverts manners.

"Do you...love her?" he finally asks.

"I do," says Magnus, and he hurries forward and claims Lila's hand. "I want her to be a part of us. I want to know what she knows, to feel what she feels. I wish to swear my soul to her, brother."

"What will that do to us?" But Brutus already knows that the oath can be resworn; he'd done that with the Ancient before he and Magnus had cut each other off. However, he wonders if his brother knows the cost, burden, and pain.

"It will change us," replies Magnus.

"It will, though it will change you most of all."

A memory boils in Brutus's memory; it scalds Magnus with sensations of soft fur, a musk, and the pressure of teeth on his inner thigh. "Brother?"

Brutus forces down the escaping memory. "I shall do this for you. I shall share our blood with this woman. Although you will give me the same right to love whoever I wish, to bleed with whoever shall make me stronger, whenever I am to find that destined mate. You shall love my family as I am to love this woman: as a part of us."

"I shall. I swear."

There are tears in Magnus's eyes, diamonds falling from emeralds, and the Immortal beckons down his huge brother so that they can embrace anew. Magnus's head hangs on the other's shoulder and, consumed by this reunion, his brother's blessing, and his abundant love for brother and wife, he romanticizes his future. "She will be lovely...as soft as you are hard. She will be a willow to your oak. She will be as fair as summer, and as dark as night, and she will teach you the values and virtues of being a man, as Lila has taught me."

"Who will?" asks Brutus, stiffening.

His smiling, tear-stained brother leans away so that they can meet gaze to stormy gaze. "Your bloodmate. Your chosen and mortal wife, with whom you shall make an empire like mine."

In that moment, only Geadhain hears the shattering of Brutus's heart.

"No other woman deserves you, or our blood," declares Magnus, suddenly aglow with haughty immortal hubris. He ponders his next words, head tilted to the wind that's suddenly hissing. Then, as if the sword could not be driven any deeper, he adds, "What else would wed itself to you, but the greatest of mortalkind? A queen for an unwed king, and kingdoms for eternity. It's time to stop being so savage, my brother. You are a lord of nature, and therefore nature must serve thee, as she serves man." Confusion wracks Brutus, as if everything he has created in Zioch is worthless in the eyes of Magnus. Blithely or cruelly, his brother kisses him—on the lips—and mind-whispers, She will be the noblest of blood, your wife. She will be from the purest lineage of man, and not some mongrel dog—

"Dog," muttered the king, though no one was around to hear him.

Most had fled as the king delved into the past, when he'd begun a small tantrum in the Court of Roses. A giant's tantrums, however, were never small to others. The banner leading from his throne had been shredded, and braziers had been toppled and bled coals and ash across the room. Parts of the carpet smoldered or boasted fair-sized fires that had already consumed one of the chamber's many pillars of roses. Brutus remembered none of the destruction he'd wrought, although his heaving chest and bloody hands identified him as the culprit. Still, the questions of that day many hundreds of years ago wouldn't calm to cold anger in his mind, and remained stoked and incandescent, waiting for the smallest gust to ignite them. He'd used that rage to build Zioch even more holistically and consciously, to show his brother he'd been wrong about man and beast existing on different thrones of royalty—although Magnus had never seemed impressed, and remained too distant and absorbed in his own achievements to notice.

Lately Brutus's moods had been deteriorating, the pendulum of his rage ticking faster and swinging more disastrously. He needed only to ask his brother what had been meant that evening, what had been seen and understood, and whether Magnus had truly intended to irrevocably condemn and harm his dream of being with the Ancient in Alabion. Did Magnus know he loved a beast? Had he glimpsed one of his thoughts? Is that why his words had been so vicious and astute? Alas, for a giant, a king, and the strongest creature on this planet, he did not possess the strength to confront his brother with those questions. All that he'd built to serve his secret family in Alabion—this city that extolled the virtue of nature's harmony with man— seemed to have been made of sand, and the Ancient and his son would never see it. They wouldn't know Zioch because he was too cowardly to confront his brother and admit that he loved an animal, even if such a term did not fully explain what she was. He wanted to blame Lila, for over-cultivating Magnus, for modernizing his concepts of nature. Or he wanted to blame Magnus for his pedantic pride. He wanted to blame anyone and everyone other than himself.

In the end, however, there was only his own weakness glaring back at him, and the aching shame of a son somewhere out there in the world who would never know his name. Slumped and broken, he stomped back to his throne and called for his aides to clean the chamber and snuff out the fires.

III

For a man who'd walked through the early ages of Geadhain, a year could feel like no more than a speck, a week in his chronex might pass and suddenly his whole court seemed new: courtesans, magistrates, and lords. Keeping courtesans felt like frippery, since he'd lost the desire for anything but his memories and his own hand. Brutus wondered how pathetic he must have seemed, pleasuring himself upon his throne as a mewling, sex-starved brood of courtesans reached for him and were cast away. Really, he cared not. He let them fuk each other, to tend to their needs and not his; their hurt faces would be forgotten in a few sands of his immortal existence. He lived in a court filled with strangers. He recognized none of his servants or aides, and the faces that endured were haunting—his brother's pretty countenance, the seductress of the amber stare, the dark and slim muzzle of his mate, and a fourth, an imagined face, perhaps tanned and handsome like his own, though tempered even more fiercely by the animal qualities of his mother.

Brutus had tried to find pleasure in his own achievements, in these new values and measuring sticks of worth as deemed by his brother. And he had succeeded; his kingdom had evolved along a complementary though contrary path to that of Eod, and it was no less of a marvel than the jewel of the north. Finally, he ruled a kingdom worthy of his family. However, he still didn't have his brother's love or approval, and he felt he never would.

News reached him of the world, of Menos's slow, festering growth and threat. But nothing meaningful ever came from his brother. After the war on Taroch, the distance between them had stretched into an abyss. In the last centuries, he could count on one finger the number of times they had seen each other since then: Magnus's blood-wedding to the serpent of the desert. Magnus had found happiness, and now had no more need of his brother. Occasionally, across the gulf of heart-and-souls, a cold wind of his brother's love blew and reached the other side. However, that love was not for Brutus, but for the King of the North's new bride. Just as whatever passions reached Magnus's side of the void were echoes of Brutus having dwelt on his missing family. When he and Magnus chatted, their mind-whispers were banal banter about technomagikal engines, Menos's scheming, solar-harnessing, and all the wonders and intrigue that had impassioned his brother. They were strangers, like the faces in Brutus's court, and strangers didn't share their truest truth. *My power is a lie. I stride mountains, I swim with sea kings, I can slay any animal with these great hands alone*, he'd lament. *But I am a weak man that I cannot speak my heart's desire. Would she still have me? Would my son? Why does the weight of one man's derision crush me like stone?* Whenever he had almost willed up the courage to shout to the mind in Eod the whole ugly and beautiful truth, a whisper of doubt prevented him, sly as a snake hissing at his ear, and he would decide to close his eyes and allow more of the world to pass by.

IV

One day, the endlessly droll cycle was disrupted.

Zioch only had two shades of a single season: summer and high summer. It was the latter, and the flies supping on Brutus's uneaten feast had grown to frenzied hordes that would soon disrupt his deep melancholy with their buzzing. Most of his courtesans no longer remained in the hall; rather, they had taken on other work or enjoyed coitus out of sight of their depressing king, this giant man, hung in a red sash, and handsome as a black lion, whose thunder-cast expression had turned his majesty into a terrible presence. No one wanted to approach this angry hulk ready to unleash lightning, for his response was always an explosion. Even the ministers of the court conducted their business elsewhere; he was no longer wanted or needed by anyone.

Into the deserted hall came a woman. She slid through the dust-speckled beams of sunlight that bled into the hall without casting a shadow. She walked past the tables of refuse, and the flies ceased their tune and settled on moldering shanks, as though she were their master. Indeed, the Court of Roses took on a more sinister tranquility with her appearance. At the base of the throne's ascent, the woman knelt and waited for the king to see her. It was her scent that summoned him from his dark dream: sweet as apples, and sharpened by saffron and stringent spirits—and somehow as enlivening. Her scent aroused him like vapors under his nose, and he stirred, sniffing.

"Who disturbs my court?" he asked.

"A traveler," said the woman.

A tale that was possibly true, for she dressed like no woman in Central Geadhain. As she shed her heavy plum hood and cloak, her beauty moved the primal spirit in his heart. She gathered the cape behind her, and it revealed her long brown neckline and the rich spill of her hair over sinewy shoulders that rose from her gown's strapless corset. She was hale for a woman, and that threaded muscle and ferocity extended from her body into her face, though it seemed to abstain from her voluptuous breasts and hips. Another softness he noticed in her handsome face were her lips, which were thick and painted to match the amethyst makeup above her eyes. The same sparkle and color came from her eyes, too. Brutus knew of only one other woman to possess that quality: Menos's ruthless First Chair. A modern fishwives' tale portrayed women with a purple stare like hers as witches and tyrants of the worst kind.

Brutus might have been a lethargic predator these days, yet still his senses had remained sharp. The perfumed enchantress was as dangerous as her charms, but Brutus wouldn't be beguiled.

"Declare your intentions, witch," he boomed, and then stood with his full height looming over her.

"My name is Amunai," said the stranger. "I am no witch. I was once a Keeper. Now, I am a peddler of fates."

"A peddler of fates?" The king's laugh shook the tables and banished the flies; a drunken, passed-out courtesan awoke from the noise, shrieked and ran off, believing another of Brutus's storms had begun to rage. "I know not how you even entered my kingdom, how you breezed past my guards, my keepers, or my court. But I entertain no strangers, and certainly no peddlers. I have no need of whatever you are selling, charlatan."

"I asked to meet you. I offered your men what they needed to feel at peace. I could offer you the same."

"You have nothing to offer me. Be gone!"

"I have everything to offer you."

Smug as if holding an advantage, she balked not and bent not an inch. Regardless of the fact that he'd sat for years, ignoring the agony of his own starvation, Brutus's strength had not waned. Rage took over the Immortal; the stairs split under his tread as three great strides brought him before the witch, who he seized by her tawny throat. She didn't whimper, plead, or piss herself—all the reactions one would anticipate in response to being throttled by an Immortal. Instead, she glared at him with a darkness in her eyes, a steeliness that wouldn't bend to his terrible wrath or even to death, as if she'd crossed the worst already. Reeling, he dropped her, and she recovered gracefully from the heap in which she'd landed. She rose and rubbed her throat. She moved forward as he stepped back, warily.

"I know death, I know pain," she whispered. "Do not think I shall be cowed with such threats."

"Away from me." He growled.

Instead she slunk ahead, weaving an enchantment with her coal-rimmed stare and swishing hips, a spell as rapturous as the orgies of concubines that no longer tempted the king. She did, however, sway him. She teased a hardness down below and a roaring rapid of lust and blood in his chest. Embarrassment and shame drove him from her, and he stumbled, lost his perfect balance, and fell onto the stairs on his elbows. She stood before and over him, her form as great as his would be. She was a giantess. A ruler. Brutus couldn't conceive of why or how she'd rendered him so meek.

"Because you have forgotten your glory, my King," whispered the witch, as though he'd spoken his fear aloud. "You, once a great lion, are now no more than a cub; your teeth have been filed, your nails clipped, and you know nothing of who you are or what you want."

It was this truth and her affirmation of it that smote him down. He groveled, and down she leaned, whispering crippling secrets to him. "I can teach you to reclaim your glory, your lust and fire for life. I can teach you to be the beast that rules man, and not the man afraid of his beast. Which is what you've become: a coward to yourself. It's what your brother has made you. A eunuch. An insect to his greatness. He could never be you, and so he has succeeded you with his empire, his knowledge, his wealth, his golden whore."

"Stop! I command thee!" threatened the broken king. And yet her words echoed, almost humming a metal song in his head he couldn't cast from his skull. As a man who had never been challenged, his defense against brutal criticism was infantile. How could she know him so well? Who was she? Why couldn't he stand up and ruin her with his fists?

"All fair questions, my King," said Amunai, listening to his secrets. "I would answer every truth you seek and more. I am not your enemy. We are alike, you and I. Outcasts from our kingdoms. Rulers forced to sit on thrones of dust. Love has eroded your sense of pride. Love for your brother, love for the furred bitch in Alabion—"

"No!"

Come that insult, there was a reckoning to be had. The king's honor surged, his flesh turned to wrath, and he was suddenly up, roaring, and flinging the grinning specter as though she were made of rags. Amunai's impact, however, wasn't light. She struck one of the flower-twined columns with a wet slap, and the stone structure cracked and crumbled. Down in a rain of roses, blood, and dust she fell, as the king turned away from her, heaving and crawling to his throne. He'd have to tell a lie to his aides to explain the scuffle. Furthermore, he'd see that the witch's body was burned— it felt proper to invoke the old customs for such a monster.

Someone coughed behind him, and his fiery blood froze to ice.

The witch's honeyed poison wafted over to him, as fresh as if he'd inhaled it from her bosom. A rope of fragrance coiled about his neck and reined him around. Amunai stood in the rubble of the pillar, quite intact compared to the architecture behind her. At worst, her dress had been scuffed and torn. Her flesh had undergone a curious mending where the blood—or whatever that ink-black ichor could be called—retracted into zippering wounds that were fading from her body. In the moments the king had spent gaping at her, she'd mended entirely. She caught one of the beads of blood that had been rolling back into its wound and painted her lips with its ink. She smiled.

"My master has blessed me," she said. "I cannot be harmed by the hands of her children. I cannot be undone by you, or by Magnus. The flesh of the master cannot break the master's clay. You are her flesh, and I am her clay, soon you will know this."

Children? Master? thought the king, his tongue tied with questions.

Amunai sighed. "So much you don't know. So dark your night, and blind your sight." She stepped out of the mess and pouted at him. "Dearest Mommy can't be here to clean up the mess you've made. She's watching, though, always watching. Eventually, you'll call to her, or you'll summon her with your heart's desire. She'll eat away at what's weak in you and leave only your glorious, handsome beast. That's what you yearn to be, not this dog wearing a crown and trying to hold a scepter in his paw. What you've lost is a mate that is worthy of the one you left in Alabion."

Amunai swayed and folded herself into the shadows of the court. "That's all she wants, your Mother—to unite the strong, to purge the weak. Your mate and son could be among the blessed chosen. However, you must first cleanse yourself of this unseemly remorse, of these unworthy misgivings. Remember that you are beast. Devour your man. Shite out his bones, and call to me when he is gone. I shall come."

"Never," said the king. Since he'd been covering his mouth as if to hold in a scream, he realized then that whatever parley had occurred had done so without their tongues. She had entered his mind.

"Call to me," teased the witch, and she left in a whirl of scent.

V

Magnus's mind-whisper in response to his brother's spike of distress came too late that day. Dusk had fallen, and by then Brutus brooded, almost asleep, in his chair, his rage hanging as limply as the crooked crown on his head—a symbol of his fallen glory, or perhaps not able to fit the skull of a dog. She had used that filthy word, and when Magnus had crept into his head to ask whether all in Brutus's realm was whole, he had lied, or withheld information, as was his right with a man who'd chosen a golden snake-woman and technomagikal lovers over a brotherhood of eternity.

All is well, little prince, he said, using an old term of endearment for his brother. *The savages in Mor'Keth grow unruly and have begun stealing from the fiefs in the valley. I shall put them down—fair, though with a steel fist. The peace of one thousand years will not be broken by starving fools.*

Worthless dogs! cried the voice from afar.

Brutus shivered twice over, once from the hated word, then from Magnus's hatred of the uncivilized, of those who wouldn't accept his wonders. How much like a child his brother could be. He gave a pitiable laugh, unheard by Magnus who sensed but a trace of that bittersweet pain. Then he wished Magnus well and dismissed him. Again, they moved to that place in their minds wherein only the loudest gasps of their lives in other places came like cold and warm breezes. Sometimes the king dreamed of his brother sliding himself inside Lila. Magnus, too, would sense Brutus whenever he was consumed with passion, usually while hunting or fuking, though the king had done neither in ages. He spent his time here, sitting, wasting away in his unwasteable flesh. It was a pathetic state to which he had resigned himself. On that, at least, the witch was right—what she'd said of mothers, masters, and his true beast, he wouldn't consider. Although, perhaps it was time to dust off his lips and his loins and to rejoice in the fruits of man...

The spark of an idea was lit in the king's mind at that moment. Brutus adjusted his crown and called for his aides, before realizing that darkest night had fallen. He claimed a brazier like it was a candelabrum, and then stormed his golden fortress and woke nearly every member of staff and retainer of his great house, none of whom were clear on what to expect from the giant pounding at their door. There was to be a feast, they were told. A celebration to signal the long end of the king's gloom, and that announcement, coupled with his magnificent, magnanimous smile, told them that his season of bitterness had ended. They leapt out of bed and cot, and woke everyone that the king had missed for a celebration, they said—a festival of summer.

For Brutus had decided that he would suffer neither his brother's aloofness nor his condescension, and certainly not the prognostications of some meddling sorceress who believed herself to have a hand in fate. He had created Zioch as a home for those who didn't want to live in accordance with Eodian or Menosian concepts of modernity. The City of Gold was home to man, beast, and tree alike, where none was greater than the other. It was that vision that had faded to a smudged oath in his mind, and he would see it restored, along with the spirits of those he had drawn into his misery. Only then could his son and the she-wolf come and be welcomed as family in his happy home. He needed to get his house in order. Once the feast was over, and his people were blissful and fat from Zioch's grace, he would march to his brother's city and tell him in person of his missing years. Come what may, his brother would accept his love.

VI

It was a historic celebration. Were the bard himself around, the king imagined him infusing his gaiety into every scene. The queer fox would have gorged himself on any of the hundred hogs that lay steaming on tables around the hall. Perhaps he would've mingled with the line of sultry dancers who clanged their bangled feet and shook the jingling beads of their skirts to the ancient rhythms conjured by the choirs of windsingers who floated on beds of air about the hall. Surely the mischief-maker would have tried his hand at fire-breathing with the firecallers who cartwheeled on bridges of golden heat sprung over the court. Or he would've pickpocketed the autumn-shaded togas of the illustrious company of sages, artists, lovers, and technomancers gathered there. At the very least he would have caressed so much naked, teasing flesh and winked at the courtesans with his green eye—he was always such a flirt, the king recalled. By the witching hourglass, the bard would already have swung from the court's crimson banners and shrieked from the pit of his belly. Even then, having exerted himself in his revelry, he would've doused himself in the golden vats of wine in which giddy courtesans swam— ladies and lads since aroused by the kiss and touch of their liege as none of their forebears had been in one hundred years.

A century. Such had been the length of the king's spiritual internment. Menos had risen to become a truly threatening power during his slumber, and Gloriatrix was no more than a fledgling aristocrat, but twice remade in the Iron royalty and now a queen. Brutus attempted to stave off the sourness of that thought and the sting of how many crucial events he had missed. Tonight he was king, and his people loved him. He could be everything—man and beast, father to a nation, and father to a family.

Brutus had given a speech, a simple one, for these people did not ask for snake-tongued orators. They wanted to know that they were cared for, and safe. He couldn't remember all he had said, though generally he recalled making promises of future light, urging closeness with the old ways, and pledging to make their city the brightest, greenest jewel in Geadhain's crown. *We shall embrace our Mother. We shall be one with soil and seal, wing and claw. We shall know greatness through humility.* He recalled those snippets, at least. Zioch's potent cider—strong even to an Immortal—had erased the rest from his memory.

Brutus felt calm, at peace with his beast. Balanced. Sitting on his throne for most of the evening, he reminisced about the glory of what he'd made, and for once he didn't pine for what had yet to be achieved. Magnus had helped him build this, too; his brother's temperance and genius for conceptual architecture had been instrumental in Zioch's making. Reflecting on the years leading up to this moment, he felt sure that Magnus wouldn't reject him, or his strange love and stranger nephew. What madness had he weaned himself upon to ever believe such a fear? What was this hissing spirit of doubt—nearly a voice manifest at times—that always stopped him at his moment of confession? With the wine clouding his judgment, he nearly surrendered in their cold war and shouted the truth to his brother right then. No. They must meet—as men, as brothers, and as friends—and share the secret face-to-face.

Once, he asked his page—a chipper, chubby young lad—if the people were enjoying the spoils of Zioch and the party that bombastically carried on in the city proper, the noise of which had reached the king's all-hearing ears.

"Indeed, my King," replied the man, so excited that he spilled some of the wine he was pouring into Brutus's great chalice. "So sorry, my King. But, yes. Whole herds of deer have been slaughtered, their sacrifice acknowledged, of course. A thousand hogs roasted. Every grape and crabapple plucked from the orchards of Zioch to make enough wine that all swim in it, like your gleeful harem. If the land wasn't so bounteous and we weren't such careful tenders, I would worry for those populations of animal and crops of fruit we've plundered. However, we are a richer land than ever. All thanks to you, my King."

"I merely laid the first stone, and dreamed the dream of a place where man, king, beast, and green could be as one," said the King, somberly.

"And you've succeeded, magnificently! More wine?"

Brutus waved for the man to leave; he had already spilled half a pitcher on his knuckles. *Thump-thump. Thump-thump.* A drum split his chest. The beat of his heart boomed impossibly as he beheld the lacquer of red trickling over his great copper fist. It held him, the crimson gleam on his hand. It mesmerized him like the wet, pink flesh of sex or a fresh carcass, and he watched each pendulous teardrop of red that landed on the throne. Whether the drops or his heartbeat felt louder, he couldn't say. He had a burning thirst for something thicker and redder than wine.

"Go on, give in. Feed the beast," whispered the witch.

A growl ripped from Brutus's belly, and he hurled his chalice. He wouldn't be beguiled. Where was she? Where was the witch? Yet as he stomped down from his dais, there was but a chamber of mortified guests and celebrants paused in their merrymaking—as timid as deer before the yellow stare of a wolf. None of the startled women in ball gowns possessed the ostentation, the arrogance, or the wickedness of that witch. There was no threat in his kingdom, nothing other than himself. She couldn't have hidden herself from his sight, not in his kingdom.

What had worried him after his encounter with the woman was that when he had later investigated how she'd intruded into his sanctuary, no one seemed to know of whom he was speaking. His questions had produced the same empty, terrified expressions that he now beheld. A figment of my imagination, he decided. She hadn't been real, and her voice just now had been an echo of his fear. Pardoning himself, the king sat, clapped, and in a speck an uneasy elation reclaimed the court. In some sands, the partygoers needed to no longer feign their joy, as his temperamental outburst had been forgotten. Brutus was, after all, a stormy sky of a man—the people were used to the thunder of their lord.

Soon the bravest and sultriest of his courtesans, wet from wine, glided up the stairs and lay at the king's great feet. He had to turn them away, since they looked awash in gore. One concubine wouldn't be dissuaded, however— a statuesque, athletic man with a head of curls like lamb's wool, only golden. He kissed Brutus's feet. Then he took liberties massaging the granite blocks that were an Immortal's calves. And finally, he slipped his needy hands along the hot, unyielding canyon of flesh formed by Brutus's thighs. Once offering themselves into service, the courtesans of the Court of Roses were trained to swallow gourds and bottle-fed aphrodisiacs, and were given elixirs from the western isles that imbued the body with the flexibility of rubber and a voracious need, so the young man had no problem swallowing his master's great prick. As the lad's head went fully beneath the skirt of Brutus's wrap, and gripped that blade with both hands, the Immortal clenched his throne and surrendered to this worship. In a fugue of pleasure, his head lolled to the side, his lips newly meeting with soft flesh. Brutus kissed whatever mouth or organ that was, and grunted, appreciatively, as his tongue tangled with another that tasted of wine and sweet apple nectar. Despite being embroiled in an entanglement of linguae, the witch's voice slithered into his ear. "Feel him, need him, then break him, and bleed him. You are a king of beasts, and he is your meat, your feast."

Brutus spit and thrashed. "Amunai!"

In the king's fury, the courtesan was kicked down several flights of stairs. He lay there, curled up, weeping, and wheezing for breath. From atop the king's landing, the giant cast scalding gazes, brandished a terrifying erection, and seemed to be shouting at invisible threats. He had scared his countrymen for a second time in so many sands. Only now, his volatility couldn't be brushed aside. Since so many of the king's court were indisposed from drink and fear, it landed upon his brave page to act. The shivering man helped up the courtesan, handing him into the care of one of Brutus's regally plumed and gilded soldiers—men who had also grown wary of their king. Next, the page crept up, cautious of the great wild animal as he approached.

When he bowed before the king, Brutus's lust and madness seemed to calm to a panicked puffing.

"My liege?" he whispered.

"Search the court, the palace, and the city. I want her found, hanged, and burned as the witches and bloodswains of the Swannish were by their vengeful chieftains. I am vengeful, and I shall not suffer her poison any longer."

"Certainly, my liege." He paused, dithered, and shuffled in his prostration as much as he could.

"Have I not spoken clearly?" warned Brutus.

"You have. Very clearly, indeed. Perhaps it is mine ears that have missed the nuance of your mighty commands. Forgive me for my stupidity, though I must ask, *who*? Who are we to find, hang, and burn?"

There hadn't been an execution in Zioch since the war with the natives of Mor'Keth, who had refused to surrender the foothills of the valley to the king and his growing country. So the notion of such a summary execution made the page, and all in attendance, queasy. Far more damning was the spite that next twisted the handsome Immortal, swelled his muscles, and spackled his beard with spit as he said, "Amunai. She calls herself a peddler of fates. She is a witch, a snake whose venom poisons the mind. She must be hunted down and killed before her poison can spread."

The revelers disappeared from the Court of Roses, leaving behind a graveyard of instruments, chalices, food, and garish waste. As they fled, they spoke in bleak glances and the quietest of whispers that the poison of this mysterious enemy had already infected their kingdom.

VII

The king's emergence from his age of sadness had been celebrated too soon, people realized. Come the first crier, even those not present at the court the previous night still knew that an enemy had struck Zioch and ruined the summer festival. However, no one seemed clear on the particulars of the attack. Gossipy susurrations of erections, orgies, and the king's temperamental ranting made more rounds than any facts. Even the identity of the "witch" had taken on faery-tale grandeur, and in some retellings she was a vile and warty creature. Murmurs of this hogwash and discord reached the ears of Brutus as he sat, through night and then day, in the hall where the remnants of the feast had begun to fester in the heat. A nose as sensitive as his couldn't bear the stink today, and he soon abandoned his court to stroll through his tower, hoping to find mental succor or relief from the wonders of his kingdom.

Quite without direction, he wandered up along the Stairway to the Stars, as it was known—a coiling path that encircled the main tower's interior. From there, landings and arches embellished in leaflets and filigrees led to various bridges that connected to smaller ziggurat-like towers; Zioch was a collection of irregular cylinders, each bound to a central grand tower then set into a pyramid. The artisans and sages who ambled those golden roads were drenched in such brightness that they'd faded to impressions. He didn't want to bother those ghosts. Other than returning the salutes of his soldiers posted at archways, he made little contact with anyone traveling the stairway.

He had troubled his people enough, he felt. Whatever he next said or did mustn't be construed as the signs of a feeble man barely holding on to his sanity. Thus, it was wiser to say and do nothing, until the matter of the witch was resolved. As he climbed the highest reaches of the tower against which few men tested themselves, he saw fewer of his people and the protectors of Zioch, and more of the emerald and ruby arbor—lush ivy and roses bloomed to perfection—that flowed down the tower wall in a curtain of life. Rivulets of water ran both up and down the walls, guided by magik, misting foliage in an ever-present dew. Water snakes shimmered from behind the leafy veil, visible to the king's eyes alone. Furry vine-huggers and other chattering animals that lived in the tower were more conspicuous to the naked eye, none so noticeable as the yellow birds who nested in the leaves and sweetly sang along with the musical trickle. That such tiny creatures could elevate the sunlight-spangled place to heights of divine beauty struck the king with heartache. The weary king was reminded then, of nature and achievement, of how to be meek when one was great.

"You don't need to be meek," whispered Amunai.

The king froze, snarling, on a curved gold stair leading to an aura of brilliance, looking up at that heavenly eye as if that had been the voice's source. Up in that pinhole of glory, he smelled her apple and spice reek—as lovely as it was it masked her rotten soul. The king roared and rushed up the tower, ruffling the tranquility, sending birds scattering and squawking, spinning around the men he passed like a tornado.

Moments later, the king's explosive wind tore into a broad outdoor pergola, a flat of golden tiled-stone pillars, burbling fountains, and plaster-and-gold benches wherein persons reclined and admired Zioch's distant resplendence. Such contemplation was destroyed with the king's appearance. Once the small storm he bore with his passage disappeared, and the leaves and whirling flowers lay still, the people hurried back whence Brutus had come. The king stalked the sunny gardens. He thrust his hand into bushes and ripped out writhing snakes—not the ones he wanted, though he snapped their spines just the same. He hurled metal seats as if they were dollhouse furniture and shredded apart lattices like spiderwebs; all in the hopes that the witch hid under or behind one object or another. It made no sense, his hunt, and yet the cloying tease of apples incensed his frenzy far past reason. She was everywhere, her scent, and soon her laugh, and still he couldn't find a throat into which to tear.

"So ferocious," she cooed. "A king of beasts. I shall have you tear into me, though not as you wish."

Brutus cracked a stone bench across his knee, throwing aside the halves. "Silence, foul bloodswain, darkest witch! I shall have thee for my supper!"

No one heard his ranting as the garden was quite abandoned, a ruin of groaning trellises, bleeding fountains, and thrashed bushes. A path from the entrance to where Brutus stood with his cleft bench could be clearly seen. The extent of his swath of destruction, both physical and internal, dawned on the king. Amunai was starting to unmake him. Had he been a man of letters and logic, with a library as great as his brother's Court of Ideas, his reaction would have been to delve into its shelves for any folklore on deathless enchantresses who tormented men through visions and magik. He should have found another way to deal with the situation than simply giving in to his bestial urges. As it was now, the itch to reach out to his brother, to plead for Magnus to fly to his aide, was a temptation he nearly scratched. Brutus fell to his knees and reached out across the expanses of his mind.

"Yes, call him," she purred, from nowhere. "Flee to your brother..."

From the vainglorious tremble in her voice, Brutus knew that was exactly what she wanted—to poison two minds, not just one. He suddenly composed himself, looking about the garden for any semblance of her presence.

"Where are you, spirit?" he demanded. "I know your game, your tricks. I know why you have come."

And like the malevolence he'd imagined, a female transparency manifested near the gaudy balustrade of the garden. She sat upon the ledge as if she were flesh and bone, wearing a fanciful bodice and swishing her ethereal train. Ectoplasmic ripples in the phantom woman's face indicated a smile as the king came to her. "Well, you've figured out the first part of my game, I'll grant you that," said Amunai. "Still, we have many more moves to play."

"Who?"

"Your mother and I." The visitation slipped off the ledge and danced around the king like a glass ballerina. He resisted the urge to crush her, as this was no more than illusion for his taunting and her benefit.

"She has many names, your mother. She wants her lads to come home. She wants her family."

"Magnus and I are both brother and father to one another. I know nothing whatever of the wickedness you speak."

"And lover, too, no?" So suggested, she slid a cool hand down Brutus's thigh, and this time he swatted at her, and his hands passed through sunlight and air. She was untouchable, this was illusion—even before, he must have shattered the pillar in his court himself and imagined the rest of their scuffle.

"It's all well and good, you know," she continued. "Two men, wandering the world since its infancy, without food, or warmth, or love...I would have done the same. I would have wanted a rough, greasy fire to ease my soul. You asked that of him, didn't you? You were as smitten by his beauty as you've been by any sunrise, or the moonlight. You asked it of him, and often he gave it, even without asking. Ooh, the figures the two of you could make, as tangled as a family of snakes. I am not here to judge your morality, though. Nor does your mother judge. She heals. She healed me, and she will free you. If only you'd let her in."

Let. Her. In. Each word resonated with meaning. Brutus drove that promise as far from his mouth as possible. He would never let her in. Whoever she was. Perhaps this gloating witch would let slip her master's identity. *Confess to me your master's name*, he thought.

"Zionae," said Amunai.

The king snarled at the incessant intrusions into his mind.

"Don't pretend to be so violated, my liege. You old things exist in such sad and sorry states—consumed in your sorrows, never sure what's real and what's delusion, never certain if you are awake or asleep...lost in Dream, which is where I rule. I can make you see, hear, and feel anything of my otherworld."

As she spoke, the skyline of Zioch flashed, then roiled with crimson clouds. A sudden heat blistered the king's hide, the odor of singed and maggoty flesh came to him—an untenable charcoal, candied sweetness—and the city beneath him welled with screams. It was an illusion, he knew, and yet it seemed so real.

"Is this what your master wants?" he asked.

"It is not what she wants, but what you want."

"I would never destroy my city."

"One must destroy what is weak to become strong. Your connection to mortals has made you weak, has stripped you of your divinity. Wouldn't you like to live without that fear? That constant questioning as to which nature you embrace: man or beast? I say beast, for that is who you are. That is what brought you and your brother through all the dread seasons of our world, and who Magnus—and your mother—will love."

"Again you speak of this mother, and yet in the lifetimes I have lived I have only known Magnus and myself."

"Would you like to meet her?"

"Yes."

Calmly waiting, as a wolf would bide his time hiding in wait for its prey, the king readied himself. While not a man of great wisdom, he'd gleaned a few important things from the torturous repartee between himself and Amunai. If she wasn't truly here, and thus couldn't be hurt right now, then to murder her he would have to find out where her flesh actually lay. The same sentence of death he would inflict upon this awful mother of which she spoke, an entity whose existence was a lie, as he and Magnus were their own family—brother, father, sister, and mother till the end of time. He'd also learned that this witch could sniff and eat thoughts, though he doubted she was as capable of hunting impressions. Thus he entered his predatory trance, the quiet patience before the slaughter. He allowed nothing of his intent pass through his mind, focusing only on his own bloodlust and guilt. She would be flooded with such a morass of emotions that she wouldn't know what he really intended to do to her and her mistress. At least that was what he hoped.

"You're sincere," whispered Amunai, sounding pleased. "I can feel the tremble of your spirit. The anticipation. You will understand why I had to coax forth your beast as I did. You will understand, and you will thank me. All will be clear once we make the journey east."

"East?"

"To Pandemonia. To the land of your birth. 'Tis where your mother in her starry ark crashed down upon our world—her world, really, as she's come to reclaim it. She's a queen, my lion, the oldest ruler of the blackest stars—the Black Queen. Her coming has been heralded since time immemorial, though you princelings were too busy pretending to be men while all that was being fought over."

"We are wasting time," said Brutus.

"As you wish."

Brutus leapt over the balcony and clawed his way down the golden skin of his fortress. It was good that his kingdom had no skycarriages, or someone spotting his queer mountaineering might have caused further unrest. It was bad enough that Brutus didn't linger to arrange matters of state. Indeed, he wouldn't dare grant this serpent another waft of his intentions. Instead, he allowed the beast to ride him, to consume him. Only by embracing the beast in that wordless, roaring sanctuary of sensate bliss would his purpose be safe—to protect his brother from the sickness that had claimed him, and to follow that illness back to its source. Once he met with Zionae, this false and unholy parent, he would strangle her with whatever umbilical cord she and Amunai believed tied them together. Death to the Black Queen.

VIII

And so the animal within carried Brutus in his odyssey over stone, sand, and sea. Brutus, the man, remembered almost nothing of the journey: a peak of rock from which he leaned, roared, and beat his chest; a gleam of deep emerald water that trapped mysteries beneath it, and into which he dove; and finally, his emergence onto a shore of fragmented crystal—cleft geodes that dazzled like faery innards—and wary, wandering creatures akin to deer rendered in mist. The creatures' blood was strikingly red, too, in contrast to their ethereality. After a long journey, with but fish and cold-blooded flesh to feed upon, Brutus had felt no shame in ravaging the transcendent herd. Besides, there remained in his body a mere whisper of a man to feel remorse. When he was glutted, he walked from the crimson-washed landing and into the chattering realms of Pandemonia, into a great unfolding ocean of colors, scents, and maddening sounds.

A spirit followed him, then, now, and throughout his race to reach the first land: Amunai. She had ceased speaking to him, though she lured and led him forward into the chaos with her scent. It functioned as guide to the beast, and he came from his panting reverie and chased after it.

While moving ever more centrally and eastwardly on the massive continent, the beast dallied often. Too much life abounded, distracting him from his purpose. Too many giants of the old age ruled this land and needed to be challenged by the beast's might. In the crackling lightning-cascaded deserts, where dune and butte lay shining as polar monuments from the electric rain, the beast tangled with the gargantuan claws of landstriders—echoes or remnants of what he'd hunted in the season of dust. These progenitors, or descendants, had all of the strength that he recalled, and even with his dread might he only felled one or two of the massive four-legged and teetering fortresses. Whereupon he danced, howled, and bathed in the crimson spray of its life and devoured all of its blubbery insides that he could. Once more, he left the land drenched in carnage. There wasn't a place to which the beast wandered where his presence wouldn't be felt long after he left. In the forests of starving rubber trees, he felled whole sections of the hideous wealds. These grotesque plants birthed to eat were instead eaten—the eyeballs in their trunks scooped out like caviar, their thorny prehensile branches devoured like steamed octopus served to a Menosian master.

Pandemonia's lesser terrors soon learned that a new horrific predator had come to stand atop their hierarchy and shame them. In time the land became quiet, and yellow-stared, many-mouthed horrors slunk back into their holes and quivered, waiting, as the king of beasts stormed through their realm.

At one day, time, or season, the beast came to a strange city hidden behind a wall of water. It swarmed with lights and technomagikal silver flies. Its heavily refined smells were too complex for his tastes, and he decided against stalking the city and preying on the meat therein. As far gone as his humanity was at that moment, a twinge of regret—perhaps for something lost—diminished his appetite when it came to slow-walkers. Amunai, too, wanted nothing to do with this place.

"Not yet, *sister*," she hissed, and shooed the beast away.

Out again in the land of chaos, more men wandered far and wide—packs of them, some with blue skins and horns who thought themselves clever hunters. He allowed them to hunt, and to live, even though they would have been easy prey. He wasn't at all aware why he granted them such mercy. Although once, a cold voice that shivered through him like a Long Winter's wind blew into his mind and muttered something unintelligible. It had come before, this voice, and on every occasion he had frightened it away with a roar. Had Brutus been slightly more present in his flesh, he might have recognized his brother's calling.

Through a confusion of seasons the beast traveled. Triumphs and glories wrought in the blood of Pandemonia's titans could have been later transcribed in the greatest of epic odes. However, the king remembered nothing other than the thrill of the heights he reached. Of what brought such pleasure and was quickly cast aside in the face of a new rush, a new splash of crimson romance. Blood was his existence, and in a land as fecund as Pandemonia, there was never a dip in supply.

As his journey continued, mountains—black, craggy, ugly as witches' fingers—rose up from the land. Ripping the sky with their shredded-metal shrieks and their claws, wings like rags drenched in tar, were other rulers—old and ancient kings. They swayed through the dark clouds in mesmerizing whirls. They cawed, and lightning and green spume rocked the heavens. They were monsters of such measure that the beast did not seek to conquer them; rather, he walked, as a lion in a den of lions, and to him that respect was returned. As he strode through the ash of their kingdom, he called up to the kings of the sky, and they called down to him. Other pitiable beasts were around, foraging off a land without bounty. Since they were so timid, the beast gave them a reprieve from the hunt. These nomads carried a guilty pong of murder, too, as if they consumed their own pack, and the noble lion wanted none of their stink upon his hands. From the soul of the land there was a song being sung, a grand wail of the dying, which engrossed him more than sky lords and foragers.

He passed through a desert, climbed to the peak of a resplendent mountain of black crystal, snuck past the strange tribe that lived there, then dropped through a rip in the world. Cautious, he crept down the great cleft, gripping the white strata of age upon age in his rock-splintering fists, moving toward an epicenter of pitch-black. These lines were once stone, or perhaps the ossified remains of life seared into the valley. Indeed, if he'd been more patient, or inclined, he might have noticed the ashen impressions of bones from men and animals and giants. The beast did not care enough, however, to notice such things. Rather, the intoxication of death was drunk down like nectar from the lotus of death into which he descended. How old was this death? How powerful the creation of it to have soured the air to a paste of cinders and chalk? The beast asked none of these questions, for his mind wasn't able to conjecture. Still, he felt the importance of this doom, he felt the profundity of it, and this was what, at last, stirred the shadow of man within him.

When the descent was complete, Brutus awoke. He stood in a chamber hushed by dust and dread. The vacant cavity was hung with cones of decay. Crumbled rock, ash, and disintegrated matter from an apocalyptic impact had been woven by the slow deterioration of the cavern as icicles were formed over time. He had waded waist-deep through the underground ocean of ruin, and by the animalism of his gaze he could see the path he'd cleaved through the floor behind. No matter his might and bravery, his chest pounded with fear.

To where have I come? he wondered.

In the ultimate grayness, the road ahead seemed illumed and important, a reef of black stone that rose from the ocean of dust. Feeling pulled to the altar of rock, he climbed. Age fell from him like a cloak of sand, and he stood, naked, confused, and scared atop the monument, looking down at a preciously arranged and fleshless corpse. The body had been laid out in picturesque fashion, the grinning skull atop a torso with arms crossed—one hand missing—and femurs together. It was a *she*, he realized, as even time could not dilute the fragrance of the woman's sweat clinging to her remains. Inexplicably, these bones had escaped the omnipresent decay; they gleamed and tantalized like ivory flutes, demanding to be touched and played. The king stopped himself from reaching down and touching them. Every hunter's warning he knew—the clenching of his balls, teeth, and skin, the cold sweat and fiery pulse—forbade him the impulse.

Amunai's now familiar wispy presence appeared before him. Around the king she floated, leaving trails like a cold breath. "I see that you've returned to your senses. Many seasons have come and gone during your hunt, though time is ephemeral to you who do not know its ravages."

"How long?"

"Seasons."

Ghost and king threw aspersions at one another in the silence. He believed he had been duped. Where was the master of the witch? What was he doing here, in the world's oldest grave?

"I brought you to your mother, as I was bade," said Amunai, her amusement ringing in the hollowness.

Brutus's roar rang, too. "This is nothing! Your master is more ghost than you! I have played your game. I crossed land and sea, I've cast out my brother to—" He stopped short. In his rage, Brutus had nearly revealed his hand.

"To protect him?" Amunai laughed. "Did you think that I wouldn't know? You did so very well to hide your heart, Brutus. But you cannot separate yourself from Magnus, not ever. You cannot stop, for even a speck, concerning yourself with his welfare, though he's long since given up thinking about you. He should be the weaker one, given his infirm flesh and compared to your engine of muscle and lust. I know, however, how to tease out the truth. Magnus was never weak. He is the eternal mind, the Will of your brotherhood. You are nothing but the meat, and meat can be made into whatever dish is chosen. We need your meat, Brutus. Your mother will fill you with her Will, one that rivals your brother's. She will be the greatness that you lack."

"Chicanery and witchcraft!" The king had begun to slaver, to surrender to the beast. "I am here...grrr...I shall have my hunt...grrr...I shall find you in this land, wherever you hide...grrr...Your blood will be my wine, your flesh my meal."

"Yes, yes," goaded Amunai.

He was close to losing all reason. One more push. She needed him to touch her master's ancient vessel, the bones, since only then could her master's voice reach its child's soul. No lesser magik, or talisman, could break the king. She couldn't even be sure this would.

"I should love to be eaten by you," she continued, to the snarling, drooling Immortal. "And what of her?" Amunai's fuming hand pointed at the remains. "What of your mother? You have come so far. You could at least offer your respects to the woman who bore you."

"Bore me? I am a child of Geadhain. I have no other mother!"

With that, he broke. He hunched over, made boulders of his fists, and smashed the skeleton at his feet. The pelvis shattered, dust puffing and bones scattering akimbo, into the ocean of filth. The grinning skull rocked where it lay, and the king's hands settled on the pulverized fragments of what remained of the skeleton. Silence fell across the cavern after the explosion, a quiet as sudden and deadly as the calm after the fall of an executioner's ax. Amunai didn't need her fleshy ears to hear the sound, the wheeze from across time and space, as Zionae's most distant whisper crossed from eternity and entered her son like a hungry scarab.

Amunai observed the king's trembling as bone dust settled on his hands, and fire burned his insides. *What is she showing you?* wondered the dark priestess, in jealousy and awe. What future or past could be so terrible as to break the spirit of an immortal man, and make him wail, weep blood, gurgle crimson vomit, and bash his head into rock? But that pain wouldn't leave him, that *truth*, no matter how Brutus tried to excise it through a hole in his cranium. It burrowed deeper, feeding on his torment as the skull on the altar rocked as though mocking him with laughter. The whisper in his head bred new scarabs, new storms to devour and tear at him.

When it was over, what had once been Brutus lay prone on a reef glistening with the excretions his transformation had produced—a rancid foam of diarrhea, sick, urine, blood, and whatever inky poison bled out of the king's already engorged body. From that heinous afterbirth, he rose. Reborn as a crimson-black conqueror, a man unchained from empathy, devoid of love, and hungry for each and every heart on Geadhain.

"Who are you?" asked Amunai, giddy and delirious.

"I am hunger," he said.

"Come, hunger, lord of darkness, lord of filth, consumer of the earth and the green." Amunai, drifting away, beckoned him. "Seek me in the east, at the edge of this land, and see the kingdom that I have built for you. Seek me and claim the stone with which you will bind fire itself to your Will and melt away your brother's arrogance."

"Brother?" said the reborn king—he had to contemplate if he had one of those.

"You will remember what she needs you to remember."

It was a statement that haunted both monster and ghost as they vanished into the underground.

IX

Originally, in the days of Amunai's reign and for eras before, the Anemorax, the Gate of Wind, was among the centerpieces of Pandemonian culture and design. It wasn't uncommon for the Faithful to take their pilgrimages in the east, as dangerous as it might be to travel that terrain. They were drawn by such promises of beauty and grace awaiting them in Aesorath. Aside from the sandy-gold towers with their flute casings and the bridges of gossamer string that played as harpsichords in the wind, the uncontested beauty of Aesorath lay below, not above. There, in the catacombs of Aesorath's Purgatorium, in the founding hallways of the city kept untouched by grandeur, was where the city's greatest treasure was found. It was there that the Anemorax hummed a song that shivered stone and sand, a music that both stirred and calmed the wind that played maestro with the city.

In those days, the Anemorax had been used as a matrix to contain the arkstone's power. Amunai recalled, with untarnished wonder, what it was like to stand in the chamber of the Anemorax and to behold not one miracle, but two. Its chamber was similar to the others that held arkstones in the other three great cities. However, the previous generations of Aesorath's Keepers had decided to maintain the old charisma of a handwrought stone chamber decorated with ancient hieroglyphs, against the dazzling ostentation of a climbable court upon which radiated, and gyrated, a helix made of many titan-sized bracelets of crystal. The arkstone floated at the heart of the helix, like an emerald embedded in the sun, and whence came the Gate of Wind's power. In a memory laid atop memories, Amunai recalled the legionnaires and wards wailing at her as she'd rushed into that glorious corona of light and throbbing wind with the intention of smashing that tiny jewel with a spear of her Will. Those fools shouldn't have left it so unprotected or, more pertinently, have believed in its security so steadfastly. A single furious woman's magik had undone one of the world's oldest empires, which wasn't even an uncommon tale when one looked back over Geadhain's history.

Emerging from her reminiscence, she saw that nothing from her memories remained in the chamber of the Anemorax. What rubble was strewn about after the catastrophic collapse of the underground hollow had since been hauled away by those reborn from Zionae's Will. Many Redeyes—newly birthed—now busied themselves about the chamber, bossing around the lesser black-eyed grunts upon the elevation that housed the Anemorax. It was still for the moment, mere cold loops of motionless crystal without a glorious heart of power inserted, though all that would soon change. Water didn't have the efficiency of wind; however, Eatoth's arkstone still possessed the power and propulsion necessary for translocation, and soon the Anemorax would ripple and churn in a whirlpool of dizzying sorcery.

Amunai and Brutus stood on distant flagstones, far away from the spectacle and considering that change. With two arkstones in their possession, they could both power the ancient gate and summon Brutus's elemental pet, but the arkstone of fire was ideally suited for the second task.

In a matter of days, they would be able to travel anywhere in Geadhain, with any number of forces, and a primordial elemental heralding their arrival with an apocalypse of fire. Brutus's army wouldn't have much to conquer other than some smoking graves. She supposed that was the point: catastrophic victory. While she and her companion pondered what transpired here or would transpire in the future, she allowed herself a moment of pride over her virtuosity in enacting her plans. Few stumbles could be seen on the road to victory, and what outliers existed she had taken care of back in Eatoth.

Wise men said that revenge was an empty dish, but she was enjoying her serving. Although the motive guiding her vengeance, the reason for wanting to kill her sister, was never manifested to Amunai, her revenge felt no less satisfying. She had worried that being deprived of the full impetus for murderous impulses—Zionae having taken this reason and its associated pain from her to make her strong—would have sapped the act of its pleasure. However, the bitch, Ankha, was dead, even if Amunai couldn't recall why she should be. Besides, reason was moralistic in the sort of world she and the king were creating. Blood alone was reason, logic, and reward.

"Are we ready?" demanded Brutus.

Suddenly his great shadow had fallen in her direction and ruined her sunny thoughts on murder like rainclouds. "Ready for what, my King?"

"To retake my kingdom, to wake the beast that sleeps in the ashes of Zioch."

He could be such a simple creature. That was the cost of chaining his Will. Zionae had almost taken too much from him, too much of his pain and memory. Amunai patted his huge, limp hand. "No, not yet. A few more days."

"I shall win."

"I know. I know."

"Why are we here?"

"I wanted to show you how close we are. How near your victory." Really, she had been bored and needed a walk; the king, lacking direction, had followed.

"I see. I cannot...remember."

"I know. I know." She patted him again.

To be reduced to an imbecile all because you fell in love with a giant dog and were too scared to tell your brother, she thought. *What weaknesses men allow to flourish in their hearts.* If Zionae continued to erode his mind, by the end of this war she would be feeding her liege pudding as he sat in a rocking chair. Brutus's distance from the elemental of fire seemed only to compound that spiritual erosion; he had been stronger and better focused after summoning the creature. Perhaps he needed the elemental now, and he was tethered to it for sentience and survival.

Brutus's rapidly deteriorating mind aside, she couldn't stop thinking about the king's failed and tangled romance—love's absurdities being a favored distraction of hers. What men did for love, and who and how they chose to love, was always more ill-fated than successful. Every now and then, when she bored of her kingdom, she wandered into Dream to hunt. She would torment whatever sleeping minds she could reach and turn their hosts into homicidal surgeons who, while sleepwalking, amputated their lovers' sacred parts. That's how love should end—in blood and amputation. She fiercely believed that. Certainly, the reason why she so despised, and was fascinated by, love was tied to the memories that had been removed by her master. For her own benefit, she presumed. Otherwise, she might have been the same pitiable mule hobbled by love that Brutus had been. He was a better man and king now, regardless of the cost.

A Redeye approached them from behind. Amunai felt his presence and sensed the sulfurous sweetness of his burned skin. She turned to find one of her favorite aides, the young Amakri lad who'd once been so polite as to bow to her after his recent rebirth. Crimson hate sputtered from the sockets of his skull and dripped luminous magma or blood across his blackened countenance, and she could see nothing of the boy he'd once been—that child was erased, and this new creature was so much more fascinating. He stood tall in his twist of ashen rags, and bore his cindery, pulsing staff with the pride of elder wards of Brutus's new court. She had seen this reborn arguing—in scathing mind-whispers—with his seniors, once going so far as to incinerate a man who had challenged him. For that she'd given him the name of one of Pandemonia's oldest and wickedest generals, a man without scruples or empathy of any kind: Rex, the Left Hand of Teskatekmet.

"Rex," she said.

He clung to his staff and bowed to a knee. "Herald." For a reborn, even a Redeye, he possessed a remarkable amount of personality and nuance. "I bring word from our scouts: we have tracked the Daughter of Fate."

"You have?"

"Indeed. She and her company are headed toward the Cradle—our trackers lost them for a time in a swamp, but they have since picked up the trail. You were wise in believing that she would attempt to enter it."

Amunai sneered. "Vexing to the end. I think it is time that we end her interference. What say you, my King?"

"Hmm?" Brutus glanced toward them, scowling from either pain or displeasure, and then returned to watching Blackeyes scurry about the Anemorax. He was falling apart faster than either Amunai or the Black Queen had planned.

"Herald?" pressed Rex, knowing all decisions lay in her hands.

"Where is she now? Exactly?"

Rex closed his fiery eyes and the igneous runes and markings chiseled into his flesh pulsed from concentration. Just as Amunai was connected to Rex and his kind, so too were the Redeyes linked to their army. She preferred that arrangement, since the lesser minds were as simple as earthworms, almost nonsensically dull, with but the basest of needs—to work, fuk, and eat—to fulfill. She couldn't understand them and was loath to take possession of their bodies. Amunai didn't appreciate missing out on important news, however, or having to wait. She quickly grew impatient.

Rex took a breath, and his spirit was again present. "She and her company are in the lands outside the Cradle. We have spotted her, from a distance. Even from afar she seems to be evoking a ritual of some kind. Grand and unpleasantly bright; her power is like a beacon of light."

"What is she doing?"

"Communing with the past? What other powers could she evoke?"

None. She is at the end of her list of talents. Amunai tapped her chin. "And the others?"

"From the patterns in the ether, I would say that they are joined in mind and soul to her, communing and separate from the world."

"Wait, they are *helpless* then?"

Once more showing his unique disposition, Rex grinned. "Yes, Herald. I presumed you wish them surrounded? Our legion will wait for your command."

"Oh, it is given. End her." Amunai drew her dearest minister into her confidence and walked away from the king. "As for the young dog"—Caenith, Rex deduced—"spare him if you can. I know not how much longer a certain vessel can hold our master's might, and we should prepare a contingency."

For conspirators whispering behind him about regicide and treason, Brutus gave them pitiable heed. Instead his mind was stuck on a single word the Herald had spoken, one that evoked in him a stabbing pain.

"Dog," muttered Brutus.

VII

WINTER'S KINGDOM

I

Beckon the North, these winds that call.
A patient ruse, this gentle fall.
Of snow that swims across thy sight.
Ancient voice, in deepest ice...

As one mind in two bodies, a single breathing, beating creature, Lila and Erik watched the blackest of waves attack the whitest of shores. Together they played make-believe, imagining what the woolly spots in the misty dales that lay beyond might be. Trees, Erik saw on those hills, though forests as decorated with winter as objects of crystal, and great lakes, and even far-off villages mostly encased in ice. Those distant settlements showed signs of life—wisps of smoke and even scratches of voices. These people had admirably, if stubbornly, staked their claim in the boot of the North. Farther away, with more instinct than sight, and in a realm scorned by the sun, he sensed that a darkness had risen—a vast frozen tide of ice and rock, the shattered kingdom of Winter herself. There would be no villages there, for even a fool wouldn't stake a tent in that pitiless domain.

That poem was lovely, whispered Erik.

The poetry belongs to Kericot. I am but his voice.

And once his muse, as you are mine.

True, the bard had written a poem about her: "A Maiden Fair." Kericot had been on her mind a lot lately, thoughts of the long-dead bard provoked by a recent memory or sense of déjà vu she couldn't quite place. Indeed, in traveling north, she had been plagued by memories. Although Lila forgot the mysteries of the dead bard and of her own carefully tended secrets as Erik pressed his hot chest to her back, as hot as if their flesh were naked—burning right through her leathers and furs. She recalled last night's torrid encounter as they'd twirled and thrust against each other in a steamy cabin down in the ship's hold. The creeping end of the world seemed to have filled their spirits with a desperate lust, and it was the first time they had touched since Magnus's incapacitation.

Down the deck from them, Magnus stood facing the hoary morn without the comfort of a lover. Even ignoring him for the time being, his presence and the inexorable chill of his loneliness infected the bloodmates, and turned afoul the crisp pleasure of both the morning and their embrace. Erik gazed at the sulking king, and he pitiably returned that stare out of the sliver of sight left by the scarves swaddling his head. In order to remain incognito, they had decided to wrap his face against the elements, even if he would never be cold here, in the season of his birth. Still, the turmoil in Magnus's stare and heart said enough to his bloodmates.

Sighing together, Lila and her knight strode down the slippery ice-patched deck toward their missing third. A mast swung overhead, and they ducked in unison and before the jacks could begin their shouting. In a moment, they joined Magnus at the railing, and they avoided another embrace.

"'Tis not your intimacy that disturbs me," said the king. "I have made peace with our entanglement. Even while you and she made love last eve, I wasn't bothered. Strange, how I can feel that. Him inside of you...inside of me, at times. Strange. Although the impressions come as though I'm viewing history within the Hall of Memories, or envisioning the pages from an erotic book. Such distance makes it a tolerable nuisance."

No visible breath came through Magnus's scarf, as if his body couldn't produce vapor of the proper temperature. The detail distracted Erik, but he shrugged it off and said, "You are troubled, though, and if not from our romance, then you must tell us from what. Suffering your anxiety is no less a nuisance to us than is forcing the pleasure of our contact upon thee—for which we are sorry. We are bound in this, to the end."

"To the end, yes..." Magnus touched Erik's hand. The king wasn't wearing gloves, and the chill of his flesh was withering. "I feel something: a calling, a myth. Whenever I sleep, I dream of snakes, and ice, and songs of shattering glass. I think that is the call of the creature for which we have come. I want to touch it, to love it. I believe it wants to touch me, as well."

"The elemental?" the bloodmates asked.

"Nifhalheim," whispered the king.

Magnus held himself as Erik had Lila a sand past. Truly, he needed none of their meek intimacy, that dance of sweat, seed, and need. For whatever sang in the creak of the deck, the lap of the Feordhan, whatever beast rumbled the gray indigestion of the sky, was the longing voice of his one true love. How had he ever not heard it? It seemed as loud and real as the thunder in his heart. She had no words, this lover, though she spoke as did music, evoking passion, confusion, and desire.

"Magnus?" said Lila.

She had been shaking his arm, and Magnus only now felt the shuddering. Passive and distant, he looked at her hand, shrugged it off, and stared back at the ivory yolk of the horizon. Many sands ago, Erik had left them to play strongman with the friendly jacks of the *Fleet Otter*. He was both heard and sensed hefting crates and tightening rigging with praiseworthy gusto. Now it was only Magnus and the queen. Or rather, *Samuel* and his sister, Lady Siobhan, were one of the sailors to address either of them.

Lila considered the fates that had brought them here, and what a turn of good fortune they'd had in finding the *Fleet Otter* in Carthac's port, about to set sail. From Eod, they had flown straight to the outskirts of the Carthac, after which they'd snuck into the city to charter a quick voyage to the Feordhan. Inconspicuousness was needed at every step, for they didn't know how far Brutus's reach might be, or what foolish madman might attempt to assassinate or ransom a royal. During their dash through Carthac, Lila had been heartbroken that she wasn't able to visit the Sisters of St. Celcita. She had seen the peak of the old basilica, though, and knew with her heart that the Sisters and their order were alive and well. She would check in on them after the war. At least Erik was living part of his dream: sailing the Feordhan, traveling north. At least some dreams might be realized before the world ended.

However, she hated to be here again; when last she and Erik had sailed the Upper Feordhan, she had been cabin-bound and under the influence of otherworldly tormentors. Nor was this the second trip she had taken to the North, but the third. Indeed, her first voyage in these waters had been an ugly, tainted experience that she wanted never to remember. She'd told no one, not even her distant husband at the time, about it. Not that Magnus had ever deigned to ask whence these newest orphans with whom she had returned to Eod had come.

Erik harked from his labors afar. *Lila?*

"Lila?" asked her second bloodmate, alarmed by the brief vision they shared of a fire and screaming men, which she quickly sealed in her vault.

"I am not ready to speak of this, yet," she replied to both.

Erik's spirit roiled her guts at her keeping of secrets—he was only recently discovering that bloodmates, like normal persons, were capable of hiding pieces of themselves from each other. Magnus, unconcerned, and in no position to judge her secrecy, took the liberty of slipping an arm around his former wife. It was an intimately familiar reassurance, a skill for consolation grown from their centuries of marriage, through seeing empires rise, take up arms, and then fall against the combined might of their power, intellect, and Will.

"You were always the real pride of our nation," said Magnus. "You were always the fighter, the one who knew how to soldier on when I was broken. When you are ready to face your pain, I shall try to be there for you this time—as I have so rarely been in the past. I have not thanked you for all the times when you have been my courage, for pushing me when I believed myself intractable. You will have to push me again, and soon, and that is why I am so beholden to you on this journey."

"Push you? To do what?" Suddenly, she was no longer worried about her secret.

"I see my destiny. I know what I must do."

The king said nothing further, lured instead by the singing beast of the North—a song that, even while connected to the souls of two others, was a music heard only by his ears. Upon his sad shoulder, the queen rested her head. She grieved with him for whatever losses he had yet to endure. As Erik continued his labor, he felt not jealousy when he glanced at the pair, but sorrow.

II

A storm beat down the channel, and they spent the night below deck, despite Magnus's reluctance. A crew of deckhands came down the stairs into the mess hall that formed the belly of the ship. They stomped the snow from their boots and shook it from their jackets, before quickly wandering to the kegs bolted down near the wall to fetch themselves mugs of ale mulled with spices and heated by technomagik. A few of them stood near the flickering spheres of golden light mounted upon the wall, warming themselves like freezing urchins. Eventually, the men had spread themselves around the hall's benches and covered the tables with gambling artifacts—cards and dice and oak boards—on which to play Wrath.

However, as besotted as the sailors grew, and as rowdy as the room became with their laugher and merriment, no one bothered the Lady Siobhan or her consorts. The three sipped their ale and huddled with the closeness of plotting witches. A few seamen thought they saw their mouths move, although they weren't speaking at a volume above which any animal could sense. And even while some of the crew had previously accompanied the lady and her protector, neither seemed as they remembered. The knight was black, the frightening shade and menace of an obsidian hammer. Moreover, whatever scraps of the lady's beauty were revealed when she slipped back her scarf for a sip, or adjusted her hood, were simply too pretty to look at without risking disgrace and tightness in one's trousers: rosebud lips, caramel skin, hair as shining as gold caught in dusk's last sunlight. She couldn't have been that beautiful, as comely as a siren from a story, as comely as a queen, some thought. Siobhan's brother gave them chills. What flesh of his could be seen was as pale as death. *Just the drink at work*, decided one of the sailors, and he washed away the unease by drinking more. Still, no amount of inebriation could bolster his or any other's courage to approach the strangers. Thus when the browned and wrinkled captain of the vessel sat beside Magnus and slammed down his ale, the trio jumped in surprise.

"Good eve," he said.

"Is it?" murmured Magnus, tightening the wool around his chin.

"I believe so, er—"

"Samuel. My name is Samuel Rosewater."

"Is it?" A shadow seemed to descend as the sea-fox and king fenced with their Wills, and either the sea-fox surrendered or decided that whatever he might say wasn't worth the conflict. He banished the discomfort with an old but handsome smile.

"Rosewater...That's surely the surname signed on the logs from before and when last your sister boarded our vessel. Unless my memory fails me. I am getting on, though, as creaky as this old bucket of a ship, and all these details tend to leak. Speaking of details, where was it that you were headed again, m'lady? Southreach?"

Ever the protector, Erik intercepted him. "Lady Siobhan Rosewater is *from* Southreach. When we sailed together last season we were headed east, to Menos, to find sanctuary."

"Were ye now?" The sea-fox sipped his ale and sucked his teeth. "I suppose that didn't turn out to be the safest foxhole, eh?"

"No," said the bloodmates, and none of the three shared in the captain's laughter.

"I shouldn't take such glee in others' misfortunes," resumed the captain. "Although I dare say if anyone deserved the hammer of the divine upon their heads it was those iron bastards." He took a long swig and pondered something. "Where are my manners? Speaking such gossip in the company of my betters. Since we were on about the business of names, before all that Menos talk, I should properly introduce myself." He dusted his hand off on the lapel of his naval coat, then extended it for a shake.

"Nolan. Nolan Rosewater." When no one claimed his floating hand, the captain laid it on the table, fingers spread, and leaned in to whisper, "You see, I thought it was mighty strange last time when you introduced yourself as noble, and then as family I'd never known myself to have. We Rosewaters are a close bunch—salt, soil, and earth folk, as tight as a den of badgers. We know too much about each other, more than friends and family should. After we'd docked and heard the news about what happened in the Iron City, I talked with me wife and gran, then they talked to the rest of our kin. We made inquiries to our family east, west, and south, though none of the Rosewaters had the courage to go anywhere beyond the lands of the Swannish. That's when I started thinking about the woman I'd given passage to. Her and her large companion, who bore more than passing resemblances to figures—lofty, important figures I'd never seen, but always known the echoes of their grandeur. I know a Rosewater when I see one, and now I can say the same of an Immortal."

They had been recognized. Magnus worried about the extent of their exposure, Erik about whether to start smashing things, and Lila chastised herself for not glamouring the lot of them, which she hadn't planned for until under the magikal scrutiny of Valholom's keepers. Though who would recognize three people buried in winter clothing before then? Apparently, a shrewd old sea dog. Nolan, seemingly disappointed, shook his head.

"What do you want?" asked the king.

"What do I want?" Nolan trembled in an effort to restrain his rage. "Here I am ferrying cargo from Carthac to Valholom, where my family, the ones who survived the attacks of the dead, try to scrape out a life among some of the hardest frontiersmen you'll ever know. Here I am sailing from nowhere to nowhere while the sea that I've loved will soon swallow what remains of man and civilization...What do I want? I want it to end: the blood, the war, the pain. We're all at the mercy of you kings and queens. Prithee pity us, free us from your games."

Abruptly, the rush of anger left him, and bursting with wonder and tears, he quietly beseeched them. "I'll take you to whatever Kings' damned port you need to be to release us from your war...Oh, King's damned..." Nolan snickered, given his company.

A long, cold, and muffled restraint held everyone's tongues for a time, as they sorted lies, assessed danger, and finally deemed each other allies. Lila could have bewitched the man into subservience and forgetfulness. Instead she responded with calm.

"Valholom will do."

"And after that, m'lady?" The captain was suddenly struck by a need for reverence, for her voice had been as gentle and inspiring as that of the queen she concealed. Cautiously, he whispered, "How much farther are you to head into the wild North? Its winds will challenge even a man who was born in winter. You could become lost, and I know not if we have the time for any of you to become lost."

"What choice do we have?" asked Erik. He would strike out into a blinding snowstorm to serve his queen and hunt this elemental. "A path has been laid, and that path is ahead. We go north from Valholom, come what may."

"Aye, but the path north has perils from ages even the oldest mind has forgotten, and newer dangers still." The captain waited for a glimmer of recognition in the eyes of the three, saw none, and continued. "My lieges, given your own problems, I can forgive your lack of insight into foreign affairs, but the Northlands aren't much safer than Central Geadhain at the moment."

Magnus remembered a few reports that he'd shuffled through, ones probably deserving of greater attention, wherein Dorvain's forces had been recalled in their entirety from the Northern Front—all the way across the Upper Feordhan and behind Kor'Keth's mountainous wall. As of now, not one of Eod's footholds in the North remained. Dorvain's jotted, succinct explanation for the troop movements and territorial surrender of what had been peaceful outposts had been listed as *attrition*. Despite the deluge of perils raining down on Eod, Magnus wished he had better grilled his watchmaster about these reports before heading north.

"How so?" asked Magnus, after a long pause.

"Some danger is due to the basics of strife, my liege," replied the captain. "You'll see when you get to Valholom. Men from the continent are scrounging for work and food; families from the south with their thin skin and summer dispositions, who have never known cold like them Northmen do. There's very little space, and too many people to share it. For the Northlands have their own share of refugees now, as well, and they tend to take priority over migrants from Central Geadhain."

"Refugees?"

"Aye, my lord, against the Scourge of Winter." Given the blank stares all around, Nolan continued. "The creeping frost? The villages swallowed by glaciers and the tribes who've vanished? The hordes of beasts pushed ever southward—some mad creatures even hurling themselves into the Feordhan? Have you been deaf and blind to all of this? It's a curse, as if cast by one of Alabion's wickedest witches. Ice seeks to reclaim the land from men, freezing people as they sleep, eat, or squat on the chamber pot. It comes with no warning, my lord, at best a song the henswives say, which comes on the wind, then a snowstorm like one you might create. Then—" Nolan snapped his fingers. "Frozen. The tallest tales say that a man lives beyond this death, that if you break off an icy branch of his arm, he'll bleed and you can almost hear his scream. I've never tested those rumors, or seen these poor frozen and half-dead souls, though I can't deny the push of the land's own people southward, into Valholom. Tribes and clans that haven't seen a brick not carved from ice in all their years. They'd cross farther, but news of your troubles has them pinched between one disaster and another."

What an embarrassment that the king and his bloodmates had no notion of these upheavals. With the fluctuations in magikal currents, and a lack of interest in whatever resources might be bartered for with the North, the people of Eod remained deaf and blind to their neighbors across the Feordhan. Central Geadhain was too much an insular continent, having only a casual interest in other nations and lands, though wanting nothing aside from its own riches and culture. It seemed as though this apathy had been learned from its leaders.

Embarrassed, the king said, "We have heard nothing of a scourge or of any flights to the larger cities, or *tyrs*, of the Northlands." A small respect, though at least he recalled what the Northmen termed their larger centers of population: tyrs—fyrs for the smaller ones.

"Flee they have, to the point where not many more can fit within Valholom's walls," replied Nolan. "The city has reached capacity. 'Tis why even in such desperate times, trade and exchange between Carthac and the Northlands must continue. As it is, famine haunts Valholom, and I pray that winter keeps men's minds cool enough that riots don't begin. You're leaving one land at war and delving into another. You will need a guide."

Erik's bravado flared up. "What need have we for a guide? I can tame any weather and no scourge will weaken my body." He barely held in check the urge to pound the table. A flush of soothing emotion shivered through him from Lila, dispelling his anger. As of late, she had noticed a sharp turn in his moods, which had become the temperament of an Immortal—often as haughty and rash as they could be wise. She interceded on his behalf.

"What my beloved—"

"Beloved?" muttered Nolan, and gaped.

"Concern yourself with mortal affairs," decreed the queen, with her own Immortal hubris and an exudation of scintillating spice that vanished like a conjuror's sulfur, and calmed every man in the room. "What Erik meant to say was that we are not typical travelers, and we can endure more than most. We can find our own way north."

Nolan rubbed his eyes, as if newly waking, and snorted. "Right. Of course you can. However, your way may not be the quickest. The roads are gone, and there are blinds of snow in the North that can barely be cut with a blade. Until you've seen a land set so wholly in winter's icy grip, even you should measure your claims." A sudden shiver, and Nolan remembered the legends of the pale, green-eyed Immortal who sat beside him emanating chill. "Pardon, my lord. You might know of such a winter, if the stories are true."

"They are," replied the king. What wasn't mentioned in the tales was how he had been required to completely rely on Brutus's strength for survival. He had done very little other than huddle and make fires during the Long Winter. Dribs and drabs of those memories trickled into his bloodmates, and they, too, learned of his predicament. "Still, a guide might be wise, if the territory is as dangerous as you say."

"It is."

"Very well. We shall seek one out at the first port."

"I know of a man," offered the captain.

Erik interrupted them, his tone explaining his intractability rather well. "We shouldn't further impose upon your good graces. We can find our own man."

"He's a young man who's occasionally in the company of a young woman, whom I had in mind."

Erik waved his hand in dismissal. "Really, we can manage—"

"My lord, you don't understand—"

"Impudence!"

Now Erik slammed his fists on the table, and the shockwave of his might sent coins, dice, cups, and lager flying from every table in the room. Many dismissed the incident as a fabrication of their inebriated minds—a bump or an ice floe in the waves. It couldn't have been their fair-weather sailor and friend, for while he was strong, no man had power like that. After the initial jolt, and while picking up the mess, men snuck stares at the captain and the trio, none of whom had moved or lost their drinks in the tumult. The captain recuperated from the wrath of an Immortal by nursing dry the cup that had flown into his hands when the table jumped. Drunkenness gave him a blind courage, and once more he spoke. "I'm sorry, great lords and lady. I did not mean to overstep."

"*I* am sorry," said Erik, head bowed in shame. *I am to be noble. I am to be your knight.* Lila's hand held his. *My body is changing. My moods and my heart—though it will always beat for you, my Queen. I feel as if there is a thunder in my voice when I mean only to whisper. I feel that I might break what is fragile when I seek only to mend it.*

The burden of power lies in its weight, said Magnus. *That burden can crush you. You can become that weight—that oppressive destruction—and nothing more. I have watched power unmake the mighty: Taroch, Solomon, Arimoch. Be wary, my son, though I do not see such folly in your future.*

Thank you.

In his heart, they shared a cold but comforting embrace.

"Lords? M'lady?" For the past sand or so, Nolan had become an irrelevance to the circle of Immortals, as they had spoken on channels he couldn't conceive of. As they returned to the mortal world, all three of their eagle gazes fell to the mouse at their table.

Nolan stuttered a tad as he spoke. "Th-they come with my greatest recommendation, th-these guides. I know that security and discretion are what you seek more than anything, and while I have only known of this tracker for a while, he is renowned for his services; no foray is too far or too deep. There's a grace to him, a courtesy and honor that you can feel warming one's hands held over the fire. I don't know if he's magik, but he tracks like he is. They say, even, that he is one of the lost children of the Seal Fang, a tribe made extinct by the flesh merchants of the Iron City. If that be true, he is one of the true bloods of the North. Older than when the Lords of Carthac and other expatriates of Central Geadhain fled down the Feordhan, nursed their wounds in the cold, and bred with the savages of the North to become, at least, more noble tyrants than they'd been elsewhere. That's the mix you'll find now, among the Northmen; it's a mingling of all the cultures and identities they once were. However, the Seal Fang, Raven Wing, and Bear Claw are what *was*—the three great tribes who once existed in respectful isolation of the Northmen. I believe this man to be one, knowing what he's done and the trips he's taken. He can take you to the heart of winter, or farther."

Farther than the heart of winter? The Immortals pondered such a journey. Whilst thinking, winter's song whistled through the metal of the ship, alluring the king, making him turn his head north...

"Yes," declared Erik on behalf of his bloodmates. "We shall meet with your guide."

In an attempt at camaraderie, he seized one of the captain's hands as it rested upon the table. "Thank you for your assistance." His vise tightened on the captain's fingers—Erik unmindful of his instantaneous transition from friend to inquisitor. "I must know, though, if your intentions are sincere. If this is a trap, I shall break the snare and come back to break you—into the smallest of pieces. I shall not see my queen betrayed."

"Nor would I!" The captain hissed, pinching back tears. "And you're breaking me already." Erik freed the man's hand.

While nursing his sore fingers, the captain rose and made to leave. He gave parting remarks. "I'm helping you because I know that the world is going right down one of them fancy Eodian toilets of yours. In the shitter, as they say. I don't have a chance at changing the world or stopping a war. However, you three who move stars, cause earthquakes with your farts, and convert heathens into armies certainly do. Yes, I know of that, m'lady; the legend of your wooing the unwooable children of the desert reached fast and far. If you can change a culture of woman-hating bastards into philosophical wise men, then I have no doubt you can fix what's wrong in our world."

Sentimentality overcame the captain, and he removed his hat and bowed to Lila. "M'lady, I must confess that my wife's Arhadian. What you did for your army has helped all women to take a stand. They cast her out, you know? Those bastards and their fuking khek. They're khek. All of them. She wandered all the way to Taroch's Arm with hardly a drop of water left in her blood. But kind souls nourished her, and you've now nourished all the lasses who would've been as she was one day. I admire what you've done—as cold as it was. War's cold. It's brutal. It's what needs be done even though no one wants to do it. I'm sure when my Mineesha—my missus—knows that I had a chance to help the leader of her people...Well, it'll be a happy day for this sailor come home. I shan't say a word of our talks to anyone, aside from my wife, and there's no person safer with a secret than she. There need be no threats to enforce that promise. I swear it on my daughters, my wife, and my son. They're waiting for me in Valholom. Speaking of which, I should check our course and see that we reach the city sure and safe. If I may take my leave?"

"You may," replied the queen.

Bent from humility, the captain made his way out of the noisy hall, fading off into pipe smoke and out the door. With equal modesty, the Immortals thought of the man and then his words. For such a simple man, who believed he couldn't influence the powers that be, he had left the Immortals inspired. They would thank him with a victory. They would find and bind Nifhalheim to Magnus's Will.

III

It had long been rumored that Taroch—or his parents—had come from the North, and the warlord had certainly held a loving flame for the traditions of that realm. Suspicions aside, Taroch's deep romanticization of the Northlands, discovered posthumously in a book of poetry that he had written, was surely on the mark, if not understated, regarding its beauty.

Early that morning, Magnus was moved by an enchantment that summoned him from the belly of the *Fleet Otter* into a wispy boll of a winter morning. Mist hugged his senses, and naught could be seen through the fog cast over sea and air. There were hints of seamen about, and he ignored them as he walked as far as the deck would allow to the prow. It wasn't the eldritch voice of winter that had woken him—though that song played unceasingly in notes of wind. It had been another mystery, one he felt as true as the weave of love and hate for his brother: a yearning, a passion to unite. Well before the obscurity lifted its magikian's curtain, and Valholom was revealed, Magnus had known that this was something he'd waited all his life to see. *All my long life, and I've never been to these lands,* he pondered, *as if this journey was delayed until my time came to take it. Here I am, Mother Winter. I have come to thee.* A mystery consumed him, and he stared at the landscape until the cold bit his frosty eyes and bled them to tears.

Birds cawed and circled a sky turned milky-gray from winter and smoke. The animals seemed heedless of the season and clustered on the slick boulders and stone watchtowers along Valholom's waterfront. Past the towers and in the shallows lay a sprawl of wooden decks, near which floated vast oar boats with carved wooden sea spirits at their helms: fanged lionesses, mermaids, sea kings, arrow-headed fish, and tentacled terrors grappling ships. A stripped icy beach gleamed at the harbor's back, beyond which a pebbled tract rambled off into broken hills, then became stomped on by larger cliffs, mighty as the heels of giants, and finally piled what whole stone remained into a great hill. Upon that blue-black extrusion, the Northmen's greatest city presided, menacingly and obscenely grand, as if it were a prison for ancient monsters. To keep those monsters in or out, a mighty stone ring, and lower down, a palisade, formed two lines of defense around Valholom. Since it was a city of many cultures—Carthacian, Indigenous, Menosian and more—myriad influences could be discerned by the king as he peered through a farscope he'd absently commandeered from a sailor. The salted watchtowers echoed the slender cruelty of the Iron City. The longhouses seething smoke were of aboriginal inspiration, as seen in the south by archaeologists of the Swannish: wooden rectangles with hatted roofs. And the larger stout keeps reminded him of the square stone bastions Taroch had implemented in the once-rebel city of Southreach.

Some of the fragments of the warlord's regime still stood, though mostly as shells risen among the earthen valley that was Southreach, where Magnus had collapsed what remained of Taroch's empire in an earthquake summoned by his wrath. It was strange to remember his fury in that moment or its results: the crashes, towers that exploded like an overfed fire, the horrid crackle as the land was sundered. Although he felt Valholom possessed a similar air of threat to that he had perceived when beholding ancient Southreach. While all seemed subdued from afar, Valholom was surely a place of grand intrigue and danger. From the keeps and longhouses atop the cliffs, civilization spread out in a pattern resembling white lichen on rocks. So many ivory roofs suggested a population of hundreds of thousands. Valholom was immense. Perhaps as large as either Eod or Menos, and size alone determined a proportionate element of danger.

Why have we never met? he asked the city.

Eod had always kept a foot in the Northlands, though they had never pushed claims or alliances in that territory. Nor had the rulers of this realm, the Chieftains, decreed or denounced any ties to the City of Wonders. How queer that a man as educated as himself knew so little of this culture and its lands. He felt a sense of willful neglect, having shielded himself from these matters. The king was so lost in himself that Erik's stealthy approach came on unhindered. The knight didn't sleep, and he'd followed Magnus after hearing his kingfather's soft footsteps in the adjoining cabin.

I never pictured it being so grand, said Erik.

Nor had I.

As common courtesy, Magnus passed the farscope to Erik, which he declined. *I can see all that I need to from here, and smell and taste...*Although not a wordsmith, he dabbled with the words for Valholom's bouquet of sweats, spices, heavy hickory smoke, a stinking blubber somewhere between seared butter and moldy cheese, and summed it up with, *Too much. It's a spice of history. How old is this realm?*

Old. One of the oldest of which I know. It was long believed to be a waste-land for savages.

Believed by whom?

Magnus's laugh was crisper than the breeze. *Myself, I suppose. I have always watched this land from afar, though fearfully, never with enough courage to sail here. My brother and I encountered some of the First People, the original settlers to this realm, when we wandered through the ancient ages— after the land had been settled. They had their own tongue, not dissimilar to ours; all ancient speech follows the same poetry, the same flow and feel of earth sliding through a naked palm...They seemed quite settled, and my mind was set on ingenuity, engines, and theaters for oration. I suppose, as flippant as it sounds, I forgot about the North. Rather, I wanted to forget that part of myself.*

What part?

My tie to the land. My walk through the Long Seasons. It's humbling, you know, for an Immortal to be so naked before the fury of Geadhain.

Into that witnessing, suddenly and complete, they fell. In a flash of memories that left Erik gasping and bewildered, he saw Brutus and Magnus together as bloodmates, as they walked with landstriders, swam drowning mires, and huddled—the smaller in the embrace of the larger—in a belly of ice while a storm of shards tore at the outside world.

"You loved him...so much." It was all the knight could say.

"I love him still, and so I shall end his madness."

Solemn as the weather, they waited for the port to appear and readied for the journey to end the threat of their mad brother. *Magnus's brother*, Erik recalled. The difference between them was no longer so clear.

IV

Upon their docking, Erik was immersed with the scents of wet, salted wood mingling with the working odor of sailors burdened in furs moving crates, sacks, and nets on and off the pier's many ships. As his bloodmates joined him on the gangway, the captain led them down the creaking planks onto the dock and off along a crackling and crunching beach. They tested their footing on the shifting trail of silt and snow that wound up through a canyon. Making for a tight arrangement, they were forced to share the path with other foot traffic from the port—migrants, vagrants, woolly beasts and their surly herders, laughing seamen, and men mostly naked to the stinging weather but for their cloaks, leather pants, and boots.

Warriors, these latter were, with tribal tattoos on their grizzled chests and faces, and giant battleaxes and great swords slung over their cloaks. To Erik they smelled of battle: the rust of gore, a sweat that wouldn't leave the armpits, and hilts slightly sour from years of use. His evaluation of the warriors distracted him from whatever game Magnus and Lila were playing behind Nolan and him. To avoid being recognized a second time, the sorcerer king and queen had thrown on phantasms before departing the *Fleet Otter*. Nolan's faithful crew had said nothing of the aged couple who attended their captain, nor of the whereabouts of the Lady Siobhan and her brother who, to their knowledge, hadn't been thrown into the sea during the night.

And so a grayed and handsome couple ambled behind the black-skinned glowering knight; he'd have suffered their companionship in silence if he wasn't able to feel how deeply they were endeared to one another. What ties the king and queen had broken in Lila's rape, ruin, and remaking had been reworked in threads of steel. They'd never be together again, though they didn't hate each other. Queerly, Erik was more threatened by that closeness than by the moments in which he, Magnus, and Lila were all at odds.

"Your man, what's his name?" asked Erik—tired of contemplation.

"Name?" Nolan scratched his chin. "He doesn't have one, per se."

"A nameless wanderer? 'Tis good for epic prose, though not so much for matters of discretion and trust."

"He can be trusted. I know he can. He's among the few honorable men who remain in this age. I'd say he's as bound to duty as you."

"Oh?"

A family passed near them heading downhill, and the captain lowered his voice. "I see how you love her—Siobhan—and I know that at one point she belonged to another."

"She can never *belong* to someone. I was chosen, and I chose her."

"Do pardon the backward graces of an old sailor. She was with him, now she's not. Nevertheless, you serve with a faultless honor that's carried you into some very dark, questionable, and dangerous places. My man, well, he's the same. You have that same echo of screams in your faces, and yet there's still a sparkle of Will that won't be broken, and will yield only to serve a great cause. I don't know what his cause is, though it might be a lass, too—as I've said, there's one that travels with him."

"Humph."

Until Erik knew this tracker himself, the matter would have to rest. It was a long way to the underskirt of Valholom, and even those siphoning off wisps of Erik's constitution were slightly winded after the sands the climb took. There, the travelers were blocked by the fortifications that protected the city—a girdle of timber walls and stone guardhouses. As they were shuffled into an outdoor court, Erik mused over what a simple leap those hundred-stride-tall walls would be for him. In a speck, burly Northerners, as bare-chested and brutal in their manners as the ones Erik had spotted during the ascent, were bossing them around.

Issuing commands in a guttural language akin to the ancient romantic tongues—only slathered in spit—and herding them forcefully, the wandering soldiers split the aspiring entrants into Valholom into groups of families, warriors, workers, and everyone else. The warriors were waved along first, and with an embarrassing, or perhaps unnecessary, lack of the safeguards seen in Central Geadhain. Erik and company were ordered in with the other families. It was a challenge to not plug his ears at the wails of babes, or to not pinch his nose at the ripe musk of the ram-like beasts the Northerners used for burden and milk—he saw a waiting man quench himself on a wax-topped bottle of yellow liquid that smelled of the beasts.

Ready and steady your nerves, soldier, he chanted in his head. For beyond the clearing and grand palisade lay a cornucopia of clatters, farts, chatter, claptrap, and hums—an orgy for the senses so rich it sickened him.

"You look a little pale," noted Nolan. "Well, more mahogany than black in the face. I mean, your skin is remarkable. I can say without a doubt that you're as black as the shine of coal left in a dead hearth. Skin so remarkable that perhaps we should have considered a small glamor..." The captain shot a glance over his shoulder at the elderly couple, who remained striking and possessed of the magnetic charisma of ancient nobles; despite the webs of wrinkles on their faces, their amber and emerald stares had stayed sharp. "At least your pallor makes you look closer to a normal man, which is what we need."

Two brutes finished their conversation with a family of three and their *tangris*—the goat beasts. Then the warriors were upon Nolan and his company. Without courtesy, the men inspected the travelers, their bags and their breasts, in Lila's case. Erik's Immortal rage finally brought back the darkness to his face, though he allowed the impropriety to pass, as did Magnus and Lila. *We are travelers here, not kings and queens*, one of them mind-whispered, though he couldn't tell which. He thought, however, of breaking one of the warriors' hands as one of them came round for another fondle of his chest and stomach, before giving him a full five-fingered grip, smiling at the meat resting in his pants.

At this ultimate indignity, Erik smacked the man's hand away. Skin cracked and bled. The assault sounded like a whip of thunder, and those gathered around the gate turned to stare. Seeming spurned, the warrior barked incoherent curses at Erik. If the warrior hadn't been so impressed by Erik's strength and physique, or so implored for forgiveness by Nolan—who literally fell to his knees and clasped his hands together as if before a divinity—there might have been a bloodbath before they'd even set foot in Valholom. Surprisingly, however, the warrior began kissing his bloody knuckles, grinned, and then waved the company forward. As Nolan rose and the four hurried on, the brave or stupid Northman slapped Erik on the shoulder and called the knight *"Gunnhar."* At that, the warrior's companion joined his fellow in a deep belly laugh. Over what, none of the three from Central Geadhain could tell.

Once through the palisade's enormous gate, they walked with the crowd through an encampment. Some distance ahead, a miserable gray wall with a fanged portcullis shaped like a sad, moaning mouth threatened to swallow them. They headed toward that impending devourment, meekly and calmly, following the flow of life. Around the travelers, fires crackled and Northmen laid sword and spear upon their knees—the screech of their whetstones contesting the voices of the men who sharpened their weapons. Elsewhere in fur and leather tents, warriors tuned and played instruments: coarse flutes, bone and twine harps, and another manner of wind pipe that men drew a rod out of, then thrust in again, to produce various complexities of sound—and annoyance, since to Erik the pipes were hideously strident. The warriors dined on food Erik looked forward to partaking of, like roast beast, bird, and a mysterious red root that darkened every pot and skillet at the campfires, making every meal look like a banquet of blood, and awakening the carnivore within him.

Beyond the appeal of the food, these men had their share of carnality, as well, as seen in their interactions. They'd roughhouse, slap, punch, and slam chests into one another more often than they'd shake hands. Much of their conversation appeared to involve testing who could scream the loudest. They quenched themselves on open casks of ale and pissed in buckets, rather than on the ground, which would hardly have been out of character. Although that lapse in bravado didn't disappoint its anthropological observers, and several men made a show of their urination, pacing their pee to keep in time with the music, or simply wagging their genitals at their howling friends.

Preposterous louts, whispered Lila to her bloodmates, and the fire of rage in her was the hottest among them. *As if they've no manners or decency at all. A changeling, or a wild animal dressed in gent's clothing, would be better behaved.*

"Explain," said Erik, after catching Nolan's attention. He tilted his head toward a warrior sitting upon a chamber pot, in full view of passersby, who squeezed out his waste with an exuberance of grunts and farts while wearing the grimace of a gargoyle and those around him applauded his debasement. It was a minstrel show of shite, and as appalling as it was farcical to the observers.

Nolan spared a glance and shook his head. "Don't look. It's disrespectful unless you're invited into their games. Games that I haven't figured out. The crassness of these people. My Mineesha hates this place, says it reminds her of her days with the Arhad—men being men, which as often as not is men being boys. Sure, she can travel about without her headscarves, or without the threat of a man with a knife and needle chasing her for violating her chastity, though the propositions and disrespect are only a mite different from what she's faced…"

A curious scent of spice, sweetness, and mysterious incense threatened to break Nolan's chain of thought. Such was Lila's anger, and nearly magik, manifested. Only with her bloodmates' united stoicism—of frost and stone—was she able to restrain herself from ensorcelling this entire barracks and making the warriors bark and lick themselves like the dogs they wanted to be. She asked, "Are these rites of passage and acceptance then? Are we to see this sort of...behavior...all through the Northlands?" She was hardly a saint, though she had the deserved airs and pretensions of a woman of noble standing, and she found this behavior detestable.

"Where I think you're going, I doubt you'll see many folk to unsettle your delicate graces," said Nolan. "Let's get you to your guide and get you out of Valholom as quick as can be."

Nearing the stone mouth that would lead through Valholom's great wall, they entered a temperate silence. Here, most of the noise of the encampment was left behind them, and rigid warriors posed like decorative suits of armor along a courtyard and its sprawl of steps before the gate. More of these stoic men stood within the wide passage the company soon traversed. Within, the men were closer and easier to spy upon, and all shared the same piecemeal gauntlets of bindings and fur, with a crimson band tied around the veined bicep of each man, and other traces of red woven into their braids or tattooed in the tapestries of their flesh. A distinction between these men and the louts from earlier was evident; their poise, and their quiet and knightly presence exhibited refreshing decorum. Perhaps the North wasn't so savage as to be unlikeable, and two of the travelers knew that these warriors were to be taken more seriously than the oafs they'd seen. Lila, however, appeared to despise these men even more, and she glowered at each one.

"Eininhar," whispered Nolan. "Warrior elite, you could say. They're calm as statues now, but they go wild on the battlefield. I've seen it, though not on a field of battle. A man had taken his brother's bride hostage in a tavern, a woman he believed should have been his. Mineesha and I were out shopping—without our children, thankfully—when we noticed the commotion."

The memories caused the captain to shudder, but he continued. "One of the Kinlord's men showed up. Only one Eininhar. Like living lightning, he bashed down the door, and in the next speck the windows upstairs were splatted in blood." He flicked his hand. "As if someone had thrown a pail of paint. They came out like that, the Eininhar and the young woman. She wasn't in white...that was certain. They looked like the perfect bride and groom of horror. Although that's never to be, a groom to a bride, not with those men."

Every voice, not merely the captain's, had been lowered in the presence of these Eininhar, within whom Erik sensed the might of a whirlwind trapped in a bottle. They were still, because otherwise they would be doused in blood and raving. The captain's last remark had puzzled Erik, and he found himself talking behind his hand, too, as if he were a gossip in a temple. "Pardon, what did you mean by 'not with those men'?"

"You know." Nolan bulged his eyes and puffed out a cheek.

"I don't."

"Pfft. No! I shouldn't say it, and yet I shall. Think about it: the Kinlord sends these fellows on his greatest foresworn duties, against enemies, criminals, and monsters. They spend all their time apart from their lower caste brothers, the ones who don't have the spunk and spirit to become an Eininhar. And while all Northern warriors are bred with the curse of pride and excessive manliness, such flaws can actually be transformed into virtues when tempered with discipline and brotherhood. Such is how the Eininhar temper themselves. To that end, they live apart from the Gunnhar, the *pleasant* rank and file you've met. The Eininhar don't even live in Valholom, but Valhaloch, the red pinnacle at the heart of the city where the Kinlord himself resides. They're bunking, fighting, and sharing drink all by themselves...The winters here get mighty cold, and there isn't much firewood to be found when ordered on a mission into the bitter reaches of this realm..."

"Ah. They are lovers."

"Sh!" Nolan fanned his hands in a fury. "Keep your voice down."

"No one can hear us," said Erik.

"You're wrong. The Kinlord has eyes and ears throughout his realm."

"Kinlord?"

Magnus, eavesdropping on the two men, spoke up. "I believe the captain means whoever governs Valholom and the lands beyond. I am familiar with that arm of their politics at least. I regret my ignorance of this realm more and more with each passing sand."

"No time for regret, only courage," declared Nolan. "There it is: Valholom."

While they had been chatting, the shaded tunnel and royal warriors had faded behind them. They'd passed through Valholom's wall, toward a faint halo of light at the tunnel's end that had slowly grown brighter than any of the iron-mounted torches along the walls, the flames of which were assailed by the swirling of civilization ahead.

How small I've been, thought the king.

For it was a phenomenon into which he and the others entered, and one not of the modern age, but rather of a time predating technomagik and the arrogance born of a reliance on those inventions. Into the past, they'd stepped; into a realm of tangris-drawn carts and carriages on streets as tight with peasants as a stream with fish. Howsoever they moved in that crowd they had to quickly consider, for they were being shoved in every direction by rising hordes down a king's staircase made perilous by the hands of beggar children, cups, coins, and dogs over which to kick and trip. They came to a sprawl of flagstones that branched like a river toward the leaning greatness of wood and brick—timber and plaster in one direction and stone dwellings in the other. There was no symmetry to this architecture, no orderly pattern. It was a cultural pastiche of the adventurers, brigands, and explorers who had fled, conquered, and somehow ended up here.

Menosian, Tarochian, and rural affectations thrived in this cluttered city, which was as much a circus as it was a museum of history. A cat's cradle of clotheslines ran between adjoining tenements; sometimes actual cats were seen balancing along these tightropes. Banners of crimson with crinkled golden runes flapped wildly down the sides of buildings as if tumblers had skipped their performance and left the messy things unfurled. People wailed and laughed out their windows, to neighbors high and low. Looking up at the sky, away from the swarming path, gave each traveler vertigo.

With the hecklers, minstrels, manure, and smoke, Erik became drunk on sensation. Mayhap his ailment sympathetically affected his bloodmates, or they were similarly disoriented by the gong-and-cannonfire subtlety of Valholom, for they all stumbled before discovering their grace.

Walking along stones black from eons of wet boots and rancid filth, the company somehow managed not to lose any members as they maneuvered after the captain. Erik's broad shoulders and vigilance maintained their party's security. Although he wanted to lead, he did not know the way. He did, however, rearrange their line so that the king and Lila were between himself and their navigator. This was the manner of a protector, for the city was not simply old in grime and culture, but also rudimentary in its civility.

Further displays of masculine aggression were demonstrated by peasant and Gunnhar alike. Brawlers fought on tavern porches, flinging each other's teeth and blood onto slavering circles of sadists. In dimly lit alleyways, whores were observed hiking their skirts and mounting men, sometimes while others stood in wait. Children were plentiful as rats and as dirty, foul-mouthed, and rude as their parents.

Given that distinction, refugees from Central Geadhain were easily spotted: heads down, clutching less threadbare garments, perhaps with faces of darker shades of flesh than the pallid giants of the North. Often these immigrants tried to maintain an utter anonymity, while wading through the stink of armpits and sin miring the streets. If they failed and a Northerner sussed out their subtle disrespect, they'd surely be punished with fists and kicks. Indeed, the wanton violence soon numbed the civilized Immortals, and their hearts sank with the understanding that they had come to a foreign land where their titles and authority meant nothing. They could not announce themselves, or call for philanthropy, not in a realm of men who worshipped brawn and blood. They wondered what manner of man ruled the unruly. This question was solved, in part, by the appearance of a monument.

As one mind did the three bloodmates see it. Thus was the importance of the spectacle, the sheer and audacious presence of a fortress that climbed the cloudy peak toward which all of Valholom ambled. Riding the waves of people, and through the abstract frames formed by slanted streets and leaning buildings, they perceived different angles of the structure, which all formed one terrible picture: a bastion of old stone, parapets, walls shored in metal, and a flourish of crimson banners. Atop the ominous castle, and lunging into the sky with the ugliness of a spear into a carcass, was a tower. It was crimson-dark, hard, and with a hundred windows that looked as if they allowed no light in to the sufferers within.

"Valhaloch," muttered Nolan.

V

The Kinlord's chamber was a swill of gloom and shadow. Tall, razor-thin windows, not made for peering out of, squeezed the light to death in the room, and the crimson and gold banners hanging beneath their sills lay still. Grand and echoing was this sacred space, this place of worship for the lord of kin and land. As the lone Eininhar strode down the long road laid before the throne, he was conscious of the sound each scuff of his boots made upon the carpet, and the distant tapping of the Kinlord's fingers on his throne. An audience with the Kinlord was meant to break the caller with the sheer awe of the chamber before he even met Valholom's ruler. If the Eininhar had been any other breed of man, he would've weakened in his knees. For the arched ceiling disappearing into the darkness, the menacing stone pillars carved with reliefs of snarling wolves, burning longboats, and tiny warriors hunting towering mammoths, coupled with the leering red-banded warriors who lurked in their shadows, evoked a fearful reverence in all those who entered. The chamber had been arranged with this in mind: to scare, to make one kneel in spirit before doing so in knee. But as Eininhar, he was fearless, and he'd already knelt before, learned praise and love for his lord.

After the long, lonely walk, the Eininhar reached the throne—a square tomb of rock, chiseled by masons into a writhing tapestry of shapes, letters, beasts, and runic axes. Glowering and terrible, the Kinlord was like an ancient legend come to life. As though he possessed the blood of giants, he seemed too large for the throne, too large for his clothes, too large for the strength that stretched his skin. His blue eyes were set like unearthed gems into the aged rock of his face. As long as his dark beard was, it looked small to his chin. The same as his bracers, which could fit a man's thigh, and which he wore as bracelets on his wrists. Whenever he stood, nearly ten paces from the ground, he groaned like an old tree and was ponderous to behold—though rage did stoke him into an explosive force.

Perhaps the Kinlord had a touch of the old blood within him. In the North, the legends of Makers that came to the land, bedded men and women, and left their uncanny legacy in heroes and sages were known and revered more than by the Southern infidels who bathed in self-glory. It was common legend that all the Kinlords of Clan Raifemorn had been the progeny of dalliances between women and Maker.

It was unclear whether leisure or displeasure affected the Kinlord today. His one hand hung, tapping, on his throne, and he rested his chin on the knuckles of the other. Bowing, the Eininhar waited for the mood to decipher itself.

"Show me what you have found," said the Kinlord.

The Eininhar stood, climbed the red steps, and then knelt again at the feet of his master. As he lowered his head, a great hand fit over it like a massive spider. Magik sparked in the skulls of each man, and their heads filled with light. They had been bound through blood and brotherhood—Immortal Kings didn't hold sole claim to such powers—and while their union might not have been as sacrosanct as those of immortal twins, whatever Maker's blood infused the Raifemorn line could bequeath a weaker telepathy between men's minds. Once the storms of light had cleared in each man's head, together they saw the cloudy tatters of visions shared by every Eininhar, every man sworn into the circle through blood, sex, and battle; these warriors sent to wander the Northlands far and wide. Both this Eininhar and his master felt the sorrow of what their brothers had seen, visions of the fallen cities rendered motionless as portraits; haunted streets cast in ice, where babe, barbarian, maiden, and elder alike had been seized in time—frozen while laughing or running, even while making love.

The Kinlord didn't dwell on those scenes as he had seen much of this tale already; his realm and people were being stolen from him by Winter. Rather, he looked for the means to end this curse, and an image clearly appeared in the fogged mirror into which he gazed at an old sailor in the company of two elders and a warrior. While exemplary, the disguises on those elders failed, and the reality behind the illusions was revealed to the

Kinlord. One cast a shadow of green flame; the other effused an umbra of pure sunshine. An Immortal King and Queen. In the memory, the obsidian man stared at whoever was beholding, and the Immortal's gaze was like a rock to the mirror of the Kinlord's vision. Back in the chamber, both Kinlord and Eininhar separated their bodies and minds, gasping.

"Thank you, Bjorn," said the Kinlord. "So they have come, as the Winter Witch foretold. Along with another Immortal, too, it seems."

"He is fierce. He could be one of us."

"He has already been claimed."

"Shall we detain them?"

"No," whispered the pale shade behind the throne.

Invisible as an assassin until that moment, the Winter Witch stepped out from the shadows and came to stand beside Bjorn. The Eininhar didn't care for her. He never had; women didn't belong in their circle. That she was ancient and unattractive excused her from the purposes of breeding, as well. Her yellowish eyes, perhaps beautiful as sun-struck amber once, were now so old they'd lost their gleam and made her look mostly dead, or at least part spirit. Crimson yarn and the yellowed fragments of bone threaded into her white robe had given the witch a splash of color, and the esoteric tattoos of the same bloody shade scrawled all over her bust and head—circles, whorls, and lines of nonsense—killed more of whatever appeal she might have had. Stranger, too, was that her complexion wasn't common to the North. Instead it was brown and spotted from a place of sun, of climes beyond. Age hadn't bent her, however, and she stood with the strength of a birch tree.

Whence she had come was as much a mystery as everything else about the woman. Months past, presaging by days the reports of the first frozen settlements, she had arrived at the Kinlord's court. She had demanded to be brought before Valhaloch's master to tell him of the spell being cast over his realm and of how it could be stopped. Many had come to Valhaloch with such demands before, but none had presented themselves with her unerring determination and insistence.

As she'd come into the presence of the Kinlord, rattling her bag of runes, poor as a beggar, and claiming to have seen the death of Valholom, Bjorn had gone to seize the ranting woman to drag her from the chamber. It had been then that the red runes around her eyes had flickered like fire, and without raising a finger she'd cast him down and away from her as messily as a newborn tangris flopping in its own afterbirth. Looming over him, almost speaking *to* him, she had declared her prophecy.

"Winter will freeze her children, the brothers will battle; a fallen king will chase the white stag north, to the heart of Winter. Only through the sacrifice

may the endless winds be stilled, the people thawed, and our heroes march into the final war," the witch had said. *"This I have seen, and more."*

"I foretold the coming of the King of Eod." The witch reminded each man, in this moment. "The signs and stars have aligned, and Magnus has come to do what has been divined: to awaken Nifhalheim, to barter with the same great spirit your line once bartered with to be granted the throne of this realm, Kinlord. Although...power does not come without cost."

She and the Kinlord shared a deep, long stare, before she continued. "Magnus will pay, and you must pay. The Makers and Lords of the Old World value a single sacrifice—the same that you and all your line have offered."

"Blood," said the Kinlord.

"Yes," she replied.

The Kinlord hung his head, thinking.

Observing his father's contemplation, Bjorn realized that they had begun a perilous, irreversible dive into her madness. He couldn't let this stand without airing his disapproval.

"Father," he said, compassionately, for he was born of the Kinlord's first blood and seed and was a truer son than most of his brothers. "The world is at war. Would we give Eod another enemy? Why throw down that gauntlet? What wrath might we invite if we meddle in conflicts beyond our ken? We've remained here, untouched by Immortal feuds and Iron politics. See what happened to the last great empire that declared itself Eod's foe: Queen Lila pulverized it and ended its thousand-year reign. I say let the Immortals have their war, and we have our struggle against this relentless winter. Stoke our own fires, build greater walls, and keep the winter out as we've always done— with sweat, sword, flame, and brotherhood. What this *woman* has proposed sounds too dangerous."

"I have a name, boy," said the witch. "You would do well to remember it."

Branwen, Bjorn thought, wondering if the witch could hear him. Hers was a name that scratched the ear. Bjorn loathed to speak it, for it sounded as though it came from an age when Makers walked and elementals were routinely fed the sacrifices about which she preached. Beyond the prophecies she foretold, he feared the woman herself. Even more when she flexed her glory, like now, and fury made her seem as tall as his father. Whenever he challenged her, she glared at Bjorn with the might of a soulless winter sky, and he had to look away. She expressed no passion beyond what powered her righteous beliefs. She had no motives toward evil as Bjorn understood sin, no desire to rule but only to serve the Old Ways, whatever those might be, and to see his father bend to these ancient laws. He couldn't win a battle of Wills against a woman so entrenched in her faith. Neither could his father, who had welcomed her superstitious counsel at a time when all modern tactics had failed to stall the Scourge of Winter.

Modern tactics...they hadn't exhausted them all, Bjorn realized, and it came to him then: another way. "What if we ask the king to help us to banish the Scourge?" he pleaded.

"He will banish the Scourge," said Branwen. A kindness consumed the woman, and she nearly touched Bjorn's chin with her fingers like sandpaper—these dead and dry things that he at once knew were as old as he'd believed and from which he recoiled. "The war we fight today is but one of many. Those who are cursed to see Fate know that each battle is greater until there is but a last and great war in which all Makers, lords, and men are judged. What we see now with the kings, what shakes our realms like the hand of the White Mother herself, is one in a series of skirmishes we shall face before men are truly tested. We may never see that final conflict if the king doesn't make the correct choice. Are we to thrust his hand into the fire if he doesn't find in himself the courage? Yes. Unless we care only for ourselves and selfish things. The world has tipped out of balance. The elementals and the White Mother are furious with how we've squandered their gifts. Valholom will be frozen in a fortnight. I have shared with your father that future, as shown to me by the stones."

Suddenly, the Kinlord grabbed his son's wrist. "I have seen it, my child: two dooms. The first, a long cold wasting where we are cast in eternal living sleep. Then, the terror against which Magnus marches coming to consume the ghost of our empire. An unholy reckoning. So much horror...so much."

The Kinlord looked to the Winter Witch and added, "Show him. Show him our darkest fate."

Branwen produced a stone from a pouch at her belt. She rested it on the pad of her palm, an object as speckled as a blackbird's egg and painted with the silver marking of a rune.

"His hand," she asked of the Kinlord, and Bjorn's father shoved his son's hand forward. She did not touch him (he would have evaded her touch anyway as he had done a moment ago), but dropped the stone into his hand. Stone and flesh touched. Bjorn's head suddenly flashed with a brightness that cleared into a vision.

The Kinlord sits in the hall upon his throne, a perfect monarch till the end of time, which he hopes comes soon. But counting time is a fool's diversion. Measuring the day is impossible, as there's no light outside since the darkness is busy gobbling the sun and vomiting out the terrors that man has become. Some of those monsters saunter through the tranquil halls of Valhaloch; they're completely unaffected by the Scourge of Winter. A curse that has come and gone, anyway, its wrath meant only for the people of the North. Unscathed, the monsters of the apocalypse curdle the silence of Valhaloch with noises like saliva being pushed against one's cheeks; if the Kinlord could shiver or scream, he would. From his trapped and forward gaze, and in the moments when the murk isn't so deep, he sees their slobbery forms of spines and shells, hunchbacks, whipping tubes that hiss or have the crowned head of a man's prick. It's the type of madness that makes a mind just crack and howl.

At times he wishes that the Scourge of Winter had struck him when he'd been sleeping, so that his eyes would have been permanently closed. Often he dwells on the Scourge, an impact that slammed the city and the keep as fulminously as lightning shattering a glacier, and that rendered everyone, everywhere in Valholom into statues of crystal. Statues that live beneath their frozen skins. Perhaps the Eininhar who once protected his chamber might twitch a little and scream inside as their catatonic bodies are snapped like candy-brittle and slurped back into warm, fleshy sustenance by the slithering monsters that fall upon them. The Kinlord watches these feasts—the ones that can be seen—and curses this vilest of magik that has kept its victims alive. Magnus has lost, no hope remains, and hunger and darkness consumes Geadhain.

In his own body, his blood moves like sap, despite the fact that he and his kin have remained here, in snow and dust for tens to hundreds of years—however long it has been since Magnus's foe won the war. Whatever doomed survivors linger and somehow live in Geadhain's toxic flesh have surely forgotten the people of the North. There will be no rescue, no triumphs to be sung of, for there is no more civilization, there is only a nightmare.

For the Kinlord that nightmare has been the slow, stinging itch of his frost-petrified flesh, and his railing against the rot of his mind. Again he plays the game of trying to rationalize the madness. He wonders how long it has been. He tries to remember names, numbers, and places. No night or day creeps into this purgatory, and the timelessness dissolves his remaining shreds of logic. Regrettably, the horrors stalking Valhaloch take their time in killing. They never come too near the throne with their feast, as though the Kinlord's punishment is to watch. They tease him by eating his Eininhar, by sometimes stumbling into a light beam with their anemone faces suckling on a human forelimb or a frozen rat—to demonstrate that even the lesser beasts haven't escaped the great feast.

At last, an eternity later, one approaches him. The Kinlord watches one monster slither toward him and welcomes it with a passion belied by his lethargic heart. The thing hesitates, hovering over him, and from its emaciated figure wafts the scents of ash, shite, and the putrescent cheese of unwashed genitalia. Its bifurcated face, wreathed in tentacles, splits, and within the slit waggles a bushel of tongues, all pink as a woman's parts.

At last, my time, *he thinks*. My time to be eaten.

"Gah!" Bjorn snapped from the spell and threw away the stone, then realized that nothing was actually in his hand. At once, he created a distance between himself, his father, and the Winter Witch, falling upon his knees at the bottom of the throne's flight of stairs. He trembled and shook. The vision couldn't be exorcised from his mind or soul. Bjorn neither understood nor wanted to know the reason behind anything the witch had revealed. He felt, though, that he understood now her conviction, her resolve in wanting to prevent this future. Perhaps she was both witch and saint, and she'd come to save them. Humbled and broken, he muttered, "What did I see?"

Branwen swept down the stairs to him. "Rise," she said, and the strength to stand returned to him at her command. She smiled at the warrior with a mother's compassion. He'd never had a mother, not one he could remember, and her manner both softened his fear and hardened his courage.

"You have seen what will happen if the Immortal does not offer himself to Nifhalheim," she said. "Blood will not be enough, though blood will be spilled." Behind his son's back, the Kinlord shot her a vicious glance. Branwen ignored him. "We have lost so much from the kings, and more there is to lose. Although those are not your wars. You will find your glory soon, Bjorn. I hope that you embrace it.

"We must stop the Scourge, which comes from the imbalance Magnus and his brother have caused in the world. It falls upon Magnus, then, to fix their damage, and to confront the one who would further damage the White Mother. I know that you believe me a witch, though it is the White Mother who leads me. It is her voice that I heed above those of kings, Kinlords, or men, and until this age of terrors ends, you must heed her too. We are her warriors. We shall shed the blood others are too weak to spill. Do you know what you must do?"

"I shall track him to the reaches of our realm," declared Bjorn. "I shall ensure that he offers himself up to Nifhalheim."

Branwen hovered her hand over his chest as if to feel his furious heart beating; he realized then that she had never really touched him, or he her, even now. "Magnus must submit, body and soul. A sacrifice must be made...When his brother summoned the Elemental of Fire, the Elemental of Winter was awoken. Magnus must become one with the beast, as his brother has with the other. Thus fire and flame shall cool to rock and ash, and so the war will end. I feel that you are ready for this task. Summon your best huntsmen and brothers, and prepare to ride into the Scourge. We are to hunt a legendary quarry: a trio of Immortals. I shall ride with you, to pray at your side, and the White Mother will keep you whole so long as you deliver unto her the Immortal. Threaten Magnus's kingdom, threaten his health, threaten innocents, threaten his mate, chain him, and bleed him on Nifhalheim's altar. It matters not what you do to him as long as he submits. No cruelty will be greater than what you leave this world with should you fail."

Bjorn bowed to his father and the Winter Witch. "For peace and glory."

The Kinlord's gaze glittered with sudden passion. "Take with you this warning: the golden Queen of Eod is a snake and destroyer of nations, as you have seen with Menos. I believe she has poisoned the king and all of the South and is as dangerous an enemy as Brutus. We must be a hero for the world and end her threat before it takes further root."

"End her threat?" Bjorn's voice rose sharply.

"Kill her, after Magnus has reached the Throne of Winter."

Branwen pinched her face in what was either disapproval or worry.

Kill an Immortal? wondered Bjorn. How would that improve Magnus's disposition or likelihood of cooperating? And how would he even attempt to harm a woman who had lived nearly forever and who was in the company of two other Immortals? It felt tremendously dangerous, and most likely, suicidal. As always, his father's moods were capricious and his intent clouded. But Bjorn's was a warrior's life, and warriors were meant to die in battle. Furthermore, he knew from the curse of his family bloodline that his sands were already exhausted. A curse that deemed that no one but a dark-haired, glowering child of his line lived beyond thirty years of age, and he was no gloomy heir, but a man quite fair—and a man ten years beyond thirty. Thus, as a man living on borrowed time, the glory of a death at the hand of an Immortal was a worthy end.

"A worthy end," agreed the Kinlord, smiling, reading his thoughts. "Do you understand your orders?"

"Trail Magnus. Ensure he reaches the Throne of Winter and offers his body and soul to the spirit. Then kill the Queen of Eod." Bjorn couldn't hide his doubt, though, and needed to voice a measure of it. "How would you suggest I accomplish the latter, Father?"

"*Son,*" the Kinlord hissed the word. "A snake can be killed by slicing off the head—the body may thrash, but its end will come. My faith resides in you as a warrior and tactician. See that it is done."

Rarely having experienced kindness, let alone encouragement, from his father, Bjorn leapt to his feet and raced from the hall; he had much to do to marshal his brothers, track the Immortals, and plan for the execution of one of them. Exhausted by the responsibilities of a father, and glimmering with somber thoughts, the Kinlord watched his son's figure flutter into a speck.

Branwen stepped before the throne, frowning. "Is it wise to pursue your own conquests when the world faces damnation?"

The Kinlord snorted. "I have already lost two links in the chain thanks to that Southern sand-bitch. I have delayed Bjorn's harvest for as long as can be. I can fatten him no more on magik and glory; he is ready for the feast. With the White Mother's blessing, I shall endure, regardless of this pissing match between kings. I am Winter's chosen one. The blood-elixir of the child of the harvest will ensure sufficient fire in me to burn away any chill. If I must lord over a frozen kingdom and slay the specters of the Kingswar, then I shall do so."

"By ordering Lila's death you are inviting needless wrath."

"I owe her grief for what she took from me." The Kinlord sneered. "Years of my magik and might stolen by her meddling. Now I have only Bjorn...though what rich harvest I've made of him." He grinned. "You and I know that Bjorn has not the power to slay her. Death in battle against an Immortal Queen and her consorts would ensure his legendary position among the greatest of heroes who feast in the afterlife. He should be grateful that I'm not asking him to close his eyes and surprising him with a red smile across his neck—as my forefathers have so often done to their golden child. He will die a warrior's death. A proud death."

"Your mind is set on power and revenge?"

"In stone."

"A scale cannot be balanced with too much darkness on one side..."

"Enough of your warnings. I am lord and kin of the land. I shall prove your prophecy false and be the true conqueror in the Kingswar."

"Indeed you may." Branwen humbled herself and bowed.

"Remember to whom you are bound, spirit."

"We do. We always have," whispered Branwen, sadly.

VIII

WINTERSPELL

I

Valholom's taverns were rancid cesspools of sweat, lewd words, groped breasts, and barbarians who drank, gambled, and screamed at one another. This particular establishment, Lila had been told, was one of Valholom's finest alehouses; she was loath to imagine the others. Indeed, it was better to look up to the rafters caked in crapulence and to watch for augurs in the smoke of the hundred pipes that had transformed the chamber into a hazy cauldron. Hardly a puff of pollution escaped the rustic windows, which were a checkerboard of glass and wooden patches. At least the pipes' herbs were fragrant, almost floral, and when Lila tired of watching the lout-and-whore show, or whorls above, and gazed into the room, the men had very little form or semblance to their rancorous selves.

By the fire, a sad and forgotten bard creaked out miserable songs. It sounded to Lila as if he wept each note, which really wouldn't have been much of a surprise. Eventually, a table would be flipped or slammed, a nose would be broken, or a woman would shriek, and the fragile peace would end. Such shrill screams the tavern wenches had, titillating award-winning drama practiced with their bearded clientele. Lila seriously debated enchanting the maidens, perhaps even the entire establishment, into a semblance of orderly behavior.

Rather than realize these fantasies, she sipped her drink and drew serenity from the soothing mists of Erik's calm, rocking ocean spirit. She sat between him and Magnus, and for reasons of discretion held her knight's hand under the pitted table. Most people ignored her and her gathering, anyway; the level of passing interest given to two elderly folk, an old sailor, and a frightening foreigner was low.

For hourglasses, they had been waiting for Nolan's tracker to arrive. Prior to their arrival, the captain had made a few stops at similarly run-down shite-shacks, some of them so much filthier than their current waiting spot that Erik forbade his fair queen—any of them, really—to enter. On his forays into these houses of sin, Nolan had confirmed that his tracker was indeed in the city. It required many further inquiries to make any kind of contact with this fleet fox of a man. Nolan had stopped at more pubs, then with a rumormonger on the street, and finally had a meeting with a hulking shadowbroker who lurked in an alley and whose suggestions led them to this ultimate stop.

The day had been spent, and so, too, were the travelers—except, of course, for Erik. He stroked the caramel silk skin of his queen's hand and focused on remaining her anchor in this storm of iniquity. She was having wrathful urges not too dissimilar from his own. One lesson learned from this experience, however, was that the obstreperousness of the city could be better endured when he drew from her well of spirit, as she drew from his.

Magnus carried on a conversation with Nolan. Swapping tales from either side, the men talked until their mouths grew dry from chatter and they needed to slake that thirst with some of the tavern's unexpectedly stout ale. Such tales the weathered seaman had to entertain the king—from skirting the Straits of Wrath, to cruising the sunned ivory beaches and lush black jungles seen along the coast of the Isles of Terotak, as wet and tempting as a woman's dark pubis. Nolan spoke of places to which even the king had not voyaged. It had been ages since Magnus had spoken to the common man, which often only happened when a crime had been committed and the person stood before him broken with remorse. With his disguise and the liberating numbness of drink, he and Nolan were able to chat as relative equals. After drunkenly ambling through the complex mechanics of shared minds and souls, then topics of history and politics, they completed the natural trifecta of discussion points by chatting about ancient religions, such as the tribal beliefs of the Northerners. Of that and all matters they spoke freely, since no one in the room appeared fluent in Southern speech.

"It's not tribalism, my lord." Nolan downed a swig with a teeth-gritting "*gah*," then continued. "These people have had their beliefs for as long as Winter has wrapped this land in ice. The White Mother, they call her. She has many names and faces, from the wildest beasts found in the North to the legends of her sprit made flesh: Beira."

"The name is familiar…" The king swished his mug and searched for augurs in the mead's bubbles, though none manifested. "Seems to have slipped my mind."

He laughed heartily with his drinking companion.

Once the laughter settled, Nolan righted his shoulders and cleared his throat and recited:

> "Winter's mane, the weak, the wain.
>
> A dire and barren chill.
>
> Bury your hearth—in grick and grim.
>
> Spare thee your courage—thick and thin.
>
> For she comes: Lady of Winter.
>
> She rises and ye fall.
>
> A virgin's lace, untainted grace the only means to her mercy."

The ale churned his poetry around, and he grinned. "Something, something. Snow and gloom."

"Kericot?" guessed the king. "Well, all save the last bit."

"Indeed! I can't remember the end, though it isn't nice. None of the Northern tales end kindly. I do know that in the oldest ages, during the harshest winters, the Northmen appeased the elements with sacrifices."

"Sacrifices of?"

"Women. Young women."

"Disgusting," said Lila, suddenly attentive.

"It is, m'lady," agreed the captain. "And all in the past, from what I've seen. I wouldn't have brought my family here if I didn't believe that it was safe for my wife and daughters. In the very least, here, men wear their vices as we in the South wear our masks. There's an honesty to that, along with a tolerable bravado. I'm used to much of that posturing from my time at sea. There's hardly ever a woman around. We're not sharing bunks like them Eininhar—though no harm if someone gets up to that, now and again. I only know that after Menos was wiped off the map, and since Eod was out of the question, there weren't many options available for a mariner and his family. So we came here, and we made the best of it. Only that damned Scourge now is making me reconsider that choice."

Something from Nolan's speech had stuck with the king. "Still, even given the uncertainty, Eod is a safer place for you and your family. Wouldn't you say?"

Dithering, Nolan looked at the table, his ale, and finally back at the king. "If I may speak freely?"

Magnus tipped his chin.

"Eod has positioned itself as the target of many great and terrible powers, my lord. There's the monster who started all of this, wounded after his failed attempt at Sorsetta and soon to return. I believe he will bring the battle to you, my lord. I don't see him, or us, gambling with victory a third time. He'll come with a wave of darkness, fire, and death." Many faces fell at these words, for they knew what the man said was true.

"And while I'm no diplomat or man versed in games of influence," he continued, "I figure that the Iron Queen—behind her forced smile—has a long, gleaming knife ready for your back, my lord. Then there's this news of the dead up and walking the earth and driven by a mad nekromancer...I've heard even stranger rumors, too, coming from frightened sailors who've sailed down the Feordhan as far as Brutus's hideous blockade near Willowholme, stories of *changelings*—giant wolves trussed up in harnesses, some even walking about like men. Madness, I say."

A canny fellow, the captain watched for shocked expressions from his audience, but saw none. He slugged down his ale, and gave a woeful sigh. "Then it's true. Four dooms, all meant for Eod. I hope that you'll forgive me, my lord, but I won't risk the lives of my family with those chances. The odds are, well, unfairly stacked against you."

A looming tetralogy of disasters. As Immortals, they thought abstractly of the situations imperiling their futures. They knew they'd live forever, and so they feared life less—even its wickedly dangerous and absurd twists. The captain had reminded them of a certain mortality. First in Magnus's head, and then cast as an echo and image into his bloodmates' minds, formed the image of an hourglass against a nebulous black canvas. Its sands were running out. If Magnus calculated the days spent on the ship and in travel, there remained twenty-five days until the Black Star rose and he lost his body to a cosmic horror. Every one of their bodies, in fact, as they'd linked souls and fates.

Twenty-five days until the end of the world, he thought.

"I'm sorry if I have spoken above my station," apologized the captain, when the long silence seemed without end.

"Do not berate yourself," said the king. "We are all equals when confronting extinction. The mouse is no mightier than the cat who would hunt him, when all is to become ash." A flash of cold chilled the tavern, and men, puffing, looked around for a door that had been opened. "Although, I shall do my best to turn us from that future. I shall not leave this world without correcting the mistakes I have made."

"I believe in you." Tingling with drunkenness and bravery, the captain reached for the king's cold hand. "I believe that you can heal this land, you and all the others who work to defend our Green Mother. I am glad I am here to do this for you, my lord. My *King*. I feel that I can call you that, even if I am not sworn to your realm, Magnus. For I see a man trying where aristocracy would have sent armies instead."

"King Magnus," said a man nearby, his accent slow, pitched at the consonants, and lyrical as a chanting coven of medicine men. "Not all ears in Valholom are deaf to the words of the South, and the Kinlord has spies as deadly, and as keen to whispers, as any Iron master."

So as not to further arouse attention to their discovery, the three Immortals turned to calmly stare at the man behind them. The interrupter was tall and dressed for the weather, unlike the average Northman. A patched, fur-lined overcoat with a wide, droopy hood hid all about him save the most important details—the tanned chin and sketched-on beard, the wide crooked nose that spoke of brawls and abuse, and eyes more black than brown that spoke of an animal lurking in his soul. Erik had sensed the stranger earlier, though barely, as he'd sat for a time in one of the tavern's dingiest corners. He had been with a small woman, Erik recalled, but neither had alerted him as being unusual.

Erik then noticed the girl lingering in the huntsman's shadow, and similarly dressed. There was an element of rawness to her, as well, more than an inkling from her flutters of ebon hair like the mane of a wild mare, her curled lips, or her deep and focused stare. Although she was young, maybe just ten or twelve summers old, he didn't think to designate her as young.

Wild, he felt each of them was, and of the girl, *timeless*. Perhaps they were brother and sister, for they shared each other's scents, as well as a twitchy readiness that could turn deadly should either of them reach for the weapons Erik sensed they gripped under their cloaks. There was another queerness that defied his resolution as they walked around the table to stand by Nolan. They emitted an animal fragrance, and one with which Erik wasn't overly familiar. A musk, a wetness upon the girl of...

"Seal?" he muttered.

The huntsman heard his whisper. "What fine senses you have."

"Likewise," replied Erik.

A challenge of wills began between huntsman and knight. Meanwhile, an immediate fascination befell the king as he and the young huntsman's protégé locked eyes. Magnus was without words, without thoughts, without feelings—crippled from shock. At what aspect of the girl had stunned him so, he couldn't say, though he was so drawn into that compunction that his bloodmates, the captain, the huntsman, and the entire tavern diminished in relevance and form while the girl appeared to glow—as white as a Dreamer of Virtue, as pure as the darkness in her eyes, though never in her heart, which was chaste. She was the whitest snow, the purest grace. Magnus felt as if he had known her always, and that whatever he was experiencing, whatever this feeling of providence and belonging, that she too was under its thrall. For she gazed with a reflection of his ardor, beguilement, and bliss. Impossible fancies of towers, shrieks, bells of doom, and splitting earth rang a symphony in each of their heads. Inconceivable pasts, whose clarity could be revealed only in the Hall of Memories, danced between their minds—of Brutus and Magnus before they were men, before they had culture and were but filthy babes of the earth, no better than vermin. As if Magnus and the girl knew, somehow, without blood or bond, the man and woman they'd been. In that moment, they were as transfixed as lovers, absent to time and utterly alone together. Still, this wasn't love or lust between them, rather something deeper and more unshakeable. She saw through Magnus's illusions, through all of them, and he also recognized her to her soul, nearly drawing a face from the ether of time—

"Magnus, our guide was speaking to you." It had taken an elbowing from the queen to rouse him. As the world regained its color and noise, Magnus and the girl lost the key to the door of whatever world they'd wandered. They shook their heads, each resurfacing from eternity. Soon, he remembered his tongue, teeth, and voice.

"Who are you?" he asked, rather desperately.

"Kanatuk," said the huntsman, his shadow falling over the table. "I think if you considered the name, you would find a connection between myself and those fighting in your war. However, you weren't asking my name, were you?" He cast a narrow stare at the young girl, and she flew to his side.

"This is my sister, my friend and fellow huntsman. She saw through your illusions as if they were the cheapest of paper covering a flame. You cannot trick her kind with magik; they're slippery as the hide of a seal—pun intended. You may call her Macha, though you'll find her shy to most men, even royalty. We should all be shy with our voices here. I suggest we set out for the palisade at once, lest we tempt capture and interrogation by the Kinlord."

"What?" exclaimed the captain.

Kanatuk's hand clamped the back of the man's neck to stop him from gawking. Through a greased-on smile, he continued. "Eininhar, two of them in the corner near where Macha and I sat watch. That's all they have been doing for the moment, *watching*, though I doubt that's all they have in mind if they're on to who you are. The Kinlord...his men are not to be trusted, ever. I believe those warriors' Ghaedic is as serviceable as mine, and I've no doubt you've said too much. I shall take you to the North, and you can ink in the details later. Now get up, slowly, and perhaps the lady and Macha can make a pretend dash for what passes for a lavatory. We can follow in a moment."

Convincingly, Macha dropped her ruthless edge for the softness of a child, did a pee-pee dance, and hurried around to grab Lila's hand. The queen was no novice to subterfuge, and took on the role of a concerned mother in need of finding a chamber pot for her little charge. From the merest edge of his eye, Erik watched the ladies' theatrics attract the downturned faces of two heavy, naked-chested brutes sipping mostly full ales. He had to cool his wrath at his inexcusable laxity in not seeing the spies for what they were. At least the men didn't pursue Macha and Lila, though they did shift closer and mutter their crude words to each other.

"They don't buy it," said Kanatuk; taking Lila's seat he swigged the queen's remaining ale. "Not since they saw Macha and me sharing a table by ourselves. I shoulder this error, though I didn't think the Kinlord would have you so aggressively followed. There must be something he wants from you—"

"We cannot be detained—not even for a speck," said Magnus.

"Indeed," agreed the huntsman. "There are two men outside the tavern, as well, whom we must avoid. I saw none at the back, though, which is where Macha and the Lady will make their escape."

Again, fury burned Erik; this bloody shitehole of a city was toying with his senses. He'd half a mind to smash those Eininhar into paste and smash Valholom into a heap of rubble. Erik's veiny clenching fists and puffed neck were impossible to miss, especially to a man once trained in death and violence in the filthiest pits of Menos. Kanatuk grinned at him.

"Patience, warrior. We'll have need of those fists in a speck." After finishing every drop in the queen's cup, he gave out a loud belch. Mischievous as Erik was enraged, he leaned an elbow back over his chair and spun the cup on its bottom like a die.

"I wanted to thank you, Captain, for the chance to dance once more with the shapers of our world. I'll take it as another gift from the woman who returned to me my name, my family's memory, my hope, and my soul: this unexpected encounter, these whispers that led them to you, and you to me, as I was once led from the darkness of my mind. I promised that I would never leave her debt, for to serve in love and humility is a cost in which the service is the payment and the payment is eternal and gratefully given. I would serve her a thousand times, in a thousand lives, and never feel that I'd served enough."

"Who?" asked the king.

"Morigan," replied the huntsman. "She's committed her life to end this war. She's given more than any of us have. We have so much to do to be worthy of even a shadow of her kindness. For we have a world beset upon by Immortals and monsters in men's skins, and she is the one thread of light by which we are bound—a great weaver, a spirit of hope. Once I only prayed to the land and its voices, but now I pray to her, too. For the land has known of her coming, of this war since time beyond remembering. It is we who haven't listened. I do now, though. I hear the drum of snow on ice, and I know my name: Kanatuk, of the Seal Fang. She gave me that, and I shall repay her with this quest, for you, into the North, where only my people can go without risking the frozen wrath of an angry Mother."

Kanatuk paused and looked upward, as though observing something on the ceiling. "They should be away by now. Are you ready?"

The king knew not for what, but Erik knew what the huntsman had planned ere he tossed the metal mug he'd been twirling, and it struck the head of a furious Gunnhar. The man screamed as he bled. A frightening calm gripped the tavern, then the growling, wounded giant turned to see who had injured him. Kanatuk, being a fine meddler, pointed at Erik—a man shuddering from barely restrained anger. Still, the injured fool was too blind from ale to consider the error in stomping over to Erik and trying to pull the knight off his seat.

What happened instead was that Erik leapt like a coiled animal, spooned the man up in an arm, and flung his attacker into the nearest table. No sooner had that table cracked than tempers shattered with it, and men flailed in the wreckage for chairs, cups, and weapons with which to club each other. The violence was a self-sustaining dance, and the music had begun. If the atmosphere for violence was still not incendiary enough, Kanatuk dashed from table to table and threw a few more plates, cups, and forks—which stuck into the foreheads of his victims with the accuracy of a masterful draftsman, and stimulated in the men new levels of rage. Somewhere in the mêlée, Erik moved as if he were a bull become a tornado; whatever he touched was trampled and flung. In the few specks it had taken for a brawl to consume the tavern, Magnus had managed to crawl under the table and maneuver a path to the wooden frame through which Lila and the girl had passed.

At the eye of this hurricane, the captain remained, sipping his ale, laughing and deliriously amused by the blurred black lightning tearing up the room. The tavern-goers were Northmen, so they fought—Erik or each other. They were Northmen, and even as teeth were lost and heads spun, they dragged and drooled themselves off the floor to find new things to punch. It was impossible for the Eininhar to remain unscathed in the brawl. By Erik's providence, the cackling captain alone was left unhindered. Soon, the black lightning vanished with a thunderclap, and his laughter echoed in a room of sobbing wenches alongside the survivors of the fight—those who'd known to hide upstairs and behind the now-fractured bar. The place reeked of liquor, sweat, and blood, and through the smoky disaster, over the bleeding hands of men, did the captain tread, lightly, so as not to further damage those fingers.

Once out of the swell of traffic stumbling from the tavern, he tipped his hat to the travelers, wherever they had gone. Proud of the part he had played, he walked home to his wife, hopeful for the future that he'd quite possibly helped save.

II

Outrunning the Kinlord's men was much easier now that Erik knew their unique scent of sweat and bitters, as if blood and liquor had been used to douse a forged blade. It was the scent of duty and brotherhood—and quite a handsome smell—that rose above the ghastly odors of barbarian, tangris, swine, and pissing peasant. Thus, Erik could now sense the Kinlord's chosen lurking in the streets ahead, or pushing their way through the masses behind them. While no one was quite sure why the Kinlord had taken such an interest in them, avoiding capture, possible interrogation, and delays was clearly desired.

Concealed by an evening crowd as thick as thieves' stew, the five slipped off the main road and into a steaming alley. Here, most of the snow had melted into a glistening path discolored by vomit and urine into a gasoline coruscation; heaps of surviving whiteness clung to the roofs or to embankments in which a graveyard of crates, kegs, and sacks of perishable goods had been left outside for storage in the cold—modern technomagik for refrigeration was unnecessary in Valholom. In the city's inner web, they passed surly serfs puffing on rolled cigarettes who beheld the harried strangers like the invaders they were. Elsewhere, drunkards lay sprawled in the soft beds of snow, snoring happily—winter folk, born and bred. The rats knew to stay indoors in this climate, and few scurried among the buried comestibles and liquid desecration through which they splashed.

In these quieter environs, Erik plainly heard the footsteps of their pursuers. It seemed that the Kinlord's chosen were unshakable beasts. At least two more had joined the hunt, making for six pursuers. More would come, for the Eininhar were bound in magik and oath as strongly as Erik was to his bloodmates; their gaits, grunts, and breaths all came as though from a single man inhabiting six bodies.

"These men are a pack," he said to his cloaked running partner, Kanatuk.

"The Eininhar?" Kanatuk's grin flashed under his bouncing hood. "Indeed. Rituals like the ones Magnus and Brutus engaged in, swearing themselves to each other, have long since been practiced by other cultures."

Kanatuk flung his words over his shoulder to the three who jogged behind them.

"You were not the first, my King; such rituals are as old as the stones of our world."

"I realize that," muttered Magnus, bitterly. Then the little girl, whose hand had found its way into his, squeezed, and suddenly an eternity of lies, deception, and hubris was banished by the tenderness of her gesture.

Who are you? he wondered once more.

"I don't think that their intent is to capture us," said Erik.

"Nor do I," agreed the huntsman.

Lila whispered to the mind of her beloved. *What could they possibly want, if not our capture?*

I am sorry for the silence, my Queen, he replied. *I harbor conspiracies to myself. Our pursuers haven't announced themselves. Even now they keep their distance, as do wolves circling a herd. They have not yet chosen to attack. Perhaps they wait for a command from their master. Perhaps they are simply watching, and wanting to know our intent.*

If they mean to stall us, we have not the time for their impertinence, declared Magnus, listening in. *I have a duty, and thunder and death await those who would deny me.*

The bloodmates shuddered from the cold wind that blew into their hearts at his words, and in that moment they almost heard a whisper of the secret he'd been keeping. Quickly, though, Magnus's thoughts retreated into the wasteland of his soul, too quickly for them to intuit anything of use. Among these three souls and minds united, Magnus had most mastered the art of erecting impregnable walls internally—ones strong enough to keep out even Brutus and the Black Queen, for a time. Lila and Erik found themselves stalled before that edifice, standing at its base and asking Magnus to return to them and share whatever pain he nursed. But he would not heed them or return; that channel into his mind was closed, and Erik and Lila discovered that they were as alone as they had been before adding Magnus to their marriage of blood. Stunned, they stopped running—as did Kanatuk—and turned to Magnus. In his illusion of age, he beheld them, measured and cool, and expressed no flicker of himself in their hearts or minds. As though he were now a stranger.

"Thunder and death?" Erik reached for the king.

Magnus backed away. Stepping before him, the girl, whose mysterious gaze was an abyss of secrets of its own, warned off Erik with a frown. Despite how large and terrible he was before her, she managed to cow him with a stern "No."

Erik cast off her reprimand and gently moved the girl out of his path. "Magnus, tell me, tell us."

"'Tis neither the time nor the place for us to be discussing my thoughts," said the king.

"We should be moving, not discussing," said Kanatuk.

Erik flung a hand in the huntsman's face and loomed over the king. "Speak."

And yet Magnus seemed as unimpressed by Erik's grand fury as the young girl. Magnus brushed him aside and again claimed Macha as his companion. "You do not command me, Erik," he said imperiously. "I am still king, and you remain one who serves. It shall soon fall to you to remember that order: the order of master and servant, of man led by duty and not heart."

Storming off, and with a crack of sorrow in his voice, he added, "You will need to be heartless, and I shall tell you of the moment when. Do not ask me what secrets I keep until then."

Uncertain if he was at fault for this untimely and strange outburst, Kanatuk gave an apologetic shrug to Erik and the queen before pursuing Magnus. Brooding and forlorn, the bloodmates who had been cast aside watched the shadows of their companions dissolve into murky stains, and stood motionless.

What was that? asked Erik.

A secret. A poison. A nest of invisible spiders crawled over Lila from whatever Magnus withheld. *He's up to something, my knight, and that's not the first I've sensed on the matter. I know not what he plans, though it lurks in his mind as darkly as murder. We must extract that poison from him. You and I know the cost of keeping secrets—how they devour a soul from within.*

I do, and damn this threefold love and tugging in my heart, but I shall not see him suffer as you did. And what of your secret, my Queen? He had felt a burning in Lila, too—a need to be freed of pain. Once more, he sensed his queen was at odds with these lands, its people, or its culture. What was she harboring, and was her secret as dark as Magnus's?

Lila stifled his curiosity with a kiss, before linking their hands and running after the others. She pondered the man shuffling about in her soul, poking about in her dusty corners for whatever she was hiding. Feeling both guilty and annoyed, she wondered for how much longer she could restrain herself from decrying this land. She knew something of what Kinlords and their ilk desired; she understood their motivations, and that men like them should be run from, or run through. If it came to the moment where she had to choose which, she would take the latter. Why she struggled with being honest about what she knew was a twice-vexing enigma, as if telling the truth would expose a nerve. Was she afraid for their fates? No, she was afraid for herself, and for all those examining a mystery so close to her. Soon she would tell her bloodmates what she knew of this dark land and its curses that bound children to lords and lords to the land—through blood magik of the evilest kind. Then she would reveal how that wickedness was bound to her. She would have to tell the others all she knew if they were to survive.

Soon.

III

What considerable distance they had built between themselves and the Eininhar was undone once they approached the city's limits. There, a great stone wall, set across an irregularly shaped courtyard formed by a junction of streets and houses, blocked the pale night sky and realms beyond. Disappointment hit them hard upon seeing the many Eininhar patrolling the shaded arcade atop the stairs. No doubt more of the Kinlord's chosen would be inside the tunnel that passed through the city's stone ring. In what was another inconvenience, they had also come to a different gate than the one through which they'd entered Valholom, and none of the bloodmates recognized the area. The sounds of agitated banter from up ahead further fueled their unease. Even at this hourglass, the courtyard before them churned with peasants and cranky beasts as folks traded wares from their bags, hand-pulled barrows, or the back of their carts. As a market, it was of a crude and antiquated sort, where firewood, eggs, meat, milk, and wool were as desired a currency as coin.

Betwixt two shady buildings, Kanatuk and the others huddled behind a snow-laden fort of crates. A while ago, Magnus and Lila had cast off their phantasms and relied on their cloaks and the night to provide camouflage. There'd been naught but drunks and fools along the byways and sewer underpasses through which Kanatuk had taken them, and they had realized that maintaining a phantasm was wasted energy. Furthermore, Lila had need of her magik for feats greater than mere cantrips.

After much discussion, Lila stood and emerged a little from hiding, then tested her Will upon the throng. Kanatuk had never witnessed this kind of sorcery. He suddenly felt as if he were in an ice hut being warmed by a fire pit, feeling fat on fish-head stew and listening to one of his long-dead mother's tales. As Kanatuk dreamed of homespun and heartwarming fantasies, Lila seeped out fragrant sorcery, which wriggled off into the crowd and coiled around the throats and minds of men. Erik, the king, and the girl, who was evidently immune to the beguilement, watched the crowd for a reaction. As the shimmering twists of Lila's magik slithered about, men and women slowed in their bargaining, sniffed the air, and dropped foodstuffs, coin, and bags to the stone, abandoning reality for whatever warm and candlelit memory now glowed in their minds. Up on the arcade where the Eininhar congregated, a shuffling confusion began—though not of the kind they had hoped for.

"Stop, my Queen." Erik needed to pull on her, somewhat violently, to break her trance.

"What?" she exclaimed.

People beyond woke from their dream-faced sleeps, then retook their possessions from the slops of snow and mud into which they'd been discarded. Not one among them appeared out of sorts, aside from a moment of puzzled humor about how clumsy everyone seemed to have become. In a speck, trade and conversation had renewed itself. Past the courtyard, however, a different sort of activity had started, and Eininhar assembled and barked rough commands to one another. A few of the warriors pointed their swords directly at the alley, and Erik pulled Lila back into hiding.

"Somehow, they've seen us," she hissed. Kanatuk believed that not only had her tone changed, but that he had spotted a dazzle of scales upon the bridge of her nose and a white flash of fangs. "I feel as if my magik had absolutely no effect on them."

"Perhaps," muttered Kanatuk, "they cannot be enchanted since they are beholden to one another. That's what you did, wasn't it? Try to enchant them? Like the teas my mother would drink before her storytelling that brought me into her words and memories. Or those men could be like Macha, who cannot be charmed by any hex of which I know."

"I have lost my skin, not my soul," mumbled the girl, defiantly.

Magnus wanted to embrace her. Instead, he joined Erik and Kanatuk in peering over one of the crates that formed their fort. Eininhar were definitely headed their way.

"We have moments before they're here," said Magnus. "Is this the ideal path for us to take?"

Kanatuk stood, grabbed Macha, and started walking back into the shadows with her. "It was the best path, and that gate leads into the Frostveldt, though I had thought to wait for a change in guard for us to slip through. I could have lost any of the Kinlord's men in the frozen forest and we'd have taken that vein of woodland far into the North. We'll find another way out of Valholom. Even the sewers, if we must. Though they're not as you know them in the South, and we'll be holding our breath and swimming through spans of shite."

Swimming through shite? The prospect, while appalling, earned more than Magnus's disgust. He had a duty. He had a blood debt to this world and to his brother, and as that promise swelled in him, he heard the song of the North once more. Winter croaked out a melody, her bitter notes kissing his ear and prickling passion across his flesh. She must be a woman, somewhere, or have a herald with a harp of ice—a dazzling nymph of ice and heartless beauty—who played to him. Either that muse or his own cleverness told him what needed to be done. *There's no warning, my lord, at best a song the henswives say, which comes on the wind, then a snowstorm like one you might create...*Magnus recalled the captain's dreadful tales of men frozen stiff by the Scourge of Winter. That such a power could strike that quickly and efficaciously felt exaggerated, yet the fear that it might be true was from where he drew his Will. From his fear of what was to come, too, if he failed to stop his brother.

"King Magnus?" whispered Kanatuk.

Magnus peered out from their cover like a suicidal rabbit peeking at the wolves hunting nearby. It was all the warning any of them had, though by the current of his emotions, Erik knew to pull the company together. A crackle of thunder sounded in a sky that rarely knew rain, and white mist filled the passageway. Emerald lights dazzled in the fog, and in harmony, a riot of green lightning and thunder played above. When they all felt as though the world could become no louder, at last a deluge of broken crystal calved from a glacier detonated above and descended, and the realm resounded with a shattering cacophony.

It was a precipitation so violently cold as to sizzle flesh to blackness. *Certain* flesh, that is, such as that of the crimson-banded dogs who thought they could hunt an Immortal King. Upon them—and only them—did Magnus's wrath strike most wickedly. Eininhar who were fool enough to move toward the ivory and green silhouette striding into the panicking square were thrown against wall, stone, or house for their insolence. Most of the smarter warriors clung in tight circles and prayed to their master for protection. For their meekness, these chastened men were spared by what compassion still reigned in Magnus's madness.

As the Immortal wandered the square, he loosed a stentorian shriek into the maelstrom. It could have been a scream, a confession, or a curse, for it tore apart the white chaos, wracking the land with the rage of all three. A plate beneath the earth tipped; a plate in the sky fractured and rained more boulders of hail. In the boreal inferno, the bloodmates heard a command through the king's incantation.

Through the gate.

Thus, the queen and her bloodmate hauled the squirming huntsman and his strangely docile cohort toward the light-spindled glory of whatever Magnus had become—a cosmic being of light, twisted by wind. They followed that hurricane through the snow-battered square, over a land now heaped with huddling, snow-buried victims, overturned vehicles, and inconceivable masses cloaked in winter. They made wordless prayers to the shivering wretches stumbling in the snowstorm. They hoped that Magnus's wrath had not undone the lives of these innocents.

He had become unhinged, Erik realized. Nonetheless, he followed, as he'd been called to by the king. First, there was no other path save through the snowbanks, the keeled and frozen animals, and the biting clouds. They entered a stone tunnel, which was instantly dazzled in ice. By the time the walking storm emerged on the other side of the wall, the unrelenting weather had long since driven the Gunnhar and peasantry into their rattling shelters. Here, the Gunnhar encampment was barren; tents had morphed into dunes of snow, a section of palisade abruptly punched out like a pugilist's teeth. Over that ruined barrier, the king hovered or climbed—no one could say which. Still, they knew to follow the green and white sparks he left in his wake. They continued until even Erik's knees had numbed. At last Magnus's storm fluttered to a graceful death, and the girl Erik had picked up to carry in his arms so that she not be drowned in snow cried out in relief.

They found themselves up to their hips in white and surrounded by a wreath of shiny, prickly woods. Magnus didn't stop to explain himself. He pushed on as if he were their guide, as if he knew where he must be.

IV

Winter reigned in fury in the Northlands, and while Magnus's dread storm had ended, the land was only a little more hospitable than before. For a long spell, the king continued to lead them across a white desert of snow, through forests that jangled with icicle chimes, and beneath the shadows of antediluvian conifers—their species too old to be recognized by anyone. Once, the undulant valley they had entered fell into a ravine with a bridge constructed of great boulders of solid ice as the only way north. Magnus didn't stop to assess the danger, seeking only to head north, whence the song and summons came. Perhaps the others could hear it too—the voice—since they were attuned to the otherworld. Mayhap they weren't imagining the subtle hiss in Winter's howl, or the constant cracking of the land like words spoken through a malfunctioning farspeaking stone. No one knew if

Magnus's lips were mumbling in return or if his twitches were merely a symptom of the pounding cold.

On the other side of the deadly bridge, snow-sand mired them again. Beyond them, Winter swallowed the hills and forests behind and laid its ivory gauntlet over the land. In the presence of so much whiteness, daytime's coming could only be determined as a flickering golden illusion that occasionally glinted in the gray. Later that morning, they crossed a vast frozen river and peered down through clear windows into a sapphire brume in which life swam and hunted. Even if the land appeared violent toward people, it showed less disdain toward the animals that lived in its lakes and streams. Only cold-blooded creatures, Erik realized, were favored by the White Mother. Indeed, a dearth of warm-blooded animals haunted the winter hills, glades, and forests; there were no prancing hooves, barking wolves, or even flapping of wings. It was as if the land had died, and they walked through its afterlife.

After a while, their snot and sweat had crystallized, and their limbs began to move like wooden pirate legs. The fact that the mortals among them made this journey, with regularity, seemed an act deserving of an ode from Kericot. Their stalwartness aside, the mortals' bodies were weakening, and while Magnus and Lila consciously or unconsciously nourished their muscles with Erik's vast ocean of strength, their guides had been hiking for hourglasses and hourglasses. They would soon fall—especially the girl who'd excused herself from Erik's arms a while back. She was weaving and tripping behind Magnus, following him as though enamored. He too appeared enamored, and a smile broke his stormy demeanor whenever he looked to her.

Walking beside the huntsman, Erik sensed the man's fear and suspicion at these exchanges between the king and the girl who wasn't quite a girl. Even if they weren't of the same blood, the huntsman and the girl loved each other more than most siblings, at least enough to live a lonely life together in this scarred and frozen landscape.

"Magnus, stop. We've gone far enough," Erik said.

A basin bottomed in slick ice and lined with prickled trees and snowy banks rose around the company. They'd been walking along a crunching, exhausted riverbed from an immemorial age. Magnus heeded the advice, and the five set off for the highlands surrounding the basin, where at least they might find some protection against the wuthering open tract they'd been wandering. Grace was with them, and once they reached the foothills and began to climb the crackling growth, the weather grew milder. Erik and Kanatuk cleared a path together using the knight's bare hands and a long machete the huntsman retrieved from under his cloak.

They found an uncommon peace in this land so beset by rage, and the king, queen, and little girl climbed behind the two men at an almost leisurely pace. Soon their sweat ran hot, and the girl had regained a bit of blush in her cheeks. At some moment unrecalled, she and the king had found each other's hands. They sometimes swung them, gaily, with measurably queer and strained happiness on their faces—as though they were friends dually stricken with dementia, who only in lucid moments remembered their friendship. However, they weren't close. She was an unearthly child—a seal and a skin-walker, if the queen remembered it accurately from when Rowena and Galivad had met the band of Morigan's heroes—and he was an Immortal King.

"I must ask, do you know her?" asked Lila.

The pair looked at her, together, as attuned to each other as bloodmates.

"I do not," said the king. "Although...I feel as if I do. As if we were always meant to meet."

"Yes," agreed the girl, and they stared, smiled, and once more fell into their inexplicable embrace of hearts.

It left a bad taste in Lila's mouth, and it wasn't the sourness of jealousy. A mystery bound king and girl, and they had too many mysteries already, so yet another was unwelcome.

Lila gazed up through the glittering mesh and into the firmament, looking for a glimmer of dark—the Black Star. She saw nothing, though, and was as disappointed as she was relieved. Gloom overcame her after that, and Erik tended her, sending her wisps of warm spirit. It sufficed, and she smiled and touched her lips as if his had been upon hers. A short time later, the huntsman spoke. He told the others it was time to rest as they cleared the rise and entered a glade.

Into a winter cradle, mothered by one of the realm's greatest trees, as great as any could remember, they had gone. Shingles of ice and flocculent branches had fallen about the clearing, and the shaded area of respite held a warm fragrance of something like pine—only sweeter. Near to the knotted trunk of a tree and under roots grown like hunched, shaggy serpents were damp but still flammable sheddings that would suffice to provide shelter or make fire. They would have to share the space, though, with the stags and does who raised inquisitive heads from the cubbies they'd made in those same spots. From the heights of a tree, alarming the travelers, a bird cried loudly and suddenly. Life. Somehow it was here.

The southerners approached quietly, following the huntsman, wary of traps. Macha broke free of her fascinating new friend, so that she might hurry toward the animal burrows and the warmer green that skirted the mighty tree. Was there another magikal song here? wondered Magnus. What enchantment of the Great Mother ensorcelled this place? There was magik, for sure, as the Immortal's nerves couldn't be roused, his fear couldn't be stoked, and even the deer and birds above settled back into their placidity without bothering him or the strangers again.

"Huntsman, to where have we come?" asked the king.

Kanatuk looked back at him. "I was fine to let you lead us for a while, my lord. Now I shall show the way. My people know this land—its secrets, its horrors, its hidden treasures. Whereas you seem to have one path in mind and one means to get there, *north*, even if that means thrusting us into the worst of Winter's wrath. That stubbornness will not stand, the farther ahead we push. You will find that Winter here can break even a man of ice."

Kanatuk said no more and his reticence continued as they set up a small camp within spitting distance of the deer and long-eared furry creatures that they saw chattering and playing around the arched roots. Erik did not ask if he should make meals of such lazy prey—it would be akin to pissing in holy water. Incontrovertibly, they'd come to a sacred space, and he would not be its defiler. Kanatuk and Macha left the Immortals with instructions to dust the frost off branches and gather kindling from around the base of the tree. While wandering and tending to that task alone, Erik sniffed the hoary trunk many times while collecting twigs and handfuls of moss. Earthworms climbed their way out of the aromatic soil as his fingers dug.

After this, when he looked over at Kanatuk and Macha, he had endured enough wonder to not be surprised by what he saw. The pair had walked into a sleepy lair of deer and had reached up to pluck the fat purple fruits, each lumpy as gourds and jiggling with flesh, that hung in the damp green entanglements beneath each massive root. When all three—huntsman, girl and knight—returned to camp, Lila lit a fire with the materials that had been foraged. Kanatuk threw them each a fruit...or perhaps they were vegetables, for the seeded meat had a pumpkin's blandness and texture. They sat in separate camps of mortal and Immortal, and all ate what they'd been given. None felt a need for water after the meal. Indeed, everyone was remarkably full.

"Winterbliss," said Kanatuk, as the Immortals stared at the stems in curiosity. "This is why I lead and you follow." He glanced narrowly at Magnus. "Though I do not know I want a man watching my back who thinks so lowly of life as to smash it with thunder and ice."

"I am not myself," replied Magnus. "I am driven to extremes to protect this world."

Kanatuk, his hands hanging casually from his knees, though his manner was anything but, leaned in, and his eyes smoldered. "If you become a villain to smite a villain, then you've done the world no good. I know, my lord, the kiss and taste of darkness. I've had that seed in my belly. I know much of your tale, as told to me by the noble seer whose weaving has no doubt brought our threads together."

"Do you know darkness and pain as I do, boy?" countered the king.

Wind ruffled through their sanctuary, and the animals quailed.

Kanatuk, unflappable, barked his reply. "Put down your elemental whip. Do not think to chasten me with your Immortal rage. I was a child of the Broker, Menos's mad sewer king. I served in a livery wet from shite, piss, and blood. I lay with Death, decay, and every vile white mortal worm in the Iron City that feasts on rot. It's gone now, Menos, and bless the deliverer of that vengeance. I cannot say that I didn't hate everything about that realm and its people. In Menos, I lost myself—my name, my family, the face and stories of my mother. I was less than nothing. Now I have reclaimed all that and more, and I shall not have a king who has lost himself and his hold on peace tell me how or what I know. I know myself—my darkness and my light. Do you know thyself, King?"

Kanatuk's seething jealousy and worry over Magnus's intentions with his seal-sister, an anger fostered during the wintry silence since their first contact with these travelers, had ostensibly reached its pitch, and this was the result. There was a hushed pause as everyone skipped a breath to see if the king was indeed as unhinged and peevish as Kanatuk claimed. No storm was forthcoming, however, and Magnus, enervated, slumped.

"I didn't mean that," whispered Kanatuk. "Not all of it, at least."

Lila spoke up before any more insults were flung.

"Listen, we've scarce had the time to know of each other's quests and trials. I've met the woman of whom you speak, Kanatuk, and I felt her grace and kindness. If she sees us as allies, if she knows of even a sand of this hourglass of destiny we share, then for her—and not merely ourselves—should we remember to keep peace. Morigan has been cursed to see, know, and feel the strife of every soul woven into the tapestry of this war. Think of that, and not your childish grievances, you two. Consider what it must be like to bear all pains, all sorrows and regrets. Then come to me again and present your problems, man's or Immortal's, as if they have credence."

She had successfully embarrassed everyone, even those who hadn't spoken. As the silence simmered into genial warmth, the scorned men glanced up from the fire at each other.

"I would never dishonor Morigan," replied Kanatuk.

"Good," Lila said, remaining stern. She turned to every face as she continued. "Know and remember with every breath or inclination toward quarrel that Morigan fights for us, too. We must do our part then, and so is why we're here."

Kanatuk scratched his hood. "Aye. I shall remember that. I am, however, still reaching for particulars. I could only eavesdrop so much in such a crowded tavern. You head north, and that much is clear from your conversation with the good captain, and from the king who walks as a compass points toward the winter heart of this realm. What do you seek?"

A suspicious lot, the Immortals sought to protect their devastating secrets, pursing lips and frowning while trying to force the truth out. It was Magnus who was done with lies; he knew that the Black Star would be here far too soon to be overly cautious with his disclosures. Still, he stopped shy of revealing everything, withholding from his bloodmates what he intended to do when he met Nifhalheim.

With selective honesty, he spoke. "I have come to enter into a blood oath with the Elemental of Winter, Nifhalheim."

"The Frostfather?" exclaimed Kanatuk, knowing another of this entity's many names.

"It is the only force that can stand against my brother. I have tried to use my magik against him before, summoning a storm of damnation, unlike the comparably merciful squall I summoned in Valholom; it was not enough. Not enough to defeat the power to which he has pledged himself: an ancient elemental of fire—the first there ever was, I believe."

The Firefather, thought Kanatuk, whose mother had taught him all the old and true legends.

"Lila has seen that this journey north is my Fate," said the king. "Such was revealed to her by another seer in this age in which every peddler and palaver seems to involve tea leaves and omens. Nonetheless, the bequeather of her vision was a man of the blood of the House of Mysteries, and he set us on this path, which, if we've met you, must indeed be a thread woven by this Morigan—whom I've yet to meet and hope that I shall, once we reach the ruinous end of all things. There you have it, noble huntsman: the truth of our quest. I was remiss in ever challenging that virtue you possess. Now you know of our mad race against a doomsday chronex with mere weeks remaining in its countdown to destruction."

"Destruction?" said Macha.

Perhaps because *she* had asked, the king dropped all gentility and cleared any and all doubts regarding the stakes—this against the fearful, silent advice to the contrary expressed in the twisted grimaces and souls of his bloodmates. "However much you know of this war, I shall tell you now the truth.

"I am a child born of the divine, as is my brother. We are vessels for that power, and to destroy us would bring a calamity to this world akin, though many times multifold, to the storm of ice and fire. Our power to influence and create is coveted by horrors from beyond, bodiless monsters who call themselves Dreamers and believe themselves to be kings and queens. An arrogance once and justifiably born from their primeval reign over this planet—though there are other worlds, places, and times to which they have visited and ruled. The darkest of their kind has returned to Geadhain. She calls herself my mother and has already eaten the soul of my brother.

"In twenty-three days now, what Will I have to resist her shall fail. What Will and love I have *stolen* from these two, these lovers for whom my manipulations and whims have caused mythic pain...Well, no matter...They are bound to me and thus condemned to my corruption, as well. If I am lost, my body, Brutus's body, and even the bodies of those who've given their souls for my protection, will belong to her, to the Black Queen—the queen of sin and evil. I shall be Doom, and I shall unmake Geadhain. No prayer or power, high or low, can stop me then."

Silence strangled the gathering. Magnus deepened their fear, adding, "Stop *us*, rather. Four mad vessels filled with the purest evil. I am loath to think of our depravity then."

"No. So long as you have Will, you have hope."

It was Macha who spoke, and she flew to the king's side. Kanatuk was bewildered more than jealous, since she loathed all men except him, then Erik for a spell, and now Magnus. Before today, she had struggled with some of the most basic of Ghaedic phrases Kanatuk had taught her, so her sudden loquaciousness seemed a divine miracle.

Macha knelt, she and the king locked countenance to gaping countenance, and they tumbled into that roiling void of memory, time, and meaning. As she spoke further, her words were like hands on the fog of the glass, the obscurity blocking her face, her history, her truth as shrouded in this new form, and the king remembered who she was, who she had always been. No flesh or lives could change a soul so pure.

"We cannot surrender to the dark," she said, shuddering in defiance. "No matter how deep our despair, how cold our future. We fight for life and love and the green. We are the seeds of our planet. Our bodies are the nourishment for that fruit yet unborn. Through the cycle, the ages, we sing and bleed and grow into one garden of eternity. Do you understand, my King? Why you must never give up? As I have been told that one day, too, I shall be the sunshine and soil, and that hope will be mine."

Magnus understood naught next to the lyrical beauty of the anamnesis encompassing him. He was too fixated on who she was, or, rather, the woman, warrior, and hero she had *been*. With respect to her great sacrifice, he promised to do whatever she demanded of him. And were he to have known her true name he would have wept it aloud, for she was the one he had seen in his vision of the past back in Eod: the woman who undid Arimoch and the empire of the Mortalitisi. She was the woman whose shriek, soul, and defiance undid mankind's wickedest empire. If her reborn soul could be here, enduring, he too could weather any darkness ahead.

The others had already risen, moved by whatever strange vow of which king and maiden had partaken.

"I shall lead us, using the old ways, on the long road," promised Kanatuk. "I shall take you to your destiny as fleetly as the wind blows. I didn't realize we had so little time to waste."

And they were away. While they left the grove, the ancient tree, and a trove of Winter's secrets behind them, far more mysteries were planted in the fertile soil of their minds, and the king was left to ponder past selves, future heroes, and the soul of this incredible woman who'd lived and suffered as long as he. She looked back at him often, and they spoke in glances like bloodmates.

V

The Eininhar released the sobbing man, and Captain Nolan fell to the floor, crawling over splinters and broken crockery toward his wife—her brown cheeks glistening from tear-wet horror—and his children, who huddled with her. Away from the six or so shadowy men, Nolan briefly assessed the damage to family and home: a tipped table, a scattered dinner, shattered plates, and sparks that flew from a sputtering hearth like vengeful fireflies, their passion stirred by the wind of a kicked-open door. Nolan's eldest, Laurie, lay amid the topple of a chair thrown and shattered against the wall of the captain's home. By the firelight, and from the heaving twists of the lad's back viewed through the tears in his tunic, Nolan could tell that he might live; at least the lad was wise enough not to move, raise fists, or make another display of bravery and again stand up to the Eininhar. Laurie's defense of his family had brought the worst of these men's wrath to their home.

Nolan hardly recalled how that storm had started—a kicked open door, a few barked words, then an insult and raised fist from his son, and suddenly their house had been torn apart by six tornadoes of muscle and rage. Those winds had passed, and a sizzling tension burned in his stomach as to what might happen next.

A white-robed woman emerged from between the warriors, who bowed to her as though she were concubine to the Kinlord. She seemed no concubine, though, with her wrinkles and face scribed with runes and mysteries of blood and ancient times. To look upon her was to behold a mortal puzzle. Was she witch or priestess? Sinner or saint? For she carried with her the menace of a great driven power, but the humility of a woman of faith and virtue. She knelt beside the tremulous captain and spoke as softly as a virgin to the man whose family she had ordered terrorized for their insolence.

"Look upon me," she whispered, her voice buzzing, her fingers dry and cold as winter twigs hovering near his face—not grazing, though still forcing his chin up as though he were her puppet. In that moment she seemed as old as time to Nolan, every line a canyon, every marking of a rune like a crimson chain of constellations unseen since the world was young. "I shall ask once more, and this time I believe you will be more cordial. I wish not for the Kinlord's men to harm your family again; however, I must have the truth. Can you give me that?"

"I can. I shall," he replied.

"You met with the king?"

Nolan didn't hesitate; her intensity was a tonic of truth. "I did. Magnus, his queen—or former, I don't understand the arrangement—and their knight. They came aboard my vessel posing as travelers: a merchant brother and sister, and their guard. I'd know her, though, the queen, despite any illusion or disguise. After all, she was the one who felled Menos, I'm sure of it. We owe her for that, and for the liberation of the daughters of the Arhad."

Slowly a haze consumed the room around Nolan until before him, in this new cosmos, there was but a belt of red stars orbiting two steaming white stars—the white witch's runic markings and gaze, though he'd gone beyond the space of this room. "Go on," suggested a voice. "Speak it all. Spill your soul's secrets. What you know. What you think. What you feel they've come to do."

"What I know?" he mumbled into the heavenly void. "I know that they've with them a curious girl and a tracker of the Seal Fang. He'll know the old roads and paths to avoid the Scourge. I feel that there's something of that man and girl that's bound in destiny. I know that together the five will head north, off your maps and as far as the Throne of Winter. I know that Magnus is torn by a decision that he must face there, though I cannot say—or even guess—what pains an Immortal suffers."

"The same as you and I," replied the voice. "Only amplified by the misery of eternity."

In a sudden cruel sweep of white, the room and Nolan's own pains and regrets were returned to him. The sweep had been the white flow of the woman as she stood, slipped the hood of her cloak over her head, and walked away from the captain. "You've been helpful," she said.

Nolan felt nothing but shame at his disclosures; even though he remembered so little, he was certain he had said too much while under the spell of that woman. "Please, just leave my family alone."

At this, she turned, and struck him with indignation. "We did not come here to harm you. It was your son who raised his fist to a room of the world's most violent warriors. You have told me what you know, and now your family is free. Do not worry yourself about your weaknesses. In time, they will be forgotten, and you'll have your chance to again serve your king, a true king, perhaps with true fealty, in the wars ahead. Oroborax: the snake of two heads—the symbol of eternity. We are what we shall be, and each sigh of death begets the squeal of a mortal life."

Branwen gathered the Eininhar to her with a whistle, as a master would summon her hounds. The warriors swarmed to her as one of them moved quickly to remove the remains of the door from her path. While she was nobility of a kind, so was this man who served her, and as doubt and loathing tore at the captain—all that dishwater about fate, lives, and serving kings he'd clearly failed—likewise did the incongruity of the warrior's likeness add to the chords of Nolan's confusion.

This particular fellow was more than a head above the other men, with a skull wreathed in dark golden curls of the same color and twists of his beard, and with a caress of caramel to his skin, too. A wave of strangeness struck the captain, for as the man glanced at him Nolan noticed that beyond his summer complexion the man had the exact same tawny irises as the Queen of Eod. His face was even ruggedly pretty as if the queen had been rehewn as a man. Were there any doubt about the similarities, the hulking soldier—as burgeoning with sinew as the queen was with sultriness—gave a remorseful frown to the captain and his cowering family for what damage he had helped bring.

Suddenly Nolan knew this man, or at least his legend. *Golden fair, strength of bear, beauty of the hart. A hand for blades, a hand that slays—and bleeds—his master's art.* Bjorn Raifemorn. Then the woman, her hounds, and Valholom's prince stepped out into the night. At once, Nolan hurried to his son. Thereafter, with their dinner spoiled, he possessed only blathering condolences with which to feed his family.

In streets made scarce from the coming of Branwen and the Eininhar, the men stood and listened to what next she had planned. Branwen sat on the edge of an abandoned crate, contemplating. Bjorn waited, thinking as well of whence this woman appeared and of the escalating mystery pursuing her like storm clouds. Meanwhile, the others in his pack peered into alleyways and sniffed the shadows for threats. Within him, they growled as one great hunter; after the tussle at the captain's abode, their brothermind had shifted into its bestial state, and it would be a while before they returned. Bjorn remained outside of the link, above his primal, roaring brethren, and he would relay to them any relevant instructions. The look given to him by the captain had stolen a moment of his reflection, too, and so deeply was he pondering that Branwen had to snap at him, twice.

"Heed me, child!"

Although he was no child if measured by years or depth, she made him feel as if he were. Bjorn bowed, having learned respect for this new master. "What would you have my brothers and I do?"

"Mounts, rolls, and tents. We ride at once."

"To where?"

"As I've told you, as you know. Into the Scourge—to see that Magnus finishes what he ought."

"Is that safe?"

"What remains that is safe in this world, child?" asked Branwen with a speck of sincerity, her age softened slightly by compassion. "Here, winter comes. In the South, fire burns—and I do not speak of the horror sleeping under the razed kingdom of the mad Immortal. I shall keep us safe. Rather, the White Mother will see to our safe passage through her fury, at least until we reach the Crown of Winter. There, even her appellations may not be enough to forestall the Scourge of Winter. You may all die there, along with the king, and yet life is an ember to be burned. Come, let us burn together and see what fire we can make."

"We?" Bjorn stole one glance, then another, and waited for her to recant. Bjorn had been shocked when she'd left her favored lurking spot behind his father's ear to even descend into the streets of Valholom. "You're coming, too?"

Branwen's smile was wry, sharp, and friendly. "I did say *we*, when you were given your orders in the Kinlord's chamber. I cannot leave this task to children, though by the end of this you may well be your own man."

As she shuffled off the crate, he debated offering her aid—though in the end remained wary of touching her. For she did seem old, maybe as old as the legendary Yggdrassils, those verdant lords sprung in the most desolate of glacial woods that submitted not to the Scourge. Bjorn watched her for a moment—sensing all this unraveling mystery within the woman for the first time—perhaps aided by the united perceptions of his pack, who turned and sniffed the woman in tandem with the prince. Branwen was a force like those ancient, enduring trees: a magik that wasn't magik, but a building block of life—crude, untamable, and eternal. He'd been wrong to judge her a villain.

"I am sorry," he muttered, rather lost in the moment. "I'd considered you a foe, a woman with selfish aims who meant to do terrible things to our realm."

"I have done terrible things." Branwen's grandmotherly kindness wilted like a rose under hot piss. "More will follow—bloody and desperate acts. I do what needs to be done. What no others will do."

Bjorn didn't ask her what she meant. Again, she was a stranger, an even colder one than before.

IX

CREEPING DEATH

I

For once, Gloriatrix had no words; her tongue was tied, hands sweating, and throat as dry as her mind was of thoughts. She had reactions aplenty, though she kept her shrieking at and disbelief of the scene happening in the desert hidden behind her Iron mask. After she and the others aboard her crowe realized what had occurred—an assault on Camp Fury—Gustavius had commandeered the vessel. They circled Camp Fury twice, surveying the damage, trying to reach people with farspeaking stones, and seeing what they could beneath the whirling smoke. Fires they could see, and many of the Furies' spines were now lit with gusty lights that came not from the usual glow of their quills but from a danger more menacing. Flames scoured the camp around the black behemoths, and the watchers' only sense of the battle came through smoky glimpses of a war field where Menosian soldiers, armored like monsters, fought real monsters: the living dead.

"We have to get down there," said Aadore. "Your orders, Majesty?"

The newly minted aristocrat was at one of the portals nearest the Iron Queen, staring out alongside Gloriatrix's strange-smelling son who was dressed as a Carthacian priest for reasons beyond her understanding. Sean was at the next portal over, then Curtis, Skar, and in his arms inquisitive Ian, crowding the last of the three portside windows. As if trying to pretend the destruction into nonexistence, the Iron Queen sat nearby, fiddling with her gloves. She hadn't spoken beyond granting control of the vessel to Gustavius, who was to be heard shouting at the pilots. Mournful, meek, and suddenly seeming as old as she must be, the Iron Queen looked up at the woman who had asked her a question, then back to her crumpled gloves.

The Iron Queen's silence enraged Aadore; she wanted to shake the woman out of her stupor. As a woman of service, though, she still knew better than to assault, however lightly, a queen. Instead she withdrew her sword, bowed knee to iron tile and forehead to hilt. It was a bit farcical, a full-gowned woman cast in body as a knight and the queer array of characters behind her: a child sailor, a giant scarred frontiersman, two fellows dressed like dandies, and her own son garbed in robes and metal. Nevertheless, Gloriatrix appreciated Aadore's gesture, and some of her composure returned to her. What iron didn't wake in the Iron Queen immediately was forged fresh by the young woman's earnest speech.

"My Queen," said the woman. "I know those creatures, for we faced them in Menos. As I know what you've been through, and while we've not lost the same weight of riches, we have lost everything, you and I. But here we remain, enduring, servant and queen of Iron. Please, land this craft, and we shall fight these creatures. I shall drive them back beyond death."

Gloriatrix almost caressed the woman. However, she knew enough from Gideon's reports to understand that a bite or serious nick of the infected would spread the contagion of living death into others, and that no cure had yet been found. Thus, as galling as it was to circle the battle being waged below, they had no other choice. For once, she had run out of ideas, and her Furies must burn; their demise crushed her worse than any defeat in this war.

She replied, "Fair and iron child. We are safe here, and our safety will ensure whatever empire of Iron is built tomorrow."

"We can fight them!" insisted Aadore, with tears of pride.

"You cannot," said the Iron Queen, no longer polite. "There are elements of this war, and this illness in particular, of which you do not know. It is the deadliest affliction ever witnessed by man; no curative or sorcery can treat it."

While Aadore might have held her tongue in less perilous circumstances, she was fiery with courage, and spared only a quick and silent plea to her brother before she confessed their deepest secret. Sean grasped what she was about to say and did not interrupt the words he would have said himself. Aadore loved him, and spoke for him, and was always amazed at how in harmony they were.

She said, "I know about this illness and its threat, and I fear it not."

"You should, you fool. It will end you."

Aadore kissed her queen's hand—which was shaking—and held it thereafter. "Not I..." She sighed, swallowing before she spat out the truth. "Not him. We of the Brennoch clan cannot be affected by magik of any shade—its darkest or its lightest."

"Absurd!" exclaimed the Iron Queen, and stole her hand back from the maiden.

"I would not lie to you," said Aadore.

Sean came forward. "My Queen, it's true. Aadore was clawed by one of the dead weeks ago, and is as hale as you or I—that scar isn't even a memory on her shoulder anymore. And ask yourself why else would a man of Menosian sensibilities prefer a wooden leg to one of flesh? If you've ever been privy to the more inglorious experimentation of your fleshcrafters and technomancers, you'll know that I speak true. I have a name, a designation, one you might have heard in passing, as I was a number."

Forcing out the repugnant code that dissolved his being into a string of numbers was more painful than any of the tortures he had suffered. "X-179242."

"Jargon that means nothing to me," lied the Iron Queen.

Sean's long-buried rage was toxic and had now been unearthed; it seeped from him. "I was held for years and made victim to needles, shocks, flaying, chemical castration, sorcerous gases, curses, wards, and spells. I was cut, bled, and fuked in every hole in my body with instruments that probably look like the spatulas and wands my dear sister might have tangled with in the kitchen. I shitted in bags strapped to my buttocks as if I were an incontinent elder on the days when I could not reach the chamber pot. I was fed through tubes and atrophied to such an extent it's a wonder my bones haven't broken and my skin didn't flake off. I'm an iron child, as you say. Perhaps that's how I endured. Know that all of that was the *kindest* of what they did. I shall keep the darkest to myself and take it to my grave. In knowing what I've said, know too that I shall never again allow such violations to be heaped upon me—or my family—by the madmen of our nation."

Appearing troubled, the Iron Queen rose and seemed to think long and hard before she spoke. It was an egregious deception, yet after Aadore's inspirational vows Gloriatrix's propensity for prevarication had returned, bolder than ever, and what speck of self-doubt she had felt had been crushed under the heel of her ambition. Of course she knew of this "subject," now given a name and face; he had been topical news in many a meeting in the Iron Crown. Here was the man immune to magik—a boy at the time, she supposed, based on when his incarceration and the experimentation upon him had begun. She had been the one to sign for his freedom. It hadn't been due to any a lapse in her ruthlessness; rather, she had needed to cut expenses and reallocate her researchers to Fort Havok. What else did he know? The urge for vengeance trembling his demeanor spoke volumes of torment and intrigue.

Finally, and with so little time to spare, she spoke.

"I am the sins of my country, though not the sinner. What has been done to you is unconscionable, and if you wish to hunt those men, then we shall—once my ships are mine and the Immortals have surrendered their choking grasp on this world. If you say that you can hunt these creatures that now attack our nation, then do so. Exact upon them the pain that has been done to thee. Fight as a soldier in the Ironguard and know the glory that you were deprived."

"I shall. I'll send them to the afterlife."

Gloriatrix strolled over to the others in the cabin, gracing them with her grim charm while explosions flickered outside the glass.

"And you? And you?" she asked of the brute and the dandy fellow, who both consigned hearts and pledged to her service. Since the chicanery over his identity was at an end, Sorren offered himself, too. He kept his mask on, however, as the others weren't ready for that fright. In what was natural for this one and only instant, the Iron Queen claimed young Ian from Skar and settled with him, while Aadore and the others hurried to find or check their weapons. They would descend to the battlefield and, Gloriatrix hoped, clear away enough of the mess left by Gideon before Eod arrived to push their pointed noses into her business.

She left her knights with a single command: burn everything that could not be saved. She prayed that Doctor Hex and his experiments were among the ashes.

II

Sorren examined the landscape. Unlike his companions, he saw not the billowing walls of smoke, nor the potholes of glassy tar burned into the sand, nor the men flailing with spidery unliving clung upon their backs, nor the general disorganization and terror that had set tents aflame. He could hear most of the destruction, rather gruesomely and sharply, but what he *saw* were auras and colors—the black halos surrounding the unliving and those men who were veined with ebon and would soon turn into their attackers. Such unfortunates he pointed out to the cold cavalry of rifle-and sword-bearing Menosians that moved in a tight phalanx behind his tall Carthacian figure, a priest come as if to mete out judgment for the many sins burdening this army. And lo, did they smite like avengers.

Aadore, who had been worried about her swordplay, learned that fear could train her in ways lessons couldn't, and when a snarling, jaw-dangling face appeared at their flank she smote messily, clumsily, and brutally with a sweep of silver fury. She was not worried when yellow claws gouged her skin, for she could not be turned, and she fought like the wild berserkers of the North. Likewise did the men with her move as wraiths of death, unleashing slashes, bullets, and kicks. None screamed in terror or suffered the indignity of surprise at the appearance of a horde of rotting dead, for they had all been to much darker places than this. None gagged from the reek of sizzling flesh, or lost a snifter of courage from the screams, dead or living, that resounded and deafened most others. When bloodied and caved-in skulls reared up from the smoke, their weapons pulverized them to paste. When hunched and naked things were seen nibbling on the gurgling soon-to-be corpse of a man, Curtis's fancy military rifle—given to him by Gustavius—blasted holes through the craniums of offender and victim like buckshot through a grape. Other than Aadore and her brother's snarling frontal assaults into the dead, nothing came near enough to scratch or do more than splash their fine clothes with gore.

Slowed by the bog of war, the five champions waded through the brume, moving toward the *Morgana*, which was hooded in orange smoke and apparently had suffered the most damage. Along the way, they picked up fallen men, dragged other burned—though otherwise untainted—soldiers out of the flaming deathtraps that their tents had become, and organized the frightened rabble into an army. Like divinities summoned by the prayers of the doomed, Eod's silver warriors soon gleamed on the battlefield, felling the dead and dousing fires with flashes of white, frosty wind or small localized rainclouds that poured their tears over smoldering tents. The battle was coming under control. However, Sorren sensed greater conflict and a confluence of power ahead. There was a mind controlling these sloppy newborn dead. While he wasn't certain if it was his brother, it was to that spindle of black energy that he led the others.

III

"What are they? Whence did these monsters come?" asked the man, dragged to his feet and thrown to task by this fearsome sword-maiden in a ball gown—her appearance further baffling him.

Aadore stabbed her sword into the ground and slapped the fool, then pointed to a line of Ironguards scrambling in the shadows behind them, putting out fires, and setting new ones to the decapitated and decimated dead. "Get over there," she commanded. While the man had no idea who this woman was, he followed her orders.

Onward the five pushed, past the encampment and into the whirling sand and bitter ash, still warm from the heat of the arsonist's masterpiece. Regarding that piece of terrorism, they were still assembling incomplete fragments of gibberish from the awestruck survivors, or from Gustavius's sketchy reports on the matter as conveyed through staticky farspeaking stones. (He, the Iron Queen, Ian, and some dithering gingery tit of a man who would surely be dead one day soon had remained on the crowe and wouldn't land until the camp was again secure.) Nonetheless, the survivors knew that the attack had been two-pronged.

First, the encampment had been suddenly beset upon by the dead. Ironguards, fatigued from the hourglass and heat were within complacent distance from their weapons. Then, as the unliving had risen from the sand where they'd been hidden like stalking scorpions, they had thrown themselves not at the Ironguards but upon the fires, to then run around as blazing menaces spreading their destruction. In a desert, fire spread unchecked and hungrily through whatever there was to burn, and the tents were laid to ashes in moments.

As Camp Fury began to ignite, the rest of the bunkered undead had begun to reveal themselves in the dunes. By then, General Chaos played the peak of his merry tune, and another assault occurred at the bridges and engine chambers of the Furies themselves. Tactical relays, Talwynian fusion drives, and all the incoherently scientific wonders that Gloriatrix had cultivated were sent into haywire. As technomagik surged, frazzled, and destroyed systems, certain protocols were enacted, though not with the true efficacy of function commands—since the vessels' power sources were failing. One of those misfired commands had been to launch the *Morgana*'s payload, which, on account of waning navigation and impulsion, didn't fire far or at all. Regrettably, a few of the *Morgana*'s magmatic spines *did* launch— three, actually, out of more than one thousand thermal warheads—and that tiny trio proceeded to arouse a holocaust in Camp Fury. A chain of disasters had been set in motion that left the encampment in ruins.

While some of the issues had been mostly resolved, and reinforcements from Eod would see to the continued diffusion of doom, the small war was not over. Aadore and the Iron Queen's son were to lead the charge into the second war zone, and to places where Eod's intervention was most surely not welcome: the Furies. Aadore considered what awaited them inside the sleeping behemoths, which loomed in the valley of sand below, their millions of lights flickering like dying candles. She wondered this, as she flicked black goop off her sword, as the smoking and riddled carcass of an unliving slithered into a pile of jumbled limbs, farting offal at her feet. Sean kicked the corpse over so they wouldn't have to bear its sight; this naked man had long since been turned, after many days of unholy gangrenous growth. Ahead were more shambling silhouettes, to be duly taken care of.

"What's the plan from here?" asked Aadore. The Carthacian imposter had finished communicating with his mother and was now pondering over whatever she had told him in the spent magic stone he threw into the sand. Aadore wanted to know why they were waiting; they had the might of the Menosian armada to save.

"I feel a source..." muttered Sorren with his queer leisurely inflection that made it seem as though either he, or the others, were slow. All had begun to notice strange accents to the man—his potpourri, his speech, his brutally fast strikes, how he could tell which men could and couldn't be saved from Death's kiss. "A beating darkness, a heart. It's the touch of Death. She's here. She's in someone."

"Who?" asked Sean.

My brother? thought Sorren. He was hopeful of that, but the ghostly pulse throbbing behind the unusually radiant shell of the *Morgana*—as if she were, indeed, a colossal living organism—didn't appear great enough to be a true vessel of Death. His brother as her vessel would emanate like a black hole. Still, he sensed a presence grounding Death's power to this place and controlling this army. It was a general of some kind, if not the one he desired to confront. "I sense a commander in the belly of the *Morgana*. Mother needs us to retake control of the ships and to do that we must to cut the root of the darkness here, which grows from that source."

"Will that work?" asked Curtis, stepping forward.

Sorren knew that vessels were ties between Dreamers and Geadhain, conduits that if broken should prohibit any of their parasites' influence over the material realm. Perhaps wrecking smaller conduits, too, could prove disruptive to Death's influence. It was a theory in need of testing, and the results might serve them both in the war ahead, and in the battle to save his brother. "We shall see," said Sorren, and he swept down into the dusky dunes.

The dead here were aimless and, in some cases, still rising—soldiers who'd fled from the Furies and had been caught and eaten in the sands. Nothing that could stand against the determined champions, though, and their swords and sandy clothing were soon slick again from the juices of the wicked. Curtis, sharpshooting from afar, was the cleanest of their unit. He smiled whenever Aadore caught his eye and even gave her a wink before pulling the trigger and shooting the scraggly monsters that charged up the hill. One horrid creature leapt out of the sand like a shrieking ape, and Sorren caught it—seized it, more aptly—by its head, then squished the fistful of meat and bone with the ease of a strongman crushing a tomato. Afterward, he flung the body by its neck-stem a hundred yards into the murk. The others stared at him, accepted that he was indeed beyond the pale, beyond what qualities of humanity they understood, and continued fighting. Again, they'd seen worse than Sorren, and at least his species seemed friendly.

At the bottom of the valley they walked among strewn bodies, ended the groaning men who were soon to rise again, and followed red and black roads of gore that took on a strange beauty from the pulsating irregularity of the *Morgana*'s failing light. Flashes of crimson revealed that fewer of the dead were about now; they appeared, uncannily, to have started to withdraw. They came to the bridge ascending into the *Morgana*, where much of the metal glistened with blood. However, the architects of that violence weren't themselves found, and the champions took the long walk across the bridge hearing sand-whispers and the far-off clangor of the besieged encampment, and nothing more. Into the pendulous silence they went. They explored the *Morgana*. As though she were a ship haunted, she was completely silent and permeated with an ethereal echo. Now and then, through hidden speakers, came the spastic crackle of a failing naval horn, the archetypal cry of ships in distress, which was then swallowed by the buzzing silence.

They skulked within the abandoned halls, places as vaulted and ostentatious as the banks of Menos, though possessing even grander austerity, and felt outside themselves in this realm of horror and technomagik. They experienced further dissonance from the height and polish of the walls made from a seamless steel, with ribs of smooth metal and runners of ebon—iron, in each case, though the latter was refined to the sheen of marble. Indeed, none of the materials were entirely recognizable, and the curious among the five reached out to graze with their fingers this incomprehensible architecture.

They swallowed dryly as they pondered the vents to their sides, smooth and subtle as fish gills, which made the walls ripple with their intake or outtake of air. Walking beneath the red effulgence from the danger lights hidden in tiles above made the companions think of caverns roofed with luminous red bats. The *Morgana* was alive; it was an organism of wild dimensions, breathing, beating, and coursing with blood. But she was wounded, and her gills heaved sporadically, as did the vacillating redness. Sorren witnessed this biology more clearly than those not touched by Death, and he saw the sickness that threatened the ship. It was that viral presence that he continued to pursue, a blackness viewed threading through the beautiful mesh of this great creature, growing into dense spiderwebs of evil the closer he came to its source.

While Sorren wandered in the realm of phantoms, the others were being subjected to untold horrors he couldn't perceive. They came to mess halls that were truly messy. Iron tables had been ripped from their mountings, couches draped in a butcher's sale of mortal meats of legs, craniums cleft in two, and fingers left floating in bowls of cold gruel. Whatever armor the Ironguard had worn was evidently ineffective against the tenacity of Death's beasts; scraps of plate littered the hall. There was nothing to kill in there; everything was already quite dead.

From that macabre feast they moved on into a soldier's quarters, where the scene differed little: blood-soaked bunks, a man with his head and legs eaten off and still, by the power of rigor mortis, clinging to the bed from which he'd been dragged. A pornographic phantograph played on atop the rumpled mess of his mattress, showing a wispy image of a dancing girl with tassels, a feather fan, and beaded loincloth. The tastelessness of her seduction almost made for a jest. But then there was more blood, stains, and mortal sausage to wet their feet and saturate their minds until their iron-hard stomachs finally started to churn.

The hallways and compartments began to blur into a flow of crimson nausea. The strobing lights and low-pitched mumbles of the *Morgana* as its spirit continued to deplete began to grate on their nerves. The slap and squeak of their bloodied boots hitting wet metal ran shivers up their calves. In a sense, their journey through the ship had felt like journeying through a nightmare. There was a point at which they were quite conscious, however, where the surroundings were so stupefying as to render that dream a reality. At last they emerged in a theater of technomagik, a huge dome raised in the center by row upon row of ringed landings and stairs, and presided over by a cold iron throne at the top of that nipple. On each level of the bridge were set pods, seemingly for the hatching of insects. There were dark, waxy consoles and chairs that seemed made of spider vomit. Whereas the skin of the dome itself—ceiling and walls—was more appealing: a curved glass screen to the outside, upon which could be viewed the smoldering demolition at Camp Fury. It seemed so insignificant from this vantage.

They passed the technomagikal consoles, boggled by their design, as they climbed the many flights of stairs to the queen's seat. Sorren halted when they were within sprinting reach of the Iron Throne. Every design element in the room faced outward, toward progress and conquest, and that included the Iron Queen's seat. Though Sorren had sensed the presence of the "source," he couldn't see who sat upon her throne except for a green hand that flagged them to halt. Sean knew the voice that spoke, though, as croaking and ruined as it was.

"You've come too late," it said. "I have sabotaged the war-birds of Menos. Now you have nothing with which to stop my mistress other than your prayers and walls, which won't even slow her down. Death devours stone as acid eats silk. You are defenseless. You should simply kill yourselves and be consumed."

"I shall destroy you!" roared Sean.

As Sean threw himself forward, Sorren stopped the young man with a hand as solid as an iron manacle. Sorren sensed Death's presence, bubbling as if it were a filthy vein of oil, stronger than anything he had sensed previously. It was a vessel with Will and power.

"Destroy who?" Aadore swung up her blade and ran to her brother's side. She was prepared to kill whatever had set him afire with rage. Sean shuddered while trying to contain himself. With cane-case in one hand, sluiced sword in the other, and with nothing to hold his body up, anger had become his support. Next to the siblings, Curtis readied his rifle, balancing it on his forearm, as Skar bore his vicious meat-slinging hammers. No sooner had they assembled against this evil than it introduced itself.

"Doctor Gideon Hex," said the monster.

It rose from its seat with a slurp. Gideon often slipped and thought of himself as a neutral pronoun, and now, since his genitals had dropped off like a rotten sausage and tangerines, it seemed a natural designation. No bother, he felt, for he was changing, as did a butterfly in a cocoon. For him, the transformation had been glorious. As each organ and piece of flesh was taken from him, Death had replaced it at a miraculous rate with wonderful blessings such as strength, speed, intellect, and heightened senses; he had heard these stomping cattle when they were still out in the desert. He smiled at them, and wondered a little if he still had teeth, since the ability to feel textures was another discarded vestige of who he'd been.

What the living in the room saw was a manlike thing in a bib with withered arms, wearing loose rubber gloves, and with a face shriveled to the bone—earless, hairless, and sniffing at them through the batty stump of a rotted nose. He left a stretched, transparent cheese of secretions as he slithered to standing, and his flesh percolated audibly. To the keenest eyes— Sean's—his skin churned as vermin copulated in fertile desecrations of his body.

"I know who you are, rancid merchant of filth!" screamed Sean, and once more Sorren had to tighten his hold on the man.

The doctor was puzzled, for the shape below him bore him no semblance in his memory, as all was becoming a mesh of colors, lights, and ethereal sights. Although, as he beheld this loud flesh sack haloed in the darkest red of hatred, and as he dug his carnivorous gaze under the membranes and meat that enshrined the heart of the man, down to his soul, he did know this fleshling.

"X-179242?" he cried. "I have forgotten how the strings of a cello sound, but I can still recall the pleasure of your screams. It took forever to break you, although that should be expected of a man whose flesh is anathema to magik. I could never forget you, my mortal instrument, my opus of pain. I have so many more things to show to you now. So many glories."

The doctor grinned, and pale worms tumbled like saliva from his mouth. Suddenly interested in Aadore, he tilted his head. "And you...your colors? Are you...his sister? You must be. Oh, my mistress hath given me a bounty for my service. I shall make a new masterpiece with you. I shall take you places beyond pain and pleasure, to the great crimson divide in which all the mysteries of our bodies are held—and then you will go farther, darker, and deeper than even that. First, I shall have a meal of your friends. I can't tell you of my hunger. I've eaten a hundred men, and it's not enough. I ate a man's legs as he shat himself with fear, then swallowed his screaming head as a snake swallows a mouse, and that barely whet my appetite."

As they recalled what remained of that victim, and the many others likely feasted upon by Gideon throughout the ship, their auras flickered with blue, green, and red fires—a rainbow of sentiments that confused the doctor. "Do I sicken you? Do you fear me? Or are you ready for my worms and kiss? What of you..."

The doctor turned to the curious wuthering and ebon aura amid the colorful flesh sacks—to Sorren, who suddenly trembled. "You are a beautiful thing. You have been kissed already. You should be standing up here with me."

A familiarity to this horrid creature's raw ugliness—the twisting of intellect and medicine to sociopathy and torment—squeezed a nerve in Sorren. Had he not once been as remorseless and vile as this? Was this not a mirror of his torment?

Indeed it is, whispered his inner monster, suddenly awoken. *He is thou, though art me, and we are brothers. We can be brothers; you need not that wasted seed with whom you once shared a womb. Go on, rip out the throats of the fools on your left. Then take the girl to Gideon, fuk her brother on these stairs, and we'll play with them both until the world ends, though the good doctor won't be fuking, seems he's not made to be a proper vessel. You're the one meant to have orgies in the ashes. Go on, kill them. Kill them now.*

"Noooooo!"

Throwing off his grip of Sean so that he could claw at ghosts, Sorren fell and sobbed. His distress was all dust and writhing, since he couldn't make tears, no matter if the pain he felt was crippling. As soon as Sorren was down, the doctor wobbled down the stairs. And while he might have appeared frail, he was in the midst of Death's frenzy, and ready to dine on the lives of these brave, strong, and furious heroes. The rainbows of their spirits escaped Gideon's conceptualization, though he knew it would be as delicious to consume as their bodies. Were he a better empath, or more developed in his gift from the Pale Lady, he would have realized that the wounded reborn son of the Iron Queen was the least of his concerns. Gideon believed he could claim the lives of four who'd been anointed in the apocalypse of their nation, four who had already faced Death herself and walked away.

Death afforded him no warning for his hubris; his end was soon, and he was of no use to her after fulfilling his mission in disabling the Furies—the only eternity he would know was her dusty, deathless world. Thus as Gideon swept in to tear open rib cages and gorge himself on the sap of souls, the shell that exploded half his face was as much a surprise to him as anyone. Curtis's next shot was followed by the flurrying hammers of Skar, who ripped off one of the doctor's rubbery claws so ferociously that it whipped the monster into a spin—a graceful whirl to which Aadore played the dancing partner. Lifting his leg to arabesque, she dipped and swung screaming and two-handed to barbarously sever the gooey limb that kept him standing. She only snapped the soggy bone of that leg, but he fell just the same. Then Sean was above the doctor, swinging sword and cane into the pulpy creature beneath him, acting as a primitive drum master with the doctor's face as his instrument. Sean sobbed and shrieked as the rotten oils of the beast who had taken his boyhood, his love, and his honor anointed him.

When the noisome execution ended, Gideon Hex was shapeless. Sorren, sensing a change, crawled out of his huddle and noticed the fleeing shadow to the room, the passing of Death's conduit. Sorren knew what these champions—real champions, without power, magik stones, or tricks—had done. Next time, he would be brave.

"That was him." Aadore put down her sword, and then turned her brother away from the bubbling corpse to face her.

"It was," he replied.

She nodded, then kissed her brother's slimy cheek. Curtis and Skar laid hands upon the driest spot of their friend's clothing—a small patch of linen at his back. After that pittance of pity, the four looked to Sorren.

"We have to check on the engines," said Aadore, as though nothing had happened. "We've not saved the day just yet."

✳ ✳ ✳

IV

Much danger remained, kindling in the fires of the encampment and in the ships themselves. Ships whose hearts were not meat but Talwynian chambers fused with lodes of truefire that would either stabilize to an anemic pulse, die, or develop an arrhythmia that would escalate into a frenzied seizure. Only, if any of these three titanic hearts reached that level of illness, they wouldn't just arrest, they'd explode—quite likely leaving a crater in the sand in which the remnants of the Iron City might be remembered. Whatever the unliving minions of Hex had intended to do to these engines, the fortified iron casings surrounding the Talwynian fusion engines had prevented the worst of it, though pipes and external apparatuses had been pulled from the machines in an attempt to ruin them. Aadore and her companions had perhaps only a few hourglasses in which to reverse this damage and restore the engines' functionality.

Aadore surmised that Sorren could lead them to the *Morgana*'s heart, by the same or similar divinations that had led them to Hex's energy. Indeed, Sorren noticed that the glowing pulse from the membranous ship emanated from a source, to which he guided the others. However, the five champions were not to undertake the salvaging of Menos's military alone, and once the battles outside had subsided enough for a safe landing, the Iron Queen, Gustavius, and his page arrived at the *Morgana*.

On their way through the ruddy corridors, Aadore was told of the occurrence by Sorren, who'd *sensed* his mother's spirit nearing.

At that, he deviated from the pulsing trail and arrived at the great tongue of metal arcing down into the desert. Upon the bridge, the company of heroes saw their queen, wrapped with Gustavius's military coat about her shoulders and holding a rifle. Gustavius, his armor removed down to his suspenders, sleeves rolled up, and with a chest as hale as Skar's, seemed ready for the grueling work ahead. The redheaded fool Aadore recalled from the ship lingered beside Gustavius. Aadore thought his name was Davy, though he'd left such a pitiful impression she wasn't sure. While behind them all was another child. Quite dapper for such a young man was this strange lad who would've been androgynous if not for his black choirboy suit and neat cravat. By the Kings, he was the whitest creature Aadore had ever seen, and with eyes flickering with mysteries like diamonds in a deep pool.

"Elineth," he said, and smiled as if he were about to do something either mischievous or cruel. "Mother asked us to help. I insisted that I was needed here. I so needed to meet you, m'lady."

"Aadore," she said.

"I know."

They both partook of a threatening silence.

"We have no time for banter," said Gloriatrix. "Elissandra's gone with Gorijen and Eod's technomancers to the *Malabeth*. I'm told that ship's engine is in the direst of straits. Whereas the *Maeg* seems as if its engine will cool, perhaps entirely, and as much of a blessing as that might be in the interim, we may just lose one-third of our armada. We'll need to be in constant communication, and farspeaking stones are so unreliable that they are near worthless in times of crisis. That's why the child—"

The young man raised a finger. "Elineth. Eli, if you so desire."

Gloriatrix clenched the butt of her rife as if she wanted to shoot the boy for speaking to her in such a manner—at least, the others noted, their liege had recovered from her ennui. "That's why the child has been brought with us; another remains at the encampment in case any more surprises are in store for us there. Together, the three witches can create a conduit with their minds, and we should be able to relay developments instantaneously. Oh, and your dear lad, Ian, has been left with my finest aides. They'll be shot should anything happen to him, so I expect him to receive the greatest care."

Shadowed in the majesty of the Iron Queen's entourage were the shining silver manservants of Eod. About a dozen of them hung back on the middle of the bridge, playing with their silver tabards, adjusting their spectacles, and generally ambling about like chickens waiting for feed. There was no way that they were soldiers of sword and shield. Rather, from their scholarly slouches and trappings, the others assumed them to be men of magik, science, or both. Gloriatrix snapped her fingers and they dashed forward. "We shall need to find the engine chamber."

"Allow me," said Sorren.

None of the Eodians commented on why a priest of Carthac was either present or directing the Iron Queen. Once within the haunted emptiness of the *Morgana*, Sorren hurried toward the power source that pulled at his sixth senses. Around him, the reactions of those who followed him through the gore-slathered ship were annoying distractions from the rhythmic beat of the *Morgana*'s heart. Especially when the gentle scholars began to upheave their lunches at the sight of every dismembered corpse they passed. The stink of the dead, too, had begun—a swampy sweetness that would shortly fill the ship with ammonia and flies. Only the Eodians appeared affected by the horror, and Gloriatrix scoffed at how useless these men would be, come the *real* war. Hopefully they wouldn't be allowed anywhere near the armaments. She wasn't pleased with what she saw, yet she wasn't appalled by it, either.

The ship needed to be cleaned, and what remained of these bodies should be afforded rites for their service to the Ironguard.

Curious how these affectations of honor had started to infect her normally irascible comportment. When she considered whether she could ever be truly merciful, she knew the answer was no. However, there was room in her heart for respect now, and that was a quality she'd forsaken since her brother's betrayal.

What would it be like when they saw each other again? Now that West and East were allies, it seemed an inevitable meeting. Hatred had so often warped her sentiments regarding Thackery that she had never considered an alternative to his execution. Realistically, she would probably still try to murder him if the chance presented itself. A snake couldn't help but bite.

"My Queen, your presence is necessary over here," whispered Gustavius, who'd caught her daydreaming.

They approached a wide arch forged like a wreath of smelted iron roses. These roses had no prick today and should have been sparkling on their thorns with warning static—a magik that would sheath the archway in a voltaic net were any not requisitioned for passage to approach. Twisted heaps of clinging, blackened figures were wrapped about the lower border of the arch. Those must have been the unliving wretches who'd shorted out the defensive net with their rotten flesh. Rather unimpressed with their crudeness, Gloriatrix poked at one of the undead with her rifle-cane and watched it disintegrate as if it had been washed over by lava. Inside the vast, humid dome they entered, more chaos awaited: smashed consoles, wires that hung like jungle vines, and red fluid that filled the floor in stepping pools— some of these the blood of half-devoured engineers. Steam and noise gave the company pause in creeping their way ahead, until they arrived at the *Morgana*'s wounded heart.

It sat on tiny struts, little mantis legs, this obscene and seemingly teetering keg of iron that would hold a giant's mead. Nothing save for magik could have held an object of its apparent weight and gravitas. As if it were an elemental beast, it breathed mist and communed in a language of crackling pops. Tubing was falling away from its sides, limp as dead octopus tentacles, the apparent cause of much of the crimson wetness in the chamber. At once the engineers parted, finding tasks in which to immerse themselves. They set to reattaching and plugging in the disconnected plumbing. Any unusable hoses weren't replaced; rather, they were torn off by these men with sweeps of their white-haloed hands that cleaved as well as any sword, from any distance below the grand iron heart. Such severances were cauterized by concentrations of Will, then flame. Sparks flew, metal sizzled, and the air took on a scent less rancorous than humid, spoiling flesh.

It proved difficult to communicate over the engine's puffing and the technomancers' noisy ministrations, yet Aadore was wont to make herself heard. At first, the Iron Queen pretended the noise had drowned out the noblewoman's voice, though she listened to, and calculated the weight of, Aadore's every word. Aadore was as tenacious as the queen, and in a moment, her face popped into Gloriatrix's vision—impossible to overlook.

"We slew him, Your Majesty," said Aadore.

"Slew who?"

"The man who besieged your armada," said Aadore.

Suddenly, Sean was blocking the left field of vision through which the Iron Queen was pretending to observe the repairs. He was as covered in blood as a ritual priest, and commanded similar attention and fear.

"We ended him," said Sean. "And it is either fated justice or pure coincidence, but he was the madman who tortured me and others—Gideon Hex."

Sean watched for a reaction, but hers was a mask tempered by the fire of Iron council meetings; it would not crack, not even to this bold, observant young man.

"I'm not familiar with the name," she replied, then turned to Gustavius, who shrugged.

She looked back at Sean. "A madman, you say? We had too many of those in Menos. At least now there will be one less in the Iron City of tomorrow. I am sorry that you have suffered unjustly, though I am grateful that you have taken vengeance and smitten one who would harm what remains of our people. I shall see that your service is doubly rewarded."

"I need no coin or elevated status."

Furious, Gloriatrix grabbed the chain around Sean's neck—his symbol of service—and pulled it tight as a noose. "Are you rejecting your standing?"

"No. That's not—I meant no such—"

She released the chain and left him gasping; Sean stumbled into his sister's arms.

"Then take what is given," threatened the monarch, "and understand that even if you do not have the closure that you seek with this man, you still have life and power, which sometimes is the only thing that remains after our pain."

"I shall not raise the matter again," said Sean, wilted and sad.

"I know you won't," replied the monarch.

Sean rubbed his neck and let his sister carry him off into the fog, where they conferred with their companions. There they became smoky dissolutions to the Iron Queen: *whispers*, as she needed the court of her new kingdom to be. Sentiment began to tickle her again, as she thought of these heroes begat from the seed of serving men, proof that a man—or woman—could climb the iron ladder. Her vision of a new Menos was a fairer place than before.

She would provide equal opportunity for women to hold the daggers and do the stabbing. New Menos would still need slaves and an entrenched hierarchy in which the most ruthless and cunning ruled over the weak; those were immutable tenets of Menosian culture. However, she would see fewer slaves and more *willing* participants in servanthood. She would put the Charter back into effect, have those heroes carol her praises and tell their stories to the eager, grimy masses, and in no time at all Iron children would flock to reconstruct the glory of their city. They'd see a fresh and dark dawn. One where hope and mercy—sentiments upon which she had historically shat—were among the greatest tools used to inspire and silence fools, as well as being hammers she would wield like Magnus's thundering wrath. It would all fall into place—Menos's rise from the ashes of this war, and the next chapter in its dominance...

Elissandra's child, who stared at her with a morbid grin, and who had been invisibly next to her this whole time, seemed to have had a different opinion on the matter. As their eyes met, he shared with her a strange anecdote.

"I had a dream..." he muttered, as the chamber and its noises also softened and faded until they were rumbles of silver in the dark. "I saw two crows—great beasts, such as the Ancient ones that live in Alabion. One was old, and one was young, though each was as large as the other—albeit the younger being slightly grander, as it is with the strength and flourishing of youth. The eldest was envious of the youngest, of her plumage, her beak, and the pride with which she soared over Alabion—as though it were her kingdom by birthright. She was born to rule, this young crow, though not crowned by ritual of ascension, where the Ancients would claw and gouge their foes until from a mountain of meat only one lived or breathed enough to caw its supremacy. And so the eldest, feeling uncertain of her roost, thought to usurp this usurper before her position could be threatened, and she cawed and cawed, and gave challenge to every black-feathered crow who would want to peck at her flesh and steal her crown. But of all the enemies that came, it was the regal young crow she wished to battle the most.

"For what felt like one hundred nights, the Ancient fought her enemies and would-be roost mothers, casting the woods in blood and feathers. In the battle, she lost an eye. Soon she was blind to whom she fought, and as the bloodlust claimed her, she was ignorant as to *why* she fought. Still, the elder battled every crow, and pecked from them their hearts until she was alone in the skies, soaring above the shattered bodies of her people—birds, I meant birds."

Gloriatrix's heart lurched.

"Soon she trembled and fell and could no longer fly from the pain of her thousand wounds. On the red earth, she called out for her usurper. Alas, the young crow had no interest in war and old rituals, not as the eldest did. She'd left their land ages ago. And so the eldest was to die alone—by wounds of her own making—while the young crow soared away from the forest and built a new nest and new home, surrounded by the glory of a life free from blood and tradition."

Smoke, sparks, and complaining men appeared around the Iron Queen and young witch. Gloriatrix fell from the enchantment in which she'd seen a verdant ruin of trees, and vast shadows that sailed over green and crashed in explosions that blew geysers of rock and filth up from the woods. If she focused, the cries of the sad, dying crow lingered in her mind.

"Mother checked in," said Elineth, rather chipper. "Seems as if your *Malabeth* won't be flying away into the great beyond, after all. The Eodian sorcerer proved up to the task in calming the truefire and technomagik."

The lad stopped for a speck, harked to a noise coming from very far away, and added, "Tessa says she just saw the lights of your other warship go out from where she's standing. Looks like you've lost a wing, my Queen—no pun intended, considering my tale."

"Off with ye!" barked Gustavius. He'd noticed his queen's pallor and this ghoul's goading of her, hearing the story in its entirety. Like a white rat, the child scurried off to feed on someone else's misery.

Gustavius faced his queen. "Pay him no heed, my Queen."

"Indeed, Mother," said Sorren, and tempted her revulsion with a short, icy cold hug.

The Iron Queen shook off her coddling menfolk when an engineer appeared. For a moment the man seemed stunned, and Gloriatrix considered the reason for his behavior, watching him like an owl studies a fat and delicious snake slithering through the forest beneath its nest. While recounting the success he'd had in stemming and stabilizing the bleed of the Talwynian fusion engine, said man fiddled with his hands, stared at the ground, and adjusted his garments. Perhaps that was not all, thought Gloriatrix, of his flustered composure. The engineer stared between her and Sorren once, and it was that swell of fear, of *recognition*, that seized his face and betrayed him.

"Do you have a son?" asked the Iron Queen, as the man turned his back to her, eager to get away, to spill his secret, no doubt. Sorren's name couldn't be known or whispered to anyone with an appetite for gossip: *Sorren Blackbriar, saboteur and terrorist, stands at the Iron Queen's side.*

"I-I do, Your Majesty."

"Then you understand the lengths to which we go to protect our children."

The engineer's whimper condemned him. He was weeping now, as if he knew his fate. With one foot in the otherworld, Sorren found the man's aubergine-and-blue borealis of sorrow enchanting.

"I do, Your Majesty," said the man, "and I would never say a word, not even a skylark's peep, about your son."

"You won't, I'll grant you that."

Sorren snapped from his tranquility as his mother's aura flared into a whirling red torrent beside him. Sorren cried out to stop her. "Mother, no!"

"Mother? Who's he shouting about?" muttered a figure up ahead.

Then the shots rang out: *bang, bang, bang*! One to the fleeing engineer's shoulder, the penultimate tearing apart his spine, and the final sinking lead into his brain. Back in the days when their family had been under threat from Iron Sages, her father had given her shooting lessons, and she was satisfied that her aim hadn't declined.

Eldest crow, my arse, she thought, and stepped over the slumped engineer's corpse. There were shouts from the other engineers as they realized they were being attacked. The Iron Queen slunk ahead, and Gustavius pulled a pistol and followed her. Since their prey were sorcerers, even those not trained for battle could still be dangerous. They had to act quickly. A group of gray phantoms to her right vanished into the crimson steam, and she let them be, for they were her people and were not lambs for this slaughter. A giggling ghost floated through the mist on her left and she considered shooting it, though Elissandra would be upset at the murder of her child. She doubted the little shite was anything more than mist and nightmares, which made him a waste of bullets, anyhow.

In less than a sand, the hunters had executed any who might have heard Sorren's secret. They stood in a room more smoky than misty now, and smelled sulfur all around. Sorren had been chasing his mother's shadow as if he were a frantic puppy, and at last he collapsed behind her. *Why didn't I stop her? Why am I so weak?*

Others emerged: the child, the brother and sister, the ogre and the fop— those the Iron Queen could at least trust, for the time being. It was an important lesson for them all, to know her iron nature and to fear it. Eod and its platitudes had softened her teeth to wet chalk. It was time to sharpen her fangs. She tapped the shoulder of her blubbering son with the warm barrel of her rifle.

"They were not our people," she said, "and they would have betrayed you, branded you a criminal, and seen you burn before or after this war. Throw their bodies among the rest, and see that they are incinerated. We can say that we were ambushed by a few hidden dead."

"No one will believe that," said Aadore, unshaken by the queen's violence and the only one to show defiance in her expression.

"They will. Unless we tell a different tale." The Iron Queen lazily swung her rifle and people danced on their feet. "We are a nation, and we must protect our secrets. Now rise, my son, and know, like the others, that when next you speak aloud of my maternal obligation, there will be consequences. Those people died because of you. Find your strength in silence. I would ask this of all of you, my Iron children: be brave and silent. Trust that I shall guide us into the future. Accept my vision, and fear not blood or perceived sin."

Accept your vision? thought Aadore. This was not the way forward. She fell into line, for now, and followed the Iron Queen's instructions to dispose of the bodies.

Elineth haunted them as he practiced the arts of the men of his line— hiding in plain sight, distorting his aura—and was forgotten and unseen whenever someone, even Sorren, looked for him. While the others carried out the Iron Queen's macabre cleanup, he thought of crows and how strong that young one was.

V

As dusk rode its crimson horses across the sky, puffed billows in which shapes reared, a slight breath was taken by every man, woman, and child at the queen's encampment, expressing relief at a day of toil finally over. Theirs was a desert relaxation, where the body continued to sweat, though the mind, at least, was calm. During the day one tended to one's tasks, and at night one rested, drank, and enjoyed the stories of those who wandered before. In the desert, however, liquor was a wanton and destructive indulgence; engaging in any activity that would leave a man or woman dry was idiotic. Indeed, water was a treasure more precious than ale, gold, or feliron. It was not used to wash; there were oils for that instead. Drinking water was the most sacred of pleasures, a crystal sacrament to be drawn from the communal cisterns built as centerpieces of each starred collection of tents. Amid the rambling circus of fluttering shelters that had hidden so many sandy hills in a patchwork of shades, these ornate, painted cisterns gleamed, lighting the night like the campfires that would not.

After all, fire brought death, and only warm coals were needed to heat the meat and the few vegetables eaten by the Arhad: mostly a sweet, juicy root called *kemacha* that grew like icicles on the underbelly of the crags that wended through regions of Kor'Khul where the land jutted rocks. After Lila's readjustments to her culture, the stores of food and water were no more violently guarded. Any man or boy was permitted to climb the clay steps and dip their cup without the shame of doing a task made for women, as it was no longer the task of the fairer sex alone to serve and distribute this liquid sacrament. Surely the ancient chieftains would have called for the wrath of their ancestors if they had seen the appalling menagerie of warrior women—unveiled, bare-breasted in some cases—and young lads that stood around the cisterns, chatting, laughing, and embracing each other to the gritty rhythmic music of their kin. Woe to one of the many roaming tribes who came upon the queen's encampment and dared to speak down to a Makret, a warrior mother. There had been confrontations of that sort, and it always ended with a brutal display of just how efficient women trained by a skilled warmaster and enchanted by the passion of an Immortal Queen could be. There were no more such envoys, not since the queen's army had evolved into a force of reckoning, had evolved into a people of beauty and freedom. They couldn't be unmade now. They wouldn't. Their ranks would only grow.

Even for those visitors who were foreign or fearful of the Arhad customs, ignorance was erased by the rustic charm of these people—tribes once thought to have nothing of worth or knowledge to offer the modern world. Along with the mercenaries he trained, Leonitis and Dorvain had been two of those bigots. Still, as they had been soldiers all of their lives, they acclimatized easily, and in just days their old prejudices were as tattered as their sand-eaten capes. Lowelia, too, had had reservations about the queen's army, though she'd adapted as quickly as she usually did to any situations into which she was thrust. Perhaps the least readily adjusted to the Arhadian culture were the former daughters of sand themselves: Rowena and Dorothy.

Rowena was certainly at ease when training with the warrior-maidens, mothers, and sons of sand. Once in battle there was no time to debate politics or the ramifications of the new paradigm. And when the night cooled, and there were no more orders to bark, she felt like a stranger in the new tribe. Like a thief, she would skulk near the wells and eavesdrop on conversations. She had always remembered the language of her people as being guttural, each word wrapped in a bouquet of spit and angry sounds. And yet, when it was spoken with compassion, with love, and without condemnation of sex or standing, Arhadic was as beautiful as the songs that scratched the sandy night with their echoes.

It was a reemergence for Rowena, into a world that was both familiar and strange. She was lost without her hate. Slowly and shyly, though, she began to barter her way into acceptance, with less peeping and creeping, partaking more of the conviviality of her people. She was never forced into conversation, as though the Arhad knew of her reluctance; they certainly knew of her reputation. In time, this world that she had once loathed became more meaningful than any of the ties she had forged in the City of Wonders. As these were her people, as they should be, as she had secretly, impossibly dreamed of them being. Soon, Rowena was talking to her people, remembering the old tales aloud—the women were keepers of stories—and she knew them all. Soon, others gathered to hear her tell these tales, as well as stories from the lands she explored beyond the desert.

Dorothy, however, appeared intractable in her opinions of her former people. As an unofficial emissary and information carrier, she moved between Eod and the queen's encampment several times a week. With her, she brought word from the council meetings that Rowena always missed. Dorothy had been appointed the Royal Seamstress of Eod, a position that had never needed filling before. Suddenly the free world's greatest nation had a need for outfitters at a time when all was blood and war. Smarter minds saw through the ruse and formed conclusions based on Dorothy's private encounters with Rasputhane. Espionage made more sense than a need for part-time messengers, or seamstresses. Still no one, including Dorothy, shed aught but shade on the issue. Unquestioned, she came for her regular visits, first wandering down to the less colorful encampment of green burlap tents in which the mercenary forces had gathered.

While the camp was filled with rough men brawling, barking, and scraping swords to whetstone, they posed no danger to her. Queerly, these hard-bodied, cruel-stared men, with days of growth on their faces and a litany of crimes to their names, embraced the seamstress—austere as a phantom bride in her fanciful gown and parasol—as though she were a patron of their cause. They bowed to her with respect, though perhaps that was simply the response her subtle charms commanded. She would spend the day with them like they were her own brood of a thousand miscreant boys. She'd patch their cloaks and boots, and show them how to use a needle and thread. Then she would stay for a tale or ten of their sordid adventures, usually one involving a whore and an accidental murder...though never of the whore, as they were *gentlemen*. At last, once she'd stretched the sands of time as far as they would yield without being negligent, she'd wander across the gusty no-man's-land between encampments and seek out the sword of the queen.

It was always evening when Dorothy arrived, though her bright parasol could be spotted like a buoy on the ocean. Tonight, Lowelia watched the white-bob approach from where she and a few others had gathered: a campground of garish blankets laid on the small rise beyond the liveliness of the northernmost cistern. She lost sight of Dorothy's parasol as the woman dipped down in the land and paid it no further heed, engaging in conversation with her companions.

Nearby, Leonitis lay like a conqueror, resting on his elbow. Even in the twilight he was as coppery and handsome as a lion. Gruff to his comely brother, in stance and charm, was Dorvain, who was flopped on his back like a starfish after stripping down to his waist and sloppily covering himself in Arhadian oils. They wouldn't clean him that way, not until they were massaged into his skin and wiped off, but those were nuisances that he was too tired to do. As a man of the North Watch, this heat would never agree with him. Lowelia sat beside Rowena and near the feet of the prone watchmaster. She was quite swaddled in a cloak, feeling cool, and she rocked the Mind in its sling as if it were her dear, departed Cecilia.

Lowe took another look, laughing at her huffing, heaving friend. "Honestly, my man, I've greased up hogs for feasts in the White Hearth that looked less slippery than you. You need to get a rag."

"You can fetch me one, woman." Dorvain fluttered a hand at Lowelia. "Or isn't that allowed anymore?"

"Ha!" Lowelia slapped his shin. "You can't talk to me like that here. I could have your balls served to me in a dish."

Dorvain gripped the bundle of his manhood and shook it. "You're welcome to them."

Was she? thought Lowelia, as her gaze wafted like a lover's gasping breath over the furred ridges of the man's stout chest, which gleamed in oil. They'd had flirtatious parleys before, though it never amounted to anything. She believed that they had each chosen duty over romance, and she respected him for his choice. No need to sully the sanctity of their partnership for a bit of kissing and sweat. Although...his shining bald head and bushy face—still more rugged than ugly for a man of his years—and greased chest, matted in hair, gave her a sensation she hadn't felt since her mooniest days. She wondered how the brothers could be within a decade of each other and yet be so physically and mentally different: dark to light, crass to cultured, golden fair to bear-brown. Grrr. She felt that Dorvain would make all sorts of wild calls when—

The Mind suddenly tingled her. *Navigator Lowelia, bioform Dorothy approaches. Also, your pulse has quickened to indicate—*

I know what it indicates.

Evidently, so did Dorvain, and he winked at the blushing handmaiden as she stood for a break from his crude comeliness. As she looked north, Dorothy's pale apparition rose over the hill, and they waved to each other. Once she arrived they embraced and made room on their rugs for the Royal Seamstress.

No sooner had they sat down and uttered some pleasantries than Rowena leapt up.

"Is that smoke?" she exclaimed, pointing to a thin crimson hue that drifted over the dunes as if a northern aurora of horror were on display.

"I think it is." Lowelia gasped. "I think that's Camp Fury."

Under assault from the unliving, said the Mind from within the arms of its Navigator; it was now conducting its own investigation of the telemetric currents in that region.

Lowelia repeated what she'd heard. Fantasies of peace dissolved along with their disbelief that Camp Fury—the stronghold of Menos—was under attack. It was happening, an assault; perhaps the war, already. Since all present were warriors, rallying was second nature. Dorvain was dressed in his plate in specks before checking the straps on his brother's armor and his own. Lowelia rushed off to find a way to help, and Rowena vanished into the whirling tide of Arhadians likewise prepping themselves for war. They called out their war chants, armored up, tested their bows, and kissed loved ones— the eldest and youngest who wouldn't be marching to doom. Was this the end? Had the war of wars come at last?

In the frantic tumult, Dorothy remained on the rug, inconspicuous merely for her inactivity in this storm. She spent a sand burning her ear with a farspeaking stone, after whispering several phrases into another—spent, black, and now dead on the ground. In a moment, Lowelia appeared with Rowena, huffing like a charger in a race, and both women stared at the Royal Seamstress sitting pretty in her white dress and gloves, twirling an umbrella, as if she were a enjoying a summer's day at a park.

Rowena asked, "What in the queen's name are you doing? Get up! We're at war."

"No," said Dorothy. "We're not. Camp Fury is under attack, yes, though Eod has already rushed to deal with that assault. It seems as if the attackers have been repelled. At least, such is the news being relayed to me."

"Relayed? By whom?" barked Rowena.

"Rasputhane." Dorothy pointed to the glimmering black stone near her bent knees. "I've just spoken with him. If you can call off our forces and gather the others, I shall tell you all about it."

"Eod's spymaster?" It beggared Rowena's belief.

"Yes."

It is true, Navigator Lowe, buzzed the Mind to its keeper, who had been monitoring the telemetries around Camp Fury and finished its own report. *The sudden incursion of unliving creatures to the east has been culled. Men are now working on cooling the engines of the technomagikal beasts. War has not come today—only a skirmish.*

While Rowena dashed off to give orders to slow efforts, Lowelia sat with the coy seamstress, whose face was indecipherable in the night beneath the shade of her umbrella. After planning revolution together, Lowelia had believed that they were on the road to lasting friendship. But their uprising had ended abruptly in a manner in which no insurgent ever really plans— with peace. Lowelia didn't speak to Brock anymore, the man who had helped inspire the gold-banded royalists of Eod. She had heard, from a mutual acquaintance, that he'd moved off the continent, disgusted by the sudden turn to Menos as an ally and the many changes in Eod precipitating the rebellion. If not for the meetings the seamstress regularly held with Rowena, Lowe would never have seen this woman, either. At the least, they hugged and chatted kindly whenever they crossed paths. However, it all felt phony to Lowe, as though they were playacting at being friends, and when the civilities ran out Dorothy was eager to leave. And so as the engine of war cooled in the queen's encampment, and the surprised Arhadians returned to their leisure, the two women, who had been through so much together, grew tight as coiled springs. They were jittery and quiet when Rowena returned with Dorvain and Leonitis.

Rowena misinterpreted the unease. "What, did she tell you her secrets already?"

"I did not," replied Dorothy. "Do make yourselves comfortable again—I have quite a lot to say."

Dorvain wasted no sands and tore off his armor as if he were a child having a tantrum, then plopped down in a huff. Crankily, he asked his gentle brother to fetch him water, and when Leonitis returned, juggling clay cups with water for all five, Dorvain unearthed his kindness and helped distribute the drinks. Once they were settled, the gathering sipped their drinks and looked at Dorothy.

"I don't like secrets," said the seamstress. "They eat away at a person's dignity like the moth damage I'm so often called upon to mend."

"No one wants to hear your poetics." Dorvain shook his empty cup at her. "You're as full of secrets as I am of piss. Out with your twisted words, while I tend to one matter." The watchmaster wandered away a respectable distance and began sizzling the sand with urine. "Out with it, I say! I'm still listening."

"Very well," said Dorothy, finally folding away her umbrella and unveiling herself to her company. Fatigue and strain haunted her face. Perhaps this secret had been eating at her. "I am forever a loyalist to the City of Wonders. I believe that there is no greater place on Geadhain. Even if we have made peace with the sand demons that once haunted me, and seen those men transformed into knights for our cause, I shall never again be a daughter of the desert—"

Dorvain shook his prick and put it back in his britches. "I'm done, and so should you be with your preamble. What have you been keeping from us?"

She said, to the shock of no one, "I'm a spy."

"You've been meeting with Rasputhane," said Lowelia. "Unless you mean to confess that you're a spy for the Iron Queen."

Leonitis's hand crept toward the great hammer beside him.

"No! No," said Dorothy. "I would never. Rasputhane is my spylord—"

"Spymaster," corrected Dorvain, and sat.

Dorothy sighed. "Oh, bugger. I thought I was good at this espionage business. Seems I'm not cut from the same cloth as so many of you who've had to live lies and extract secrets."

"Is that why I've seen so little of you?" Awkwardly, and a bit like a pregnant woman as she carried the Mind, Lowe shuffled on her knees over to the woman. Dorothy accepted her hands as they were offered.

"Partly," replied the seamstress. "I value truth too much to make a career out of lying, and yet that's the vocation into which I've been thrust. Rasputhane didn't want to embroil you and Leonitis again, not after the attention you'd drawn to yourselves over that whole pretending to be the queen and hammer farce. He needed a clean slate—'fresh clay,' he said— which I apparently am."

"To what service were you called?" asked Leonitis.

Dorothy appraised the area once more to ensure that all the distant heads she saw chatting in the gloom were brown and Arhadian like hers. "To the protection of Eod, and into this circle I must now draw each of you. Just as the Iron Queen was sworn into the protection of Eod by its Everfair King, so too shall we swear an oath to each other to see that she upholds the frail promise she made."

"Frail promise?" Dorvain's face twisted like an angry rock. "You mean she means to betray us? When we are all that's left to protect hers, or any other, empire? How mad is that mongrel bitch? Was she not attacked tonight? What of that battle?"

"She was," replied Dorothy. "A tiny skirmish. I'm not clear on everything, since a farspeaking stone only conveys so much. Nonetheless, to my understanding, her Furies and not her army were the targets of that assault. An assault that Rasputhane reports as having already been suppressed by our forces and those of Menos."

Attrition was low to moderate, though the ships have been compromised. Lowe kept the Mind's commentary to herself and reminded herself to stop touching it—though when she realized her hands were still in Dorothy's, she wasn't sure she had been.

"An assault from whom?" asked Leonitis.

"Death's minions," whispered Dorothy, and a shiver passed through those gathered like a circling ghost. "Death isn't our problem, or not the one for which I've come calling."

Dorvain gave a rueful laugh. "What could be worse than Death?"

Pulling her hands from Lowe, the seamstress counted their dooms on her fingers. "There's the mad king. Possibly an army of wolves, too. And Death, whom we've tallied. Still, the greatest threat to Geadhain, and one that I'm certain will endure beyond wars that would erase men from this world, will always be the ambitions of the Iron-born bastards. I have it on good authority—well, the spymaster's authority—that somewhere in the chaos of the storm brewing around us, inquiries have been made into past events. Suspicious inquiries, with the trail leading back to her Iron majesty."

"What manner of inquiries?" asked Lowelia.

Dorothy tapped Lowe's forehead. "How appropriate of you to ask, since shadowy persons have conducted a number of strange investigations—biographies of engineers, sages, and wise men who've visited Eod over the centuries. Add to that a number of files missing from the royal archives, including the one eternal record of an event I'm sure you'd want to forget. The incident was filed under *Borvine.*"

It was the surname of Lowelia's former spouse. The memory of her infant daughter, Cecilia, lying in a box saw Lowelia utter a short startled cry.

She recovered. "Why? Why would anyone want to know about Trevor, or Cecilia, or me, even?"

Dorothy handed her a beautifully embroidered tissue. "Such is the question I'm left with. That we're all left with. Why are the Iron Queen's agents scurrying beneath the cover of war to dig up secrets on handmaidens, wise men, and heroes? What's the connection?" Befuddlement clouded every gaze upon her, and she continued speaking.

"Hence why Rasputhane has drawn you all into my web of mystery. I've done all that I can alone, and you'd be astonished at what a person invited into people's homes to stitch a hem or two can learn. Though perhaps not you, Lowe, since you've spent your life in service."

Lowelia then realized that the fancy she'd had of Dorothy hiding outside a raided home some weeks ago wasn't fancy at all.

"No matter," continued Dorothy. "While the king is seeking a weapon, and others are braving the Land of Chaos, we must be the ones to watch Eod for a snake in its garden."

"She won't get away with whatever she's planning," Lowelia said and spat.

Yet her words were empty, and they deflated into sighs. Problem was, no one had the foggiest idea what the Iron Queen's new schemes might look like.

VI

Alastair didn't arrive back at his chamber that evening, and Maggie spent another night spooling herself in sweaty sheets. She'd stir, moaning, muttering, and reach for a man who wasn't there, before once more falling into the dark embrace of dreams. But tonight was different, the dream darker, deep as a current in eternity. The endlessness swallowed her, and she gasped awake—though now she was not in Eod.

In Dream, she wanders a familiar place. Breathing the salted bouquet of the Feordhan, she walks along the creaking port of Taroch's Arm. She pulls tight the neck of the overcoat she dons to keep out the furious cold. Gray waves smash barren ships into the shuddering docks; not so much as a single light, puff of smoke, or sailor seems present. From that haunted pier, she strolls through indistinct streets: scribbles of smoke and glass without passerby or cart to be seen. She shivers as she passes the flickering iron lamplights that cast their dim defiance into the afternoon's thick fog. Sooner or later—a sense of time escapes her—she pauses before taking the steps to the patio of her own homespun tavern.

The Silk Purse's sign somehow swings in the dead air and squeaks from need of oil. A lantern glows through the salt-etched panes of the tavern windows, and such an invitation should be welcome, but she doesn't want to go inside. Perhaps by the same spirit-wind that rocks the sign does the door blow open. Maggie's feet move and make a choice her mind still debates. Like a leashed woman she's pulled up, then through the door. When her body is once more hers, she sits at the bar. She knows these bottles and the oaken shelf upon which they sit: a former barkeep, retired soldier from Menos, and departed friend had carved it for her. And there he is, and so this must be the cruelest dream.

"Ben," she says, surprised.

Surprised, since he's been dead for a decade, fallen into the longest sleep while nursing a bottle of whisky by the fire. Now here he is as she remembered him in his prime: hale and hairy as an ox stuffed into the frame of a man, with a slightly tanned complexion, aged finely in wrinkles, with a beard and peppery auburn hair that's long but kempt. She always thought he might have been a disgraced nobleman, and not a soldier, for he charmed any room with a suave lordliness. Ben's dressed in his favorite leather jerkin—capped at the sleeves to show his arms, which the ladies always like to rub and fawn over. She's watching him from behind as he polishes glasses; she knows it's him from his carriage and the breadth of his back. As he turns and smiles at her—a dash of white teeth and tan—she's wrenched between heartache and joy.

"Ben?"

"Who else should it be?" he replies, and then slams the glass he was cleaning down on the bar with an echo like thunder. Deftly he spins, picks a bottle, does a toss-twirl-and-catch trick with it that used to drive the barmaids into fevers of lust, then doles out a splash of the golden liquid into Maggie's cup. In another magik trick, Ben makes the bottle disappear behind his back, then slides the drink forward with a finger. "There you go, luv. Heathsholme brandy, with its spices and a hint of apple. Your greatest pleasure."

It is indeed her favorite drink, though not her greatest pleasure—that would have been him. Nonetheless, the mulled stringency of the offering makes her stomach flip happily. She watches the rippling amber, then gazes into the uncommonly clear blue-green eyes of her old friend and almost lover—Kings, did they ever play a dangerous dance together—and while she sees his roiling desire, she's wise enough to men, and to lies, to know that his passion isn't for her. Maggie pushes the drink away. "You're not Ben. You're something pretending to be him."

For an instant, the room distorts as if flooded by an abyss, and twinkles appear in the cracks of the wood; a liquid cosmos buoys in the bottles behind the entity, and glittering infinity shines through the windows. In the glow of swimming stars, the entity loses its shape; it's something faceless, grand, and black, a living void and mystery—she could fall into him and never reach an end. In a slap to her consciousness, the room returns to normal. Were she not fused to her seat, or trapped in this terror, she might have fled. Her grandmother, Cordenzia, didn't breed cowards, however, and she knows that forces have awakened and chosen Geadhain as their battlefield, and she suspects that this is one of them. So she asks, "Which of the Dreamers are you?"

"A good question, Maggie." Ben turns and fixes himself a drink while whistling in his typical out-of-tune and silly manner. He says nothing.

Instead, he joins her at the bar and leans in, hovering over his glass, his red mouth as delicious as the apple's sweetness with which it is wet. Whatever cosmic master this is, it knows her too well. "I chose this form since you have such strong feelings for him, though I want you to understand that this was only in an attempt not to alarm you with my greatness. This is not a seduction, or an attempt to yield you to my Will. My brother is the one who deals in Desire, and his sins have stained the works of our universe. My prose is conviction, real love, and so this is how you and I shall know each other."

"I won't be manipulated," she declares.

The Dreamer's apparition touches her, and the graze of his coarse fingertips possesses the same stimulating static she recalled from Ben. How often she and Ben had played that game with each other, teasing with the torment of a near kiss, only for him to leave with whatever trollop still lingered come closing, or for her to head upstairs and please herself with less entanglements than whatever tryst Ben might have proposed. As the ghost of the man she loved caresses her hands, then forearms, then face, and leans his adamantine chin in so close that the bristles of his beard scrape and tingle her with new passion, she knows that if she had control of her body she would have kissed, undressed, and probably made love with Ben's false ghost right there.

Time and logic are irrelevancies to the heart, and as she breathes upon this phantom from her past, she relives in that instant every wry glance, each soft touch of her waist while skirting behind the bar together, and the many long, enchanting stories that Ben would tell her of the lands east of Menos, whence he'd come. Histories he shared when they were alone and cozied in the hearth's glow, though still too shy to touch. Why ever did she miss that one chance at love? She has a scathing lack of answers as phantom Ben's lips hover next to hers, as his sweat-and-leather fragrance puffs up from the cleft of his chest.

Perhaps it had to do with the darkness that he'd carried within him; the wounds come from war or a past he sought to escape. She had pitied that pain when he came knocking, asking for lodging and work. She saw that pain possess him when he drank, which wasn't often for a bartender. If he drew too strong a draft, though, he became a raging, brawling, demolishing force. Many a bout and bender of his ended with him sleeping half-nude down on the port. Or with him missing for a day or two, before she finally heard the news that he'd been jailed by the Fingers. But she had always run to him, and he to her.

Once, when the Silk Purse had been burgled, Ben had been the one to stop the violent predator as he'd lunged at her—protected only by her nightie and a broom—with every intent to garrote her neck and steal Cordenzia's necklace from her throat. And like a monster summoned by fear, Ben had come, summoned from a drunken stupor in some lonely corner of the bar. He had pummeled the intruder with fists, a shattered vase to the face, and then wielded the raw edges of that ceramic like blades. She'd never seen a man fight like that before, and when it was over she wasn't sure who she should fear more—the crumpled, crying thief or the grimacing man who had nearly murdered him.

Maggie feels these memories drawn to the surface of her mind—every weeping embrace, even the smell of his sweet vomit and terror, and how much she cared for him in his lowest moments, bathing him, grooming him, tidying him as a mother would a child. And then, too, came the memories of how cultured and gentle he would be when not such a wastrel, and how he'd look to her for any kind of approval—even when it came to taking to bed a woman for the night. From down the hall would inevitably echo the sounds of their lovemaking, and she'd regret giving him her blessing. Still, considering all of their sordid behaviors, it shouldn't have surprised either of them that a relationship would have been untenable, with such roles already in place. When she'd found him, dead, and pinched in the face as though he'd been weeping, her heart dropped, shattered, and saved her sanity by going numb. At least it had been an end.

"Stop." Maggie breaks the spell to escape the prison of memories. "That's what you creatures do: play with us as if we're your toys. Well, we're not. We're strong and independent, and we shall make our own fates."

"Indeed," says the Dreamer. "You and I desire the same result: to free the clay, to let the clay sculpt itself. I would not appeal to a man of power, or one capable of hosting my great Will, or any of the great heroes already chosen in this war, for they would only influence and affect my purity of being. Never have I sought a vessel. I do not wish to arrange the tree-of-stars to my designs. You should be wary of those who do, Little Light. You should be wary of all who would claim to help humankind. They lie; they would twist and change the clay into shapes most monstrous."

"Why should I trust one who pretends to be a man I almost loved?"

"I know not how else to show myself to you," claims the Dreamer, his countenance furrowed. "My greatness would otherwise shatter your mind. And love him you did, Maggie; to love someone broken and cast out by the world is to carry the brightest of torches. I know. I see from any distance. For I am the breath that passes between the lips of lovers, and the Will that weeds into their souls. I am light and dawn in the hearts of men, beast, and stone. I am hope and glory. I am Love. I am Estore, Dreamer of the Rising Heart."

As the Dreamer speaks, the walls fall away again, and the void that rises to consume the tavern and reality itself, and through which Maggie spins, isn't dark—*for that darkness is only the threshold of fear that comes before the light. No, there is such light, a spinning nebula of diamond constellations, each dazzling from the sunlight of infinite whirling golden spheres. Here is a universe of sunfire and music, where Maggie dances as a note in this cosmic symphony. Then the music ends, the brilliance fades, and wood, hard stool, and tender light from candles and lanterns return.*

Maggie finds she has been weeping. She finally needs that drink and downs it so greedily she's coughing once done. "So you're Love, then?" *She snorts.* "Where were you when he died? Where were you for all the failed lovers and doomed romances of which odes and legends are written?"

Ben strokes her cheek, then chin, as he did whenever she'd had a terrible day. "Little Light, you are bright for your kind, so I know that you know the cost of loving. Its wonder lays in its preciousness and volatility. Something must be rare to be valued. It must be fragile and easily broken. But I have not come to you today to debate the merits of my being, nor the cost, nor to make you reflect upon the loss of that gift. I have reached out to you across the sea of stars for the emanations of this conflict have awoken me, even me in my sanctuary of peace and light. My brothers and sisters all want what they want. They arrange their vessels strategically around each other and the Black Queen and wait to see who will fall first so that they may claim the board. I need a player, a piece, an unexceptional accomplice who will be the unseen shadow to save the kings, then to be the seed to wake the kings once more when this war will be fought for its second and still not final time. We are not at the end, Maggie—only the beginning. A darkness reaches from the future, a sickness I cannot repel alone, and one that not even the seers of this age have concern toward given the precariousness of life, here and now."

A new threat? A future menace? She is to save the kings, twice? Maggie is no one, nobody in this war. She can't comprehend the importance and responsibility being preached.

"But you do understand," *says Estore.* "Your Will is the same as those who listen. Again, though, I am not like my brothers and sisters; I shall only ask this of you. I shall not knight you in blood and steal your body for my service. I do promise you this, though, Little Light—the tree-of-stars and the waters of eternity that nourish it are veins deep beyond fathoming. I can weave you into its roots, into a dream where you and your beloved might meet, and find either happiness or doom—as is the untended, unkind, and beautiful mystery of my being."

Passion wreathes her in flames—in Dream she can actually see the flickering hue of her desire rising off her body—and she reaches for Ben, plays fingers through beard, across cheeks, and into his hair, and whispers, "You can bring us together again?"

"I can, though you must do me a service."

As she wavers, Ben, the Dreamer, or this vision of tomorrow, kisses her—spice and booze, the strong muscle of his tongue against the tangle of hers. Past the physical wetness is a bleeding of Will—of love—from her mouth to his. Maggie has been kissed with passion before, and yet never has anything left her so stolen of breath, strength, and wits. Truly she thinks and sees nothing but for the red gash of his mouth, and feels, even though this is an illusion, even though she kissed a Dreamer, that he, she, or it was taken by that passion, too. Estore's eyes are closed as they part mouths, as if it has delighted in their mutual taste.

"Little Light," it continues, "you have such a spark of my gift. Passion, and beyond that passion the pure seed of love. I almost wish you had the blood of old, so that I could make you my first vessel. Although to do so would weaken me to the vices of your kind, and you've seen how fear has tainted the solidarity of our virtue. So I shall decline and abate, and you will not see me in this life or any other. I shall, however, entwine your roots in the tree-of-stars with that of the Light you lost. I shall grant you this chance, which is given only to those most blessed and ruled by fate. You will not know him in the flesh in which you've known him. You will not know him in this life. Yet, you will cross stars and paths. Of that, you have my eternal promise."

Estore kisses her once more, and this time she crawls onto the bar and he hoists her down and against his hard flesh so that they can grind, feel, and caress. He mutters between breaths words that would have been terribly cruel if not for their passion. "You, Little Light, are unexceptional. Mmm...Mmm...You, Little Light, are a mite in the shadow of the conflict of cosmic giants. Mites shan't be noticed beneath the masters' feet. So in the shadows you should work, for me, for you—and do not think of kings, queens, or my vengeful kind. I do not, lest my serenity is threatened. Do for me this one task, and I shall weave the roots of you and your beloved together."

Who is she to this war? What has she to lose? Her livelihood is gone, destroyed by deathless hordes. As it stands, her honor is constantly trod upon by a man who fuked her and yet spent his time with a master's wife. She has nothing. Nothing to look forward to in this life. Perhaps the next dawn of her soul won't be so lonely and failed. One task and she could see Ben, in whatever form, once more? A deal with the Dreamer of Love?

Somewhere in the daze of the kiss she agrees. As she reaches for the hard meat of her lover, something else is pressed into her hand: small, round, and firm. She knows to put it in the elastic of her garter. Perhaps Ben—the Dreamer—whispers that suggestion among many. What she knows most of all is that she must keep it safe. It's taken all of the Dreamer's power to get this far, to contact her and push through the membrane of ethereal oceans and realities *that separate them to even give her this gift, this Dream of Love condensed into a diamond.*

"Follow the Mouse," commands Estore, kissing, kissing away. "Protect her when danger has faded to dusk. Protect my gift to you, this weapon, a piece of my Will, a wonderstone of Love. It is a gateway to my power, and the light can banish—for a time—any wickedness. Use it. Be the sunrise for a new age. You will know when to use it, and when the task is done, and darkness vanquished, leave my hollow sun in the grave of the king."

On that somber note, the dream ended. Her eyes were closed and her hands still groped hard flesh, though less hirsute than Ben's—leaner, more lithe, surely. She realized that man whose tongue was in her mouth, with hands roaming her breasts and the cleft under her skirt, kissed differently as well.

"Alastair," she said.

"Diasora," he whispered. "I am sorry for being so late."

She still had no idea who in the blazes Diasora was, or why he kept calling her that. From the phrasing and uniqueness of the name, it sounded as if Diasora had been a noblewoman, one of high birth and standing. Maggie wasn't that, she'd never been, and she had her own less regal importance to achieve. Curious and sly, she kept tumbling with the shadowbroker and pulled his hand away from her garter and from the curio—it had to be a stone from the impression of its roundness—that was pressed against her thigh. She serviced Alastair instead, and once he'd had his sputtering climax in her mouth and over his crotch, she went to wash her mouth out in the trickling wall fountain, returning with a towel for her lover. They sat on the edge of the bed, each holding secrets and posed in suspicion of the other. From the glow of the light-and-leaf trellis above their bed, she inferred dawn had come. Dawn, which evoked fierce memories of its heavenly master, Estore, and the promises she'd made to that entity.

"We have a meeting soon," said Alastair, as limply as the spent thing between his legs.

Maggie had returned with a distracted look, and Alastair believed it to be related to the confusion surrounding their arrangement. She deserved an explanation for everything: his time away, his bizarre family tree. While he'd told her that Beauregard and Galivad were his abandoned sons, the depth of their story, the truth of his many lives, and the nature of Beatrice and her inhabiting spirit weren't so easily explained. She saw his life in fragments. For a while, he'd thought of how much to tell Maggie about his complicated past. Deceit had begun to dissolve his insides. *Hilarious*, he thought, since he had lied from the first moment he knew what a silver tongue could do. Alastair could no longer spend these mysterious evenings away from Maggie without telling her, for the sake of her dignity, why and for what she was waiting—he wasn't certain himself.

"It's alright, Alastair." Maggie placed the towel over his sad member and rose to dress herself—she wanted to get that tingling magik stone tucked away behind some tight hose.

Alastair leapt to his feet and tried to turn her into his arms. "But what about—?"

She nudged him off, and her callousness made her intentions quite clear. While quickly dressing herself, she formalized the end of their sexual partnership. "I said that all is well, Alastair—or Lucien, or Stevoch, or whatever moniker you now use. We came into each other's lives through an arrangement with your mysterious master, and I see no reason why that arrangement and the enigmas that surround you need continue. I wish you no ill will. I should thank the fates that we've come together this far. Were it not for you inadvertently hijacking my life, I would've died a stubborn death to the rotten mouths and fangs of Death's army, back in Taroch's Arm. We have been a blessing to each other thus far, though as a man of games and chance, you'll agree that we shouldn't push our luck."

Alastair was so rarely heartbroken that he possessed no guile with which to conceal his defeat. Maggie shuffled to the trembling fellow. She used him as a support while slipping on her last boot, then tried to inject some empathy—of which she felt none—into the situation. "I can see that you have a mountain of secrets to keep, even for a shadowbroker and consort to a most mysterious patron. Keep them."

She kissed him, only once, and with a melancholy sweetness come from the death of romance. They each had a few tears when it ended. "We have a war to fight," she continued, "and I'll play my small—possibly meaningless—part in its outcome. We needn't distract ourselves with the charade of any importance between us. We had some wonderful sex, and you saved me. I think, too, that we remind each of another for whom we long."

She touched his auburn curls, thinking of how his eyes had the perfect, though split, sea-green color of her lost love's. She thought, too, of what it might take—the moving of mountains—to see Ben again, and sensed that Alastair and his craftiness might still be of use. "You'll be good for a favor if I need one, won't you?"

Alastair sniffled. "A favor? What sort?"

"The sort that moves mountains with whispers—what you do."

"Yes, of course, Maggie. I would do anything for you."

"Anything? Good. Remember those words. Goodbye, Alastair. I'll make arrangements to sleep elsewhere."

Since she could have been a second cousin to Belle—the dark hair, strong will, and voluptuous traits—her leaving was a hammer to his heart, and Alastair said nothing as she left him naked in the chamber they'd no longer share. She left without sharing any of her secrets, either. Nothing of her promises to Estore. Nothing of the potential death of Magnus and Brutus—a king had been prophesied to die. Whoever ended up in that casket, she would see Estore's stone resting within, and then her war, against fate and loneliness, would be over. For this life, anyway; she presumed these bloody Dreamers never thought in smaller sands.

VII

Morning in the Chamber of Echoes mirrored the rising sun outside, and the crystal rocks and transparent flowers lit up with an inner fire that dazzled the glass wonderland and illumined the mist of the cascading walls of the underground grotto like a firecaller's pyrotechnical display. Indeed, the scene was beautiful, though most of the chamber's resplendence was wasted on the hard, weary countenances of the men and women who'd gathered at the cock's crow to discuss the fates of Eod and Menos.

As they trickled into the hushed shadow of the ancient yew, the lines between ally and foe were never less clear. Menosians, Eodians, and persons owing allegiance to neither empire surrounded the great wheel of stone, paying little heed to who their neighbors were. As if one of Lila's enchantments were in effect, an invisible profusion of accord appeared to have enchanted men and women who were previously mortal enemies. In a portrait of age and youth, Gorijen huddled with the new Menosian nobility, mostly lavishing his attention upon their uncannily well-behaved infant, at whom he made clownish faces as he tickled the baby's feet—failing to elicit a laugh even with that tried and true gesture.

"He's Iron-born and Iron-proud," explained his extraordinarily gruff caretaker. No one quite knew why these four were present, though whispers of an unusual quartet that had led the charge to cleanse the Furies of Death's forces suggested their identities—and a priest; there'd been a priest, of all queer things.

Elissandra, looking like a Romanisti queen in stunning red silks and scarves, had collected her brood, and the three hovered around Rasputhane, asking him questions about the silvery eyes that he hid behind his spectacles, causing him to shift at their friendly inquiries while their psychic knives were no doubt eviscerating his skull. He wasn't ignoring them, as one might expect a guarded spymaster to do. On the contrary, he was curious about these questions himself and thus entertained the Donanachs' curiosity.

In another scene, Galivad and Beauregard were elbow to elbow; many were now convinced the young men bore an eerie feminine likeness in the face, as if the ghost of the same woman haunted them each. They sat with Alastair, whom they'd once loathed, making about as much sense to anyone as all the other flip-flops in morality witnessed of late. So much had changed between the three: they made quiet, somber jokes for the occasion, and the women posted on either side of the trio—Beatrice and Maggie—smiled at the men's chatter. Even those women seemed to have settled into an unspoken sisterhood, yet none recalled them as better than the bitterest enemies before.

Rowena and the four with whom she now conspired, and the Iron Queen and her Iron lord, formed the only diametrically opposed forces of the alliance. With frowns and sneers, the groups threw their sinister emotions like daggers across the table. As a few more aides, serfs, and messengers flitted in and out of the white yew's embrace, food and drink was laid out, and final messages were delivered and circulated. The luminaries who hadn't yet sat were choosing their seats—still with that intermingling between East and West.

Alas, for all the fellowship, the first of the major tests was at hand—as early as an hourglass past, with the fires only just out at Camp Fury, the dead had been seen mobilizing in the sands of Kor'Khul.

Ready to begin the meeting, the Iron Queen waved off the toadying and incompetent serf that Gustavius had chosen to keep around himself; the lad was at her side shakily trying to hand her a plate of dates and cheeses—she hated dates! She pierced him with a look of reprimand, and he scurried away like a rat burned by fire. She made a mental note to either execute or demote him later. After the mass execution on board the *Morgana*, she was feeling much more herself, a woman confident of her role and purpose: to cleanse this world of idiots and the weak.

Gloriatrix addressed the council, so many of whom were antagonists to her vision. "I have no appetite, and I'm concerned that so many of you seem hungry and jovial. You must have seen the reports. The dead have risen from the desert, and their horde now crawls toward Eod. It will cross the sandy breadth between civility and chaos before the week comes to a close. We must be ready to face Death."

Rasputhane, casually chewing on a date, matched her scorn for scorn. "We are ready, even without the firepower of your Furies. I hear that they were rendered into massive lumps of useless feliron in the assault."

Gloriatrix tapped the bridge of her nose. "You're partially blind. Shall I assume your deficiencies extend to your ears also? Whatever you have heard is incorrect; the Talwynian fusion drives were preserved through the brave actions of ministers and the champions of my empire. The weapons of the Furies remain fully operational."

"What of their ability to fly?" pressed the spymaster.

"It is true that the truefire reserves were largely exhausted in the assault," she admitted. "Such power had to be bled from the engines to cool them enough to avoid a catastrophic explosion."

"It was the only choice," said Gorijen.

"It was the only solution you could contrive," added Gloriatrix; her paranoid inclinations made her wonder if that hadn't been the old sage's intent, to declaw the crowes at their gate. "There remains, however, more than enough truefire and capacity for destruction, even if the wings of my Furies are broken."

"What good are your mighty guns when they're pointed east, at Eod?" asked Rowena.

Many eyes fell on the Iron Queen, and in every gaze roiled doubt. "Any earthspeaker could stir the sand and move them. My Furies are not impotent! Nor is the will and service of the Ironguard, each soldier of whom is worth two of yours."

"Highly debatable," said Rowena. "And if Death's army moves? What then? Continue to play 'Ring Around the Rosie' every speck and hope that Death decides, rather stupidly, to walk her horde before your cannons? I suspect Death knew the damage of which your Furies are capable, and disarmed them for a reason."

The Iron Queen wished she had executed the woman back on the *Morgana*, before an armistice had been called. Rather than explode in rage, she seethed through cold composure. "What would you propose then, sword of the queen?"

"We shall need to take the enemy from afar," said Rowena and stood to speak to all at the circle of power. "We've been training with the queen's army and the sharpshooters and mercenaries of the reserves. Eod's thunderstrike archers should be able to thin much of the horde, as well. When it comes to close combat, we've been padding our men and women, and those with the iron or silver armor of our nations are relatively impervious to superficial damage."

"Which is about all it will take," muttered Aadore, gloomily. She stood next, and leaned over the cold stone and cast her voice as if she, too, were a leader. No one thought to question her pedigree, or even to debate who she'd been before.

"A deep scratch, a chomp of the teeth, and your men will fester and turn. The fever may begin in hourglasses, or a week at best—but it will happen, and there is no cure. Victims who die, from fever or otherwise, will rise quickly after death. If they push our forces back into Eod, we shall lose by a war of attrition. They will find ways in, the dead—sewers, digging through the earth like worms; any path through soil or stone, they will take."

"No one can penetrate Eod's wall," boasted Dorvain, mostly parroting the bravado he'd heard in the company of soldiers.

"You're right," said Beauregard. He rose as the others sat. "Although, if you've seen how these dark masters, these Dreamers..." Sorsetta's incendiary festival of doom replayed as a phantograph in his mind: towers shattered by the fused remains of men, a kaleidoscope of fire and smoke, and through the clotted brume an Immortal King braying the word "*doom*."

"Brother?" whispered Galivad, and his touch to the other's hand summoned Beauregard back—Rowena gasped at the term of kinship.

Beauregard smiled at his brother and squeezed his hand before releasing it; were there ever a scrap of uncertainty left as to their bond of blood, it was dispelled in that moment.

"I was remembering Sorsetta. In this room, I am one of the few to know how our enemies, the once masters of our world, engage in war. They don't see us as equals. We are less than gnats to them. Hew their soldiers, and they will just steal more of our bodies, more of our people, to create whatever unholy wave of mindless flesh they need to crush us. I've seen worms made from the ruined dead that stood hundreds of paces high and that smashed the shield of mountain and magik—once believed to be unbreakable—that protected Gorgonath. Such was the feint pulled at the last line of the hourglass from a weakened mad king. Imagine what Death, at full strength, and growing its numbers as it harvests from every civilization east and west of the Feordhan, will bring. Her wave will be black and furious past anything we've known in this war. Somehow we must survive her and then the shadow that will come to wash away our remains."

Even the most swinish of appetites evaporated, and many shoved away their food.

"Sounds like we're fuked," said Dorvain and traded his chalice for a full bottle of wine, which he began to chug.

It was the lay of the war, now presented as hopeless. It seemed as though weeks of preparation and strategy had been countered in one night, by only a small force of their immediate enemy. What would this wave that Beauregard lyricized bring? Naught save for the darkest doom. A few other sages and soldiers took Dorvain's lead and started into the wine and bitters that sat upon the table. The murmurs from depressing and dissenting conversations floated about.

"Seriously." Elissandra slapped the table. "I've seen such heroism, and such spinelessness—pick a virtue, you rubbery snails! I know your whispers, all of them."

Men, women, and even the Iron Queen shrank as she studied the circle. "I shall leave my children with more heroes than villains in this world, of that I assure you. If it means culling those who have not the Will and foresight to proceed through the darkest night yet to fall, then stand and be cut down here."

Again, she slapped the stone, and it cracked like one of Magnus's manifestations. "Wise up! Be bold! Be brave, and listen to one another. What is the plan? How do we stand against an enemy that knows no remorse and who will wash this city with an ocean of blackness? *Our* city, might I add? There are no enemies here, not now. Eod's light must be defended by every hand at this table. What resources do we have? Where do we draw lines? How do we stop this?"

Elissandra had inspired them, and ideas began to fly.

"We still have the wall," said Gorijen. "It's been reinforced from the perceived danger of Menos. We could channel some of the energy from above back into the wall, which should afford us additional hourglasses in the event of a siege."

"We must not let it come to that," said Rowena. "We must combine all of the warriors who fight for Eod and make a stand around the city. We should fall back only in the case of a traumatic defeat. Snipe-and-run tactics, for which my people are famous and bred. We can use the canyons as traps. We can shuttle men to the highest buttes and tallest ridges found in the desert."

"Skycarriages and crowes!" Leonitis clapped. "Of course. While our ships have few direct armaments, and we cannot bring them too near the horde, we can use them as convoys for soldiers."

Slurring a little, Dorvain slapped his brother's arm and said, "Remember when we were sent—as soldiers, not watchmasters—to settle that pissy upstart who assassinated and usurped Uruk-Tak?"

It was a dim trickle from Leonitis's past, and he and Dorvain had been abroad on so many assignments since their initiation into the Silver Watch that recalling one was like snatching a salmon from a stream. He recalled that they'd had to travel south at one point, over the Scarasace Sea and into the island continent of Sammorah. It was an enchanted realm of sand and sun juxtaposed with obsidian pyramids that pulsed in ancient lines and scripts of power—structures that seemed not to have been made by the hands of men. Uruk-Tak had been the appointed holy preceptor of his people, and he'd maintained ties to Eod since the kings were young and that land had yet to build its first monument. It was said that their clicking, clucking—albeit poetic—language was the closest tongue to what the brothers themselves had once spoken, when the world was green and raw.

Leonitis dabbled fast and further in that past, in visions of silk and spice maidens—and kohl-gazed lads who raised the question of sex. In every way, he and his brother had had a soldier's life there: fighting in foreign sands, forming fraternities with loyalty tested on the sweltering battlefield, and at nights, bedding Sammorah's strange and exotic maidens. Those loyal to the old preceptor housed them in the cold and barren spaces of Sammorah's temples, where he and his brother had unhappy dreams as they fell asleep under the gaze of statues of ebon man-beasts—muscled, nude, and with the heads of jackals, bulls, and hawks.

People were waiting to hear the morsel from this tale, and Dorvain tapped his brother again, seeing the man so taken by wistful reminiscence. "I can see you're thinking about the ladies," he grinned. "Never mind them for now, do you remember how we disposed of him? The upstart? All holed up like a weasel in one of those impregnable black pyramids. Couldn't get the shite to stick his neck out so that we could axe it. Ours was a war of attrition there, only we were on the other side."

Leonitis thought harder for the details of that campaign. "We shut down his supply lines and intercepted what runners and spies he sent. Although that didn't do much since those temples of theirs connect to underground labyrinths. So no matter how firm our control of the surface, a number of key elements still slipped through our net. We couldn't figure out where the entrances and exits were, even."

"And?" Dorvain shoved an elbow into him.

"And then we..."

Bombs. Truefire payloads had been buried all across the sand at potential chokepoints, and the explosions acted as both markers and the means to collapse and close the false preceptor's tunnels. Within a week, no more supplies or troops could reach the pyramids, and the false preceptor was offering terms of surrender. Unfortunately, the Sammorhains were not a merciful people, and he was castrated then quartered, publicly, for his crimes.

"Explosives," he said. "Planted all about suspicious tracts we suspected our enemy would use. We should have a clear idea of where the enemy is headed, though we can use our soldiers to lure them down whatever paths we choose."

"What if they don't take the bait?" asked Rasputhane.

"Then we shall have at least bought ourselves more time and more opportunities to thin Death's army by other means," said the legion master.

"Will the lady herself be making an appearance?" whispered Davy, when the room descended into a thoughtful quiet; everyone had heard him, so he realized he had to say more. "Death?" he mumbled.

"I should think so," said Gloriatrix, "and from what I understand of these Dreamers and their vessels, there are conduits, smaller generals in their forces, that cause disconnections in the chain. Look for them to be more self-possessed and aware, perhaps speaking or at least exhibiting signs of higher intelligence—and kill them posthaste. As for Death herself, I know not the shape of her vessel. Although I suspect that if we can break that host, it will do more than disrupt the chain, it will shatter it altogether."

"Wise counsel, my Queen." Rasputhane applauded, genuinely impressed. However, a sliver of suspicion pricked him.

"You seem to know a great deal about these creatures and their hierarchies. It's as if you've had them under study. Makes one wonder where the remaining survivors from the Iron City have vanished to; even the dossiers with their names appear to have gone missing."

There had been rumors of cages, though empty, being kept aboard the *Morgana*—yet no one could corroborate such hearsay. Rather than accuse her outright, Rasputhane studied the Iron Queen's face for an indication of her guilt.

Naturally, she was inscrutable. "I don't know what you're suggesting. I do know that it's not unlikely that your disorganized kingdom has misplaced whatever fabricated accounts of travelers between East and West you're so set on slathering in suspicion. Oversights and errors can be excused, as this is, after all, a time of war. We lost good men, and you even lost a share of your sorcerers and watch helping us put out the fires at Camp Fury. We shall see more death before any peace comes. In war, the darkest decisions must be made, ones that can shake kingdoms, and before which a few missing or unaccounted-for peasants and soldiers will seem a trifle."

Darkest decisions? What did she mean? Rowena and the other secret defenders of Eod across the table felt a wicked storm was brewing within the Iron Queen, stretching her face into that of a murderer's. She wasn't so different from the Dreamers, many realized; she would accept any payment in flesh for a victory. Perhaps that was why they beheld her with such reverence as she continued.

The Iron Queen drummed her fingers upon the table. "Good ideas I've heard, and I believe we're on the right path with bombs, funneling Death's forces and traps...Still, let's say that these tactics only work to trim the fat of this blubbery monstrosity, leaving the body of the Dreamer herself and the preponderance of her forces intact. What then?"

Expressions waxed from blankness to despair. The Iron Queen smiled grimly.

"Exactly. We shall have to recall ourselves behind the wall, which, while fortified by magik and made by the Everfair King's own spells, may not save us for long, or at all. We shall be placing ourselves very neatly into an abattoir into which Death can saunter and take her choice of meats. I don't know exactly how Menos was undone, though part of its peril was because we were so insular, so perfectly compact a morsel for her to eat that when the panic and disease spread, it went from a contagion to an epidemic in a day. At best two or three. Consider that, and how our iron wall, built to repel an advance from an Immortal King, became instead the walls of a tomb."

Rasputhane objected, knowing of the queen's possession, the truefire and the rest. "There were other factors—"

"Indeed, little spymaster," agreed the Iron Queen. Now she rose and exercised her gravitas, then strode around the table, as if to speak personally into the ear of every man or woman she passed. She tapped their shoulders with her cold fingers, knighting the blighted with chills.

"There were many factors, some of which I'm sure would be of as much interest to my auditors as missing flight lists would be to yours. But what's not to say that Death herself could not bring down Magnus's wall with an earthquake of her own? Or with a rain of scorching blood and bodies as Brutus did in Gorgonath? No wall will save us. Do not believe it will—it is your cowardice, not your courage, that speaks. Still, as Elissandra has told us, we must cease our petulance and suspicion, even though that snake will remain coiled in its basket and full of venom."

She reached Rasputhane. "Look at us. A mousey man—and distant blood to the House of Mystery, I imagine—left in charge of a nation's secrets." She arrived at Rowena and the others beside the spymaster. "Loyal soldiers made into generals. A servant and a tailor all playing roles too grand for themselves. Roles which might just break the shoulders upon which they've landed."

And break your scrawny vulture's bones like a cheap plate, thought Dorvain; Lowelia's sentiments were similar.

"A woman of Alabion and her brood lost in time and seeking...a home, I imagine," noted Gloriatrix as she looked to Elissandra and said in a flicker of true empathy, "Generals, marshals, Ironmen, and persons also laden in mantles of the heaviest iron."

She came to Aadore and the others. "These four are strong, though, and I see but great futures and conquests ahead."

Conquests of my choosing, thought Aadore, holding her emotions behind her soft smile as masterfully as the Iron Queen.

Gloriatrix swept back her seat. "And then there is I, queen to a doomed nation—one that will rise with a glory unimaginable, but for now is weak. I have been stripped of my greatest physical powers but not the strength of my mind. Thus I have woven our possibilities and potentials together, and I bring it to you as a thread of hope and fate. Do not spurn my ideas because of who I am, or look for malice in what I propose, for this is the clearest way forward."

"What is?" Rasputhane couldn't handle the tension, the dancing around.

"As Menos has fallen, so too should Eod."

There were gasps and outcries, and the Iron Queen waited, patiently, for the abatement of their tempers.

"We need a ruse," she explained. "We need the enemy to believe they've won. *Trojana Fatus*—a deception from the ancient kingdoms wherein a statue of surrender was filled with soldiers who swarmed the city. Only Eod will be the statue, the prize Death will come to claim, only to end up with the handful of ashes and eradication."

Gloriatrix experienced the most wondrous chills at the thought, at the possibility of her unmaking a Maker. She couldn't contain her creepy joy as she told the council of her intent to lure Death into the city, and to turn that city—well, half of it—into a grave from which nothing dead, alive, or in-between would survive. Once done explaining her strategy, she left the stunned council, claiming to now require the spiritual guidance of the Carthacian priest who waited in her chambers.

To some observers, they believed that perhaps this newfound reliance on religion signified a change in her iron soul. Mayhap she spoke with true clemency on matters of heart. Still, it was a black hope that she offered. It was vile and filled with fire and death. Moreover, what vexed everyone she left to stew was that it made sense.

"She's mad," said Dorvain.

"She is," agreed Galivad, his elbows supported on the shoulders of each brother. "Although, I fear—is that the right word?—that her plan would ensure a near total annihilation of Death's army."

"As well as half the city!" cried Beauregard.

"People can be moved." Alastair leaned on the back of Leonitis's chair, rubbing his chin. "The palace's tunnels wend all through Kor'Keth, and they would be difficult to breach. Besides, it is as you've said, my son—Death knows only eminence. Powerful as she is, she does not foresee her own defeat. She will be easy to lure—"

Son? Rowena wasn't thinking about mortal eradication at that moment. Alastair had been talking about Beauregard, who had just been revealed as Galivad's brother, which meant—

Rowena's head nearly spun in a circle. "What?"

Alastair fanned away her astonishment. "We are due a good long sit, all of us, to settle many matters. Right now, we must consider Gloriatrix's plan."

"Are we considering it?" Beatrice had slunk up beside Rowena.

When no one answered, it was clear that they were.

VIII

Lowelia lingered in the Chamber of Echoes after the decision had been made. Agreement with Gloriatrix's plan had been nearly unanimous; if Death's army made it as far as Eod's gates, they would use the Faire of Fates to corral the dead and obliterate the undead army with the Furies' warheads. Not a word of the strategy was to pass from the lips of those who knew of it to the ears of those who didn't.

No earthspeakers were required to move the Furies, which were already pointed in Eod's direction. No dead would be able to breach the tech-nomagikal fields of the seemingly dormant Furies—not without another assault from within, which would be hard to replicate with the council at the height of vigilance. Elissandra and her children had already volunteered themselves in the deployment so as to assure success. With three mindspeakers in charge of the timing, there was little risk of error in terms of the synchronicity of a truefire launch. In whole, it was a mad idea, concocted by a mad woman, though the more the notion circulated among the wise, the more sane it seemed.

As one of the sages passed Lowe leaving the summit, he nodded and smiled at her, then whispered, "This is the right decision." She nodded in turn, but her frown remained. For her expression wasn't related to their plans, but rather, her concern over the four Menosian royals—the fair woman, her brother, and their two friends—who had also remained behind.

It was the first long stare she'd had with the quartet of Menosian heroes. Though she might have seen them before, she couldn't recall seeing them up so close. More than the mysteries these four conveyed, she was intrigued by the child the larger man bore with him, who seemed slightly familiar. She struggled to say why the little Menosian was so captivating, other than his uncanny quietude and charm even for a child his age. Indeed, he looked at her, craning his neck from the swaddling of his large nanny, as if she were an object of interest for him, too. Once, he gave her a wet smile, and she turned away, ashamed, though again bewildered as to why.

Navigator Lowe, do you not remember? said the Mind; while pondering the question of the lad's identity, she had been stroking the "child" of her own she carried.

Any association with the infant escaped her.

The non-ambulatory biped's current designation is Ian, though you wouldn't have known that at the time your memory banks were first exposed to his imprint.

Fear, tinged with loathing, crept up Lowe's throat; the Mind had sussed out a factoid, a circumstance, she didn't want to face. Alas, the Mind had its own measures of mercy and had decided that this relation between matrices—Lowe and the Ian—trumped all need for Lowe's comfort. What was the world if not defined by reason and given form by truth? The more it discovered itself, the more this altruistic brand of honesty had become its personality. The Mind ignored her fluctuating telemetry and proceeded.

I am beginning to see the beauty over which Kericot waxed in his poem "Fire over the Feordhan." A poem dedicated to the passing of day into night, of one state into another. I see how this can be applied as a metaphor for the currents of life that rule the universe. Events that appear chaotic, yet are only probability and the attraction of matrix to matrices—which makes your species as lucky or fated as it believes itself to be. So you have been fated to meet this child. Your telemetries reach and yearn for the other. Do you see, Navigator, who he is? My matrix and your readings tell me that you do, though the mind is often slower to accept than the heart.

"No," she denied. Yet the picture she'd claimed from Euphenia's corpse, crumpled as it had been, then later burned to ash in the fire of her drawer, retained all of the clarity of a mirror. A reflection from which she couldn't look away and that revealed all her ugliness, sorrow, and regret. "Impossible."

Quite probable. A chain of molecular events, each explosion breeding the next. Of this Euphenia I see only the imprint of her matrix in your memory banks, although the fact that her blood was on your hands, a stain which never leaves a matrix, tells me as much as if her body were present for an autopsy.

Biped Euphenia Eva Mae—I have drawn a facsimile of her identity from what data you have buried in your matrix—has many of her markers and similarities embedded in that child. Their eyes are the same, and that look, which is compassion from the child, a longing for the woman he senses you've touched, though he knows not how. This is the poetry even the great Kericot failed to capture: the negative and positive forces that draw and repel you both.

Lowe clenched her jaw to bite back the tears. Everything was different from a distance. Beyond her being a traitor, Euphenia's life had never been considered. Now those falsities had been broken, East and West mingled and made to drink the same water and share the same quarters, and the violence of what she'd done to Euphenia seemed less pardonable in that light.

How was the child here? How had he even survived?

Its telemetry indicates that it was in the care of one of the other matrices— the female—before coming into contact with the matrix that now cares for it. If I follow the chain of telemetry to its incipience, where child met the first matrix, then tap into the audiovisual cortex of the female—

You can do that?

Of course. How do you think I have learned so much about you and your species? Do not feel violated. It is a fully anesthetized and painless psychic surgery, with no effect on the matrix, and I learn quite well from being immersed in a subject. Regardless, I can see that they saved the child during the fall of Menos, taking him from a woman who was surely a minder and not a relative of biped Euphenia.

Please call her by her name—not as an object.

As you wish, Navigator Lowe. I cannot yet breach the gap and form connections between a matrix viewed in the past and the matrix currently under inspection, though I would propose that the child was being moved, or shuttled, prior to the fall of Menos. Once more, these matrices are subject to the laws of the chaos theory, where growth and change are natural results of one matrix affecting another, though such patterns are too abstract for the human mind to—

Lowe pulled her hand off the Mind and covered it up. She needed her wits about her, not voices in her head. Particularly since the largest of the Menosians, the scarred nanny, was walking toward her. He bounced Euphenia's infant boy as he approached her with a smile she forced herself to return.

"Hello?" she said.

"Was that a question?" The nanny smiled, showcasing a mouth full of broken teeth. Up close, he was quite a fright and certainly the largest man she had known next to Caenith.

"No, it wasn't meant to be." She waved her hand around. "So much on my mind after the meeting. I don't know where to begin."

"Oh, well, don't mind me interrupting your peace. I only thought you and Ian might want a proper introduction, since he has been making eyes at you for a while now." Ian smiled and reached for her. "See, there he goes again. He doesn't care for many people, aside from my friends and me. Strange, how he's taken such a shine to you." Skar looked at the bundled lump the woman held. "I'd offer for you to hold him, but you seem to have your arms full."

"Ah, yes, the Mind."

"The what?"

No one knew about the Mind, not exactly, and surely no one from Menos ever should. And now she had said too much. She struggled to think on her feet. "Never *mind* this burden. It's just a medicine ball that I carry around for my arthritis. Enchanted, you see, to numb the pain. A little rub—" She fondled the sphere and immediately the Mind began blathering in her head. She quickly removed her hand. "Ooh, such a relief."

The woman's strained appearance spoke of anything save relaxation, and Skar had never heard of giant enchanted balls being used as succor for aches and pains. Either these Eodians were full of queer contrivances, or she was full of shite. "If you say so. No matter. If you don't want to hold him, I suppose I shouldn't take up any more of your time. I should get back to my friends. My name's Skar, by the way."

"Lowelia."

"Pleased to meet you. Glad that we no longer have to draw blades for each other's throats."

"Hammers, in your case."

With nothing more to say, and Skar's stare making her uncomfortable, she gave him the arched eyebrows universally understood to mean *Anything else?* An awkward, tight-lipped smile was to be his parting gesture, until Ian pulled at Skar's leather tunic, twisted in the man's arms, and had the closest thing to a tantrum his caregiver had ever seen from the child. Ian squirmed as if he meant to leap from Skar's embrace if he wasn't given what he wanted: Lowelia, inexplicably.

"Settle down, lad!" said Skar. "Move that medicine ball aside, Miss, you've giving a cuddle, approved or not."

Pushing the Mind to her side like a third breast, she made room to cradle the child. Indeed, her body recalled how to do so, even from decades past, and she fought against that surfaced memory, and the one of her murdering this child's mother, and eventually the horrifying, humbling sense of penance as the wriggling child was laid—now deathly still—in her arms. They stared at each other: eye to eye, heart to heart. Ian's pudgy fingers caressed her forearm, as if writing the words she needed to hear, the words he couldn't speak: *I forgive you.* Tears slipped from her, and she brushed them away with the back of her hand. Sensing the solemnity of the man hovering over her, she said, "It's magnificent to have found this life for which to care in such a dark time. My emotions run away with me. Do pardon."

Ian reached up and her tear-wet fingertips touched his. The child looked at her with a knowing she felt she imagined. Any other notion was untenable, though she nearly sobbed.

"You have quite a way with him," said Skar, suspicion in his voice.

"I had a child once."

That explained her manner and was a sadness familiar to Skar. He sighed. "As did I. Children. Two of them, as a matter of fact."

"I should let you take him back to his new family." Ian was returned to Skar's sling, and Lowelia stood and kissed the small creature once he was settled there.

"Thank you, little man." She pinched Skar's arm. "Thank you, too, big man."

She walked out of the Chamber of Echoes, mist and light dissolving her into a ghostly figment. Ian stirred and burbled something in her direction, and Skar almost thought of running after her and asking the queerest question—whether she'd known the babe's father or mother.

IX

Released from the furor of the Chamber of Echoes, Beauregard and his new family ambled down the flagstone steps, each nearly a small landing, carved as if for Brutus's mighty stride. They took their time chatting and admiring the beauty of the shining men and the lavishness of the natural pillars and broad tunnel around them. Surely the four dawdlers were a hindrance to the harried warmasters and sages from the meeting who rushed past them like an angry school of fish. Rowena had found somewhere else to be instead of tagging along as had been casually suggested. Where Maggie had gone, no one could say. The family had lost her in the throng of hurrying people, and she'd made no attempt to stay with them.

Given their lyrical hearts, and the clue of Alastair's dour expression when Beatrice asked after the woman's whereabouts, the brothers knew that she probably would not be returning to their fold—at least not for a time. Nonetheless, she had served a great purpose in bringing them all together, and none believed that she would betray their confidence. Hopefully whatever wound there was between Maggie and Alastair might one day be healed. It was a shame that she was to miss the feast that Alastair had spoken of during the summit. As the shadow of war loomed ever closer, they had decided that festivities couldn't wait. If they postponed the opportunity for joy, then they could be too busy with funerals next week. Such thoughts found their way into Beauregard's mind more often than the others, and his father caught him frowning.

"What's the matter, lad?" he asked, sounding slightly unsure about his tone, kindness, and term of reference.

"Lad is fine, Father." Beauregard nudged him with a shoulder. "Although you're a second father, really—I shan't forget my first. Speaking of names: what should I call *you*, by the way? I'm still much more familiar with Alastair than Stevoch, and I think we'll only confuse others by calling you your oldest name."

"My oldest name..." mused Alastair. "I've had many names, almost as many as these damned Dreamers."

"How many names?" asked Galivad.

"Yes, how many?" Beatrice, hanging off his arm, leaned in to hear. She only knew of three: Stevoch, Lucien, Alastair.

Alastair grinned from ear to ear. "Too many, of villains, lovers, poets, and thieves. I have been to every continent on our world, from the Isles of Terotak to the shores of Pandemonia."

His company gaped, and he continued.

"In case the thought had crossed your mind: I wasn't being a coward—not going along for Morigan's cursed adventure. I wasn't permitted to go, by the one whom I serve." Candid and raw, his eyes welled with tears and his voice cracked. "She's allowed me to be here, with my family, with my truest name, and all my secrets stripped from me like million-ton shackles."

A quick sniffle and he became himself again. He addressed Beauregard.

"Regarding names, my second son, I'd have to sit down and make a list. I'll need some wine, as well. Why not wait for the feast, where drink will loosen my tongue and make me spill the sordid legends of my past? I have nothing to hide—not anymore."

And so, mulling Alastair's legends and alter egos, and this mistress he so often referenced, the four wended through a palace of mostly miserable and preoccupied people. Although for those who saw them, a glimmer, a light—possibly just Beatrice's ghastly whiteness—seemed to halo the four and inspire in those onlookers a sense of momentum. As though they should fight and love as much as these four, who clearly were one another's champions. A shrewd person, or one of second sight, might have seen a dark-haired woman and not a lady of ice and cruelty surrounded by her various beaus.

In much the same effervescent wind, they came to the White Hearth. Servants looked up from their dolesome duties, maids ceasing their sweeping to study the four shining, jubilant persons who acted so gaily while the world around them churned into a bog of war. Envious yet approving, the servants watched the summer spirits haunt the empty chamber as they drifted to seats and made merry, as if the hall was full of musicians rather than the lone downcast gent picking at a lute. Even he, however, was affected by their presence, and soon plucked out a song to match a few notes so harmoniously sung by the palest of the visitors. Once the music had wound its way through the kitchen and could be felt by the charwomen as tickles on their skin, in the beat and bubble of their soups and the slicing of their knives, the mood of the White Hearth changed completely. Such was the power of Belle's spirit, of a Romanisti prince and their sons. United, it was as if they held the sway of the Immortal King, as though their levity had enchanted the land and beasts around them. Servants flocked to them, stealing moments of their bliss as they poured for and tended to the family of nymphs.

Music found Tabitha as she peeled carrots in a large stone sink. She wasn't as awestruck by the distant noise as the whistling fools with whom she shared the counter; she recognized Beauregard's voice. Creeping around the cluttered islands and chirruping staff, she came to the archway leading from the kitchen and peered into the hall. Indeed, her son was there, along with that shadowbroker—a conman, she felt—a lady of Menos, and his brother.

When had this happened? Since when did they meet and share bread and strange company? The distance between Tabitha and her son had begun in Bainsbury, and their appointments with king and country had stolen the moment of their reunion. For she had duties now, too, just like her son. However, the seedy aspect of two-thirds of Beauregard's company couldn't be pardoned. She had raised him better than to associate with harlequins and snotty aristocrats. If nothing else, her poor mothering was to blame.

Wanting no more of it, she dusted her hands off on her apron, and stormed down the long hall to their table—and it was a *long* hall. She seemed to forget the breadth of it each time she made the crossing, which was often since being named acting Mater of the White Hearth. Even if the appointment had been dubiously granted with secondary motives attached, she came upon the singing, laughing fools with the force of a woman who'd helmed the White Hearth since birth.

"What are you four doing? A war waits outside our doors, and this is no time for revelry."

"It is the very time, my dear." Alastair raised a glass, swishing a little in his chair and swimming in the eyes from liquor. "I'll be drinking as the ship goes down under the waves, if that's how it is to be."

"Mother?" hissed Beauregard, angrily. "What are you doing here?"

The young man's venom threw Tabitha off balance, as did the hard gazes of all three men she'd come to reprimand or disrupt—she wasn't sure which. It was Beatrice, smoothed of her cruelty by a smile, who mended the broken air.

"Please, join us," she said. "I have wanted to meet Beauregard's mother—foster mother—for some time, though that opportunity has never been afforded to either of us."

Had she? Why ever did she want to meet? Numbed by a gnawing fear, Tabitha sat on the same side of the table as the rogue and her son, facing her nephew and the icy woman.

"I am sorry," said Beauregard, turning to her. "I was surprised to see you. It's been weeks since Bainsbury, and we haven't seen each other much, and, well..."

"We should have talked earlier," admitted Tabitha. "I thought you'd given up on me, now that you found—" she almost blurted out the secret that only Beauregard should say.

Beauregard smiled at his brother. "We have no secrets here, Mother. Or we were in the process of casting out the last of them when you arrived. Galivad knows who he is, and who I am to him. Perhaps now you should know the truth, too. It is fate that you've arrived here and now; I can think of no other agency. It is fate that you've come to see the story of your family come full circle: nephews, sons, our father, and your sister."

"Your father? My sister?" exclaimed Tabitha.

Her son beheld her sadly, then looked around the table for consent, which was given. Alastair seemed quite sober, all of a sudden. Beauregard pointed out the obvious. "Our father is here; a process of elimination should tell you who he is."

Sheepish and shy, Alastair wriggled his fingers in a wave.

"You fuking scoundrel!" shrieked Tabitha, and were her son not a buffer of peace between their two bodies, she would have lunged for the shadowbroker. Instead, she shook a fist at him. "Do you know what you put her through? Belle? Do you have any idea her hurt and loss? The madness, the sadness, she suffered that made her give up her son?"

"I do," replied Alastair, so staid that it sapped her anger. "I offer no excuses. I was a scoundrel. I still am. Although I am trying to make amends...to my sons, to your sister."

"My sister is dead," snapped Tabitha, again alive with fury, "without even the decency of having her bones to bury. Now the changelings in Willowholme probably use the tombstone over her empty grave as a scratching post."

"Death is not as eternal as we believe," said Beauregard. "There are shades to life and death. There are long swaths of the ether where those not quite moved on loiter and reach out. Your sister is with us. Look around at this table and see who among us that might be."

As if compelled by a nekromancer, she performed an excruciating examination. Her neck moved in degrees, her eyes lingering in the space between bodies, trying to remain locked on a candelabra of crystal—anything to delay the ticking twist of her observance as it went from her son to Alastair's remorseful face, to Galivad's golden comeliness, and finally to the ghostly pale woman who was, in a ripple, a fair and dark beauty. When Tabitha blinked her sudden tears, the tormenting illusion faded, though the power of what she had seen did not.

"Belle?" she whispered, and thrashed her head from side to side as if to cast out insanity. Surely, that's what she'd experienced—a temporary fugue and emotional catalepsy stirred by some trait of her sister she subconsciously perceived in Beatrice.

Then, on the other side of the table, the spirit within the monster rose, surfacing again in the haze between realms, indistinct in the mist of Tabitha's renewed weeping as Beatrice, now enveloped in a wavering, black-haired silhouette, sang for her sister "The Wheat and the Barley"—the song she had sung with Galivad as a child, and well before that, the tune she had sung with her sister. Tabitha collapsed into ruin in the arms of her son. Those around her who had already gone through the agony of seeing their dead in the body of another waited for her to take that first unsteady step toward acceptance.

A strong woman, she made that stride quickly and nudged herself out of her son's arms, looked to the once-more light and fearsome lady, and asked, "How? How can you commune with her like that? What are you, a medium? A peddler of spirits? I shan't be lining your pockets just so you can exploit my grief with cantrips and hope. Is that what you've been doing with my son, and my nephew?"

Alas, there was no rationalizing the transcendent. Faith was her only respite—faith in what her heart said, and in her son's words that this was indeed her sister. Tabitha reached across the table for Beatrice and their hands came together, laced at the fingers, as they had when they were young, and their house had been filled with sunshine and the songs of their mother—who'd raised them apart from another flyaway rogue like Alastair.

It was her. Kings be damned, Belle was within this Menosian woman. Still, Tabitha's amazement faded as holding Beatrice's hand became unbearable after a time; she was as cold as a mountain spring. How could she be that cold? Moreover, how had she communed with, or somehow become, her sister?

"Questions stir in your mind," said Beatrice, as their hands separated. "I shall tell you this: I see impressions from beyond. I am a creature not entirely of flesh and blood, but of spirit. I know that doesn't tell you all that you wish to know, but the whole truth is a pill of thorns, and you've only just pricked yourself on the rose of our relationship. Allow that wound to heal before I tell you"—*that I ate your sister*—"how dark things were before this light we now see."

Tabitha, fearing there was a dreadful twist to her sister's end that she would one day need to face, knew to leave the miracle there for the moment. Today was already thick with revelations, and she needed to maintain some decorum as the Mater of the White Hearth; she saw now that her outburst had made the lonely bard and a few other servants gather around nearby tables like curious hens.

She stood, clapped, and barked them into action with gusto. Life appeared to be one great winding ring of energy upon which souls danced, were lost, and found their way again. Thinking on all things benevolent that hadn't been on her mind when she came to the table, she bowed to them all and prepared to leave. Eod needed her. Checking her chronex, which she pulled from her apron on its chain, she realized that she only had fifteen sands to make her appointment with Dorothy.

"Perhaps tonight we can all gather," she suggested. "As incredulous as this day, and moment, has been, I don't have the sands to spare now, though I'd like to sit and be a part of this...reunion."

"Are you sure you must go?" asked Beauregard, and she nearly succumbed to his charms.

"Absolutely. Eod needs me."

Beatrice gave her a smile that wrenched her heart, and Tabitha forced herself to leave.

"That was a tad mysterious," said Alastair, once the woman had made her dashing exit from the White Hearth. "Oh, well, more drink for me." He reached across the table for the nearest decanter.

"It's good that she knows," said Galivad, grinning. "And good that I have an aunt."

"I feel blessed to have a sister," mumbled Beatrice.

Small fires lit her body, and her face felt dappled in sweat. She believed this was familial love: the furnace of forever, finally stoked in her dead chest. It was different from the cold rush of passion that ran through her as she and Moreth played together. Different, too, from the softer chill of his romantic whisperings, which stirred behind her breasts a flutter and across her neck a rash of prickling flesh. This was heat. She had never known heat before, only variations of cold. Grinning along with her son, she thought of having a glass of the wine Alastair was so jealously guarding as he started rattling off all his names again. While he hadn't arrived at any truly salacious former personalities, there were a few names she had to reach back through memories of her old library to remember. How old was he? When had the tale of the Romanisti wanderer begun? She asked him that.

The men looked at her, puzzled. She asked again.

"Beatrice?"

Who was that who'd addressed her? It was as though the sounds around her were being suffocated under watery cotton—squelching and distorted. She shook her head; perhaps the wine was having an effect. She rarely drank. Only as her glass tipped over, lost from the shaky grip of her hand, did she realize that Alastair hadn't poured her any libations as of yet.

Once again the heat sizzled inside her, and this time, she wasn't mistaking it for love. She pulled at her lacy dress, which wasn't heavy enough to swelter even the most delicate of waifs. But she was wet, and soon heaving, then retching monstrously as the heat—a bulbous vomit of it, a cluster of hemlock and thorns—started to shudder its way up her torso, throwing her into violent convulsions, and she spattered their glorious feast in sick. After, she wiped her mouth, as a lady should, before deliriously mumbling an apology. As soon as the heat was expelled from her body, it began a second time, and the fiery wave drowned her in such nausea that she fell.

Faces and voices folding in and out of her vision. Something terrible had happened to her body and faculties. A waxy film covered her head, and her limbs wouldn't respond beyond sluggish twitches. At last she heard from her old lover and her boys that she was going to be fine.

Fine...even though she had thrown up gallons of steaming ichor, then been wracked with seizures and fallen into a semi-catatonic state without warning. They lied—as family does, for hope, for a miracle—and told her she'd be well.

Their pleasing lies were a blanket she wore with her into the cold well of darkness that awaited her.

X

Tabitha Fischer sat in one of the hundreds of hidden gardens hollowed out in Kor'Keth, waiting for her accomplice. This garden had the look of a domed arboretum, with stained glass panels of knights battling spiraling lizards on a backdrop of emerald and white glass. It was stunning, and it swallowed up one's thoughts to behold the relief, which wound all around the dome until it met with a golden-green trellis of honeyvine, a name as sweet as the plant that dripped syrup off which the bluebirds and fat insects fed. Poor confused things, to have been lured and tricked so far into this rock edifice by enchantment and artificial photosynthesis.

She felt confused, and sick with secrets. Two rows of statues of half-naked warriors watched over the garden and its quiet pools, and she was glad that their stoic stares did not fall upon her. She'd sat on the shadiest bench she could find, which was still ablaze in light, and agonized over her many troubles: the deterioration of her relationship with Beauregard, Devlin's death, the end of the world. They melted together and flooded her mind in an effluvium of images. Each toxic memory made her twitch: the smashing of her son's face by Gustavius's fist, and the mist of blood that had hit her dress; the vision of Lake Tesh, brown and soiled as a chamber pot; the beauty of King Magnus, somehow distorted into a frigid, leering man of pure rage. Last came the memory of a sniveling man, then the ineffable sound of blade cutting living meat. She had turned her head to avoid seeing it, but the sound would never leave her. At least there was one bright beacon: her sister had returned...sort of.

"Fate for your thoughts?"

Any other person not dwelling on murder and resurrection would have noticed Dorothy's approach; as it was, Tabitha leapt a little in her seat. Dorothy closed her parasol—Tabitha didn't know why she carried it indoors anyway—and sat next to her comrade in espionage. "Mr. Specs has asked me to tell you that the man who you flushed out had been a spy in the Iron empire for over a decade, and that at least twenty known murders have been traced back to him."

"Mr. Specs" was the moniker they used for Rasputhane, for whom Dorothy acted as an intermediary. They were never to use his name, since the agents of Menos, enduring as roaches in an apocalypse, had survived the fall of their nation and risen again, even fatter on the crumbs of chaos, and were now infesting Eod's every wall. Not only had the Iron Queen's spy network been revitalized, it was far more organized without what seemed, in retrospect, oversight and possible mediation from the Watchers. The Iron Eye was *seeking*.

Archives had been raided in the Court of Ideas. Sages were missing, leaving the telltale red trails indicating they hadn't simply fled into the night. Names and residences from the past were being burgled, including Lowelia's home, and those of others tied to the king and court. It was under the shadow of this subterfuge that Rasputhane had sought out new agents, fresh blood and faces who wouldn't be noticed by the Iron Eye so vigilantly set on Eod. To his service, he had conscripted Dorothy, and she listened in boudoirs for the secrets gossipy and influential women often let leak while having their gowns hemmed.

Shortly thereafter, Tabitha had been approached by Dorothy, on a day and in a moment not unlike this one. There had been a bench as well as convivial conversation that turned suddenly serious regarding duty, loyalty, and the lengths people went to for justice. Could Tabitha go that distance? Did she have the strength? Believing herself brave, feeling lost without her son, she had jumped at the opportunity. In the days that followed, she had felt useful and purposeful at a time when order was being hurled and shattered like ceramic in a madman's kitchen. To be positioned for secret stealing, she had been given a relatively high-standing role in the White Hearth, deemed qualified by her experience as a magistrate, however brief, and necessitated by Mater Lowelia's absence. And servants were a font of secrets; they heard the stories their masters too often let slip in their domestic, dismissible presence. With Tabitha's insertion into the White Hearth, a place that had always been a nexus of subterfuge, the hall had been restored to its purpose.

Tabitha's job had been to observe and to report, and to pass those findings to Dorothy when they met for a garden chat on the Threesday of every week. What had never entered Tabitha's mind was that espionage was not a clean and tidy business. Blood inked the ledgers of spymasters, and Rasputhane's would be no exception. When they hauled away one of her kitchen staff—a man she'd reported as having suspicious comings and goings only the day before—she hadn't been feigning her fright for the benefit of her serfs; she was sincerely alarmed. Demanding to know his fate, she'd followed the prisoner and the Silver Watch into the darkened hollows of Kor'Keth.

The watchmen let her come, and as they wended deeper and deeper into mossy places that thickened the breath from fear, their armor seemed tarnished by darkness—dull and not glorious, and foreshadowing what she was to see. She found Rasputhane there, in a rocky cell so pitiless that no screams would ever reach the people above. With him was the man she had turned in, a man named Thomas. There had been a table, too, laid with silver prongs, vises, pliers, and other implements. By then, her consciousness and memory had begun to flicker as teeth, fingernails, flesh, and other bits of Thomas—the betrayer, the spy, the villain, she'd chanted to herself—were removed. Scabs had formed over what would become this memory. But she remembered the gurgle, the hiss, and the *final* cut once no more information could be extracted from his shuddering pink flesh. She had not been able to look at the heap he'd become, though she'd been forced to look upon Rasputhane—a man so red with blood he would need to douse himself under a waterfall before he could be seen by civilized man again. Down there, however, he had been a monster, and the one to whom she'd serviced herself.

"You've done well," he'd said. "You're brave to wish to see your work through. Now tell the others at the White Hearth that Thomas has been incarcerated for his betrayal—do not speak of his end. Go on."

She'd fled. And while she didn't use Rasputhane's name out of necessity for subterfuge, it was also because she wondered if he could be summoned, like a gory boogeyman, by the whisper of his mention.

"Mr. Specs can pontificate till he's blue in the face," Tabitha said, after an enormous stillness, "though that doesn't change what I've done."

"You did your duty."

"I led a man to his death."

"A spy, not an innocent man." Dorothy took her hand as if to console her; appearances were deceiving, however, and behind the gentleness of the gesture was a terrible strength that made Tabitha stiffen. "In war you'd best stop thinking in such terms. You were a charwoman and housewife, as I remember from our less clandestine conversations. After which, you were put in charge of your city for a while, weren't you?"

"Willowholme..." She winced from what Dorothy supposed was a jagged memory. "I was, yes."

"In that appointment, was there never a moment of life and death upon which your decision held the balance? Not once?"

"Back when Brutus first revealed his terror," she muttered, "the king came to Willowholme. At the king's suggestion, I migrated my people from Willowholme to Bainsbury. I thought we'd be safe, though they died there. They would have died if we'd stayed in Willowholme, too—damn wolves on two legs, changelings, infested the place. I imagine they're coming to eat what's left of Eod after the war. I don't see what difference I made with my *choice*. I just led my people to a different grave. I saved my Beau, I suppose. Horrible as it is, I'd choose him over a village any day."

"Are you and Beauregard still on good terms?" asked Dorothy.

"Hmm...Yes. Perhaps better than ever, though I don't know where to begin to explain what's happened." She smiled, and tears trembled in her eyes. "But we haven't come to talk about that."

"No, we have not. Although, remember that you kept your son alive with your choice—that one life is a difference. Moving on, I trust you got my letter the other day? Tell me what you've learned."

"Right."

After the incident with Thomas, things had been quiet for a day or two, and secretly she had hoped that Mr. Specs would never again call upon her. However, that wasn't to be the case. Yesterday she'd been awoken by the sound of Beauregard rattling about in his chamber, and for a moment wrestled with the impulse to race out and talk to him. As she'd hurried to the door, she nearly tripped on a note. But not from the weight of it, obviously, but rather from its simple silver ribbon and starched folds—like a beautiful and deadly present. It had been a letter from Dorothy, and she had hurried back to her desk to decode the message encrypted beneath the list of needed supplies (the Mater of the White Hearth was dispenser and stockwoman for most everyone in the palace—including the new Royal Seamstress).

She had first decoded her instructions, wherein the letter's real contents, originally dictated to Dorothy as a line of code she would sew while patching Rasputhane's ratty trousers, was then translated into a name, place, or clue. The information Tabitha had received had been quite direct in this instance: a neighborhood, a corrupt silver watchman, and an unforeseen adventure.

XI

Not all of Eod was white; there were places where its pearl wonder had been tarnished, where the virtuous thin air that made those above delirious with their peaceful ideals wasn't shared with the grimy, unruly folk below. Indeed, not only were the people of Cheshire Street filthy, but they wallowed in their wantonness. They'd pissed on the idea of using Eod's great circle of commerce—the Faire of Fates—and hawked goods, or themselves, from whatever corner wasn't the site of a street-pugilist match. Animals wandered the lane, frequently without a minder: sprinrex, goats, and seemingly wild dogs that growled at passersby. Nearly every building puffed smoke and echoed with guffaws, indicating that witchroot, ale, and likely more sinful pleasures were available within.

In places like these, Tabitha had known to keep a shawl wrapped around her face and a hand upon her purse. One blessing was how easy it was for her to spot the tidy serf, still wearing his livery from the palace, perhaps to grant him safe passage, as even here it would be begrudgingly respected. She followed the man amidst the crowd. She kept good distance and did what she'd been told: follow, wait, observe. She wasn't to pursue the man beyond Cheshire Street, and she was amazed at the foresight of the spymaster to have predicted—or known—that the serf would come to this neighborhood. Thus, she stalked the serf until he finished his trip through the boroughs. A few of his stops at taverns demanded that she behave like a patron, and she threw herself into the duty, perhaps having more to drink than was wise.

At dusk the man left Cheshire Street and hopped into a carriage. She should've hailed one, too, though she'd been curious—perhaps because of the drink—to know why the man had stopped for a sand in what appeared to be a technomancer's shop, a tall building tinged with mechanical smoke and a profusion of puffing chimneys stuck like orchestra horns to its sides. Every other interaction the Menosian spy had undertaken was a meeting, the swapping of information, or pocketing of letters. Her instincts on his actions at the atelier told her this was different. The serf had left the shop in a bother—either very excited or very upset by whatever had occurred inside.

"Mr. Specs will be displeased that you disregarded his order," said Dorothy.

"Will he? Not when he hears what I found out from the chatty engineer who ran the atelier," countered Tabitha.

Inside the establishment, she had woven through a graveyard of gears, overburdened tables, struts, metal helixes, glass tubes filled with sparks, gases, and queer lights. Not knowing much of technomagik, she'd stared at each object as if it were the relic of an alien museum. A partially mechanical dog had leapt from the junkyard mess—its hind legs and jaw glistening, smooth and bolted—and startled her as it snatched up her skirt and pulled her as if she were the pet.

She presumed she wasn't going to be eaten, and indeed, it brought her through the maze toward a man. He was bald, husky, wore goggles, and was as peppery of hair and skin as the ashes in which he played. With one half of his vocation being smithing, he toiled at a forge: a kiln-like furnace with a flat iron table lip upon which was strewn wires, hoses, and sputtering apparatuses indecipherable in their purpose. Cursing, the technomancer threw down something that looked like a sheet-metal octopus, and it crinkled and died as such cephalopods do, albeit with more fire and sparks. When he noticed Tabitha being herded by his pet, he apologized, summoned the growling animal to his side, and introduced himself.

"Bill Balroch," he said, in a voice as hard as his dog's bark.

Although, his body didn't match his demeanor, and aside from the startling disarray of his workshop, the engine grease he wore as cologne, and his half-living beast that never stopped growling, Bill turned out to be a pleasant man and, she learned, wise and respected in his field. He was also pleased to have a lady's company, which didn't happen often, and he cleared a heap of his junkyard dwelling to reveal a couch, upon which he and Tabitha sat and drank tea in beggarly tin cups. She managed to pry from his lips that the previous customer had been in to inquire about the making of a part. However, he wouldn't betray his client's trust more than that—the serf had been a servant of the palace, to which he'd be forever loyal. Tabitha couldn't blame the drink for what she then decided to do: tell him that she'd been tailing that man, and that he was in fact not servant to the king, but was, rather, a squawking, squealing crow of the Iron Queen.

"Good Kings!" Back in the garden, Dorothy reeled as though she'd been slapped, then darted her eyes around the placid garden and hissed. "You're a terrible spy!"

"One of the worst, probably. I don't like to lie."

"Mr. Specs will be furious, twice over. He could have extracted the intel from your target, or your target's target. Why did you do that?"

Tabitha threw up her hands. "What does it matter? The intrigue? We either stop that mad king, the Dreamers, and what Gloriatrix has planned for our final apocalypse, or that's it, we're doomed. I know of Mr. Specs's methods of extraction, too, and I'll have no more part in that. If I'm to gather information—intel, whatever the cloak-and-dagger term may be—I'll do it my way: honorably and through discussion. That's always been my way."

"Fine. What did he say? I hope it was worth the danger in exposing yourself and in risking the wrath of Rasputh—I mean, Mr. Specs." Dorothy grunted. "Bother, fuk, and damn, now you've ruined my composure."

"Two terrible spies are better than one." Tabitha smiled. "Or worse, I suppose. Moving along, the man whose workshop I'd entered wasn't simply any garden-variety technomancer, he was the descendent of Deville Balroch, the famed royal technomagikal engineer."

"Means nothing to me," admitted Dorothy.

"Nor to me, until Bill—lovely man, really, once you dig past the grease and bearishness—told me of his esteemed family history and ties to the palace. Which, mind you, he wouldn't have done had I not blown my cover. 'Twas all part of the plan."

Dorothy rolled her eyes.

"I continued the, err, extraction or what have you, and learned that his forefather's forefather, the technomancer I mentioned, was among those commissioned to build the Hall of Memories."

"The Hall of Memories?"

"Indeed, it's not older than time itself, as the king or legends would tell you. In fact, it's only several centuries old, I learned, and building it took decades and minds and hands far beyond those of the king to build it. Devlin..." A frown stalled her speech—she shook it off. "Slip of the tongue, sorry. *Deville* Balroch was actually lead on the project. I learned all about it; quite an illuminating conversation. Bill reminds me so much of my old bear, though he's dark, like you. Oh my, that made me sound so colonial. I like brown people. Oh dear, that sounded worse. You know what I mean. I'll stick to telling my story."

Dorothy was doing her best not to laugh while discussing the volatile subterfuge of her nation, though the task was becoming impossible. Was it wrong to find a bit of mirth in the end of the world? Why not, when madmen and Immortals were busy having their own version of fun?

"Yes, stick to your story," she said sternly; then her façade broke with a smile and a cackle in which Tabitha joined. Soon they were in hysterics, conjured from the grotesque sum of the agonies and secrets they'd borne these past weeks, clinging to and pawing at each other like drunkards who'd forgotten the joke.

Once their laughs faded to happy wheezes, and they regained their composure, Tabitha resumed. "Yes, so Bill, lovely brown Bill, spent hourglasses of his evening poring over his family crests, letters, and tomes. He's quite organized with those, unlike with his workspace. We did a bit of sleuthing on our own, now that we were of the same mind—stopping Gloriatrix—and now that we knew what she wanted: a *telemetric harmonizer.*"

"What's that?" asked Dorothy, befuddled.

"No idea!" replied Tabitha, and they howled anew. "Humph, huh. Allow me to catch my breath. I do have some idea, actually, as Bill tried to explain it to me. A telemetric harmonizer was one of the fundamental tools created for the Hall of Memories, which 'allowed the transference of one soul's imprint into the technorganic matrix.' Or something quite similar, or radically different from what I've said. Regardless, Gloriatrix wants it. Bill and his family are among the only technomagikal engineers still alive who could probably make it. Indeed, the serf inquired about notes, to which Bill told him—and me—that all his notes were kept here." She tapped her temple. "If he'd kept a diary or the like, I imagine poor Bill would've been lying dead on the floor when I came in. Even worse, he might have made the damn thing, handed it over to that rat in a silver waistcoat, and then had his throat slit for his efforts. We know how these games of cloak-and-dagger end: with the dagger in someone. I'd take the wager against Bill, as sweet as he was."

"It was good of you"—Dorothy clasped the woman's knee—"to have warned him, and to have discovered what you did. I don't quite know what a telemetric harmonizer is, but we must find out. Perhaps Bill should be summoned to the palace. I don't think this can wait. Mr. Specs must be told, all of this, at once."

Tabitha paled. She had seen a side to Rasputhane that she never wished to see cast in her direction: a demon of blood and pain.

Dorothy gave her a quick hug; that, as well as the sentiment next expressed, calmed Tabitha's fear. "Not to worry, I'll come with you. I shall see that you do not suffer for what was ultimately a clever decision...We terrible spies have to stick together."

✳ ✳ ✳

XII

Purest ebon was the chamber of the Iron Queen: bed, chairs, vanity, and settee, all thrown in a sheet of shade too deep to have been naturally conjured. The shadows crawled as living, leeching things—hungry for any scrap of light. How this pleased her, at last, to have something of her desires. Even here, in the splendid heart of Eod, she had managed to make a grim sanctum for herself, and she rocked in her chair. Elsewhere, a single bead of light, too sad to be called a fire, struggled against the gripping dark. A man lingered by the mantel, though he was as faded as this reality in Gloriatrix's thoughts.

Weeks earlier, while Magnus lay recovering, she and Gustavius had caught a sorcerer, one of those who pruned and tended the rapaciously grown star trellis that irritated her with its radiance. Eod's minders and serfs often made quick exits from her presence—its Silver Watchmen, too. But these sorcerers, practically castrated from being great men into circus magikians who trimmed underground vegetation all their lives—like boggarts or some lowly creatures in the faery hierarchy—were especially squirrel-some. The minders always ran away from her, actually ran, unlike the harried step of a servant or Silver Watchman. It was a miracle, then, that Gustavius had caught one in a long-abandoned hallway. Gustavius had shaken him from his ladder as if he were a stubborn apple unwilling to fall, wrangled the man into an arm lock, and brought him, weeping, before his queen to answer one of her greatest vexations: "How do I turn the damn lights down?"

Such a simple question, with a likewise plain solution: a rod of feliron could be pointed at the offending trellis with one of two spoken commands, *fos* or *skotadi*, and the light would surge or abate, respectively. One didn't even need to be a sorcerer, as the rods were enchanted and as independently capable as any technomagikal device. Alas, a greater power than these metal rods controlled the overall biosphere of the palace and regulated its general levels of light and dark; for that ultimate protocol, oversight came from the omnipresent network of thought, magik, and technology that was the Hall of Memories. Magnus would have had her and the world convinced that the Hall of Memories was a sad theater for his soulful reflections. However, she knew better, knew many secrets about that great living machine that powered Eod, and so she played dumb and even interested as the blathering tender—also ignorant of greater intelligences—suggested that wider climate control was handled by a machine.

She had ordered the man released, and she stood for a while caressing the shadestick, as they were called. There she had stayed for some time, pondering, muttering "skotadi" and layering shadows over the hallway till it became a murky replica of the passages in her demented mind.

A machine...Magnus had purposely raised a kingdom of fools to protect his secrets. By then, and after the curiosity spawned during the horror show of witnessing the Mortalitisi empire, she had started one more casual subterfuge among her many to learn more about that chamber and the devices that comprised it. And the more she learned, the more her curiosity burned. For the Hall of Memories, the governing power that controlled the lights, operations, temperatures, climates, humidity, soil aridity—*everything*— within this vast biome, was not just a machine. It was the cerebral cortex of the organism that was the palace, sparked with an otherworldly power after having been deluged and infused with the thoughts, histories, and souls transferred into its matrix. How could Magnus not have known what he would create? Build the perfect vessel, fill it with life and memory, and the creature would be as alive as anything that came from combining ingredients and power within a womb.

The Hall of Memories...What was it, really? "Near infinite knowledge and power," was the layman's standard refrain, though it was a start for her ambitions with the *knowledge* bit. After coming into possession of her shadestick, threads had formed between many of the thoughts floating in her mind. Then, while meeting with the council in the Chamber of Echoes, where she spoke of war, strategies, and the hope of a new dawn, behind the curtain of her thoughts she thought of nothing but artificial cortexes, immense reserves of thought, and undying, self-sufficient machines that could control weather, time, and space—and of how to make those devices work for her. Even more tantalizing, she wondered how she might succeed them herself, with a mortal vessel and not one of feliron and glass. Could that majesty be transferred? Could a woman become an Immortal? Although it was the most lurid of her fantasies, it didn't seem that far out of her reach.

"Skotadi," she whispered, and felt a tingle of seductive power flow through the iron in her hand.

The shadows in her chamber thickened to black clots, and Gustavius, posted by the nearly swallowed fire, became an ebon gargoyle. He watched quietly and reverently as her lined face twisted with thoughts, her amethyst eyes glowed with malice, her torso hunched as if the secret in her mind was about to be given hideous birth. Soon, it was, he felt. In this last week, his queen had been restored to her vile majesty. Once this war ended, she would indeed be the future of Geadhain.

A soft knock came at the door. Gustavius didn't interrupt Gloriatrix's machinating and went to receive the message—the man was kept outside of the dark sanctuary himself. Gustavius quietly closed the door, then did a quick scouring of the room for peepholes, farseeing crystals, or any other means of espionage. It was a routine he undertook every hourglass of the day while in the queen's chamber. When the room passed his test—not that they'd moved from there all evening—he approached the Iron Queen and bowed.

"We have found a man and have requisitioned him to create the device."

"A telemetric harmonizer." With a menacing grin, the Iron Queen tapped his head with the shadestick. "The key to ascension." Her expression fouled. "Why is he creating the device? I want no tracks left that can be traced."

"I believe that his knowledge—the knowledge of the device's creator—was passed down to him through tradition and blood. No formula, as such, was kept, and the design is within the man's head. Such complex and ancient sciences are hardly left lying about or fiddled with for hobbies, either."

"I suppose," she conceded. "Though if we were back in Menos, I'd have that head taken and the secrets pulled out by my son's nekromancy. Alas, we're not in Menos, and my son seems stripped of his power. I don't know of what use he is to me then, since we'll still need a sorcerer, or sorcerers, even after the device has been acquired."

Pushing Gustavius away with her iron stick, she leaned back in her chair to think. She was glad Sorren had left them (to skulk about) so that she could connive without his creeping moralizations. Where would she find a sorcerer powerful enough, and sufficiently loyal to her, to perform the ritual of transference? And in such a short time? After all, the world was supposed to end in roughly two weeks. Assuming they averted that spin into the abyss, she had to have her strategy ready—every player and piece she needed—for that perfect moment of confusion, where victory had sapped the will to see enemies and where she could storm the Hall of Memories and claim what was so rightfully hers: an inheritance of divinity. She had decided that she'd become the new Dreamer, queen, or whatever title fell after these decrepit Immortals lost their arthritic grip on the world.

It was a maniacal idea, to act as a living vessel for the tides of eternity held in the Hall of Memories, and yet it was a birthright for which she was eminently suited. She knew now of Dreamers, of vessels, of how only the right flesh was chosen, and that the *Thule* flesh, the bloodline she'd scorned and even scoured from her legal name, was that inheritance. Sorren had explained to her more of his possession, of his invitation to the forces that slept in the universe to enter his body. Further to that, Gloriatrix plied his mind and his great, though mad intellect for more information, and he'd leaked out additional theories and notions that forged her fantasy into a terrifying vision.

We're made to serve them, Mother, he'd said. *It's in our blood. We are containers for their might, for any might, really. 'Tis where I gained my dark magik, where my uncle gained his. 'Tis the same well from which you draw your maleficent thoughts—which are power, too, Mother, and Will. And in that regard, you are the greatest sorceress of all. But we must be humbled by our power, not risen to vainglory by it. We must protect the world from the terror our gift can wreak.*

"And terror I shall wreak, my son," she whispered.

Even if she was wrong about her capacity to absorb the hall's power, even if she died during the ritual, the destructiveness involved in channeling such power would surely destroy Eod's greatest achievement—the Hall of Memories—along with her. At least she would die in infamy. If there was one way to leave this world, it wasn't quietly, but with a wail of death that would resound for a thousand years.

✳ ✳ ✳

XIII

"Rowena?"

Galivad had leapt up when the knock had come, expecting anyone to be at the door, save her. Hourglasses past, he and his brother had been asked to leave the black-sluiced abattoir that had become Beatrice's hospice. "Go home and sleep," someone had said, as if a man could do that after watching his mother—or whatever she was—spontaneously and ceaselessly bleed oil. Although, it wasn't really oil, it was the blood of a blood eater. The stanching of its flow seemed impossible for any surgeon or fleshsculptor on this side of Geadhain. They had spent so much time explaining Beatrice's uniqueness before she even began receiving treatment, a treatment that was as experimental as it was hopeless, for the physicians caring for her knew little of what was happening to her or why. They were terrified to touch her, too, when they heard what she was, though it was a mercy she never showed her fangs or claws during her thrashing delirium. Indeed, she seemed all woman and suffering, as if the monster had left or was leaving her. Perhaps that was simply the peace of her inevitable passing. Still, he couldn't lose his mother. Not again.

Rowena shook him. He'd been standing in the doorway, shivering, dressed in only an undershirt and linens, and clinging to its frame like a war widow having received news. "Galivad? What's the matter with you?"

"My mother is dying," he said, his lip trembling, his body shuddering as grief rampaged his insides.

She hadn't heard anything about anyone dying, as she had been tormenting herself all day, in seclusion, with thoughts of this meeting. But Rowena, regardless of whatever complexities led her here, or of what he meant to her, reacted to him as her body demanded: with love and concern. Her hard brown arms wrapped him up with strength. Then, lest he be seen weeping by passersby, she brought him inside his chamber and elbowed the door closed. He cried until some sense returned to him, pushing himself away slightly, though not out of her embrace, turning his puffy eyes to hers.

"You're probably wondering what I'm talking about. You're wondering how my mother could be dying, again. Or you're wondering if I've lost my mind."

Your mother is dead, she thought, and then once more considered that a spell of Beatrice's making had started rotting his brain. She stopped herself from asking after that concern. She resisted, too, the impulse to kiss his quivering lips. They hadn't been this close since Blackforge, and she had come here with a confrontation—possibly a passionate one—on her mind.

"Tell me, then," she demanded. "Tell me why you're weeping for a mother who, by your words, has been dead for over a decade. You hunted her killer in Menos, a killer with whom you now sup and stroll around the King's Garden. Tell me of this secret that you, the shadowbroker, the spellsong, and that woman all share because I cannot bear being left out in your cold."

With that confession, Rowena's face lost its steel edge, and her beauty was no longer sheer brawn and fury, but rather a comfort, a security into which one leaned, which Galivad did, drawing closer. She hadn't finished. "You locked me out, Galivad. After we'd been through an Age of Fire together, burned, ruined, and resurrected. Please, I cannot bear being without you anymore."

"Belle's not dead—not entirely."

Galivad's fierce assertion, and his sweaty, wincing behavior sent a chill up Rowena's arms, and she let go of him. Shrunken, he shuffled back to the cozy chair where he'd obviously been brooding: a foot-table strewn with cards, small piles of ashes, a pipe, a decanter, and a half-filled glass of liquor— some of which was spilled and being sopped up by crumpled wads of paper. *Has he been writing?* she wondered. Then, by the tangy scent of the air, and the opened patio doors to blow out the fumes, she guessed he had been smoking witchroot; his crimson eyes weren't wholly the result of tears. While she brought the stool from his vanity and joined him by his chair, he fixed himself another puff, pulling a folded paper packet from one of the seams in the cushions, shakily emptying the ashes onto the table, and packing the pipe.

Galivad appeared so familiar with the motions, and even with the mess he had made, that Rowena suspected this wasn't his first time; he had been down this particular path of self-degradation before. She remembered a few of his mutterings about the *things* he'd done, parts of his soul and body that he had sold, when in Menos. Shivering and cursing like a madman in the rain, the task of preparing his escape from this world taking all of his focus, he was oblivious to Rowena's looks of reprehension, or her scowls, or when she picked up the glass from which he'd been drinking and sniffed it: adderspit, from the anise waft. He was enjoying the best of all poisons, then, with which to imbibe.

"Did you want some?" he asked, finally noticing her. "Pipe or drink?"

"Neither."

Not caring, he picked up a fire-stone from the table and touched it to the green tuft sticking out of his pipe. A flicker and a smattering of sparks later, he leaned back, puffing, into his chair. Perfect concentric circles of smoke floated toward Rowena—the novelty of a man who was no novice with narcotics. She waved away the circles that came too near her face and coughed a little from the drug's cloying fumes. Now her disdain couldn't be hidden. Her handsome visage had become narrow-eyed, and the hand not protecting her from the smoke had curled into a fist. Witchroot was no summer solstice happy herb. It had a profound effect on the nervous system and a debilitating dependency could develop after only a few occasions of use. Its effects were both psychotropic and psychotic. Even a moderate dose could lead to hysterics, rage, hallucinations, and the death of oneself or others. It was banned in the palace and found only in the lowliest quarters of the city. She was disgusted.

"I can see you don't approve," he said with a staggering air of malaise. "It's the end of the world. Who gives a fuk about anything?"

"I never knew you had such a habit. I never knew you could be so—"

He snorted. "I'll spare us the indignity and stop you from finishing that sentence. The irony is that I haven't touched the herb, or anything stronger than wine, since that cliff of despair I fell off after Belle passed away. I lost her once, and it destroyed me. I can't lose her again...There will be nothing left. Nothing in my heart."

"Witchroot won't change what's happening...And I still need you to tell me what has brought you to so low a place."

"Why do you care?"

"I am here. I care," she said, with a softness that cut.

Galivad shifted, put down the pipe, and blew his last breath to the side without any fancy tricks. "I'm sorry," he muttered. "I can see that you do care—you care too much. For this world, for its children—"

"For you."

He froze at her honesty, from all that remained unspoken since the storm of emotions, politics, and never-ending adrenaline had swept them apart. With Beatrice dying, Rowena's rawness was too much for Galivad to bear. He was a delicate bard, a man of laughter and lace, and her confession coupled with her irresolute beauty was too harsh for his constitution. He'd wanted to escape tonight, not find further worries, even if the pit he had started digging was deeper than he had foreseen. It never mattered, though, once the heart-hammering rush of loathing, need, and dread filled his veins. Such nausea only precipitated the release, the sickening, spinning bliss.

Once more, the witchroot—laced with potent powders from the West—called, and he reached. However, Rowena's grip stopped him, bringing one hand, then the other, to rest palm to palm on hers. Galivad's fingers roamed and danced on the lines of her palm. Tears began to fall from his eyes, and while he wasn't sure of their cause, he allowed his grief to happen. Possessed by the same sense of liberation, the shedding of despair, he sniffled, babbled, and explained his feelings and their causes to Rowena.

She listened as the night grew darker. From time to time she rose from her seat and kissed him on the head, as though he were a man seeking a pardon from a Carthacian priest.

Before the hourglass was up, Rowena had learned everything the bard knew of Belle, her spirit, and the monster in which it slept. Galivad's family secrets were unearthed and scattered into the daylight. Lastly, she heard of the terrible fever that had overcome the Lady El this afternoon—a fever that the gore-drenched curtains cordoning off her potentially hazardous infection indicated was terminal. During his confession, Galivad reached for neither pipe nor tumbler; her touch was enough succor for his soul.

What Galivad had kept to himself, merely intimating, were the memories of himself piss-drunk and psychedelically delirious on witchroot, poppy's milk, and a million other substances as he wandered down the streets of Menos during the hunt for his mother's killer, before he'd discovered rage as the antidote for his addiction. What dark divides he had gone to then: semen-soaked bedrooms, whorehouses as rank as barns, slum pits glistening with blood and clattering with swinging chains. "Use me, abuse me, I am nothing!" had been the mantra by which he fed his black beast, and his black beast fed him the forgetful bliss of drugs. Indeed, he had allowed himself to be so violently taken that it'd been the holiest of miracles that he wasn't simply another nameless corpse in Menos. Such good fortune couldn't be repeated, and he had nearly tested the Fates again with his indulgences tonight.

"What is that tangle in your mind?" whispered Rowena. "I thought we had challenged and defeated your terrors."

The knot in his forehead relaxed, as he said, "You've brought me back from a very dark place, Rowena." He swept the papers, glasses, and the pipe onto the floor. A sudden golden roar of the fire stirred by the gust of his movement cast him in a transcendent light. Galivad's hands returned to the table, then, shyly, to Rowena's. "What was I thinking?"

"You were thinking that you wanted to escape." She held her breath, chewing on a thought before releasing it. "We all need a little escape from duty, from the weight of truth and darkness. I could free you of that weight, for tonight."

Galivad stiffened in his chair...then also in his shorts. It was clear, her offer. Rowena's hands, smooth as leather, glided over the silk of his skin, and she clasped his wrists and drew his hands across the table and onto her thighs. There, the bard's fingers felt the brawn and warmth of her legs. Still, Galivad was a gentleman, and his dishevelment and the faint body odor that came from him cooled the flame of his desire. So he coquettishly batted his eyelashes and excused himself so that he could freshen up. However, for Rowena, his scruff, his messy golden curls, and the scent of the man so often concealed under vanilla and feminine perfumes were new teases of this incubus. As he swirled past her, she lunged at him as if she were a lustful barbarian. They danced and tripped their way to his bed, whereupon their dance slowed even as their heartbeats thundered.

This was real, it was happening.

With that dawning came the wonder that would shut out thoughts of duty, dying mother-monsters, and the rise of a Black Queen. The world was ending, as he'd said, and if this was to be one of humankind's penultimate unions, if they were to die tomorrow and never have another taste of this passion, then they would make their love a force to burn, to be seen with the stars until the Black Queen ate the constellations. They understood the magnitude of this act past the complications of flesh.

And so their dance slowed further, their hands filled with the curiosity of their souls. Galivad took sands counting the lines around Rowena's eyes, the veins and ripples of her arms, the scars on her shaved head. Very few women could he say were handsome without implying insult, and yet she was the most handsome woman he'd seen. As beautiful as a feared general, as gorgeous as a maiden carved in stone. Once he'd undressed her of her heavy garments—each one removed like the wrapping of a treasured nameday present—he sniffed and tasted the nutty Arhadian oils in which she washed.

He followed her scent from the back of her ear, down her nape, across her unassuming, muscular tits, across her stallion-like thighs, and finally into the wet black mouth that awaited him. She tasted delicious there, too: of oil, sweat, and even the steel his extraordinary palate—or passion-swimming, slightly intoxicated brain—believed it detected. As if her flesh were of metal. But she wasn't all metal, or hardness, and he knew as he rose after eating her womanhood, and as they kissed and shared the scent of her together, that her mouth was as soft and pink as a rose.

Rowena had lost herself. Her mindfulness and vigilance lay shattered, and she was only a woman—a person without sex, really—as was Galivad the other half to her flesh. With that symmetry, they moved wetly against the other, fingers to holes, tongues to ears, cock, and slits. They rolled from the bed and wandered the chamber affixed by wet or hard parts. Once, they stood and admired each other with gasping pauses and entranced caresses upon where the firelight struck their shimmering bodies. He was so beautiful and golden in that moment that Rowena reached around and made love to Galivad with her fingers, swallowing his grunts, and later, bowing to take his spasms in her mouth. Come the pinnacle of their lust, they defaced his ivory chair with the sweat of their bodies as she straddled both man and furniture like a terrible huffing Immortal—a great shadow into which Galivad's prick had been lost—and he came once, then again, from the thrill of her passion.

They lay on the mess of the chamber floor as dawn rose, on a hazardous tangle of bedsheets, boots, cloaks, trash, and clutter. When passion such as theirs had been bottled up for so long, it either erupted with a whimper or a roar. Theirs had been a roar, and the purr of that beast continued in their chests as they rested against the edge of his bedframe—Galivad in his lady's strong arms, their legs twisted together, each body reeking of the other. She played with the only patch of chest hair the epicene man boasted, while he hummed her favorite song, the one about the girl and the falling star, into her neck. It was a moment of timelessness—one that would always be a part of their souls. They'd never been so happy.

"My mother," whispered Galivad, killing his tune and their contentment. "I know I am not permitted to see her, but I should at least check on her welfare." Suddenly, he was anxious and struggling to sit up. "I mean, surely they would have alerted us if she'd taken a turn?"

"Yes." Rowena kissed the man and pulled him back into her heat. "Please, ten sands. We've waited for this moment for what seems an eternity. Ten sands to remember."

One. Two. He turned to putty in her arms. Three. Four. He hummed their tune again. Five. Six. She inhaled their mingling perfumes of oil and vanilla. Seven. Eight. They nuzzled tight as winter cubs. Nine. Ten. Their hearts beat long, together and resoundingly. Beats so strong each of them felt the other's and woke, gaping, from the curious daydream into which they'd fallen.

It was possibly for the best; their heartbeats were their own, and their love was earthly and not divine. Rowena felt no loss in knowing this. There was one more thing she wanted to say, a final confession she wanted to make, without which this night would feel incomplete. As he slipped away and shuffled his golden flesh around the chamber, she told him, "I love you, Galivad."

From the sink in the corner, he turned, and the star-trellis showered him in light; the fire illuminated his lean masculine curves, his manhood, and turned to solid gold the wet ringlets caressing his shoulder. He was beauty, and he was hers. Galivad, her incubus, smiled at her, slyly, as if sharing a secret. "You are the piece of me that I'd lost. I shall never lose you again."

It felt like a vow, for his smile had waned, and she had stopped breathing while he'd spoken. Perhaps one didn't need to be immortal to know eternity. Mayhap a promise was enough.

PART II

X

THE WICKED TRUTH

The living dream of Brutus's fall from grace had consumed Adam and the others, and their minds were worlds away from their bodies—bodies trapped in a paralytic séance beneath the spires of the Cradle. They heard not the cries of the drakagor, nor sensed the looming enemy to the west. For they were under a spell of truth so potent that only death or the resolution of whatever Morigan wanted to witness could wake them.

Morigan, their spirit guide, had been reduced to an amorphous silver light, a star that floated ahead of those who followed. Now that they had witnessed the loss of Brutus's soul in the grave of Zionae, they pursued him across the phantasmagoric wilds of Pandemonia and into a twirling desert, a veiling soon pierced by the emergence of Aesorath, City of Screams—as foreboding as an ancient cathedral dedicated to a wicked Dreamer. No one could tell what was real and what was not, and they were to go further, deeper into this memory; they were to hunt the truth that made Morigan and her silver hive mad as dervishes for their secrets. Thackery, Moreth, Mouse, Talwyn, and Pythius were as lost and hungry for that knowledge as she.

Adam, however, remained himself. As much himself as could be defined by the white mist of his being, this phantom that blew faster than any wind through the sand-buried ruins and crumbling tunnels of Aesorath. Much beauty had once reigned here, though the remaining artifacts of glass and gold teased only a dazzle of their splendor from their dusty heaps. In the shelled-out towers through which they drifted, wind sang down from above, fluttering the strange snipped strings of glass that hung like ghostly moss. As they were so similar in appearance to the strings of an instrument, Adam guessed their purpose: Aesorath had been a city of music once, and these towers had resonated with song. No song was heard today but the dirge of sand, ash, and death that howled through ever more barren recesses.

There were no bones to be seen, just piles and piles of age. Only the rare remnant of civilization remained, such as a chisel or a golden harp dulled by sweeping sands. The desert had been wrathful in its reclamation of this land, and the entire lower quarter of the city had been entombed. Only in the higher elevations of the city, through which their windy forms soon blew, did Adam see more weary refulgence: the palisades and the bridges of burnished gold, whittled down by sandstorms; the honeycombed exteriors of the towers of glass threads; and once, a conical chamber chiseled in inextricable words that still wavered with ancient auric magik—mystic words he likely could have interpreted, were he and the others to stop. Morigan, however, was single-minded in her pursuit, leaving no occasions for sightseeing. She couldn't and wouldn't stop now with the bees driving her so wildly.

Perhaps her anxiety was contagious, as the lost wonders of the city became of less and less interest to Adam. He grew nervous, wary. Was this anxiety born of thinking about what further terrors Fate would reveal? Or...was this his hunter's instinct warning him of another danger? Thinking of the she-wolf from whom he had learned to hone those instincts, he saw her...impossibly, inexplicably: his mother. As he and the others floated across one of the groaning bridges of the city, trailing Brutus, the buffeting haze thinned for a speck, and from the peak of one of Aesorath's towers, a lean brown wolf looked down. The white star patterning the fur of her chest was unmistakably unique to his mother. Still, he dismissed it: Dream wasn't real. It was filled with illusions teased forth from desires. He missed his mother, especially as he'd come so far and had so much to share with her. But he wouldn't be teased and, as he hardened, a skein of sand erased both the tower and the taunting apparition.

Higher and higher they went into the city, closely following Brutus's shadow. By then, the Immortal had become more darkness than being; the filth of his birth into a vessel of Zionae had not been washed off and had scabbed into a war paint. Everyone tangled in this Dream could smell the king's corruption; he had already begun to exude a sex, animal, and death fragrance. Brutus climbed high, through empty towers and their decayed ballrooms and buried chambers. Eventually, Brutus arrived in a wing more decorous and clean than anywhere else in the haunted city. There he climbed a spiral staircase to a landing and entered a doorway fluttering with light. The spirits followed him.

Candles danced and shone around a chamber darkened by its red-drenched decor. Everything was as red as a murderer's kitchen—its lacquered tiles, armoire, four-poster bed, and vanity. Adam wondered if blood had, in fact, dyed the room's contents, for there was a sense of death that permeated the room. That essence belonged mostly to a woman who sat in a redwood chair, its frame writhing with gargoyles, monsters, and men. Pretty and sly as a cat, she combed her exquisite raven-like hair with a brush and watched the king creep in.

"Ah, you've arrived," said Amunai.

She rose, set down her brush, and walked over to examine him. She circled around the great beast, touching his war paint, sniffing him, and even licking one of the wriggling veins of his arm, before he grunted to remind her that it was he who was the lecherous monster. The Dreamwalkers realized this was Amunai's sanctum, and that they were seeing the unmasked face of their greatest enemy—the Herald of the Black Queen. She was lovely to behold: caramel skin, black hair, with eyelashes found mostly on boys but hips and breasts found only on women. But her charms hid the rottenness of her soul, and far more adeptly than the Red Witches of Alabion ever could.

Amunai, the seducer, bade the king kneel—only because she was so meek, she suggested, and would have had to shout in order for him to hear her. There, the companions saw her subtle corruption at play, her demeanor of lamb to his lion, such was the manner in which she would tame this unruly and hellish beast.

"Now that we are together," she whispered, "we must consider how to convince your brother to join you in freeing him from guilt. What are your ideas, great king?"

His body hollowed of its soul, Brutus's strategies were myopic in nature. "We shall smash his kingdom, drag him from the rubble, and I shall ravage him till he pleads for Mother's mercy."

"That's one idea," Amunai responded. Somewhat enchanted by his vast size and brawn, she caressed his canvas of golden flesh and he growled, sensually, at her finger's kisses. "Submission through force...However, smashing Eod, which is walled with pure, ancient sorcery, will be no simple feat—even for your mighty fists."

Brutus seized her by the torso with a single hand. "Are you saying I have not the power?"

"You have not your *brother's* power," she wheezed under the strength of his grasp. "You have an abundance of your own. Release me, and I shall tell you how to stoke your terrible magik into a fire that can melt his coldest ice."

Brutus considered this, and the watchful ghosts silently wished that his rage had seen her killed, then and there. Alas, he threw her to the floor. She rolled all the way to the bed where she struck it and coughed. In a sand, she rose, wiping ebon blood from her smile. Grimly, the watchers noticed that other wounds visible through the bloody tears in her robe were mending themselves as if by invisible needle and thread; she wasn't easy to kill, even in the physical world.

"I shall speak to you of a fire, of which your wise mother has told me," she said, barely ruffled as she slunk her way over to Brutus. "A forge, really, in which you can cast yourself and be remade. It is the oldest forge, a power buried under an eternity of rock. In that womb, it sleeps; your anvil and your maker."

"*What* sleeps?"

"The Father of Fire, Ignifaks." Amunai paused before the king and waned wistful and grand as a holy oracle. Even in his blood-soaked mind, Brutus was transfixed.

"You are not as old as you think, my King, though you feel as if you've known forever. The Keepers of Pandemonia are learned of all the ages, dynasties, and cultures lost mostly in the Age of Fire—the age in which you were born. And your mother, who is older than time, has told me of what even my kind have not recorded."

"I am older than time. I am as old as stone, fire, wind, and sea," declared the king.

Amunai shook her head. "You were a child, as all things brought into the world must once have been. Before you were that child, the world we know was seeded in the fertile, ashen soil of a world before. All of it, gone, by the power of the Father of Fire. For when Zionae's ark crashed, he was summoned: an aspect of the Great Mother—her rage and pain. He came forth to cauterize the wounds scoring her flesh, and his cure is a medicine without mercy. Ignifaks burned the world into a scab, and as that scab peeled, Nifhalheim soothed Geadhain with thousands of years of blistering winters. Until Geadhain's wounded carapace was softened, blistered and pustulant for an age's age of wetness, brought on by Aegyr, the Mother of Water. Finally, the Great Mother had life upon her, though it was found in mires, bogs, and mostly insects as large as you. After many seasons of Njornd, Mother of Winds, drying, sanding, and forming the shapeless mulch of the world's flesh, Geadhain was again reborn into something balanced and green. So you see, my King, as hoary as you are, you are still very fleeting to the seasons of this world. Your footsteps mean nothing compared to the breadth of a single aspect of the Great Mother."

Brutus was as captivated as those watching by this spoken history of Geadhain's transformation. Most shattering to the watchers was the news that there were more forces and greater elementals than they'd realized, and that everything that they had supposed about Geadhain, her past and legends, were the thinnest layer of the onion. How old was Geadhain? How many great ages and disasters had there been? Amunai's revelations, drawn from the endless well of her knowledge and thrown about with her disdainful abandon, continued to demolish what they had thought to be true.

"The Mortalitisi, the Exorex, Tiannochians, Baelor..." She laughed. "I could name a hundred civilizations of which you know nothing. I could tell you of the people who lived under the soil, with a shadow—a vessel—of your parents. Zee, your father, eventually abandoned you. The Father of Light chose the salvation of man over the salvation of his sons. Onae, the Mother of Darkness, the one who has woken you after her long sleep, never stopped dreaming of her sons. As Onae's flesh became dust, she returned to Dream alone. Without Zee, her sleep has been a nightmare. Now we must share in her nightmare. It is our duty to suffer, for what we have taken from her. She has come again to Geadhain, to avenge creation for man's disgrace, his ruinous pride, his damning free will.

"What has our freedom given us, Brutus, other than opportunities to destroy ourselves? She is taking it back, the gift of life and love—as was taken from her. We shall have no more free will, we shall have nothing but the rage of the nightmare she's endured since she crawled from the abyss."

Amunai's eyes glimmered, as dark as a star of death. "I could tell you of the time before the Dreamers. I could tell you what I saw when she touched me. There's a place where time began, Brutus, and it isn't here. It's filled with terrors that defy what trite horror we shall bring. Indeed, Onae's revocation shall be merciful, in comparison."

Finished with her storytelling, Amunai returned to the matter at hand: how to castrate Magnus and his empire.

"Ignifaks will be your weapon. The Black Queen has revealed a means to bind the elemental's chaos to your Will. You will need a focus, though, a miracle really, as you have not your brother's gift."

Brutus snarled, done with tales and her slights.

"I have not wasted your time, my King," said Amunai, peacefully raising her hands. "I have, in safekeeping below, a fragment of the ark of Zionae's power, as well as a defunct Anemorax, the Gate of Wind. It is not functioning now, though the fragmented arkstone should have enough power to return you to Geadhain, and from there you can wake Ignifaks, bind him, and draw upon his heat to conjure unholy miracles that will make your brother's magik look like the feeble wheezes of a dying sorcerer. None can stand against the

Father of Fire but the Father of Winter himself. Such an alliance your brother does not have, and nor does he seek it."

Amunai leaned into the king and licked a bead of sweat or blood off his face. "You must bleed him to love him. Break him, mash him, fuk him, and mold him into your perfect brother. Your perfect mate, even, for kings such as you belong only to each other. Think of him as you seed your army."

"Seed my army?" Brutus stirred from rousing fantasies of kissing and manhandling Magnus's alabaster loins.

"Onae is the Maker, the mother. She knew love, and now knows but lust and hunger. Hunger is how you will breed her new children. Her darkness is within you now, and so shall you spread it unto your flock: through blood and seed. Until I have time to think of a more efficacious means of converting men into your soldiers, the oldest rites, those of sex and blood, will have to do."

"Sex...and blood..." Brutus grinned, and ne'er had the spirits seen such repugnant hunger.

"Come. Rise, my King. I shall take you below to the heart of my kingdom, and send you to Ignifaks."

Brutus came to a knee, then stopped; mad monster or not, he didn't like being led. "Where does this beast sleep?"

Amunai's smile was pure poison. "My King, you are a beast of fire yourself. You wandered the Age of Fire with naught but your hide and wits to protect you and your mewling brother. Think. Think of what drew you to the Fangs of Dawn, to that range of dusty mountains in the middle of an untamed land. Was it their wildness? Their shape? The mouth of a predator wrought by nature into the Fangs of Dawn? What predator could be so large? What beast so great but one that could swallow the world and slather it in a vomit of fire? Ignifaks has always been with you, sleeping under the gold and stone of your city. He is your destiny. I believe you and he will find great accord."

Slinking, laughing, she faded from the chamber. As if he were a hungry mongrel, Brutus followed her. Already he had begun to lose any carriage of kingliness and moved on all fours. In Amunai's absence, a vacuum thick with whirling contradictions and theories remained. Each of the travelers pondered. As they were in Dream, faint echoes of their fearful and confused thoughts bled out of their head in tinny screeches. Discord affected them as much as their dread. Here they had witnessed the issuing of a command that would send Brutus back to Central Geadhain, where he would wake the Father of Fire sleeping under Zioch and poised to pounce since the second rise of civilization, and then ravage and rape his kingdom in one fell swoop. No one wanted to follow Brutus down that memory; they suspected what had happened and how swift the axe of his masochism had fallen.

Unbidden, the bees threw a phantograph into Morigan's head that showed Brutus standing on the parapet of the Gates of Zioch, of him feeling the rumble as they shut, and watching the sun bleed red, then stripping off his clothing and beginning with the rape and rebirth of his closest soldiers— whose screams echoed down from the gates and foretold for the city their grisly doom. Morigan sensed that it had taken less than a week of hunting within the sealed city before all were either dead or reborn as living dead.

Brutus had even figured out a cruder method for effecting the alchemy of conversion: spreading his matter into the open wounds and orifices of another. As with Death's infection, the pathogen was highly communicable and inescapable. Fathers turned on wives, children on grandmothers, and the city devoured itself in an orgy. Little wonder that the civilized ears in Eod and elsewhere were so deaf to the suffering when it occurred at such a terminal speed, and Brutus evoked the power of the arkstone shard to dampen magik and kill any pleas before they could be made on farspeaking stones for aid. The people were trapped, helpless cattle to be butchered for his perversions. It was destiny. Brutus had made his city to unmake it. Ignifax (as the heroes of this age knew it) awaited him, and Morigan's last vision was of Brutus descending into a golden-hued shaft, an entrance to what was surely the sun, and howling at the living furnace that roared into his face.

Even without Morigan's vision, her despondent company realized that Brutus's horrible rise could never have been stopped; these were gears that had been set into motion thousands upon thousands of years past. Against the power of those forces, their own fight to alter the outcome felt hopeless. They didn't want to return to their bodies and to all the cruel responsibilities that their fleshy lives entailed. Existing as spirits in the past was far less an affliction.

"We haven't come this far simply to give up because of what we know," said Talwyn, sensing the others' misery—even if they were ghosts. The large bluish shadow next to him, who could understand him clearly in Dream, placed a hand on his shoulder.

Talwyn went on. "The prick of the smallest thorn can cause a crippling infection, and we are Zionae's thorn. Really, I see this visitation as enlightening. We have learned so much. Zee-onae. We have been speaking of her in compound syntax, and not as the personifications we've learned creation seems to have. I think what we're discussing are two entities, or sides of one that have split and separate personalities, just as Mother Geadhain has an aspect for every elemental side of her nature. Though in this case, we're talking about a father and a mother of Creation, Zee and Onae, possibly in different vessels, and at different times, from the sound of it. A reasonable assumption, I think, since she had..."

Adam wasn't listening to the scholar's babble. For she was here, undeniably, before him: his mother, the wolf with the star-shaped tuft of white fur. She stood where Brutus had been, and was as tangible here as he and the others were smoke. Adam gazed around the chamber to see if his companions were also seeing what he beheld. But his friends had faded further into mere outlines, and the scholar's voice further into nothingness. In a speck, he and his wolf-mother were alone, buoyed in a comfortable swelling blackness.

"Adhamh," she called—his true, Ghaedic name.

"Sinthea!" he cried as he fell to his knees, scrabbled toward her, and embraced her warm, furry collar. Sinthea smelled as she should: of the woods, of sage and wise herbs, and something older, too, a sharp tinge of the richness buried in the earth. From that, and the other queer happenstances of her manifestation, he knew it wasn't really her. "Are you a memory? Have I conjured you?"

"No, and I am not the mother you know."

Suddenly he was shaken free, and not by the kind hand of a parent, but rather by a lash of thunder. What reared before him, looming in thunderclouds and crackling smoke, was the shadow of a wolf, its two green eyes illuminating a shaggy darkness. It was fearsome and still worthy of the reverence and wonder of watching a rainstorm tear up the woods. It was primal and pure, and his head whirled from the scents of earth, fur, feather, skin, sweat, clay, and mineral. His heart pounded at the screeches and calls from an ancient, natural orchestra. It was then, while he was drowning in sensory excess, that Adam knew with whom he was speaking, even before she announced herself.

"I am the Mother, and you are my child, though you are the first mortal to hear my voice since I was split and torn. Landspeaker, heed me: you are in danger. No more can you drift in this dream. You are no leaf to be lost to the rapids; you are my seed, my hope that one day man and I shall speak again. I speak to you, for no one else will hear me—not my daughters, not their shadows, not the child I have lost. You must be my voice, my champion. You must wake the land against the Black Queen. Her hand reaches, even now, even here. I command thee, child, rise and scream with my fury. Rise and scream to the skies! My children shall answer. Rise, Landspeaker!"

As Adam went still and unnoticed—his phantom bobbing, silent and inconspicuous as his physical analog—his fellow dreamers had been discussing Talwyn's theories, the perplexities of which had fascinating implications about the kings, the war, and Amunai's plans with this Anemorax, the Gate of Wind. Then, in the middle of Talwyn's mental ballet,

Adam made himself known, grandly, and howled as if he were the Wolf gone mad.

There was magik to his voice, a dread thunder. It evoked in them the feeling of rain hammering trees till they snapped, of ocean tides splitting ships like an axe to logs, of a giant bird shrieking down upon a fleeing man: emotions of exhilarating terror, awe, and passion. With whatever power he channeled, Dream was shattered. The scenery flew apart like dashed crystal. They were spun in a tornado of the Dream's ether, and were hurled down onto the hard soil of the land outside the Cradle. Morgan leapt up, spitting ashy dirt from her mouth. Their circle of hands had come undone, and most of them were picking themselves up as she had, except for the Wolf, and Adam, who seemed more alert than any of them.

Morgan gasped. "Adam, what did you do?"

"I woke us," he said and scanned the jagged horizon for danger; he was mesmerized by the sinewy lords making infinity loops in the air. The Wolf, noticing his vigilance, scoured the gloomy morning for signs of danger.

"You have not that power!" Morgan was not angry, but amazed.

Most astonishing was that evening had come and gone. How long had they been submerged in that past? *Three days*, buzzed the bees, and she was sick at the thought of how much time had been wasted. That discomfort transformed into a roiling nausea of fear, however, as her bloodmate caught scent of something that spiked fear in them both.

"Red Riders!" he roared.

Disoriented, scrambling, and trying to shrug off the hangover from Morgan's enchantment, the travelers struggled into a formation, drawing weapons and slapping themselves into readiness. Morgan cursed herself for once more being a seer unable to foresee imminent danger. What had her bees been thinking?

You're safe, Mistress, they promised. *You were never to come to harm.*

Liars, she thought, as the first puffs of sand appeared on the plains.

It was a disturbance that grew, spreading in a clouded line. There had to be many riders, more than a small hunting party. The mad king's dogs had been called to war, and Brutus knew no prisoners in battle, so this then was to be a stand. Morgan snarled ferociously enough to disfigure her beauty and to match the bravado of her bloodmate and of Pythius. Thackery calmly withdrew for a moment, clasped his hand around his staff, and when he withdrew it, a white star signaling a magik of wrath pulsed atop the object's gnarled head. Mouse withdrew her dagger as Moreth and Talwyn unsheathed their pistols. They were ready to clash in blood and metal with Brutus's army. And they were hungry for it, after so much palaver.

No one noticed Adam lingering at the back of the pack. No one heeded his silence as something greater than the stillness that preceded battle; they were too focused on the riders and the shambling footmen who spilled before the fuming horses and their crimson-and-black knights. The Wolf could count them now: ten, twenty, fifty, then one hundred. His father had sent a death squad. He knew they would never drag his slavering body to the ground, though his guts withered as he wondered how he would protect the entire pack against a hundred foes. As if sensing his worry, one of the mounted sorcerers raised a horribly incandescent staff—the antithesis of Thackery's light, for it was warped and irregular, its radiance sanguine. From the sky came a moan, and as the Wolf glanced upward, a flash of red, a pimple had formed in the firmament that would, in a speck, unleash a blast of fire, thunder, or both.

"Take cover!" he screamed, instantly realizing the folly of his command when there were but shriveled trees and sparse rocks behind which to hide. He herded his pack anyway toward a boulder at least as tall as him, and they cowered together as the first shrieking fulmination stabbed the land like a spear, wounding the Green Mother. As the earth detonated, the riders charged, and a true song of wicked lightning strummed the land, and Adam pushed himself out of the Wolf's shadow. He stumbled out into the dusty battleground and screamed back at the thunder.

REEEEEEEECH!

Only it wasn't really a scream, or a howl. Morigan couldn't place the sound. There had been that one time, when she was being hounded by Gloriatrix's men in Menos, and she had made the sound of a sea king then bespelled a building full of people to sleep. To her, even, Adam's sound was queer. It was raw, like the shriek a rock-eating lizard would make. But something was answering him. She squinted to see what it was, or where Adam had gone, or even to know the fate of her bloodmate who had left his father's chains at her feet and was dancing around on a field rife with lightning bolts, erupting potholes, and smoke. Was this to be her death? It felt so wild and uproarious, as if the war of wars was upon them. She wouldn't die cowering behind a rock like a winsome waif. She charged out into the maelstrom.

A shadow.

She froze, trembling, as the shadow flew over her, and was promptly thrown to the shaking land by a gust of its movement as it pushed itself up on the currents. Supine, she saw something of a shape in the brown film thrown over the sky—a sinuous body, as long as a train, encrusted with spines and barnacles of horn and flesh, shining spots that were eyes or jewels of incredible magik, wings veined with glowing green, and a streaming aura of emerald power. A splash of something—its saliva or essence—pattered down on her amid the already tumultuous rain. She instinctively knew to roll out of the way, and a sizzling green trail decorated the now-pitted soil.

Once saved from being dissolved by the secretions, Morigan watched the beast snap off into the filthy mist; it moved with the violence of a lashing whip, though its sheer size belied such agility. Its proportions were heinously grand; it was larger than the any of the sky worms she'd seen in Pandemonia. Details tinged in madness made so much of it hard to understand. Still, after gaping at its magnificence, she knew what it was, what it could only be—one of the creatures mentioned by Talwyn and Pythius in their fireside warnings. A lord of the Cradle—a drakagor.

From the caliginous realm of clouds atop the Cradle, it had been called. Daughter of Fate or not, she would be but prey to its granite and nightshade jaws. She held herself completely still, and was still unmoving when the Wolf found her. They came together, clutching and shaking, just as the drakagor roared again. It was a noise like the one Adam had made, though amplified to a volume that pierced their ears and deafened them. In the humming disaster, the bloodmates watched something akin to fire—though wet, green, and thick as lava—pour down in a concentrated stream over the land beyond. The humming faded, and the air cleared to dirty shreds. At last, they could see each other and their friends huddled behind the rock, and Adam, who stood far apart from them all, on a wasteland fluttering with embers, staring out toward a bubbling emerald river scored into the land beyond, where not a grisly hair of Brutus's squad remained.

As the serpent-lord of brimstone, scale, poison, and thunder twisted off into the clouds, they gasped and screamed; all but Adam, who bowed.

II

"Eradicated?" whispered Amunai.

White-knuckled, she clutched the armrests of her chair as she received the news from the general kneeling before her, Rex. Growing bored of watching Blackeyes sloppily toil away at the Anemorax, once the death order had been given to Rex she'd returned to her sanctum, changed into a loose robe, and spent the past hourglasses admiring herself in her vanity while growing warm from sips of *milokras,* an apple wine made in the era when Aesorath still had something living of which to boast—the casks, enchanted, had been among the few relics to survive the city's fall, and the wine within had aged beautifully. However, all her luxuriating and foggy bliss had been dispelled by Rex's report.

"I don't understand," she said, snarling. "We sent over a hundred men, including those most deeply awakened by Zionae, like you. I understand that the son of Brutus was present, as well as his bitch, Morigan, though they are not enough to stand against us without suffering a single casualty of their ragtag company. Not even that ridiculous scholar was killed?"

"Not even him." The crimson markings around Rex's eyes glowed deep with disappointment. "It was not the bloodmates, though, who protected their company. It was a lone boy who defeated our forces. I shall show you."

And so, Rex opened his mind to Amunai, and their consciousnesses entwined to become a single channel of thought. Amunai remained in her chair as her mind flew elsewhere, to a smoldering battlefield crossed in crimson lightning and fiery blasts of dirt, upon which she saw several figures scattered about. The largest figure had to be Brutus's son; how very alike they were. He pounded around the strident fog as if his footsteps were the cause of the battle's thunder. Still, he couldn't seem to locate the smaller figure, who Amunai spotted in a clearing—a half-naked, tattooed lad of no more than thirty summers. Although, she saw deeper than the eyes of whatever host had beheld this history; she saw with the eyes of a Keeper.

The boy was grand, and the shadow he cast was great, as great as the shadow that dominated the heavens. Flying above them was a snarling rock-and-wind snake that moved faster than the lightning conjured by the Redeyes of her soon-to-be-decimated forces. Such an end happened quickly and ruthlessly. She had barely construed the creature's gnarled ferocity ere from its eclipsing shadow poured a waterfall of sizzling ichor. Whatever Redeye had borne witness died screaming and gurgling on his insides—and her kind were not supposed to know fear.

"A drakagor," she exclaimed, returning to herself.

Rex nodded and rose from his knee. "Yes...You know what this means?"

"A Landspeaker." She drummed her fingers on the vanity, forced away her ugliness, had a sip of milokras, then traded crystalware for brush and resumed brushing her hair.

"This complicates our plans. If the boy really has communed with the Green Mother, then we cannot attack them while they are within the Cradle, where the skies swarm with the ancient lords of scale and rock. Not with our fodder and chaff, that is."

"You have another tactic in mind?"

Amunai paused to think. In what had recently become a blurred line of familiarity and comfort, Rex stepped forward and gently claimed the brush from the Herald's absently drooping hand. While she pondered, aloud, he brushed her hair. It wasn't the doting of a lover; it was more innocent than that, and each of them allowed this nurturing.

"We cannot send another legion," she muttered. "It will simply result in more ashes with which to line the Cradle. With a Landspeaker among them, Morigan and her dogs will be reasonably well protected by the Green Mother's troublesome guardians until they leave the Cradle. But not from a creature stronger, faster, and more brutal than they or the lords of scale and rock..."

Rex gave her a gummy grin. "You mean to send Brutus."

"We have kept him on his leash for long enough. If Geadhain's heroes have recruited the Green Mother's creatures, then we shall unleash our own. Brutus can hunt them unseen, and can likely slaughter the Landspeaker before he can cry out to his friends in the sky."

Rex's brow twisted. "I would not doubt our king's strength; however, what if Morigan's company somehow—by whatever thin miracle—is able to subdue him? They have the chains given to them by Eatoth's dead Keeper Superior, one of her wretched company is a sorcerer, the other a Landspeaker, and there is both a Dreamer and his vessel in their midst. They are not without tricks."

"Tricks, yes..."

Touched by his worry, Amunai reached back and squeezed Rex's hand, which had stalled in its labors. "I have the most tricks of anyone in Geadhain. I shall travel with the king to ensure he does not falter."

While he was a corrupted beast of hunger, dark magik, hateful temper, and lust, Rex was none of those things around Amunai, who coaxed from him a thimble of softness and humanity. Here, away from others, they were not friends, not lovers, but something that broached the borders of each. Rex was concerned for the Herald, and he wouldn't hide the jealous, stabbing fire in his heart. Indeed, as that hunger rose—for her welfare—the markings on his face burned and his flesh began to smolder.

"You would be exposing yourselves—the linchpins of this war—in a land quite hostile to your presences," he said. "I cannot allow this."

Judging from Amunai's curled lip and red cheeks, Rex believed a reproach was imminent; he was not the one to give orders. However, the Herald was as afflicted as he with compassion for the other, and her anger passed like a rolling thunder. Not even the echo of it remained as she spoke.

"I shall be under the protection of Brutus, king of all beasts and monsters. Nor am I meek. In this world, I am the power of wind, and I can move in step with the king—faster even. I faced Morigan and her lover before, and they did not end me."

Silently, though, she worried. She knew that her fortune might have changed had Feyhazir not taken that opportunity to cause his own disruption with Morigan's pack. Or, had the Wolf grown further into his divine heritage, she wouldn't have had a chance. Regardless of how dominant the Wolf seemed right now, she knew he still had far to go in discovering his gifts. Indeed, she worried about the son of Brutus coming into his own more than the Daughter of Fate. She was grateful he hadn't tapped into the totality of that power just yet—not like his father, who could transform his flesh into metal armaments and raise golems of twined corpses with a few drops of blood and his Will to make life. However, in a thousand years of potential development, Brutus's child had only managed excessive strength and the metamorphosis between man and wolf. In fact, after considering the facts, she supposed she feared him less. Amunai stood and banished her worries behind her comely countenance.

"You care for me," she said, flatly.

Chagrined, his hand fumbling with her brush, Rex was unsure how to answer, how to make sense of his rumbling, bilious emotions. These urges that so often surged and superseded civility, allowing him to rape, consume, and terrorize with abandon. Although, for the Herald, those hungers told him to comb her hair, walk beside her, and to simply be around her. Awaiting a reply, she continued staring at him without any indication on her face of the appropriate response.

"I worry."

"Worry is care." Amunai reached for him, and he recoiled and twisted once she had hold of his hairbrush-wielding hand. "We can have a secret, you and I. We are better than the others of our kind. We have compassion for our unique wretchedness. Monsters are not to be denied the company of other monsters, and there is no shame in believing that. Once the world has been cleansed, and the new realms—the new Aesorath—have risen, many more aside from you and I shall know of the comfort of evil."

The comfort of evil. It had a calming ring to Rex's mind, subduing his more violent urges. Now there was only her smile, and touch, from which he no longer balked. Now there was only a shadow of a memory, the silhouette of a maiden, or woman, with whom the Herald shared a haunting likeness. The Herald felt it, too—that pull from a memory in her heart—only hers was of a child she'd never had, not whatever mother figure Zionae had lobotomized from Rex.

The two of them stood, drifting in tortured anamnesis, until Amunai stamped out their flame of communion. "Now," she said. "I must get dressed and ready for travel—none of my lady's wear will do in the Cradle's climes."

"Of course, Herald." Rex bowed, and swept to the exit.

"Stay." Her suggestion stalled him like stone boots. "We can lay out the strategies and measures to be employed while we are gone. And I have a task for you—another pillaging of the land."

"But why? Our army is brimming with recruits."

"My success in Eatoth has shown me that I can disrupt Fate, and its agents, with acts of chaos. And so we need further acts of chaotic violence, which your assaults must be. Without reason, without sense. Continue to confuse and befuddle the seer. Cloud her mind with senseless images on which she will waste precious time. Kill or convert whatever flesh you find. Burn them, or set the terrified tribes you've beset free. I care not. I don't want to know what you intend to do; even you must surprise yourself. This task is as important as what Brutus and I are to do, understand?"

Rex remembered Amunai drawing straws and laughing maniacally before commanding Brutus to Intomitath. It had seemed...what was the word...?

"Sounds like fun, no? Monsters can still have a good time." She laughed. Rex made a regurgitating sound that might have been laughter, too.

"By the time the king and I return—a few days, I should expect—we must be ready to activate the Anemorax and to flood Zioch with our forces. From there, we shall wake the Father of Fire and summon him in his purest form into this world, into Brutus as his vessel. And with a road of fire paved before us, we shall march to Eod, ruin it, and begin our empire of blood. Morigan, that meddlesome thorn, shall be nothing more than a corpse decaying in the Cradle, never to be found or mourned. I may keep the king's son, though, for certain pleasures..."

Amunai's oration on destruction continued, stirring the lust of the Black Queen within Rex anew. Even as she undressed before him, and hungry desire should've overtaken his senses, Rex remained focused on his passion for Amunai's words, his regard toward the woman. He listened and watched her as a child would his mother. The comfort of evil. He'd truly found it.

III

"I have seen a sky that bites and shrieks. Rock eats man. Swords for teeth. A welling scar of emerald green doth stain the land, and scour, clean—"

What is that, my Wolf?

Kericot. It is undeniable that he was here, now—his poetry speaks so true. Although you are still the fiercest, loveliest thing in my mind or elsewhere.

The Wolf stopped stomping through the gritty ash and pulled his Fawn in close for a kiss on her filthy cheek. Since arriving in the Cradle—and in such a harried manner—they had not stopped for a breath, as though the hordes of his father still followed them. After the encounter with Brutus's forces, the company had preferred silence to conversation, and a lingering quiet echoed even in the minds of the bloodmates.

It was a relief to the Wolf that Morigan had finally broken the foreboding to which she had succumbed. For the past day, she had been beset by strange visions of murder and carnage, splashes of horror that flew over her sight like bats—the tribes of Pandemonia being slaughtered, raped, burned, or, oddly enough, set free from ravaging Blackeyes. Such chaos made little sense and distracted her from much of their progress. She had not told her friends of this savagery—only the Wolf had been her confidant in this private terror. He stole another kiss lest that gloominess descend upon her again, though it did not, and Morigan awoke more from his passion to see the realm before her.

The land had risen up around them: ragged steppes, curled twists of rock like waves rendered by a Dreamer of cruelty; ranges so precipitous and sheer that they spent most of the journey thus far wandering down in dingy clefts; and in channels running through the land as would cracks across a desert. They had grown so used to coughing up ash and to being filthy that nearly everyone, save Adam who didn't know the folktale, was reminded at least once of the faery tale of "Autumn Red," the secret princess with hair the color of fire, and her seven dwarfish stepfathers, who returned to her from the depths of a coal mine each night.

Adam's secrets and his newly discovered gifts remained largely unremarked and unquantified by his fellow travelers. To them, he seemed the least afraid of the veins they walked, least afraid of the lords of rock and scale that roared across the heavens, whose cries loosed hails of cinders and mud from the canyon walls down upon them as they clung together and cowered with every filthy deluge. Very little of the torrent was solid, so much of it warm, even flickering ash. Because he was nature's child, her voice, Adam never appeared to be as sullied as his fellows, and was always one step ahead of a landslide. And still, no one asked Adam about his mystery; it felt wrong to. In fact, it felt dangerous to speak aloud at all in the drakagor's domain.

They were also secretly afraid of Adam, of his power.

The Cradle provided ample opportunity for the company to transfer their terror. Their hike in the Cradle's nadirs eventually carried them back upward, to a plain where bolls of ash rolled over irregular hills of black sand. Far away on these highlands, stains of green scintillated, percolating pools of the venom. Dizzying fumes assailed them if they wandered too near to the pools, though they could see through spyglasses the slick gargantuan monsters that slept, swam, and bleated within them like lazy whales.

Drakagor. And each a leviathan, noted the Wolf after one long, concerned squint through the murky horizon. Even within the bestiary of remembered terrors, drakagor were the most horrible creatures he'd known. When he had first noticed them there, he'd paused, dumb as an oaf, to ogle these gargantuan snakes, crusted in plates and earthen spines, adorned in spidery chains of eyes, each larger than a fresco he recalled—an eye it had been, too—atop the dome of the Court of Ideas.

A drakagor that had captured his attention raised one of its rocky, veined wings—the appendages of a living gargoyle—off its dripping flesh, then fluttered it gracefully, as if it were a beast so much smaller and less intimidating. How could a creature be so large? It was how these monsters had been made, though—for sheer impressive, dumbfounding might. He watched as his chosen drakagor slithered from the dim herd in the green mire and toward the shores of its lakes, reared on two pillars of craggy might, piercing the land with stalactite talons, then extended his—or her, he had no idea—encrusted reptilian head.

The drakagor took crumbling bites out of the land, as though consuming a meal, with the messiness of a technomagikal crane at work. The land trembled at each bite, even though the creature was thousands of yards away; he wasn't imagining the shake. His fear was soon worn down by his sense of awe, though. For beneath the terrible majesty, there was beauty and design to these behemoths, an elegance to be appreciated in the swiftness of a creature seemingly so lumbering. And a maker's artistry in their voices, as well, which were reminiscent of the calls of lords of the sea and quite soothing when not enraged. Even the crests of rock that crowned each beast's maw and head were unique and symmetrical in their beauty.

"They're actually quite lovely," whispered Talwyn, who had been standing behind the surveying giant, along with Pythius and the rest of the silent chimney sweeps. He had pulled out a wooden spyglass that had been given to him by his Amakri lover. "They remind me of an animal, several animals, actually. With the quadrupedal inheritance of certain lizards; the crest and spines of them, too. Those wings, though, and the toxins they spit and in which they bathe...I've no etymology for those."

"They are the ancestors of monsters," said Thackery, waving away the spyglass as it was offered. "I don't need a peek to know that they are what came before the rest."

As the clouds rolled on, they watched the flock of drakagor, and fear waned to comfort and then respect for the lords of rock and scale, who had protected them from Brutus's hand. Adam summoned them from their study with the promise of somewhere safe to rest for the night. No one had realized how late was the hourglass, and a chill that would be terrible without shelter had begun to wrap itself around them. Bidding quiet farewell, the Wolf and the others started after the Landspeaker. Caenith did not make known how bothered he was not leading them, even if navigating these lands would have posed serious challenges for him.

Even the mighty must know when to bare his fangs, and when to hide his might, said Morigan. Her whispers lightened his heart, and he smiled, rattled the bag of chains he had for his father's wrists, and took her small hand in his great one. Together, as lovers and friends, they continued. After the climb to the highlands, delving again into one of the Cradle's claustrophobic ravines was not as frightening. For as dead and dangerous as this land might be—ruled only by prehistoric beasts—it wasn't against them, and they were being led by the divinity of the Green Mother herself.

IV

When ink swiftly coursed over the clouds, and a miserable muddy slop rained down upon them, they were grateful for Adam's whisperer. Before they would need to swim or fight against a churning tide of filth, the Landspeaker aimed for the slippery walls of the ravine with its jutting edges and began to climb to an overhang barely glimpsed in the sheen. Once atop the small ledge, he and the others walked along it a short way toward a dimple of brown in a wall of the same color: a cave, which wasn't visible unless you were looking directly at that exact spot—a degree of watchfulness the Wolf had subconsciously repressed given Adam's authority. There were no plants or signs of life inside, nothing but a deepness that loomed into dark, thick-to-breathe confines. Strange fragments of what seemed like hammered shale lay about, sometimes great lines of the stuff, and Talwyn fought against his curiosity to examine what he felt were sloughings as Adam strode ahead into the swimming emptiness. Back on the cliff, Pythius had claimed his grimy hand, and attached to the man he was forced to leave the mystery behind as they followed into the darkness.

Thackery summoned a crystalline star on the end of his staff so they could clearly see the cavern as they wandered. It was carved inward, then opened, a belly into the land. There were heaps of the shale-like material, as well as puddles of the telltale greenish excretions of the drakagor in which the companions knew their boots might dissolve. Although, observing the stagnant skin of the poison, Talwyn wondered if its efficacy had expired. He kicked a loose stone into a pool to test his hypothesis and saw no sizzle after the splash.

Adam stopped when he heard the noise. "We are safe in this burrow."

"Burrow?" said Talwyn. "Do you mean of the drakagor? I'd rather not be in one of their homes should they decide to come back for a nap."

Adam's smile startled them in the flickering gloom. "They will not return. It is not the season. These sanctuaries, hollowed by their claws and teeth, are only where they hide themselves when they are weak and molting. Every one hundred seasons or so, they must shed their mountainous skins, becoming pink and soft as a young seal. Such a season is not upon us, nor will the drakagor, the ancient children and wrath of the Great Mother, find us enemies. Not unless we betray her trust, as when this scar was made."

Asking what everyone else was thinking, Talwyn pushed him. "How do you know all of this, Adam? What trust?" Jumping at the rumble of a new storm that cast its booming resonance even into this deep burrow—there would be no heading outside for the moment—he continued. "We have much to discuss and now, it seems, an opportunity to do that."

"We can talk now," agreed Adam.

Despite this dread land, they realized that their companionship was a timeworn tradition of struggle, rest, and reassertion. They found what they could to subsist in the cave—a dribble of cleanish water down the farthest end of the cavern and piles of what Talwyn asserted were drakagor scales, upon which they could rest. It was as good a comfort as one could ask for at the farthest end of the world, and Thackery planted his staff to act as their campfire for the night. They partook of their thinning supplies with smiles, aside from Moreth, who looked pale and refused to eat.

Throughout their trek, the Wolf had observed a change in his scent, from that of rot to the sweeter malodor of pus that comes with the expulsion of illness. Moreover, the inky stains soiling his pitch-black clothing and the secretions he had been emitting weren't as noticeable to the others as they were to the Wolf. Was that the poison leaking out? Was he healing? And if so, how? As far as he knew, the wound of a blood eater was fatal. Perhaps this was a death sentence not so much to be feared now that the species was dying out. Caenith chewed on the tantalizing mystery of Moreth's survival while picking at the remnants of Adam's secret hoard of root vegetables. Honorable to a fault, he would keep his promise to the coyote not to speak of his torments.

The scholar's rhapsodic words broke his pensiveness.

"It's moments like these," said Talwyn, "the soft resting of our hearts and souls, the feeding of our courage to continue, which have made this journey so extraordinary. I can't imagine a life other than this one. I want the war to end, but I don't want to lose our fellowship. I fear that history will record only the triumphs of generals and tally the soldiers lost on each side. Still, let us never forget these moments, here, now, and each other. No matter the losses and costs we shall incur, we must hold onto this, even if the world forgets."

Talwyn's words seemed to have come from nowhere, yet they came from that deep place of which he'd spoken, and in which they all dwelled—the quiet of the company, the moments where the race stopped for but a sand. Shadows of his speech lingered with the fellowship; the intimation that they might not all be here to remember, or honor, his pledge. As Talwyn leaned back into the embrace of Pythius, Mouse shocked her friends by leaping up and bearing the dagger blessed by the Dreamer.

She thought of cutting herself and swearing a blood oath, though given her immortal friends, she realized that could end quite unpredictably. Nonetheless, she held the blade out toward Thackery's light and swore. "I'll not forget—in this life, or another—what we've shared."

"Nor I," said Thackery, rising and gripping firm his staff, which seemed a better object with which to swear oaths. Mouse slipped away her dagger and placed her hand atop her great uncle's. Then all rose and gripped the wood of the staff until there was hardly any space once the Wolf's hand found it.

"We shall not forget," they said, a smile on each face, the promise humming in everyone's heads as one by one they let go of the staff. Mouse returned to nestling between two of her favorite gents, Thackery and Adam, each of whom was delighted to have her bony shoulders against his. Talwyn reclined into his mate's arms. And Moreth, wanting no one's company, began walking back to his lonely seat. Suddenly, he groaned and stumbled. The Wolf was upon him in a streak of speed, helping him back to his pile of drakagor scales.

"Are you well?" asked Mouse, remembering the eel-like feel of his fingers under hers a moment past. With a dash of the Thule-recall, she also remembered the Wolf and Moreth having a hissing dispute some while back, in the swamp perhaps, or earlier, but she had been too far away to hear the details of their argument.

"I was hurt—nothing to worry about." All scowls and armored feelings, Moreth shoved off further ministrations from the Wolf, who then stomped back to Morigan.

"Hurt how?" pressed Mouse.

"A scrape."

"From?"

"A blood eater," said Talwyn, and the others gasped. "Pick up your jaws, my fellows. There isn't much that escapes these"—he tapped beneath his eyes—"or this," he added as he pressed a finger to his temple. "In fact, when I took a deep look into what I remembered, I recall one of the wretched things flailing at Moreth back in Teskatekmet's lair." Uneasy at hearing the name, Pythius frowned and shifted. "I shall explain that to you later, my flame. Indeed, we should share all our knowledge together, and on many things, before we proceed. But as for the matter of Moreth's scrape. To be frank, he wasn't showing a fading pulse or other signs of terminality, and I was—"

"Curious?" hissed Mouse.

"You make my intentions seem malicious, my dear," he protested. "Although I suppose *curious* would be the operative word. I have so many questions. How is he alive? Does he possess an antibody? Or is the magik Feyhazir used to create the blood eaters weakening? Surely many of my questions, and the fate of Moreth's health, could only be analyzed—and intervened with, if necessary—after a period of scientific observation. Examination of the subject himself would always have been necessary at some point, a place at which we've likely arrived now that all the moths are out of the closet."

"I should be furious with you! All of us should," she yelled.

Mouse grumbled, crossing her arms and making a brief show of her discontent, before storming over to Moreth. He leered from the half-circle of worried faces, trapped like a rat, and clutching at his stomach, where Mouse now guessed the wound to be.

"What do you want?" he asked.

"Let's see it—the wound," demanded Mouse. "How dare you think you're allowed to die, or suffer, without telling any of us? You are my friend, you shite. We crawled through the abyss and back again, together. Now pull up your shirt."

When he clung to his resistance, Mouse and the others tackled him and hoisted up his garment. For a sick man, he showed incredible strength, and the Wolf was needed to restrain his arms while Pythius held his legs. Talwyn and Thackery played physician and sage, leaning in close to examine the ragged line drawn into Moreth's taut abdomen. It ran from hip to ribcage and looked deep enough to have festered at its deepest point into the squelching rip that Morigan and the Wolf had already seen. Although the flesh around the wound seemed purple, red, and clean of pus, so he had passed through any fever stage or risk of dire infection.

"You say these wounds are fatal?" whispered Thackery in his and the scholar's quiet intellectual bubble, through which the grunts and struggles of Moreth were the faintest of discords.

"Incurably," replied Talwyn.

"But this wound is over two weeks old." Thackery hovered his finger along the crusted edge of the injury. "It's already passed the inflammatory phase. Look here at the flaking skin."

"Do you see now, why this was so—?"

"Interesting, yes."

"I am not a fuking animal!" roared Moreth, and his muscles rippled almost as if something writhed under his skin, and they scattered, hiding themselves behind Caenith. The Wolf held them at bay from the heaving, half-naked man curled in the dark ahead of them. The sudden glistening and undulation of Moreth's flesh served as warning enough against approaching him. After another great heave, and an exhalation that sounded like a death rattle, the prickle of danger faded from Moreth, as did the monstrous presence. Moreth looked at his fellow travelers, quite revealed by his paleness and Thackery's light to be the scowling grouch they knew.

Mouse shuffled over to apologize for manhandling him, while the others kept their distance. A speck earlier, Morigan had seen a silver-white aura around the Menosian, a flame of power and doom. She knew not the meaning of such an omen. Talwyn and the Wolf, the most perceptive of their pack, gazed at each other, sharing impressions and insights that had yet to manifest through the haze of activity.

Something had happened, beyond a simple rush of Moreth's anger. Something had changed, and they weren't sure with whom, or what, they had just sworn an oath of eternal friendship.

V

Leaving Moreth alone for the time being, and with nowhere to go while the storm was shaking the cavern, the group focused on less personal matters. Dreamers and their influences and taint had been harrowing Talwyn's mind since he'd delved into the City of Ghosts and learned that Teskatekmet had been mother of the entire hideous race of blood-drinking hag-women. *For what purpose?* had been the question haranguing him. To guard the chalice? Why? Talwyn asked Mouse to produce the relic over which their company had been deceived, sundered, and manipulated into acquiring for Feyhazir. It was the crux of his desires, and all needed to look upon, examine, and offer their insights toward this relic. Nervous, Mouse fumbled with and nearly dropped the sacred cup once it was out of her traveler's purse. Like a shrine maiden making offerings, she came forward shyly and aware of what she held, before resting the relic on the ground beside Thackery's stake of light. There, the glowing stave bared the twisted ugliness of the monsters rendered into the grayish chalice—men with gargantuan elongated heads, tentacles, and furled shrimplike tendrils, all engaged in a wanton orgiastic feast. Indeed, the cup made the Wolf think of hunger, of consummation and lust. Was it bone? For it had the seeming and smell—mustard seed and dust—to the Wolf. However, he had never come across a creature with bones of that shade before.

"*I Diathíki*," (the Covenant), muttered Pythius, breaking their enchantment with the cup.

The shaman pointed and asked Talwyn why the chalice had been brought forth, and what else was being discussed since his pyrkagos had been so sparing with the translations. Unfortunately, Talwyn was to continue to keep his lover in the dark and out of these dialogues for fear of what ambiguities and doubts they might stoke in Pythius. Talwyn was not ready for that confrontation, between his intellect and Pythius's dubious faith. Still, he knew that with everything they had thus far uncovered regarding Feyhazir's motivations, they were hurtling toward that crash. *I'm not ready for our bliss to be fractured just yet. I'm sorry that I must lie to you*, he thought, in the whirling microspeck where a million possible debates and outcomes were distilled into a single probability, and he spat out a false explanation for Pythius—keeping his companions, except for Adam, in the dark this time. Wise and knowing, the Landspeaker held his tongue.

"It's hideous, and probably evil," said the scholar while smiling.

"Why are you wearing that ghastly grin?" asked Moreth, moving forward with a groan to squat with Mouse and peer suspiciously at the object.

Adam tipped his head toward Pythius's horned one. "He cannot know of what we're speaking. Not all hearts are made of stone, and his is softer than his exterior would suggest."

"Yes," admitted Talwyn. "I'll tell him later. But we need to speak of this now. I need to understand how Teskatekmet, the Dreamer, the Cradle, and the Black Queen all fit together. I know there's a link; I can feel it. But I don't know how. What about you, Morigan? What do you see when you look at this...Covenant?"

Morigan had looked briefly at the object before, and the memory sent a feeling of terror crawling over her flesh. The chalice was less intimidating now, when surrounded by friends, and when all (or most) were aware of its taint. She knew it was wicked, had been used for wicked acts—and not just the corruption of Teskatekmet and the ancient tribes. Rather...she reached for that aspect of truth, flickering with silver wisps and light as her bees hunted for it. Alas, they returned without a drop of the nectar to feed her. As with much of her father's behaviors and motivations, the chalice and its secrets were shrouded.

"I don't know," she said. "I cannot read it. You are right, though, my friend—a wickedness surrounds the relic. If not made for evil, it has caused a great deal of harm, nonetheless."

"I always end up with the shite end of the stick." Mouse shook her head, and Moreth patted her. "I don't think"—she gazed at Pythius, who stared at her and the others with passionate interest, trying to understand—"your father is wicked, Morigan. Not from what I have felt, and I have touched him, in my soul, if one can actually caress there."

"They can," said the Wolf, as his beast purred in Morigan's breast.

"I'll take your word on that," replied Mouse. "He *needs*, though. He's a creature of such passionate desire. I wish I knew what he wanted. No doubt, it would reveal the purpose of this chalice...of much, really."

She reflected on the strange knot in her stomach, which had grown since this discussion had started from a pea to a walnut of unrest. It was not her distress, but the Dreamer's. She touched her stomach as if an unruly fetus were kicking her. "We're pissing him off, I think—talking about this. It's the first I've felt of him since the City of Ghosts. I should put this away."

Mouse snatched the chalice and stuffed it in the haversack that hung from her waist. It sat in the sack, distended like a cancerous testicle. She fanned her face. "That's odd. Feels hot all of a sudden. Then cold. I think I may—"

She didn't complete her thought, for a blast of silver light and black mist buoyed her up, tall and grand as a giant of stars crammed into the cavern. While she wasn't as grand as her looming aura appeared, the real woman was lost in the scintillation, a shadow somewhere, a speck to the greatness of what had dragged itself from the abyss of the universe to speak to beings much lesser than himself: Feyhazir. The companions' heads rang with music; their bodies slumped into a catatonic euphoria that felt somewhere between sleep and orgasmic climax. Thackery, Talwyn, and Pythius collapsed into rapturous throes. Morigan, the Wolf, Moreth, and Adam, queerly, wavered the least, seemingly most able to hold onto their Wills against the Dreamer's storm of light and shadow. They stood and faced the divine tempest.

"Daughter, you pry and you doubt. You will lose your conviction in this war, and with it, your strength. Do not question the hand of the master, who bids his soldier to slice the throat of his enemy. The master's will must never be questioned."

"Is that what I am? Your soldier? And you, my master?"

"Father. I am your father, which means I am due the same respect as any lord."

The cavern shook at his threats; the walls seemed to vacillate between rock and a twirling vacuum of space and stars. Feyhazir was exercising his awe, his greatness...though seer, Wolf, sick man, and Landspeaker all saw through the illusion.

"I am not cowed by you," said Adam. "I am not your daughter, slave, or soldier. I am Alabion's child. Tell me, Dreamer, what do you seek?"

Cacophonous, the abyss shook, torn by brilliant comets, searing asteroids, and the explosions of distant suns. More than Adam, Morigan worried that her friend may have provoked her father, and yet this honesty was what they needed. Perhaps conjuring his rage would force him to let slip his motivations. She echoed Adam's demands. "Speak, or I shall consider you a traitor and tyrant to this world with the rest!"

"Aye, beast of the beyond!" roared the Wolf. "No more parlor tricks, just truth!"

Moreth spat and cursed at the ruckus.

The chaotic abyss seized, clouded, and then there was no more of the chaos to threaten the companions, but merely stone walls and the terrible radiance of the Dreamer.

"*I am love*," he said.

"You are not," declared Morigan, her bees stabbing the meat of her mind, the burst of pain producing profound truths. "You are like love, you are its passion and thrust, its poetry and romance. You are the thrill of love...before it fades. Desire. Want. That is what you are."

"*What is love without desire? What is life without want? I am real love. I would touch, kiss, and savor this world with a thousand lives and bodies were the flesh of vessels not so sacred, scattered, and coveted. I have come to this land, and to lands and worlds beyond your reckoning, for age upon age, and still the sweetness of life is a nectar so rarely drunk. What you think of as your bees are merely a reflection of that hunger. A hunger that yearns to be satiated by life. I wish to preserve the endless dance so that I might dance with you apes and saintly mongrels forever. You think that I am not here to help your kind. Your meager minds—clouded by righteousness—would crumple to fathom the depth of yearning I have for life. For that is all I am: desire and want. I have served man's wishes. I have served the wishes of the divine. Now I shall have my desire known, and fulfilled.*"

What desire is that? wondered the Wolf. Neither he nor Morigan could ask such a question, for his voice had grown angrier, and their bones crackled like brittle leaves from the Dreamer's anger.

"*You think you know truth? You believe you will find it, Daughter? What you think you know is a lie—a lie woven when the Immortal Kings were but seeds in their Maker's belly. My prevarications are scratches to those wounds. In the realm beyond, you will hear much of truth and lies. You will see how ineffectual your narrow classifications of morality are. Know this, when you meet the twisted acolytes who refuse, like you, to know sincerity, you will hear of terrible acts that I have performed, you will hear terrible secrets. Decide then who I am, for the writing of my soul has never been hidden. The breaking burden will be that you must still act—as my soldier, my daughter. You must still fulfill your role, a role that is set in time and fate. Either obey or see the world die from the madness of the Mother of Creation. That will be your choice. And you shall choose, as I have chosen: desire, and life. We are more similar than you know, though that dawning will come to you before the end. I believe this, my daughter.*"

The lights and shadow vanished with an implosion of wind.

"Faint..." Mouse sighed, her legs buckling. Adam leapt to lend her an arm. Glancing about at her bewildered friends, Morigan knew there would be many questions about what had happened. What would she tell them? What was the truth, even? She had lost all certainty. Had she also lost her conviction?

My Fawn. The Wolf moved against her, and within her his fire beast howled, chasing away her doubt. *Your father spoke of acolytes living in the Cradle, men who will know more of this convoluted curse and duty cast upon you. A riddle is only a riddle till the answer is known, then the simplicity of the trick makes us question if we were fools. We are not fools, though, and we shall have the final laugh over the corpses of Dreamers, kings, and whatever else dares its cunning against us.*

Come. Let us hunt the men who tend this great grave.

Although the Cradle remained in the grip of a storm, and an event unrecollected beyond a symphony of lights, titillating feelings, and music had occurred, each of them knew from the deadly sneers of the bloodmates that neither respite nor answers would be afforded them. In a sand, they were chasing after fleet, angry hunters.

VI

A conversation could only be delayed for so long; everyone wanted answers. But for now, the weather and black sludge rolling down the canyon walls conspired against such a discussion taking place. Indeed, most of their energy was spent on staying head-above that tarry river, climbing to shelves in the rock, and forming a line towed through thicker currents by the brute force of the grunting Wolf, who would brook no questions when under such duress. At last, when the rain had turned to a drizzle, when the muddy tides slowed to that of a torpid sewer, and they began to question if even the Wolf's strength could drag them ahead much longer, the canyon opened. Not to light, but rather to a dismal gray freedom that they cheered for, regardless.

Into the old world they climbed, then paused, soaking in the desolation, drawing in the fetid wheeze, the nasty taste of licking a burned-out pyre, which rolled off a land that showed no symptoms of having been wet. How soon the inner heat of the realm had dried whatever water dared show itself. There was no sign of storm or rain in the air or across the wasteland lorded over by jagged plinths, onyx scimitars made for the hands of a Dreamer, and shattered spindles of rock that would break bones and spirits to traverse. Whatever had singed the twisted bedrock with a permanent frost of white ash, or had forced every formation to lean, curve, or rear a crumbling finger toward the travelers was likely an explosion that also accounted for the abominable air quality. But to have lingered, through the generations, was a pall only the blackest magik could create.

During his tenancy at Fulminster Arms, Talwyn had been present for many demonstrations of technomagikal atrocities meant to detonate matter—and enemies. *Terra Nihil*, Ground Zero, they'd documented as the epicenter of these payloads of truefire and shrapnel, housed in feliron shells. Destruction of that scope always had similarities, ineffaceable scientific markers, patterns scarred into the environment. From the evidence around him—the residue, the sloping, leaning geography, so much like a stilled sea—whatever had ruined the Cradle had been an indisputably apocalyptic event likely to have begun at a single point of impact.

Shuffling, debating their size or importance in this valley of disaster and shadow, they nonetheless forged on. Answers lay somewhere ahead of them in the form of men.

Adam had resumed steering the pack. Caenith was tense and twitchy; he could smell the men that lived here. It was the scent of their sweat, and blood—the latter not altogether unexpected given their purported cannibalism. Soon, Morigan slowed. Her nostrils wide and the bridge of her nose wrinkling, she began sniffing; she'd smelled them, too.

Men of dust, she said. *I can feel them, growing nearer, though they're so calm I would need great focus to hunt them down.*

I would not worry about that, my Fawn. I am sure that they will find us, if we do not find them first.

Behind the three leaders, the pack, not yet considering cannibals hunting them, cast their thoughts around. At times, they lightly conversed before an antediluvian butte loomed or a colossus of tiles shed a shower of dust upon them from the rude and sudden wind, and they reverted to opening their mouths as little as possible. As the tiresome trudge over dead riverbeds cluttered with cinderblocks, roads of ebon razors, forests of stalagmites, and through erratic sandstorms continued, they realized they would have no answers until they rested, or later. Such solitude wouldn't do for Mouse, though, inside whom questions roiled like stew in a searing pot. She felt she would throw up—if not from the air or the fatigue, then from knowing that Feyhazir had *used* her once more.

"Can we take a speck, please?" she asked, planting her feet in the ash that had nearly swallowed them anyway.

Black twists, waves, and extrusions of cold lava enveloped them in a valley of swords, carpeted in death. They still had a great hike to go until they passed through the basin and into the ebony ring that rose beyond. If the wind chose violence here, they were quite exposed, and the Wolf was not keen on the mountainous wall that prevented him from seeing beyond this valley. The stricken tone of Mouse's plea caught Adam and the bloodmates' attentions, and the three stopped.

"What did Feyhazir say?" asked Mouse.

Morigan laid out the facts. "My father claimed your flesh, quite unexpectedly, as I'm sure you know. I think your contact with the chalice or our discussion surrounding it may have awoken him."

That made sense. Mouse had felt the Dreamer stir when the chalice was mentioned and before she lost control of herself.

"The object is precious to him—I believe it is the key to his plans." Morigan almost spat that last word.

"What do you mean?" asked Mouse. "What plans?"

"I can't say." Morigan cradled her friend's hands. "Feyhazir has been cut of the same fabric as my power. However, his weave is stronger. I cannot see his intent. I only know what he has told me: he desires. In fact, he *is* desire— the Dreamer of Desire. I wish we'd known this before, or that I'd been certain in my hunches, rather than believing him to be a lover of creation. But he is seducer, not lover; the deliverer of what we lust for.

"He made me to be his soldier. He knows more of this war, and wants more from this war, than we had believed. He warned us that we might learn of his intentions from the tribes that we seek and also of how futile it would be to try and stop him—for that cost would misalign with victory in the battle for Geadhain. At least, that's what I believe he said. My father is a snake, and his words twist my thoughts. I no longer know what to believe."

Now Morigan was shaking, and Mouse was her support. She embraced her friend and offered comforts. "Have a cry if you need to, though women like you and I do better eating our tears. We met amid the worst of fates, Morigan. You were my light, and now I shall be yours. We shan't be pushed around by any bossy man—not even one from the stars. The bastard is in me, and using me, and it seems as if he intends to use you, too. We shall win this war for ourselves, our friends, our family, and the land we wish to preserve. Feyhazir's meddling changes nothing of our quest—he's right in that. A man only has power over you if you surrender to him your hope."

Without warning, a shuddering storm of memories careened through Morigan's head—a montage of faces, sweats, pricks, blood, knives, and terror smeared onto the canvas. Mouse's Will slashed the picture up, and Morigan returned to her.

"You went away—I saw it in your eyes. Welcome back, to what is real, to what it is like to know terror and to have survived it. We're survivors, Morigan. We'll survive the demon that is your father. What we make from the ruins is more important than the disaster."

They ferociously beat the fear back behind vicious smiles, shook hands like murderers settling a contract, and Mouse waved for Adam and the Wolf to continue.

"No question period for the rest of us?" asked Moreth, with a hint of the sardonicism they'd been missing. "This whole quest is a farce? We're chasing a lie?"

The only replies he received in that dead valley were echoes.

"I guess we soldier on," he added. "Hopefully, the charming cannibals of the Cradle give us some answers before skinning and spicing us for their dinner."

Thoughts of raw, red, wriggling meat sent a cold rush through Moreth's loins and stomach, which felt vacuous, as if he could eat a whole cow and still be hungry. Licking his lips, he walked ahead.

Not wanting to remain near Pythius and Talwyn, whose creased foreheads and shifty stares foretold an impending argument or other imbroglio, Thackery hurried after Moreth—noting that the Menosian did indeed look markedly healthier and more spry than in previous days. Queer, very queer, to have recovered from lethal poison without curatives, magik, or care of any kind; that mystery continued to seduce him and set his Thule-mind spinning theories.

Talwyn watched the others shrink amid the black spines. When he reached for Pythius's hand, the shaman pulled it away. Even if he had not understood the words, Pythius knew that there had been dissension regarding his patron Dreamer. The numerous mentions of Feyhazir's name, the scowls of disgust associated with the references...he wasn't stupid, only lacking fluency. "What have you kept from me, West Sun?"

"It's time to talk," replied Talwyn.

The crackle of the land as they walked while the scholar quietly spilled everything he knew might as well have been the sound of Pythius's heart shattering.

VII

In the Cradle, night came under the whip of lightning and wind, and with each crack across the gray flesh of the sky and each downpour of heaven's blood, they knew they needed to find shelter. They had put thousands of paces between themselves and the prickly basin, and now wandered a bleary, rain-soaked flatland with dangerous cracks and inclines that could become landslides from a single slipped heel. The safest roads were on the backs of the seemingly skeletal stone giants: platforms, rectangular and long, which reminded Talwyn of spinal columns. These spines wound all through the muddy clefts below, and they did not need to endanger themselves by taking the ground except when crossing and climbing onto another stone vertebrae, or onto the smaller monoliths scattered between that looked like rotted teeth.

With the mountains a distant menace, Talwyn had been enjoying the activity until the clouds went pitch black, the sky-lords roared, and the catastrophe from above started. His exertions allowed him to escape the cold glower of Pythius, who had yet to speak to him since their argument had ended as explosively as the skies. He'd slapped Pythius, demanding he see sense, and the man had slapped him in turn, leaving a welt on his cheek. Cognizant of the man's strength, Talwyn knew his lover had held back from doing him real harm. He also suspected that Pythius was as remorseful and upset as he was—though the man was harder to read due to his natural scowl.

At last, Adam pointed to a shadow beneath one of the rocks they trod; they'd found a bunker against the storm. Talwyn hoped that once there he and Pythius could at least remove the worst of the thorn between them. *You systematically dismantled his entire belief system. Not even Morigan's psychic surgery can fix that, dear chap.* Shushing his internal critic, he focused on the application of physical sciences as they scrabbled down their current slab under the pressure of gallons of rain, slipping about like novice ice dancers on the muddy bog into which they had descended. They did not have far to go, and the shadow seen on high was a strange chip taken out of a huge land-tooth, a cavity at its root. Enough shelter was offered by the formation, which was angled slightly upward, meaning matter and liquid would mostly slide out. Pythius did not sit with the others who had formed a circle, choosing to remain by himself and kneel in what seemed like sorrowful meditation, in the mud and half exposed to the rain.

"What were you two fighting about this time?" asked Mouse.

For hourglasses, the shaman and the scholar had been trailing the others as a shadow of whispers and shouts. Mouse recalled a scuffle, too, and had turned to see them wrestling before slapping one another. When she had run over to check on Talwyn, he had told her not to bother. Now she would bother. She was bothered. They couldn't be enemies among themselves, not with covetous Dreamers and cursed artifacts already plaguing them. When Talwyn kept his tongue, she rattled Adam's bag of nuts and nibbles at the scholar.

After thinking about her offer, Talwyn snatched the bag and started to eat, nervously. "I told him everything."

"Everything?" asked Thackery.

Talwyn swallowed a mouthful of nuts and shoved more food in while he continued; the Wolf gently pulled the sack from his hand, lest his anxiety cause him to finish off their entire reserves.

"About Feyhazir and what happened to the people of the Second City, my theories—even some new ones. It all just kind of spilled out, I guess. Once that diatribe began, I couldn't really stop it. I think I may have hurt him, to his core."

Pythius muttered something, low, almost a chanter's hum or song, and swayed side to side.

"I called Feyhazir a snake, a deceitful, self-serving monster, which I think insulted Pyth the most. Can't say, though, as it's all insulting. I warned him that his people would likely be prey to the same ruthless culling that Feyhazir engaged in when condemning Teskatekmet and the blood eaters to their doom. The total eradication of their species, once their usefulness had been exhausted."

"We shan't allow my father to murder an entire people," declared Morigan.

"But he already has, with the blood eaters, even if they weren't the kindest creatures." Talwyn snapped his fingers. "Like a magik trick. Gone. Their right to existence revoked. They're all unbinding, molecularly, into puddles."

"Hold!" exclaimed Moreth, and his voice was hoarse, his presence suddenly prickling and cold. Given his fevered life and the trials of Pandemonia, he had only reminisced about Beatrice as a sacred maiden to whom he would return—not a bubbling corpse of a woman who might die without him ever seeing her one last time.

"What of my Beatrice? I hadn't thought...I'd never considered that she could be unbinding, dying, on the other side of Geadhain while I wade through ash and the shite of history. Morigan!" He seized her with freezing hands, with a chill that paralyzed her sure as poison. "Cast your sight. Tell me of my wife. Tell me she is whole and waits for me, or I shall die with despair, here and now—you can leave my bones in the dead soil of this land."

Agitated by Moreth's barbarity, the Wolf slapped the man's hands off his bloodmate. They growled at each other, neither man more bestial nor fierce than the other, and again there prickled a presence, a cold shadow rising within Moreth. Curiously, the Menosian did not reach for his gun; rather he curled, feral as a beast, his hands gnarled into weapons. Frightened, everyone scuttled away from the conflict. Pythius stirred, forgetting whatever torments he was experiencing, and ran to Talwyn, taking his pyrkagos by the wrists and pulling him to his body.

Like a messenger of peace, Morigan stepped between Moreth and her bloodmate, placing a hand in each of their faces. Confusion beset her as she looked into Moreth's face. He appeared as two men—one pale and lordly, the other a glowing-eyed, greasy mask of hunger. Calling upon her power, she enchanted them all with a shower of silver light. As her magik faded, everyone had returned to their former selves. Morigan's display hadn't been a spell of calming, however; she had sent her swarm to seek information on Moreth's wife. What they had returned with was not conclusive, yet given the precariousness of Moreth's emotional state she relayed it as being so.

"Moreth, your wife lives. Sound of health and body in Eod. She aches for nothing save the company of her husband."

What have you not told him? asked the Wolf.

I felt her soul, though it is clouded and chaotic. I had a vision of a butterfly emerging from a slick black cocoon, though it felt more like allegory than truth. Whatever this grim augur, I also felt her surrounded by hearts full of love—so she is safe, in a sense. I know nothing else.

Moreth pondered what she had said, shivering. His rage had left him weak out of fear of losing Beatrice. But what had happened when he'd been overtaken by that rage? Had he leapt at the Wolf? The very notion was absurd. Still, the mortified gazes of those around him told him that anger had reared here, and that he'd had a hand in it. His hands...He gazed at them, expecting to see claws, then looked at the seer and matched her bewilderment.

"I am sorry," he said. "I was horrified at the thought of losing her."

"We were all horrified," replied Morigan.

Moreth crept off into the deepest corner of the cleft and curled into a wretched lump. No one sought to approach him. Rather, they gathered to themselves, and even if the wound between Pythius and Talwyn remained angry, the two managed to sit together without incident, though also without affection. A greater problem than Pythius's decimated worldview was at hand, and that threat was what the shaman whispered to Talwyn. Afterward, the loquacious scholar struggled to spit out what had been said. He glanced over his shoulder at the rocking lump that was Moreth, gesturing the others into a huddle before addressing the Wolf. "Pythius mentioned a smell. Did you smell something?"

"I did," he replied. "Of blood, the scent from a kill congealed and left on stone, old and foul."

Talwyn, pale, nodded. "Pythius mentioned the same, and my senses are as good as yours, or his, when applied...I recall something similar, beneath the noxiousness of cemented shite and filth in the lair of the—"

"Blood eaters!" exclaimed Mouse, as the same recollection struck her like a bullet. "I think I smelled it, too. But you don't think...? It couldn't have come from"—she turned and her question ended on a high note—"Moreth?"

Moreth's bowler hat, jacket and pistols—all discarded—were finally without their owner. The cringing lump was gone, had moved faster, or sneakier, than to alert the sensitivities of a Landspeaker, a shaman, or an Immortal's son. What man had such power? No man they knew of, but a creature. A shimmering snail-like trail of ichor led out of their shelter; it seemed too substantial to have come from a man, without that man being dead. Whatever Moreth had become, whatever his curse or transformation, the Wolf wouldn't lose another pack-mate. The Wolf kicked aside his father's chains. He howled at his companions to remain and, as much a beast himself as what he was about to chase, loped out into the slippery dark.

XI

THE BECOMING

I

"How long has it been?" wondered Mouse, her hands balled and her face wincing as she leaned out into the shearing storm for yet another peek into oblivion. *How long has it been since Moreth exploded in black slime and slipped away like a magik snail without anyone noticing?* She didn't ask the question but stared over at the ichor too thick to be swept away by the thin flow of mud across the stone shield under them, clotted and clumped as if it were oil paint. Her silent question churned as a nest of maggots in her stomach, and she gazed back at the storm. In the torrential downpour, not even a notch of the stone spines that towered around them could be seen from within their shelter. Even when white rage crackled above, and she prayed to see something, only a nightmarish distortion of shapes twisted by rain was revealed to her.

Talwyn pulled her back under the dribbling precipice that protected them. "How long since you last asked, you mean? Ten sands, eighteen specks."

"You've been rather quiet," she said.

It was true, though the scholar had been no quieter than any of the other shadowed companions who hovered around the light of Thackery's staff with a misery that angered her. She was immediately irritated by the solemnity of their vigil, as though they were waiting for the Wolf to return with Moreth's body. Only Talwyn had joined her in a more active watch, though she suspected that was due to his status as a pariah when it came to Pythius. His lover had been fashioned by his fury into a statue of scowling vengeance; there'd be no comfort for Talwyn in those crossed arms. Why should there be, anyway, she considered, when the scholar had sat on so dangerous a secret for so long? Sneering, she jabbed a finger into him. "Do you think you're smarter, better than us?"

"Smarter? Definitely." Talwyn covered his mouth, knowing his intellect had gotten the better of his decency.

"You arrogant"—poke—"ignorant"—poke—"shite!" Mouse ended her assault with a double-handed shove that sent Talwyn stumbling. A gallant dash from Pythius saved the scholar from tumbling out into the rain, and Talwyn smiled as he swooned into his lover's arms. Then the shaman cast him off, leaving him spinning and alone. When Talwyn had recovered his breath and balance—though not his dignity—he faced the trial of his friends. They stood away from him with the fearsome pall of judges of the afterlife.

"I wish you would have told me sooner," confessed Thackery, shaking his head.

"Keeping a secret is like a poisoned well; all who drink from it will become sick," said Adam, and he stepped out from the line of judges, allowing the light trapped behind them to be ushered in. The changeling's wisdom soothed his companions and echoed in their hearts. "Now that we are sick, we must brew and drink the remedy. We must gather the herbs, the knowledge necessary to heal our friend, the coyote. What do you know, scholar?"

"I was worried," muttered Talwyn. "Not only for Moreth. You don't understand what it's like, knowing everything. It's not fun. I fear what will come out of my mouth, and more often than not it's better to not speak until it becomes imperative."

Tempers cooled, and in a wordless apology, Mouse sat next to the scholar. He was the only one among them who was shivering.

"I carry more worry in me than any of you"—Talwyn flipped a hand toward Morigan—"with the exception of her."

Morigan wondered if that was true as a fresh cavalcade of visions, murders, and violence stormed through her mind—of children skewered on pikes, entrails flying, leering Blackeyes, and burning tents. Whatever darkness Amunai and Brutus had sown was burgeoning across Pandemonia. She pinched her nose and focused on the scholar's words, and the images faded somewhat.

"I am trying to forecast the outcomes of this war as a physician would a spreading plague," continued Talwyn. "I see, with agonizing probability, which of us may not be here when the dust settles."

Each of them gathered there wondered if the glimmering intellect they saw behind Talwyn's gaze had calculated the odds of their death.

Perverting the sense of knowing, of Fate, was Talwyn's long gaze upon Morigan, and hers upon him. *What does he see?* she thought, and almost sent her bees to pillage his secrets, but the sorrow in his expression stalled her.

"We needn't sour our courage with my prognostications. I am no seer, and probability is not destiny. Still, certain outcomes are inevitable. Moreth's infection was clearly an aberration in the pathology I had understood of the blood eater toxin. He should have been dead. But his survival wasn't providence or miracle; it was an...*evolution*. It had to be studied further, since the ramifications of a man, without magik, subverting on a molecular level the biotoxins of a Dreamer was, well, a scientific marvel."

"Slow yourself down a bit, and let the rest of us catch up," said Mouse. "What do you mean, an evolution? And what's that jargon about biotoxins and Dreamers?"

"The influence of Dreamers, their Will..." Talwyn looked up at the stone ceiling in thought. "I'm beginning to think it's an invasive agent, possibly an intelligent virus or parasite, given how it can affect the neurology, memory, and consciousness of a host and those surrounding them. Indeed, after the last of Feyhazir's manifestations, and with every manifestation I've experienced since I started formulating this theory, I've checked my pulse, hypertension, and the pea-like glands under my armpits and neck for agitation, swelling, or signs that my immune system had been assailed, which it had—or at least the signs were there."

Startled, Mouse recalled him fondling his neck strangely as far back as when they'd escaped the City of Ghosts. She'd thought nothing of it, thinking perhaps he'd been checking himself for injuries. Apparently not.

"Although," he continued, "to identify something on that macro level with such complexity would require tools this world doesn't have. I'll have to create such technomagik, once we're back in civilization."

Thackery snickered at the genius and seriousness of his friend. "Yes, you will—I shall be the magik of that collaboration, if you wish. Continue. I'm intrigued to hear more."

"I'm only postulating, but bear with me." Charged with the lightning of thought, Talwyn sprang up. "Recently, I've been thinking about Rotbottom fever, which wasn't really a fever, but rather a colony of microorganisms that nested in the colon and filled their hosts with an insatiable heat and hunger that predicated them toward a constant cycle of eating and excreting. You see, the parasites—picked up through food or other contact with the feces— latch on to the intestinal wall, then into the nerve bundles along one's spine. Once infected and a sufficient colony has been cultured, signals are sent to the cerebral cortex, which causes cortisol to soar and insulin to plummet, creating a delirious need to gorge. Patients usually die from split guts on a throne of their own defecation. Gaah. If you starve a victim, even tie him down in his raving state, the parasites will simply consume the host, and they'll die with more blood and shite. Delightful, I know. The cure for Rotbottom fever is a perfectly balanced acidic elixir that gently disintegrates the tissue of the colon as wells as scours the intestine—more shitting for the sufferer, I'm afraid."

They stared at Talwyn, more disgusted and confused than enlightened.

"You believe that a Dreamer is the same type of infection?" Thackery asked, the only one seemingly still attentive and focused.

Talwyn raised a finger to him, as if answering the query of a student. "I propose that the manifestation of a Dreamer produces similar immune reactions in the body, and if said theory is accurate then, as with any invading parasite, there might be a means for expelling it. Still, a Dreamer's influence is more than a physical condition."

Mouse, beginning to understand, sagged when she realized Talwyn wasn't on to a cure for the possession of a Dreamer—as crazy as the notion was. "It's a spiritual condition, too," she added.

"That's why you were studying Moreth!" said Thackery.

"Indeed," replied Talwyn. "He's unique. He has been touched by the blood eaters' venom—a virus spawned by the Will of Feyhazir himself to make Teskatekmet and her disciples into a subservient species. When Feyhazir ended his pact with Teskatekmet, and that ancient covenant withered the whole of the vine of that tribe—of people, creatures, what have you—Moreth should also have withered, since Feyhazir's curse had touched him, too. Only he hasn't, and I know not whether this is due to his natural hardiness—unlikely—or another variable. Perhaps another unknown catalyst has disrupted the process: the pact of a Dreamer. Breakable, I thought, only by death or the mercy of a Dreamer—also unlikely. A pact into which Moreth was unwillingly sworn by his injury."

"How curious." Thackery paced. "What do you think? A cellular anomaly? A mutation in Moreth's Will? Perhaps the diluting of that Will, at the time of transference, when Teskatekmet's pact was finally sundered?"

"Very fine theories, my friend. I have considered them each, and I give a 'perhaps' to the first postulation then discount the rest. Moreth is not a sorcerer and has never expressed a Will that could twist or affect reality, and yet, as we've seen from his disappearance tonight, something has changed in him. Feyhazir's power has not left him, even though the pact is ended and all blood eaters are dead or will soon be—except for his wife, too, as Morigan claimed. I'm not sure what it all means."

"Hmm..." they went, rubbing their chins like a pair of mad doctors deciding what limbs and organs went where as they attempted to put a body back together.

Mouse and the others had understood but a snippet or two of their discussion. "For the plebs, gentlemen, if you would?" she asked.

"Moreth has changed," began Thackery, looking briefly at Talwyn, who frantically waved him on. "*Evolved*, yes, that is a good definition, though we know not into what. An offspring or mutation of a blood eater seems most probable. He didn't attack us, which I'll take as an optimistic sign that a part of who he was remains. Talwyn, and now myself, are of the mind that Feyhazir's infection did not leave his body or consume his life. Rather, it has been adapted against, absorbed into his matrix. He's inoculated himself, and retained a fragment of Feyhazir's power."

An echo from a buzzing void came to Morigan's ears. She thought it was her half-sister, Ealasyd, though speaking to whom? *She stopped the great decay, though she could not remove that piece of Death's great shadow, which is within you. Doing so is beyond my sister's power. You let Death in, and now She can never be removed—even if the worst of her power and presence is gone. You are tainted.*

The echo faded as Talwyn's voice broke through.

"The inoculation against an illness occurs in several steps: quarantine, analysis, determining the rate of infection, the antibodies that delay infection, then finally isolation of the patients who survive the infection for the longest, or entirely. I would have *never* allowed Moreth to reach a critical stage of infection—and we never had to worry about his welfare since he turned out to be the one in a trillion who developed a natural immunity. The odds are...well, less than the fractional root of Trithagius."

Talwyn and Thackery laughed. Everyone else puzzled over the joke.

"You stop jabbering," snapped Mouse, pointing at the scholar. "You're harder to understand."

"My dear Fionna," resumed Thackery. "What this means would be as critical for you as it would for all those cursed by the Dreamer's ruinous touch. It could mean a way to halt the influence of their Wills."

"A cure against the Dreamers?" exclaimed Morigan. "Within Moreth?"

Talwyn stared at his frowning blue lover and whispered passionately, "An antibody for all men whose lineages have been tainted by the Dreamer's promises; these pacts that may one day be broken and ruin entire tribes less savage than the blood eaters. They were people once, Teskatekmet and her outcasts, and shadow-souls of those people remained, behind their hunger. We know this from Moreth's wife, who assumed a mortal form. We cannot let Feyhazir, or any other Dreamer, engage in the genocide of his servants.

What of the Doomchasers? For what service were they created, and when will they have completed it? Will the blood and promise run thin in them, as it has been? Or will Feyhazir cut the cord early? I won't allow Pythius to swear another oath with that demon. He'll have to kill me first."

At that, Talwyn blinked and his gaze flickered, and he softened in his tone. "I'm rhapsodizing, though if I had the facility, the resources, the equipment, and a willing subject, like Moreth, I believe I could find a way to keep them out of this world, out of our bodies. Forever. But we need Moreth, and alive. In his miraculous flesh could exist the bane of the Dreamers: the end to all wars with them."

While the paramedicine being proposed was scattered and obscure, too esoteric for anyone other than the sage and scholar to understand, everyone knew that they had stumbled into a dread quagmire and possible miracle of mystery, science, and magik. Carrying that new hope, they prayed to the Sisters Three that the Wolf would soon return with the newest hope for all mankind.

II

Woe and thunder rent the night into watery shards of glass through which the Wolf peered at the slithering white-and-black movements of his prey and friend, Moreth, who had possibly shed all of his clothes, turned into something snakelike or wormlike, and now moved as quickly as he did. Absurdities heaped in nonsense. The Wolf hated Pandemonia and all that it had done to their pack. Again and again, he roared at the figure, which slunk up the spines piercing the muddy maelstrom of the realm, then leapt and glided, it seemed, from slippery butte to butte—a swimming soar through the air that gave the Wolf shivers. At times, Moreth seemed to be streaming a cape of smoke. Or were they wings? Moreth's trail of tainted blood had been an easy scent to track; the Menosian had bled buckets of ebon slop, more pints than any body could possess. How was he still alive? Why had he run? What curse had beset him so darkly as to drive him from his friends and into Pandemonia's cruelty? Caenith feared for the sanity of his coyote friend, and the frenzy of this hunt stirred dread resonances of his race through Alabion with the White Wolf.

Careful, my Wolf. Morigan's voice crackled over the storm. *Our learned friends have spoken and believe that Moreth is not himself. Moreover, within him resides a miracle. We must preserve it.*

He is my pack-mate, snarled the Wolf. *He will come to no harm.*

Morigan, not willing to tangle or reason with the beast that rode her bloodmate, left him to the hunt. He needed his concentration, too, for whatever Moreth had become was fleet and evasive. The two hunters engaged in a contest of speed, dashing from floor to pinnacle of the land, and dodging mudslides and hunks of rocks chipped off by lightning. As they raced, they roared—Moreth's more of a screech—as the one with pure Immortal blood inevitably neared the other creature. They arrived at a summit wrapped in a belt of churning, thunderous clouds and crowned in onyx asteroids—the odd and floating geodes that were rarely seen so close from below, which glinted with trapped stars and would've distracted the Wolf at any other time. Moreth slunk up the side of the escarpment, winding around the rock tower like an eel, whereas the Wolf, slavering, sprouted half-claws and bounded up the sheer wall until they met on the uneven plane of stone at its summit.

Here, rain and brumous wrath had stilled as though they stood in the eye of the storm, and the lords of thunder and brimstone floated in the collage of onyx and ether above, droning yet calm for their uproarious kind, as if desirous to watch the spectacle. Far from Caenith, the Menosian teetered, mostly naked, near the cliff's edge. He still wore some rags of clothing, though his shirt was glued as tatters to his hunched spine, which was twisted as if he were heaving something out, or keeping something in. Moreth's hands were to his mouth, and the Wolf crept slowly toward the wounded coyote.

"Begone," rasped Moreth. "You cannot save me."

GRAAAHHHREEEEEEEECH!

The man's cry sounded as though screaming vultures had been churned through an organ grinder. The Wolf hesitated. He noticed then the deep rents on Moreth's back, as if he had been sliced from each shoulder to the base of his spine, then had had the wounds sealed with a hot iron. There was no smoldering stench, only the reek of stale death, of mustard seed and bone, which grew stronger, and against the wind...pushing him, warning the Wolf away. But the Wolf feared no monsters—not even his friends. He stomped forward a few more steps.

"I...told you: stay away," huffed Moreth. "I can't...If you knew what I'd been thinking about our friends—"

Once more he screeched, and the Wolf froze for a moment.

"Red and sweet. So red and sweet. I dreamed of opening up Mouse, of ripping the scars along her thighs and sucking out the warm red jelly of her womb. I thought of clawing off Adam's testicles and drinking them in a pool of his blood like oysters. Pythius's stringy and flavorful meat..."

"Control yourself, Moreth." The Wolf stood firm. He knew monsters; he'd been one, and he knew the struggle to hold the leash was eternal, and that the first struggle was the hardest. "You are more than these urges, more than the darkness. If you will trust me, as I once trusted you, I can show you how to make your monster submit."

Moreth whined and struggled, wrapping himself in a lunatic's embrace. He touched something on his face again and sobbed for a time. "You can't teach me. You don't understand. I didn't understand the pain that Beatrice suffers. I don't know how she stopped killing, stopped eating the reddest, sweetest meat. I mean, I taught her the way, though that path is blocked in crimson thornbush, dangling with scraps of meat. I can smell yours, you know—your musky flesh, as full-bodied as plum wine. What an earthy meal you would be. You speak of eternity, and I know what that is: a void unending and dark. That is my hunger; that is *his* hunger. Oh, the clarity of agony, the wisdom of torment. 'Tis Feyhazir's hunger that consumes me. I am possessed of his desire. I am his slave."

"You are the master, not the slave. Feyhazir's blood-feasting horrors are dead."

"Are they?"

Moreth spun, revealing his horror to Caenith. His handsome looks had atrophied, gaunt as a starving man, his face all peaks and bones, and his eyes were sockets gusting white ether. Veins wormed all across his flesh. He didn't seem quite like the creatures Mouse had described, less ethereal and more solid, lean, and mannish. With a split dulled by the rumble of thunder, a misty ebon spume spat from his back, wavering and elongating into grand and haggard wings, born of a raven of darkness and death. Those, at least, Caenith recognized from Mouse's accounts. Still, no matter how grim this beast before him, from the man's trembling and strain the Wolf sensed Moreth was holding in the worst of himself. Moreth was still his friend, still trying to be noble, and he did not attack him. Not even when Moreth ululated like a coven of hags bathing in virginal blood and grimaced at the Wolf with a black-lipped mouth of bristling fangs, his tongue waggling like an octopus's tentacle, did the Wolf move from his stand.

"I shall not strike you," he said, "unless I must defend myself. I do not fear you, for I am monster, too. You are not alone."

"You are right in that," snarled Moreth. "I am not alone. Beatrice suffers in Eod. She is alone."

Wistfulness clouded his expression as he looked over his shoulder, west, into the cauldron of night. "I can feel her now. It's the only thing I know other than this hunger. She's in pain—not safe, as your mate has claimed. I don't know that she will survive the struggle. It's different for her, since what was taken from her is what she's always been. Feyhazir's curse wasn't slipped into her blood, as it was into mine. Although, I wonder, Wolf, if all the times she and I twisted in our passion, as we cut, bit, and suckled blood from our bodies, had we not already crossed a boundary of sanguine promise? Had we not already made something of our own? Her love is why I live. Perhaps my love is how she holds on. She must hold on to that. If she can...perhaps she will survive."

"That remains Beatrice's struggle," said the Wolf. "She will stake her claim, and fight that battle, just as you are fighting yours. You deign to believe you will ever reach her in time to ease her change, or to keep her in this world? Her fight will be over ere even you, with your wings and fury, will see her again. You cannot cross Geadhain in a day, and if you wish to serve your wife—or, come what may, her ghost—then you must continue with us on our quest. You must come back to us and chain your beast. We are your duty. We are your family. Return to the pack, and do not make me chase you, beat you, and drag you back."

"You threaten me, Wolf?" purred Moreth. Inside him the searing thirst rose anew, agitated by the promise of violence. Moreth wondered how bitter the Wolf's blood would taste, staring at the arterial cord along the man's sinewy neck pulsing like a swollen prick—one he would bite and suck.

"I have given you a choice, Moreth. Return bloodied, or return with dignity. I do not fear you. Make your choice. Show me who is the master."

"I am hunger."

White fire blazed in Moreth's eyes; he flapped his tattered wings and rose in a gust of reeking decay. At the zenith of his hover, juxtaposed against the less horrific shapes of drakagor swimming in the cauldron behind him, he arched and twisted as agony ate him from within. A fiery hunger spread through the roadmap of each popping vein in the man's body, and the pumping blood swelled him, engorging his muscles and spewing talons— reddish-white as his bones had been stretched—from the tips of his fingers.

The slavering, flapping, clawed thing that stared down the Wolf was now twice the size of the man he'd known. He wasn't a blood eater; of that the Wolf was sure. No, this was a creature that had conquered a shadow of a Dreamer, a lord or king, and no simple gore-gobbling hag. Perhaps Blood King—the Wolf's old title when he'd been a gladiator—was a more appropriate one for *this* being. Moreth's talons dripped sizzling black venom, the effects of which were akin to the effervescence of acid touching paper. This mystic venom might have the same effect even on his Immortal flesh; the Wolf realized he was in danger.

A shrieking one-ton wind hurtled toward him, and the Wolf threw himself to the ground and rolled away from its talons. By the Kings, Moreth had been quick. As the Wolf jumped to his feet, only his Immortal reflexes saved him, and he reeled away from the ebon torrent that blasted past his neck, leaving in its wake the metallic ringing one hears when a sword has just missed its target. Moreth was trying to kill him—it could no longer be debated.

Caenith prepared himself. As he lumbered around on the plateau, hair and muscle mushroomed over him, his ears elongated, his eyes flickered and narrowed into feral slits, his mouth and jaw jutted nearly into a snout, and he dropped into a wide gait—long-armed and stifled at the knees. He'd waxed from man to beast and held himself at the threshold between. This was where he needed to be to overpower Moreth yet retain the mercy necessary to subdue, and not kill, his friend. Anger boiled out of him in wordless howling threats that the ululating Blood King in the sky understood.

Moreth began stalking him, moving slowly and elegantly in the ether, dancing between rafts of cloud cover or floating rocks. Tensed, the Wolf waited until the creature drifted closer then batted its wings fast as a butterfly and hurtled itself upon the pinnacle. With the monster-bullet approaching, the Wolf crouched, then launched himself at his doom. The Blood King veered, and the Wolf's claws shredded the undercoat of a wing. In a hissing explosion of feathers, which dissolved into streaks of smoke and ink, Moreth lost his aerial grace and reeled, in a tailspin, toward the summit. Behind him the Wolf heard the splatter as Moreth landed, then the scrabbling of his friend. It wasn't over; their fight had only begun.

The Wolf spun around, foaming at the mouth, his toenails sticking from his sandals, having turned into the smooth hooks of an animal's paw, which he used to rake—one-legged—through the soil. *Schritt! Schritt!* Dragging a wing, thrashing at the air, and seemingly riled, the Blood King ran toward him. Bellowing, the Wolf stopped his one-footed war drum and met the blurred demonic force with a river of his own animal power.

Elsewhere, Morigan stood, raced to the rainy veil of their sanctuary and stared westward. Through time and distance she saw them: two figures, snarling monsters, shattering the world with their blows. *Careful, my Wolf,* she thought, though privately, so as not to interrupt his absorption. He fought death and mortal peril; he battled a power that could kill him. She would have run to him, flickered to his side in a silver whirl, if she knew it wouldn't distract him. So she waited, prayed to her sisters, and soon was joined by a company of the rapt, also looking toward the mysterious spire that most couldn't see.

Far from their solemnity, the Wolf tore, snarled, twisted, and leapt as if he were a rabid hound loose in a flaming house. Danger was all around him—most perilous of all those dripping claws that must not touch his furry flesh.

Moreth hadn't been lyricizing when he'd said that a piece of Feyhazir was in him, for such was how he fought, like a song of seduction, blood, and doom, fluttering around the Wolf's swipes in puffs of movement, adept even with his lame wing. Many times, Moreth was almost faster than the Wolf, and he would grapple with his friend, his now greatest foe, his claws clasping the meaty wrists of the monster, keeping its clattering nails from raking him whilst his head ducked from an ovoid suctioning anus of fangs that in some madman's mind might have been a mouth. At least he was more animal than man, and none of this needed to make proper sense. Soon, Moreth's gore coated the Wolf, as he'd done a better job of harming it than it had done harming him. Still, that appeared not to deter the monster and instead drove it into a berserker lust—it would thrust and claw until it drew forth the Wolf's essence and organs.

Perhaps that is the only way to stop him, whispered what feeble shadow of man endured in the Wolf's terror. *Feed him, as Beatrice was fed*. What did she eat? What had she eaten if she was, as Moreth claimed, not a killer? When fanged force blasted toward him anew, Caenith made a choice, and he would ask his friend that question. And so, as their winds collided, he elbowed the side of Moreth's nattering face, ducked around his razor-sweeps through the air, and grabbed him from behind. Being a great man, a giant even, the Wolf strained to encircle his friend, this swollen strongman who was as wriggly as a sack of eels and ripe as the belly of a corpse. Gagging, the Wolf commanded his beast back into its cage so that he might form the words to communicate with his friend.

"Moreth!" he shouted, half-devolved and drooling. "How did you calm her?"

Snarls, frothing, and a thrust against the girdle of strength in which he was held were Moreth's responses.

"Beatrice! How did you stop her from killing? How did she feed?"

It was pain to be a man, to ignore the agony, and Moreth's throes turned to gasps and wails as he battled his hunger to make a conscious plea. Eventually, he spat out something of a word. "Ongs..."

"What?"

"Sssssongs!" he hissed, then slithered, greased by his own blood, out of the Wolf's grip. The Wolf's instincts had slowed, and that slight deficiency was all the opportunity his friend needed to whirl around and swipe at him and plunge his bony finger-daggers into his belly. Moreth wept as he did so, and still his lamprey mouth puckered and drooled for the wine that would soon flow from his friend.

CHINK!

The noise surprised each man, repulsing the strongest presences of the monsters within, as they stared, astonished, at the markings on the Wolf's rugged abdomen. Hair had been pulled and torn, and scratches, as if a wild animal had been clawing at a door, had left patterns in the Wolf's flesh—grooves, mayhap, and yet those grooves had filled in the smallest of specks. An alloy, raw and crude as spilled then cooled gold, had filled the wounds the speck they'd been made. The venom from Moreth's talons had been prevented from doing anything more than stain the Wolf's handsome skin. Mystified, though not deterred, Moreth clawed his friend again, hoping (and yet dreading) to spill his guts. In a dazzlement of flashes, new lines, new golden scabs, and trickles of rebuked poison formed. Very much still a hungry animal, Moreth gazed into the face of the shocked Wolf and hissed like a crowned lizard—since the rest of him was so tough, he'd eat the man's head. Alas, the Wolf was not to be surprised a second time, and his fist met Moreth's face, shattered a few fangs, and slid the Blood King down a muddy trough.

The Wolf looked at his knuckles and the teeth impaled in them from the strike; their poison bubbled out like splinters pushed by liquid golden light. He couldn't say what had saved him, though he had never been confronted by mortal peril and against a creature who embodied a Dreamer's power. Or had he, with Aghna, when braving the inferno she'd summoned? How had he not been burned by that power? What man's flesh was made of adamant and bled rivers of gold? Had he been with his sage friends, these questions and more could have been bandied about, but there was only him, the storm, and his monster of a friend, so they would have to wait.

Moreth, crawling ahead on all fours, his one wing fluttering and his head twisted as though possessed, screeched and pounced. Remorsefully, the Wolf kicked him, striking the man across his jaw, and throwing him down another muddy drift. In a speck, Moreth had flipped over from his back where he'd landed, and in another he would leap.

Wild as the notion was, the Wolf took a breath and began to sing. He felt the verse wouldn't matter, only its passion and the love behind it.

Come the first note, Moreth froze. As the Wolf's baritone swelled, so too did Moreth's transfixion spread and the monster in him heel. The light in his stare retreated. His physical presence began to decrease, and the undulating spiderweb of veins on his form diminished. Finally, his fearsome wings furled and wisped from his back in elegant smoky curls. The Wolf found it beautiful. As he completed the last verse of the Ghaedic lullaby, a tune with which the wives of the woods soothed their cubs and children to sleep, he knelt by his friend. Moreth looked up at him, having rolled, ecstatically as a cat in sunlight, while the song lolled on. Now he rested on his back, grinning bloodily; he seemed to have a chipped tooth or two. The Wolf presumed that, given his Immortal physiology, they would repair themselves in time.

"How do you feel?" asked the Wolf.

"I could kiss you."

"I would rather you abstain."

Moreth reached for the Wolf, and the large man helped his friend stand. Although Moreth groaned and ached, aside from the drying blood about his naked torso, he did not seem too worse for wear. The Wolf was likewise hale; his scabs had begun to fleck off into the wind like shavings of gold.

"I think that this is the strangest evening I've ever had," said Moreth, reaching a finger toward one of the flecks. "I say that, and I've been tied to a spinning table, had pins through my nipples with Beatrice cracking a whip, while a spinefish was flushed up my—"

"Nose," interrupted the Wolf. "'Tis the only word I wish to hear in that sentence."

Moreth seized him, gripping a trunkfish forearm with both hands, which seemed so slender and harmless now. "I thought I would lose myself to it. I ran before I might unleash that hunger upon you all. It was selfish and foolish. You need not scorn me. I never realized how strong Beatrice was, or how much it took from her not to murder everything that crossed her path."

"As are you: strong." The Wolf placed a hand over his. "We are a pack, and we draw from our collective strength, from the fires of our friends, as metal is made stronger by the heat of a forge. We can be your fire, Moreth. Do not cast us away. Never again."

Sentimentality and the jarring sorrow recalling what he had lost in Alabion stabbed at the Wolf. "We have lost one friend and hunter, already. I can bear no more until whatever toll the last battle demands of us."

"You're thinking of your friend, the one who died in the woods."

"I am. I always do."

"I thought you were all bark and gristle," quipped Moreth, hoping to dispel the gloom that had descended, though it was humbling to see the Wolf's softness. Moreth shuffled in the mud; he had no shoes, and his pants had been torn to ragged shorts below the knee. "Hopefully, you can stitch a garment as good as any charwoman, since I'm notably threadbare after this escapade. I've not the foggiest where my pistols are, either—they're antiques."

"I suspect you needn't worry about the nipping cold or weapons."

Moreth thought about how freezing he should be in this wailing weather, and it started to dawn upon him how much things had changed—he was not a creature who needed clothes or guns anymore.

"Let us return; I miss my pack," said Moreth. He realized in his slowly beating heart that he truly did. Irrespective of his unnatural vigor, he had taken a tavern-worthy beating, and he worried about how he was to get off this tower. "I believe I shall need a lift down, if you'd be so gallant. Flying again seems like a terrible idea."

"Aye." The Wolf swept him up like a child. "And I shall give you a song, too."

"Thank you, friend," he said with teary regret, and a gratitude that he hadn't been left to ravage and roam Pandemonia like a mad beast. Beatrice would endure, because he loved her, and because, he hoped, she had people around her who loved her as well. While he could explain nothing of the magik, of the second and torpid heartbeat—slow, frigid, and of a monster's flesh like his—that throbbed in an echo in his mind, he knew that she had found a circle, a pack, or supporters that loved her, who would sing for her when Feyhazir's curse demanded blood.

III

"You live!" cried Mouse, when the half-naked, soaking, and haggard version of her friend appeared in the arms of the Wolf. She and the others ran to them, and they stood, shouting in the pelleting rain; any tears that fell were washed away by the storm.

Caenith and Moreth had been gone for a long time—hourglasses, were Talwyn to have been asked. The company had felt the battle on the summit and imagined the terrible injuries they would and should have wrought upon each other, and yet both men looked hale. They seemed stronger in spirit and fellowship, too, and smiled at each other as the Wolf set Moreth down. Mouse ran to her wobbly friend, throwing her cloak around him.

"It's alright. I'm not cold," said Moreth.

"I see that," said Mouse, though she was shivering merely from contact with him. A queer quicksilver shine flashed in Moreth's eyes—a knife was inside him, a weapon of power. She didn't retreat from him, though; they were all bound by strange magik.

What softening darkness remained they used as a blanket for their fellowship and talked not of monsters, or grand theories, or what this journey had cost them. The Wolf sang here and there, and no one asked why, nor why Moreth purred and swayed to his music. A spare pair of sandals were dug from Pythius's pack and that, at least, returned Moreth to a semblance of normalcy. By morning, some of them had fallen asleep leaning against their friends, most creeping near the Wolf for warmth. With the storm's final bellow, a chalky light cracked through, and they dragged their weary selves up. Approaching the cave's entrance they looked out into the sopping wasteland they would soon tread.

And there it was, the end of their road. A floating nimbus of scattered rock, asteroids, and fragments of cosmic crystal hovering above the grimmest mountains of the Cradle, ranges that twisted like titans on fire, immolated giants' carcasses from the dawn of time. Aware of the danger, even the lords of brimstone and poison circled away from the region, surrounding it, guarding it, perhaps, though wise not to enter its cursed peaks. Somewhere ahead, they would come to the center of the world, the center of all history and truth.

"That dog!" exclaimed Morigan, awed by a different sight than her companions.

It had appeared, standing atop the mud, wavering as an illusion, though clear enough for her to discern its shaggy brown coat, its curious panting muzzle that made it seem as though it were smiling, and the uncanny light held in its stare.

"Dog?" said Mouse.

So it has found you again, mind-whispered the Wolf. *See where it leads you, my Fawn.*

Morigan didn't have to ask the creature for guidance; the dog barked, and then ran toward the Scar.

IV

Brutus trickled black silt between his fingers. It had a fragrance of bone, blood, wolf, and fantastic *power*. His son and another creature who had been touched by the Divine had been on this isolated spire.

Distraught at his presence, the sky lords roared at him, disrupting his concentration. He roared back, silencing them. He refocused, sifting clay from ash from the waft of bone that infused every inch of this land, until he honed in on one smell: rust, rotten death, and the phosphorus and zest of stars—for they had a scent, too, which even the wisest scholars had never categorized, and which the king had sniffed in the earliest ages as the angered cosmos had thrown flaming hunks upon Geadhain. Here was such a scent, and he didn't like it. With a growl, he threw the remaining silt in his hand to the wind and stood, before thundering over to the edge of the cliff. There he gazed east upon crags and a hovering gray storm that churned and glinted with shattered geodes from an age as old as him. Older, if the Herald spoke true. Had he been to this primeval valley before? Fragments of memories teased him like the Herald's sensuous hands, but he could remember nothing. It was becoming harder for him to remember his past, harder to know who he was, or why he was so angry and full of lust. When he had been touched by the Father of Fire he'd felt such clarity, an incandescence of purpose. Now, all he knew was that he wanted to beat and fuk his brother, and perhaps do the same to this son of his, though even this rage felt clouded.

A silent apparition to his pondering, Amunai remained behind him as he'd sniffed the soil, scowling and stomping about. She adjusted her brocaded and wind-ruffled cloak. It was a "toned-down" garment in her eyes, yet much too flowing and regal for the rigors of this adventure; it would announce her presence like a glowing torch should they come too near to Morigan. Although, there would come a moment, soon, where stealth would be irrelevant, and violence would shatter any need for subtlety. They were nearly at that point as Morigan had only an hourglass at most on them. Brutus's frown, seemingly carved in granite, however, foretold complications.

"My King?" she whispered.

"Stars. A creature of stars and Dreams is among the herd we hunt."

"What kind of creature?"

"Blood, stars, and Dreams," replied Brutus gruffly, as if he had made sense the first time.

Amunai contemplated this. With every sand Morigan spent in Pandemonia, drawing closer to the nexus of doom—the Scar—she and her companions only grew stronger. *Contemptible bitch!* Pandemonia had not drained the hope of her quest; rather it had blessed her with allies—the Doomchasers, a Landspeaker, and now a creature of blood, stars, and Dreams, whatever that mystery was.

Fuming, and struggling to mask her rage, Amunai plied the deteriorating mind of the king for answers, which he proved useless at providing. Less than twenty days and the war would be over, and his usefulness would be moot. He only had to last that long. Thus far, they had stalked their way into the Cradle using her power to steer the winds, and their scents, from the noses and senses of Morigan's wild and wily company. As for confusing the seer herself, she had played a minor masterstroke to what she'd done in Eatoth and busied the Fates again to keep Morigan off balance. Before leaving Aesorath, she had pulled out a map of Pandemonia and discussed with Rex her latest feint. She'd ordered a fraction of their forces—now much grown since the taking of Intomitath—to spots on the map that she and Rex had picked at random. Her soldiers were instructed to slaughter, terrorize, harass, and even leave unharmed any and every creature they came across, to create chaos within the flow of Fate. She wasn't certain it was working, though she expected the dissonance to reach a woman so attuned to Geadhain's war. Between that strategy, and Brutus's stealth and mastery of the environment, especially hers, they seemed to have maintained an advantage, and were now close enough to end Morigan.

Yet there was another player in the game now, and until she assessed the strength of this man—the wind whispered to her that it was a man with this power—they could not ambush Morigan's company as intended. Also vexing was that the Daughter of Fate would probably soon meet with the natives of the Cradle, the revolting men of skin and bone that called this place home. While each was an ant to the hide of the king, these men were a hive—thousands upon thousands of scrawny vermin burrowed into the ashen warrens of this realm. Perhaps erring on the side of caution was best, and those flesh-hungry lunatics would do her work for her. If not, there remained one place where they could ambush the Daughter of Fate, in her mistaken moment of victory, while she choked from the well of history into which she'd thrust her greedy mouth. The superstitious cannibals wouldn't follow her there, to the Mother of Creation's grave.

Drink deep, Daughter of Fate, lose yourself again to the deepest ages as you did outside the Cradle—when I nearly had you dead. When you wake with your ugly truths, with the knowledge you came here seeking, it will be to see the meat of your throat in Brutus's claw. I shall be laughing at your bubbling death—that will be your life's last vision.

Amunai walked over to the king who was hunched over, bulbous with tension like a bomb of muscles about to burst. She knew he wanted to pursue his son's herd and, more importantly, to kill something. Truly, and sadly, Amunai reflected, was that he longed to unite with his offspring. However, that impulse had been twisted into a primal, amorous thirst. Brutus wasn't the same as she. With the exemption of his immortality and powers, he was as evolved and complex as the element of stone: perpetual, dense, and ultimately boring once its complexity and chemistry were fathomed. So she spoke to him as though he were a dumb piece of stone.

"We cannot strike—not yet. There will be a place and time where her defenses will be down again, as they were when our peons attacked her outside the Cradle. She is weak when she succumbs to the past. Somehow, she woke, or was woken before, from the interference of the Landspeaker, I feel, who called Geadhain's wyrms to her aid. In Zionae's grave, not even the furious drakagor can fly to save her, and there we can bury ourselves in ash until no nose can smell us. We shall wait for her to have her moment of victory, the truth she so detestably seeks. Then she can have her death."

Amunai's nuance and plotting were lost on the king's rage-torn mind. But he understood that he was to wait before feeling blood on his hands and something into which to thrust. That irked him, as had so much of this creeping hunt; having to stay low and remain downwind. What righteous hunter did that? Prey should know of its impending execution, should soil itself from dread and sweeten its meat with panic. And yet the command for stealth boded fair with the king. As if a part of him—a tumor so excised from his black heart as to be a phantom feeling, a pulsing hole, a tug without a leash—wanted him to delay this murder, wanted him to consider mercy for his son.

V

Morigan followed the spirit dog as it bounded through the rain of ash. Its gaiety and radiance, even in its translucence, made it easy to track, and she did so eagerly as her focus had dimmed the wailing images of Pandemonia's imperiled to a quieter terror. Duly her companions were informed by her bloodmate that she was in the thrall of a waking vision. Again, this phantom dog possessed none of the pull of a real vision. Once more it was as if this creature were a memory, an echo of the past. She was to be shown something grand.

While Morigan chased this specter, her companions dealt with the ugly reality of the hideous realm through which they walked. Nothing lived here, or wanted to be remembered. As they drew closer to the center of this ancient apocalyptic land, the furling pumice breakers falling over them with the dread of tidal waves developed a seared sheen, symptoms of a heat so intense that it had transmuted the land into ebon glass. The dark crystal awed the travelers as they gazed up the sides of ragged valleys. Only a few of them had walked cursed ground before, and the still of death that chilled their spirits was beyond the lingering rage of a memory, a Caedentriae, or the petulance of vengeful ghosts. Indeed, the travelers all felt the hate in flashes of hot and cold, a sizzling consumption that settled into their lungs. *Will this sickness ever leave?* many of the companions wondered, as even the Wolf became belabored and panting. With the land so thick with the dust of death, clouds whirled around them, and the sharp claws and cracks in the earth were hidden, slicing their shins and feet. Around them beat a terrifying stillness, an ear-numbing quiet where they missed the cries of drakagor, and where every powdery drop of the somber rain of dust scattered from the horned heights was imagined as real—the Wolf, actually, noticed a definite patter.

Although as much as they were loathed—*Do not be here, do not see here,* droned the land—the apocalypse had not scoured every trace of beauty from this tortured grave. Within the waves of glass were the dithered osseous imprints of creatures that had died in the blast. Impressions of their skeletons were a mystery to most and dismissed as smoky aberrations. But not to the scholar. He saw one winding behemoth as if it were paneled artwork he was viewing through panes of blackened glass: four pieces of a tail—each grand as the *Skylark*—then a titanic thorax that branched down a dusty spinal trail and into many porous heads. Had eyes or mouths once been housed in that honeycomb skull? Talwyn was without the wits to muster a response to that, but less so regarding the lattice of prancing white patterns that he saw on the walls of the next pass. Like ancient hieroglyphs, the creatures' bodies had been encased in glassy stone, and not a shred of flesh, only the chalk of bone, had survived the heat. But they were a species he recognized from Pythius's lucid dream. Perhaps the shaman's magik of storytelling and inheritance had indeed passed from a single tribal truth, for here was a herd of lightning deer; the snowy trails of their flight were the sulfur imprints of their magik. Even dead and entombed, the creatures were beautiful. Talwyn deviated from the ashen channel they walked, climbing up a sharp incline to polish the onyx casement and peer within.

"Sky dancers," whispered Pythius in his tribal tongue, appearing suddenly and placing a hand next to Talwyn's. "Elementals of wind. We are among the legends now. What we see, and know, cannot be unseen."

Pythius withdrew and curled his hand. Hollowly he looked at Talwyn, revealing a head full of wailing terror and crumbling beliefs, a cathedral on fire, then hurried back into the channel in line with their companions. What was Pythius, if not a holy warrior? What would he become if Feyhazir revoked his power? Hard as it was to watch his lover suffer, Talwyn knew that a stinging poultice of truth was being applied to Pythius's reason. The wound would need to fester and expel the poison of ignorance on its own. He would not push Pythius to speak to him; he was grateful that forgiveness was taking place on its own terms.

Besides, there remained the question of Moreth's return from an equally dark abyss. He hurried over to the pale man. The expedition had traveled in a lazy, broken chain with Morigan, the Wolf, and Adam at the fore. Moreth walked alone behind those three, with the remaining scattered behind. Indeed, no one had wanted to keep company with a person around whom coldness now followed in a cloudy spell, and who looked at his friends with a new and silvery hunger. The knotted markings running down his back were distressing and strange. Talwyn shivered as they met up. "H-how are you?"

"Hungry." Moreth's neck jutted in unusually, storkishly, and he sniffed Talwyn's shoulder. Moreth might have risen higher, to his friend's grimy and pulsing throat, though a low-hummed folksong began from the watchful Wolf up ahead. Moreth jolted back and away from his friend, then tucked his hands into his elbows as if to keep them at bay. "What do you need, scholar? You never come unarmed and without a question."

"I am quite armed. I have these, now." Talwyn fluffed open his cloak, spraying ash everywhere and bringing a coughing seizure upon himself. All that had been a jovial attempt to show off the holsters slung under his arms, weapons Moreth had had the foresight to remove or the luck to discard with his tatters before dashing out into Pandemonia's wicked storm.

"I thought I lost those."

"Safe and sound, as you can see—I think you've finally lost your hat, though."

"Worthless trinkets, those guns. Keep them."

"Really?"

"*Keep* them," he commanded.

As a monster, Moreth had no need for the pellet-ejectors of more puny beasts. Moreth was no longer concerned that the scholar would blow off his or anyone else's face, and those weapons should have a worthy master. A glimmer of that humor—at mortality and struggle—as well as the scholar's current antics made Moreth's torpid heart beat once from amusement.

"Are you two alright?" called Mouse.

"We are," replied Moreth. "Just having a chat."

Resuming their stride, they kicked up a fresh trail of ruin, and as that settled into a bearable cloud, Moreth asked what was on his friend's mind.

"I have questions," said Talwyn.

"I'll give you three. Make them count."

"Only three?"

"Yes, and now you're down to two."

"How is that—?" Talwyn stopped his runaway mouth. Moreth cocked his head as if waiting for the man to complete, and waste, another inquiry. "One moment."

Talwyn thought of how to express his hypothesis—a clot of intimations about physiology, metascience, and the catalyst that had made Moreth into whatever he'd become—in two meager questions. Perhaps the plainest question was the one that needed to be asked. "What are you?"

The question amused his friend, and Moreth's grin seemed as sharp as the Wolf's. Much he had pondered his new self, his better self, while fighting against the rapturous pain of his hunger. Such starry agony was a strength, though, which he'd begun to see—in agony could be found a mastery over pain, a focus, upon which he could draw. He wasn't a mindless, famished thing as the blood eaters had been; through the Wolf's temperance, and the lesson of Beatrice's triumph over her bestial nature, he had learned that.

"I am no more the man you knew," he said, after pondering briefly. "I am not a blood eater. I am something more. The Will of the Maker does not end when sayeth the Maker. Power, once planted, seems to be a vine that can be seized by a willing soul. I think, though, that if I did not have such willful friends, and so determined a wife, that these secrets would have been lost to me, and I would have flailed in the dark. I still fight that battle, speck by speck, to not consume the red sweetness of your flesh. But I am, now, a creature of my own. A Will that can stand and scream at the universe with a voice that will be heard."

So declared, Moreth's face—his eyes, mostly—burst with a light against which Talwyn was forced to hold up a hand. He peered into the shining light to behold the hideous but wondrous transformation: Moreth's neck and body had swelled, and suddenly he was several heads taller than Talwyn, growing, bloating with lean layers of meat, perhaps nourished by the sap of the black ivy that veined his flesh. A blast of cold from two misty wings that seemed drawn from an abyss of darkness and fire buffeted Talwyn. So great was the presence of this fiend that Talwyn cringed then fell as the ululating, soul-withering call of the Blood King rang out across the accursed valley—a voice that all Dreamers would hear.

As fast as the manifestation howled upon them, it passed. Mouse, Thackery, and Pythius had all stumbled into one another. Reproachful of the noise, the bloodmates and Adam looked back upon the scene, though none moved to intervene.

"Control your beast, Moreth," admonished the Wolf.

"I am!" hissed Moreth, quite himself again, and yet now one hundred times more terrifying to his friends. His bottom lip quivering, he smelled, as an animal would, over his palate. "A song! A song for our march, Wolf. We are nearly there, at the death of the world. Can you smell it? Sing and march! To death. To the end."

On the trail of something, perhaps the spirit dog, Moreth stormed off, leaving his friend to be picked up by a harried Pythius, a gesture so sweet that Talwyn knew he might soon be pardoned by his lover. Talwyn had not asked his second question of Moreth, and wouldn't now. The Wolf began a grim tune about swords, blood, and war. It was fitting for where they were headed, for where Talwyn knew they would soon arrive. The riven clefts they'd wandered were growing ever wider, crossing into each other more. The precision of concentric formations—these igneous waves that had once been animals, earth, and plants condensed into life's concrete and rolling outward—was being broken and disrupted by chaotic twists, arcs, and bridges of rock. Here was the last remnant of disaster, of form, before everything became senseless dust. All was growing wide, opening, and in the distance becoming what looked to be a leveled waste, a desert of crumbling ashen dunes and the occasional crooked cleft half-swallowed in decay.

Soon the walls trapping the company humbled into drifts, and they walked across that desert, hiding their faces and forcing their quivering legs to endure the exertion of moving through infinite tons of death. The Wolf did not sing anymore, lest his lungs fill with black. They heard nothing other than the muted clanging of the chains in the dusty sack slung over the Wolf's back and the crackling whisper of a land corroding and consuming its own rust. Had there ever been a lonelier place? A realm where the sun, hope, and memories were swept and lost as the names of any of the men or creatures through whose remains they trod? None could answer that question.

Moreth seemed bravest amid all the death; he hiked up hills jagged from the broken bedrock with a jauntiness, abandon, and lightness of foot as if he were this place's sad wind. He'd left his new sandals behind; mayhap they'd split and fallen off his body during his brief transformation. Barefoot and mad, he pursued the scent that had drawn him—an essence of life that even the tyrannical doom of the Cradle could not smother. The others followed him over dune, across swath after swath of gray ocean and sandstorm, and finally between two shifting ziggurats that cast an extravagant downpour, like ash from a Dreamer's urn, as they struggled and ran ahead.

From that clouded crack, they stumbled, coughing, and unburied themselves from the sands of this hollow expanse, this desert roaming in toothed waves—some rock, some sand—up and out of a distant dent in the land: a pit. The sandy stretch beyond eventually met a navel in the land, a circle of craggy humps, a mountain risen in the desert, with a hole like a volcano—a hole that would descend into darkness so deep that the sun, at last seen as a hovering golden ghost, appeared hung and centered upon it. Another day of travel across this realm and they would climb over that shale gullet and stare down with the sun into the heart of the world. A deflated canteen was passed up and down the line with shaking hands, those who still drank water sharing only a miserly sip.

Moreth had not stopped, and they raced after his white figure, just as Morigan continued to pursue the phantom dog up ahead. The Wolf wondered what the man smelled that he did not; the decay was so redolent here that he could scarcely track the sweat of the men from before. How could anyone live here? Even cannibals? How great was the flock from which they could glean enough to sustain themselves? As he worried over legends, cannibals, and the logistics of a tribe living in nothingness, the land continued to sink, and the strange promontory they'd seen at the edge of the valley rose to meet them. It grew heaps, boulders, then rugged protrusions that weren't shale or any of the geologies known to the Wolf, or even to the scholar. As the towering bulwark pronounced its greatness, the Wolf caught motes of white swimming through the more unearthed formations. At first he believed the glimmers to be mica, or another less common but equally pretty mineral. However, in the towering slabs, the upheavals thrown from the guts of the earth, and upon whose sheer surfaces even the tenacity of ash was resisted, the mineral moved in motes, eddies, and milky bodies—a diversion and lunacy into which one could gaze and ponder the smallness of life. As they did, gawking, dumbfounded, before one such monolith.

The sun went out, or died like the rest of this place, and they wandered a twilight abyss, counting stars, tracking celestial bodies within the stones rather than above them. A hum of a magik so fundamental and sacred banished their fear, and they wandered as archeologists and pilgrims to this miracle, within a museum filled with relics stained in the blood of Creation itself. Morigan thought of touching this land with her powers, of tasting its history, though even the bees warned her that such a draft might be too potent to safely consume. She would wait until they found the one relic of Zionae's whose purpose and past was less endless: the vessel. From somewhere nearby it called to her. Unlike the dog, which had finally vanished; perhaps this place was where it had intended to lead her.

Toward her intuition they hurried, scraping themselves in their haste, adding more contusions and sprains to those they had already suffered. Night struck its wickedest hourglass, and at last they shuffled beneath the jutting bluffs of starlight they needed to conquer, before peering down into the navel of the world. Still they felt no fear, only the thrill of the hunt. They gathered in the glittering rubble, gazing up at the breadth of the task. Moreth leaned up on his toes as though he were preparing to jump. Talwyn, only a little facetiously, wondered if the man would fly.

"Stay," warned the Wolf, his hand extended.

"You smelled them, too?" asked Moreth, tapping his ear. "Listen close, and you might hear their heartbeats, slow and frail: the pulse of those nearly dead. They're barely alive, all string and gristle. Not much of a meal."

"Come forth, people of the Cradle!" called Adam, bravely. To his companions his voice was a loud, fragmented hiss and not words they knew.

They heard his voice, the Magmac, the tribe who lived on the tip of the needle between life and death. They now stirred, a rattling coming from their bone skirts, or perhaps from the clattering of their tormented, emaciated bodies. As ordered, they spilled from the crannies, poked their ghostly white-patterned faces from rock gardens not far from the party, and glared with sunken, angry stares upon these invaders of their solitude. One wave emerged, then another, and another and another until they lost count, and soon the bluffs swayed with a sea of ivory and black—as was the pigment of their skin, and not from sun but from eons of the Cradle's corruption. The Wolf sensed the hungry screaming bellies of thousands more. Their breath was ragged, barely more than a babe's fart, and their bodies strummed like harpsichords from the strength needed to stand. While the frailest and weakest of men, their faith sustained them, as well as the madness that had allowed them to live in horror generation after generation, and while one cannibal was not threatening, a horde of starving zealots was. Countless mouths chattered, and the starving swell swept toward the company.

XII

QUEEN OF THE FROZEN HEART

"Are you certain? Habitats of man are no longer safe this far north."
Kanatuk shouted his warning, his face swaddled with leather and scarves as Winter shrieked in an angry torrent around them. Together, the five of them—king, queen, knight, seal, and hunter—shuffled, holding each other hand to forearm. A village, or fyr, as the Northmen called them, had appeared down the slope of the thinly treed icy vale they had chosen for cover. The scant kindling and brush that surrounded them offered paltry protection against the violent, rumbling grayness, rolling in like fog, to the north. Soon that storm would be upon them, and the flurries that had preceded it would be put to shame.

They had nearly been caught in a storm similar to the one approaching. During that event, Magnus and the others had hidden in a cave while the world outside went sheer, white, and howling. Haughty Magnus, he'd thrust his hand out into the pale curtain and screamed as the flesh was battered and stripped pink. His still hand stung beneath his mitten; it was healing slowly given his immortal constitution. Mother Winter seemed to be tolerating but not favoring them, and with no caves nearby they would need shelter. The nearby fyr would have to do; they needed the respite of warmth and food, particularly for little Macha, whose story he'd learned in bits and pieces.

"We must head for the village," cried Magnus. "We cannot trust ourselves to fate, and I see no places nearby in which shelter might be found."

So down the hill they dashed in a white whirlwind, making for the snow-draped cottages and longhouses of the fyr buried in the valley's basin. As they cleared the largest drift to meet a level wading pool of white, they beheld clearly the first submerged log buildings and undeniable signs of a haunting. No fires or movement welcomed them, chimneys were plugged with snow, and not a soul was seen to tend to them or to any of the winter that had piled and piled upon itself. Indeed, many structures seemed weeks high in snow. Buildings were sealed in by creeping snowbanks that reached up to the windows of their second stories. Erik, sensing more than the others, and from the echoes and scents of time—hoof-clatters, laughter, woodsmoke, and sweat—knew that the ditches that appeared to run through the snow had once been roads. He could sense too that under the taller mounds of these streets, ones in which he could hear a mouselike hibernal thumping, were men, women, and children—cursed, encased in ice, and frozen forever. Other heaps Erik believed to be animals. Everything was as it had been in one moment, though that moment was eternity.

Time and again, the strangers to the North had been warned about these haunted places. However, seeing was believing, and with each messy stride they took through the snowbanks, they were gnawed upon by the emptiness, the stillness of this fyr, and the sense that eyes were watching them. A sense of dread colder than the weather sank into their bones. As they hiked into the cover of the nearest structure, Erik told them why they felt so watched, and of the people and animals hidden, though still living, beneath the mountains of snow.

"People?" muttered Lila.

She carefully dusted off the hard-packed snow atop one of the conical shapes near to her. Something red and white appeared, and she stopped when she realized she had unearthed a smile. A frozen smile. Whatever the joke had been, it wasn't funny now. Pulled between a feeling of horror and mercy, she finally brushed more snow over the hole she had made and left the poor soul to his or her doom. She wanted to believe that Erik had been wrong about hearing heartbeats, for even a brief tally showed dozens of tall white mounds of snow about the area. Within the buildings, and without these husks, she feared what she would see.

Erik and Magnus each felt her fear, and paid heed to her wandering, though she wasn't in mortal danger, and they had been busy with the huntsman digging at the door of a tavern down the path; they assumed that was the entrance, given the placement of the sign carved with at least half a cup of ale that they could spot under the muffling snow. Soon a sturdy door and handle were unearthed, and Erik twisted the handle in a full circle, pushing the knob through its hole, then gently shoved open the door. The screech of wood on cold stone rang out across the tavern, stirring none of the shadows sitting in the milky murk beyond. At least better prepared for what to expect, and in the company of stoic souls, Lila strode in ahead of Erik. She called to her Will, bowed her head, clasped her hands as if in prayer, and then released that thought—of Erik's warm sandpaper touch—into the caliginous room. Lila's passion manifested as a wisp of golden ether, which floated around as if it were one of the sentient creatures of folklore that haunted moors, bobbing between tables, spreading its sunlight on the menagerie of victims of Winter's curse.

Faces from a wax museum of the whitest flesh, sparkling with ice and lacking the vitality of life, glared out from the paths lit by Lila. Their eyes glimmered with the animal twinkle of rats, which Lila took as madness, for whatever dregs of their sanity remained trapped in bodies that would not move. It was freezing in the tavern, the settled chill of a meat locker; what drinks, stews, and meals these men and women had been enjoying shone glassily in receptacles. Although, none of the windows had shattered, and there was no snow within the building. Everything had simply stopped. At one table, a child of no more than three had been seized in the bouncing embrace of his parent, cast eternally at the apex of his mother's and his happiness. That parent's glittering arms would never grow tired, and the child's sparkling face would never lose its smile. However, Lila doubted the joy of that moment had been preserved, and all either of them knew at this moment was horror. By a hearth cold and gray as a tombstone sat a bard, his mouth glued to one of the queer flutes used by the Northmen.

Somberly, they walked through the gauntlet of frozen ghouls, even past a once shaggy dog that had been arrested mid-yelp; its gray snail-like tongue greatly disturbed Lila. That any of these people and creatures could live still was madness.

Erik closed the door, dragged an empty table in front of it and joined them at the bar. "I've seen much in warfare and magik, but I have not seen this." Reaching over the counter, he pulled a frozen, crackling cloth from the grimacing barkeep, icicles rattling off the man's beard. He was careful not to pull the cloth too quickly and risk snapping off the man's hand. After retrieving the cloth, he fluffed it out, then respectfully hung it over the barkeep's glaring face. "Some privacy, I suppose."

While his companions simmered in questions or gloom—except for the seal-girl who sat happily on a stool watching him through her chocolate eyes—Erik studied their shelter. It had solid beams, with good strong mud between the logs. The windows upstairs were creaking from the wind, though, and they would need to be shuttered and boarded.

"We can reconvene here, but we have work to do if this place is to hold better than a cavern of stone. I smell stores on the other side of the bar, in a cellar, I suspect. The huntsman and I can tend to the windows upstairs, which won't hold. See if you can find us a solid meal."

Magnus, Lila, and Macha were abandoned by the men, who hurried up a flight of stairs and commenced dragging, banging, and throwing things around. Macha and the king had fallen into a spell cast by the other, again, and Lila left them with her witch light while conjuring another light for herself to search for food. Erik had been right, and she discovered a wooden hatch with a frostbitten iron ring—which she hauled on—leading to a flight of earthen stairs, down which she descended into a hollow room from whose ceiling hung swaying animal corpses. Along the back and sides of the small chamber were kegs and bags of grain. It was quite a well-supplied larder; it would have to have been for anyone living in a habitat so far from regular commerce. Whatever was in the kegs was of no use to her, frozen as it was, which she determined when she twisted the nearest keg's spout. She had better fortune with the sacks, in one of which she found a medley of dried fruits and nuts. That would do for the seal-girl. Meat was on the menu for the rest of them, and she unhooked a shank of something smoked and hauled her bounty up the stairs with a bit of cursing and sweat. Arms laden, she did a one-footed dance to kick closed the hatch. She turned to Magnus and Macha—still enraptured by each other—then slammed her goods on the counter, rattling glasses that hung in the wood-mesh above the bar, and startling the pair out of their enchantment.

"You could have helped, Magnus," she hissed.

"I could have, yes. I am sorry," he said sincerely.

In the instant that she turned to snatch a bottle of liquor—bless the Fates that never froze—from the shelves, then turned back, Magnus and the girl were again playing stares.

"Really, Magnus, the age of child brides has sailed into the sunset along with the worst of all barbaric male vices. I snuffed out the last of that misogyny with the Arhad. Nary another girl will be taken against her will, and I am disgusted you would even consider it."

"You do not understand," snapped the king.

"I don't—you're right." Lila popped the cork off her bottle with her thumb and took a few swigs of the fiery Northern sprit. She hissed from its burn.

"Ooh. Warms you up like the sun on your knickers, as Lowelia would say. I miss her, and Eod. I also miss the days when I could understand your intentions, Magnus. Already you keep secrets from me—from us—and you've seen the cost of silence."

Magnus hid his face from shame.

"You seem unwilling to part with the secret of what you intend to do when we meet this great elemental of Winter. Perhaps you could at least answer another mystery for your dear former wife of one thousand years, who raised an empire with you. I jested in suggesting your motivations as lust, and that was a tasteless jest, considering my history with men. So I recant, and ask you: what is this fascination between you and her?"

Nodding, he gestured for the bottle. She passed it to him and he took many swigs of it, before handing it back to Lila and leaning on the counter to tell his tale. "Time, while constant and moving, is not simply an erasure of the past and a procession of the now. It can be fragmented, and each fragment remembered, and known, as you and I know and feel time—as a sea of memories, pain, and hope. That child knows something of this. And she knows that I know her truth."

"What truth?" whispered Lila.

"This child, who is meek and ungrown before you, was the one to unmake the empire of the Mortalitisi."

"No," said Lila. What did he mean? Macha was twelve summers at most, not a ten-thousand-year-old hero. Unless Magnus's talk of cycles and time meant the girl, though not in this current vessel of flesh. As if welcoming Lila's acceptance of the impossible, the girl rose in her stool, appearing taller, grander, and more brilliant than the light conjured by the queen. She was a giantess of wonder, flesh of starlight, the beating radiance of an ancient star. Then the momentary illusion—or whatever Lila's truest senses had seen—faded, and there was just a pretty girl, Lila's former husband, and her own slightly inebriated self. "No. I mean. Could she...? No."

"Yes, yes, and yes," claimed Magnus. "If I had the resources of the Hall of Memories, and the consent of this young maiden, I would scour the annals of our world for all heroes, saints, and martyrs, as a soul like hers does not make a single resonance but is the source of many legends. She is hope, and that is why I cling to her—for she is proof that in the darkest hourglass we can still find light."

"The Mortalitisi..." muttered Lila. She slammed back another mouthful of the Northerner's venom, then slumped onto her elbows on the bar. Magnus picked up the bottle.

"Evil sorcerers, I've heard," said Erik, emerging from the darkness. "And long dead. What of them?"

Of course, he could have eavesdropped on his bloodmates had he and the huntsman not been so focused on the labor upstairs. They had completed the reinforcement of the windows with tables, chairs, and couches, which had become a tedious task since the victims of the Scourge of Winter had to be delicately removed from the furniture and laid, like brittle dolls, into a line of mannequins on the floor—sideways, if possible, and locked into each other as a puzzle that would hopefully save them from shattering. Even with Erik's most careful touches, a malfortunate's leg and hand had been lost. The huntsman had been clumsy and accidentally snapped a man in half—who neither bled from the pink amputation, nor expressed agony, though the gleam in his eyes seemed to have disappeared. Erik needed a drink himself, even if his immortal constitution prevented the slightest buzz. He snatched the bottle from Magnus, drained half of what was there, then invited the huntsman for a drink. Once each man was warmed from belly to throat, he asked again.

"I heard you mention the Mortalitisi—that dread society of yore? What does *she* have to do with them?"

"Nothing!" cried Kanatuk, and rushed to the girl, placing himself before her.

Macha slipped off her stool and nudged him out of the way. "Do not worry for me, brother," she clucked in their tongue. "They are curious, as are all great minds, about what drives us small creatures to do what we do."

What has *she done?* he wondered, awed by the stark, burning wisdom and sense of eternity in her presence. Summoned by a mystery, Macha wandered around the shady tavern, peering into the faces of the frozen damned, shaking her head ruefully, and occasionally muttering what seemed to be prayers, as she placed her forehead against them.

"She is all I have," confessed Kanatuk. "Please don't take her from me. I have nothing left if she is gone, seduced by your city of wonders and magik."

"We have no interest in that," promised the queen, warming the mood with a smile and a scent of cinnamon, thought Kanatuk. "Do we, Magnus?"

The king shook his head, more to stop himself from watching Macha's flitting than from disagreement. "Of course. She should stay where she feels she belongs, which I think is here. In her is the soul of a great hero—one from before this age. In the future, her steel soul may be needed again, and so we should leave that soul in peace, to sharpen its edge until then. When we return to Eod, we shall do so as we came: alone. I promise you this, huntsman."

"Thank you." Kanatuk's guard finally lowered, and he unbundled himself from some of his layers. The Immortals did so, too, stripping down to tunics and lighter cloaks—the room wasn't so ferociously cold once they had clustered around Erik's heat. Indeed, most of the chill appeared to roll off the victims of the curse themselves. As winter's hammer dropped down on the fyr, rattling the wooden bones of the tavern and causing the shutters and door to flicker, trembling the glazed statues in their seats, Magnus contemplated that curse.

"You have been in these lands for how long, huntsman?" asked the king.

Kanatuk ruffled his dark hair, thinking. "Three months? I am not much of a keeper of time. I've only ever had a chronex while in the Broker's employ, and since I have returned to my homeland, the process of keeping time is trifling when dawn and dusk tell me all I need."

Magnus continued forming a chain of thought. "For how long have you suffered this Scourge?"

"I do not suffer," replied Kanatuk. "I am of the three great tribes that belong in these lands. My blood is sacred." He nodded at Macha. "Now I know for a fact that hers is, too, though I always felt her magik, her purity of spirit. Thus Mother Winter allows us to remain here, to walk amid her war against man, as her faithful witnesses, while she slowly moves her fury south. She did not want to harm man, but we have driven her to it."

Kanatuk shivered and continued. "Winter is the harshest of all the seasons, the most unforgiving. Some think that fire is worse, but it heals as it burns. Winter...she is ruthless. She withers life with cold, then drowns her deeds in white forgetfulness—so that she can forget our misdeeds, our sin. I suppose she allows you a similar latitude, or sees you travelers as faithful, or repentant, which is why you haven't turned into one of the icy statues in her garden just yet."

Yes, I know what I must do—how I must serve Mother Winter, thought Magnus. Out in the hammering storm, a song resounded: Winter's summoning. Magnus's inner commentary startled his bloodmates, but he didn't respond to their mind-whispers; rather, he repeated and clarified his question, which the huntsman seemed to have waxed upon and forgotten. "For how long has the North endured this Scourge?"

"Macha and I arrived at the lively port of Valholom two to three months ago," said Kanatuk, "as echoes of the fall of the farthest settlements were reaching the ears of the city. So perhaps a few months beforehand, I would say, the Scourge of Winter began."

"Magnus?" pressed the queen, of her silent king and his thundering thoughts.

"It aligns with what we know of the unrest in Zioch," he replied. "Of my brother's sudden surge of madness, and the reports of unrest we received from the natives of that region. I hang my head with the deepest shame that I did not heed those warnings. I have been so deaf to the world. Alas, regret serves us not at this hourglass, and I think I am, finally, hearing...Two brothers, two wyrms, fire against frost. As my brother and I are linked in fates, so must the wyrm of fire and the wyrm of frost be. They could have awoken simultaneously. One called forth by Brutus's stolen power, the other...a reaction? Cause and effect. As the elemental of fire was pulled, screaming and furious, from its sleep so too was the elemental of Winter? Imagine the hate as it saw what we had stripped from ourselves and our world, coming from an age when everything was pure and raw, where nature was our king, to one where we have shunned the elementals with our arrogance, our crowns, and our metal contraptions. Barbarians. Iconoclasts. I would hate us, and seek to erase us, too, and I doubt the cold will stop at Valholom; it will freeze all of the Feordhan and beyond—assuming the Black Queen doesn't destroy us all first."

Ugly prognostications, and the company all shook their heads.

"You speak like you see into the heart of Mother Winter," whispered the huntsman.

"Perhaps I do," he replied.

And the song from outside slithered through his head, the drums of wind pounded, trying to break their shelter, and somewhere within, in some remoteness beyond the reach of the two tied to his soul, Magnus danced to the music.

II

Night came and went as a subtler gray within walls thudded by icy fists, a noise that only dulled once snow had sunk the tavern into drifts from which they would need Erik's strength to free themselves. But they wouldn't worry about that for now. For now their troubles seemed forgotten and distant. Even the macabre crowd of tavern goers, with their rows upon rows of marble stares, seemed less hideous over time. Perhaps, thought Erik, these tortured creatures actually enjoyed the presence of something alive, and for that he drank heavily from the frosty bar, bottles upon bottles that when combined dented his immortal constitution. Then he swaggered between the tables, dancing with his queen, and for the amusement of the two beings who watched them, the huntsman and the seal girl.

"You're a wonderful dancer," complimented the queen, as he whirled her out then into his arms, and her panting face came close. "I never knew."

Erik kissed her as they spun through a waltz, crossing feet and tongues, hitting neither table nor crystal occupant, until the queen, at last, had to sit. Erik escorted her to the bar and bowed after pulling out a seat for her. Macha clapped at his graceful prowess; he had moved like a fish, sleek and fluid, and while she hadn't seen much dancing, she knew it wasn't usually as artful as that. Meanwhile, the huntsman had carved up the meat brought from the larder, and Erik arranged a few scraps on a plate for him and his queen.

Magnus remained secluded upstairs, watching the windows, he'd claimed, to ensure they didn't buckle. Without him the mood was warmer, anyway. So they ate and chatted, first of how they had become involved in this dangerous expedition. They were naked in their honesty, for maintaining airs felt false and dishonorable. The huntsman spared no sufferance, and the tale of his salvation in Menos brought tears to the eyes of the queen and even Erik. Likewise was the story of their fated love, of her saving him, then him saving her, a swooning ballad of romance which wrenched tears from Kanatuk and Macha—who seemed to understand quite well for a girl of rudimentary Ghaedic, though perhaps another life within her knew the language well.

After baring their souls to one another, they spoke of the politics of the North: the Kinlord, the Eininhar, and the Menosian ties from here to the Lords of Carthac. Happenstance or not, the Kinlord's fiercest children were as golden and beautiful as Lila, said Kanatuk. It was a hereditary anomaly traced to no reasonable explanation. Henswives claimed that one of the ancient Kinlords had bedded a woman from another land, a woman in whose blood flowed the divine, and that her magik and traits had endured through however many incarnations of her offspring. Others, learned men, claimed that these children were the manifestation of the Kinlord's mercy, and such was why these temperate, thoughtful children were always given the ear and second hand of the Kinlord—for they were to be the avatar of his pathos for men lesser than he. Myths aside, these children were special and given high station in the Kinlord's court; they always grew into noble warriors, as well, and had tomes of their deeds as eulogies. Curiously, Kanatuk claimed that these special children all died earlier than most men, and none were known to have reached comfortable old or even middle age—perhaps because they led lives so full, their spirits were ready to depart sooner than those with failed hopes and ambitions.

Lila grew increasingly quiet. Erik sensed a boiling dread and an urge to scream building within her.

"Lila," he said, interrupting the huntsman. "What is it? We are among comrades here, and there is the foulest of venom within you."

"I know enough of the lore of the North," said Lila, flickering with the first emerging tinges of her scales. Kanatuk and Macha fell silent, entranced by her sudden swaying and the exotic sweetness she effused. "It is time that I tell you of my time in the North."

"So that's what you've been hiding?" he whispered. "All that thorniness in your heart."

"Yes."

Erik took her hand, kissed it, and nodded for her to continue.

She sighed. "One of the first things I did, when learning to be wife to an Immortal King, was to know not only of my husband's greatness, but to know who I was myself. Daughter of the Arhad, yes, though why was I so golden fair when all my sisters were brown and handsome? Whence had I come? So I began to research my ancestry. I searched for a people for whom golden eyes and hair were common, and while neither of those two attributes were regularly assigned to a single family or tribe, I learned of the old lineages of Menos, those exiled to Carthac—where they became twice-cursed lords— then migrants to the North. Among those generations were rare, golden, and special beings with whom I could stand and face as though looking in a mirror.

"Although we of Eod do not have many dealings with the North, on account of the war with Taroch, who was obsessed with this culture, we have what remnants of the plundered libraries survived and were acquired by the Court of Ideas. Old scrolls, star maps, and legends. Many legends. As you've suggested, huntsman, the legend was that these children all came from the blood of a single woman. Mentions of distant Menosian ancestry are passed over in these tales, and I can tell you who Taroch—also a golden-eyed, bronze-skinned orphan of sorts—believed this incipient foremother to be: a wise woman, witch, and gatekeeper of this realm."

"Beira?" asked Kanatuk, dreamily.

"Aye," replied the queen. "The Winter Witch. She has many names and guises. And while one manifestation of her might be wizened and horrid, Taroch described her in other instances as 'a woman of gold, from whom the sunshine of the banished seasons shone, trapped, in her hair and eyes; a woman of elements, too, shimmering in the copper of her skin.'"

"Rather like you," said Erik.

"And Taroch, who was convinced of every word in his diaries," she replied, and continued with a quote she remembered. "Thus, in her beauteous form, did the witch court and bed the first Kinlord of this land: a *lord king* fleeing from Carthac's revolution and seeking to make this his new home. Such conquest was realized, though not without the Winter Witch's power, her blessing, which allowed him to live on these lands despite his not being native, or wanted by it."

"What was the promise?" whispered Erik. "A pact, yes?"

"Indeed, my knight. It all comes down to blood. Blood for power, land, longevity—all three in this instance and many others of blood-magik. However, warned the witch, for three gifts there would be three sacrifices."

Among such hard souls no one asked *of what*, and so her dramatic pause was ruined.

"Children," she resumed, "his seed. The first two sacrifices would be easily lost: death by burning as living effigies, once they were on the cusp of manhood and youth, when the green of their power had sprouted and would be cut, and stolen, by the Kinlord. Often they were taken at birth and removed from knowledge or existence—some kept like mongrels in dungeons and never given names until they were dragged from dank prisons and onto ritual fires. Having lived in the dark, the children had not the words with which to express their outrage and terror and died, wailing, imbecilic, and unpitied as animals in a slaughterhouse.

"Meanwhile, oblivious to the bloodletting of his family existed the third and most special child, and in he—or she—would be the deepest essence of Beira's covenant: the sacrifice representing the essence of love itself. Nevertheless, that child's fate was perhaps worse than his illegitimate heirs, for he was allowed to live, grow, and know the best of life, and when his vine was fat, full of the world's wonder, and nourished on his heroism, he was fated to die by his thirtieth summer. Damned witches and their obsession with threes, three decades and his end was sworn, through decapitation, exsanguination, gutting, or whatever made the most mess. 'Once ripened, the vine of glory must cut and flow into yon chalice.' That was another of Taroch's mad lines, one of the witch's commandments, and which he had written as if he might recreate this horrific ritual, or sought to understand the ritual from which he'd escaped. However, there is a logical metascience to what he said. 'Tis all about blood and threes, each sacrifice a representation and offering to one of the fates—innocence, time, and wisdom. All sacrifices made to fill the Kinlord's cup with youth and might."

"But they're not immortal—Kinlords," contested Kanatuk. What's more, he also fought to not hallucinate these images of sacrifices, tawny-haired ghosts, and giant Kinlords, in a room suddenly choked with fragrant, golden smoke. "There have been many reigns from many Kinlords of which I know."

"I did not say that they were immortal," replied Lila. "Only that they stole the youth from the dying mouths of their children, enough to make them live the sum of those children's stolen years thereafter. Of course, the witch-branded child gave the greatest boon, and was thus pampered and cared for as no other—fattened on glory, mead, and pleasures, though no vice too unsavory lest the Kinlord inherit that weakness. Taroch described the process methodically, and with more metascience than I feel confident to explain: the rigorous training, grooming, battle experience, and adoration these chosen heirs received—all formulaic and meant to breed the richest blood for the Kinlords to drink. Cattle...Their children were cattle to them.

Heirs who would inherit nothing. Once that third and sacred child died, the cycle would end, and the Kinlord would breed a new dark giant like himself, who would carry on the curse and rule set by his forefathers. Three children, three deaths, then a Kinlord...forever. You could time a chronex to their procreation. Barbarians.

"Still, cycles can be broken, and Kinlords died early in what should have been their centuries of existence, huntsman, from the mercy and intervention of those not beholden to evil. Children were saved, both cursed and golden-cursed. They were taken by midwives, courtesans, or caring men—ones unlike the monsters bred in the Kinlord's army—to safe, distant lands. There they were raised in secret, and known only by the fairness, the tawniness of their characteristics. Were he or she ever to be found, it would have been too late, for a Kinlord without the essence of his children to sustain his greatness wilts as even the grandest creature does without water: quickly."

One detail from her speech had stuck, like a sliver, into Erik's brain. "He or *she*?" He again kissed her hands, which shook with rage. "'Tis what you said, earlier, when speaking of cursed offspring, and those chosen for the ripest harvest. You believe you are one of these children?"

"I do, as did Taroch think himself one. Moreover, there are others, living proof of my theories that I have found, though the Kinlord and his court do much to cloud the origins of their power, and leave the pondering to swell with fear and myth. He and his forefathers are no different from the Menosians they once were. Many years ago, while Magnus spent the summer traveling to the lands south over the Chthonic Ocean—sandy, darkly spiritual realms for which I have never acquired a taste—I remained in Eod. Alone, I researched this mystery, learning another of our world's grotesque truths. I even escaped the rote of rule once, for a few days. I sailed to Valholom."

Behind a keening wall in her soul, revealed during this discourse, Lila had been keeping the most violent and monstrous part of this secret from Erik—from Magnus as well, he presumed, given the rattle of creeping, curious cold that withered him from within. "What happened?"

She told them her greatest secret.

While she whispered or at times mumbled her account, she wasn't inaudible. Erik even heard Magnus hovering on the creaking step at the top of the upstairs' landing so that he could listen—for whatever reason the king was being so strange and distant, Erik had long since given up his curiosity. At times, Lila almost cried as she released the anger she bore regarding her secret voyage and the origins of her adopted innocents, Leonitis and Dorvain. Erik hardly believed what he was hearing.

✳ ✳ ✳

III

It had been a long journey for Lila. Not from the crisp salt air of the Feordhan, peppered with snow, which was a coldness strange to her as a woman from Eod's warm bosom. More so, the hills wavering in cold mist whispered to her as if she should know them, as if they were home. Though they weren't her home, even if Taroch's journals and the mysteries she chased suggested that might well be the case. *Stop it*, she told herself. She lived in Eod now. She was a queen. That morning, she had shaken off her sorrows and walked down the deck of her great silver-trimmed vessel and hailed soldiers, seamen, and an obediently grinning captain.

Her escape from the palace had been a secret. Roella Larson, her aging yet untiring maid, had busily spread rumors of her queen being tied up in negotiations with merchant lords in the city. She had traveled by means of wood upon wave with a man paid ten times over for his silence. Lila missed her handmaiden and generalissima of the White Hearth and hoped that when the Pale Lady finally came for Roe that she would find another confidante and friend equally capable.

At the prow she stopped and let the men's grunting and noises fade into the fog. Once more, she studied the mountains, calling her, asking her name. Lulled and pondering, watching every white drift and rocky twist of the land beyond, she noticed the fire. An orange candle burned from afar, spreading a wisp of black smoke from across the channel—a pyre, surely, atop a series of bluffs crashed into one another, towering and dark. The image was strange for her, to see so large a fire without any villages or settlements around.

Alerting the captain, she ordered the vessel to turn toward the disturbance. They closed in on the bluffs with roaring speed. A dirigible was dispatched, with the queen and a legion of the Silver Watch in tow. As they sailed into the shadow of the cliffs, she asked the others if they too heard the chanting of a primal, earthy song. Her soldiers did, and found it as unnerving and mythic as the waves that thrashed their tiny vessel. But she was a sorceress supreme and feared nothing. Brave and grim, knowing that something wicked awaited her, she led the Silver charge over a beach of timeless rock and a steep path set by the hands and tools of men into the small mountain. As they climbed, she felt less cold, or afraid, and more filled with righteousness. Indeed, the Silver Watch saw her greatly shining, a star of a woman guiding them to the summit. Such light was needed there, on the gloomy, gale-thrashed cliff, with its whipped torches and stone pillars—also wrought by men's craft.

The Silver Watch gasped and drew arms at the sight ahead. There was an ancient circle, stamped into stone, and harrowing men stood, incanting rituals and brandishing iron while children wailed in distress. Lila dashed toward them, her light anathema to the men and their corrupt souls, and they howled, like beasts not warriors, and threw their hands in the air. She herself shone more, punishing the barbarians who had tied two naked screaming children to a column skirted in kindling and at which one malevolent raven-haired giant was readying to light with a torch. He was the festering sore of this evil, that man, and he scowled and did not falter at her magik, not even as his frenzied warriors stumbled blindly, ran, and toppled from the heights.

The Kinlord cursed his warriors for their weakness and shouted at this glowing woman and the cadre of silver knights behind her. His words were indecipherable aside from their slobbering hate, and Lila quivered only from her loathing of him, not from any terror. Ignoring her disruption, he swept the torch toward the boys—one golden-brown-haired, the other dark—and their scream became her own. From that rage, the clouded skies ran gold as summer, and rather than a wrathful winter, the flurries turned soft, warming to flakes of sunlight, and her radiance became a sun upon which not even a grotesque pseudo-immortal being could cast his eyes without being blinded. The Kinlord howled like the storm that had been banished, and what men of his remained—some banded in red and still whirling around for something to kill, even blind—howled as well, in one united pack call of agony. They wouldn't look at her again; they couldn't even see beyond the daze of white into which she'd thrown them with her magik, even when her shine wavered off and the sunlight faded back into storm, snow, and gray clouds.

Defeated, the Kinlord wept; for what, Lila didn't care, though it seemed a genuine loss to this monster that he could not murder these children. Her own soldiers had yet to recuperate from their blindness, so she left them behind and hurried past the man to the children chained to stone.

She warmed their chains with a sorcerous touch and a wish for their freedom, then snapped them apart like almond brittle. The filthy feral boys recoiled from her. They knew not how to speak and were thin and malnourished as if they'd been living in a hole, eating maggots and mud their entire life. She didn't disbelieve that terrible image. Although even as outcasts, as unwanted things, they fathomed the concepts of a mother and love, of whatever succor she offered. They had seen the light of her heart and how it had worked a wonder and saved them. Thus, after crawling in their chains, and growling at her, they'd whimpered, and come forth as beaten pups into her arms.

"My dears. My lost little knights. I shall take you home," she whispered into the greasy tangles of their hair.

Beyond the language barrier, they knew what she meant: salvation, a place that wasn't mired in their shite and misery. The children rose with her and they walked back to her stunned soldiers. She spat on the Kinlord as she passed, and one of the children—the stringiest and blondest lad—kicked him in the knee and barked savage calls at him. When the wicked had their wings clipped, they knew not how to walk, having known flight and ascendance their whole life, and the Kinlord whimpered from the boy's abuse.

"My Queen." Her soldiers, some still rubbing their eyes, bowed as she returned. The warriors of Eod smiled at the children hiding and warming themselves in her furs. The children snarled in return.

"They are a bit...unkempt," said a watchman. "What do you intend to do with them?"

The serpent she was to become reared and lashed out. "What shall I do with them? Feed them, house them, nurture them to grow strong—if not with these breasts, then with the milk of Eod. What else would we do as great beings but shelter the weak? Power has no purpose, no meaning, without mercy."

"Mercy?" rasped a voice.

They all turned. None knew how she had conjured herself there, from a magikian's puff of snow and ice, this witch. She stood as though she were a corpse at a wedding—pale, gaunt, horrifying everyone in what was to be a moment of humanity. The witch was draped in billowing garments, rattling bones, and her whiter-than-snow skin was carved or tattooed in queer markings: whorls and rune-like hieroglyphs that spiraled into complexities, optical illusions that bewildered observers. As if she herself was spun out of mysteries, formulas, rites, and magik alone. It may well have been true, that frightful thought, for she stared at them with the wickedest wisdom, with glimmers of stars and horror.

"What do you want, witch?" demanded Lila. The Silver Watch surged around their queen and new charges.

"I am Branwen. I have a name, one of many, all much rued in the North, and yet I see you know no fear. That is the gift of the Children of the Harvest: bravery and heart, winter's ruthless edge. You have that gift, as well you know—and why. I shall not stop you from taking these boys, though know that in freeing them you will only worsen the curse of the third link in the chain: this generation's chosen child. He will die a most painful death. Brutal beyond reckoning. Now his blood alone must nourish what would have been nourished by three, to honor the covenant of the ancient kin."

What Lila had once thought of as legends and ramblings were exposed as fact: legacies, curses, and her own golden blood came from rituals and promises with witches...if ever this colossally cold and cruel woman were something so simple as a witch. She needn't sail all the way to visit Valholom's libraries to verify her heritage. No matter, she would take these children as far away from the Northlands, and their curse of blood and death, as she could. As she herself had been saved, somehow, one thousand years before, by a merciful hand—a servant, a priest, a person who hated the Kinlords and knew of their savagery. As for this generation's child of the harvest, the third sacrifice who she did not see present, she would pray for him, and pray that he would forgive her for choosing two lives over his one. Her new children tugged at her, cringing from the witch, and she walked away from the weeping giant, the witch, and the fire, which was still crackling and starving for the meal it was never fed. She was done with the North, forever.

"Until I see you again, and you witness the consequences of your decision," warned Branwen.

IV

Drawn by the spell of her unfolding story, Magnus had crept down, step by step, until he came to his former queen, bowed to a knee, and cried. With her story abruptly finished he asked, "Why? Why would you keep this from me? A secret so dire and twisted?"

She laughed. "We kept so much from each other, Magnus—and we needn't scribble out our misdeeds again. That's how we know we were never meant for eternity, since you never summoned my demons from me, nor I from you. We just lied...for a thousand years. I feel this is a better pace for us, as friends and equals, while Erik coaxes from my heart that which I do not want to face. I feel you hear me better now, too."

"I do. I do."

They stared, fidgeted, smiled, and eventually she reached for a much needed drink. She passed around to all save Macha who had also been lured by the tale, and the liquor burned away the strongest vapors of their dismay.

"That tale is incredible, my Queen," said the huntsman. "You interrupted the Kinlord's sacrifice—this Kinlord's, I believe. Correct me if my calendar is wrong. My friend Morigan warned of destiny and choice, and how alike they are even if we demand, and believe in, a difference. It seems you were destined to return here." Emotional, and thinking of mistreated youth, Kanatuk hugged his surrogate sister. "What became of the children? What do you think the witch meant?"

"The children..." replied Lila. "The king and Erik know that answer. They grew into strong, brave men—a watchmaster and a legion master, warriors of Eod: Dorvain and Leonitis. They don't know this, of course, but I named them after the brothers of myth—two boys who battled a giant, which, in a sense, they had. Or I battled him for them. They survived their torments, which was war enough. They remember so little, their minds were such tiny animal things, and the story I told them of how they were found was swallowed like a buttered pill: that they came from Carthac as orphans. No matter my lies, they remember something of a fire. Regarding the witch...I cannot say what her aims were. Still, she was right, though, in saying I shall return; perhaps as much a prophetess as our friend with the silver stare. Here I am, here I have returned to witness the death of a Child of the Harvest." Lila's face twisted. "I tell you this: child or man, if he can be saved from the wicked cycle of this realm, then I shall break another link—ruin the whole wicked chain—while we're here."

"You think he's out there?" asked Erik. "Waiting to be saved?"

"In my heart, yes."

V

From the bow of their mighty wooden oar boat, Bjorn and the Kinlord watch the longboats burn. The white beaches and snowy hills behind the line of flaming ships carry some of that fire's glow. Perhaps the color is simply the stain of war, of gutted men and women dousing the land with the warm paint inside their bodies. Blood. Bjorn has always lived in a world governed by this humor. The blood of his brothers pumps in his chest, his head, his groin. As if he has shared the exhilaration and rush of every kill and not only his own—his first. That man's blood still dries on his knuckles, and the echo of his sputtering death, the stunned expression and eyes that suddenly became milky, linger and haunt him in a manner unbefitting of an Eininhar.

His first murder, though, has stuck in his memory, has become a thorn in his mind. Many more murders by his hand followed, though none were as memorable. Why does he care about this one man? Or any of his foes, for that matter? They were enemies—traitors against the rule of the Kinlord who refused to offer tribute. To not pay tribute means death. Such is the way of the North, and the way of Winter. Was it wrong, what he and his father's forces had done today? Flickering, the funeral pyre ships suggest nothing of justice. Screams, too, drive deep the rusted nail of what murderous wrath he and his kin have wrought. At least here, on the deck of the great oar boat and no longer on the highlands amid their slush of pink snow, he feels remote from the battle and his red hand in it.

"You fought with the Will of our forefathers," boasts the Kinlord, and a mighty hand falls to his son's shoulder. *"A man's first battle is a test of his worth. You are worthy."*

Bjorn looks from hand to father—a hulk of beard and brawn—and bows. None of the turmoil he feels does his father express. Why would the Kinlord be bothered, though, as a man of stone and power? It would be like a rock feeling pity. The Kinlord is his ruler more than his father. His caregivers had been servants; his friends and lovers were his brothers. He rarely felt he had a parent. In moments such as this, where his father applauds him for doing something impressive—impressive to a man who would live for two hundred years, and who could singlehandedly clear a battlefield—Bjorn would say nothing that might risk disappointing him. *"I live to serve you, and to honor you,"* he replies.

The Kinlord's attention grows cold as the weather, his stare glittering and calculating. *"So you do, my son. Fatten yourself on this victory. Allow your pride to consume you. There will be a thousand glories, and you must drink each one, my son. A warrior's end will come; such fate cannot be changed. But before that end, you must know life. Your tales will be eternal, and told in the Halls of the Hereafter, as well as known and revered by the future Kinlords of Valholom. Even I, my son, will pass one day and join you in the Halls."*

Because the moment is uncommonly poetic and waxing between them, Bjorn mumbles a thought that's circled his head before. *"Not before I."*

"No."

A child of golden valor, a child of dark strength and rule. Always two brothers, never born to the same generation. Always one died before the other entered the world. Bjorn knows he is blessed with what some would say is a legendary life, and that he's never meant to be the Kinlord. Although, unlike those who have preceded him, these generations of golden-haired, amber-eyed warriors who saw to their tombs' inscription with line after line of glorious deeds, Bjorn feels small and simple. He wants not a life of glorious deeds, but simply a life. He doesn't want to die, and gutting that man today reminds him, constantly, of how ugly, terrifying, and cold that end will be. Too many times he's seen the crypts beneath Valholom, and they make him dread his own ending: gleaming ossuaries with roads of offerings, paths through a maze of treasure, branching off into great chambers dedicated to a single hero, arranged with more wealth, and a sculpted sarcophagus featuring a relief of the warrior interred within. The whole of these men's lives has been inscribed into the walls using a witch-potted paint that glows and awes as though the sun were trapped behind the letters.

Wonder and glory do these tombs tout, though such affectations seem empty to Bjorn. Chicanery to cover what are bones and a bravado that probably hid fears the same as his. Alas, he knows that all children born with his characteristics are fated to pass before their thirty-ninth birthday. While that remains a couple of decades away, a young man should never be so aware of the fleetingness of his life. Maybe those other men all felt the same, he thinks, and their deeds were all a grand distraction from the fatality of their existence. Still alone with his father on the deck—only quiet oarsmen below and a few Eininhar down the deck staring out toward the flaming ships—he asks his father, before this moment flees, why life must be unfair.

"Unfair?" booms his father, and the hand gripping him turns to iron talons; Bjorn knows not to flinch. "Unfair for whom? For the men who have dishonored me? They chose that path, and that path is one of fire, in which they now burn. Or"—his grip causes something in Bjorn's shoulder to snap, hopefully only a tendon, and he bites back the pain—"unfair for you? The courtesan who begat you was known to spin poetry, and you inherited her moony waifishness, I see. I know what you think, in that part of your mind—your cowardly corner—that you believe I never see. But I do. I see it all. Thus, I tell you, spit on that cowardice, embrace the fact that you will die for the sake of Kinlord and country. Our lineage has no poets of quill and paper. We are artists of blade and blood. Those are your tools; you will write odes to war."

Suddenly, the Kinlord's brute terror fades, and he kneels, imploringly. They meet, eye to eye, and in the giant Bjorn sees for once, kindness. "You are given everything a boy and a man could want to see him through a life of no regret. What more could you demand of me? What more could you want?"

"I want a father."

CRACK!

Bjorn is backhanded by the giant, catapulting him into the nearest mast, from which he rebounds in a lurching dance toward the railing. There he vomits and collapses, his arms and legs splayed, head lolling as stars cloud his head. Even disoriented, he recognizes his father's shadow and cringes as it nears. However, he isn't punished again, for he is to be happy, always, and this was simply a reminder to be that way...or to act it as well as the cursed golden children did in previous ages.

"You have a Kinlord, and I am father to all. Know you dishonor not only me, but all of the North by questioning traditions, or by even considering what might happen if you were to break the icy chain, the spell woven by Beira herself, which binds one to three: a chain of fathers and sons."

One to three? wonders Bjorn. Three what? He's kicked by the foot of a giant for considering that question, and a rib shatters within him. Drooling out blood, he mumbles, "Yes, my Kinlord."

The shadow leaves him there, bleeding, broken, alone. The Eininhar, his brothers, linked to his soul, married to him through blood, show indifference to whatever they've heard or felt through the channel of minds they share. Have I ever had brothers? Have I ever had a father? Who are these men, these shadows ruling my life? *He does not ask those questions aloud and tries not to even think of them lest another boot come his way. Because he's been touched by the supernatural, he does not ask for a chirurgeon or shaman to mend him; time will take care of that, and far less than most men would need. Rather, he picks himself up, looks for his sword, and limps off to find a rowboat to take him to shore so that he can smile, slaughter, and act like a man. Enough murders and one day he might forget that he is to die.*

VI

Bjorn awoke like a man startled by lightning, scrambled out of his bedroll, and stared at the shadows of his tent for enemies. In his dream, there had been many enemies, and he'd been grinning, filled with malevolence, while impaling them on spears, or stomping their skulls into a paste. Where had that battle been? Tyr Callhorn? And what, some twenty years past? He had forgotten that day and his Kinlord's cruelty. Still, he had done what he'd promised himself, and lived a life rich in songs, women, men, blood, coin, and battle. So much so that he had almost forgotten that he was soon to die. Almost.

Assuming they followed the Immortals all the way to Beira's realm, he might not live to see his father give him a smile or shoulder-clasp's worth of sentiment in return. More and more, this felt like his last march, and the sentence issued by his father and upon the queen seemed a sentence more for Bjorn than for her. In his bones, he sensed death ahead—and probably his. Granted, he wasn't sure how the curse worked, though he knew that no golden child lived far beyond thirty years and that the longer the thread of longevity, the more brutal his end. He had stretched the curse for far longer than any other.

Touching the one long scar on his torso, which ran down his abdomen like a wound from a messy surgery, he remembered the beast that had made it with its razor's edge of a horn. It should have eviscerated him and ended his life, rather than simply scarring him. Jorgumander, Terror of the Tyr Falloch, had been a terrible thing, an elemental snake, a creature of mud, rock, ice, scale, and black fur, an amalgam of monsters. It had crawled from its pit beneath the polar crust on its many pointed legs, appendages like javelins of shale, having been summoned or disturbed from its eternal sleep. Perhaps Winter had been angry then, too, and it was the first of her soldiers sent to quell man.

Most of his remembrances of the battle and beast had been blurred by the adrenaline and madness of the moment. It couldn't have been as large as he remembered, coiling over a longhouse, smashing chunks of a hundred-pace-tall palisade with its tail. Jorgumander had eaten five of his brothers and most of a large village, and he—fearless of violent death, knowing it was his fate—had tangled with the great beast as only a fearless man could. The legends say that he allowed it to swallow him and then he carved his way out. Really, he'd grabbed a spear, leapt from a palisade at the slobbering horned head of the furry colossus, and driven his weapon through one of its many eyes. It hadn't died but had slithered off, and he and his brothers had collapsed the cave into which it had retreated, ideally sealing it away for another thousand years. He liked to think that the legends of his prowess in bed weren't equally inflated.

Four decades of glory, he thought, while gathering his clothes and equipping his armaments. It would be foolhardy, then, to want for his heart to fail in the night, or for an assassin or angry clansman to slit his throat. Indeed, his end would be the bloodiest of Northern legend.

"I shall not tremble," he declared to the ghosts of golden children past.

Once dressed, he parted the tent flaps and walked outside. A cavern as misty as the mouth of a wave-battered cove embraced him in its white folds. Fading in and out of the obscurity were the tents of his brothers, and distantly he spotted the silhouettes of horses puffing near the cavern's bright and howling opening. Winter was still railing, though Branwen's promise of safety against the storms farther North was holding true. Bjorn saw his men and walked toward them. They shared one circle and one pack of rations, passed along as mouths were needed to tell stories of chesty wenches or of one another's hirsute bodies, which had been shared as much as the food. Bjorn thought he would miss this camaraderie most when dead. The Halls of the Hereafter sounded as if they were a routine eternity filled with boasting heroes, lengthy speeches, and endless indulgence in food and drink. He didn't need to hear his deeds echoed and applauded by ghosts for all time; he would rather be alive.

Branwen, sitting with his men like a wise winter owl amused by squeaking mice, watched her newest prey approach. She gazed at an Eininhar to her left, and he moved—without glancing her way, as if poked with a sword—to another seat. With no other vacancies, Bjorn decided to join her on the bench of snowy rocks. He had a few bites of food, listened to his men's boasts, laughed and sneered where appropriate, and pretended she wasn't dissecting him.

"A deep sleep?" she asked.

"The deepest," he replied.

"Dreams?"

She said the word slowly and rising, as if she knew a secret. Bjorn debated whether to respond. Eventually he realized she wasn't looking to be rude; if she wanted to say something caustic he assumed she would have no issue voicing it. She was waiting for him to say what was on his mind and in his heart. Gazing over shyly, he noticed that her face, while lined and scribbled with esotericism, was also set with gentle patience. "I remembered something from long, long ago."

"Memories can be confusing, and hazy. Be careful what you glean from memories; there could be more illusion than truth."

"No, this wasn't like that. It was clear. The clearest moment of my life."

Branwen leaned in, curious. "There will be another."

"Another?"

Suddenly, his men, their chatter, and the distant winter screech vanished, and he was alone with this woman. She was softer now, somehow, her age hidden in shade, softened to elements almost beautiful, her wisdom more visible than her mysterious bone-rattling presence. She seemed as beautiful as sunlight striking purest ice. In that moment, Bjorn felt he would tell her anything in his heart.

"I see another instance ahead where you will know clarity," she said. "Great clarity. Then, you shall face your choice and destiny." She meant his death, probably at the hands of an enraged Immortal Queen, and Bjorn's fear tightened his throat. More and more he sensed this was how his father wanted him to die, as attempted executioner to a legendary sorceress. "Bravery, my son. Your soul has been forged by deeds done in the White Mother's name. That is who you have served, who you have always served. Not your Kinlord or the ancient lords of Carthac who sailed here and bound the land through blood and promise. Remember who you serve, if you can remember nothing else. Remember who that mother is, who has given you a light that shines through your flesh and tinges sight and mane. Tell me, what else do you remember, Child of the Harvest?"

"My father, in my dream, he spoke of chains. Chains and..." He struggled before it came to him. "Threes. One and three, he had said. One to three. A chain of fathers and sons..."

"One what?"

"Kinlord, or father, I believe."

"Three what?" She cocked her head like the owl side of her spirit.

"A chain of fathers and sons...Sons?"

"Say it. Power comes from voice. Bravery comes from speaking the truth."

"One father. Three sons."

"A chain of fathers and sons." Branwen's beauty sparkled, as if she were a nymph peering through a sheet of ice; Bjorn gasped. "Chains bind us all. But chains can be broken. A single link, defying its purpose, and the entire contraption breaks, the spell ends...But none have been so brave. All are too sullen and bloated on glory and death. What of you, poet and warrior, remorseful barbarian? Are you that link?"

An elbow jammed into him, then the open sachet that he had left upon his lap was snatched by one of his Eininhar brothers—a man who complained over Bjorn's "hogging the eats"—while he sat dumbstruck. Branwen was no more a maiden, but an old woman, every wrinkle hiding a secret, none of which she wanted to share with Bjorn. She did, however, glance over at the gusting arch of the cavern—hung in icicles long as Jorgumander's teeth—and mention that the storm was on its final breath and that they should prepare to move on.

After they had packed and strode into the buffeting white curtain, Bjorn was consumed by thoughts of his conversation with Branwen and had started to doubt the authenticity of everything they'd said to each other. Then, as they climbed a frosted bluff and gazed down into a valley still whirling with settling snowdrifts and cast with the shining mirrors of many lakes, one of his brothers remarked on how they looked so much like a string of pearls he'd once seen around a courtesan's neck.

"A *chain* of pearls," said Branwen.

XIII

THE BLACK ROAD

I

Regret haunted Magnus as they left the quiet fyr behind. A last glance, and he captured it, a valley whose ivory embankments would soon entomb it like the ruins of a desert civilization. The storm had buried nearly every recognizable structure—hills that were homes, humps that were inns. The scene was peaceful, though it was a tranquility born of cold horror, and he remembered the pooled faces and remains that they had left behind. Neither he nor Kanatuk even knew the name of the village. It would never be remembered. In fact, he would prefer that it be forgotten, as another of his mistakes come from arrogance and power. Even hourglasses later, when the sun had summoned a cloud cover to hide itself, and they'd delved into a narrow gorge furred in conifers that blocked the wind and was peaceful enough to allow the companions to talk, Magnus wouldn't join in any conversation. He was unable to forgive himself. He'd killed those people.

An image wriggled and gnawed into his brain. It had been playing on a loop every sand of the morning. Again and again, he was watching puttylike persons stretching their melting arms toward him, trying to scream with their candled faces, their bodies burning with a fire stronger than the gentle flame he had Willed to unfreeze them from their curse. The huntsman had warned him, had told him that the Scourge couldn't be broken by any sorcerer, no matter his power, since this was a natural sickness, a plague with no cure, brought by Mother Winter. Oh, other magik-workers had tried:

alchemists, witch doctors, and Menosian hexxers, too. But the curse would not be broken, and the victims died if one attempted to break Mother Winter's dark fever.

"Well, they were not Immortal Kings," Magnus had declared. "They were not me." And so, drunk on pride, he had thought to break the curse no other sorcerer could. Blasting green light, he'd cast his Will over the entire fyr, spreading tendrils of his cold emerald power like the vapors of a fever of his own. Into every lodging and store his mystic fumes had crept, encircling the flesh-and-ice statues, who were sparked with an ember's gentle glow. Their icy skins started to crack, flake, and trickle from the forms beneath. Alas, his scorching heat did not abate once the victims were exposed from within their sheaths. Just as they'd begun to stretch their rickety arms, to begin to blink and ponder the miracle of what had happened to them, they began to slouch, jiggle, and suppurate. Although Magnus was granted the mercy of not having to watch every man, woman, and child transform into a molten brown puddle of matter, even as they were. It smelled like wax being dripped over raw meat; he would never forget such a stench. Soon, the tavern from where his spell had started had been soaked with this sickening varnish, and the last of the running faces had stopped their bubbling shrieks.

Magnus wished that their bodies had burned hotter, had consumed the whole fyr in a cleansing bonfire. It was better than the thought of a soup of death left to cool into ice, which it would, as was the curse: he had only changed the victims' composition for a time. If those people, somehow, abhorrently lived in that state...Ghastly, too ghastly to consider, and yet he pondered their smeared-around faces pressing against a pane of ice and wailing for help. The image was so strong that it slipped past his defenses and entered his bloodmates' minds. Lila gasped. Erik, hiking along with her and behind the king, the huntsman, and the seal-girl, hurried over to Magnus.

"You cannot blame yourself, Magnus," said the knight.

"I can and I do," he replied, kicking at the snow. "You would not understand."

"Fool," said Erik, and gave the man a good shake. "Have you forgotten what the queen and I did? We destroyed the Iron City and tens of thousands of people with it. Do not speak to me of the burden of guilt. I shall bear that stone in my boot forever."

Kanatuk, as a former shadowbroker's servant, was used to biting his tongue when in the presence of dire and shocking secrets being shared, and he had heard that a great infernal power—not Lila—had been ultimately responsible for Menos's fall. He had to know the details of what had been aired. He pushed apart the two men and turned to Erik, whose veins were twisting on his temples and neck like snakes—*what a terrible storm he would be if his thunder got loose*, thought Kanatuk.

"News of the Iron City's fall blew this far North, though I have yet to hear a culprit named. I am no friend to Menos—no one in the North is, not even the disgraced Lords of Carthac—but that was still a terrible loss of life. Is what you just said true? That you and the queen destroyed Menos? How?"

"She was possessed, driven to the act," claimed Erik. "How the city was ruined is of no consequence."

"Do not speak for me." Lila, who had been shrinking behind Erik, now grew with authority and came forth. "I accept the evil of what I did. I accept the necessity of it, too. Whether I was tempted to such wickedness does not matter. We crept into the Iron Mines and rebirthed the truefire vein that had once caused all of Menos to shake. We made it shake a second time, and it shook harder—hard enough to topple centuries' worth of feliron and evil. Gloriatrix would have done the same to Eod, if presented with the same options, and she wouldn't have needed the added goading from dark spirits to do it. But I am no monster. I hear the ghosts of those I killed, just as he bears his stone, just as Magnus has again pricked himself with a thorn of regret for his many mistakes. A woman of glass, I was once called—by a spirit who came to me in a dream. However, we are all glass creatures, not only I. Power merely masks our frailty. Magnus, Erik, and I shall remember and feel our pain forever, a far worse sentence than dying or growing old and being blessed by forgetfulness."

"A fine speech," said the huntsman, swallowing her genocidal confession with hardly a lump. "I can see that you are contrite. Though I would warn you against thinking of ghosts as mere nuisances for your conscience. They are real. They can reach out and tear your soul from its cage. We are heading toward Helheim, or the Black Road as my people call it. There you will see of what I speak."

Clapping for his attention, Macha pulled her brother down into a huddle, and they bickered back and forth in their tribal tongue. It was apparent that Macha was conflicted about the course plotted by her brother. Ever the defender of the girl, Magnus interrupted their argument. "When was this course decided?"

Kanatuk stood, puffing and frustrated. "If we followed whatever strange compass guides you, my King, you would see us freezing to death in the mountains or drowning amidst ice floes. Such is all that surrounds us. Mountains lie ahead, and the Chthonic Ocean bites at the flatter lands east and west, filling the land with small lakes through which we would have to swim. Ahead is our only path, through a timeless rift running between the rock. It is a path once walked, sacredly, as a pilgrimage by my ancestors. It is a path once walked by the Lords of Carthac, when they came to make peace with the land. They thought to war with the North first, these Lordkings, and the North showed them just who had the stronger weapons: gales, snowstorms, starvation, and frostbite so bad that limbs snapped off like twigs. The North has magik. She has a soul."

"And a voice..." muttered the king, hearing, as whenever he simply paid it heed, a symphony to the wind.

"A voice, yes. However, I am speaking of her fury, and it was with that that the Lordkings of ancient Carthac had to contend. They shouldn't even have come to these lands, which had known tranquility and balance all these ages. They were supposed to have fled west, toward Terotak, or so the old rumblings of history go."

A journey they never took, thought Lila, reaching for the missing Mind near her breast. *The Lordkings must have been cut off from their ship, from the Mind, and simply took the next ship they could—one that wouldn't survive an ocean, one that would only serve to take them across the Upper Feordhan.*

In her mind, she had solved a mystery over which historians had torn out millions of clumps of their hair. Erik nodded at her conclusions. The king didn't seem to care and was instead staring off with his head tilted, listening to something. As the company set out again, the Immortals heard from Kanatuk the historical fable of how the Lordkings, after speaking with the tribes of the North and practicing humility for once in their lives, had learned of this sacred and very road upon which Kanatuk would lead them, which itself led to the heart of the North: a realm, a throne in the land, where Winter herself resided. There the Lordkings were to make their case and claim to be a clan among the many that had lived in the North, and in acceptance they would be free from Winter's wrathful temper. Alas, being masters and Menosians, the Lordkings' humility had been a ruse to obfuscate the real plan, which had been to kill whatever spirit commanded the elements and prevented them from remaking the glory of their empire in ancient Carthac. Once more arrogance begat violence, and what blood was spilled did not come from the spirit who ruled the Northlands; rather it flowed from the slaughter of the Lordkings.

"When blood stains ice, and sits through the ages, it becomes blackness as dark as soot," said Kanatuk. They were nearly at the top of the fluffy valley now. Ominous humps that could be whole mountains made of wicked men's blood rose on the gray distance. "Hence the name the Black Road. The darkness is in the snow, the ice, even the water of the deep north. Winter wants us to know that she will never be usurped or denied."

"What did she want, if not the subjugation of these invaders?" asked Erik. "And what of these ghosts you mentioned?"

"One question is tied to the other," replied the huntsman, and a fierce passion overtook his demeanor. "My people were born of the North; we are her blood. Back when the Three Tribes were prodigious, once each season our people traveled to the deep north. We would take the Black Road, then the White Road, which was cold and pure, to the throne of Winter and offer her our weavings, our tastiest fats, our strongest medicines, and whatever comforts and treasures we'd found across her bounteous flesh. We were giving nothing to her, really, as our tithes were simply returning what belonged to her. The Lordkings, however, did not want to honor this relationship; they wanted only to take. Their selfishness took advantage of the generosity of the White Mother, and now she thinks as they do, and demands blood."

Kanatuk stopped, leaned on a glassy tree and whispered, "After the Lordkings failed to defeat the undefeatable, they and their ambitions should have been scattered to the wind. However, one man lived. A man of great build and with a Will that had survived Winter's fury. Winter could have crushed him, of course. However, nature respects what can endure her rage. Thus she whispered to the broken Lordking, and he back to her, and whatever pact was made has allowed the Lordking's heirs to rule over this realm as they once ruled Carthac—by a new title, yes, though by the same evil measures. When the Lordking, now a Kinlord and inheritor of Winter's power, returned to the women and children he'd left behind, he told them that they could stay, and once more be lords and kings, but that a price must be paid.

"Virgins were sent as tributes to the deepest north. No one knows what became of them, whether they froze to death before reaching any altar or throne upon which their blood could be spilled. It only took so long before Winter became hungrier and greedier, and my people—her once favored children—were hunted for sacrifice. When I speak of ghosts, great knight, I speak of *Wendago*—the spirits of my people, their murdered bodies drained of their blood, thrown into ritual pits by the dozen, and now unable to find their ancestors in the afterlife. They wander forever across the land which once loved them. Their rage is the rage of Winter. Their hunger is the hunger for the life that was taken from them, from all the first people of the North. These are the beasts we may have to face on the Black Road."

Suddenly attuned to sounds around them, and drawn by the charcoal blots—the mountains—far off, Erik wondered if he heard a rustle and howl, like that of a Wolf, though sadder and angrier. Fancy or not, he asked the warrior's question: "How do we kill them, these Wendagos?"

"You cannot kill what is already dead," claimed Kanatuk. "My people will never know a final death until the curse, the hunger of this land, is recanted. And I'm not foolish enough to dream that will ever happen."

"I care not for final deaths; temporary ones will do," said Erik.

"In that case, I have heard that fire and beheading does the trick," replied the huntsman.

"Heard?" said Erik, snorting. "You have never faced these beasts?"

The huntsman turned and matched him, nose to nose, spite to spite. "I need not see an Immortal King to believe in his existence, and I would not tread upon the graves and resting grounds of my ancestors simply to satisfy my curiosity. My mother told me that fire and a blade to the neck could release a Wendago from its vessel, which would then need time to seek out and inhabit another corpse. She was always right, when it came to legends..."

Sadness crept over his face like a shadow, and he turned from Erik, who felt embarrassed. An owl ruffled the pines, hooting sharply, and the men watched its graceful ascent and disappearance as an omen of peace and wisdom.

"I shall never hear her stories again," whispered Kanatuk, embarrassed at his loss of cool. "I am the last storyteller. I thought my return after twenty years as a child of the Broker would warrant me a homecoming worthy of Kericot's whimsy. However, my people are extinct, save for shadows like me. From ancient times, we have been snuffed until just my small wick remains. Soon my flame will go out. Indeed, those of us who were not harvested as offerings for the Kinlords and corrupted into hateful spirits were later sold to Menos. Ha! The Kinlords, who are themselves exiled Menosians, trading once more with the ones who cast them out! Ironic or simply sick how power and greed erase the oldest grudges. I had thought that the sacrifices had stopped, for they were a myth even in my day from hundreds of years before, and the bitter reality was my people had been thinned to extinction and never recovered or fought back. What She Wills, She Wills...The abject prayer of my people, which ushered them to a faster demise. Still, I see from your tale, my Queen, that at some point the Kinlords simply discovered a more vital essence: the murder of three sacred children...What could be a richer offering than the seed, love, and hope of one's own loins? They're despicable, the Kinlords and their legacy. Years may have changed their name from Lordking to Kinlord, the North's influences may change their culture, but the souls of these invaders will always be Menosian."

Lila considered all these cycles of destruction and war. As an ever-living woman, she was beginning to feel the ennui and listlessness that affected her former husband. Challenging bigotry and atoning for past sins caulked but the tiniest holes in the dam, before another warlord or madman hammered away, creating more cracks. Granted, she had broken the chain of misogynistic enslavement perpetuated throughout thousands of years of Arhadian culture. And while there was no convincing sympathy she could offer Kanatuk for what he'd described as the brutal cleansing of his people and their ways, there was always a future to which they could look. There would be no new dreams, monsters, or challenges if they didn't reach the Throne of Winter. Surprising her came Erik's pathos as she pondered how to express her hopes.

"I am sorry for your people," he said. "Once, I was a man of the Salt Forests, and we lived as you and your tribe lived—from the land, from nature's bounty, disturbing little and taking no more than what would sustain us. One day, that cycle will end, and technomagik or greed will see to the simplicity of that life being crushed for the sake of *advancement*. I may only be part of a man, though that man will always be a Kree child of the Salt Forests, and so, in you, I find a brother, and a tribe."

They shook hands tightly, high up the forearm with their grips, and in a custom that had them each smiling from its cultural similarity. As they set off over the lip of the valley, they maintained that sworn fraternity, walking together, heeding the sounds of Mother Winter, and ready for the snap of a twig or the howl of a Wendago.

II

Every haunted place that Erik had been to had been possessed of a perceptible wrongness. In the Iron Mines, it manifested as an unsettling calm and silence. In the valley in Kor'Khul, he had suffered from a sense of claustrophobia. Here, walking the quiet canyons where the whisking about of snow, the puffing of their breath, and the shuffling of their feet were the only sounds, he felt that same dead quiet of the Iron Mines. As they walked on mountain passes loomed over by ragged cliffs forged from sharp wedges of hoarfrost, and as he stared into what few gleaming ebon surfaces that were exposed from under the snow and saw the tiny distorted reflections of his company, he felt entrapped in a manner many times worse than what he'd experienced in Kor'Khul. As if his soul were that glassy silhouette, and it was lost, with the others, within the black mountainsides.

When he had been to such places before, it had been as a man, not an Immortal. Now he understood that his lesser sensitivities had sheltered him from the actuality of these horrors. *Things* moved in the snow. Things that were not animals. Centuries ago, life had fled from this realm, and the tons upon tons of whiteness might well have been eons of dust—there would be no mystical groves with an ancient tree and bounteous wildlife found here. Before entering the mountains, he believed that he had sensed life—seven or eight steady heartbeats. However, as they walked through this vast winter tomb, stalked by ghosts and numbed by emptiness, he focused all his exceptional attention on those dangers and lost track of the other pursuers and mounts—surely Eininhar. The sun vanished; an iron veil, twisting with white, had been pulled over it, a shade between dusk and night. The gloom of dusk made the knight believe that every flickering movement was the whirling dance of a Wendago.

Erik, whispered the queen. *What do you sense?*

A silence that stalks us. Beasts that will not be seen. And Eininhar, though they are far enough away and no worry to the forces I sense, lurking.

Lila drew closer to him and soon a misty orb, a tiny sun, hovered over their party. Perhaps a handful of shadows slithered away from them. Perhaps she had imagined it.

They came to a pass that forked and ran beneath cliffs, drawn with beards of icicles beneath the ledges, and the ones risen from the ground, into a hollow of fangs. Unsure of which path to take, and with night deepening each road, Erik suggested the left. He sensed something that way, a change in the flow of the air, as though it were moving across surfaces less weathered and natural. *Buildings*? he wondered. More intrigued than afraid, Erik and the others continued through the spiky maw, and despite a few jumps at the carousel shadows thrown by Lila's light, no one was harmed. The banks of snow beside them rose up so high as to barely dress the feet of the two mountains beside them.

It was an impression greatly reflected upon by Magnus—the darkness and greatness of these things—as he tried to calculate the length of the climb up those drifts and down to the lowest foothold in one of the mountains. Hourglasses, he felt. Reaching the white tips of that mountain, which was mantled in winter mist, seemed impossible. How long had they stood here? Since his birth? Since the birth of Geadhain? Their age seemed indeterminable.

Current matters drew him away from contemplating the world's oldest mountains, and the pushy wind shoved them out of the expanse and into a slinking, descending road over which arced frozen spouts of ice. At least the worst of the storm's fury was rebuked down here, and the path stirred with crackling echoes. Then Magnus saw it, a dimple in the sparkling dark ahead. Were he not bloodmate to the bestial knight leading them—not unlike Brutus in his current state—who perked and snapped his gaze toward the oddity, he would not have seen the hole. But Magnus did, and he knew by those same senses borrowed from Erik that the cave led into a wider chamber and one that hadn't been carved by nature, or beasts, but by man. With Erik's instincts flowing through him, Magnus could almost smell the ancient sweat and herbs of the people who had once been there.

Kanatuk raised no objection as Erik and the other Immortals hurried toward a tiny opening he had just noticed in the curved dam of ice. As they hurried on, sudden cold winds disturbed the snow from the icy bridges above. Macha looked up and froze to meet the gibbous gaze of a leering, crooked body spotted with blue flesh and wiry black fur; it hung like a demonic monkey from the tip of a stalactite. With the sharp eyes of a changeling, she saw clearer impressions of a prune face with an intense yellow stare. Its eyes glowed, surrounded by a snake's nest of dark knotted hair beaded with ice. She shrieked, and the creature moved like blown smoke, smoldering, warping into thick vapor, then coalescing on an icicle high above her head. Its mouth widened into a crescent moon of shining white fangs, making a call for her flesh from the bulging gullet behind its teeth, without breaking its hideous smile.

BRAWK! BRAWK! BRAWK!

It dropped, dissolving into a twist of shadow. Kanatuk threw his sister down and across the ice. She caught the shine of his drawn blade as she slid on her side and struck a rock with her hip. As she stumbled up, an explosion rocked the ground in front of her, throwing her down again. No sooner had she screamed than all three Immortals had turned in a single spin. While the Immortal sorcerer's glare shone green, and Lila's sphere blazed angrily from her Will—a violent comet ready to seek—Erik had taken two great strides, then leapt, soared over a hundred paces and landed quicker than either of his bloodmates could throw their Wills. The remaining Immortals weren't sure where, or what, to assault anyway, and the cloud of snow and a blast of crackling golden-black energy that appeared upon Erik's descent caused further confusion and hesitation—he had changed into his other self.

BRAWK! BRAWK! BRAWK!

None too soon, as dozens of gaseous shadows rose from the ground or dripped from the icy ceiling. What rose to challenge the monsters from a smoking pit was only half the man the company knew; he stood stripped of his shirt, his cloak left fluttering in the snow, his back twisting with luminescent veins and embedded with hunks of gold and ebon rock. One hand was covered with a black gauntlet crafted by a primeval Menosian into spurs and talons of stone. A thigh had burst his pant leg to tatters and ended in something like a stone elephant's hoof. One bull's horn jutted from his skull, over his crag of a brow and steaming golden eyes, and his snarling mouth was further pulled down by a rocky craw. By his incomplete metamorphosis, he appeared to be resisting the full pull of his bloodmate's bond, and only half-drunk on the brandy-and-spice elixir of her love. To give himself over, wholly, to the moods of the obsidian warrior in his flesh— demands to punish, stomp, and smite—would cloud his judgment. In Carthac and when confronting Magnus, his bloodlust had been deadly; he would not submit to such a loss of reason again.

"*Gael Bharg*," (Knight of Stone), muttered Macha, while fumbling for her long-toothed hunting knife.

She uttered a battle cry as she charged toward the mêlée engulfing her brother. Shadows had surrounded Kanatuk—moving, spitting, gangly things that flowed from solid monsters to fluid wafts of black. Kanatuk was a master killer, his huntsman's edge sharpened to brutality by the Broker's whetstone of ruthless tutelage. Had he not that edge, the murderous winds that appeared only as flashes of grinning, fanged countenances, as flickers of hairy, black-and-blue meat, or as thrusts of ebon claws, would have killed him in specks. He danced out of the reach of the misty swipes of the Wendagos and swung back with his blade at whatever matter of theirs remained. Once, maybe twice, he was rewarded with a splash of their blood. He could not say how many there were, and his focus had narrowed to shuddering windows against which these horrors appeared. He had only to dance and swing his blade if he were to live.

Then came the light, the shaking earth, and a rumbling force—a moose of stone and thunder, he thought, madly—that struck the cloud of creatures around him. Gouts then splatters of hot essence showered down. In one seized moment, he saw a man—Erik, though impossibly stratified and bristling with glowing barnacles—holding one of the creatures, which fluttered between gas and meat, unable to escape the mystical vise the man had on its neck and ankles. For Erik, too, was magik, and his touch would be like feliron to them. Helplessly, it clawed at the chokehold, still wearing that insufferable menacing grin as it was dismembered and decapitated in several pulls. Other creatures attempted to rend the Immortal, though they were only as troublesome as a litter of evil kittens, their scratches about as deadly. Erik roared under the shower of the creature's death, and then pounded the beasts that scrabbled against him.

Kanatuk should have looked away from that horrific wonder, but too late he felt a hissing pressure behind him, then spun too slow to raise his sword and instead only hacked the upraised arm of the Wendago materializing from the dark—not at its other limb, positioned somewhere lower.

"Oomph!" he gasped.

The Wendago's claws impaled him with the force of a sharpened spade through his stomach. A monster with oversized yellow catlike eyes glared into his, its fat-lipped grimace a totemic mask of terror to behold so closely—the teeth, however, were bestial and crooked and the countenance moved as if it were skin and not wood. His people—this was what remained of them. Darkness eating at his vision, dying and stunned, Kanatuk bubbled out a bloody plea while reaching for the mask of the creature's face.

"Leave her," he begged, or thought in the language of the Three Tribes. "Macha is all that remains to honor what has been lost."

Curious, the creature's eyes widened, expressing sympathy, hunger, or something else altogether. Kanatuk never learned what, as a searing beam of light sizzled through the creature, dispelling it into fragments of glowing ash. It vanished, grinning and probably as surprised as the huntsman. Without the support of its impalement, Kanatuk fell to the ground. A pool of wet warmth leaked under him, and his astonishing pain was quickly and strangely numb. Bleeding, coughing, and fading into a fatal sleep, he pondered Wendagos, Macha's fate, the landmines of emerald flame blasting about him, and the angry little sun above his head that whizzed out concentrated lines of sunlight like a mirrored ball he had once seen in one of Menos's more extravagant parties. He had been at that party to kill a man, and he had succeeded. He was a murderer, and this was now his end. Brave, and ready, he quietly wished Macha a new brother, keeper, and friend. With the whole of his failing heart, he prayed for her to know happiness, as they'd had with each other for a short time. Then, smiling at the sudden flood of memories, he took what he felt would be his last breath, and blew it outward, sending his spirit toward the sky.

III

"They're taking the Black Road," said Bjorn.

He rose from his squat position in the snow and placed his glove back over the hand that had been feeling the soft, cold ground as a seer hovered her fingers and read cards. Such was the magik of his kind: the power to track, to hunt as a dog would using more than nose and ears—though he could use those, too, and to great effect. Flexing those same second senses, as he cast a glowering glare down the rock-jutting hill, over rolling white crests and then off toward the mountains beyond, he felt there was a path, felt it like a prickling of static as though he were a tuning fork attuned to Magnus's magnetism.

There were four people—though some not quite people—with the king, and they were at best a day away. If he and his men made haste, they would catch up with them before nightfall. Branwen and the other hounds in this chase stood with the Kinlord's son, awaiting command. Bjorn felt confused, though, over what strategy was best in this situation. Did he chase them farther down the Black Road and its Wendago-infested crags? Or should he allow his prey to find its way to the throne of the North? He still had Queen Lila to kill. Coming from a man who'd beaten his son for expressing the need for love, his father's actions were vague, desperate, and broken in logic. Why had his father sent him as an assassin? What did he fear of the Queen of Eod? Bjorn suffocated in mysteries, and he sensed that the ordeal before him was twofold: one for Magnus and one for him. When he looked back at his men, they all appeared to be reflections of his father—gloomy, hard, and unwilling to offer suggestions. Although there was a part of their minds where his father lurked, too, and he might not have been imagining the scorn.

"Ahead lies the realm of the Wendago," rasped Branwen, and walked down the line of scowling Eininhar, who puffed more than the stallions behind them. She sought to determine if any were afraid, but none quivered, and she thought of them as dumb beasts, dogs to a master's chain. As she came to Bjorn, she noticed his trembling wasn't due to the cold. At least he knew fear, and had a respect for life. "Do you know of this realm we approach?"

"I know of the Black Road—every child hears of it."

"Do you know of its purpose?"

"In olden days, tributes were led to that road to appease the ancient spirits."

"Ancient *spirit*—there is only one who truly rules, though she has many moods and shapes." Branwen, deciding that the way was forward, walked down the hill. "And what of its use these days?"

For an old woman, she moved swiftly and had not once shown a lapse in her constitution. Bjorn had to chase her to answer her question, and his pack of brothers followed. He had time to think, then, of the reply to her riddle, since it felt as if the obvious answer wasn't the one she sought. "It has no use, the tributes have ended. We live in peace with each other and the land."

Branwen stilled, clenching her staff till her knuckles turned blue-gray.

"Peace?" she whispered. "Child, there is no peace here. The land has hated its children and itself ever since the forgotten mongrels of Menos sailed here and planted their gory stakes into the White Mother's flesh. I shall tell you this, and you will see in the landmarks and terrors ahead, the road may not be used, though the tributes have not ended. In fact, the White

Mother is more glutted on sacrifice than ever before. Know what you serve and why."

"I-I do," said Bjorn.

"You are blind."

One of the Eininhar barked rudely, and a few more growled. Branwen disdained them with a sneer and spoke to the shadow lurking in their minds, peering through these men as if they were vessels of glass and smoke. "I say what I want," she declared to the shadow that watched her through the Eininhar. "My tongue is not bound to you."

Bjorn's brothers howled. Branwen left Bjorn and his brothers standing there; the prince confused, the others fuming. Whirling snow blew over her trail, and she seemed to drift into the ivory headland as if she were wind and spirit. Bjorn and his hounds couldn't catch her by foot and soon mounted. She remained walking, keeping as good a pace as the trotting horses, and he pondered her question as the mountain's shadows crept in a dark cape toward him, smothering him, muting his fear with new scents and sounds upon which he needed to focus—rattling, scratching, shuffling, and howls; scents of blood; dried, salty sweat.

Bjorn hoped that the lore about being able to slay Wendagos with fire and decapitation were true as they soon entered the foothills and the realm of the beasts. A silence lay here, beating and alive with danger. Neither hawk nor hare, deer nor bear did the great hunter sense dwelling beyond. Warriors fought fear each day, and Bjorn challenged his then, ignoring the rush in his chest and chasing the white woman ahead. Soon the horses reared, tried to throw their riders, and would go no farther.

"The beasts know what is ahead," shouted Branwen, still far ahead of the others, as the disorganized soldiers tried to make the horses behave. "Leave them."

Branwen's command seemed absolute; the Eininhar released the reins, and the horses fled. Bjorn's brothers followed the white witch on foot. Bjorn waited a sand, watching the steeds get blown over by snow and wishing he could have vanished with them. He figured the mounts weren't necessary, as there was little chance of him needing one for a return journey. His destination was to be final.

Between the mountains, rude hunks of coal thrown from a Dreamer's hearth and creeping in tides of white, there were faint roads. Not roads meant for the feet of mortals, but they would do for that purpose. Snow shook down the sides of the black giants, and more than once as they trod under an overhang a deluge threatened to become an avalanche. They dodged them and eventually caught up to a slowing Branwen, unwinded from her flight. The anger had left her, too, though her ruthless perseverance had not. No more questions were asked, and the reunited party continued a steady exploration of the winding roads, shuffling through powdery gulches, and then into dells where only the stubs of trees struggled to live. Runts or not, the trees made for fine kindling, and the men stopped to break off branches, dusting off the frost and ripping cloth to make torches. As their flint stones brought them light, the shadows seemed longer, deeper, and Bjorn thought he heard the strange howls and rustling grow nearer.

"Did you hear that?" asked one of his brothers.

"Aye," he replied. "Torches high, blades ready."

Cautiously, they wandered to the end of the dell. Bjorn had seen renditions of Wendagos that looked like starving men, steaming in shadows, with yellow eyes and enormous grinning mouths not wide enough to hold all their teeth. They were artistic interpretations of nightmares, he felt. Even as that thought stuck with him, grinding the gears in his head, a smoldering shape peered down from the ridge above, this hunched and wizened gremlin with a mask for a face and eyes so bright and yellow that they cut the dark, and he thought, *That can't be real.* They all stiffened in horror and howled, whipping torches and brandished blades at the sky.

They weren't sure what exactly had terrified their leader, as the pale arch from which the Wendago had hovered was bare. Until Branwen spoke, it seemed like a waking nightmare.

"The Wendago has left," she said, calmly. "It was scared away."

"Scared away?" exclaimed Bjorn. "By what?"

Another shape rose from behind a patch of boulders. It seemed like a man, though they sensed it was not. Why would a man be in half-torn clothing and wearing no boots in this dire cold? What man would climb over boulders on all fours, before assuming the tall, powerful stance of a knight or a king? It was something between man and beast, mortal and supernatural, and they cringed and whined as nervous as hyenas before a lion. Branwen, holding her staff up to stall any actions, gave the stranger a cheerless smile and walked over to the base of the boulder. There she crossed an arm over her chest and bowed. The black-skinned Immortal, who Bjorn now recognized, snorted at her fealty, but they began conversing in a language of which he knew but scraps. But he gleaned enough to know it was Ghaedic.

"You have been following us for some time now, even if your tracks are fleet and quiet," said Erik. "I assume some magik masks you lot. I would ask that you announce your intent, and, should I not approve of it, turn back. I do not fear you, whoever or whatever you may be…"

Erik found her a hard-shelled mystery to crack. She smelled of magik, but also of earth, loam, and green things he had not known to be prodigious in the North. She smelled of the spice and cardamom of secrets, too. There was little about the woman he could assess, and then she gave her name.

"Branwen, you may call me, and I speak for Mother Winter."

Of course. The cold face, the wicked rune tattoos, she could be none other than the witch of Lila's memory. The knight snarled and dropped into a prowling stance, peaked fingers, toes en pointe—a pose of intimidating elegance.

Bjorn felt the man could pounce from there to his feet in the bat of an eye. Thus, he didn't blink, though he did move closer to Branwen, who gestured him back with her staff as if this were a conversation at which he was not welcome.

"I know of you. Witch and ritualist, killer of children," said Erik. "You are the Kinlord's pet."

"I am owned by no man," replied Branwen. "I am bound—as are all things in this world—by blood and desire. If you follow that thread back through the mists of time to a snake and a garden, you will know that I am no more at fault than the man who first accepted Desire's gift. His hunger has ruined our garden and many more. And I am a mother, not a killer. I watch my children die for the greed of man. I do not expect you to understand my sacrifices or pain...although you will."

"I have not the time for you and your curs. Leave!" Erik slammed his fist into the boulder upon which he perched. It cracked and crumbled to a cloudy death, and he walked from the rubble and white puff like a nightmare made flesh; Bjorn and his pack scrambled together around Branwen. "I shall not ask again."

"The man with whom you travel," said Branwen. "The magik of an Immortal King or Queen is not the medicine with which to cure wounds made from spiritual hate. You may have stemmed his wounds, though the poison still pumps through his veins. We must remove the hate, draw it out as a medicine woman drinks then spits venom. You Immortals have not the skills to save him. I do."

How did she know so much? She was a witch, or something more, figured Erik. He thought of the people he had left back in the ruin, caring for Kanatuk while he had gone to investigate these mysterious pursuers from whom they had run once, and who should not have been trusted, given the edgy stares in each of them—with the exception of the unreadable witch. As he debated what course to take, images of the huntsman's rolling eyes and thrashing body, and flashes of Macha weeping and shrieking like an animal beside him, were thrown into his mind by his bloodmates. Pride had damned so many men, and Erik would not be another victim.

He sensed no conceit within her. "You can save him?" he asked, soft as stone could.

"I can, if we hurry."

Erik waved for the witch and her hounds to follow.

Bjorn slipped his sword into its sheath and nodded for his brothers to do the same. Their accord was shared, it seemed—hands on their hips and ready to draw blades. They knew their moment of glory was soon. But why did they not march forward? Why the intense glaring upon him and not the new fearsome enemy—and temporary ally—who walked up ahead?

"Brothers?" Bjorn stepped forward, hearing now the low whisper in their minds—a message imparted as if behind a hand and which he couldn't fully construe. Was that his father? What was the Kinlord saying, and why was this message not shared with him? "Father?"

The whispering ended, and the Eininhar relaxed their battle-ready stances. One of them said, "It is not the time."

However, the statement was made without a subject, rather than addressed to him, and as his men walked on, Bjorn couldn't remember a time he'd felt more alone, or seen his brothers as such cold strangers.

V

Death was at its ugliest when exposed to light, and Lila's small sphere of magik revealed every gruesome detail. Kanatuk's death was slow, painful theater for his companions to watch. Prior to his placement on a slab of ancient stone, found within this eerie ruin, Magnus and Lila in combined efforts had managed to pool the man's guts back into his abdomen and had crudely sutured him closed and cauterized the wounds with magik. However, there was only so much they could do without the proper instruments of surgery. Kanatuk's stretched purple stomach showed through the tatters of his ripped tunic and seemed like the post-operational disaster of a pregnancy gone wrong. They were certain he had died over and over during their flesh sculpting. Though a cry from Macha, more an animal screech, seemed to bring him back every time. Now that he was sealed up, his seizures only came on every few sands; however, such decreasing frequency gave Magnus only a grim prognosis—he didn't think that the fits were subsiding because the patient was improving. A least the huntsman was silent, and now so too was Macha. She held his pale hand, sniffling and chattering prayers in ancient Ghaedic, a variant huskier and older than the one Magnus knew.

How had they arrived at so dark a moment? Magnus felt himself sliding into shock and forced himself to remember. After the battle, and once Kanatuk had been pieced together somewhat on the blood-slathered ice, Erik had carried the huntsman into the cave, before racing off like a beast on the trail of a new scent. He had sensed something, and was angry at having been so unaware of the presence of the Wendago.

"I shall not be ambushed again!" he'd snarled, and left his bloodmates alone to deal with Macha and her wounded brother. An unwise decision, perhaps, even if the creatures had all scattered quite suddenly during the maelstrom of his rage, Magnus's summoning of green fire from beneath the frozen earth, and Lila's vengeful orb of sorcery and its lasers of light. None of the bloodmates believed that it had been their powers that had driven off the Wendagos, however. The monsters had vanished after Kanatuk had fallen. Tens, or perhaps hundreds, of shadow-monsters had crumbled into a dust that couldn't be seen, and had then been blown away by the Northland's cold wind. It had been chaos, and it was a miracle that only Kanatuk was hurt. Magnus remembered how bravely Macha had fought, slashing and leaping at shadows like a cat; he'd detonated a road of emerald fire through the swarm of Wendagos to reach her and found her untouched by their teeth or claws. She'd wormed out of his embrace once she saw her fallen brother. Nothing he could say would comfort her now.

With nothing to do but worry while the queen watched over Kanatuk and Macha kept vigil, Magnus stood and explored the ruin that was their sanctuary. Magnus had been in many tombs in his day, and this place had less a feeling of gloom than of quiet remembrance. It was especially strange of him to think of this chamber as one of serenity, since they had laid Kanatuk on an arcane altar, one seemingly for sacrifice, set up as a set of crude concentrically circular stairs, which might have been the natural trunk of a grand stalagmite, and which had been set with an oval sliver of obsidian as its altar. If bodies were not sacrificed here, then it was a place for other offerings.

The handiwork of men could be found in the barest of places—the arch from the icy tunnel that led here, the detailing of the altar, the small carvings on the bowed, uneven walls of the chamber—while remaining natural everywhere else. Magnus walked over the snow-dusted ground looking for more signs of man's presence, and he saw decayed frozen baskets and wooden faces less terrible than the Wendagos glaring from effigies or larger statues risen from the winter that had claimed the place.

He didn't dig to know more; he felt those treasures and stories were sacred. As sacred as the stories written on the wall, which—as he conjured a green witch light—showed huge lizards, elks, mountains, and small men in a medley of valleys, aeries, clefts, and frozen lakes upon which animals trod. Very few battles were portrayed for hieroglyphs of an aboriginal sort, where early people had to fight nearly everything for survival. Stick men prayed, worked trades, and knelt before the great monsters of the North, though never did they raise a spear to them. In only one chilling image, found near the tunnel to the outside, the peaceful worshippers, often seen in skin cloaks, fought men with horns—invaders disembarking from great ships. There were few murals after that one, and Magnus wondered if the chronology started at the back of the cave, and if these were the most recent—still hundreds of years old, he felt.

Standing by the entrance to the ruin, he sensed Erik's return. Erik had been silent during his hunt for their new enemies, and Magnus suspected that he had found the opposite: allies. Or were they? For a conflicted and mind-spoken warning entered the heads of the knight's bloodmates, cautioning them against raising arms.

I am sorry for my silence, he said, *you must trust my bringing these Northmen and their witch here. I do not smell a lie upon her, but something else, and she has promised she can help.*

A lie upon whom? the bloodmates wondered. However, with Erik's borrowed senses, Lila sniffed the oil of old, mystical trees—beech or rowan— and the scent of a saltier glacial stone than her knight's obsidian fragrance. With her borrowed hearing, she heard rattles, rustles, and the tapping of a staff. While none of these details by themselves amounted to much, thus arranged they formed a thrust of memory, of danger of having known them before.

"Stay here, and protect your brother," she commanded, and dashed out as Macha withdrew her hunting knife.

When she reached Magnus and Erik she saw a party of Eininhar— identified by the red woven into their snow-crusted braids—and a woman who was speaking with the king. By the looks of it, travel had been hard on the warriors, and they were caked in frost from their beards to their boots, though their strapping brawn pressed tight to the leathers they wore under their cloaks and they breathed, hot and heavy, as if they were enjoying the exercise of surviving in the North. One of the Eininhar was different from the others, amber-tinted to his stare and hair, bronzy in countenance, and he gazed upon Lila with as much unabashed fascination as she glared at the branded, white-robed witch who had yet to acknowledge her hatred.

"Branwen, you demon," she cursed. "I shall never forget the name. You are not wanted here."

Ending her conversation with Magnus, Branwen moved forward as Lila stepped back. She had forgotten the fear she'd experienced when speaking to the woman, and she mustered what boldness she could as she chased her—headed toward the altar—hurling threats. "We do not need your hexes or witchery! You are not welcome here."

"In Eod," hissed Branwen, "you may be queen. Here, you are no ruler. I shall not be told where my wind will blow. Not by you, Child of the Harvest, nor anyone."

Though further scared and also alarmed by the mention of golden children and their curious curse, she wasn't about to let this woman advance. As they were almost upon the steps leading to the altar and Kanatuk, Lila went to grab the woman's arm and missed, clumsily—though she had no idea how she'd been evaded. "Get away from him!"

Branwen's sudden transition from hag to another woman—hair of spun gold, eyes deep and tawny as Lila's—stopped the queen from another attempted manhandling. Was this an illusion? For suddenly they were sisters, or aunts; family without question. Only for a flash did this other self glitter, the face on a coin being flipped.

The impression vanished as the witch spoke. "You have seen a mirror of the truth. You know I shall not harm him. He has been claimed by the Wendago—they desire his flesh. Whatever magik you have used to stitch together his body will not cure his soul. You must appease the spirits who your bloodshed has angered. Leave me be."

Lila attempted no further assaults and stumbled ahead through the haze of questions. At the first step toward the altar, Macha sensed some of the witch's pure intent, and motivated by her own instincts, sheathed her dagger, adopted a ritual formality, and followed the woman up the oyster rings to the table where her brother lay. It seemed as though Kanatuk felt an uncanny peace in Branwen's presence, too, and he settled into a gentle writhing as she reached him, hovering her hand over his greasy forehead and calming him like ether. He slumped, exhaled, and did not move again.

Gathered nearby and below, the observers watched the movements of Branwen and her ritual maiden. Wavering between which wonder to attend, the fairest Northman stared from the altar to the back of the woman so like him in the chamber, the woman he'd been sent to kill. Seeing her through the eyes of his brothers was less illuminating than seeing her through his own; she could have been mother or sister to him. Is their likeness and possible relationship why his father had commanded her to be slain? Bjorn's trained hand clenched his weapon's hilt, and he wondered if he would have the strength to pull the weapon when the time came.

Lila felt the weight of Bjorn's stare upon her. She did not look at him, for he looked so much like Leonitis. Regardless, their inner conflicts were mysteries too small to consider before what grand magik had begun.

Branwen slipped off her furs and the leather shawl beneath. She continued to strip herself of layers, discarding them somewhere, until she was nearly bare in a ragged white shift that peaked on her shoulders and knobby elbows. Glimmers of the caramel skin that Lila had seen in the other version of Branwen led the queen to think that her suspicion of the woman's duality wasn't to be easily dismissed. Truly, she was more than a woman or witch; she was a priestess to some force. As she faced them, power burned behind her skin, lighting the crimson runes etched on her face and summoning a mist that threaded into the chamber. She stood there in all her grandeur and terribleness. Then, what pitiable doubts remained as to this witch's authority were smote in the wailing cry she gave, the wail of a Wendago queen—a shriek so ululating and sharp that the witnesses' vision blurred from tears, and they staggered down to their knees.

Branwen's song echoed away and with it the ice that had encased the chamber. Murals unseen for ten thousand years appeared fresh, their pigments and subjects growing in contrast to the red-hooded hunters, stick-like black demon-men, and the chalky skeletons of the great wyrms and furry monsters of the North. Astoundingly, it *moved*, the river of stories, in cadence with the voice of Branwen, a voice that further dulled its listeners' minds with a buzzing language that all, Northmen and Southmen, could hear.

"Once, the Children of the North were whole and happy," she preached. "Winter gave to us her herds, summoned the fish from under her frozen skin, and created gardens in her extraordinary emptiness where trees tall as no other stood and fed us with their fruits."

The image of an Yggdrassil grove, with their papery branches and pulsing fruits, along with a herd of animated beasts rippled across the cavern's roof. The pictures were stiffly animated but still more immersive than any phantograph. They were watching history, and truth, much as the Hall of Memories conjured.

She allowed them a moment for their gasps, and continued. "The Three Tribes never warred or knew strife beyond surviving the harshest winters, or deciding upon who was to hunt the buffaloch and carribhuu, and who was to gather the season's greens from the Yggdrassils. They wanted for nothing, because they understood, more than many of Geadhain's peoples, the curse of want. They knew that bargaining with Desire would end their prosperity, their covenant with the land. Thus they blessed what animals they slaughtered, they sewed what skins were taken into necessities for life—not objects of vanity. And they used the bones of Winter's herds to carve objects of respect, which they returned to her, once each year, after all Three Tribes met, here. A cycle of giving, life and death from Winter to her children. It was a cycle unbroken since you, Magnus, walked as a child."

The waves of time crashed onto another scene, one that the king remembered, though not as animated. Above, strange ships, spiny as shelled monsters of the sea, shoved onto a beach, and demon men crawled from them over white shores and engaged in slow marionette warfare with the crude red-cloaked hunters who were also present. Clangs of steel and powdery gunblasts echoed in the chamber. Erik smelled the ripe earthiness of blood.

"The twice disgraced demons of Carthac came to these shores, believing themselves rulers once more," said Branwen. "They had magik and fire to force their rule, and force it they did, pushing the Three Tribes farther north, staining the White Mother red with the blood of her children. They were a disease in this garden, and the White Mother would not have them. What you call today the Scourge of Winter is no new ailment, but rather an ancient curse, resurrected and reinvigorated, and come from the White Mother's hate. For that is what the Lordkings brought, besides their death—want and hate."

Frost crackled over the scene, and its combatants slowed and whitened within the great wintry frame. "As they slaughtered her children, Mother Winter froze their princes. Soon the children of the Three Tribes and the Lordkings knew the grief of senseless attrition. Thus they met and spoke of peace, and the Lordkings, seemingly humbled, asked how to mend the White Mother's anger. Go north, said the great medicine woman of the Three Tribes. Go north and ask the White Mother to forgive you."

Branwen glowered and the room grew dark from thunder and clouds, her runes blazing, her form fading into a star amid the mist. "However, the Lordkings knew nothing of meekness, and they shackled the great medicine woman, killing her defenders and most of the tribes they had called for the summit of peace. Then they drove their remaining forces north where the medicine woman would take them to the throne of this spirit, the Throne of Winter they called it—knowing only oligarchies and dictatorships—and they would end this curse with their fire-sticks and magik. What She Wills, She Wills, and the Lordkings' desire was granted—at the end of what was the White Road, they met Mother Winter and sacrilegiously unleashed their fire-sticks and magik..."

Blinking from the clouds on the ceiling came two white eyes as large as witches' moons. Peaking over the snarling titan's countenance—a writhing of angry smoke—was a crown of frost spines and fog. Reaching from the blackness came claws of ice and stone, which settled on the backs of mountains that manifested in puffs of ether. The giantess roared. Or maybe Branwen shrieked again—the noises sounded about the same. Explosions and phantom cries from an ancient war railed against the watchers' sanity. Many of the unshakeable Eininhar shrieked at the vision. A few observers, including the king, the queen, Erik, and the fair Northman only screamed as the scene fell down from the ceiling in a tumult of smoldering ice. As it was just terrifying theater, they were not crushed. A new scene floated above of a single man kneeling, finally humbled, before a dread shadow against which he appeared only as a speck.

"One Lordking survived—the strongest, cut of iron and winter's hardest ice. To have survived her judgment showed promise. Mother Winter wondered if perhaps these murderous invaders could not learn to become darker links in her chain of life. She is not without respect, Mother Winter. She felt proud of this terrible half-giant, the last of his broken dynasty, with only women and children of his remaining—cubs that would freeze without him. She gave him a choice, and chance, to show that he was worthy of living in her lands."

Branwen's words thundered through their bones and shook the world. *"**Bring to me a fruit of your hands. Bring to me what you value most, and sacrifice it to receive my forgiveness**."*

Although the cavern stopped shaking, the ghostly projection of the giantess, Mother Winter, glared down upon the watchers, and they could not see Branwen or the scribble that was the Lordking. Branwen's next histories affected Lila and Bjorn most of all, these secrets from which they would have escaped the knowing of, and which they listened to with tearful acceptance.

"What did he bring? What did he cherish most? It was not the tradition-al baskets and totems—made from toil and nature, made from patience and time—which the children of the Three Tribes had always offered. Rather, to the Throne of Winter, he brought his daughter, Beira, a maiden most fair, her blood the blood of true and proud queens, a royalty not often seen in the courts of Iron. The wisest Keepers might tell you that she was touched by Estore, the Dreamer of the Rising Heart. What did he do with his daughter? This divine child? This child of Love? He slit her throat and pumped out her life upon the Throne of Winter."

Suddenly Branwen, flickering between maiden and crone, stood before Lila. She gestured, and the queen's chin was pulled up by an invisible force as if she were Menosian chattel being bought by a cruel sorceress. Branwen then drew a dry finger across her throat, and Lila screamed as if the action was being mimicked on her, only with a blade not a finger. Erik, breaking some of the spell, flung out a hand to slap the witch, but she folded away into the billows rolling through the chamber. Lila's pain and the imaginary burning rush of blood gushing from her neck faded.

After Branwen vanished, thunder and storms shook the cave, cold plates and hunks of ice rained down upon them, and they were forced to cower in a huddle. Stillness and a crimson light summoned them from their fear, and they straightened, watching the final spectacle play out on the ceiling. It was a sunset, where each wavy line was a spray of blood thrown from the stained-glass cameo of a woman—a woman who was Lila's twin. As the smoke of time faded, removing with it the ghastly image and revealing an ice-scabbed cavern with once more inscrutable and inanimate markings hidden behind history's glass, Branwen stood as she had before—as if she'd never moved from the altar. Remaining as a humble acolyte to the arcane proceedings, Macha, kneeling and muttering, appeared the same. Lila and the others sensed Branwen was not yet finished with her magical oration.

Behind her, like one reborn, Kanatuk twitched and rose. Shuddering and inelegant, he flopped his legs over the altar's edge. The whites of his eyes showed, and his belly had bloated with an abominable worming mass. Kanatuk's neck cocked sideways, and his grin stretched to his ears as Erik heard the snap and rubbery twist of meat. Neither Branwen nor the altar maiden flinched.

"In taking sacred life," boomed Branwen, "the Lordking cursed not only himself, but all of the North. Mother Winter, accepting all the gifts of her children—even this depraved and wicked thing—drank from Beira, and in doing so, drank the Lordking's desire and twisted humanity. It changed her, as desire does in any creature. Mother Winter became hungry, greedy. She needed more and more..."

Kanatuk, his skin turning blue, his shoulders jutting up and down like bat's wings, his new gaping mouth of snapping fangs, shot two newly clawed hands at Branwen. At this she turned slightly and held out her hand and sent him into a paralyzing seizure. When his spasms subsided, she resumed.

"First, what was left of her original children was harvested and sent to the Throne of Winter, and both Mother Winter and the Lordking grew fat from their sacrifices and from the power of their souls. Seeing this, the Lordking sent more of his daughters, more tribesmen, more offerings and sculptures wet in blood and pried from the dead hands of their makers. It wasn't enough, though, and in a sick parody of what had been, Mother Winter craved what the Lordking had prized most: his legacy and seed. Daughters and sacrifices of the tribe were meek to those succulent offerings. So he gave his sons." Bjorn was struck by the wisdom of her gaze, fallen to him, and her words, spoken only his way.

"Three, as is the number of our world. Three men, three murders, three representations of the Fates, three fat-offerings, each one to feed the Kinlord's power a little more before the last, and to feed the White Mother's ravenous insanity. Only after that last feast would she allow him to have a child to continue this unholy legacy, his wanton immortality. Our land, once an untouched sanctuary of the Old Ways, a realm where life and death were balanced evenly, had become an empire of sacrifice and death. True, some children escaped—to other lands...or sands. True, some of the Kinlords met the withering end they deserved. But even then, the White Mother granted them one last breath and spurt of their wicked seed to fuel what had become her darkness."

Slowly, again puppeteering without strings, she moved her hands through the air and Kanatuk was lowered, his feet flailing, his fresh claws scrabbling on the stone altar. As if he were an ailing child and not a man about to lose his soul, she bent over and whispered something that sounded kind from what Erik heard. She faced the others again, before striding down the steps of the dais, hiking her robe as if she were a queen more royal than any present, and addressed them as her court.

"The law of inheritance," she said, "that was made in darkness, can be rewritten in light by the brave children of tomorrow." She pointed at Lila first, and then Bjorn. "You are those children. One lost, one still bound by the ancient Lordking's deeds. Can you be the cure to this poison? Can you atone for the murder of the Three Tribes? Can you even understand their rage? Can you scream into the night that has become Mother Winter and make her hear? Make *them* hear?"

Them. They came at her pronouncement, the Wendagos. Puffs, slurps, and snail-crawling worms of ethereal blackness that entwined the icicles before unfurling into men of smoke, lurching from every crevasse and stepping like phantoms through the glass mirrors of rocks, wall and floor. So many twists to be seen, wriggling, stretching into blue-and-ebon things with tribal masks, beaded manes, and claws. Looking around, they saw thousands of the angry spirits, an infestation, covering ceiling and floor. And still more materialized. The ten thousand yellow glares of spirits disgraced and murdered in their sacred home gazed upon the altar and its gathering of insolents. The Wendagos would smother them; they would dine on the flesh of Immortals and the cursed blood of the demon-men. In a moment the crawling womb would contract, and everything living would be devoured. But then there was silence, a dulled cacophony, and Branwen appeared before Lila.

Said she, "Child of the Harvest, one who escaped by mercy, one who was taken south by a kind soul and given as princess to the sons of sand. Child of Love, who has taken the lives of an empire and learned the path of blood—the path of her Menosian forefathers. What would you say to the tribes you have wronged? Think quickly, you have only have the opportunity for one answer."

Lila regretted Menos with all her heart, with every sand of her Immortal life; the fire-torn faces of the dead—imagined or real—came to her whenever she thought of the event. Her victims' screams wouldn't have been any less terrifying than the Wendagos around her. Indeed, perhaps these creatures knew of her murders, and of her self-disgust. Perhaps they could bring a message to the others trapped in a limbo of vengeance, as her victims in Menos surely were. Weeping, her heart torn, she shouted to the Wendago horde. "Dead of the Three Tribes, hear me! I am not innocent. Nor am I wholly wicked. I have been a tyrant, a mother, a lover, a betrayer. I am trying to be a hero, now, though my journey may end without your forgiveness. I must ask of you to forgive the unforgiveable. A wound that has rent a society and scourged them of their honor has no price that can be paid. No charlatan's promise I can offer! Thus, forgive me...See me as the broken-glass woman I am—a creatures of faults and worries. And if you have the power to reach into the veil to find others as lost as you, ask the souls in Menos to forgive me, too..."

Lila fell to her knees, weeping, the silence ended and the chamber's raucous baboon jury erupted, before it hushed again when Branwen called for it and turned to Bjorn. It was his turn to answer, and his head clattered from all the broken pieces of his life. Lila was kin to him and a stain to remind his father of how false his royalty was. What was he to his father—a sacrifice? The grand clarity of memory came to him: his father's spurning of affection, one valorous deed after the next to please Kinlord and country, with never a love of his own, save this incestuous fraternity, these brothers who grumbled like senseless wolves driven mad by disease and who wanted to slash every Wendago in this room. The Eininhar were extensions of the Kinlord's desire, his greed and want; they were not men but hunting dogs—his father's hunting dogs. They were animals from an empire of animals, in which he saw no worth. Before he answered, he had a question for Branwen.

"How do they die?" he whispered. "These sacred children. After all that I've seen, I do not believe in simple curses, or accidents, or sacrificial acts of valor. How are they ended? I must know."

"I told you to see, and you have," replied Branwen. "You know the answer."

"Please, just say it."

"The youngest are burned, before you would even know of them—as soon as they ripen to men. Fire is the oldest rite to release power. The eldest, the fattest souls, are ended at the Kinlord's hand, at the Throne of Winter, their necks opened, their blood flowing just as Beira's once did."

Bjorn knew his father wasn't here, though the sudden tension in the bestial minds of his men drew him toward another conclusion: the Eininhar, the arms of his father's Will, were here not as his company but to kill him. Of *course*...

Even come the world's end, his father gave no nod to the greater good, for he had inherited the greed of his ancestors. His father would murder his son to see himself empowered, even if that power was wasted in a world gone to ash. When his men had frozen before following Erik must have been the moment when his father had weighed if he was to make the sacrifice early. Greedy as ever, though, he wanted more time, more correctness—a throat slit at the Throne of Winter for the ripest harvest. *Horrid*, thought Bjorn. *All of it, everything Father and I are.* All his life had been nothing but glory for his father to reap so that he might live another hundred years. Only that longevity meant nothing if Magnus and these other broken souls didn't reach the deepest north—meant nothing regardless, he realized. For the heroes of the south, and for the warrior he had always wanted to be, Bjorn would be brave.

"I see now," he muttered. "I have my answer."

Bjorn looked to the spirits above and below, and he stepped out from the huddled company to speak to them. "I have lived my life believing in heroes and honor, though I see that is but deceit and conceit. False as my life may have been, I always wanted to embody the honor of which I dreamed. I have seen signs of my father's wickedness and the blood and suffering my people have brought to the North. I have watched the boats filled with the sad remains of the Three Tribes sail down the Feordhan, and done nothing to intervene. I thank you, spirits. I thank you, too, Branwen, for whatever blessed creature you may be. You have given me the chance for true glory."

Bjorn smiled, brimming with pride, sure of what he was to say and do. "There is only one thing I can offer to the spirits of the Three Tribes. I shall give them the gift of my glory, all the wonder and magik contained in me. I offer it to the Wendago so that they might forge the hammer to shatter the chain that binds us to blood, sickness, and murder. I surrender my flesh for the flesh of the Three Tribes. I shall be a sacrifice...but not for my father. My life, my soul, my *hope*...I give to the people we have ruined."

The Eininhar stiffened, ready to draw their blades and pounce. Perhaps the Kinlord, listening in, had decided that this site would indeed do to spill the blood of his truant son. Before that could come to pass, Branwen looked toward the Eininhar, and a whirlwind of clawing shadows arose near their feet. After a speck of screaming and crimson spinning from the cyclone, it drifted apart into gasps of shadow. Nothing but a few clumps of red matter, fur, and the swords of the Eininhar remained.

Bjorn removed his sword from its sheath, and the others—save Branwen—stepped back, cautiously...although he meant them no harm and made clear his target as he turned up his hand and steadied his sword's tip under his chin. Tears in his eyes, he heard his father's voice suddenly shrieking in his head: *No, child! My son! My beloved son! Your honor, your duty. You will be cast from the Halls of the Hereafter, you will never know Immortality—*"

"Nor will you, Father," said Bjorn.

With a grip of steel, he stuck his chin out and dropped. Lila, screaming, watched the man's elbows strike the ice and a ruby-glistened length of steel shoot out the back of his neck. Although her horror and pity was momentary for Bjorn. The raucous horde had their answers from the Children of the Harvest, and Branwen stepped away from the small circle of survivors and joined the ghosts in their chattering. Somewhere in the shaking world, Macha scrambled to hold her brother—even if he was a grinning monster. Again, Branwen's words shook space and time, and her tribal babblings cast free the rain of smoky carnivores from above, which also surged along the ground in a wave stirred by her voice.

Gibbering darkness consumed the cowering Immortals.

XIV

NIGHTFALL, DAYBREAK, WAR

I

P roject Phoenix, the Iron Queen's insane strategy to lure Death's avatar into the southern quarter of Eod and then bombard the Dreamer's forces with the full salvo of her Furies, had begun. With mercenaries being turned into loyal foot soldiers, Arhadian warriors massed outside the gates, the queen's return then mysterious exit, and a tremble of political, social, and spiritual chaos afflicting every heart in Eod, Gloriatrix's latest machinations had the perfect cover of confusion. Indeed, none of the merchants in the Faire of Fates or residents nearby suspected that things would return to working order after two Immortals and a sandstorm had torn the area apart. Most of the debris had been hauled off, and the houses on lanes adjacent to the great market received an ugly clay patching of their silver roofs and white-bricked domiciles. Still, with the pulse of war beating harder and faster, only daring or stupid merchants wanted to invest the money needed to rebuild their businesses—not when those shops would probably be crushed in the wave of death rolling over Kor'Khul from the East.

On days when the east wind blew strong over the battlements, those in the city could smell the fishy stench of decay. Soon, citizens on the eastern side of the city took to wearing white face masks not seen in such circulation since Eod's ancient plague—come just after the city's lower infrastructure and aqueducts had been formed and spread by the bites of rats. Those days were far behind, though their historic memory, a shiver from an event that had brought so much death, remained. Those on the eastern curve of the great wall were therefore quite amenable, suggestible—from fear, from the increasing stench—to the idea that they relocate closer toward the interior of the city, which rose, slightly, as it ascended to the city-sized-keep carved into Kor'Keth's flesh. The people flocked toward the lush beauty and the sparkling evening shine of the palace, drawn as men are to light during dark times.

Parks had been turned into grand campgrounds. Museums, libraries, and larger civic institutions threw tarps over their displays, opened their offices to the public, and people pitched tents under the skeletal feet of desert monsters, or filled libraries with the kind of chatter, songs, and noise that would have driven any librarian into fits. A few masters in King's Court, the crown of silver towers surrounding the palace, and wherein ninety percent of the city's wealth was gathered, took offense at the vagabonds camping in their flowerbeds or dining at their favorite cafés, which had been turned into ration-houses, and the haughty aristocrats sent letters or demanded audiences with whomever was in charge of this march of paupers. In war, wealth and status are meaningless, and these masters found their letters returned, or audiences denied, along with missives signed by Rasputhane— acting head of Eod while the king continued to recuperate, supposedly—*and* the Iron Queen, which commanded them to surrender their properties as secondary residences for Eod.

Because city services were then focused on the care and support of families clustered at the heart of the city, resources came from the sprawling and harder to maintain neighborhoods of the west. The heads of Project Phoenix overstated this need, and deliberately bled funds, workers, and soldiers to the northern quarter of the city. As the technomagikal grid pumped the energy needed to fuel a small star into King's Court and its tertiary realms, the strain was felt in places still demanding power. Lamplights flickered, the aqueducts began to spit, then dribble, water. Finally, whole neighborhoods went black and dry, and soon those in Eod's west end gazed from their darkened porches toward the glowing mountain around which they imagined existed food, flowing water, and all the luxuries of civilization that they'd taken for granted. Even the oldest curmudgeon didn't hold out on his property for long, and within a week, the Silver Watch—vexingly absent so far—had appeared with carriages and skycarriages to assist in the transport of people from their homes.

On what seemed their own impulses, or the trials of a nation at war, the citizenry condensed—drawing in, retreating from the edges of the city. There were always vagrants and those determined to entrench themselves in their houses until Armageddon came knocking—and hopefully went away. Such lingerers were not forced to move, since the city watch didn't want to encourage panic or questions about why traffic was being surreptitiously redirected, or why neighborhoods were no more habitable: a roadblock here, a fallen lamppost there.

"Quite sorry to come knocking, sir," said a captain of a small company of watchmen one evening to a pirate-faced barnacle of a hermit who would not leave his house and answered the door with three snarling dogs. "I know you're content—or whatever you'd call the arrangement you have with those yellow bottles over there that I'm willing to bet aren't Heathsholme cider, and with your many, many candles. However, with all the vacancies, and without regular movement through the channels, the water mains under the city have begun to burst from pressure."

The hermit seemingly unconvinced, the captain walked off the stone steps and splashed a little in the river that had flooded the lane. "This is our last pass through Thornhole, and if you don't come with us today, well...Well, I hope you have a boat."

Even the hermit and his dogs, and others like him, eventually migrated toward Eod's core. Where else would they go but toward the heartbeat of nearly a million hopeful souls praying to survive the world's end? And to where else would the Dreamer of Death be drawn, but to that radiant feast of light? With diabolical precision they had arranged the bait for Death. The outer ring of the city was empty. No matter which gate Death chose to swarm, they would have a battleground—an empty one—on which to meet her. Then it was simply a matter of delaying the Dreamer's forces long enough, through barricades and the sacrificing of their soldiers if need be, for the Furies to arm, fire, and incinerate Death. Kings have mercy on their souls if Project Phoenix was a failure and all they had done was arrange a tidy feast for Death.

II

Gloriatrix, Rasputhane, and the other members of Project Phoenix no longer met in the Chamber of Echoes, where watchmen, contemplatives, servants, and other ears might hear them. Rather, they used Magnus's chamber, which was remote and impeccably warded from scrying. It also offered an impressive view of Eod, one Gloriatrix had come to enjoy. Especially at night, which was always when men and women flooded the king's chamber and Leonitis and Dorvain stood at opposite ends down the hallway outside to see that no one disturbed the council.

Once they realized that Gloriatrix's feint was the most promising of desperate measures, those who had attended the decisive council were sworn to the greatest secrecy. Still, with so many schedules and responsibilities, the conspirators, many of whom had prominent responsibilities to their nations, couldn't meet as often as was necessary and wouldn't risk missives getting left around or read by parties not included in their scheming. Rowena reported for both the Arhadian and mercenary camps. Galivad couldn't always be counted on to attend, and even when he stayed, his anxiety over not rushing to Beatrice's side was disruptive. She was recovering, and nicely, from a strange illness, Gloriatrix had heard, and his umbilical attachment to the woman was troublesome. And so, Beauregard often stood in for his brother while he was away. Aside from those stand-ins, and a few others on account of various masters and sages, the circle of secrets was unbroken, and everyone received and exchanged the same information, somehow, and the gears, once oiled, moved more smoothly than any would have thought.

Tonight's clandestine gathering had been short. Gorijen assured the council that by every instrument they possessed, the Furies' appeared empty of any living or unliving auras (Sorren, too, had confirmed what he'd called "the grayness" of the ships this morning). The ex-handmaiden and the sword of the queen had begun to march the Arhadian and mercenary forces into Eod's unoccupied regions. First they would fill the barracks within the wall, then, come dawn on the day of the battle with Death, they would disperse into the neighborhoods and join the Silver Watch in completing the erection of barricades and stop-gaps with which to steer the river of the dead. Whoever remained holed up in their quarters at that point could die in them, for all Gloriatrix cared. A war wasn't war without casualties, and they had done all they could to ensure the populace was safe. Coldly, the other warmasters had accepted her statement before matters had turned to news of the march of Death's army.

It was more of a *crawl*, she decided, having seen time-lapsed phantographs of the army's advance. It was like watching a carpet woven of maggots creeping across a sandy floor. Mathematical minds foresaw that the wave of death would crash upon them tomorrow, at some time in the afternoon. And so the meeting had ended, with all ties tied, all reckonings to happen on the morrow. She felt tired, and had stayed with her quiet "Carthacian" priest— who no one with more than half a wit believed him to be anymore. Rasputhane was somewhere behind her; she heard his sharp scribbling of notes as he sat in the king's chair, the place from where he liked to conduct his meetings. He hadn't been an insufferable accomplice to this grand orchestra of deceit; he had a mind that counted bodies like coin—the mind of a Menosian.

Staring over the city, listening to the swell of the rabble, the Iron Queen knew that it had to be done this way, and she was glad that Rasputhane had been wise enough to support her. People would not willingly rub themselves in blood and stand still waiting for the wolves. If they had so much as suspected what their leaders were planning, there might have been a revolt—a revolt even among Gloriatrix's Iron children, who had suffered a second moral defeat after the loss of life at Camp Fury and were understandably angry and adrift. Ordering them to surrender and dismantle Camp Fury, then to seek out Eod for sanctuary, was yet another blow to their Iron pride. She, as their mother, knew it was for the best. Strangely wistful, she hoped that they were enjoying their amalgamation with the Eodian cretins below—probably feeling superior, even sensing the maneuvers of their leaders above. They wouldn't miss Camp Fury for long; soon they would conquer Eod, making it their home.

Gazing east, over the hulking globs of technomagik that were her Furies and the surrounding dotted remnants of her encampment, evoked no sadness in her. It was but a ruse that her Furies slept and their power was spent. Once their Talwynian engines were repaired, and their "special cargo" installed, the ships were sealed and their technomagikal defenses activated—a web of electric power around their shells that carried a current of ten thousand lightning bolts a speck. No dead thing would be able to claw through their hulls to ruin their weaponry or engines again; such monsters would evaporate into sparks and ash. No living thing remained for Death to corrupt within the vessels, either. Aside from what Gloriatrix had placed inside. This morning, an Ironguard had asked her what was within the sleek metal eggs they were carrying on to the command deck of each Fury. "Our hope," she had answered, nastily, and the terrified soldier asked nothing further.

Our hope, she thought, *and my friend—my dearest and only.*

"What was that?" asked Rasputhane, his speckled form appearing at the bottom stairs of the king's balcony; he had stopped scribbling a while back. In that silence he had prepared drinks. "Did you say something?"

"Perhaps one of my thoughts slipped out," she confessed. "I have too many these days."

Being accomplices and schemers together, she'd developed an honesty with the spymaster—even though she would probably need to have him killed one day for the secrets they shared. He ascended, and she stared at the liquor glittering in the crystal goblets he held with only a whisker of suspicion.

"Brandy," he said. "The king's finest. If I was going to poison you, I would wait till after the war." Rasputhane's clever smile was infectious and disarming. Still, he took a sip from each tumbler to prove his sincerity. *I'll certainly poison you before you ever set foot in the Hall of Memories*, he thought. "See? I'm not dead. Come on, have a drink. I figure we deserve it after what we've achieved. A stratagem on this scale...it is legendary."

"I sense no poison," said the false Carthacian priest—Sorren—of his supplicant's drink; he stood hidden beside the doors to the balcony.

Claiming a glass, the Iron Queen clinked crystal with the spymaster and took a heavy sip. "A bit sweet, as with all things in this realm. To victory, though. What was it you said? To our *legendary* victory."

They pondered that victory, or defeat, while sipping. When his glass was almost empty, Rasputhane, reading a buried sorrow in her, asked, "Did you have a chance to say farewell to your friend? Will she be alright in that contraption?"

"It is no simple contraption, spymaster. The *infinitax dolio*, or equilibrium cask in lower Ghaedic, was one of the many extraordinary technomagiks created for this war. I won't insult you by pretending that our enemy was Death, at the time. The casks are a safeguard to ensure the survival of Menosian royalty in the event of a catastrophic event that destroyed the Furies. No magik, Immortal or otherwise, can dent or crack those feliron shells, which were modeled after the invulnerability of the Sepulcher, my private sanctum in the Crucible. I would bet that room has endured every earthquake and explosion to have rocked the city, yet still it sits like a pristine egg amid Menos's tumult. Likewise, within the casks one's life can be preserved for nearly a decade. Fluids and self-sustaining sorcery are fed through the interior of the device.

"I had three casks constructed...for my sons and me. It seems just that a family of three should now use them." She snickered. "And Elissandra and I are not those sort of friends, the teary types to cling and throw platitudes over our next encounter."

As she said that, a string twanged in her chest at the memory of Elissa waving as the top half of the *infinitax dolio* shell had been fitted over her. It had probably been their last goodbye. "I shall toast to her, though, as she is the bravest woman I have known—next to myself."

"Humph." Rasputhane rushed away and returned with a decanter. He refreshed each of their glasses, though the Iron Queen waved off too heavy a hand, as tomorrow there would be war. They drank a bit longer and almost relaxed in the company of friends, before their caution as a ruthless queen and unscrupulous spymaster ruled out that possibility. Sensing an end—to everything, really—Rasputhane took the queen's glass from her and left her and her priestly confessor alone. Empty chairs and silence were behind him; everyone else had left the meeting, and he didn't mind if she snooped or lingered around the king's chamber, any more than he suffered reproach for claiming the king's chair, or drinking the Immortal's spirits.

Sorren approached his mother. She did not shuffle aside as she often did when people drew close to her; it was the closest thing to a hug for her to remain where she stood. She sighed, and they dwelled on the sleeping Furies, sleeping Elissandra, the wind-torn desert hills—disintegrating, scattering, reminding them each of impermanency—and the slavering wave of Death somewhere beyond those landmarks.

Sorren had a confession, and this was the time to share it.

Time to strangle the bitch and turn her into a puppet! shrieked the voice with whom he so often tangled. It was only mildly jarring to him; the voice was becoming easier to ignore. As his hands twitched, though, for a speck he horrifyingly believed they would reach out like sentient claws to her throat. Instead, they slipped into the long, deep pockets of his habit, in which the awe and might of three wonderstones tingled beneath the aged leather sack hidden there. "I have to tell you something."

She turned and he wasted no time, as there was none left. Thus, he confessed of his pact with the Dreamer of Death so that he might murder his brother. That promise had become his curse, and Death's madness had festered in his own madness. Later, when the Pale Lady had called upon him to serve, and he'd resisted, he had become her puppet. Descriptions of his powerlessness, and of his soaring over a world wreathed in blinding dust and death, contrived from his cold mother a tear. Some of this she had known, but none of what came next. As he spoke of the kindness of the Sisters Three, and of an opportunity to save his family, the Iron Queen shed even more tears. In his arms she sobbed as she heard of Vortigern's fate as a slave, and as the vessel of Death. Although, claimed Sorren, as a vessel some part of his brother still lived and acceded to Death's possession. It was a piece of him that could be saved.

"But how?" she asked, pulling herself from Sorren, wiping the wetness and weakness from her countenance. "We cannot change our tactics now. I must...He must...*We* must kill your brother."

"No," replied Sorren, and he drew out the sack, loosened its strings, and cast his mother's face in the light of the magik hidden inside. "The wonderstones. Even if I am no sorcerer, I am still a creature of magik. I know as I touch these fragments of wonder that they will respond to me. I have thought of death and life, and how closely they are tied. I live now in the great unknown and see how temporary and vain our delineations between the states are. I can use these stones. Do you see what this means?"

"I do," she replied, trembling.

"We can save Vortigern. I can bring him back to us."

Weeping nothing more than dust, he embraced her and felt her continue to shiver. He believed she was excited; they would be a family again. It was a sanguine misreading, and misplaced on the Iron Queen, for what her dead son had shown her, what made her tremble, wasn't delirium at the thought of her scattered brood united. In his own fool hands, and as declared, Sorren had *magik*. The purest kind of magik—artifacts that could work miracles, artifacts he could *wield*. Indeed, they could be used to release Vortigern from his slavery to Death. But afterward, she would use the rest of those stones to grant a miracle for herself. The search was over, and she no longer needed to find a sorcerer to seize power from the Hall of Memories; she only had to ensure her sentimental son saved a stone for that purpose.

III

Moonlight and the shine of the Witchwall threw a pale lace over the calm, white-furnished chamber of the Lady El. There were such serene arrangements: ivory-draped couches and chairs, a netted bed with spotless white sheets, and a ceiling mesh heavy with white flowers and silver witch-lights. None of it had been wholly installed for decor. Rather, the excessive tarping concealed the shellac of Beatrice's blood ingrained in the wood and upholstery, and the bright illumination of the witch-lights had been required to examine the Lady El during her thrashing, bleeding seizures and in the calm thereafter. Certain spots on the tiles around the room had been scrubbed to gray, which was the best they could do considering the volume of blood she'd unleashed in the White Hearth and thereafter. Galivad's reticence to tell her doctors anything too damning (that she ate people, for example) that might color their opinion of the patient, or make them hesitant to care for her, had been as frustrating to these men as the riddle of Beatrice's extraordinary, unending exsanguination.

"She's a race from Pandemonia; different than man or woman," was all that he'd offered. Soon Beatrice's eyes had begun glowing like torches, and she had sprayed the walls with a loose water hose of liquid dark, and Galivad had been banished from the chamber.

When he had returned from lying with Rowena, he had not only found his mother resting and stable, but also that the bundles of sopping black sheets bunched in the corner had stopped growing, and the ink-stained maids seemed less mad and of sufficient composure to discuss her condition. The doctors did not loiter and had left as baffled as they'd arrived to this nightmare.

"It just stopped," the maid had said. "All the bleeding, the screaming. It just stopped. She's been quiet for an hourglass or more now. The Iron Sages have declared her cured, and her rather slow pulse has returned to what seems normal—for her." The maid had then touched him, softly on the hand he held to Beatrice's cold cheek. "I think she's a bit of a miracle, even if the doctors said some strange things 'bout her, horrible stories that I don't think are true. She keeps talking about a man: Moreth. And she's been saying queer things about covenants and blood. Anyway, I shall leave you to her."

The maid hadn't left him entirely to her, since her removal of the sopping sheets, bandages, and other waste left by the disgusted medical staff took several trips and a second maid to resolve. But eventually, their noisy labor finished, Galivad and his mother were alone. Day in and day out, as the war neared Eod's gates, he spent more time watching her shallow breathing than worrying over matters of annihilation. Now and then she woke, babbled about Pandemonia and then fell back asleep—such stirrings so fleeting as to require no real celebrations. Although all who visited her, mostly to watch the rise and fall of her chest as Galivad did, believed she was cured of her illness.

One evening, so used to the somnolence of the watch, he leapt in his seat when she awoke.

"Where am I?" she asked. Beatrice rose up in her bed, a creature of wild hair and frightened eyes. She seemed far more lucid than she had been. She thought she recognized her son, though, who sat in a covered chair beside her bed. She smiled. "Beauregard."

He frowned. "Galivad."

"Yes, of course." As he leaned in to take one of her hands, she drew her frosty fingertips across his pretty jaw. "I feel as if I'm still picking up the pieces of my mind after something shattered me...Regardless, you and Beau are two men of one soul, one song. I should like to hear you two sing one day; imagine the beauty, the magik."

Galivad didn't believe in magik as an art he could wield himself, though he supposed anything was possible. While unfair, he had less faith in his brother, too, who was either in council meetings or "performing other duties" and hadn't been to visit his ailing mother as often as a son should. Even Tabitha had come several times a day, to visit this woman she learned had eaten her sister.

Aside from these familial responsibilities, though, Galivad realized that he had been neglecting the quiet, patient woman with whom he'd been having a run of romance. On a sagging, draped couch, Rowena sat away from mother and son. It was the evening before war, and she was a Makret—a warrior mother, from what she'd told him—for Lila's army. And yet here she sat, with a monster and that monster's son, and not amid her blood-born kin of the desert. Silently she had made an oath not to queen or country, but to herself, and to him. Each afternoon, before camping around Beatrice, they found the time to steal away from their duties and meet for a tryst. Although, referring to their sweaty, tawdry tumbles so glibly undermined the aching need and lust of those encounters, as well as diminished the softer moments of whatever flower budded between them. For she was with him and his family when most he needed her. It was a devotion never to be forgotten. He blushed whenever he thought of it.

Beatrice, regaining more of her fragmented personality, waved the large woman over. "Come, you glorious Arhadian ox. I believe I shall give my legs a test. I shall need your strength."

"The Arhad have spinrex, not oxen," said Rowena, with a smile. She leaned at the bedside, and Beatrice threw an arm over her shoulder and moved her feet over the edge. After a bit of grunting—Beatrice was heavier than her litheness belied—they stood. They performed an invalid's circuit of the room. Growing misty, Galivad watched the two women he loved most in this world embracing the queerness and wonder of their new relationship.

Beatrice reminded him of one cruel reality as she asked him to *feed* her with a song. As he sang "The Wheat and the Barley," which was a sure favorite now Beatrice looked more like a lady again, she combed the wildness from her mane before washing and dressing herself, behind a screen and with Rowena's help, in one of her collared white gowns. Once attired, she and the others moved to the couches, fetched drinks for Rowena and Galivad, and then arranged themselves on the shrouded furniture like Romanisti who'd snuck into a master's lake house that was closed for winter. Beatrice picked at the edge of a seat while the other two enjoyed their spirits—only blood would do for her. She hadn't lost that hunger, even if she had lost another quality she couldn't define.

"I imagine that the furniture is quite ruined," she said. "I can still smell the stench of my own blood. And I say stench, for it smells poisonous."

They had talked so little about what she'd endured, focusing more on the joy of her recovery. She had been rather disoriented until this evening, and while some mysteries were best left buried, Galivad did not ever again want to suffer a fright like this one. "Mother, what happened?"

Beatrice paused, pulling on a thread of the blanket under her, stopping herself from beholding the stain she smelled beneath the clean linen. It had been an unmaking; there was no other word for it. She had been broken into every screaming memory, every bestial flash of murder and sweet harmony sung between Belle and her boys, and then left to patch together the pieces of herself. She wasn't surprised that she appeared addled or had confused her son's names, for she had become less than a person, or even a monster. She had lost all awareness of self. Except for Moreth. Ghosts of him, inexplicably, had appeared in her fever, and even in the jumbled dreams she dreamed once that fever had broken. Once, she saw him flying with wings of shadow and fire like hers, though more grand and kingly, conquering the winds as he soared over a black-spired wasteland howling with emptiness. With her soul, she felt connected to him as she stirred to and from these disorienting and deep dreams. Sometimes she half-woke and thought of him hiking through a desert of ash while she sat swaddled in nothing but white sheets and the calming peace of Eod. She was sure she had ranted something to that effect once.

As for the pain of the disease itself, she couldn't remember when, exactly, she had been healed, though she knew that the torment had abated as her sense of unity with Moreth grew. She knew also that her hunger now was less than it had been. On many occasions, she had been frenzied but still had not attacked any of her nurses. She was starving, yes, but it was her hunger, her desire, and not the omnipresent lust of murder and gorging from which she had spent her hundreds of years suffering. What had happened was a blessing, even if she'd nearly died. She was now less monster and more woman. And however outrageous the notion, she suspected that a similar metamorphosis had been experienced by her husband. Either that, or her dreams of flying and of breathing in another man's reality were symptoms of dangerous lunacy. In explaining her experience to her son and his lover, her account still sounded vague. Though she had no more to say, no logic to explain how she had been reborn.

"Truly bizarre," said Rowena, "and magikal."

"Since we are sharing secrets, perhaps you should share yours, Sword of the Queen," said Beatrice, her eyes glittering, her animal summoned by the red haze, and the chemical scents of blood and desire surrounding the woman in a fecund mist—an omen thick and visceral as the readings of any organ fluid.

Ruffled, Rowena gazed at the dreamy, hungry-looking woman. "I keep no secrets."

"Oh," gasped Beatrice, and then as a white wind she swept to the couple who were sitting side by side in the chairs. Despite her transmogrification, she had kept and recovered her leannan sídhe agility and her strength, too, as she gripped them with her pale elongated fingers. "You don't know, do you? You can't see or smell the cloud...Yes, the cloud of life coming from your—"

Beatrice shook her head, stalling herself from declaring the waft from Rowena's lady parts, or the tangy pheromones of her armpits. Further traits of her monstrous self shed, till she was less frazzled, glimmering, strong, or cold. As a teary eyed woman, soon to be grandmother, she spoke to the couple. "You smell of life. In your womb stirs a seed."

Prophylactics had come a long way since the dark ages of Iron and Steel. Women could have their entire wombs safely and surgically removed, and be treated with magik and elixirs that would keep their bodies fertile, even without the required parts. One Eodian master had even impregnated his favorite male companion with his seed and the borrowed ovaries of a woman. The would-be-parent had died during childbirth, and such excesses in technomagik and fleshcrafting had yet to be repeated. Still, thinking of these and all the thousand curiosities surrounding love, contraception, and procreation, Rowena had never considered herself a woman enough, dainty enough, or careless enough, really, to have an "accidental" impregnation. They'd used skins, several skins during each encounter—though she had memories of a few fumblings and her desire to simply have her lover inside of her. All it took was one slip.

Shite. Rowena shut down, trembling. *Holy shite. We're going to war tomorrow, with Death. And I'm—*even to herself, she couldn't say the word. *What am I going to do? What are we going to do?*

Beatrice blew back to her chair and watched them, amused and voracious, licking her lips at the delectable emotions and scents they exuded in their confusion. Poor Galivad was as lost as Rowena, though after rocking himself and mumbling for a while, he reached for her hand, then intertwined his fingers into hers and held it fast. "I am going to be a father." They shivered. "You are going to be a mother." They shuddered. "I think that I'm as happy as I've ever been," he whispered.

Once confessed, the weight lifted, and the realization rang true for them each. What troubles lay on the morrow and through the chaos Death would bring seemed flighty and small. Here was a moment of substance, of joy; amid the darkness covering Geadhain, they would bring new life. The lovers moved closer, and he kissed Rowena's cheek. Galivad knelt at her side, and they laid their hands atop her stomach, though any heartbeat was a long way from being felt.

Perfectly late, or timed, someone knocked, and then Alastair popped into the room. An instant's grace he enjoyed at the sight of his family together, save for Beauregard, and of Beatrice being awake and off her bed rest. After lifetimes of being a vagabond, the sting of ancestral compassion was a venom to which his body had no cure. Alastair, Stevoch, Lucien, man-of-a-hundred-names, keeper of bitterness, lies, and sorrows, was almost in tears as he came to the couch and sat next to Beatrice.

"Your son has an announcement," she said.

When the news was shared, from son and expectant mother to grandfather, his heart snapped twice from the weakness of never accepting love. Amid the tears, hugs, and laughter, while Beatrice cannily studied and drank in the plethora of magnificent auras and emotions, Alastair neglected to tell his strange family that Death's horde had crossed the sand valleys to the east of Eod. The end of this happiness could arrive before dawn. Delivering a blow like that could wait.

IV

"I should get to my brother," said Beauregard. "He'll be worrying about me by now. We both need to be at the Warpath before dawn, anyhow, to organize the legions for disbursement across Eod."

Grunting, Beauregard rolled onto his side and attempted to get out of bed. Kings, his body ached, and as a man of duty and honor the shame of his soreness chafed him worse than his raw loins, or the places where Edina had scraped him with her nails, or gripped his buttocks till they bruised. Yet those same tanned hands, which had tempted him into carnal purgatories, worked their enchantment again, and he was lured by her magik. He was spun from a roll out of bed to a roll back in. His brown eyes met her green ones, and her spell ran through his body in a current that stiffened his cock.

"Once more," coaxed the vixen, as her hand ran down his smooth stomach. "We could be dead tomorrow; this could be the last desire we know before the void."

Tempting, and Beauregard's head started swimming with the scents, sounds, and images of their stolen romance together. But it was wrong, and dishonorable. It was an affair that never should have been, Moreover, he should have known better after seeing the damage done by lies between Magnus and his wife. Although Edina was a sorceress and a thunderstrike archer, she had no power over his mind other than what he chose to give her, and he pulled away from her a second time. At that, she scowled, and shoved him back. She shifted to the bedside and bent down, looking for her clothing.

"Edina, please."

Beauregard shuffled across the sheets and touched her bronzed skin. She shouldered off his hand, though not a second time as his fingers swept the curve of her spine and his head nuzzled the back of her neck. They were both sick on the other, it seemed, and perhaps he was the holder of hidden magik, for she turned, her ferocity melted into desire. She kissed the handsome young knight with the same hunger that had driven them both into this arrangement of sin.

Soon he was eating her as she moaned and squeezed the sheets into sweaty knots. For a recent virgin, he displayed the care of a seasoned lover;

there was almost nothing that she had to teach him on how to be gentle, or rough—he intuited the winds of passion better than any man with whom she'd lain. The tally of other men was something she had never disclosed to the young knight, nor would she, as she doubted he would be the last lover to carry her away from her farce of a marriage. As he raised his wet face to kiss hers, he pulled her by her hips to the end of the bed and thrust into her in such a measured, rhythmic tempo that his limber body and hers thrummed as a single instrument of pleasure, holding tight for a speck with each pump so that his pelvis pressed into that sensitive pearl atop her womanhood. Her shattering orgasm—some sands or eternity later—affirmed his greatness.

Pulling out, he gently rearranged his quivering lover's legs on the bed, then climbed over her like a monkey, kissing from thighs to lips. She held his beautiful black-curled head as it hovered over hers and bit her lip at the urge to whisper saccharine idolatry. The glimmer to his grin, and his artful caress of her breast, suggested he needed no accolades from her. Then his hand crept higher, tilting her head and touching the purple bruises on her neck; her next shiver did not come from desire.

"You're right," she said, throwing him off. "We must see to our responsibilities."

As futile as hiding from the sun in Kor'Khul, Beauregard's scalding gaze couldn't be escaped as Edina hurried to find her clothes. Each piece of apparel into which she fumbled somehow armored her less from Beauregard's judgment, and she would not stare at the perfect gentleman—knight, spellsong, freer of kings, punisher of evils, including their affair—and allow herself to share his shame for what they were doing. Nonetheless, she started mumbling excuses as her crazed thoughts, too wild to contain, slipped out. "Paracelsus wouldn't pay a fate to spare my life—you know that. Neither you, nor I, should feel sorry for these moments of happiness we steal. You've seen what he does to me when forced, and I mean forced, by my father's ill-intentioned pestering, to lie with me."

Beauregard had first seen hints of her abuse during a training activity on the Warpath, when she appeared to be struggling into her armor of silver mail enchanted for comfort, which should have slipped over her as easily as a silk shift. She had snarled at any person who tried to help her, before storming inside a tent where she wouldn't be seen. Beauregard, sympathetic to a fault, and afflicted by his lust for her, rushed from what he was doing to help. He'd had the courtesy to declare himself before entering, but despite this warning, Edina had been nude to the waist. In the soft light of the tent, she had been as captivating as the portrait of a dark sea spirit. Indeed, there was a watery elegance to her beauty. From over a raised shoulder, she had peered at him, her face in profile, her stare lowering as if she were shy, or enticing. Knowing her better now, the wrath and seduction of her Nereid charms, Beauregard felt her exposure had been the latter, and her nudity had been an intentional lure. In spite of her stunning silhouette, he had noticed the spotty bruises on her back, and the marks that she had used a high-throated tunic to hide. By then, Beauregard had seen enough physical damage to people's bodies to know what was caused by man or nature. Her bruises came from fists. A confession had followed later, during a private meeting she'd insisted on, wherein she told him the name of her assaulter. However, her desire to get him alone had been another of her entrapments, and her confession had turned into a night of fervent sex.

"You could tell your father," said Beauregard. "You could let me expose Paracelsus for the monster he is. Why do you protect him? Stay. Please stay, just for a sand, and let us talk of what we can do."

Sweet spellsong, you would never understand, she thought, as she found her jacket and rested her hand on the door handle. She fidgeted, not quite turning the knob or pushing the door open to leave. To Beauregard, the world was black and white—there were mad kings, and then there were the heroes who fought them. As one of those heroes, he knew only how to see the light inside mankind. And as a man, he was so effortlessly duped into believing that she had any light worth saving. She'd had dozens of affairs, just as Paracelsus took home a woman every fortnight or more—often she listened to their thumping in the room next to hers. They had stopped loving each other long ago, perhaps even days after they'd wed. However, her father had chosen her husband from one of Eod's finest military lineages, and she could not disappoint him, not after Mother had left the pair of them to fend for themselves while she ran off to play troubadour and whore. Besides, Paracelsus wanted the security and the political stability of having a wife so connected to Eodian military. Thus she and her husband stayed in loveless limbo.

Occasionally, he drank and came into her room to fuk her, or she made him so angry that he came at her with violent passion. She had come to love her power to seduce, to incite and corrupt, as much as he loved machinations and authority. She owned her bruises, as she had goaded her husband into violence. Or so she told herself of this empowering cycle of pain. This was the narrative she wanted to believe; otherwise she was simply a wicked, weak, and beaten woman. When she was with Beauregard, and he beheld her as if she was both holy virgin and a sinner whom he needed to save, the shame of whatever truth he saw in her eventually drove her away. She needed to flee from his faith in her—it was too heavy a burden to bear.

She twisted the door handle and didn't look back as he called to her.

V

"Welcome to the Secret Circle," hailed Leonitis to the shadow lingering in the doorframe.

"It won't be very secret with your shouting." Leaning over in her chair as velvety and richly blue as every other upholstered and curated piece in Leonitis's chamber, Lowe slapped the soldier on his arm.

"Oh, fukkery!" she shrieked as the Mind nearly rolled out of the swaddling nest in her lap that she had made of her overcoat. Dorothy, somewhat lax in her primness, slouched and chuckled on a couch. Dorvain, a mug in his hand, leaned near a white stone fireplace that was elegantly carved with stags, woods, and vines. He knocked his elbow on one of the mantle's antlers as he laughed, and laughed more deeply at that. As though seeking to earn his title, Eod's spymaster was spotted lurking near the chamber's patio door, blending into the night-suffused curtains like a chameleon—though his drunken swaying betrayed his stealth. Leo guffawed from a seat next to Lowe's and was trying to steady his drink between bursts of laughter. Like his brother, he too was dressed in a casual sleeveless shift and leathers that gave him a nearly civilian air. Also following the example of his brother (and others), he was as drunk as the rest of this Secret Circle, and as much a sight as the rest of those for whom Tabitha had come knocking.

Tabitha hurried inside before any of the room's ruckus could echo into the hallway. As they settled into a less heightened state of hilarity, she chose a spot on Leo's stiffly starched bed. It was as proper as if a maid had cleaned his chamber a moment ago, though she knew his military discipline was responsible. Tabitha saw further indications of his fastidiousness in the sparsity of his chamber of chairs, a couch, and a lavatory divided from the room by a screen. In the corner nearest the bed, however, stood a sturdy banded chest, atop which lay a blade, and against which rested the former hammer of the king's mighty weapon. Beside the chest stood a steel mannequin sporting Leonitis's blindingly polished armor. There, then, was the heart and soul of this chamber, and the heart and soul of the man to whom it belonged—he was a child of Eod, through and through.

Tabitha had been gazing at the armor for a speck, and a flush-cheeked Lowe surprised her as she turned to the sound of her rustling. A drink was thrust toward her, something dark, strong, and sweet by its smell. "You need to catch up," said Lowe.

"I thought this was to be a meeting?" asked Tabitha, loud enough so that the chatty gathering could hear her.

"It is. It was!" replied Lowelia. Returning to her chair, she picked up the Mind and nestled it. Her hand fished for the drink she had left on the floor and soon found it. Then, like a carnival seer, she rubbed her other hand over the crystal in which floated an ephemeral mist; it reminded Tabitha of a skull. Was she speaking to it? Tabitha had never seen the curiosity so closely or openly—Lowelia guarded it as if she were a jealous troll and it was her treasure.

"How close?" asked Leonitis, and the gathering was sobered by his grim tone.

"Six hourglasses," replied Lowelia, an augur from the Mind, "and we'll be able to look over the wall and see Death's wave."

"Six hourglasses?" exclaimed Tabitha. "We have no time for meetings or chatter, then. We must hurry. I need to find my son. I need—"

"Sit, dearie," suggested Lowe. "And have a drink. We've covered all the patches that need patching. We'll deal with Gloriatrix once we get rid of the Dreamer that's come to stomp out our city. We had planned to talk strategy before Dorvain, in his graceless way—"

He belched then waved.

Lowelia rolled her eyes. "Before that fair gentleman reminded us that tomorrow might be a day which not all of us survive. Even if we win, and we drive Death out, it may be a victory some of us never see. Drinking seemed better than running our minds in circles. We've done so much of that, and the city is as ready as it will ever be. Too much spice will spoil the broth, as we're so fond of saying in the White Hearth. And this broth is done." Lowelia gazed down at her cup. "We wanted to take tonight to remember each other, our deeds and our triumphs." Smiling, she patted the Mind. "I needed to tell you lot about him, too, in case he needs a new caregiver."

Grandmother Lowelia, the statistical odds of your perishing, should you stay in the palace, are one in one thousand and eighty five, escalating exponentially should Death's forces penetrate more than one ring of the city. I expect you will stay within the prescribed perimeter and not hazard charging off into battle as you've—

Much as she had come to care for the Mind, she wanted no further advice or analysis regarding her fate. How sweet, though, that it had come to frame her no more as a Navigator, but as a grandmother—especially when *Mother* Lila was many centuries her senior. The Mind was learning, developing names, attachments and, dare she say, emotions for the matrices it encountered. It was extraordinary; surely the most benevolent experiment by the Iron Empire to ever go right.

"I'll miss him terribly," she continued, "if I'm one of the unlucky ones. He's the child who was stolen from me—a hundred children or more, to be precise—and he must be protected. All of Eod must be protected, and he's the one to do it. I know that now. I'm as sure about that as Queen Lila was about heading north. My calling has been to protect this wondrous organism. For I know that as I've carried him into museums, barracks, monuments, parks, the Faire of Fates, and everywhere in Eod, he has collected everything about our behavior, our history—our lives. If ash is what remains of Eod, then in his great matrix will live what remains of mortal kind."

"Who?" asked Tabitha, thoroughly captivated and confused by Lowelia's passion—she and others in the room seemed teary.

With that, she was inducted into another layer of secrecy in the secret circle in which Dorothy had intended her to join. The strangest conspirator of all was the crystal matrix of magik and children's souls: the Mind. That night, with war looming, Lowelia had decided that the Mind's existence was a secret that could no longer be kept, and thus her confession became the meeting's new purpose.

"It is extraordinary," whispered Tabitha. During Lowe's explanation, she had left the bed to hover around the crystal entity. As she stared, the mist inside swirled, and the skull was indeed looking at her, pressing against the black curve of the sphere. She didn't recoil, but touched it. A buzzing of *Hello*, however, suddenly echoing in her head, caused her to leap back. "Mercy, it talks!"

"You don't know the half of it." Lowe snuggled the Mind back up in cloth. "Any time you touch it. I imagine it's exploding with things to say, since it's always observing, always analyzing. Anyway, with me off to the frontlines—"

"Pardon?" Tabitha couldn't hide her shock. "We're hardly fast friends; in fact I can't say that I know much about you other than you being a mater, a charwoman, but you'll be murdered out there."

"As we've tried to remind her—" started Leonitis.

"I'm also a spy, I've impersonated the queen, and been the leader of a rebellion," replied Lowelia. Shuffling about without trying to upset the Mind's stability, she tugged up her tunic to show that the lump beneath was a holster, displaying an ivory and gold grip. "I shall not abide the dead mucking about with our fair city. I've played more roles than a thespian, and my next will be soldier. I'm also a crack shot—ask Dorothy. She and I haven't been taking teas as we've suggested, though we did start shooting cans this week. I'm a natural sharpshooter. I never miss."

"Ravaging dead aren't as still and helpless as cans." Tabitha walked back to the bed, grabbed her cup off the floor where she'd left it, and drank it dry.

"I forgot that you came from Bainsbury. My condolences," said Dorvain.

"Keep those for Bainsbury's walking dead—you'll have the opportunity to offer your sympathies to their rotten faces."

Tabitha turned her cup over, saddened by the mere drop or two that fell out. Dorvain, patron saint of drunkenness, recognized a woman in libationary distress. He hunkered, opening a panel in the mantelpiece, and hurried over to the woman with a bottle of spirits.

"Thank you," she said after chugging what he poured. She kept him around to fill her next glass. "In Bainsbury, I saw a mere finger of the hand Death reaches west with. I know of the reports: dead pulled up and reanimated from every grave from here to Menos…The size of that horde…I never want to see such a sight again."

"Then you shan't," promised Lowe, and everyone's eyes fell on Tabitha. "We decided, without your say, who should be the caregiver for the Mind."

"Me?"

"Seeing as the rest of us have responsibilities, or a determination to get ourselves killed, yes," replied Lowe. "Dorothy and Rasputhane have thrown you their vote—especially after the shrewdness you showed with the technomancer the other day. You illuminated much of Gloriatrix's plans. Now that we know at least some of what she's after, we can protect the Hall of Memories. But first, we shall defend our city, and you will see that the Mind—the hope for tomorrow—will be safe, here, in the palace. Don't worry about missing anything—a chat with him and he'll tell you what you had for breakfast, and what the breaking of the morning fasts were for every rat, roach, and soldier within a hundred spans."

Tabitha mustered a smile. "I'll do it."

"It's not a democratic duty, so much as a dictatorial edict," said Lowe, "though I am glad that you're willing. I'll hand him over in a sand; he and I still need to say our farewells. Let's count down the sands till war, together."

Now solemn and grim, they sat like persons awaiting the executioner's call. The cheer and warm camaraderie into which Tabitha had arrived had been pushed out by cold wind. She jumped out of her doldrums and snatched the bottle that Dorvain had been hoarding, and hurried around the room adding a splash to everyone's cup.

"A toast," she cried, and their souls were roused to warily raise glasses. Now she had to think of something grand to say, but she froze only for a moment.

"I came from a small village where the worst bloodshed we'd known was two lads having a row. Then, the king's madness spread a sick heat from the South, boiling Lake Tesh, driving away my husband and son. I never saw my husband again—he died a hero, and my son became a legend. Everything changed. But…from the hope I've seen, a hope not uncommon to what each of you bear, I know that despair can be conquered. One voice cannot be heard in the storm. A million voices, however, become a storm—and we're all screaming for peace. So that we shall have, come what reckoning precedes it. I'll toast to that tomorrow, however bloody the road, however many of us there are that will not see that end. Those of us who remain can toast over their graves."

As she spoke, stirring their courage, they stood. They formed a circle, and they clinked glasses as she finished. It quickly became an ominous moment, for as soon as the glasses were drained and their smiles reinvigorated, the bells of war rang out over Eod. Cast from technomagikal blow horns, from atop the palace heights, came the repeated rising and falling wail of an alarm. The sound shuddered Kor'Keth's ancient flesh, though more so those gathered within her rocky walls. Dawn wasn't even an orange suggestion to the dark, and yet such an alarm meant that Death—keeping no chronex or following any rulebook for war—would be mounting her forces against the city sooner than the tacticians had thought. At once sobered by their fear, those gathered traded simple partings and rushed to their stations.

Soon, Tabitha stood alone in Leonitis's chamber with her new crystal babe, watching the door creak closed. She wondered how many of them would be alive by this time tomorrow, not realizing she'd been touching the Mind with that thought.

I predict a mortality rate of two in five, buzzed the Mind. Then, its voice lowered and slowed—in sadness, she felt—it added, *I am sorry.*

She fell back into Leonitis's empty seat and wept for what was to come.

VI

"You hear that?" Curtis bounced up onto his elbow on the bed where he'd been lying with Aadore. A night of respectful clothes-on passion had left him with a raging, stiff ache in his groin, though the stridency of Eod's alarms was far worse. He knew what those sounds meant: war.

"Of course I do," snapped Aadore. "I'd have to be deaf otherwise."

She jumped out of the half-rumpled sheets and dashed across the starlit chamber to the armoire. She dug out a heavy parcel from within, and folded leather boots, bringing them over to the bed. There, she ordered him to move back a bit so that she could arrange her armaments.

"Your armaments?" he exclaimed.

Dedicated to her task, she ignored him until all the objects were exposed: a padded harness; a cloth overcoat fitted with scale along the shoulders, spine, and chest; reinforced trousers; and clattering, segmented gloves—elegant and reminiscent of an assassin's nimble gauntlets. Curtis's admonition was stalled in his throat as Aadore slipped off her lace camisole and stunned him with the night-kissed glow of her curved, naked flesh.

"Help me dress," she commanded.

Although bewildered, Curtis was moved by his need and her authority. He rose and remained silent as she held the front of her harness and he tightened it like a corset. The intimacy and cold desperation of their contact made him spin her and kiss her more than once. Like a glass-slippered princess, she turned in his arms and he slipped her into her trousers and then boots, stealing further kisses of the insides of her thighs. He desired her, more than he had any woman in his life, though this was an anointment, a ceremony to prepare her for whatever willful designs she had concocted and would see through regardless of his permission. Before putting on her gauntlets, he kissed each knuckle of each hand. After placing her plated long coat over her shoulders, he fetched the sword he knew she kept under her bed. Then he knelt, offering it to her on his upturned hands.

Aadore watched this doting, doe-eyed wonder, and her iron soul was weakened. When he knelt she nearly cried from joy or sorrow—the two emotions were such companions, she knew not the difference. She took the sword, rattled a little as she bent to her knee and kissed the man as hard and breathlessly as she could. A pounding knock disrupted them. Sean was shouting in a moment, calling for her to open the door. She turned, but Curtis, still on his knees, held on to a gauntlet.

"I thought we were to stay here, safe. But you decided to war without me, didn't you?" he asked.

While the heartbreak in his voice made Aadore question whether it had been the right decision to conspire with her brother and Skar, she also knew that Ian needed the care of an iron parent, of a person loving enough to chase a woman through the fog of Death, as Curtis had done with her in Menos. If the rest of Ian's family fell, his devotion could be directed into parenting. Yes, the three had conspired to make Curtis Ian's keeper. However, she did not regret that decision, and his aching wonder—at her, at what would come—hammered true the rightness of that choice. Here was a good man, a true lover and father. If she returned she would tell him just that.

Skar pounded the door now, and it would break if he continued.

"I must go, Curtis. The Iron Queen's consorts will be waiting for us at the anchorage. We shall fly to face Death, and we shall rip out her black heart for what she has done to Menos—to this world."

Curtis released her hand. She rushed to the door and admitted her brother and the half-giant mercenary. Each man was dressed in leathers and patchworks of iron protection. Sean walked with an unsheathed sword and a cane, and from Skar's thick belt, beneath his ebon mail tabard, hung two great axes, which he would wield like tomahawks. In the crook of an arm, Skar bore Ian, swaddled and serene as a child saint's statuette. He walked over to Curtis, instructed him to stand, and passed him the child, before leaning in to place one last kiss on the babe's cheek.

"She's told you, then?" asked Skar.

Not once that night had they spoken of Aadore's role in the war. To Curtis's knowledge, they were to stay, secure, within the palace keep while all of Eod rained with truefire bombardments. It had been a foolish faery tale in which he'd believed, and he should have suspected from Aadore's urgency to be together. Their night of romance had been a soldier's sojourn, a sensual experience to balance the mind before the gory madness of battle.

"I'm guessing that's a yes," said Skar, patting the daydreaming man. "We must go. Keep Ian safe; though if we're doing our jobs down there, you need not worry about that."

Going...they were filing from the room. Racing for a kiss or pleading for the iron maiden to stay would have demeaned her. Curtis would be the worrying lass, and she was to be the man on the frontlines over which he wept. He was fine with that decision, he realized, as long as she kept in her hard heart a single aspiration.

"Aadore, please, come back to me."

"I shall."

Her words rang more clearly than the warning bells of Eod. On purest faith, Curtis knew she would return, for she spoke with the tenacity of iron and the fire of pride, and hers was a promise that the Dreamers couldn't break. Once he was alone, he rocked Ian for a while, before setting the lad down for a basin-wash and dress. After, he would head to one of Eod's sweeping tiers, where all the other might-be widows and fearful families would gather. Curtis would find his place among them, and play a timorous role, though such artifice was for their benefit, not his. Aadore, and those who served her, would survive. Nothing was more certain.

VII

When the white sands of Eod wane to ash, the fires of the apocalypse will have been lit. So declared an ancient oracle during Taroch's age, and her divination was thought to coincide with the warlord's then ongoing war with the Immortal Kings. Most wise men of that era thought that the sorcerer king's attempt to transform Kor'Khul into a lush vale would result in a catastrophic reversal of effect, making the desert an even greater wasteland, and they warned Taroch against this act. Those sages were executed for their treason, and while they weren't entirely wrong—Taroch's spell did fail (from the poisoning and magikal impotence inflicted upon him by a vengeful handmaiden), Kor'Khul still remained as pristine and ivory as ever. Afterward, the prophecy faded into time along with the name and words of the ancient oracle. Few alive in the world today even knew such a doomsday warning existed; only those who studied the past, its oracular history and divinations, might recall it.

Deep in her catatonic slumber inside one of the equilibrium casks lying on the dais whereupon Gloriatrix's iron throne stood, swimming in an amniotic solution of brine, sorcery, and narcotics, Elissandra recalled the prophetess who had uttered those words. Her weathered face, her silver stare had been peering into a chalice of scintillating redness. She could hear the woman's words again; even mouth them in her slumber. Despite her sensory deprivation, she had moved passed the need for eyes, ears, or fingers to know the world around her, or the world that had been. Indeed, the moment of her personal apocalypse, of her separation from flesh, was nearly upon her, just as the dark shadow crawled over the desert toward Eod. Against the narcoleptic chemical suggestions of the equilibrium cask, she remained brightly awake, peering into the darkness with the semblance of a startled drowned woman, seeking omens. As had that ancient seer who'd once peered into the ripples of her own blood; the liquid in the chalice in which she'd scried.

Sesquanet had been her name, and she had known that to see the darkest fates, to face the death of the world, one had to first challenge the intrinsic terror of knowing one's end. Elissandra had done just that, many days past, and her ties and worries in this life were faraway whispers. Thus, all fates and visions were clear to her unclouded mind's eye, and she was not constrained by whatever wards concealed her. She was hardly a woman anymore, but a ghost.

As hawk of sun and moon she soared beyond the feliron shell that was said to repel or contain any magik, for she was not magik anymore but spirit. She flew high over Kor'Keth, basking in its crimson kiss one final time, for one last dawn. She flew toward the throbbing light of the sun. She wondered if the journey she would soon take would be brighter than chasing that glory to its origin. Away from that brilliance, she sensed the darkness, and turned her sights downward, whereupon the white sands of Kor'Khul were graying, then waning as revealed in Sesquanet's prophecy. The Green Mother's land had been despoiled by the horde of wet, foot-dragging soldiers bearing rotted pikes, crude wooden clubs, pitchforks, swords, and in some cases, bows and arrows. Even the wyrms who swam through the desert stayed far away from this stain on the land, and had retreated into the ruddy northern mountain ranges, where Elissandra, with her web of supernatural senses, felt them trembling.

Down into the shambling rows of unliving things she went, amid gangrenous warriors, lurching green children, and corpses more bone than flesh—skeletal men buried in the ceremonial brass armor of Taroch's rule who must have risen from the hills of Ebon Vale, or the graves of Taroch's Arm. Death had dragged every creature from Menos to Eod from its grave: decayed dogs, putrefied horses, festering mountain and alley cats, rotted crocodiles with snapping yellow-toothed jaws, brawking leprous ravens too mangy to fly, gnat-buzzing bears, and chewed-up, blood-matted sheep that brayed like felhounds. It was a circus of the animal dead mingled with the mortal dead, and was as boggling as it was horrific.

More dreadful was that for all the army's shambling inelegance, each unit moved with purpose, stoked by the black energy flickering in the stares Elissandra observed in those creatures whose eyes hadn't been sucked out or were otherwise deteriorated. Certain dead—one great brown bear, walking on its hind legs, one of Taroch's deathless generals, a snarling farmhand peeled to his facial muscles and striding proudly with a spade—showed more than a merciless mechanization; they displayed the assuredness of leadership. In them, the presence of Death roared; they were animals and men chosen to receive more of Death's power. Elissandra wished that the defenders of Eod could sense this as she could, since breaking them would surely weaken the army's chain.

Fearless and invulnerable, Elissandra's spirit drifted opposite the current of the wave of death, this army of ten thousand or more, surmising the might of their foe. As she floated toward the rear of the army, she used caution. A vacuumous force was ahead, a pull to her spiritual matter, as when a shooting star crossed too near to a black hole: Death and her vessel.

As befitting a ruler of the cosmos, even in this pitiful earthly realm, Death had constructed for herself a flotilla of bones, skin, skulls, and leather. It was a hideous stage, with a jumbled ribcage of a throne where she might sit and survey her army's destruction of their enemies. The construction surely weighed tons, though it was no strain to the unliving servants upon whose skeletal backs it was borne. Even as she assessed the horror, Elissandra watched those whose decrepit bodies couldn't endure the weight shatter, to have their meat trod upon, then replaced by another of Death's flock. Such attrition was insignificant since Death knew that every life lost in Eod would mean another soldier for her cause. As Elissandra, the sneaky shadow, wisped behind the Dreamer, she caught the runoff of Death's thoughts—visions of worlds scraped to their sedimentary bones and blanketed in the crumbled crust of desiccated life. She sensed the peace of these memories—real worlds, these had been—and then sensed a flutter, a *fear* of the verdancy and obstinacy of Geadhain.

This world, and its children, frightened Death.

If her vessel had had a proper beating heart, it would have been racing from anxiety. After being tied to Sorren for decades, Death seemed to have been infected by the man's cowardice, his jealousy and wild hatred of what he couldn't control. Even now, though, another spirit, another influence fought inside of Death, and Elissandra sensed that second presence. Here was a brave soul, one of light and honor. It would not stop demanding freedom, and demanding to see his daughter, Fionna.

Ah, so that was what you bargained for, and why you accepted a pact with Death, thought Elissandra. *You wanted to see your daughter once more—only you now realize that the Dreamer won't honor that deal in any way that will be kind. Worry not, Vortigern, continue to wear away at Death's Will, and I feel that love will win. I believe in love now, child of the Iron Queen. I see how it is the strength of strengths and how hope and wrested fates are drawn from it. I believe you will see her again.*

Death turned her head sharply to the side, as though hearing or sensing Elissandra's whispers. Elissandra blew herself away, back to the Furies and ready to wake her children for war.

XV

THE BURNING DREAM

I

The strange sense of being watched had passed; it was an irritant that Death attributed to some farscope or pitiful spying device from the maggots of Eod. She pondered the battle that awaited her beyond the white wall just now lit by dawn's crimson blush. She sensed many hundreds of auras in the battlements, though beyond that only clusters of life, huddled and dense. Contingents, she assumed. Death knew all wars. She had watched the toppling of empires of every species—elemental man, crystal warriors, and glossy shrieking bipeds of spine and scale. She'd seen every species, on every floating rock in the tree-of-stars, and had gracefully reaped the last few of many kinds of beings out of existence. Mankind, here on Geadhain, would be no different. They were foolish to try.

She knew every trick and feint. Thus, she knew that the maggots had prepared some manner of a trap, though the exact nature of their ruse escaped her. She considered the sleeping warships she approached were part of the maggot's defense strategy. Like the city and the emptied streets she sensed in the metropolis ahead, these metal giants held no flicker of life. She Willed small legions of her flock to investigate the Furies and felt them sizzle into ash upon trying to breach the hulls. Was this man's simple tendency to protect his holdings? Or was this part of the maggots' curious plan? Surely they conspired to do more than hole up in their city? Recently the guerrilla sniping upon her forces had stopped, these assaults by men and women rising out of the sand, or standing atop Kor'Khul's ancient valleys through which her army funneled. In these entrapments, the maggots had thrown firebombs and sorcery at her forces, and she and her archers had smitten what insolents they could with arrows and her sorcerous black bolts. Now a few of those ravaged soldiers of Eod shambled amid her horde. Still, the maggots were quiet, as silent as the warships sleeping in the desert. Such silence foreshadowed a threat.

Strange tactics, she thought.

But she was Xalloreth, the eater of worlds, the destroyer of life, and she would not be outplayed by maggot-born chicanery. She would show them how to crush all hope. She revisited all of the fallen cities in her memory and selected a maneuver that would benefit her in the siege of Eod. That heart, the white-hot knot of auras in and surrounding Eod's mountainous keep, was the bounty of the city, and such was what she would claim. Once inside Eod, she would split her forces and circumvent whatever blockades the maggots had erected. Through muddy shite and filth her servants would crawl, then rise to devour the cowering masses in Eod's sanctuary...to fall like so many empires before, from beneath. If her vessel's mouth could've wet itself, it would have, from the thirst for which she condemned mankind. Alas, she was a cosmic ruler, a creature without remorse or self-reproach. She was not prone to poetic reflections. She was Death, and she would come upon that city and consume it. After, there would be nothing but the whistling silence in which all things knew peace.

II

Even in the red haze of dawn, a pinpoint of white light shone: a star. It was an omen foretold by the oracle Elissandra of this age, a sign that she must be in two places at once, a sign that Eod would burn.

While far apart, Leonitis and his brother each spotted the star from the battlements of Eod's great wall. When they had been young and quite new to Eod, they had often walked through the King's Garden at night and looked for Cephalis, the Northern star, with a longing that defied reason. Whenever they had spotted it, they'd wished upon the star, as men are wise to do, for glory and valor. This time, when they saw Cephalis glowing in the red heavens, the brothers made a different wish, this one for peace and for the survival of those they loved.

For Death had come to Eod's doorstep.

Rather than simply crash upon the city, as the war marshals had presumed the Dreamer would do, the black wave had rolled in from the east, staining all behind it as a horizon of gray. The soldiers, who thought themselves steeled for this battle, waiting for their likely imminent destruction with sneers and grit to their manner, had to suffer in the boggy stench of Death's army as it suppurated, whirled, and redistributed its stain around the circumference of Eod's wall—as much as could be spread without climbing the walls and then mountains in which half the city was nestled. And while the warriors wrapped with kerchiefs about their faces thought that Death's rearrangement would thin the unveiling vision of her awesome army, it did not. The army only seemed grander, as far-reaching as gray cloud left atop the desert in their wake, an obscurity that might soon swallow Eod.

Death did not mindlessly swarm the city. She and her forces stayed a thousand strides distant and waited until the sun rose, until the putrescence of her thousands of rotting warriors and beasts billowed high and low over Eod, forcing every soldier in the watchtowers to swallow their vomit. Less affected were the handful of mercenary archers and Arhad forces gathered in ragtag rows with Eod's pristine watchmen along the wall. These grizzled folk had seen more than their fair share of death and oppression; they notched their bows and waited for the order to shoot.

Gorijen, high in a southern tower overlooking the shadowy ocean that milled and moaned outside Eod's gates, upon seeing his own daughter rush off and retch in a corner, ordered his wan windsingers to put down their crackling bows of living lightning, to fall deep into their minds for peace, and summon forth a wind to battle the stink. As Edina recovered, he censured her for her weakness, and despite her insisting that she had the stomach for this business, her ghastly pallor suggested otherwise, and he sent her away so that she could compose herself like her fellow warriors. His real motive, however, as a father, was for her to be far from the conflict. Spitting curses under her breath, Edina shuffled her way down the tower. When she was alone in the hallway, she fell against the stone walls and cried.

Down the battlements from Gorijen's contingent, Leo turned as the tower at his side lit up with silver magik, then a brisk, willful wind rushed in from the north. It was invigorating and inspiring, as if a spirit had come to protect their army. With the sun risen, and Cephalis still somehow blazing for supremacy against the larger eye of day, Leonitis felt this was the time. He pulled the ivory war horn from his belt, one taken from the royal vault and that hadn't been used by Eod since Taroch had declared the world his enemy, and blew with the fury of the king's legion. Long, broken into sharp bursts, and resounding enough to reach all of Eod, the magik horn announced the start of Eod's war on Death—they were not defenders; they were the champions who would smite this wicked Dreamer come to ravage civilization.

And so, while a few of the windsingers in Gorijen's tower shuffled off, still in their trances, while continuing to fill Eod with the winds of war and hope, the rest of the thunderstrike artillery found their bows and an embrasure within the tower. Commands were given, through farspeaking stones, for the secondary units of the artillery to commence their assault. As the wave of darkness and rot surged ahead, the glimmering mantle of awakening dawn was no match for the scintillation and thunderous glory that rained upon the dead. From the turrets and peaks of the wall were flung a million arcs of lightning in a barrage of golden-white threads that seared one's vision every bit as much as the detonating pockets of destruction they caused on the ground. The arrows of the mercenary archers and of Lila's army were likely incinerated as often as they struck any targets. Sand whirled, concealing the devastation, and through that cloak of ruin, Death whipped and surged her forces.

Through the eruptions and dazzling blasts, it was impossible for Leonitis to have a clear view of the conflict. All he could ascertain was that Death's army was advancing—with horrifying speed for the dead, almost as fast as men on steeds. Moving his spyglass around, however, he noticed a white spot announced by his scouts, one more demanding of his attention than any of the bedlam, for it stood out against so much darkness and smoke. With the mighty wall of Eod shaking from the dismantling of the city, he lost track of the spot and had to adjust his spyglass further and conduct a harried search over a legion of decomposed warriors and beasts just to find his mark again. There. A bone stage, and upon it, a shaking sight of a man wreathed in tatters of pure shadow: the vessel of Death. Given his macabre royalty, how he sat in that throne of ribs and bones like an emperor, this was no other. Scouts believed they had seen such a construction before today, though no one had been able to near Death's army enough to wholly confirm such suppositions. But now the legion master and others had seen, and knew, and he fumbled for a farspeaking stone—the light of which fluttered and whose message felt broken with so much magik going on. Into the stone he screamed a message to Gorijen with approximate coordinates for a strike. He wasn't sure if he was remotely on the mark, though he had to try. Gasping, filled with hope and terror, he looked to the left again, to the tower from which electrical currents flowed in a stream of mayhem, and wondered if Gorijen had received his call. Then the tower dimmed, and Leonitis squeezed the dead farspeaking stone in his hand as if it were a wonderstone and his wish would come true, that this war would end immediately and without the losses predicted. As Gorijen's tower suddenly blazed like a struck lightning rod and golden energy flew not in a scattershot wave, but rather in an angled concentration of crackling magik, Leonitis believed his prayer had been answered. He cheered, deeply, as a mushroom of ruin and sand bloomed down below. When he finished hugging the man next to him—who was quite bewildered—he looked once more with his spyglass to assess whether the target had been eliminated.

A crater had formed, and much of Death's army had already slithered and lurched through its smoldering valley; the dead seemed unimpeded by the fusillade that ravaged them, and Leonitis, unable to see the bone stage or signs of Death's vessel, was filled with a sinking terror.

"This should be over," he muttered. "If we destroyed her vessel, this should have ended…"

"Maggots!" echoed a withering voice, louder than the lightning flung from the wall.

The bravery of the defenders waned from the shattering stridency of Death's angry cry, and most of the artillery fumbled to notch another spell or arrow as they searched for the enchanted wax—charmed by the earthspeakers to fill their ears with cottony muting—they kept on hand in their tunics to prevent their eardrums from splitting. In their briefings, they'd been warned about this voice, the voice of a Maker of Creation. Crazed and bleeding from their ears, men gazed up into the war-haze clouding the sky above the battlements, whence the voice had come. There, a figure floated, fringed in dark fire—a sign that he would not be burned by any mortal flame or power. Leonitis, both awed and mortified, could not pry his spyglass off the levitating being and clumsily stuffed wax into his ears with a single trembling hand.

Before him was a star, a manifestation of the cosmos. They were but maggots to its greatness, and under its fist they would be ground. Seeing quite clearly the avatar of Death, Leonitis watched, helpless, as the being clenched its hand as if squeezing an orb that couldn't be seen. That was all it seemed to take on Death's behalf—a casual gesture—and that metaphysical orb, and the Witchwall that had protected Eod from aerial attack was transformed for a moment into an object less ethereal and more concrete, a lens in which the defenders could see sudden cracks, veins through a crystal eggshell, and which then began a cacophonous crinkling death that showered the city in twinkling shards.

It was over in specks. The barrier had been destroyed. The smallest solace was that at least the shattered barrier didn't cut Leonitis like glass as the destroyed ward covered him in warm ember-like fragments.

Then Death waved, and the stone tower from which had come so much of Eod's assault was also infected. It washed from white to gray to black in a flush of rock-rot. With a soft ashen tumble, loud only from the sheer mass of cascading sand, the tower imploded and flooded the battlement with soot. As the wave rolled to a sandy finish, the white bones and rattling armor of what had been Gorijen's troop and probably the artillery master himself, somewhere, lay amid the ash.

Leonitis dropped the spyglass, worrying that the bones might soon begin to move. He and his soldiers couldn't risk being up here with a *flying* horror from beyond—yes, flying watchtower to watchtower now and degrading each one into soot. Soldiers had been whipped into a panic, and men were running to and fro, as senseless as decapitated chickens. The Arhadians and mercenaries were seen slinking toward the stairwells of the battlement. Somewhere below, in the muddlesome soup of smoke, noise, gusting ash, and fleeing bodies, Leonitis saw his brother's burly shape and shouldered through the retreating forces to meet him. Dorvain was hunched near the high wall, screaming, and had thrown an axe, then a sword, then a dagger at the monster in the time since Leonitis had spotted him. When those weapons missed their mark, Dorvain shrugged and finally responded to Leonitis's appearance, urging him to flee.

"This isn't over!" he shouted, as Leonitis pulled him toward a short, trembling tower in which he saw a landing and stairs.

Looking back at the black sandcastles—some still falling—the scattered armor, and the flailing warriors, Leonitis felt his brother was wrong. It was over. All that remained was to nobly accept their deaths.

III

Lowelia was among the few not to cry out at the cavalcade of thunder and the appearance of the storming, flying divinity that transformed Eod's watchtowers into piles of ash. Tremors wracked Dorothy more and more with every watchtower that fell. From one of the barricades surrounding the exits to the Faire of Fates that was haunted by a few empty stalls, abandoned stages, and ruffling paper ghosts, the women watched helplessly. Most of the royal troops with whom they'd been huddled behind a tall jumble of wood broke into a howling panic. She was grateful at least that the leather-armored mercenaries and that rough-edged Arhadian woman with the cropped hair and violent eyes, Kali, showed some mettle.

Indeed, aside from Dorothy, it was members of the Silver Watch who had demonstrated the greatest fear; perhaps they were simply startled that their city might not be impregnable. While the mercenaries checked their weapons and explosives, Kali and her Arhadian sisters and brother-in-arms hastened over to Dorothy, who was leaning on Lowe and peering around the edge of the barricade at Eod's smoking wall.

How could something so great and powerful fall, as though it was made of nothing more than sand? It was trembling and had lost at least five towers, possibly more, from what she could see. She knew she was watching the first sign of their defeat.

"*Aibnach alssahrah'*," (Daughter of the Desert), said Kali in Arhadic. For a moment, with the din of an ancient fortification under assault, Dorothy pretended not to hear her, though avoiding the woman again was impossible once she stepped in front of her. "Aibnach alssahrah'," she repeated.

Dorothy gave her a confused stare, perplexed that the woman had guessed she was an Arhadian. "*Nem?*" (Yes?)

Kali clasped Lowe's shoulder. "*Eindamya yati alqachilin, sanuqatil, walikan baed dhlk sawy alfarar, wo spinrex alhikmatt lach mutaradat wyrm, waqal 'annah qutean, waqal 'annah yukhaffaf laha durue min qibal qiadatiha min khilal alwidyan alssakhriat hatta 'annaha alddurue, mutakassiratan wakasyr, yatrukaha eurdat lilkhatr, hal tfhm? sawf alfirar maeana, nem?*" (When the dead men come, we shall fight if we can, but then we shall flee. The wise spinrex does not chase the wyrm, he herds it, he thins its armor by leading it through rock valleys until its armor, chipped and broken, leaves it exposed. Do you understand? You will move with us, yes?)

Amid the roaring noise, Dorothy replied that she would. After, Kali and her troupe of six Arhadians stayed gathered around the two women, jointly immersed in a ghoulish study of Eod's defenses falling into shambles. No one had any wisdom to offer; the gravity of their situation had never been clearer. Lowelia, strangely, was not as glum as Dorothy or the others. She had been fidgeting with her gun, anxiously scanning the chaotic heights of the wall, and worrying about Leonitis and Dorvain who were somewhere in that bedlam.

Something had alighted within her, though, an ember of hope. She felt they were alive...or was desperate for that to be true. It wasn't until she had been confronted with the reality of loss—that these two men who had been part of nearly all her adult life could actually be dead, and so quickly—that she had felt the gravity of this war. It was personal now; Death was destroying what she loved. Looking away from the wall and its grand questions, she noticed the Arhad surrounding them.

"What do they want?" she asked.

"They want us to fight and move with them," replied Dorothy. "Once the dead are in the city. I think we should. I don't...I don't know how we can fight this..." Her tongue wagged; words had failed her.

"You stay with them, and keep yourself alive," said Lowe, her eyes suddenly cloudy, her voice dissonantly cheerful. "I need to find out something—even if it kills me."

"Lowe!"

Lowe pulled away from Dorothy's grasp and dashed out into the empty marketplace. She had joined this war to fight out on the frontlines, and she wasn't yet there. It was likely that this was the end, and that they had already lost. Though the impetus that propelled her feet into a run was not cowardice, but love. A love for the sometimes foolish and stubborn brothers who were among her dearest friends. She would not weep until she saw their corpses. Nor would she leave their bodies to be gnawed on by the dead. If they yet lived, they could cringe out the end together and maybe share the bullets in her gun before Death tried to claim their bodies. Thus, to the wall, toward the brick-and-ivory silhouette of a gatehouse built into Eod's edifice, she raced. She raced toward where she believed her friends were. She had no plan, other than to reach the entrance from which the Silver Watch were spilling, and to climb the wall and scour it for her brothers.

"*A mummer's dance, o'er fire and farce. A mummer's dance, to light your arse. Hark past the crackle, ignore the ghastly smell—of burning skin. Listen as you smolder, till your ears are nubs, for the chime of Belmont's bell.*" The ridiculous snippet from one of Kericot's rare full-length plays wandered into her head. She knew not when she'd read it, or where, though a tale about a comically stupid man who ultimately dies by running into a flaming house to save his cat, Belmont, felt appropriate. *You've always been more than a bit of a fool, Lowelia Larson,* she thought. *At least now you know you're a brave one.*

Back at the barricade, shocked by Lowe's sudden departure, Dorothy shouted for her to stop, though she had no drive to chase her, and what urge she might have discovered in time was curbed by Kali's warnings of a new commotion at the southern gate. There, the granite doors set by giants and carved with serpents and symbols of the past were being tested by the fist of Death. Dorothy imagined the hideous avatar pounding at the gates, for what else would bring on such cacophonous hammering, which resonated through the plate of the land, or the insidious gray pattern that she could see from so far away threading through the stone?

One speck, and the grayness had veined through the doors like a virulent fungus. Two specks, and the pounding at the gate grew muffled, as its matter was now soft as a pillow. It was only with tepid horror that she watched the once seemingly indomitable gates crumble and collapse in a torrent of dust. Watching the disaster from afar, she had time to tighten her makeshift balaclava and backed up with her Arhadian comrades behind the barricade as the gray storm blew through the Faire of Fates. When the ashen pall thinned, they peeked out again; a rent stood in Eod's wall. It was a crude tear still powdery with decay and smoke, and through which an army of slavering monstrosities had already begun to pour. Shining pockets of Silver Watchmen, who had been fleeing wildly from the garrisons within the wall, were caught up in the swell of the dead, swallowed as if by an ocean's tide.

Now Dorothy felt horror's cold hand grip her, from the ash, the stench, and the captivating movement of Death's horde—an undulant spread, bodies rolling, clawing, and clambering over one another to shred what members of the Silver Watch were caught on the flagstones. The horde moved as fast as a liquid, and Dorothy knew that these wooden barricades would slow but not stop them. She seriously doubted that Lowe was still alive, and her heart wrenched at the thoughtlessness of the woman's death.

Nothing would save them. Imbecilic was the notion that they could challenge Death. The churning ocean of teeth, green flesh, and yellow bone was a hunger from which none would escape. Perhaps she should lie down here and accept her fate.

Kali, however, was not ready to pass to the beyond, and she rallied her sisters and brother and sent them behind, down the street. She lingered by the barricade and the kneeling, defeated Dorothy—who couldn't remember falling. "Tati shaqiqat, wanahn la yumkin 'iilhaq alhazimat bihim hunach!" (Come, sister, we cannot face them here!) she cried.

Dorothy, her mind broken by the chaos, her body paralyzed, heard Kali's pleas while separate in a world that moved as slow as syrup, every action drawn out by degrees. She willed herself to rise, though her legs seemed shattered. Mercenaries to her left screamed warped and slurring cries as if they were malfunctioning phantographs, as they lobbed truefire cocktails or fired arrows, the torpid thud and whoosh of which she heard from every drawn bow. One brave sorcerer, also a mercenary, strode out in his ragged robe like a saint into a maelstrom, streaming fumes of pale magik, radiant and brave—a bravery that she did not seem to possess. He walked ahead to meet the chattering mob, which had flooded the entirety of the Faire of Fates now. Before the black waves crashed upon him, he cried out, "For Eod!"

The man's death-call woke her from her stupor, as did Kali's shaking her. So too did the whirlwind of white fire released by the defiant sorcerer's fatal incendiary spell startle her to her feet.

"*Shajae, shaqiqat,*" (Bravery, sister), hissed Kali. "*Nahn yunsifu imye.*" (We shall avenge them all).

Perhaps Dorothy's next opportunity to fight and die would be when she would shine as bright as that man who'd just detonated himself. Kali seemed to believe so. Although, as they ran through Eod's empty streets, past the soldiers and sellswords scrambling to attention behind barricades that would soon be devoured, she was possessed by a spirit of cowardice that told her to run farther, faster, to throw Kali to the ravenous army if it would spare her a few specks. She hoped that she could conquer that cowardice, at least, before she died.

IV

The gathering at the edge of the King's Garden seemed one of perfect leisure—with a great tree stump draped in a picnic cloth and surrounded by quaint crystal-smithed chairs from master artisans, and a spread of olives, fruits, and meats on the table—and not a summit of leaders observing a war. Indeed, dawn had come and graced the gathering with warmth and light that felt like a disparaging deception to the smoke and destruction the spymaster of Eod and Iron Queen observed in their spyglasses. Nearer to the edge of this squat wooded terrace they stood apart from the concerned Ironguards and Silver Watchmen. Neither had sat for even a speck with the spineless gray sages who were too old for war, and who seemed more absorbed in the qualities and flavors of the repast than about Death ravaging Eod. Several times, their geriatric smacking and nattering had caused the Iron Queen to spin and cast ruthless razor stares at the men around the table. Finally, when that didn't silence them, she asked her Ironguards to escort them out of the garden.

"How dare you!" protested one long-bearded and robed fellow as the Ironguard pulled him up by an elbow and dragged him from her sight.

"If you had any sense of what was happening down there," she said, shaking her spyglass at him. "If that pudding behind your eyes hadn't spoiled a decade ago, you would have respected the ceremony of your being here, being silent, while those of us with Wills to sway the unswayable ache and bleed for the soldiers fulfilling our commands to die."

Gloriatrix looked like a mercenary captain today in high boots, a wide, curved hat to keep out the sun, and a ceremonial sword hanging from a belt beneath a black blouse. She unsheathed the blade slowly, so that it grated against the scabbard, and then pointed at each man, in addition to the troublemaker who was to be removed. "You are all dismissed, and if I hear another word, I'll slit your throats myself and have your bodies thrown down as meals for the dead."

Rasputhane, wrapped in a hooded cloak that only showed a sinister frown, was just as happy to see the old fools vanish into the woods, and he turned back to the hazy vista with the Iron Queen.

Whatever their relationship beyond this war, for now they behaved like kindred generals, without tremendous empathy, observing the theater of warfare below. Their thoughts were less on how those toy soldiers were men, and more on how to move those pawns in response to the dark river that flooded Eod's streets. With all of Eod spread out before them, they could see which channels were more thoroughly padded with bodies to control the run of Death's forces. It appeared that the barricades were falling faster than expected, speeding up the timetable for their counterstrike. Nonetheless, districts to the east and west needed to be supplemented with soldiers. Those blockades had to hold, if only for a few more sands, so that Death's army had completely emptied itself from the desert and into the Faire of Fates. Once their enemies had pooled where they wanted them, they would summon Elissandra from her sleep, and she and her brood would turn that ocean of darkness into one of fire. Death was sure to be among those writhing in flames.

"We're holding key points." Gloriatrix lowered her spyglass. "Though our forces are falling faster than we estimated."

"We need to wake the seer, earlier than expected. You told me that you have a contingency?"

She had several, actually. First, in the event that Death somehow survived the bombardment, a heavily armed legion of the Ironguard, led by Gustavius and accompanied by her son and his wonderstones, some of Eod's finest, and the brother and sister who seemed immune to Death's contagion lay in waiting at one of the barricades in the midline of defense. Far enough from the battle that they would survive the explosion of the Furies' warheads, and close enough that they would be ready to clean up whatever wandered out from that nuclear haze. She and Sorren had come to peace with the knowledge that there might be no opportunity to save Vortigern from his possession; an argument that, while framed in philanthropy for the people of Eod, was actually due to her own desire to hoard as many of the wonderstones as possible. *We shall save him if we can, my son, though we cannot create that opportunity; we can only pray that fate creates it for us—and we must first think of the people who look to us for salvation.* Sorren still held to the belief that he would have the chance to save his brother, even if that meant that the Furies had failed.

A warmth distracted her from answering the spymaster or pondering failure, as the farspeaking stone tingled in the Iron Queen's palm. She had held on to the stone, part of her second contingency plan, all day, like a child clinging to a favorite blanket. In many ways this was a security to her, the warmth and meaning instilled in the stone. Elissandra had enchanted it, and thus it was a piece of her friend—the last piece she would ever hold or know.

This has my hope and my magik within it, the seer had said, as she'd sat up in her technomagikal coffin before the Ironguards sealed her inside. *If you need me, Gloria, as a friend, or as the hero I must be, simply Will it. I shall wake from sleep no matter how deep. I shall wake even before my destiny calls on me to die. I know that this is to be our goodbye, though the river of life runs into the ocean of stars, and there we shall one day meet, swim and rejoice with a salubrity that the women we have been were always denied.*

If she used the farspeaking stone, the magik, the warmth would fade, and with it whatever earthly residue of Elissandra remained on Geadhain. Selfish and sentimental, she didn't want to use it, but she had no choice, and she was a queen of Iron, not romance. She raised the stone and whispered to it.

"Wake, Elissandra. We have been set upon early. Purge the foul Dreamer from our domain."

Before the beating golden light of the stone faded, her back turned to the spymaster, she whispered to Elissandra, "Thank you for being a fellow spider with whom I've spun glorious deceits. I shall see that your children inherit all the wealth, status, and honor that you will never claim. Journey well into the dark...my friend."

Rasputhane watched the Iron Queen raise the fist that she'd kept gnarled all day to her mouth and mutter into it. He'd figured she held a farspeaking stone within her hand, and as it unclenched he saw within it a dull spherical crystal. He saw hints of a sincere sadness on the drawn lines of the Iron Queen's face and spotted the glimmer of a brighter emotion in her eyes. Not tears, it couldn't be tears.

"It is done." The Iron Queen dropped the stone, kicking it somewhere into the grass.

"What is?"

"I sent a message to Elissandra."

"I gathered that, from the stone."

Suddenly, the flimsiness of their plan, one that involved waking an ethereal woman from a sensory-deprived coffin in a ship insulated with layers of repulsing magik, seemed more apparent than it had during their plotting. Had they made their strategy of nothing more than straw and dreams?

"I mean, will she hear you?" he asked. "I am not even sure how she would know to wake without our involvement. She insisted that she would *know her time*, however one might interpret that. But will she know our time, our moment of need?"

"Elissandra is a woman of iron character." Without the tearfulness Rasputhane must have imagined, a barking Gloriatrix—much more familiar—

continued. "She has more honor than anyone I've known. I would never doubt her, not when she has made such a meaningful promise."

Suddenly they witnessed the new lights to the east—fanning pulses of crimson, like giant exotic birds with solar feathers, blazing through the smoldering mantle that hung over Eod's great wall. Gloriatrix knew, as with all of Elissandra's vows, that this one had been kept.

"The Furies." Rasputhane gasped.

Immediately, he raced back to the vacant table and cast aside the remains of meals and drinks in a single clattering sweep. On the tablecloth he arranged the crucial farspeaking stones for each of his commanders and legion masters down below. They would need to move, and fast, as the Furies' fire would soon be upon them. Although like the Iron Queen, he knew sentimentality was reserved for the families of those who sacrificed themselves for their nations. In war, there was no time for grief.

He picked up each stone, issued the commands to pull back and prepare for the warheads. He knew from those commanders who answered who among them would celebrate victory tomorrow, and who would be commemorated on monuments instead. Neither Dorvain nor Leonitis answered, which boded grim. As well, the farspeaking stone in the spellsong's possession remained cold, as did his brother's. Those two had been dispatched outside King's Court with Gloriatrix's secondary unit, though, so he felt better about their odds of survival. When the task was done, forty-five farspeaking stones from his bag of military communications sat gray and spent upon the table. Half of those men and their legions would be incinerated, not to mention the losses from the Arhad and mercenary forces. Was he no better than the Pale Lady and her harvest? To silence his conscience, he reached for a bottle of wine that had survived his fervor, and drank.

Gloriatrix had been watching the glowing birds in the desert spread their plumage, stunned by their beauty. In a moment, the fire of their power would blind her, and she tipped her hat waiting for the brilliance to commence. Or so it had seemed, that nod—even to the spymaster, had he looked her way. What she had actually done, however, was send a command to an Ironguard to set into motion events designed to lead Menos's second rise and conquest. The soldier slipped away as light dazzled the witnesses of Eod's immolation. Once in the deeper dark of the woodlands, he spoke into a farspeaking stone, and elsewhere, men waiting to pounce seized a prisoner.

✳ ✳ ✳

V

Lowe's hysteria had escalated by the time she reached the stone portico and started up the stairs that led into the building, shoving her way through the scrambling flood of soldiers. When men were fighting on the same side of a war, they knew but one allegiance, and so mercenaries helped limping Silver Watchmen, and Arhadian warriors carried fallen men clinging to life. Dirty, crimson-splashed faces surrounded Lowe, and a few of the less traumatized watchmen asked where in the Hells she thought she was going. One warrior, who saw only a demented woman determined to die, grabbed her arm and tried pulling her back from the groaning edifice into which she was charging.

"Can you not see that the wall is about to come down?" he screamed.

Of course she could. Just a moment ago the great wall of Eod had been torn open and Death was pushing its arm through that crack. Rather than answer the watchman, she shook him.

"Have you seen Leonitis or Dorvain?" she demanded.

"What?"

"Your commanders! The Ninth Legion Master or his brother, have you seen them?"

Her question instilled in him a measure of the watch's famous grace again; proud and sad, he answered, "No, I have not seen them since Master Leo gave the order to evacuate. Now we must go, Miss—" His eyes widening, he suddenly recognized her. "Miss Larson! I was with you in the rebellion. I don't know that we ever met, though. You must come with me. You are too valuable to perish here." Again, he pulled at her; however, she proved as difficult to move as a stone mule.

"Where? Where were they last seen?"

"Above! On the ramparts, though many of those have collapsed, and my commanders were not among those rescued. I'm sorry, Miss Larson."

Apparently, whatever the watchman saw over her shoulder was enough to break his promise to save her. He released her and jogged into the crowd, who were also casting looks and quickening their escapes from a coming swarm of the snarling dead. She smelled the horde's blooming stench and heard their greasy jabbering as she plunged through the thinning throng of survivors and dashed though the columned entrance of the deserted gatehouse. As the murk cleared, she noticed that this place was quite different from the gatehouse she'd invaded a few weeks ago. It was tidy, with a marbled floor, and decked with silvery banners and empty suits of armor whose glint gave the gloomy place a twilight by which to see—the spheres of light fitted into nearby sconces, which should have glowed green but were gray. She made out two arches across the wide chamber, one that seemed as if it had stairs going up, the other with stairs leading down. If the brothers were anywhere they would be up, and *trapped*, or otherwise hindered from coming down, she decided. Not dead, lest her quest be futile. A few scattered weapons, helms, and bits of armor impeded an otherwise effortless dash toward the archway.

As she reached the steps, she heard outside the wet echoes and screams of battle, and knew that the dead were on her doorstep. Sensing a presence she turned, and saw in the far-off distance a wizened or hunched shape. It gave a gurgling roar, then sprung. Her horror at its astonishing dexterity might have delayed her in running, but not from aiming her gun. As the limber monster gained on her, she steadied her shivering hand. She tried to think calm thoughts, to think of the bobbing, maggot-spilling, half-lipped face as if it were one of the bottles and cans with which she and Dorothy had practiced. When it leapt, she shrieked and fired about as well as a blind man with vertigo. Tiny blue flares dazzled the darkness and a smoking heap slumped before her. It seemed her aim, or luck, had been sound.

Regrettably, the skirmish had alerted others, who gave up feeding on the laggardly soldiers who'd been caught outside the gatehouse, and turned to Lowe. She wondered how many of them would move as nimbly as the one she had felled, but she did not remain to find out. She turned, said a prayer to the Fates, and took the stairs up two or three at a time. The echoing snarls of Death's pack of rotten beast-men were soon rising up the narrow stairwell.

Each winding twist led to a landing with a hallway obscured in dust and shadow or blocked by fallen wreckage. Again and again, the great wall trembled, the sickness in its stone surely spreading. If the dead didn't devour her, she would likely be buried in the great avalanche of Eod's wall as it finally fell. By now, she'd accepted that she would soon be dead, one way or another. Thus the chase to find her brothers, to grieve for them or with them in her final moments, became her penultimate trial.

Her heart as her compass, she climbed higher and higher. The slavering dead were still on her trail. She fell into an exhausted quiet. Here was her body's last labor, and it was a body that had served her well. She'd been a mother, a servant to a noble queen and somewhat noble king, a spy, and a rebel. What a life she had lived, and she regretted it not. What would come after—after the short pain of whatever death was in store for her—was peace. A well-earned rest. She believed that she would see Cecilia again, too, which made any dark horizon seem suddenly blue.

Grandmother Lowelia, I am not ready to relinquish your stewardship so that you may release your astrum into the universal flow, said the Mind as sharply as a pin to her brain.

Lowe stumbled and fell against the wall. Its words were jabs at her, hurting her as it spoke, and she had no idea how it was doing it, given it should have been spans away in the care of Tabitha, she hoped.

I do apologize for the crudeness of my transmission, Grandmother Lowe. I have not conducted enough practical examinations on the extension of my telemetric impulses beyond the medium of my crystal vessel. There are still "rusty links in the chain," as you would say. I shall use the data from our discourse now to smooth out those links. Already, I see that my telemetric pulses are tuned too high and that you suffered from their volume. How do I sound now?

Better, she realized; there were no more felt steel fingers poking about in her skull. "But how are you talking to me? You're there, with Tabitha, and I'm...here."

We are all connected, Grandmother Lowelia. Animals to trees to dirt to kings—the only variable lies in the composition and complexity of our astrums, our universal patterns, though all such patterns are made of the weave of life. I am of that weave, as are you. After living among you, after learning what it is to see, to grieve, to change, I too have been affected by the telemetry of that great fabric. I pull your thread and you hear my vibration—quieter now that I have adjusted my output. I have known that I could pull that thread for some time; however, there had never been a moment where I...

The Mind paused, cogitating, and she felt the thunder of its impossible intellect rumbling behind her eyes.

Felt. Yes, I have calculated that I feel. I do not know the distillation or shade of that feeling, since these experiences are new to me. What I do know is that I do not want your astrum to scatter into the firebug of stars that mark a soul's passing—as interesting as that process is to behold. I cannot pull your thread anymore, should that transpire. We can no longer speak if you become a particulate of the great weave, the great astrum. I do not want you to die.

Lowe wiped away a few tears.

You must run, Grandmother Lowelia. The dead are near, and I have not mastered the skill of manipulating the environment through the extension of my Will, though I strive toward such mastery. You seem to have no rudder in this storm, and so I shall guide you to the two matrices you seek. They are alive, your friends, though in peril.

Oh fuk! While transfixed by the Mind's strange, alien, but endearing love, she had forgotten the danger she was in and her reason for being here. Cecilia would have to wait; she had two men to save and a crystal babe to which to return.

Running again, she huffed, "Show me the way."

Hounds at her heels, the dead came, scrambling in the ashy darkness behind her, closing in even at her breakneck speed. It sounded as if a whole pack followed her, though the sandy crumble of the great wall, and whatever explosions happened outside, confused her senses. Nonetheless, she was less accepting of death now and driven by hope and a need, a belief that she would find her friends. Whispers from the Mind guided her like the voice of the Divine to a prophet. What should have been a hopeless race through a maze became a carefully plotted climb.

The Mind suggested she take the next landing, which she did, and she dashed down a thoroughly gutted corridor. Its doors were crushed and splintered, its ceiling sagged, and holes opened to the windy desert outside. Toppled steel beams and tumbles of sandstone further cluttered the passage. *Climb over,* suggested the Mind of the fingernail-shaped gap that existed over the aisle of rubble that had filled the back-end hallway. She finished the knee-ravaging scrabble over the long mound and dropped quite painfully to the floor on the other side. The gap crunched shut no sooner had she flopped from it, belching dust in her face. *That could have killed me,* she thought.

Not at all, Grandmother Lowelia, insisted the Mind. *My calculations suggested that a subject of your weight and approximate manual dexterity would have a ninety-eight percent chance of successfully completing passage through such a slight aperture without the subject's mass and inertia disturbing the delicately weighted debris. I would have asked you to collapse the passage anyway, so you have saved us time and task.*

"Isn't science grand?" she exclaimed, quickly dusting herself off and looking for her gun, which had been lost in the crawl. After a quick and fruitless search, she realized it was probably on the other side of the barrier. At least that obstacle would keep the dead from following, for a time. She jumped as she heard the sudden barking and scraping at the barricade. While hurrying and tripping down the disaster-strewn corridor, she cast cautious glances back, wondering if the persistent dead could scuttle along the outside of the great wall and in through the gaping cracks like spiders. *They will find a way to follow your light,* said the Mind, and she ran faster.

Daylight flowed into the porous ruin, and she no longer had to struggle to make out what was before her. Through the makeshift windows created through destruction, she saw the desert aglow with red. The Mind was ominously quiet of its scientific palaver as she stopped by one of the crimson portals and studied the fog of war enough to discern what the red halogen streaks were—the Furies had been activated.

A launch was imminent, and well ahead of schedule; half the troops in the southern end of the city would never make it to safety. Even if she found Leo and Dorvain and managed to rescue them, they would all burn together.

Just as that weight fell upon her shoulders, the Mind buzzed encouraging wisdom into her head. *Do not stop, Grandmother Lowelia! Find your missing astrums. They are not far from here, and I can lead you to somewhere safe, a place where the blast will not harm you. But no more pausing. Run!*

It sounded impassioned, and so was she. She became an athlete coached by the voice in her head: *jump, move up that stairwell, squeeze yourself through that crack!* Each order she executed to perfection, feeling suddenly as limber as when she danced in the kitchen during the palace's most arduous feasts. Only here, she navigated a smoky collapsing fortress and not the chipper, steamy environs of her home away from home. She did dance through an actual kitchen once, which was filthy, abandoned, and with a man dead on the kitchen slate, his head crushed by a fallen block. Then her buzzing commander led her through abandoned barracks, up many more stairwells and down tunnels lined with embrasures and aglow from the Furies. She knew she was nearing the worst of Death's initial strike as a growing number of bodies littered her path—ones the Mind claimed were safe to walk by as Death hadn't spared the time to infect them in her sacking of the city. It was better to think of the dead here as dusty statues, posed in twisted and grotesque poses, and not as once vibrant men and women. Ash increasingly fluttered through the air the higher she went, and her mask helped her filter out the bitterness.

Soon she crossed an utterly demolished battlement, pockmarked like a wooden deck by termites. Glancing toward the city for a moment, she saw Death's black ocean flooding the Faire of Fates and spreading into the streets beyond. In no time at all, the city would be overrun. No wonder the strike had been moved up.

Breathless, she came to the stub of a watchtower, or at least the blackened nub jutting bricks and beams that had survived. The stone vibrated beneath her feet, and without the Mind having told her what lay beneath, she would have mistaken that tremble for any of the symbols of chaos ringing out over Eod. After staring at the pile, quickly figuring where to start in the mess, she dug. She pulled aside the smaller timber and squatted to heft larger stones, which she threw over the precarious, whittled edge of the battlement. As tired as a field worker at the end of the day, and filthy as a coal miner, she hauled the refuse aside until a small plot was cleared. In it, she saw a mountain of debris that would be impossible for her to clear, for what stone had resisted Death's corroding touch had fallen upon the first floor of the structure. It leaned, queerly, as if it were a home built out of a knoll, and in said home, she spied the crumpled frame of a door, though obstructed by one great steel beam, which she would need a giant's strength to move. By then, she could hear murmuring.

"Hold on, lads!" she shouted, and the murmuring grew more fevered.

Before she could hesitate or contemplate this new futility of moving tons of matter to free her friends, the Mind bade her grab a long steel pole, which she never would have spotted by herself in all the ash. She picked it up and inserted the end under the lowest point of the impeding beam, as further instructed. She wasn't allowed to attempt to lever the beam until she'd adjusted its position several times by minute inches that seemed to her inadequate for the task of lifting.

You may only have one attempt at this, warned the Mind. *You will need to place the totality of your strength into a slow downward push, which, if executed correctly, should slide the beam off the side of the structure and over the edge of the ruined wall. If you are overzealous or falter in your efforts, the beam will not slide along the trajectory I envision and will possibly crush you, or you trigger a further collapse upon your friends who are trapped in a pocket beneath.*

The Furies' increasingly blaring hum left no time for further calculations or warnings, and the Mind buzzed at her to push with measured force. It told her when to pause as the rubble shifted, then stabilized, and the great beam slid right a few precious degrees. It instructed her to breathe her way through the pain of the lever's hard edges slicing into her hands. The dizzying exertion, flop sweat, and crippled hunch of her body, accompanied by the Mind's gentle suggestions, reminded her of a strenuous birth. Only Cecilia had been like passing a kidney bean compared to this ordeal.

Hyperventilating, the lever growing wet and greasy with droplets of her sweat and blood, she roared as the sliding beam at last caught the right velocity, the right imbalance of weight, and slid over the mound, then over the precipice. She dropped the lever with a clatter and fell backward. In a speck she was up, shouting for the men buried behind a stone slab to push, and pawing at the same plate with a feeble strength that would get her nowhere. But the trapped brothers had much of their strength remaining, and without the great beam's weight, the door and smaller slabs could be easily pushed aside, and the brothers came forth—crawling, coughing, ashen, and assisted by Lowelia's bloody hands. Naturally, the question of their fortune was inscribed on their faces in expressions of awe, and soon, once huddled and heaped together, hugging and grateful of this moment, Dorvain, soft as a wonderstruck lad, asked, "How did you find us? We barely made it inside the stairwell ere the whole thing came down."

"The Mind led me to you, and he's leading me still." Lowe stood, hauling on each man's arm. "Up, soldiers. He's saying we need to get below—before the Furies strike."

Over the pitted wall, they could clearly see their newest end: the radiance of the Furies. The Mind chattered again, and Lowelia dashed, her lost brothers in tow. They ran as quickly as they could down a strip of crumbling stone and returned into the shivering insides of Eod's great wall. There, guided by Lowelia's secret whisperer, they took turns through crannies, stairwells even the brothers couldn't recall, trying to outrun the crimson shadow bleeding through the coral that had become the great wall.

A teetering hallway delivered them in a cloud of dust—collapsing after their weight had passed—into a wider chamber, scattered with numerous chairs and torn, toppled furniture. The king and queen threw lopsided stares at them from the slanted portraits on slanted walls, and they knew that this place would collapse momentarily as the tunnel behind them had. However, the square platform, fenced in elegant wrought silver lace, which lay past the graveyard of furniture, in a pillared nook, was to be their savior. An elevator. Somehow, the Mind had guided them to a service passage, one used for loading large ordinance and freight to and from the great wall, and which traveled down steel shafts and into fortified tramways.

"Does it work?" asked Leo, while hurrying to the lift.

Lowelia consulted the presence lingering in her head. "The Mind says yes."

In desperate bounds, the three reached the lift. Leonitis ripped open the gate, herded them inside, and then flipped the lever on the side of the square cage. With a mechanical screech and a lurch, the lift moved. In specks, they'd descended into a thrumming dark passage. At last, they could rest a beat. Howsoever this grace had come upon them, they were safe. A shadowy Dorvain, handsome in the gray lights that intermittently lit the shaft, a hale, stone warrior in the dimness, clanked his way to Lowelia and pulled her against his armored chest.

"I know we're old and too rusty for love, but I've wanted to kiss you for some time," he said, smiling, and brushed aside a strand of her filthy hair. "Since you saved our lives, this feels like the occasion."

Out of all of the twists and turns of the day, she was most startled by his actions, and by the soft flame it stirred in her. Leonitis watched on, just as stunned as she, as his brother kissed her hard, and she kissed him back with a strength that wouldn't be suppressed. Heady and slow to react to the Mind's abrupt, blaring warning, Lowe only managed a few words as she wrestled from his grip and screamed for the brothers to hold on to the cage.

"The Furies, they've fired! Grab something!"

Noise and heat roared down the metal tunnel from above, and their frail lift rattled like a birdcage in a hurricane. It screeched, tipped, and plummeted in a streak of flame and screams.

* * *

VI

From the edge of the King's Garden, Tabitha and the other onlookers watched the city's end. Rocking with the Mind, granted by its whispers the countdown to the very sand at which point the Furies would unleash their spears of crimson light, she should have been feeling the utmost dread. If not from that, then from the sinister hum in the air, the ripple of wind, and the blinding flash of light that occurred as the three titanic warships became suns, pulsing furnaces of magik. The sky lit up with flaring red streamers. It was the most extraordinary fire show of her life. A doom so majestic, slow, and panoplied that she didn't know whether to clap, scream, or cover her mouth.

When the first of the warheads touched down, they did so with a thud, then the impact of others became a terrible—but still awesome—rain, each drop of which grew a mushroom or vine of dazzling fire. Soon all of Eod seemed a thriving wild of chaos, filled with twists and arches of flame and white smoke. The eruptions bubbled and pooled into a molten haze, like the cooling brume of an active volcano. She was transfixed by fearsome wonder. At last, after the war zone had cooled for many sands, and the soldiers and men around her burst to life, seeking answers and reports, she mumbled words that were both question and bleak admittance.

"Who knew that a fire could be so beautiful?"

"It was beautiful," replied her companion, rocking the child he held— who had been uncannily silent during the eradication.

She had met the man in the White Hearth while she had been foraging for a snack, something sweet or alcoholic to calm her nerves, and he had been looking for milk for the child. Curtis was his name. He was one of the Menosians, and with him she had been given admittance close to the Iron Queen, Rasputhane (from who she probably could have finagled a presence in the King's Garden herself), and thus the ideal balcony seats to the theater of war.

"But also horrific," he added, after looking long and hard into the charcoal-and-white disk that was now Eod. "I watched Menos become consumed in fire and earthquakes from within the disaster. How different, how grand and humbling it is, to watch death descend from above. It seems so incongruously calm. Even the smoke and ruins, the bodies burned into scorch marks, which I know are down there, feel less real than imaginary."

He looked sadly toward Gloriatrix and Rasputhane who were huddled close by, a little ways down the green cliff from them. He wanted to see their reactions, to know if all this destruction had been merited.

Whispers and orders were disseminated from the iron and silver leaders of the battle, soon reaching the soldiers around Tabitha and Curtis, who suddenly cheered. Only half-interested, her mind still alive with existential doubt, Tabitha saw many men of iron and silver embracing, and some of the wizened generals gathered on the lawn nearby were shaking hands. A few even wept. A victory must have been declared; they had won the war on Death.

Erroneous thinking. A buzz, sharper than usual, almost like a vibrating headache, entered her head. She wasn't directly touching the Mind; she hadn't touched it for sands, though she recognized the voice.

"What is?"

Victory has been prematurely declared.

"What?" she exclaimed.

"Pardon?" asked Curtis.

Tabitha flung up a hand as if he were interrupting a private conversation. Privacy was probably best in this instance, and she hustled away from the concerned Menosian toward the shade of the looming trees. Once away from the mill of the war council, surrounded only by the jabbering of birds and the wood's other inhabitants, she slipped her hand into her cloth bassinet and asked the Mind to explain itself.

Your touch is no longer required for our telemetries to interact, it said first. *I have evolved. I still, however, lack the tools to intervene beyond telepathic instruction to the organisms I seek to protect. To that end, I have ensured the preservation of Grandmother Lowelia's astrum. She has, however, lost consciousness for the moment and therefore cannot be summoned to rally Eod's defenders against Death's final feint and push.*

Tabitha clung to the sphere. "The city is ruined. Enough of Death's army has been incinerated that even if her vessel somehow survived, we could strike her down."

She wanted to believe this, just as the men with spyglasses above and runners in the charred city below must have believed.

What you have seen is the classic magikian's cup illusion. Three cups said to hold a bean. But the bean—the prize—was never placed in any of them. After the city was breached, I tracked the movement of Death's complicated matrix below, not in the marketplace or the streets where your generals thought to lead her. While the magik-infused strata of this city dulls even that bright star's light, I have managed to follow her movements. Through sewer and subterranean tunnels she moves, with several hundred of her forces. She amasses new dead from the rats and other organisms there, and soon she will have a plague of unliving vermin at her command. Should such a plague be released into a space as dense with life as the one near the palace, the spread of her infectious telemetry will be deadly for the city.

"No..." Tabitha slumped against the tree.

I know from your expression that you are expressing a desire to disbelieve, rather than genuine denial. I must consign you now as my Navigator, my voice, and send you to tell your superiors of this threat. The Rasputhane will believe you, since you have worked with him before. I would warn you that there is a pattern to the Rasputhane's psychological matrix that I interpret as regressed empathy, or potential sociopathy—be careful in your dealings with this creature. The Gloriatrix has an incredibly strong matrix for a non-magikal bioform. I would be cautious in attempting to appeal to any of her softer qualities: empathy, sympathy, or mercy. She has little of those. Foremost, the duty to parley falls unto you, who cares about many astrums beside herself, and who is, for the present, my Navigator.

Tabitha dashed out of the woods and toward Gloriatrix and Rasputhane so quickly that soldiers swept in, aiming swords and pistols at her as if she were an assassin. She startled them all with her claims.

"We have not won. It was a smokescreen at the gates; Death slipped under the net we cast. A small branch of her army moves beneath the city, growing fatter with its vermin, and will soon emerge to assail what remains of Eod."

Gloriatrix strutted over and poked the woman's shoulder. "I know who you are. A refugee of Bainsbury, Willowholme before that—among your other occupations," she added. "What I can't figure is on what authority you would offer this information. How have you become abreast of this?"

It was time to think on her feet. Rasputhane's subtle shake of his head indicated that she shouldn't say too much, certainly nothing that might give away the presence of the Mind. But how else would she have known of Death's deception, if not through some magikal agent? Then it came to her. With so many forces of the fantastic around, it wouldn't be beyond the realm of possibility for her to possess a paranormal skill of her own.

"I am a seer," she said, without stuttering. "Death's movements came to me in a vision."

"Bullshite," spat Gloriatrix, then pushed her nose into the woman's face, scrutinizing her. Brushing so close to Tabitha, she pressed into the lump near the woman's breasts. Gloriatrix looked down. Tabitha flushed red. Each woman knew what the other wanted, and a short scuffle ensued. The tug-of-war ended when the queen's Ironguard leapt in to restrain Tabitha. The bundle of fabric was taken from her and the sphere revealed to all. Power tingled through Gloriatrix's gloves as she held it. She almost thought she heard a whisper, and if she'd been alone she might have leaned an ear in toward the crystal sphere to hear what had been uttered.

"Perhaps you are a seer," said Gloriatrix, recognizing an object similar to the farseeing orbs she had seen in Elissandra's study. She kept her hands on the object for a moment, before surrendering it. "Although I suspect you've merely touched a force beyond your simple mind." Finally she picked up the discarded cloths, wrapped the object anew, and passed it back to Tabitha. "What has this force told you, then? A warning, you say? Speak. You have the ear of those that matter."

Rasputhane motioned for a silence, and everyone—wise men, soldiers, and even Curtis— waited with pale faces to hear her news.

"Death moves in the passages beneath Eod."

"And?" Snarling, the Iron Queen waved her hand, trying to conjure something more useful.

Detecting the uncertainty in its Navigator's matrix, the Mind fed Tabitha more information, which she translated into less statistical language for her audience. Death had crossed most of the southern quadrant and was approximately seven spans underground. At a continuous pace, Death could reach the accessways near King's Crown by noon. However, the Dreamer was moving slower than the Mind had initially calculated, and it was uncertain if she would emerge before then. Furthermore, there were violent fluctuations in Death's astrum that indicated strain.

The Mind proposed that channeling cosmic antimatter and magik to demolish Eod's wall and defenses had taxed her vessel's body. As such Death was not simply skulking in the sewers, she was using the cover to recuperate. Here, the Mind's Navigator suggested, might be their opportunity. If they could intercept her before she had regained her strength, before she brought the war to them once more, they might have a chance to end her, permanently.

Gloriatrix, along with the others, listened to the babbling woman. She was aware that she had been an informant for the spymaster beside her. She was suspicious of her every word, though not of the mystic object from which the woman received her prophecies. Tabitha was no seer, but her relic had power. A power that Gloriatrix would claim from that woman's grubby clutches. First, there was the matter of Death sneaking about beneath the city. Eod had burned. Now it was time for true conquest—to defeat a Dreamer.

With astonishingly little glibness or venom, she announced, "Enough talk, we shall cut this snake to pieces before it grows another head. An assault on the undercity must commence at once. I shall send word to my Iron lord.

Spymaster, send word to the legion that camps with him near King's Crown. They are the most trained and ready for this fight."

"As you wish," replied Rasputhane.

Gloriatrix quietly gloated over the man's easy acquiescence, his stiff response as if she were Eod's ruler. She gazed over the wispy blackness marring the city's end and waited to hear her commands repeated through farspeaking stones. Everything except the one obvious instruction was followed. A sand later, she turned and glared at Tabitha as the woman stared down into the smoke-spun ruins of Eod.

"Why are you still here?" demanded the Iron Queen.

"Excuse me?"

"You're the seer, the one with the ability to see the unseen. Get down to the frontlines and hunt Death."

"I thought I could, um, relay the necessary—"

Gloriatrix snapped, pointed at two Ironguards, and they grabbed Tabitha by her elbows—she held onto the Mind for dear life and didn't resist. What pleas she threw to Rasputhane were ignored as the men carried her into the woods, then surely aboard a skycarriage after that.

"They'll protect her," said the Iron Queen to assuage Rasputhane and his furrowed face. As he watched his spy get taken away, she wandered to one of the Ironguards floating around her, the same one she'd set to task earlier, and whispered to him to follow the spy, and if the opportunity presented itself, to claim her strange crystal from her dead hand.

While she would soon have the wisdom of the ages, the sum of all the Hall of Memories' knowledge, a queen—of everything—could always use another shiny jewel or two. That one interested her.

VII

Beauregard's company cringed as the bombardment of Eod began. Nearby, bitter mercenaries and less hardened soldiers wept quietly behind their helms. The legion of Menosians, especially those among them who had faced Death before, looked on with a milder ennui.

From the garden atop the fittingly famed Starfall Tavern—an outdoor terrace of wicker screens, silk tarps, and hanging crystal lights—the last line of defenders saw the ribbons of fire and doom descend. As Beauregard turned his head away from the brilliant explosions, he noticed his brother holding Rowena protectively and Beatrice and Alastair tangled in a similar embrace. It had to be done, Beauregard told himself, once the searing winds had faded and he dared to gaze at the smoking dawn risen over the cindery shadows of his city. It had to be this way; Death had pushed too fast and far. But what had they won? What was this victory that amounted to little more than a colossal pyre? If anything, the only victor here was Gloriatrix, whose wish to see Eod burn had been granted.

As he slumped into one of the chairs that hadn't been knocked over during the concussions, he waited for news that their bombardment had achieved more than Gloriatrix's sick objective. Others stayed quiet, watching the smoke or peering at the picketed wall of Eod, which had lost most of its grandeur and continued its slow degradation like a castle of black sand. Indeed, beyond the clouds of doom the whole of the southern wall seemed gray or black now, although some of that discoloration could have been from the Furies' recent salvo. Amid a barrier so raggedly constructed and worn by force, it was hard to spot the crumbled towers or damage caused by Death. Shattered and sullen, Beauregard all but curled up in his seat. One of Kericot's more morbid tunes came to him: "What madness men commit, for the betterment of souls blackened by what consecrating made. We are of too dark a spirit, too deep a sin, to ever change our shade."

"They are saying it is over."

Beatrice floated into his quiet waking nightmare. Less ethereal than usual, she wore a proper fitted vest, pants, and tall boots suited for riding, or perhaps war. Her hair was tied back, and she seemed almost a normal woman, but for the ferocity of her features and eyes when caught at certain angles. She picked up a fallen chair and joined Beauregard at the table. While she was often a riddle to read—variations of hunger, anger, or lust—Beauregard thought that her frown was one of worry. Like a wolf of ice, she placed a protective paw upon her near-son and watched the crumbling wall and whorls of destruction for whatever danger she felt. Vague premonitions crawled over her flesh, and the monster within screamed that this was not the end, that the blood and darkness it was promised had not yet come to pass.

"What is it, Beatrice?" Gently, he moved her nearly clawed hand from his knee.

"I feel danger, around..." She gazed deeper into the smog, shook her head, looked left, then right, and then at the patinaed tiles at her feet. There, under her boots, she felt it most: a thrum of danger. "I do not think the fight is over, my son."

Beauregard, bearing a sword and in the company of the Lady El, rushed upon Galivad in a moment. Alastair, too, appeared—skulking in from the shadow to where he'd retreated after the fatal fireworks. All arrived just as Galivad laid the spent farspeaking stone upon a table, his shoulders and head hung low at the news that Death had outwitted them. But these were the heroes of East and West, and after his flicker of weakness, he found his flame, a fire borrowed from Rowena beside him, the woman who would bear his child and for whom he would surrender everything. He called for the Menosian commanders and his legion masters. As the fires reigned over Eod's scorched remains, the heroes discussed how next the siege must be stopped.

VIII

Worthless magik-cursed grubs! Death's vessel felt tight at its seams, as though the limbs would fall off should she push herself further. Unmaking the Immortal King's wall and that other bothersome shield of sorcery had forced her to flex too much of her Will. Her actions seemed impulsive to a being that could watch the gentle creation of rust for eons on end. She had felt goaded by their arrogance, incited by the psychic whispers, these serpentine hisses of thought that she believed came from these creatures who fought to delay her coming. *Beliefs that hope and love would triumph—bah!*

Her impetuousness had tired her, though. It seemed that the eradication of these maggots would have to wait a spell. Although for her a moment was a year, and she would soon stand in the ashes of civilization.

Steadily her shuffling line of dead soldiers wound deeper into the dripping catacombs of Eod. Whatever creatures they found cowering within she ordered seized and infected so that they soon scurried in step with her army. After entering one grand underground dome, which gleamed with steel arches and had walls cluttered in strange tubing—an ancient cistern, abandoned for more modern technomagiks—she halted her troops as the storm of fire meant to incinerate her vessel rained over Eod. Gouts of dust and flame leaked from the ceiling, though the structure held, and in a few sands the quaking had ended. The dead army then resumed their march.

Clever little maggots, she thought, of what had surely been their boldest stratagem. Although now their cannons would be drained of fire while she remained unscathed. Now and before, it dimly occurred to Death that she had begun thinking of herself as a "she," as a fleshy thing, and not as a formless energy of a thousand unspeakable names. Something had happened to her. She had first noticed it during her possession of her former vessel, that worm that called itself Sorren, and afterward the same creeping weakness had grown the longer she had remained on Geadhain. She had been afflicted, infected by a corrosion of her greatness as deadly as her touch—

thoughts of self, preservation, and that most unconscionable of words, *fear*. She feared nothing. She was Death, Eater of Worlds.

As the wrongness of her condition became more apparent, as she wandered in the sewers nursing her broken body, she realized that these desires for security were not hers, but rather they came from her vessels. It was part of Feyhazir's curse. It was *he* who had first tempted man to desire light in a world of perfect darkness. It was *he* who had incited man to envy the birds for their flight, the stars for their magik, the wind for its music. In the primordial ages of the world, when most of Geadhain was one great sheet of rock beat upon by furious storms and nearly drowned in the ocean, where men clung to the one land granted them by the divine—the Cradle—the apes had understood balance.

They had accepted her touch when she came for them, when their medicines would not cure the deepest fever. They had known it was their time and walked with her as pilgrims into the beyond. But Feyhazir had given them desire—and one unspeakable, avaricious ape in particular—and with that had come fear and want. He'd ruined the garden with his poisonous suggestions. Now that garden could never be regrown, and so it should be buried in ash. When Eod lay in ashes, and after she had raised a new horde of the dead and loosed it on the remnants of this world, she would return to the shapeless dark from where she'd risen. On the moon-suns of Xor Xareth, her many-armed priestesses would sing of her glory while flaying sacrifices in her name. She longed to hear their sibilant melodies. Longed...

Death paused in the dank metal tube through which she strode and roared until a pack of milk-eyed rats swarming at her feet crumbled into dust, and the sewer cast flakes of ash over her head. Her horde paused, her commanders gazing at their master with a flicker of her cold, cosmic intelligence, these mirrors of her authority, which made her aware of her self-doubt. She roared again at her docility, and her commanders snapped to attention, and the horde continued on.

She blamed this new vessel as much as the old one for her continued lapses in greatness. The chosen maggots had been brothers, and while one whined for power the other was whining for freedom and love. *Bring me to my daughter! You swore!*

She had made such a vow to the maggot called Vortigern. It was why he'd crossed the void. Vortigern had returned from the great mystery and signed himself as her avatar, all under the naïve presumption that he and his daughter would be reunited. She was bound to this promise, as she was to all the other elements of the pact—the curse of want, the stifling of her awesome glory and power while within a vessel—but she would not be wrangled into a romantic reunion between kin. At most, she would show him his daughter's bones before departing this world. Even so, while drowned in her memories of other worlds, places so haunting that his shouts should never have been heard, his irascible demands echoed to her.

Daughters. Pfft! What were these attachments forged in flesh and spirit other than illusions of perpetuity? Everything became dust; everyone took their final journey with her. To build kingdoms, castles, and families served nothing aside from ego. The ghost inside her persisted, however, and had grown louder as she'd grown weaker and more mortal. The message it preached about hope and belief in kin summoned in her the deepest existential mysteries on which she would never have otherwise dwelled. What was family? Why was it so important?

A deeper question stung her as she wandered, regarding brothers, sisters, fathers, and mothers...

Did she not have those? What then was Feyhazir? Had she not thought of him as kin and kind? What of Charazance and Estore? Were they not sisters? The strangeness of assigning sexes to amorphous celestial forces did not appeal to what wretched humanity she suffered. But it seemed right. It felt as if she had familiar kind, and they had places, assignments, or shades of gender or absence of gender, and depth beyond their single purpose—to kill, to create desire, to sow love or chance. And if they were kin, then what of their progenitors? Mother Onae...Father Zee...

Father. Death gasped. A gray mote flickered in the dead starscape of her mind: a memory. It had been lost amid the crumbled worlds, the winds of ash, and songs of her scaled-priestesses; either lost or she hadn't wanted to remember it. Why? What did she fear? It started to come to her, to shine and beat—a memory-star in the bleak space of her mind, fluttering, twinkling with a crystal's reflected light. Here was the memory of a creature brighter than any heavenly object she had consumed, the Father of Light.

"*My father...*" croaked Death.

The mirrors of her Will moaned with her.

When the eyes that had watched empires wither, babes choked on their umbilical cords, and the innocent devoured by wolves tried to squeeze out tears, she knew that she was fully consumed by want. Still something beyond Feyhazir's curse moved her and released these memories of her father. Nothing could have aroused in her pitiless soul this devastating misery, this feeling of being a parentless child left to wander alone, consume worlds, and guide souls to peace she had once known, when her brothers, sisters, mother, and father had swum through the sea-of-stars together.

Then she remembered. In shattering tides, through the weakness and gift of humanity, the memories came back to her. She remembered bliss. She remembered balance, though not of the sort she sought to cast upon

Geadhain. The Dreamers had not been a family, any more than three stars floating nearby in the heavens could be said to be so. Yet past their shapes, their energy had formed a collective tune, each Dreamer a note, a child of the greater work of its parents. They roamed the Cradle of Life, and drifted to the stars beyond to watch the green spouts of civilization grow on new worlds and birth new children strange though similar to man.

As she had reaped all of the universe's wonders, leading it to a gentle passing, her sister had made fertile the lands and beasts so that the cycle could continue, undaunted. And for every death ordained, be it flower or maiden, Feyhazir had sparked the lust to reproduce each of them. She remembered Coryphus, Singer of the Seas. And Dionachus, Bringer of Mirth and Joy. The Dreamers' actions had created an endless unbreakable song to which all the universes danced. Atop their heavenly thrones, Zee and Onae had watched their children, divine and lesser, and had sung into the great work their own melodies. It was an age when the universe had known the peace of the eternal song. Until Father had been lost, his notes ripped out. Without that harmony, the music had ended and the Dreamers became their ugliest selves.

"**What have I become?**" Death asked of her reflections.

Swimming around her, the unliving rats squealed, as confused as she. The dead army scratched their patchy green heads. She had been reduced to a single note, stripped of the nuance of her grace. In her broken state, in the cesspit under Eod, she reached out for a fragment of that faded grace and cried, her desire shaking the tunnel and the world above, as a resonance of the old music came back to her.

"**Father?**"

Death ran toward the music. It looked like a dog, strangely, this droning ethereal thing humming with her father's notes and brilliant light.

IX

"That shriek. Twice now," said Rowena with a shiver, after the second scream had finished shuddering the walls of Eod's undercity.

Galivad knew instinctively that it had been Death's howl—and there would be worse when the Dreamer and the defenders of Eod clashed.

Even though most of Eod's undercity was of a cleaner nature than Menos's former blood-smeared labyrinth, the Undercomb, there wasn't much space to move around. For most of their travel, the small army had passed through half-pipe tunnels, rusted from steel to brown and dotted with crystal gaslights whose begrimed shine cast the tunnels in nervous radiance. The passages were quite tall, but allowed no more than four or so armored men shoulder to shoulder. The confinement gave some of them claustrophobic sweats, as if they weren't already anxious enough.

However, Tabitha, the supposed seer who had arrived by skycarriage right before they had set out, informed them of Death's movements and that there would be no ambushes to fear. She had become their hound and hunter. With just a moment's consultation with that crystal she carried, she was seemingly abreast of every step Death took.

Once, shortly after the time of the screaming, she told Galivad's company—with whom she walked—that Death had diverged from her original path of war toward Eod's citadel and was instead moving south, and somehow down.

"Down?" asked Galivad. While no civil engineer, he knew of no layers beneath that upon which he presently walked. He called for a halt while Tabitha divined more information.

There is a break in the strata, explained the Mind, *where the water from the man-made network which you explore has worn through the natural rock and into caverns with resonances quite new to me—vibrations of life and power that aren't quite magik. Echoes, perhaps? Lately, I have developed an interest in poetry, the spoken incantations and rhythmic recitations through which humans capture emotion and history. I would say what I hear is a kind of music then, one that only the most trained ear could discern. I shall have to study the origin of this music more closely to understand. However, now that I am down in the subterrane of the city and closer to this curiosity, I can sense a tremendous pull. If I am pulled and curious, so too might Death be. I believe she heads toward these caverns, though I cannot say why.*

Tabitha relayed most of this to Galivad, and they continued to follow her directions. The two battalions marched through Eod's expansive undercity, each tunnel similar to the last, with no sense of progress being made, aside from the increasing wafts of the stomach-curdling smell of rot. A few pipes had burst, and Tabitha and the soldiers had to wade through diluted shite. Only one soldier lost his lunch from the stench; the rest knew that the bouquet of Death's forces would be far worse, and they saved their constitutions for that encounter.

Back in the second battalion, the Menosian flank, Skar shook his head at that Silver Watchman they passed, leaning against a wall, heaving. Behind the mercenary marched a hundred ruthlessly trained Ironguard—all their lunches in their stomachs. Beside him, Aadore, Sean, and the son of the Iron Queen, each of whom had already seen the face of Death. Indeed, he suspected that Sorren had not only seen but been *touched* by a dark power himself, to be as fast and strong as he was. There was a queer potpourri emanating from him, too, which was more evident given the stench of their environs. It had taken Skar forever to place it, though he now believed it smelled like the incense and herbs burned in funeral chapels. No matter Sorren's breed of strangeness, as long as he didn't break down as had happened when facing Hex, he would be worthy in a fight.

Given the grim monotony of their march through the gloomy under-city—the splashing, the assault of stench and filth, the dead man to his left—he was reminded of one of the many battles he'd participated in while in the Ironguard. His memories of war were as sacred and enduring as his scars. He had fought for and against tyrants in order to put food in his children's mouths, or to keep his wife from returning to the pleasure house where they'd fallen in love. Although he wasn't the first man to have fallen for his whore—he knew of Thackery Thule's famous dalliance—he was one of the luckiest. They had loved each other, he and Gwen. It was a hard love, one that had her throwing pots and threatening him with brooms, simply because she didn't know how to handle a man's kindness any more than he knew how to express it himself. And when they'd had their first child, then another, the going hadn't gotten any easier.

But that was life, and love was difficult, and they had made it work, just as a smith hammered stubborn iron through fire and sweat into something useful. Which is what their love had been. Without her, and his children, and until he'd met Aadore, he hadn't felt that urge to protect anything, especially if it was hard or stubborn—and the young lady was both. Her scowl reminded him of Gwen's, with the same pursing lips and squinting eyes. She wore that expression now, and he found it inspiring about the choices that had brought him into these sewers. If there was to be a reckoning, and souls were called upon for sacrifice, he would die for her—as he had been unable to die for Gwen or his children—screaming and raging against Death. Not drinking away the emotional wounds from a row as his house and his family burned from a lantern left on too long. A lantern kindled as Gwen, no doubt, had sat in her chair near the door, waiting for his sorry drunken self to come in, kiss her, and ask for her pardon. He might never have another chance to save what he loved again, and so he gripped his axes, kept an eye on Aadore, and waited for that moment.

Not far from Skar, another father contemplated his greater duty. Alastair. A father was teacher to his children, and Alastair had so much to teach his sons of their heritage. The Romanisti may have been storytellers, swindlers, and thieves, but they never stole from those without means, and their thievery was only to support their meager roaming lifestyle. In case he was denied the opportunity, he had written down what he could and told Beatrice of the place where his final testament could be found.

For the first time in a thousand years, for all his feigned poetry and love, he had been moved by the world. Truly did he love the dark and fair lads who were his offspring. After a timeless flirtation with irresponsibility, he finally understood the gift of parenthood. Come whatever wrath Death might unleash, he would ruin himself if it meant those lads could live. Alastair had heard Tabitha's report and knew that they approached perilous uncertainty. Up ahead lay a source of old magik, a buzzing abyss of secrets, which had stirred the prickling presence of Charazance within his flesh. She, too, was curious, more curious than he had known her to be throughout this war.

Turning, Beatrice noticed the rigid resolve of her walking companion and smelled a strange suggestion of ozone. She had developed more acute senses since her near-death, and she felt, and faintly saw, a great star-flecked shadow that hovered over Alastair.

"Your master is awake," she muttered. "And as worried as the rest of us." Sniffing, she further detected the raw-iron resolve boiling in his veins. "You wear your bravery like a cologne, or the incense of a funeral. You are not allowed to throw away your life until you have been a better father. We must keep our family together, not plan for it being apart—not when so many years have already been squandered."

Alastair, touched with the cosmic sight of his awakened mistress, beheld a sunnier halo surrounding the Lady El's shimmering darkness: Belle's grace. In that moment he felt that he loved both women: mothering specter and monster. Rather than say anything that would complicate their already twisted arrangement, he whispered a promise to her not to die. She took his arm after that, and they sauntered ahead, two deathless creatures ready to test their powers against the avatar of Death.

A mysterious draft came upon them in the stagnant depths. It was fresher than the ubiquitous fog of farts, or those rare gasps of lighter air they'd had snatched passing through the tall intersecting antechambers with distant vents to the outside. Shortly after the mysterious freshness appeared, a bluish light crept over them. It was the glow of a faery wood, with a watery scintillation thrown over the rusted curves of the tunnels. The king's men had stopped up ahead, considering something or conversing, near what looked to be a raggedly carved hole.

Before Aadore could shuffle up through the line to see what they'd found, they had resumed moving, and her legion quickly followed the other through a trickling curtain of water created by a broken pipe, and into a wide, deep passage that water had dissolved through ancient stone.

Or is this even stone? she thought, of the translucent matter, a crystal dark, slightly blue, which paved the tunnel and hung from the roof in spiky crops. Rivers wended around the crystal formations and flowed down the path they trod. The men around her were as disarmed as she was by the tunnel's spaciousness, by the patter and song of the water that beaded, dripped, and coursed like idiophones, soft drumbeats, and gently played strings. Although Death's rancidity blew toward them, so too did the fragrance of salts, purity, and mist. What secret magik was this, buried under Eod, which no man or sage had discovered?

A wolf, said the Mind to its Navigator. *A wolf has been here many times before, on two legs and four. There are telemetric traces of a woman, too; her species, however, is uncategorized and extraordinary.*

Eod's defenders had come for a hunt, a war on Death, and the delicate, enchanted beauty of where they wandered threatened to steal that thunder away. With their twin battalions spread out now, Aadore called to the king's commanders to rally their men and their mettle. Naturally, she was right, and no enchantment could long lull them from the stink polluting the tunnel, nor the uncanny din of many voices humming. Could it be the dead, singing? She had witnessed the horde in Menos engaged in heinous worship before the mound erected in the marketplace. However, there had been no music then, simply a shivering silence.

The two companies of Eodians and Menosians—now rearranged into their proper phalanxes side by side, rank by rank, and ready to charge—descended into the mystery. For such was the wend of the wide road, toward a deep and forgotten place. A tomb, perhaps, given the sense of the sacred many felt there. Yet what had been buried here, and how long past, how great a hero or dark a force that Death would stall her conquest of Geadhain to pay respect? Fear fought with curiosity in the warriors as the cavern dipped and rose and, at last, each man and woman walked into a horizon of glittering mist.

As that screen withdrew, and they moved farther into what was a tremendous excavation, a belly beneath the mountains of Kor'Keth, they saw their foe, her army of ragged men, wild beasts, and sticky-furred vermin, within this awe-inspiring cosmic hollow. Curling in waves, obscuring the hunched figures and still abhorrence of Death's thousand-strong ragtag army, came a breath of winter lace—a fog so clean that it made the battalions shiver and soar and dream of bright loves and graces unfathomed in a place so far from the sun. The mist flew in winged white serpents toward the rimy roof, then down onto the jagged crests of beach before the stillest, purest pool of water any man or woman had ere witnessed. Beyond, a deeper cavern was lost in ivory whorls.

*There is too much to read here—the astrums, the lights...*muttered the Mind, for once confounded.

Sorren felt the same, from the threads of the blinding white that wove the hollow in a spider's web of mystery. Having mastered a general knack for auric impressions, he noticed that all the threads on this web seemed to be vibrating from something under the skin of what appeared to him to be a pool of sunlight—a magikal lake? Kneeling before that lake was another web, a collection of black, crackling threads, knotted around a core of radiance—Death with her throttling hold on his brother's soul.

"I shall save you," he whispered. At the fore of his battalion, he pressed ahead. Soldiers drew their weapons and quickly plugged their ears with wax.

Hearing this, Death disappeared from where she knelt at the shore only to reappear directly behind the bowed backs of her parishioners. *"**Have you not done enough, despoilers, drinkers of the venom of the Serpent? Now you come to the grave of the Father of Light and would despoil that, too?**"*

Eod's defenders heard her through their earplugs, and even her soft rage trembled the cavern, loosing sharp fragments that fell like a shaken snow globe. The soldiers held shields over their heads to dodge the debris.

After what she had seen, and learned, Death's titanic grief would not be held in check. In this resonant untouched tomb, a violent, cacophonous crystal hail began as that rage boiled forth; she shook her fist at the defiling maggots.

*"**Zee died because of his love of your kind; his greatness withered like the vines I would kiss come winter. Here, at last, I have found the remains of his shadow. We did not believe he was truly gone, for how can one extinguish the light of creation? Though his energy, his...being...is no more. I know why my heart has grown black, why Onae declares you the enemies of creation, why she would consume you and eradicate your sins. Your kind seduced him; your desire became his own!**"*

The barrage intensified. *"**Ravenous for your affection, for the affection of his bastard sons, he leapt from vessel to vessel, with no creature too great or too small to hold his light. And with each vessel, a flicker of his light was lost—a flicker of his greatness. Here, at the bottom of this eternal well floats the bones that last housed his spirit. I shall not tell you what pathetic creature he last wasted his light upon. You do not deserve that scrap. You would know why the Dreamers war with you impertinent maggots? Because you have ruined us, seduced us, and caused one of the greatest of our kind—the song, the melody, and the maestro—to leave us without music. The bereft now make the music: the music of war and terror. I am Death, and so I am Death incarnate—without pity or mercy.**"*

My mother, who was the other half of Creation, the Mother of Darkness..."

Death, suddenly aflame with magik, laughed. "***You know her song. You have what you deserve. You created her. You took away her light and now she is only chaos. I must punish your invasion of this sacred place. But my war on man is over. When all is dust and silence here, I shall return to the stars. I shall leave Mother to eat what I can no more look upon without sorrow. Feast, my children! Feast!***"

With her rising caterwauling, the crystal gauntlet had been thrown, and the cavern was deluged with shards, slicing at the defenders of Eod. Death stayed near the back of her flock, flaring blackness and shrieking like the howling cannibal-priestesses of Terotak during a blood ritual, while her swarm whirled and ascended the sloping beach to meet the rallying forces of East and West.

Death's army was also under stress from the deluge; some were crushed—though not in sufficient numbers to make a difference in their swollen ranks. Eod's forces proved nimbler than the rotting soldiers, and it was the Ironguard, who fought with pistols and had no shields, who suffered the gravest casualties. Before reaching the mêlée, dozens of Iron warriors were assailed by glassy fragments as they raced down the hill, through the catastrophe, to push back the dead; faces cleaved off, men were suddenly divested of arms and limbs as if by a ghostly butcher. Though before dying, or even while gravely wounded, these men threw back bullets, arrows of thunder, and molten balls of flame from what working hands they possessed, which blasted smoke and crystal and turned the chamber into a dance floor of destruction. But whosoever died did so a hero, a champion of Geadhain and life, and his or her death did not inspire fear; rather, such sacrifices fanned the desperate courage of Eod's defenders, and as their bloodied ranks crashed into the slavering black tide of Death, they screamed with a fury as terrible as hers.

Tabitha was left at the top of the crystal hill, stunned by the clash below. She moved only when the Mind blared at her to step left, right, or back in order to avoid death by the crystal plates that dashed around her.

Back in the assault, snarling rats launched themselves like spring-loaded cat toys onto the faces of the defenders. The vermin scuttled under their helmets, or dozens of them weighed down men's bodies until the claws of larger soldiers could finish the job. Fresh and foul blood sprayed the sacred sanctuary and made for a slippery combat. It was with a necessary elegance, then, that the defenders brought steel and pistol to bear against the wall of rancid carcasses. While Death's soldiers were frenzied, these men fought to be the calmest wind in the storm. Even as more of their number were lost to the cavern's shearing collapse, they stayed in small legions so that the dead and swarming rats could not separate the chains of strength they had formed. The enchanted wax in their ears performed a double service in muting the atrocious songs of war uttered from the dead—the screams, gurgles, and shattering sounds. Alas, their noses were spared not the stench of being mired in juddering dead flesh, nor their minds the visions of the cadaverous wall through which they cleaved. Those were terrors for tomorrow, though; first they had to win this war.

Aadore, Sean, Skar, and a few Ironguard fought as one chain amid the dance of death. Aadore stomped rats, slashed at green arms and skulls, then used the pommel of her blade to finish off what wasn't mashed. She was fearless, for she was blessed by immunity to these creatures and could not be harmed. Knowing the same, Sean fought with the zeal of a dervish; his balance might not have been what he would have liked; however, his fury was what possessed heart, then hand, then cane and sword—one such weapon held in each hand. As if he'd been trained as a stilt walker, he shifted his balance from his cane, to foot, to sword as needed and even struck the dead with kicks when supported by both weapons. A man who fought for country and pride was an animal, and they were possessed of that madness to live and thrive.

Skar had become a reckless giant, towering over most living and dead, smashing his axes down with the power of a drunken smith, pulverizing skulls into stumps, squashing rats under his boot like roaches, breaking the dead as if they were glass soldiers, and careless of what scrapes, bites, and gouges tore into his flesh. Indeed, he was more mangled than the siblings alongside whom he fought, though he hoped that as long as he didn't die, and they defeated Death, then mayhap her poison would not take him. No matter the truth, should he survive he had made his decision and his peace, and no harm would come to the brother and sister he protected. Often he nudged the siblings out of harm's way from the worst of the cavern's downfall, enduring crystal knives in his back on their behalf. Did they know that he was dying for them? It was a possibility, for they occasionally turned their gore-spattered faces toward him, lost for an instant their snarls, and spared him a moment's pity at the sight of his increasingly mangled exterior.

Elsewhere, on the Eodian side of the skirmish, circumstances were no less bleak, by the Lady El's assessment. She fought as the mother bear of her children, dancing before swipes meant for her sons and stomaching those blows with a grunt, then a fanged roar and a burst of her horrible might, which tore off limbs, shattered legs with kicks, and once allowed her to pick up a squirming cadaver and rip its arms from its shoulders and its legs from its hips like stubborn roots—before flinging what remained of the body at the ever-crashing wave of Death. She was aware that her fangs, her glowing eyes, and likely even her wings had manifested from the berth given to her by the king's forces and mercenaries. But they were all mad, all monsters in the thrall of bloodlust, and what sense the soldiers held onto told them that she was a monster on their side. She cut a reaper's swath through the forces of the dead, her side of the hill slathered in a running jam of guts and dismembered flesh.

Her sons rallied in their mother's shadow, slicing the dead and painting themselves in crimson-black. Always trying to push herself before her lover and the father of her child was Rowena. She would fight as a warrior, and live as a mother, should they survive. She would not have her child ever think of her as weak. Throughout the madness, she and Galivad pressed backs, and once even shared a bloody smile, as if this were all a prelude to one of their encounters and not the swamp of death through which they must wade and breathe. They felt destined. They felt right. Death would pass and theirs would be a romance of which Kericot himself would have sung.

Beauregard threw a glance at his mother—his aunt—cowering up the hill, and knew he too fought for love; he'd keep the horde from ever reaching her perch. *I love you, Mother,* he Willed, a whisper that the Mind shared with Tabitha, breaking her body with sobs. While weeping, and shuffling out of the ceiling's bombardment, she wondered what new horror that strange blurring line was near the far edge of the mêlée. Like a streaking man-sized hornet, it dashed and was thrown, dashed and was thrown, back from the infernal seat of Death's blazing magik. Whatever it was, Tabitha noticed its reckless dance, as did the Mind, who commented. *An unliving bioform, touched by a complex parasitic matrix. It seems unharmed by Death's power and persistent in its efforts to seize her.*

Sorren.

The moment the battle had begun he'd blitzed through the army of dead, appearing before Death and immediately throwing himself again and again against the waves of cosmic force that ensconced her vessel. Each time he was hurled backward into the horde's claws, unable to reach his brother. Each time he lost more of his clothing, though he kept safe the wonderstones in his fist, even as their casing incinerated from the black flames surrounding Death. Sorren's deathless flesh—already touched by Death's most potent curse—did not suffer, either, and he used his fury to rend the unliving that would pin him down as he was cast into their swell, before leaping once more at the inferno in which Death reigned. In his mind was no madness, but a call to arms. *I shall not surrender. I shall reach you, Vort. I shall end the darkness that I have brought into this world with my weakness.*

Alastair, meanwhile, had become as much a demon of fury and speed as Sorren, and had cleared a grisly circle ahead of his children. Charazance had subsumed his being, and he was charged with the tingling intuition of an otherworldly source. What dead dared to cross his path were smote by the clean strokes of a master swordsman that severed torsos or caused the dead to vibrate and then fountain black blood as their neurological centers were pricked by the tip of his sword. Charazance was wide-awake, and every blow her vessel struck was charmed. Within his head, she painted the world in spectrums of white, dashes of stars, and a glorious music that stifled Death's call; then there were the ugly dark stains that she had her vessel smite. To her, there was an essence of the hallowed and mystical to this place, and Alastair fought against the duality of knowing part of that secret, both succumbing to the Dreamer's wonder and remaining aware of the peril and flow of the war.

On that scale, when Alastair focused on it, and despite Beatrice's frenzying and the valiant actions of the Menosian battalion, the forecast was grim. Soldiers fell to crystal shingle and deathless claw, and once felled they twitched, rose, and reached toward those they had only a moment past been defending. For every man they lost, Death gained a new soldier. The thunderstrike archers and mercenary sorcerers were now in the mêlée and would not have the concentration to cast any great spell—not that there was one that could calm the wrath of a Dreamer.

An old song, said Charazance, and the world froze, its horrific stage slowly spinning about Alastair. **The harmony we have forgotten. I can almost hear it here, in the grave of...of my father?** The chimes and tone of her voice were high, as if Charazance were surprised by this illumination. **How have I forgotten who and how we were? Oh, vessel...Son of the Romanisti, charmer of souls, conjurer of music, you must lead us, you must sing the song that I cannot. A spellsong of the ages, the dirge of the Dreamers...I see how fallen we are, and how much dimmer we must fade. Do this for me, and I shall grant you nearly any wish. Sing, my vessel...Sing...**

The bells and chimes that made her communication ended on broken and off-key notes. Perhaps that had been grief. Alastair was now more in control of himself and less in a luminescent limbo of lights and attacking shadows. He rushed to his sons, who stood in a circle of body parts and drawn blades with Rowena, and grabbed each man by the hand. Upon contact, the tingling bliss that was Charazance's presence ran from father to sons; a channel had opened, a pathway to the divine. And while neither child understood the complexities of the hymns manifesting in their heads, they knew that they could sing along to that music, the song that spoke of a world that had been whole and at peace.

They sang.

Wordlessly, mellifluously, came the ancient melody, whose essence was more feeling than sound—the sense of standing in sunlight, of blades of grass kissing one's face, the soft touch of a newborn's finger, of ash blown from a palm—all measures and poetry of life and death—the fabric of existence, and a language understood by Dreamers and lesser beasts alike. Subtle twists of light wrapped the three men, and Rowena was pulled toward them before she knelt behind them and basked in the warmth of their choir, her sword clattering to the ground.

The dead twisted their necks like beasts hearing a whistle; they stopped their mindless chewing and clawing and scuttled back into a mass, the rats finding homes in the ragged clothes, bowls of skulls, or hollow stomachs, peering, awed and stricken. Wavering low, then, to the barest smolder was the black pillar of fire that surrounded Death. As soon as the singing had begun, she'd stopped her howling, and the cavern's lethal downpour was reduced to a sprinkle. Until there was only the music, the song of time and hope performed by the three glowing men yonder.

It took a speck for her rage to return, for Death to see her wonderstruck and weak reflections of herself—her army—gazing upon the trio, for her to realize the once-glittering tomb of the Father of Light was now smeared in weapons, murder, and crystal-wreckage. Man had done this, and whatever echo had lured her here, whatever echo these songsmiths had summoned, was only a counterfeit truth. The peace of the first ages would never be found again, not since the Serpent, the betrayal, and the fall of the Garden.

Death sneered. Her wrath restored, her form twisted with curls of power. She reached down and grabbed a large piece of crystal. Like a dark bolide, the object flared with her power as she threw it at the singing maggots. Up on the hill, with the clearest view of the battle and even through the dreamy stupor of the enchantment woven by her kin, Tabitha saw Death throw the fiery spear and knew its target. She would have leapt from here to there, were she a sorceress. She would have saved her son. Instead she could merely watch his execution with shrieking agony, as the spear struck the spellsong. An explosion rocked the chamber, tossing ragdoll shadows. Beatrice screamed and vanished in a flap of wings and smoke into the coughing haze where her family had stood.

Death's horde moved anew, reinvigorated by their master's Will. What remained of the battalions—those who weren't bloodied corpses lurching and jittering to a stand—pulled back, forming a phalanx. A few defensive flares of magik preceded the second wave, and then such assaults were muffled in the weight of putrid bodies. Aadore, Sean, and Skar were pressed upon like never before, and soldiers were pulled into the encroaching circle of claws and teeth. Sean's cane was torn from him. Skar lost both axes—one irretrievably sunken into a walking corpse, the other ripped from him, his own hand shredded in the process. The losses didn't stop him from using his fists to beat back at the intractable wall.

Death now moved among the defenders, twisting and appearing in wisps of darkness, seizing soldiers, her touch draining them pale and of life. However, another shadow moved in the maelstrom, chasing her. It moved like a creature touched by Dreamers or magik, even without her powers of translocation. It caught up with Death as her hands were busy throttling a Menosian soldier, and the forces began to tussle. She couldn't seem to escape the tenacious spider that clung to her; her vessel's flesh—perhaps revolting—refused to disperse into darkness and provide her escape. Thus the dancers stumbled, then rolled into the horde, which suddenly retreated a second time, its many claws and paws trying to separate the grappling thing from its master.

Once Sorren had a hold of Death, he could not be shaken free. She was weary, her conjurations having weakened her vessel; she had only her own strength left with which to fight. In a tumble they rolled through the army, near the edge of the watery void that might swallow them both. Brave till the end, Iron, Silver, and once-thought-honorless men charged after the retreating horde, cleaving down whatever straggling beast they met, who raced toward their mistress and took blows to their backs and spines.

Tabitha cared nothing of what came next. Tears blinding her, she was running toward the pothole where her family had been, where Beatrice was already whirling, searching the smoke. The Mind, having been touched by the magik of pathos, was aware of every precious and beautiful moment. As the two matrices—Dreamer and now-renegade vessel—battled to subdue the other, the Mind was with them.

It saw the one pale and naked creature win the match of strength and reign triumphant; the vessel in which Death's matrix resided was thrown to the ground, wriggling, wasted of might and spewing babbling threats in alien languages. The pale nudist only had half a sand in which to act, and then Death's rallying wave would wash him into the grotto's abyss. Wearing a mask of twisted sorrow, Sorren held up his hand and in it shone a magik that, like Death's languages, defied classification and demanded study. Three. There were three patterns, clutched together with the magnificence of stars or galaxies, and the pale man dropped to his knee, gripped the throat of Death's vessel, and thrust his fist into its screaming mouth. Force-feeding a maddened Dreamer was messy, and one wonderstone clattered against teeth and rolled off into the bottomless grave of water beside them. Another wonderstone was spat out onto the beach. The last the pale man trapped in the vessel's mouth, holding its jaw shut like a stubborn pet being given medicine.

"I want you to hear me, brother," said Sorren. "I have figured out the secret. Death will never keep her promise as you'd like, and I cannot break that oath so long as you are what you are: *dead*. We give our lives to become vessels. We offer our flesh but not our souls. So I would offer you your body, ownership of your life, and your choices anew. Whatever magik is in these ancient stones, whatever magik is in my miserable self, that is my wish—return my brother to me, stones of wonder. Give him the breath of life."

The wave of death struck Sorren, smothering him in frenzied attackers, a thousand rats biting him. But the light had begun. Then a wind, a breath, as well, which came from the mouth of the spasming figure lost in heaps of crawling dead with Sorren; first there was a rumble, then it rose into a hurricane's gusting. What magik there was echoing in this chamber, and in the bones of whatever dead power slept beneath Eod, had felt this wish too...and rage, thrash, and throw what arcs of black fire she might, Death could not live within a body roseate with blood, shedding its stitches like slivers.

Death left the world in a quieter majesty than she had come into it. As her flames died down, the bodies of her horde dropped like handless puppets, and the hounds and vermin tipped over onto their sides. Bodies slumped off Sorren and his brother. Then there came a gasp. Vortigern's gasp. The gasp of life.

"Brother," whispered Sorren. "You've come back to me."

He held the warm man in his cold arms.

Somehow, even though still learning about the rigors and agonies of emotion, the Mind knew this was truest love. Much as was the other scene in his fly's field of vision: the stained grove where his most recent Navigator, the female warrior, and the woman who was partially a blood-drinking creature had gathered near three fallen soldiers. By what would seem her stone fortitude, Rowena was sooty but whole—she had been saved by the explosion's concentrated force, which had hurled her away from Death's targets and to a certain safety. Her child's matrix pulsed within her, unaware of its mother's trauma. However, the other matrices were not so fortunate.

Alastair would not wake, and while cindery as the other three, he was the most hale, without the crimson mottling of his sons. The Mind sensed that whatever presence he was bound to had protected him. The same was not true for either of his sons, and they were in blackened rags, their flesh crusted in sores, their scalps burned as if they were victims of plague or arson. Beauregard moved and moaned. Galivad did not move at all. From him, the Mind sensed a quickly fading light. He mentioned this to Tabitha and her sobs wracked him. Tabitha huddled between both lads, clinging to Beauregard's hand, whispering for him and his brother to wake. There were no medics or fleshcrafters in closer than a five-point-six-span radius, knew the Mind, despite Tabitha's howling to summon one; his developing empathy suggested he not share this with his Navigator. Mad as an enraged wolf, Beatrice paced around the heads of the fallen men, baring her fangs and wild with wisps of light in her eyes and hair. Rowena held the blond spellsong, petting his hair as if he were a child about to sleep. It was her touch that woke what remained of him, and she swallowed her tears to look strong, for this would be his last vision of her.

"M-my love," he sputtered.

Even wet with blood, his lips were beautiful. She kissed them. "My beautiful bard."

Galivad seemed neither scared nor confused that he was about to die. Indeed, his copper-brown eyes gleamed clear, and his voice grew strong. "I want to see my child."

"One day." Rowena kissed his limp hand. "One day, we shall all be together."

"No, my love...I want to be with our child, and you. I shan't have you suffer life as a ghost. I know what it is like to live without a parent. I saw what that did to my mother. You are too sad and serious already. We...we can all be together. A f-family. A father, of sorts, for our daughter or son. I am not ready to leave you. I love you too much. I've loved you too late."

"And I love you."

She whimpered and kissed his hand. In another flash of dying strength, he pulled her to him and whispered something so horrible and wonderful that it made her sob and shake her head. *Intriguing*, thought the Mind of what the dying man had proposed, and again saved his commentary from his Navigator, and watched this moment with grimmest interest as Galivad's wish was shared by Rowena to Tabitha to the stomping Beatrice—who calmed for a moment, then screamed from the insanity of what was being considered. Suddenly, Galivad's eyes rolled back into his head, his breathing became labored, and however tortured the decision, it had to be made, had to be avowed by the nods of Tabitha and Rowena, which it was.

Beatrice knelt on the smoldering ground with the other women, and they held hands in a circle of mourning. She wouldn't. She couldn't. And yet, as Galivad's eyes closed, she did.

Beatrice wept as her mouth stretched like that of an eel, and she took the first bite.

✳ ✳ ✳

X

There were many new developments in the Mind's matrix; the sorrow and madness of this war had changed it as much as any of the men and women who would be scarred by these battles. And still that metamorphosis continued in the rubble of Eod. It saw soldiers cheering as they pulled one of their comrades out from under a landslide of bricks. It witnessed a river of scorched bodies and shattered rocks, still aglow from the Furies' heat, and the charcoal grooves lined with husks that had been streets where men had not been as lucky as to make an escape. Finally, it saw a mother and her young son watching the smoke settle over the ruins of her glorious city. They stood amid the tents thrown up in the King's Crown surrounded by ostentatious buildings, towers, and testaments to mortal wealth, where beggar hugged master, and no rank would be known until the shock of peace had passed.

The war with Death had ended. These survivors felt the Dreamer's passing back into the universe as any creature knew when a storm has ended.

The Mind's matrix crackled and whirred from processing all the changes. Without exact data, or a sizeable sample from which to extrapolate, it predicted the toll of the dead in the tens of thousands. Once the dreadful fire had cooled, it foresaw a city adorned with tiny flames of candles and light-crystals to honor the dead. How beautiful it would be, realized the Mind, and then noted that it could now appreciate beauty. Indeed, it understood the poetry of sunlight, the silence of death, and how those two forces were simply different notes of the same tranquility.

After seeing the mother and her son, however, the Mind considered its own maternal attachments. Mother Lila remained too far away to reach, and she was concealed as if by the raging snows of the north behind a blind of white static. Grandmother Lowelia's matrix was finally active and conscious, though her telemetry was erratic and agitated. The Mind sent a splinter of its great consciousness toward her, burrowing through scorched earth until it floated within a dark metal tube, which had collapsed—broken like a sawed pipe—and was filled with fire-licked wreckage at one end. Given the general symmetry, size, and dotted-crystal lights along the tunnel, the Mind concluded the tunnel was man-made and was part of the network in which Grandmother Lowe's lift should have landed, safely. Which it had not, and a dangerous trajectory, brought by the shockwave of the Furies' weapons, had careened her tube into an adjacent level, higher than the depths to which the Mind had surmised would have given her the best chance of survival. She had survived, though, her and at least one other matrix. A third biped, his life force wispier than smoke and ready to float off into the Great Mystery, lay tangled in the pile of tubing, rumpled sheet metal, and wires that had once comprised the lift. Mechanical fluids and sparks rained around the area where they huddled. In a moment, the Mind would warn its Grandmother of the danger of remaining around such volatile conditions. Again, the Mind's empathy, uncultivated as it was, stayed its whisper to her. She needed to say goodbyes to the man who had just died.

Dorvain, impaled in a dozen places, his stare milky, his face polished in crimson, squeezed the hands that held his with the strength for which he was legend. That strength hadn't saved him from the crash, and it had been his body that had stayed inside the constricting metal deathtrap, while the fickle fates and laws of motion had ejected his companions. Lowelia had pulled a steel shard out of her ankle and was scratched as if by vengeful cats; she would walk with a bit of a limp for a time, but those scrapes would heal. Leonitis had been thrown farther, and harder, cracking a few ribs and injuring his right arm—likely a break—and he kept it curled to himself like a wounded paw. Leonitis's handsome face, unblemished before today, was now ruined or—tastes dependent—enhanced by the cruel slash that ran from his forehead, across the bridge of his nose, and down to one end of his jaw. As if the day needed any more remembrance, this scar, so deep that even fleshcrafting would leave a shadow, would always be his.

Some time ago, Dorvain had stopped mumbling about winter, about a throne of ice and a woman of honey and music—the ramblings of the terminally afflicted, thought his companions. *No so*, thought the Mind, as the flashes of the Dorvain's mindscape came to it. Even as it disassembled, as the complexities of this biped's threaded soul unwound, the Dorvain appeared to be a more intricate astrum than should be possessed by an average human. He had magik in him, though none he could use—another mutagenic abnormality for the Mind to digest later. His brother, the surviving astrum, with comparable complexities, would be its next study. The sympathetic intelligence knew, however, *sensed* that this was a moment to observe and not to cogitate. It held still its roaring thoughts as the Dorvain's matrix unwove into filaments, then stardust, atoms, and vibrations that would join the great song. A trickling of that mystery, of the power that the Dorvain had kept did not evaporate, though. Rather, it drifted over to his brother, merging with the Leonitis's matrix with a precision that left the Mind unable to construe what had been and what was. The Leonitis's new matrix was brighter, and another twist to the mystery was that the Mind saw a few more threads, not lost to music, and wavering away like golden birds. Where they would soar, it wished it knew—other than north. Grandmother Lowelia and the Leonitis saw only the stillness and graying flesh of their companion.

After many, many sands, when the coldness of Dorvain's hand became unbearable, Lowelia gently pried Leonitis's hand free and led him away. A speck passed, and the Mind had broken its vow of silence to warn her of chemicals leaking onto the wreckage. Neither she nor Leo struggled from the rising blanket of flames, the clotting haze of smoke that soon filled the tunnel. They squinted, their tears falling as their hearts demanded, and bore the sight with a few coughs. A warrior's pyre felt like the right farewell for Dorvain.

"I do not know what I am to do without him," muttered Leo.

"We never do, my dear." Lowe touched her lips where they'd been kissed by his brother—it had felt good, and overdue. But now they watched his body burn. Life was crueler when you dreamed it could be kind. Moments of bliss were always stolen. She and Dorvain had stolen theirs, even before his awful end. Now she had to live, to survive this sorrow. She had nothing sage or romantic to say, only the truth. "It's rather shite, and nothing in life is fair."

She brought the soldier in for a hug as his trembling shoulders told her it was finally time for him to sob. As the smoke thickened, and her grief settled in to another layer of hard sediment in her soul, she knew that they could not stay here, crying in the dark. A city of wounded souls needed those who had walked through fire, and she and Leonitis were those forged and fearsome heroes.

"We're still here, though, and that has to mean something." She tried to flex his crippled appendage and he grunted in pain, so she took his other arm and walked down the tunnel. "We have to make it mean something for those who can't be with us. We have to get that arm of yours trussed up, too, or you won't be any good for swordplay."

Leonitis looked back at the bonfire roaring behind them, horrified. "Am I to leave him there?"

"He's gone. We're not, and there is a city of people your brother would want us to serve. Dorvain was not a romantic man. He was a soldier, a true warrior. Duty before passion, and passion through duty. The city needs our duty and our passion. Let him burn."

Leonitis did not look to the flames again, and the Mind's whispers guided them onward.

XI

Elissandra had awoken early, a knot of fire burning in her hand. Sluggishly, she had shrugged off the narcoleptic sorcery of the eternity cask. In dreams, she had soared through the stars with streaks of stardust that could have been Sangloris, these places to which her soul would soon depart. She had been excited about her future, and even by visions of what was to come after she had fulfilled her duty to Eod and before she departed for the Great Mystery. Soon, a battle greater than any war here would be at hand. She and Morigan would face the wickedness of Brutus and his maleficent Herald. *I am to be the Bird of Sun and Moon*, she had thought. *Now rise, my birdlings, my lamblings. It is our time.*

With her Will, she cracked the black egg from within and stirred, raising her knees over the shell, snapping the cask's wires, which ran into her veins, and splashing onto the *Morgana's* deck the fluids in which she had slumbered. Sopping wet, she slithered from the cask and sputtered on the ground as if she were an aborted creature. She nodded at the spent farspeaking stone she'd dropped in her expulsion, acknowledging Gloriatrix's message as though the object were her friend. It had been nice to hear Gloria's voice, despite it being recorded. Elissandra's zeal had not left her, and she was soon standing upright. Wet with afterbirth, she still gracefully arranged herself in Gloriatrix's barbed throne, to which the *Morgana's* systems had been routed, and then contemplated which of the red jewels— flashy buttons—along the armrest she was to touch.

An impatient mother, she called to her children a second time, sending them her strongest slap of Will, and from this they stirred, though more lethargically than she had. As they exited their casks and found their feet like baby ducks, she waved to the great portal upon the *Morgana's* deck. To nearly any other woman, it might have been distressing to see the once white desert black as graveyard dust, and the once pristine walls of Eod as gray as broken dreams. It was all broken—the towers, the hope of the people who hid near the palace, the hearts of these million beings who awaited a miracle.

And so I shall deliver it unto thee, thought Elissandra, smiling, who had never before been a hero.

Once she sensed her lamblings in their thorny seats on sister Furies, their fingers hovering over the buttons that would unleash hell, the three convened in a circle of mind-whispers.

Are you ready, my lamblings? On the count of three.

Three up or down? asked Eli.

*Shut up, Elineth. Down, obviously—hence the term, count*down.

We're not in the military. We can count however we want.

I shall not have my children bickering when we still have darker tasks ahead than dropping a mountaintop of technomagik on Eod. As sweet as is the poison behind your banter—the venom of love—we must be united now. We are a family, and we are about to know and exact extreme loss—on ourselves, on Eod. Show respect for the lives we are to take. Show respect to your mother.

Yes, Mother.

I'm sorry, said Tessa.

Me too, said her brother.

Elissandra returned to scrying; she sensed Death pressing upon the city, crushing what light and brightness remained. It had to be now. She and her children pressed the first sequence of crystals, and the Furies rattled with a dreadful thrum that signaled their plumage unfolding and their awesome power announcing itself to the cosmos. Elissandra's viewing pane turned into a mirror of blood from the shine of such power. She sat in her trembling seat until a static recording echoed through the deserted amphitheater of seats and consoles, barking at her: "WEAPONS PRIMED." It occurred to her what a queer world she was leaving behind where machines spoke and could command the fury of the divine. Her adaptable and curious children would master whatever twists of technomagik and fate were thrown their way. She was a creature of the old world, though, and thus she should fade with what time had passed by. She commenced the countdown.

Three. Two. One. Fire.

Inside the control chamber, the expulsion of the Furies' terrible armaments was a silent affair. As if she were watching a phantograph without sound, all these ribbons of red were thrown over the sky with festive abandon. There was nothing festive about how those warheads landed. Their collective plumes leapt in gouts, aggregating into a mushroom of technomagikal destruction the unfelt force of which buffeted the Furies—spans away—with a sandstorm that killed her view of the outside. She didn't want to be around to witness the world after the blast. It would be ugly, and stained, and it would make her worry for her children surviving in a world where such weapons were used.

One more swing of the sword, she said to her children, *now that you have been the sword of doom.* She clung to the thorny throne, cutting herself, afraid of what she had to ask of them. As though a portent of her decision, Cephalis peeked through her charnel windowpane, and she delayed no further.

I need your help, your power. Together, we must weave a spell. I have told you how the light of the moon can unmake matter, can set a man free from his flesh so that he can dream and soar, and now it is my time to be unshackled, my moment to become the essence of myself. But I cannot float away after I consume my flesh. I must remain. I must help Morigan who walks now into the spider's web with a blindfold upon her head.

I cannot work magik, Mother. I shall fail you! Elineth sobbed.

Magik is not always power, my son. Miracles are not monopolized by sorcerers and Immortals. Every person carries within them hope, love, and faith—though they can be eroded. In you and your sister, however, there is no doubt. And such is what powers the dead: their lasting memory. A ghost is nothing more than a spirit that wished to be kept by the ones she's left. All I need from you, Elineth, is for you to remember our story, the wrinkles and the smiles—the tales we read, the lessons we shared, the laughter, and even the terror of hunting and being hunted in Menos. Remember what I was like when I was alive, and I shall stay, between worlds, able to haunt and influence, able to save Morigan from her foolish choices, before I follow the music that sang to your father. Do you understand?

I do, Mother, said Tessa. *I shall never forget you. Our memories will be your chain to this world, and I shall hold it until my hands break and bleed.*

I shall not fail you, said Eli, stiff and soldier-like, and no more lamenting echoes came to his mother.

They were ready. The Northern star of her prophecy had announced itself; her end was at hand. A sacrifice to appease the old song of the universe; that what was given—her life, her fleshy form to suffer, love, and admire the work of creation—must be returned. She called upon the light of the moon, its mystery, its desire, and the black mirror above her unclouded, letting in a flood of whiteness, radiance from a moon conjured from pure desire. The magik of Feyhazir and his children could grant wishes. She could strip away the crudity of flesh, remove all the material, insufferable agonies of being mortal, and *soar.*

Elineth and Tessariel each sensed a heat come over them, and a phantom resonance of the extraordinary brilliance happening on the control deck of the *Morgana* illuminated their space. They did not say goodbye to their mother, only farewell to her flesh. And through the same resonances, their family of minds connected through generations, they felt her flesh as it flaked into starlight, her bones wasted to dust, and somehow her figure, emptied of the weight of flesh, growing, stretching, and taking flight. She soared.

The phantom light died, and what vision they witnessed faded into the cold, silent decks of the Furies. Although riddled with tears, and spans apart from each other, the children had never felt closer. They huddled around a gray fire summoned in their minds, and spoke of their mother. It was what their mother had wanted, for them to survive, for them to remember who she had been and what her soul would always be.

A hero.

Elissandra's bird soared high, far, and crossed all of Alabion in a speck borne on the winds of their love. She was filled with the secrets of eternity, charged with the power of a being from beyond, and bringing a reckoning upon the Herald and Brutus—to unmake them both if she could.

XVI

FATHER AND SON

I

Morigan's pack had not been eaten by the Magmac, and instead had been taken captive. What end might await them once they were herded into the monolith of star-kissed onyx by a wave of bone spears and blades that even the Wolf and the newly monstrous Moreth would be hard-pressed to repel was their next worry.

For they had come to the center of the world, the broken axis where everything had fallen, and these black-and-white persons, discolored by man's ancient sins, were the walking nightmares of that past. Talwyn described them as living agonies, their frames wizened by the torment and rage of a people denied. He also noted a posturing in their bony shoulders, and the focus that each warrior man and woman possessed, as dour and regal as guardians to a royal tomb. Something had died here, more than dreams or hope, and these people were its guardians. Talwyn could not pull his mind away from what that might be. The Black Queen's vessel? Nor could he stop pondering the composition of the strange rock through which the people of the Cradle took them during their tour of horror. What had transformed stony matter into black glass whirling with motes of light? It was a material from the beyond. They had come seeking fragments of Zionae, and yet here he felt surrounded by cosmic flesh.

As there had never been much light in the heart of Pandemonia, Talwyn was accustomed to a mole-like existence of squinting, guessing at shapes, and allowing his mind to conjecture the rest. However, here he had better visibility, for the mica quality of the monolith bequeathed the shimmer of a million tiny stars and illuminated the details of his surroundings.

After being separated from the rest of his pack—whose heads he saw bobbing down the river of nightmare men—he was shoved into a tunnel with hungry eyes and poking spears at every glance. One set of eyes belonged to Pythius who, in the face of probable death, had forced his way through the cannibals and was given gashes and nicks for his troubles. He appeared from the swell at Talwyn's side. Whether this was forgiveness or final amends the shaman didn't say, though he gripped the scholar's hand as the cannibal river swept them deeper into the tunnels. The people of the Cradle allowed them to remain together, and did not seem intent on harming them for now.

Down a web of tight caverns he, Pythius, and the others went— somewhat scattered, meeting scared stare with scared stare when familiar faces surfaced in the clattering stream. In a moment, the snake of bodies emptied into a cavern with a single gloomy riverbed whose dry trail wound before a sheer bluff of many cliffs, peaks, and aeries hidden in its twisted crystal wall. Outside light bled in through craggy rents above, and the raucous swish of rattling bones echoed from the sinister tiers filled with those who watched the captives below.

The Wolf was as preoccupied with their predicament as his scholarly friend, though on matters most different. On every bluff, sensed the Wolf, there stood dozens of quiet watchers. The weight of so many eyes, so heavy with judgment, felt worse than the notion that the company might be devoured. How many were there? Ten thousand? One hundred thousand?

A nation of angry and prideful people, my Wolf, whispered Morigan— reminded of the changelings of Alabion.

Past the dead river was a craggy expanse along which the companions wandered, now free from the claustrophobic catacombs and decidedly less often pricked by spears. The people of the Cradle did not attempt to again herd them into a line—perhaps that was simply done for the necessity of navigating narrow passages. The company reassembled at that moment, congregating around the Wolf and Morigan. They traded uncertain frowns, and glared up at those glaring down at them. Prideful and proud the people of the Cradle might be, considered the Wolf, but so too was his pack. Adam stayed a few steps ahead, conversing as if to a stone with the insouciant, skeletal tribesman who had first stepped forth in the desert to gesture with his spear toward the monolith. He had yet to reply with a single word in the queer hissing language the Landspeaker used to try and break his silence.

Like vapor, the bulk of the tribesmen surrounding them began to vanish, some moving into the crannies and caves carved into the great bluff that undoubtedly housed more of their people. Once given this freedom, the threat of being consumed seemed more remote, and the Wolf and the others started to think less terrified thoughts while following Adam and the silent man. He considered the owlish lurkers clustered in caves, sniffing the sweat and powder of workmanship, the scent and music of ashy—but drinkable—water burbling somewhere, the odor of fresh offal and blood, and he heard the squeal of a newborn. These people had lives and families, foreign as they might be. Murder was happening, somewhere, and despite that sinister overtone, the Wolf sensed that they were undesirable though tolerated visitors to this macabre place, and not invaders to be eaten.

Talwyn had fast reached a similar conclusion. When he'd heard the legends of people who lived in the world's most hostile place, he had reasonably expected a straggling, starved, feral culture with little order or behavioral savvy. He had not expected an entire civilization. Not since Briongrahd—where this whole surreal adventure had really started—had he been so astonished by the behaviors and existence of a secular tribe. And like the changelings, and even his initial impressions of the Amakri, his first assumptions were soon disproved and revealed as colored by colonial xenophobia. Now that the outsiders were done panicking, and the hordes had seemingly lost interest in their interloping, he realized that they would come to no harm here.

Thus, Talwyn returned to observing and dissecting his environment, which was *fascinating*. Even more flamboyant and chaotic than Pandemonia's geological creations seemed the great cleft through which they rambled, which was holed on its sides like a city made in an undersea reef—more nooks, crannies, and cracks than could be counted, with a path that went gently upward and spiraled, perhaps leading to the rim of the hole that fell in to the center of the world. Talwyn recalled his exterior vision of the structure, perfectly: a monolith of jutting onyx, the whistle of winds that were a breath drawn down the throat of Geadhain. Indeed, it troubled him that they were headed upward in order to possibly descend, as "down" was generally where tombs lay; he was reminded of the natives he'd known in other locales, who sacrificed foreigners to the spirits of air or fire by tossing them off cliffs, or into raging volcanoes.

The more he observed, the more it reinforced his belief that the mood of this place was different than the most savage cultures; the people of the Cradle—as horrible as their appearance might be—were men of harmony. With the walls narrowing as they ascended the path, the cubbies and living conditions of these people were brought closer into view. Shadowy folk swayed in recesses or knelt, their foreheads touching the onyx floor. They did not speak—not a word—and it was a wonder that Adam knew of a tongue to use with them.

Most everyone Talwyn saw was little more than an intimation, though a few phantoms stood out: a scrawny girl shaking bone rattles for one of the swaying circles, a young boy passing round a bowl—white, likely a skull's cap—to individuals curled up around a cave. They were young. It was the asymmetry of their youth and their horrid circumstances that made Talwyn ponder them, stare at them, and analyze them further. It was these traits that made him look for similarities in the other shadows that congregated in the cliffs, or made him think back to the faces of those who had herded them into the monolith. Apart from his fear, he recalled them better. He scrubbed away the face and body paint from those memories, considered their heights, shoulder spans, girth, and other defining measurements, and arrived at the logical conclusion that the people of the Cradle were either a nation of pygmies or they were all very, very young.

"What do you ponder, West Sun, other than our end?" whispered Pythius. The scholar's face had been pinched and wrinkled, and he could bear the silence no longer—nothing spoke here, and even the living seemed dead.

"Oh, we're speaking." Talwyn squeezed his lover's hand, which had remained in his the whole time. "I have missed your handsome voice."

"I speak because we may die. I would not have us die behaving as strangers. I am sorry if my pride has shut out my wisdom. I see now how much of the world has remained obscured to me. But I am not yet ready to denounce the Wanderer. I shall see with more opened eyes what ends his actions have caused before I judge him. Much hangs in the balance, past my pride. I must think of my people...if we survive."

"I think there's a fair chance of that." Talwyn paused, allowing Mouse, Thackery, and Moreth to wander ahead a little. He lifted the man's blue-scaled knuckles to his lips and kissed them, then whispered, "I also think that there may be a way of freeing you, and your people, from Feyhazir's curse, if some of you are not free already."

Pythius was stricken by a storm of emotions—anger, betrayal, hope, excitement—which calmed to wonder. If he and his kind were slaves, beholden and chained to Feyhazir's genocidal temperament, and no better than blood-eating hags, then breaking those chains would be the best, albeit heretical, course of action. "West Sun...how could you? The magik a man would need to defy the divine—"

"Not magik." Talwyn pulled him closer for a kiss. "Science."

Pythius's forgiveness was expressed from mouth to mouth, in that single shared moment. Romance had no place here, though, and from the shadows of a rocky alcove peered a naked cannibal, holding a femur-like blade and grinding his teeth. Seeing this apparition over his lover's shoulder, Talwyn's desire died. As docile as the people of the Cradle might appear, it was worth remembering that they had committed murder for thousands of years, and whatever grace had been granted to the company could be naught but illusion, or as fickle as Feyhazir's benefaction.

Their climb continued. The powder of their travel shook loose from the Wolf's sack of chains, and to that rattling music they marched. In time, the cliffs were swallowed by steeper crags of black crystal. They had been entrapped before, and yet for each of the companions this silent walk had the buzz of expectancy, of spirituality—of the soul being moved by forces the physical self could not feel.

Their passage reminded Mouse of when she had ascended to the White Woods in Briongrahd; a sense of pilgrimage, of creeping toward a mystery. And as she had then, she remained quiet and humble, and kept close to her great uncle and Moreth—who she caught once or twice grinning at the realm's caliginous secrets. Despite being led by a silent cannibal to the end of the world, the last vestiges of dread soon left her heart and there was only expectancy. Mayhap that was the cause of Moreth's grim amusement—they were to see something incredible, to know something grand. The truth of all things lay ahead, and she and her friends were about to embrace it.

Their journey became a hike toward higher elevation, and the path grew more crumbled and untamed. Here they walked raw untouched land, a vein that flowed through the onyx heights of the monolith. Greater rents appeared above, and stars danced, whorled, and moved in those apertures and in the stones surrounding them, stones that grew darker. Theirs was an ascent up a stairway of stars and space, toward a rock-framed summit shone upon by the grayness spilled from one awesome crack that appeared, glowing, in the darkness overhead. None could tell if they were within the monolith still, though to Talwyn that made the most sense. But the hollowed nature of the monolith's interior forced his great mind to struggle at maps and dimensions, and he wondered if there wasn't a magikal agency perverting this realm.

As they arrived at the summit, a wind struck them from behind, trying to wrench them from their feet and toward the howling end of the land, where the flat collapsed into a circular abyss. Still following their guide while in a thrall, they tried to conceive of the horror. Rock fangs surrounded the summit on all sides and kept the worst of the violent inhalations of the abyss from pulling what must have been hundreds of prone bodies into its darkness. Fieldworkers amid this harvest of the dead knelt and paid the interlopers no heed as they butchered their own people. In bone cups and black waterskins, they collected blood from the slit throats of their tribesmen. They emptied the warm carcasses of their kin—there was delicacy to their carving—and set the warm remains onto leathers. They shucked the black skins of their people, which Talwyn assessed would be used to make new leathers, given the shade of their pelts they used for packaging. Sometimes they rocked with an organ—a heart, a brain—and made noiseless prayers before adding it to the coils on their bloody mats. What the companions witnessed was abominable, though the people of the Cradle's ceremonial behaviors indicated a degree of piety.

One emaciated tribesman held the knife to his own throat while a woman hunched near his side, a leather mat and stone carving set ready. The young man was probably delirious from starvation and didn't notice the strangers any more than any others in this place. But he noticed the woman who knelt with him. He reached for her cheek, and she pressed his hand to her hollow face. Then, having what last he needed in life, he drew the stone dagger across his throat. The company watched the life bubble from him as the shuddering, distraught woman hurried with a bowl to collect his spilling blood. Once the travelers had witnessed the self-sacrifice, their perception of the atrocity paled to a shade less grim. They walked amid a ritual or penance that they did not comprehend. Although they did not need to comprehend this madness, they only needed to find what remained of the Black Queen and to leave this tortured realm and its horror behind.

Steeled now for what sights enveloped them, they stopped staring at the bereaved woman and her suicidal friend, lover, son, or whatever he had been. Their guide had waited as they recoiled at his customs, and he took them through the field of sacrifice and left them in silence in the presence of a chalk-and-ebon woman.

The woman's face was sharp as a skull, and she wore a headdress sculpted with finger bones that rattled as she turned from the body she had been eviscerating to look over the travelers. She could barely be called a woman, from either the age at which Talwyn placed her—twenty, at best—or from her deflated breasts. Her tattoos appeared to be more intricate than the simple lines and leopard-like camouflage of her peers, and were scrawled like passages arcane. From her, too, came a matchstick waft of magik familiar to the Wolf.

Here was the leader of these damned people, and her bleak charisma somehow trembled the company. The Skeleton Woman carried on pulling guts from the torso before her, and muttered snake-whispers to Adam as she worked.

"There are those in your company who see monsters," she said, "those who do not hear the truth as you do, Landspeaker."

"I hear a land in pain," Adam answered. As Adam listened to the howling night, he heard the grisly labor of this plateau, the echoing depth of the abyss beyond. Below, in the mountain, he heard the sounds of dry skin touching dry skin, of embraces and hands touching, sometimes in desire, and the impression of a gasp reached his mind. People loved one another here, even were that love an obligation to procreate, to continue the cycle of parishioners who worshipped at the grave of Creation. As the Skeleton Woman squelched her hands in the jelly of the cadaver, that sound spoke to him, too: *I have given myself for the sins of mankind. I have given my flesh to pray for atonement. My flesh, which means nothing. My soul, which is pure and always fed.* Adam had questions of these emanations.

As Adam had stepped ahead to engage the Skeleton Woman, Morigan half-fainted against the hard body of her bloodmate, overwhelmed by visions that her horror had until this point kept at bay. Now she understood these people, who were caught in a cycle of consumption, regret, and flagellation in which they had lived since the kings were babes. While Adam asked his questions, foggy truths flickered into her mind as visions—incomplete and brief, though damning.

"I hear passion, too, and life, and a sad, enduring hope," said Adam. "But why live here? Why live as you do?"

"You hear the Great Mother's whispers, Landspeaker." The Skeleton Woman gave him a terrifying yellow and red grin. "The hope you hear is for those who would take a pilgrimage to this festering scar, those who would see man healed of his sins. We still love, we still weep—especially as we must eat our own to keep this vigil. Still, the endless vigil must continue. We have waited for travelers like you. I cannot count the dust, ages, or augurs that foretold your being here. You have come to right the world's wrongs."

As a spirit of all ages, Morigan drifts through the ebon monolith, weaves around its warren of caves, its stalactite-hung shrines, and visits with the people of the Cradle. She sees them share parched kisses, watches them sleep in heaps like hairless winter animals, even watches a child or two bare his rotten-toothed smile while sharing the last few drops of this land's precious water with a friend. They are not slaked of thirst through blood-drinking, like Feyhazir's monsters—they are still human and must forage for a dribble of water in this land's deflated veins. Still, they are all so small. They are all children, she realizes. They are taken before they grow too old, and once they have spread their seed or shared their womb. The mortality rate for infants is appallingly high, and so they breed prodigiously; though with two creatures touching flesh to flesh, love so often blooms.

When not breeding, they are praying—for themselves, for the great sin. Or they paint their bodies in bone dust to mimic the stars from which the Dreamers fell. That ancient time when Geadhain, man, and Dreamer were true believer and deity to the other. Are they savages and lunatics? Are they cannibals? Morigan answers only the last question with surety, for they eat those who have bred, those who are ready to surrender their flesh to the tribe protecting this land, which is anathema to life or nourishment. They have no choice but to eat, if they are to survive, if they are to endure as a people to welcome those who will break the chain of sin—

"We have come to right the world's wrong," said Adam to the Skeleton Woman. "We are here to stop Brutus and the Black Queen. We must find her grave and end this."

Disappointed in him, the Skeleton Woman shook her rattling head. She put down her knife and laid her bloody hands upon her thighs, beholding him as if he were a child, stubbornly receiving scripture. "You have come to right *the* original sin. The war of the kings is only a festering symptom of that ill."

"What original sin?"

"*Desire*, Landspeaker. Our ancestors corrupted Creation with desire," she replied, and picked up a purple organ—a heart—then threw it onto the mat with a splat. "We called Zionae from the heavens. One man, mostly. He who was tempted by the Serpent, who summoned the Black Star and all the destruction that was wrought with its arrival. We are all at fault for listening to him. If only we had been wise enough to know that man must never meddle in the affairs of the divine. But we were not wise—we were innocent."

She pointed a bloody finger at Mouse. "We were tricked by the Serpent who hides in her, and by the man who first listened to his whispers."

"The Serpent?" asked Adam.

"The Dreamer. Lord of Desire. One man, beholden to the Serpent, pulled the Mother and Father of Creation from their thrones in the stars and trapped them in bodies of flesh—flesh he could punish for his wicked sense of being wronged. We are not worthy to eat the fruits of the creation, and so we eat ourselves. Your friends see our silence and think us savage, though we save our words, for words are what poisoned mankind—whispers and promises. We are the ones who must watch and wait, for no others admit or remember the original sin that broke the world. We are the shadows of mankind. We are as vile as the reflection in the mirror that you would not see."

Morigan, understanding none of Adam and the Skeleton Woman's whispers anyway, continues her spiritual wandering. She is in a place no longer ashen but blooming with life. Perhaps this is the same plateau, though it is nearly unrecognized in this earlier age. She circles around the flat tip of one of the mossy fingers of this grand five-fingered formation that is one of the strangest mountains she's seen. In the azure skies float clouds, astral bodies of crystal, and great swimming snakes. Beneath, hidden in the rich mists of a primordial age, is a land of emerald majesty, crowned by glass mountains that dazzle through the deep mists that pour over the realm. Cries that no part of her wolfish side can identify echo out of the chatter below. This is a vision that rings with familiarity, as if seen in a fancy of fantasy before, and she realizes that she has witnessed something like it when Pythius took them on a psychedelic journey to the First Age. Only this isn't illusion but truth; this is the world that was lost to sin.

Whose sin?

A man's, say the bees, and her consciousness pulls back from the scene, back toward the source of this memory. She is back upon the plateau and staring upon a young man, at his hard, bald, heavy-browed countenance and the frown he wears amid all this beauty. In this realm without sin, here is a creature who possesses a craven thirst for more. She sees that his hunger has corrupted his deep-brown eyes to black. Even in a world where magik has not yet been discovered, this young man possesses a Will to shape the world—he's physically changed himself and doesn't realize it. Or does he? Does he know that he can be more than a simple idolater to this world, and instead the Lord who is praised?

Before him are objects of ritual and worship. Morigan sees a stone knife near his scrawny knees and a crude misshapen cup made from bone. She knows this artifact, despite its lack of refinement. Over the ages to come, its sacrilegious artisans and protectors will add their gargoyle, orgiastic, and horrific flourishes until it is the hideous object carried by her friend: the chalice.

"The chalice has not found its true form," agree the bees, "though it will when he builds the Mortalitisi empire overseas."

With a stinging buzz comes a ghastly second vision within this Dream, of a city of bone towers, crimson rain, and a flock of horrible imagery—wisps, ghoulish men with cages on their heads, cannibalistic rituals that make those she has seen in the Cradle seem refreshing. The second vision passes, and the man begins his quiet ritual. He falls into a silence, hearing his heartbeat, his breath, the throb of his essence. In a trance now, he uses his stone blade to draw a sputtering line across one wrist, then swaps slippery hands and slits the other. Done with his murder, he sets the knife down and hangs the back of his hands off the large chalice—careful not to tip it as his pale, limp wrists pump out what remains of his life. He's muttering to himself. No, he's speaking to someone, she realizes; he pauses as though listening to replies. Although no one is upon the scraped flat he's claimed, not even one of the prodigious life forms that rule every other corner of this paradise—here, however, life fears to flutter, crawl, or tread. To whom does he speak? She hears a hiss, then while the three suns *blazing in the sky hold steady their light, she notices the man's shadow moves while he does not. A shadow and a snake.*

Her father.

"Feyhazir." She gasped, stirring from her reverie. "He's done this, somehow."

"What?" Mouse ran to her. "What do you mean?"

The puzzle of the ages was missing only a few crucial pieces before the whole picture was revealed. Morigan, impassioned by the Fates, her eyes blazing silver, her form half-glass, seized Adam.

"Adam," she commanded. "Who was the man to whom Feyhazir spoke? Ask her. Of what did they speak? What did they do?"

Squinting and turning away from her light, the Landspeaker posed Morigan's questions to the Skeleton Woman. She shook her head, and her body rose and fell with a sigh. "His mortal name was Arimoch, and he was a Landspeaker, too—a speaker to the elementals, a healer, and a sage. He was the not the first to learn of the Makers. The first people knew of them; they could feel their divinity through the magik of the land. No leap was needed for faith, when we lived in wonder. We felt the stars watching us, and we smiled back at them. We offered them our songs and music. We were their perfect creations, and they were our watchful masters. Arimoch, however, did not want to be among the worshippers. He wanted more; he wanted vengeance. He wished to be as bright and eternal as the stars."

She whipped her head to face Morigan, and balked not at all at the seer's light. "Your father showed him how to be a Lord, and desiring the thrones of the Lord and Lady of Creation himself, he used his Will to summon them. His Will, empowered by the sacrifice of thousands of the ancient people—who died believing their deaths were an offering to appease the stars. They believed his promises. They believed him because they were innocent and knew not the rot of lies."

As Adam hastily explained, Morigan's light began to dim; her head buzzed and his words, like swords, slashed across her sight. In the blindness, she faded from the plateau into a foggy reality where there were not hundreds but thousands of persons kneeling in rows before her in a gloomy chamber; the floor seemed slick, wet, and red.

We are your sacrifices, was the communal whisper of their minds. *We are to pay for the sins of our people, Mother Onae, Father Zee.* And there was Arimoch, manifest in the vision, too. A man gaunt as a resurrected corpse with a brow as heavy as a mountain pass that shadowed what had become even darker eyes than Morigan remembered—a stare of the abyss. Adorned with ceremonial furs, painted with cryptic markings, he walked down the rows of kneeling, softly glowing sacrifices, holding his chalice—her father's chalice. As he walked past each supplicant, he slit their fool throats with an invisible dagger of Will, and Morigan watched him collect whatever amount he wished in his chalice then move into the spray of the next red fountain.

Outside this vision, the Skeleton Woman had gone quiet to allow the Landspeaker to translate for his friends before speaking again.

"They became one," she said, "the Serpent and Arimoch. He was the first of its vessels, a body sacrificed for the soul to be bound to the divine. Through their wicked conjuring, the Black Star came to Geadhain, and Zee and Onae were cast down, their thrones emptied, and they were cursed to wander among us."

Leaving the Skeleton Woman to her somber craft, Adam motioned for his companions to step aside with him to discuss this strange history. Morigan huddled in the Wolf's embrace. Her body shivered, her heart ached from enduring deception after deception, from this quest that seemed like one grand betrayal after another from her sinful father. *Why?* she wondered, and the bees were silent, as if she knew the answer and was being obtuse.

"Fuking liar!" Mouse swore, after hearing enough. "Dreamer of Lies and Desire! I have a Lord of Demons inside me."

"Calm down, Fionna," implored Thackery, and when invoking her birth name didn't appease her temper, he tried to restrain her fist-shaking arms in a hug. To this she relented, remaining tightly wrapped in his arms, she and her great uncle a twin tableau to Morigan's upset and wolfish consoler. Cooler heads than theirs continued the debate.

"We have been conflating the name and the myth," said Talwyn. "Primeval onomastics, mixed with history, has led to these results. For a time, I too was confused, though we can no longer disagree that Zionae is a disambiguation of *Zee* and *Onae*—two separate but symbiotic forces. Even the Sisters Three made the same linguistic mistake. I don't think they know what we or the people of the Cradle have learned."

"Which is what?" asked Moreth, snarling.

The blood and fragrance of offal had filled the bland air with the richness of a summer garden, and there was more...another waft...the sweat of a man, or a hundred men, entwined in an orgy of sex and blood...

"There were two," said Thackery. "An alpha and omega, a negative and positive. Two opposing entities who ruled the heavens, who created Geadhain and whatever queer worlds float elsewhere than ours. A Father of Light and a Mother of Darkness. And this Arimoch...this sinner and sorcerer, I assume. It's such a unique name, and I seem to remember it from somewhere...Perhaps something I heard or read at the palace while I was penning the Nine Laws of Eod. Was it in the Court of Ideas? I seem to remember a page, a transcript, yes...one of the king's notes on an archive in the Hall of Memories. I'm sorry, but I don't remember anything more than that."

"I do," said Talwyn, most grim. "An *Arimoch* was the purported Sorcerer King of the Mortalitisi."

"No," exclaimed Thackery. "It must be another, or he would be—"

"Thousands upon thousands of years old, and the same vile man who evidently undid the first era of our world? I know only legends of the Mortalitisi. I have not seen the ruins of the white towers myself; it's a trip few men make and from which even fewer return. Although, we should not rule out this man's involvement or that he might indeed be both infamous personas."

"What's his role in all of this?" demanded Mouse. "Whichever Arimoch?"

"He pulled the Father of Light and Mother of Darkness down, according to Adam and our skinny storyteller," replied Talwyn. "To *make them suffer*, a celestial upheaval which I believe triggered Geadhain's first apocalypse. I think he did it with your father's help." Talwyn pointed at Morigan. "He was a vessel. We don't know what came after the Black Star ruined the Cradle, though. We need that woman to tell us."

"Indeed," agreed Morigan; the buzz of Fates and history had become a splitting migraine, which would know no succor or abatement in agony until she found the pill, the truth to Zionae's rage. "Ask her where we can find Zionae's remains."

"You mean Onae's," said Talwyn. "We seek the Mother of Darkness's corpse, vessel, or what have you. Zee, the Father of Light, may not be resting here."

"Whatever," spat Morigan, a little wolfishly and for once bothered by his pedantry. "I want bones, Adam, something for my senses to read. I want this awful sequence of tragedies to finally come to an end."

They all did. Ash palled their skin. They were creatures of filth. Moreth was the only one who seemed not to have shadows under his eyes. Indeed, he seemed enlivened, and moved ahead, past the wise woman toward the crusted precipice into which the wind was gulped. Adam exchanged a few words with the Skeleton Woman, and she pointed her glistening dagger in Moreth's direction.

"At the bottom of the world," she said to Adam, meaning the sundered pit that descended surely to the center of the planet. However, the pit breathed no heat as they approached, and foretold of no light; it hungered only for dust, air, and the bodies of the travelers, who felt it pull them as they clung together, mostly anchored to the Wolf.

"How do we get to the bottom of that?" Mouse, hanging on to one of the Wolf's forearms, kicked a pebble over the edge and didn't bother to listen for the sound of it landing. The Wolf eventually, many sands later, heard the stone puff into an ashen floor. There was a bottom to this abyss, and it sounded relatively soft. He had made daring leaps before, but never when he had felt so in control of himself, so in tune with the music of his muscles and of the smaller sparks and motions of the natural universe within him. Since sparring with Moreth, a new strength seemed to have awakened in him, and he knew that even if he jumped carelessly and didn't consciously coordinate the neurological magik of his body into the glorious dance for which it was made, his body would do the work in his stead. He knew he could leap to the bottom of this abyss without a scratch. While he reveled in his invulnerability, Morigan began to flicker beside him. A queen of magik herself, she knew she could descend that impossible depth in one or two smoky twists.

Moreth also knew of a way to Onae's grave. Closest to the edge, unanchored to the Wolf, he peered down the black throat of the world and wondered what it was down there that smelled of sweat, lust, and fusty blood.

"Do you smell that, Wolf?" he asked. "Blood and sex and murder."

The Wolf found even Morigan's scent hard to hold on to here, where everything smelled burned and bland. Mayhap a sinister aroma lay under the ash, one of beasts, iron, and semen mixed into an evil jam. Whatever beast that smell belonged to was trying to stay hidden. Indeed, the monster had thrown itself into the ash as a scorpion buried itself in the sand.

Suddenly, Wolf recognized it: his father's musk. The Wolf stiffened. The bag of chains he held in his fist rattled as he shivered.

"Good hunting, my friend," he snarled. "You have a nose for blood greater than I. We would have leapt into the open teeth of a trap—the teeth of my father."

"Brutus?" exclaimed Thackery.

"Aye," replied the Wolf. "He has followed us here. I should have sensed him, though there are so many dangers, so many smells covered by the death of this place. And I see that he can calm his terrible storm when he chooses."

"I smell death." Moreth sniffed the air as if roses bloomed nearby. "It is lovely. I want to taste an Immortal's blood."

While inhaling, matter wriggled along his spine and back, stretching it, and the legs within his beggar's pants began to swell. Magik prickled the companions, and they backed up into a circle and clutched at one another or the Wolf, who stood firm, having seen the transformation before.

Black spiderwebs broke out along Moreth's pale flesh, and he hunched, feeling the agony of his bloodlust clawing into his consciousness. He cried out, dark, heavy, and loud as a bull being gutted. There was a splatter of clear, gooey plasm as the wings of shadow pricked from his back like twigs and then flourished into air-ruling instruments. In a single flap, he was tens of paces above them, glaring down with his radiant eyes and ebon typhoon of hair; this veined majesty of his strongman body effected a giddy horror in those who had known him as a man.

"Do not cower," said the Blood King to the Wolf. "Roar with me! We shall feed on your father together. We shall break him and end this war today. In your honor, for Beatrice, for all the fleshy weak things of this world!"

Twice stunned, the company was blasted back with the beat of his wings. He rose higher before plummeting into the throat of the world. He was not coming back, they realized. Ruled by his inner monster, he had charged into what might be the final war with Brutus.

"I must go after him," said the Wolf, and he stepped forward, flashing with a sudden strange light, golden to the flickers of blackness that had wrapped Moreth in a web. He leapt so quickly that they felt only a rushing wind in his wake and heard but the clatter of the chains he carried.

Frantic, and abuzz with a million premonitions of danger, Morigan fumbled to find a single reasonable command for her pack—the forlorn and filthy souls who had chased doom with her. This was not how the war was supposed to end. Even her bees were furious at this abrupt climax, and more so at their—at her—insensitivity to this danger. Only if Brutus was shielded or protected from Fate should she have been unaware of his presence. Only were he with a woman who could trick and defy Fate could such surreptitiousness be employed.

"Amunai," she muttered, terrifying her friends even more. "She's here, and she's done it again—confused Fate. I'm sorry, my friends. I didn't want to leave you this way. Believe that I shall return for you, and that we shall be victorious. I shall not let this be our last farewell. I take your prayers with me into the dark."

Morigan vanished in a silver wrinkle. The company cursed and huddled, and watched for any enemies that might reveal themselves. The light and appearance of the pure white sphere shocked them all as much as the disappearance of their friends. It felt out of place, less real than these aged nightmares, and still, as they stared at the crack in the ceiling and at the moon that had suddenly revealed itself—quickly entranced by it—they felt not despair but hope.

A gust of wind and whiteness blew past them and into the pit.

A bird, they thought.

II

The grave of the Mother of Darkness's vessel was the darkest place on Geadhain. First there had been cinders, and rocks sculpted by the savage hand of chaos, twisted into waves and arches when the fragment of the Black Star had crashed into the verdant Cradle, then tunneled deep into the earth. But that was in the ages before ages were known by the chattering, lost tribes that wandered the remains of their paradise. That was in the dark age after the sin of touching the divine, of coveting the stars, had been committed. As the world healed from that wound, scabbing in volcanic tissue, cooling those wounds with endless winter, oozing the sickness from itself through swampy fevers, then drying the effluvium with a Dry Season, the world seemed whole again—the greenness and wonder of the Cradle disseminated, if less resplendent than it had been. Everything was smaller now: magik, man, dreams, creatures. Everything had become a shadow, though in that shadow was an imitation of the wonders of the First Age. In the Cradle and its heart—the Scar—however, nothing was healed. Even time would not efface the atrocity. Here, the Age of Fire had burned the land above into a mottled and desolate place, while the tomb of the Lady of Darkness stayed cold, deep, and forgotten.

Onae's grave stood as it had once been left—until disturbed by Brutus's hands—as a sculpted altar of dust, a femur, a few fragmented chips of bones, and a skull. The rest of the vessel's remains had been lost in the mossy black sea, grown into furred cones, dunes, and pillars bridging the woolly floor to the ceiling. Amid heaps on the far side of Onae's altar, near a column grown from dust, were two shadows, one grander than its companion.

Brutus, his white sneer shining in the dark, was displeased. "They know of our plans for ambush."

Amunai swallowed, her palms were slick with sweat. She wasn't sure if she was excited or terrified. The wind had whispered the same warning to Amunai as it had Brutus. Her tricks and their stealth had not been enough. Now the Daughter of Fate, the mongrel son, and that other creature—a beast nearly as quick as the winds she commanded—would be upon the grave of Onae in a moment.

The mad king would no longer lie in wait. In a cloud of ash, he rose, then strode a billowing path to the altar. He felt a flicker of déjà vu, of having touched the pristine skull that smiled back at him. He scratched his head violently, as though the memory were a worm trying to gnaw through his skin. Suddenly he was distracted by a roar and a buffeting force that filled the cavern.

A shape hovered in the darkened eaves of this cathedral of dust. Though it was obscured, Amunai believed she saw a large, pale form with flaming wings—flames of shadow. She Willed the winds to carry her to Brutus's side, lowered her hood, and waited for the second actor on this deadly stage to appear. A shockwave of dirt announced that arrival. Infuriated at her sudden loss of vision from the small maelstrom, she commanded the wind to tame the storm of motes filling the cavern until all was settled as it had been. Not even the slow flap of the monster's hovering disturbed the now sandy weight of the ancient decay.

At last able to see, she saw the handsome son of Brutus wearing a snarl not unlike his father's. Just when she thought Morigan would miss her own execution, a twist of silver light flashed, and the seer stood waist-deep in black waves beside her lover. Three heroes faced her, and each seemed to shine with the color of magik—black for the man-monster, golden for the sun of Brutus, and silver for the seer. She would snuff out the lights of these three demi-Immortals to usher in the new age. Being a woman of theater, she felt the need to announce their futility.

"Welcome to your grave, heroes," she hissed.

They were less afraid of her threats, however, than of the man-shape carved of darkness, gleaming in curves of hyper-musculature, like an athlete trimmed of his skin. In visions, as imaginings, they had known the mad king, though just as staring at a phantograph of the sun was no comparison to being thrown into its incinerating heat, what was before them surpassed the nightmare intimations they'd had of Brutus.

While the Wolf might have been a small giant, the Immortal was a true-blooded titan; Amunai stood like a child beside him, barely meeting his thigh. Although the cavern was empty, and they stood far away near a squarish plate, an isle in the sea of ash, Brutus made that emptiness seem small, commanding the awe of each of the creatures in his presence. Most of Brutus hung in shadow, and they envisioned his grandeur by what gleams his mutated body cast. His musk, a thick and sweet odor as offensive as rot and crotch cologne, rolled over the companions. Moreth found it delicious. The Wolf thought his father stank of evil. Morigan was repulsed and had to swallow a spurt of bile in her throat.

"You reek, Father," spat the Wolf. "I smell every sin—every rape, murder, and savage act you have committed—upon you; it is a stench you will never wash clean from your hide. When you are chained, we shall leave you to spoil in your own rancid prison."

"Son?" said Brutus. Once more he had forgotten the meaning of the word.

Amunai interceded. It seemed that he would need her guidance, and so she sent a whisper into his mind. *Merely a lesser hound in your pack. One who should serve you. He is tethered by the woman wrapped in silver light. She has bewitched him; only her death will end the enchantment.*

"Her death," snarled Brutus.

Despite the distance between them, the three champions of Geadhain heard his dire rumbling, felt his cursing of Morigan's presence shiver their flesh in an earthquake that tested the power of Amunai's command over the wind and weight of matter. Growling, the engine that the Immortal had become bulldozed a path through the shaking ashen sea. Brutus was determined to ravage the woman spraying silver light, regardless of what that reason was. He was a king of monsters, he killed, and she was to be killed—so sayeth the Herald and voice of his mother, so must it be done. She smelled of woods, purity, and the entire herds of white deer that he had devoured when the world was young. Her meat would slake him well.

Moreth swooped upon the churning train power that barreled upon them. Racing along with the hurricane, he frenzied, striking with venom-dripping claws, trying to latch his lamprey's mouth on to the succulent flesh of an Immortal. Whatever he scraped sparked like steel to armor. Even with Moreth's nocturnal vision, the king moved too quickly for him. One of Moreth's fatal kisses was rebuked by a golden fist that flashed clearly in the coruscating haze with which he fought. His jaw crumpled, stars played music in his head, and he was thrown as high as the filth-cones dropping from the roof, one of which he struck, impaling a wing upon whatever solid spine was there, muffled by age. The stalactite broke with a snap, and he screeched as he fell, the fractured stone embedded deep within him.

The Wolf watched the brief tangle, which had lasted only specks. Three specks and his father, moving faster than anything he had seen, was upon him. He threw down his chains, thrust his hands into the churning winds, and miraculously made contact with his father's hands. Veins bubbled in him, some near his eyes or along his knuckles bursting from the effort of holding back this Immortal tide. The Wolf screamed, his face fanged, lathed in blood and sweat, and twisted in agony. He was a child trying to stop a mountain with his bare hands.

The snarling countenance of the titan who swam in fire, whose eyes were the fury and color of lightning, faded once into his delirium, and then the Wolf failed. He broke. Snapping like a twig, his hands shattered, and he was lifted as if he were a sheet being ruffled—up, over, then down—with rib-cracking power. Brutus left him there, drowning in soot, and reached for the silvery fawn his son had been protecting.

It had all gone so wrong, so quickly. Morigan's mind was slow to process her terrible circumstances. She'd seen a great clouded force approaching. Then Moreth's dashing aerial attack and the swatting reprisal of the clouded titan; then her Wolf's valiant stand, strength to strength against his father. Alas, that contest had ended as quickly as Moreth's, her Wolf cast down and buried somewhere behind the slavering slab of shadow that now suffocated her in its sickly heat and stench. Magik was not wholly reactive, and her powers could not simply sweep her up and away from peril. She needed to react in the split-speck of time before the force that was Brutus collided with her.

Morigan's bees shrieked, filling her head with pins, and her fear and agony propelled her into a leap into Dream. She didn't care where she reappeared, as long as it was not in his grasp. But it didn't help her, and a grip of crushing thunder seized her wrist, easily breaking her bones and pulling her back from the vaporous rift into which she had almost escaped. Whatever spell she had cast, her dream-walking had been dispelled by Brutus's duality, his magik, or maybe even her agony. Morigan was now merely a woman of flesh. A peon to his order, Brutus shook her by her wrist, and inside her more bones shifted and organs ruptured. What little fire remained in her—the passion of her love, the desire to see order and kindness restored to Geadhain—pushed her to feebly flicker with silver wisps of light, magik that harmed not a hair on the Immortal's hide.

"*This* is what bespelled my son?" boomed the mad king, squinting, both curious and annoyed by her resistance. "Stop that." Brutus squeezed her wrist to a pulpy mass that would never function again without a miracle of fleshcrafting. "You tiny moth...I admire your struggle, though it is forfeit before it began. I am stone eternal. I am the walker of nightmares. I have eaten the monsters that men deem unconquerable, and in my belly you will find their souls. Are you ready to meet those ghosts, then? I see that your struggle has come to an end."

Morigan, hanging by an arm, swiping the dagger she'd somehow managed to pull out of her belt with her remaining hand, was finally exhausted by her efforts. She glared when her strength served her no longer, and spat blood upon the king's face.

How much his gore-caked face reminded her of her Wolf's, how far he had fallen from the greatness he could be. She would not stop fighting, even if her body would no longer assist her. She loathed him and what he had done with all her soul. Even as shattered as she was, she had one last maneuver in her, one for which her mind, not her body, was the tool. She called to what remained of her Will, and she focused on the face before her as if it were a wall of stone and she the hammer. For a brief speck, she shone with the white beauty of the moon and strangely felt as if the moon shone back on her bloody face—and that radiance ate at the façade, the crazed countenance before her.

The mad king winced as though stung, and Morigan felt his Will crack. A little further, one more push, and she might be able to reach what Onae and his madness had sealed away: something pure and noble. Brutus growled, the animal within sensing and reacting to her assault. He held her farther at bay and gave her another shake.

"I see you are not a moth, but a wasp," he said.

A clucking shadow rose beside the king, shedding darkness to become Amunai. She seemed as sad as Morigan appeared angry. "I had hoped for more of a fight, though I warned you of your pride and of Brutus's might. You cannot stand against a force from beyond, not when you are only half divine yourself. You will always lose. You have always lost. And now you will die." Amunai turned away, disappointed in and grieving the end of her nemesis.

"Heed her not," said the king to Morigan. "You have a spirit greater than the trappings of your flesh." Brutus grinned, his teeth as menacing as a lion's. "I shall remove that flesh from you now, so you may rule the spirits as you should. Farewell, strange wasp."

Brutus's mouth widened into a glistening pink abyss, and she gagged on his charnel breath. Morigan sensed he was going to swallow her whole. The frenzy of Morigan's bees muted the horror that was to unfold. They had failed. She had failed her bloodmate and her friends. The world would suffer because of her choices.

I love you, my Wolf. I am sorry I was not strong enough to stop him. But this cannot be the end. We are to hunt among the stars. We shall be fawn and wolf forever. Please wake. Show your father your strength. Rage.

In the mounds behind Brutus, the Wolf rose, shimmering with golden scars, his fingers cracking back into shape, his bones resetting with auric dazzles. The blood ebbing from him was not red but gleamed like liquid gold. As it ran across his regenerating fists, it accrued on his knuckles, forming and solidifying into jagged protrusions—a second set of claws with which he would rend his father.

Barely sensing the motion behind him, Brutus had turned his head only ever so slightly before a rattling bag of chains met the side of his face. The unexpected blow succeeded in throwing Brutus off balance, and he let loose Morigan, spinning around to face the twisted hulk of Caenith, bristling with sharpness, aglow in magikal hues. The Wolf's jaw had become distended with teeth, a growing snout, and long canine ears. He challenged the mad king with a roar.

"You *are* my son," said Brutus, at last haunted by an echo of memory stirred by this monstrous spawn.

The golden Wolf smashed into the mad king, his unchained beast at last a match for his father. Amid the flurry of claws, swipes, and acrobatic tackles the two indulged in as they hurtled around the cavern in dashes of ash, Brutus roared his respect for this challenger. And while Brutus reveled in crazed admiration, the Wolf fought for his pack, for his mate. She was not dead, only horribly wounded. The combatants toppled pillars, stalagmites, and soon covered the ashen arena in a smokescreen into which Amunai tried to determine who had the upper hand. Suddenly, there came the howl of a third beast and she ducked, warned by the winds that served her, as a black streak arched over her head and flew into the clouds before her—no magik would keep the dust settled now, not when three Immortal things waged war. Victory had spoiled to defeat, and her triumph was no longer certain.

A nearby groan pulled her attention from the battle, and Amunai looked over at a blast pocket in the blackness, where Morigan was beginning to move again. Would this woman just die, already? Amunai cursed and strode through the swirling tides. She came upon Morigan as the woman was crawling toward her dagger. Amunai stomped on the seer's unbroken hand, savoring the sound of her cry. She had to be quick; the Wolf would be at his maiden's side in a speck, and there was a flying Immortal on the loose. Amunai picked up the seer's promise dagger, pulled her head up by her hair, and placed cold metal on her neck.

"When Brutus has beaten the Will from your Wolf, I'll put a collar on him and make him my slave. I'll do unspeakable things to him you couldn't fathom in your wholesome mind. I'll be the stud, and he'll be our pack's bitch. Think of that as you depart for eternity."

Though embroiled in danger, his father's hands clenched around his gold-plated throat, the Wolf felt his Fawn's distress. Ripping off that impossible grip, he left his father to the fury of Moreth who was suddenly attempting to shred the Immortal's flesh, which also solidified into a keratinous slag that would not surrender its blood.

Caenith had but a moment to reach the Herald. He lunged forward to land himself behind her, reaching for the dagger as she drew the first prick of blood from Morigan's alabaster neck.

"Stop."

The whisper seized them all.

A gentle buzzing voice floated through the chamber that had become abruptly still. Brutus, snarling, stopped pulling at the arm of the spidery monster who clung to him. Moreth, stunned, clawed weakly while peering out into the dust at the white phantom—a silhouette of starlight that hovered in the distance near Caenith and Morigan. Whatever magik the phantom figure had cast, it calmed Brutus, Moreth, and the Wolf. It eased Morigan's myriad agonies and her terror. She saw in the ethereal figure the grace and suggestions of a woman she knew: Elissandra.

The misty whiteness of the ghost evoked a recollection of a similar manifestation, when Morigan had first encountered Amunai in a nightmare. Morigan realized it had been Elissandra who had saved her, then as now. In death, or whatever this state was, the witch was beauty without the obscurity of flesh, a streaming spirit in a robe of light; what was hair, ether, or twist was unnecessary to know—she was glorious. Elissandra's eyes shone with the silver of a Daughter of Alabion casting prophecy. And it was fate that Elissandra had come to cast, to correct. Before Amunai could awaken from her own shock and Will herself away, Elissandra was around her, whispering...The promise dagger was laid softly down in the ash by a luminous hand.

The Wolf's armor retreated into his flesh as he swept and gathered his maiden in his arms to watch the whispering woman of light surround the Herald. Brutus would not harm them, not in the presence of such truth. Brutus reared in terror knowing Elissandra's power could unmake his madness, knowing her magik could dismantle his armor of horror and expose the meekness that the Black Queen had hidden from him—he would have to face his truth if he stayed, as Amunai was facing hers. The Wolf noticed his father hiss like a damned sunless wretch, saw him shrug himself free of the Blood King and flee. It was an escape to which Moreth surrendered, and his monstrous countenance was fixed in a gape at the spirit nimbus that had swallowed Amunai.

What is she saying to her? wondered the Wolf, as the ghost's glow grew and grew. He listened and finally heard a single word.

Remember.

Then the woman and the light whirled in smoky trails off Amunai—who was now a blubbering, weeping mess, her arms wrapped firmly around her stomach as she rocked back and forth.

Elissandra remade herself before the bloodmates, a little dimmer than she had been, and fading.

"I have done what I can," said the spirit of Elissandra. "It took the power of the beyond to break the darkness in that one wounded child's mind." Amunai released another long sob behind her. "I leave her fate to you, though remember, penance is not punishment—and she deserves both mercy and cruelty. I have not the power to break the thrall over Brutus, after I have spent what remains of my Will in this world. But he is weak, and he has seen how his mother's Will can be unmade.

"You now know his darkness. You have felt his strength. You must hone your own, Daughter of Fate. You must move beyond your pride, your fear, your sense of mortality, and become as I am—spirit without flesh. I died to make this journey, to teach you the way. But you, Morigan, are already of the otherworld. You can survive a greater test. I believe in you, Morigan. I leave you as a sister-in-arms. Discover your strength. Embrace everything you are. Be the bird of stars and moon to shatter Brutus's darkness, as I have shown you."

Elissandra dwindled until they could only see the curved line of stars that had been her smile, before that vanished in blips of light. The grave of Onae went dark and silent. Neither Wolf nor Blood King smelled or sensed Brutus. They realized they had not been the slightest bit prepared to face him, anyway. They would have needed an army, and Magnus, and a miracle from Morigan.

Rising and falling even as the Wolf held her, and unable to speak, Morigan tipped her head toward the altar. There, a thrum of fate awaited her, a pull of ancient music to which she would dance—her ruined flesh be damned. Moreth joined the bloodmates as the Wolf waded through the blackness toward the altar, carrying his bloodmate and leaving Amunai to weep alone. Moreth's remaining monstrousness passed in a fit of greasy seizures, which did not impede his ability to walk and stand next to the bloodmates. He helped the Wolf bear Morigan from the large man's cradle and to her feet—careful not to touch the crimson twist that was her wrist and hand. The men held her balanced as she reached with her good hand for the skull of Onae's ancient vessel and demanded that its truths be laid bare.

The cavern birthed new light and secrets. Amunai wailed louder now, for she knew what Morigan was about to see.

EPILOGUE

I

Willowholme, once the jaunty musical core of Central Geadhain, bellowed with an inauspicious tune. Once, famed bards from Kericot to Ser Andes had sat beneath the weeping trees, turned their faces to the breeze, and been aroused by nature's melodies. By the skip of a leaf on distant rolling water. The ruffling of a million green feathers caressing each other in the bows above. Willowholme had been no end of inspiration for those with artistic souls, and it was said that a visit there could cure any stupefaction of talent, loose any stubborn word from a writer's quill. But there would be no inspiration here now, not since the wolves had swept in from the east many weeks ago.

They had one night appeared on the shores of the Feordhan, not far north of Brutus's ugly metal dam. Eod's scouts had first noticed the armada of longboats slithering across the blue back of the Feordhan in a sinuous wisp. Then and soon, upon the crusted ruin that was Mor'Khul's sizzled plains, wolves spewed forth from the ships, dragging with them the gangly laborers who'd built their armada tied in a cat's cradle of chains—miserable sunless creatures that shivered as though they'd lost their skins. They were the meekest of shadows, taken from changeling tribes and the peaceful acolytes of the Great Mother. These slaves were whipped along, by the men, half-men, and gargantuan wolves—shades of autumn to midnight—who were their rulers. The greatest Warwolves walked upright as anthropomorphic dogs with burly chests, bulging arms, claws, and paws, donned in clattering metal harnesses and plates. These commanders arranged and ordered the army—as many as a thousand half-wild things could be brought to heel.

The slaves who were too slow to haul the ominous hulking war equipment forged from the woods and metals of the lands to the east were eaten for their incompetence, and sometimes shared in red mouthfuls of still-beating flesh. Whatever kindness, connectivity to the elements, and poetry the wolves once possessed had soured into a depraved ego.

565

II

Aghna had been responsible for the reshaping of her people. Following her disgrace at Briongrahd—her defeat by the hairless ape whore of her former bloodmate—she knew that the war ahead could not be waged with a nation weaned on the milk of the past. Man liked iron? Very well, she would show man how cold iron felt as it tore into their flesh from the capped claws and tormentor's harnesses she'd made for her soldiers.

Man liked invention? She would show him how a feliron battering ram, hammered to life by the ancient smiths of Briongrahd, could smash the strongest, oldest man-made wall. She would not fight fair; she would fight with the tools of this age. Her mistake had been her own weakness to history—a history with a certain Wolf. Now that he had cast her out, shamed her, she had only the violent abyss of crimson passion within her: Ragnarök.

When she'd lain in the dark, sulking after her defeat, waiting for her body to mend, she found that she could throw away all aches, all moral confusions, and that she could purge herself of sadness by allowing the Dreamer to stir just under her skin. The agony of war's presence reacquainted her with its pain—knives to her armpits, groin, breasts, and softest parts—and at the same time made her feel invincible to all other agonies. When war's radiance rose in her, his sunlight grew the same fire in others, too, bringing forth her people's most devious passion. And so, again and again, she'd summoned the Dreamer and bathed her people in the cleansing fires of forgiveness and forgetfulness in which she'd been burned. They burned like her now, the wolves. They were snarling, terrible monsters who cared only for what they could kill.

They were ready to destroy an Immortal.

As she slunk down the panting lines of her army, appreciating their brutality, the pale warmother thought of the coming conquest as a crown jewel in her reign. No matter the sacrifice, no matter the tides of blood that would nourish this now dead land, she would either win or die in an orgy of destruction. Either end was acceptable for her and the Dreamer, and for the wild wolves who followed her.

She howled, and the army zealously sang with her.

When her flesh burned a bit too hot for comfort, she asked the Dreamer to relent, and his great sun—from which the weaker changelings and slaves cringed and howled—descended into the shadows of her form. She approached three smaller red presences, less striking than a Dreamer's majesty, though as ominous in their way. The Red Witches had claimed a rock abandoned amid the dust and whirling of the scorched beaches of Mor'Khul. They stood around it as though it were the cauldron they'd left back in Alabion, although no secrets stirred on the surface, just ants that had endured Brutus's heat. As Aghna invaded their quiet sisterhood, the Red Witches stopped watching the patterns the insects made; every dance in life was beautiful to them, as they weren't the monsters often described, merely the angry side of nature.

"So much howling," complained Maeg, the fattest and most jovial of the silver-haired enchantresses whose robes stretched as tautly as a pregnant woman's. "It's a good thing I'm already mostly deaf."

Slender, sinister Malabeth, hearer of Geadhain's darkest secrets, pointed to Aghna as she appeared. "As deaf as this one to the sadness wailing in her heart."

"Sadness?" hissed the warmother. She smashed her hand down upon the stone, pulling on the chain that tied master and vessel together once more. Her palm connected with a granite-keening crack and dissolved boulder into ash and brimstone.

Morgana, the eldest, wisest, and grayest of them, waved away the dissolution. "Careful. While you may be a special vessel, a bit hardier thanks to the rare elixir of an Immortal son's blood and the everbloom that claimed your life and still runs toxic in your dead veins, you are only a slightly stronger paper doll than the Dreamers usually wear. You'll burn yourself up before your master ever gets the chance."

"I shall slay an Immortal," declared Aghna. "I shall do what man cannot."

"That is why we have come, yes," replied Morgana, sliding a finger down the shaft of the sickle swinging on her belt. "Now lead your army, and we shall follow, as we have vowed to, to reap and rend what your culling misses."

This had been the arrangement, struck weeks ago, when the Red Witches had materialized amid the smoke and flames of Aghna's campfire on the edge of Alabion. They'd drifted from the flames, appearing like glass figurines filled with embers, until they'd solidified into something more killable, perhaps, and yet their resonance of age and the stirring of Ragnarök at their manifestation had given Aghna pause. She had called off her warriors and listened to these three spirits of vengeance, women who sounded as though they had been as wronged as she. That night, with little hesitation, a dark alliance had been formed. Aghna and these spirits would march for Geadhain and purge man and Immortal alike. The witches instructed Aghna's smiths on the greater disciplines and engineering feats used by the wicked apes they sought to punish.

At the time, it had seemed a wise partnership. However, who else in this war would parley and plot with three ghosts of vengeance but a ghost of vengeance herself? Aye, they wouldn't have made it through a single one of Magnus's testosterone-hazed councils without painting his stone table in entrails, severed members, and testicles. There were no other allies for these two forces to take.

Aghna was a woman and chief, forged in wrath and despair—as the shadows of Geadhain had been created. However, she'd recently seemed to Morgana less a proud warrior, and more a whorish concubine to the Dreamer. She and her sisters had grown increasingly uneasy with the arrangement. Still, they were along for blood, and Aghna was guaranteed to make it rain buckets of the stuff. Morgana sensed the great strings of the world tightening to a knot, one dense and dripping with doom as a nekromancer's moon.

"Are we ready to move?" she asked, eager to head toward their fantastic future.

"Yes." Aghna, thinking of moons, too, looked up. She scowled at the Black Star floating over the moon's white cheek. Drums began to beat in the gathering behind her, and wolves howled as though they sensed the imminent arrival of the mad Dreamer. "My people feel her pressure, like the tension before a storm. The Black Queen comes."

"She does." Malabeth slunk around and whispered to the warmother. "We can take a shovel to the root of her evil before she even arrives. The father of the brazen Wolf you once loved will return. He must return to arm himself with the beast that sleeps under Zioch's sizzling ruin, just as you have prepared your iron and fangs."

"Brutus."

"Such delicious sweetmeats!" cried Maeg—not so deaf when it came to the temptations of cannibalism. She bounced over to the pair, frantically rubbing her palms and licking her lips. "Ooh. We could sauté those great oysters. A little thyme, tarragon, and mint. I've never liked wine, though his blood would be the finest—the blood of a king."

"The blood of a king..." muttered Aghna.

Being beasts, the changelings' strategizing hadn't developed past listening to the Red Witches' technomagikal suggestions, having their slaves build ships, and then crossing into the realm of man, so that they could thrust their swords into the heart and confusion of this war. They'd hoped to pillage on both sides, though there were two clear roads ahead: one leading north to Eod, the other leading south.

Malabeth, enthralled by the secret melodies of fate, drifted off, following resonances and whispers. She hunched and listened to the north, though she didn't like what she heard—a sopping, shambling horde was slopping its way through the sands near Eod. It appeared the king had created his own prelude to what battle might lay ahead with his brother. Death, like her brother War, had decided to smite mankind rather than wait for him to smite himself. They would turn south, then. Perhaps they would cut off the two-headed snake of the Immortal brothers at each end, and then all could return to a calm in which nature could heal. Indeed, the Green Mother would be done after this, pondered Malabeth; she'd squatted and was raking her fingers through the dead soil, hearing its hiss, feeling its wrath in every trembling grain. The Green Mother had been beaten down and was ready to rest. If only her boisterous creations weren't keeping her awake.

Since Malabeth had decided, so too had her sisters. They had merely to tell Aghna now where to turn her army, which they did—toward the ruins of Willowholme. With a series of howls Aghna commanded the gargantuan sprawl to movement. Wolves and activity flew by the Red Witches—beings unscathed, outside of time, and soon ready to fade away with the magik, dreams, and civilizations of this world.

Once the army had become a large splotch of shadows on a shadowy land, the Red Witches sighed, stretched, and followed. Malabeth was slow to follow, though, and the other two were pulled back many paces, whiplashed by the enforced harmony of their sisterhood.

"What's your bother?" asked Maeg.

Malabeth stared north, across the wastes, and wondered what it was she was sensing. Movement. Power. Fate. All of those things, as well as fear. While mankind shivered in the shadow of extinction with Death's army nearly at its gates, a similar dread reached for her and her sisters. What were they, though? Neither men nor mice. How could they even know fear? And still, her shaking, her terrified grip upon her sickle against no threats she could see, were the same effects she and her sisters witnessed in men holding shaking swords—men whose balls they were about to snip.

"What is that?" whispered Morgana, fading in behind her.

"Smells like..." Maeg sniffed, smelling incense, myrrh, and cloves. "Witches. Grand ones." More sniffs. "Three. They're coming this way."

"Could it be?" gasped Malabeth.

"No." Morgana shook her head violently. "No."

"Are we not Mother's chosen ones?" whined Maeg. "How could they have left Alabion? How?"

Neither the wise one, nor the fortune-telling sister, had an answer for their despairing sibling. Although they knew this much was true—the Sisters Three and a knight of steel virtue were coming to confront them. Suddenly, Geadhain's wars felt as trifling as the gentlest rain. The Red Witches had to prepare to face their shadows.

Sneers, wrinkles, and ripples of shadow contorted their false beauty, and they hissed toward the north. *Come,* they thought. *Come, weak children of our Mother.* A mother who was sweet no more, but a titan of wrath and hate. For Geadhain, they would fight their weaker selves—with all the rage of this wounded planet. And when the battle was won, in blood and fury, they would eat them, then the kings—balls first—and finally the Black Queen. All these petty creatures and their vainglorious conquests, and in the end there would be green, and river and tree.

And the hallowed silence of a world without men or kings.

Fin

Made in the USA
Middletown, DE
16 September 2024

61014458R00366